DEATH IN VENICE AND OTHER STORIES

Thomas Mann was born in 1875 in Lübeck, of a line of prosperous and influential merchants. Mann was educated under the discipline of North German school-masters before working for an insurance office aged nineteen. During this time he secretly wrote his first tale, *Fallen*, and shortly afterwards he left the insurance office to study art and literature at the University of Munich. After a year in Rome he devoted himself exclusively to writing.

He was only twenty-five when *Buddenbrooks*, his first major novel, was published. Before it was banned and burned by Hitler, it had sold over a million copies in Germany alone. His second great novel, *The Magic Mountain*, was published in 1924 and the first volume of his tetralogy *Joseph and his Brothers* in 1933. In 1929 he was awarded the Nobel Prize for Literature. In 1933 Thomas Mann left Germany to live in Switzerland. Then, after several previous visits, in 1938 he settled in the United States where he wrote *Doctor Faustus* and *The Holy Sinner*. Among the honours he received in the USA was his appointment as a Fellow of the Library of Congress. He revisited his native country in 1949 and returned to Switzerland in 1952, where *The Black Swan* and *Confessions of Felix Krull* were written and where he died in 1955.

The Vintage ♥ Film series:

Alice in Wonderland Lewis Carroll

Atonement Ian McEwan

Brighton Rock Graham Greene

Catch-22 Joseph Heller

Death in Venice Thomas Mann

* *Fight Club* Chuck Palahniuk

The French Lieutenant's Woman John Fowles

Memoirs of a Geisha Arthur Golden

The Talented Mr Ripley Patricia Highsmith

Trainspotting Irvine Welsh

* not available in Australia and New Zealand

THOMAS MANN

Death in Venice

and Other Stories

TRANSLATED AND WITH
AN INTRODUCTION BY
David Luke

VINTAGE BOOKS
London

Published by Vintage 1998

2 4 6 8 10 9 7 5 3 1

Original German publication 1897, 1898, 1900, 1902, 1903, 1912

Original German book editions published 1898, 1898, 1903,
1903, 1903, 1903 by S. Fischer Verlag

Death in Venice in 1912 by Hyperionverlag Hans von Weber

These translations of 'Little Herr Friedemann', 'The Joker', 'The Road to
the Churchyard', 'Gladius Dei', 'Tristan' and 'Tonio Kröger' were
originally published in the United States in 1970 by Bantam Books, a
division of Bantam Doubleday Dell Publishing Group, Inc., as *Tonio
Kröger and Other Stories*; this including 'Death in Venice' originally
published in the United States in 1988 by Bantam Books.

First published in Great Britain in two volumes 1990
by Martin Secker & Warburg Limited

Vintage
Random House, 20 Vauxhall Bridge Road,
London SW1V 2SA

www.vintage-classics.info

Addresses for companies within The Random House Group Limited can
be found at: www.randomhouse.co.uk/offices.htm

The Random House Group Limited Reg. No. 954009

A CIP catalogue record for this book
is available from the British Library

ISBN 9780099541561

Printed and bound in Great Britain by Clays Ltd, Elcograf S.p.A.

Contents

Introduction

The present selection of Thomas Mann's stories represents a period in his work of about fifteen years, from his first maturity until just before the First World War. This period contains at its end his greatest story, *Death in Venice* (1912, first book edition 1913), and also, near its beginning, his first and (as many would still say) greatest novel, *The Buddenbrooks** (1901). The other stories here selected all belong to the turn of the century, when Mann (born in 1875) was in his twenties; two were published a few years before *The Buddenbrooks*, the rest shortly after it. Mann is generally thought of as a novelist rather than as a writer of short stories (or *Novellen*, as they are usually called in German), and his total output of about thirty stories is quantitatively only a small fraction of his output of major novels. Mann himself, however, was not convinced that the major fictional form was really more suited to his characteristic talent than the short story. Late in his life, when working on *Doctor Faustus* (1947), he wondered, rather over-despondently, whether he would ever be able to write a better novel than his first, which had almost at once established his national fame and twenty-eight years later won him the Nobel prize. He always felt more confident, however, about the value of his short stories, stating more than once that this more succinct form, which he had learned from Maupassant and Chekhov and Turgenev, was his 'own genre'; and some at least of them bear out this judgement. *Death in Venice* in particular is

*The traditional translation of this title, simply *Buddenbrooks*, is not a translation at all: the normal German way of referring to a family is without the article, but it would not be English to say 'Smiths' when we mean 'the Smiths'.

vii

an acknowledged masterpiece of European short fiction, and possibly the most artistically perfect of all Mann's works. The short story was a form to which he kept returning between ambitious novel plans, not all of which were realized; and it is significant as well as surprising that all his major novels, from *The Buddenbrooks* to *Doctor Faustus* (as well as the long picaresque fragment *Felix Krull*, begun in 1910 and finally reaching the end of only its first volume in 1953), were originally conceived as short or 'long-short' stories.

Mann was a prolific critic, essayist and letter-writer, and among his many comments on himself and his own work is one, also made in later life, that applies particularly clearly to these pre-war stories, though it is true of *The Buddenbrooks* and most of the other novels as well. In his autobiographical essay *A Sketch of My Life*, looking back in 1930 at what was by then the greater part of his literary output, he remarked that each of a writer's works is a kind of exteriorization,

> a realization, fragmentary to be sure but self-contained, of our own nature, and by so realizing it we make discoveries about it; it is a laborious way, but our only way of doing so.

And he added: 'No wonder these discoveries sometimes surprise us.' This has been recognized as an unmistakable echo of Goethe's much-quoted observation (also made in middle life) that all his works were 'fragments of a great confession'; and although Mann's is a modern, more complicated, psychologically coloured version of the point, it remains an irresistible invitation to us to see his works, like Goethe's, as among many other things a series of exercises in more or less latent autobiography. The fact that so many critics have insisted on this view of them, apparently with authorial blessing and often to the point of tedium, does not mean that we can or should wholly eschew the biographical or psychographical approach, which at one level is a necessary part of the commonplace of general information about both Goethe and Mann. Mann transmuted his personal substance into art with a great deal more self-conscious irony than did Goethe (and irony is another word which, despite its endless reiteration, is impossible to avoid when discussing him); but he was not engaged merely in an introspective or literary game. It was more like a serious process of self-discovery and practical self-analysis, of fictional experimentation with actual or potential selves and actual or potential intellectual attitudes. Despite the cynical mask he often wore, especially in his early years, it was ultimately a quest, a search for some kind of balance and wholeness, for human values that would (by reason of that very balance) be personally sustaining as well as intellectually satisfying and positively related to the culture of his times. In most, perhaps all, of the stories here presented we can observe, deeply disguised though it may be, this process of self-educative experimentation.

Something like it is certainly happening in *The Buddenbrooks*, which stands as a monumental and dominating feature in the background of the first six of these early stories. At one level it was a vast mirror in which Mann's German public recognized itself, an ironic yet not hostile study of North German middle-class life; but it is far more than a 'social' novel. It is autobiographical in the sense that Mann was here exploring his own origins, the roots of his personality and talent as they were to be found in his family and immediate forebears. Artistically the novel is a masterpiece, but as its subtitle, 'Decline of a Family', might suggest, the exploration yielded a bleak message. The two characters most closely identifiable with aspects of Mann himself, Thomas Buddenbrook and his son Hanno, who represent the last two Buddenbrook generations, both die (one in his forties, one in adolescence) for no other very good reason than that they have lost their will to live. The positive and humane values embodied in the traditions of this great Hanseatic trading family seem in the end to be negated. Thomas loses faith in them, and his life becomes a mere exhausting keeping-up of appearances; the inward-looking, sensitive Hanno never had any faith in them anyway, and solves his existential problem by succumbing to typhus when he is about fourteen. In the closing pages the surviving womenfolk sit round like a naturalistic Greek chorus, trying not to doubt the Christian message of a reunion in the hereafter. Despite the great zest and comic verve with which the detailed substance of the story is presented, *The Buddenbrooks* in the general tendency of its thought may be described (using another here unavoidable word) as an exercise in nihilism.

Thomas Mann himself clung to no kind of Christian faith. His intellectual mentors were Schopenhauer and Nietzsche, particularly the latter, whom he read avidly from an early age; the former he did not encounter at first hand until he was well on the way to completing *The Buddenbrooks*, but from Nietzsche's writings he could have absorbed much of the Schopenhauerian message. Schopenhauer, the supreme exponent and stylist of philosophic pessimism, had published his masterpiece *The World as Will and Idea* as far back as 1818; unrecognized at the time, it had become increasingly influential in the later nineteenth century. It offered an atheistic but metaphysical system, beautifully elaborated into a symphony of concepts, founded on a deep and imaginative appreciation of the arts (and of music above all, the art Mann most deeply loved), but first and foremost on a rage of compassion for the suffering of the human and animal world. Schopenhauer regarded any kind of 'optimistic' philosophy as not merely stupid but actually wicked, an insult to the immeasurable pain of all sentient creatures. In his own later essay on him (1938) Mann remarked on the strangely satisfying rather than depressing character of this great protest of the human spirit: 'for when a critical intellect and great writer speaks of the general suffering of the world, he speaks of yours and mine as well, and with a sense almost of triumph we all feel ourselves avenged by his splendid words'. The young Thomas Mann, especially, seems to have agreed with Flaubert (and with his own Tonio Kröger) that to write was to avenge oneself on life. Art was redemptive and, so to speak, punitive. That at least was Mann's theoretical and deeply temperamental starting-point: a vision, as he was to put it in *Tonio Kröger*, of 'absurdity and wretchedness'. It is part of the essential theme of *The Buddenbrooks* that in proportion as the family loses its nerve its later members become more intellectually sensitized and inward-looking, they participate more deeply in this negative vision. The two processes, culminating in Hanno, are aspects of one and the same 'decline'.

Nietzsche's influence on Mann was more complex and far-reaching even than that of Schopenhauer. From both of them Mann would learn a high mastery of German prose and, more especially from Nietzsche, a kind of polemical, sceptical and ironic attitude of mind that was perhaps even more important to him than many of the particular conclusions of Nietzsche's thought. Nietzsche, whose own intellectual life had begun under Schopenhauer's spell and who spent much of it trying to turn his master upside-down without ever quite succeeding, had been the supreme protester not only against life and against God but against any kind of complacently rationalistic, secular ideology, to which he felt even Christian belief to be preferable. Writing between the early 1870s and his mental breakdown in 1889, he was a thinker of such radical scepticism that his thinking was inevitably fraught with paradoxes. (As a French contemporary had remarked, '*il ne faut croire à rien, pas même à ses doutes*'.) As a young man, at the same age as the Thomas Mann of *The Buddenbrooks*, Nietzsche had adopted the atheistic metaphysic of Schopenhauer's universal life-drive, or 'will to live', the 'will' that must be negated if life is to be redeemed into nothingness. But a contrary instinct in him seemed, or tried at least, to reject this nihilism. What avenue of escape from it was open?

Nietzsche utterly despised literary Naturalism but was no poet, hard and embarrassingly as he sometimes tried to be. In his youthful, incalculably influential work *The Birth of Tragedy* (1872), he had hailed the masterpieces of Aeschylus and Sophocles as the redemptive aesthetic visions of a deeply pessimistic culture and had saluted Richard Wagner as the genius in whose dramatic music the spirit of classical Greek tragedy was now to be reborn. But he turned away both from Wagner (who for Mann was to remain the supreme and representative musical genius) and from metaphysics, and set about exploring the possibilities of a modern, total scepticism, fortified by acute psychological insights of a kind that in some ways anticipated Freud. In the aphoristic writings of what is usually called his second, 'positivistic' period (though the label puts him in company he disliked, and 'second period' is also doubtful, since it never really ended), Nietzsche set out to unmask and undermine all the traditional values and preconceptions of European philosophical, ethical and religious thought. In the first Nietzsche, the devotee of Schopenhauer and Wagner, the young Thomas Mann could embrace a kindred spirit; the 'second' Nietzsche taught him that nothing was sacred and everything suspect, that an attitude of guarded self-conscious irony was constantly required and single-mindedness difficult or impossible. The Nietzschean irony was not simply a cautious pose or a literary method: it reflected the contradictions in his thought and temperament, which later became those in Mann's thought and temperament. Nietzsche's persistent polemic against traditional Christian theism as he understood it (its collapse as a respectable option for modern intellectuals was what he called the 'death of God') had shrunk from no conclusions or corollaries. The full implications of the disappearance of God must be faced, all consequential losses ruthlessly cut: good and evil, humility and self-denial, charity and mercy and compassion (although, and because, Nietzsche was himself a deeply compassionate man), must be buried with their divine inventor and sponsor. But what of the puritanical lust for objective scientific truth, for relentless fact, which Nietzsche came to see as a last disguise of God even for atheists, a last secular 'absolute' value in which 'the Absolute' had taken refuge? Must it not also be discarded, is it not in any case dangerous to know too much, unhygienic to believe too little? What positive vision can be constructed in this emptiness?

The 'third' Nietzsche, of *Zarathustra* and the 'Eternal Recurrence of the Identical' and the Superman, tried to meet this challenge. The response must be adequately sophisticated, heroic, noble and grandiose, imaginative and creative. The earth from now on must not be made merely comfortable but invested with inherited glory; man must not be made merely happy like a sheep, or multitudinous and long-lived like a flea, but develop into a 'Dionysian' higher being, dancing on the grave of transcendent divinity. Seeking an antidote or at least a palliative for the destructiveness of his own thought, Nietzsche devised an aristocratic humanism centred on the idea of human self-transcendence, a pantheistic monism affirming above all else the divine self-sufficiency and 'innocence' of the eternally repeated evolutionary cycle of history. He offered a philosophy which might be called 'vitalism' which in the sense that its supreme positive value was now Life and Life's enhancement, its supreme negative value biological decadence, and its most far-reaching corollary a critique of intellectual consciousness as such. 'Life' itself thus became a quasi-religious absolute value, relativizing the value of Truth. In so far as the critical and morally conscious intellect stands, as it stood for Schopenhauer, over and against the mindless brutality of the life-drive, judging and condemning it on grounds of compassion, that intellect (*Geist*) must itself be held suspect: it is revealed as the chief form of 'decadence', the handmaid of nihilism, an anti-vital poison. By making Life (*das Leben*) the central touchstone in relation to which everything – art, morality, science and even truth – was to be evaluated and rethought, Nietzsche was offering the epoch that followed him its dominant idea and watchword: Life would now be something like what Reason had been to the Enlightenment or Nature to the age of Goethe. But Nietzsche cannot be defined in terms of one idea, only in terms of dialectical conflict. His failure to integrate the Truth-Life polarity meant that his influence too was ambiguous, indeed paradoxical. Mann and others could find in him both scepticism and the desire to escape from scepticism, both nihilism and the struggle to overcome nihilism, both 'decadence' as a reaction against naïve complacency and the quest for 'the higher health' as a reaction against decadence. These dilemmas, in various forms, show themselves in the early stories by Mann that we are here considering.

Mann's first collection of stories in book form appeared in Berlin in 1898. Samuel Fischer, the head of the great publishing firm then still in its infancy, had an eye for 'modern' literature and for Mann's talent, and Fischer-Verlag was now to become the exclusive publisher of Mann's entire work. The firm also owned the important literary periodical *Neue Deutsche Rundschau*, in which most of these stories also first appeared before publication in book form. The first collection took the title of one of the stories, *Little Herr Friedemann*, which the *Rundschau* had brought out in the previous year; Mann had finished it in 1896. He himself regarded it as the first of his important stories, telling a friend that in writing it he had discovered the 'discreet forms and masks' under which he could communicate his intimate experiences and problems as published fiction. The story is his first fully developed treatment of the theme of the isolated outsider-type, who recurs in variants in many of Mann's works including all these early stories. In this case, the central character has grown up a hunchback as the result of a childhood accident and has attempted to contract out of 'life' by forgoing all sexual attachments; he devotes himself to aesthetic and intellectual pleasures (*Geist*), only to find them all unavailing against the sudden irruption of long-frustrated libidinal forces. We can only guess at the autobiographical basis for this tale, written at the age of twenty-one or less. What is obvious however is the parallel with *Death in Venice*: in both cases the central character's carefully structured way of life is suddenly and unexpectedly destroyed by an overwhelming sexual passion. This motif of erotic 'visitation' (*Heimsuchung*) seems, as he himself observed, to have been of some importance to Mann, in whose later work it continues to recur (examples are Potiphar's wife in *Joseph in Egypt*, Ines Rodde in *Doctor Faustus*, the heroine in his last story *The Delusion*). The point is one to which we must return in the context of *Death in Venice*.

Little Herr Friedemann may fairly be classified as a 'Naturalist' story in the specific sense that it reflects the methods of the contemporary school of literature which adopted that label, and to which Mann always acknowledged his indebtedness; a few of his first *Novellen* were, indeed, published in Naturalist periodicals such as *Die Gesellschaft* and *Die Zukunft*. The movement's chief German practitioner, Gerhard Hauptmann, also used the theme of sexual infatuation or enslavement in his stories (*Bahnwärter Thiel*, 1892) and plays (*Fuhrmann Henschel*, 1898): it was a telling way of emphasizing man's dependence on his physical nature, in accordance with the doctrinaire deterministic positivism that underlay Naturalist theory. To advance beyond Naturalism, as indeed Hauptmann himself did, was one of the young Thomas Mann's main concerns, and we may trace a 'post-naturalist' element in the opening paragraph of *Little Herr Friedemann*, which deliberately parodies the movement's other favourite programmatic theme of alcoholism. The story belongs to a further literary context as well, as an interesting creative variant by Mann of a peripheral situation in Theodor Fontane's recently published and much admired novel of North German life, *Effi Briest* (1895). In Fontane's story the little hunchbacked apothecary, Gieshübler, a modest connoisseur of the arts and a drawing-room musician, is emotionally drawn to the heroine (the beautiful young wife of the new district administrator) but succeeds with tact and good humour in preserving his peaceable existence, based as it is on renunciation. In Mann's more *fin de siècle* version of this, the sad little Herr Friedemann (his name, meaning literally 'peace man', is not accidental) is exposed to the disturbing influence of Wagner's music as well as to the attractions of a woman very different from the innocent Effi. There is already a certain Nietzschean colouring in the motif of the physically inferior type fascinated by ruthless physical vitality, though Frau von Rinnlingen is also conceived as an inwardly sick, problematic nature who recognizes in her deformed admirer a companion in suffering but at the last moment (rather like Ibsen's Hedda Gabler) is too proud to admit their affinity and cruelly spurns him.

Little Herr Friedemann, though to a lesser degree than some of the other early stories such as *Tobias Mindernickel* (1898) or *Little Lucy* (1900), may be said to reflect a Naturalist predilection for 'unpleasant' themes, but in Mann this was far more than a doctrinaire matter. Looking back on his pre-war period, he described himself in one essay as

> a chronicler and analyst of decadence, a lover of the pathological, a lover of death, an aesthete with a proclivity towards the abyss.

And it was also because he was a born storyteller that the later Mann, too, never quite lost his taste for the horrible. Another constant feature of his mature narrative writing also first shows itself in *Friedemann*, where in the already mentioned parodistic opening he uses sophisticated detachment and understatement to make the pitiable event of the baby's accident at the hands of the drunken nurse seem tragicomic. It has been said that the novel, by its realism, is essentially a comic form, whatever tragedies it may contain; and Mann's method certainly bears this out. Parallel examples occur in deathbed scenes in *The Buddenbrooks* (the clinical symptomatology of typhoid as Hanno dies) and *The Magic Mountain* (the onlooker's reflections on the chemical composition of his tears) or in the final scene of *Doctor Faustus*, where, as the hero makes his shocking public confessions before collapsing into madness, his landlady worries about sandwiches and his audience about how to get back to Munich. The effect in all these cases is of course not to destroy pathos but to heighten it, by inverse countersuggestion and an increased illusion of reality.

The Joker, another of the stories in Mann's first book, was finished in April 1897 and first appeared later that year in the *Rundschau*. The German title, *Der Bajazzo*, means literally 'the clown', being formed from the Italian word used in the title of Leoncavallo's opera *I Pagliacci* (1892), which Mann would have known; I have translated it as 'the joker' because this word also suggests the oddity in the pack, the outsider. *The Joker* strongly develops this theme and is also the most clearly autobiographical of the stories before *Tonio Kröger*. Mann, of course, used real material from his own life and family background not only in *The Buddenbrooks* but to a greater or lesser extent in most of his important early fiction. Either Lübeck, his native town, or Munich, his city of adoption, is the at least implicit location in nearly all cases; other recurring motifs are the old patrician family house and its garden, and the central character's parents with their contrasting influences on him. *The Joker* combines all these features and others. In real life, Mann's maternal grandfather, a Lübeck citizen who had settled as a planter in Brazil and married a Portuguese Creole, had returned to Lübeck as a widower with his young daughter, Julia da Silva Bruhns; she, at the age of eighteen an exotic Latin beauty with considerable musical talent, had married Thomas's father, Consul (later Senator) Heinrich Mann. As a child Thomas had felt very close to her; she would play Chopin to him (as in *The Joker*) as well as singing him *Lieder* and reading him fairytales. As in *The Joker*, too, the young Thomas Mann used to spend long hours producing his own operas on a toy puppet theatre. His father had inherited the old-established corn business, but it had done badly during the 1880s and Senator Mann had lost heart. He died in early middle age, when Thomas was sixteen, and the firm went into immediate liquidation (*The Joker*, *Tonio Kröger*). His widow settled in Munich, and Thomas joined her there a little later, in 1893; Munich now became his permanent residence until his emigration in the Nazi period.

The most important autobiographical feature in *The Joker*, however, is its reflection of the young Thomas Mann's state of mind in the years before writing *The Buddenbrooks*, and in this respect it differs interestingly from *Tonio Kröger*, which came after the novel. In both stories the central figure leads a free-floating, unattached existence, as Mann himself was enabled to do by his modest share of the family inheritance, even before his writing began to earn him any income; between 1893 and 1898 his experience of regular employment was limited to six months in an insurance office (a formality scarcely more serious than the Joker's brief apprenticeship to the timber firm) though from November 1898 he worked for nearly two years as reader or junior editor with the satirical weekly *Simplicissimus*. In the late 1890s Mann could not be sure that he was a major creative artist and that he would successfully establish this as his social role: *The Buddenbrooks* had not yet been written. Was he really more than a talented dilettante, lacking the skill and training for any serious occupation?

The Joker, written during his third year in Munich, reflects these uncomfortable doubts, extrapolating them into an experimental *alter ego*, a figure embodying the possibilities of unattached dilettantism. The narrator in this story (the use of the first-person convention is unusual in Mann) resembles in some ways the 'superfluous man' of Russian literary tradition; he is in fact just as much a marked man, a doomed outsider, as the hunchbacked Friedemann, though in a subtler and less obvious way that takes him some time to discover. He begins by thinking himself one of a socially privileged élite and ends by recognizing that he is a decadent failure – not *vornehm* (noble) but *schlechtweggekommen* (inferior), as Nietzsche would have said – with no real identity or place in society at all. Like Friedemann, he discovers that aesthetic epicureanism cannot in the end compensate for human isolation. The unwitting intervention in his life by Anna Rainer, superficially resembling that of Gerda von Rinnlingen in Friedemann's, is however not so much an erotic irruption as a critical revelation of his social nullity, reducing him to self-contempt and despair. Only genuine creative talent will redeem the 'decadent' outsider and at least to some extent integrate him with society. But Mann, in the next three years, proved his status as the creator of a major and successful masterpiece. With *The Buddenbrooks* written, the more confident 'mask' of Tonio Kröger could be adopted.

Mann sent the manuscript of *The Buddenbrooks* to Fischer in July 1900, and a few weeks later wrote *The Road to the Churchyard* as a kind of light-hearted afterthought; it appeared in *Simplicissimus* in September. This short piece parodies not only Naturalism (by reverting for instance to the alcoholism motif) but also Mann's own sub-Nietzschean theme. The boy on the bicycle is referred to merely as 'Life': *das Leben* is personified as a commonplace young cyclist brutally pushing aside the melancholic drunkard who tries to regulate his heedless progress. Mann has here deliberately trivialized Nietzsche's notorious vitalistic myth of the 'blond beast', the heroic aristocratic embodiment of ruthless energy; a similar sentimentalizing reduction will give us the innocuous blond innocents in *Tonio Kröger*. At the same time the grotesque Lobgott Piepsam represents, in the comic vein, a kind of rudimentary intellectual or religious protest against ignorant, unreflecting vitality. This protest is a recurrent one in Mann and was clearly something close to his own feelings. It also obviously contained an element of envy, plain enough in several stories including *The Road to the Churchyard*, the contemporaneous *Tobias Mindernickel* (a psychological study in which the Piepsam-like outsider kills his small dog in a rage at its animal high spirits), *The Joker* and *Gladius Dei*.

Both this last story and *The Road to the Churchyard* were included in Mann's second collection of six *Novellen*, which Fischer brought out early in 1903; it also contained *Little Lucy, The Wardrobe, Tonio Kröger* and *Tristan*, which gave the volume its title. *Gladius Dei* and *Tristan* are linked in a number of ways, as well as both having been written at about the same time (though we know more about the earlier prehistory of *Gladius Dei* from a jotting of 1899 which notes the germ of the story, the motif of a young religious fanatic in an art shop). *Tristan*, possibly also conceived a year or two earlier, was probably finished shortly before Mann's journey to Florence in the spring of 1901, and *Gladius Dei* shortly after his return. Mann gave a public reading of both stories in November of that year, and *Gladius Dei* was first printed in a Vienna periodical in July 1902, whereas *Tristan* did not appear until the 1903 *Novelle* volume. Mann had visited Florence for reasons connected with both *Gladius Dei* and a longer work with which this story had been associated from the beginning, namely the three-act historical drama *Fiorenza* (1905). *Fiorenza* has no great merit as a play and was never successfully produced; but both it and *Gladius Dei*, a brilliant story which Mann himself underrated, are highly significant expressions of a conflict which Mann took over from Nietzsche and which was also deeply rooted in his own temperament.

It may again be abstractly defined as a form of the *Geist-Leben* dilemma: a conflict between his puritanical, morally critical intellect on the one hand, and on the other the experience of visible sensuous beauty, especially as represented in the visual arts and more particularly the art of the Italian Renaissance. The hero in *Gladius Dei* rejects 'art' in this sense for the same reason as he rejects 'life': namely, that both are expressions of unreflecting sensuous vitality. He claims to represent art of a different kind: something more inward, an intellectual literary art that criticizes life in the name of moral values and religious feeling. These complex relationships and antitheses were to be further explored in a major aesthetic essay under the title *Intellect and Art* (*Geist und Kunst*), for which Mann wrote copious notes in the two years immediately preceding *Death in Venice*, but which not surprisingly he never finished. There seems to have been considerable ambivalence in Mann's attitude to the visual arts. His spokesman in *Gladius Dei* objects to them puritanically as products and elaborations of the sexual drive, and therefore as allied to 'life', which is itself a product and elaboration of the sexual drive. (Mann had first learned this from Schopenhauer, who had called the genitals the 'focal point of the life-will', and had even suggested that we are ashamed of them because of our unacknowledged moral awareness that life is an intolerable evil which should be ascetically renounced, or aesthetically redeemed, instead of merely reproduced.)

Mann's ambivalence also embraced Munich, where *Gladius Dei* literally takes place, and Italy, where it symbolically takes place. Of Italy, which he repeatedly revisited, he was to say in Tonio Kröger's words:

> All that *bellezza* gets on my nerves. And I can't stand all that dreadful southern vivacity, all those people with their black animal eyes. They've no conscience in their eyes.

As for Munich, which became his home and that of so many of his fictional characters, it was after all a metropolis of the arts, more especially of the visual arts, and never was this more the case than in the later nineteenth century and in Thomas Mann's time. There was around 1900 what amounted to a German cult of the Italian Renaissance, with Munich as its centre. Since the reign of Ludwig I, the main royal architect of modern Munich, it had been fashionable for Bavarian architects and sculptors and painters to use Italian and especially Florentine models. In the 1840s, for instance, the King had had the Ludwigstrasse built, with the Odeonsplatz at its southern end and on the Odeonsplatz the Feldherrnhalle, an imposing military monument deliberately copied from the Loggia de' Lanzi on the Piazza della Signoria in Florence. Mann refers to the Feldherrnhalle in the story as 'the loggia', and an association, indeed symbolic identification, of Munich with Renaissance Florence at the time of the Medici is central to his concept. But his tribute at the opening of *Gladius Dei* to Munich, this 'resplendent' latter-day city of art, is of course ironical. The negative side of the ambivalence, the unintegrated puritanical part-self, is projected into the dark figure of the fanatical monkish Hieronymus: and he in his turn is to be symbolically identified with the Dominican prior Girolamo Savonarola (1452–98), the fanatical ascetic reformer who rose in protest against the luxuriant neo-pagan cult of sensuous beauty in Lorenzo de' Medici's Florence, won a popular following and political success for a time but was finally condemned and executed as a heretic. Mann had read Villari's biography of Savonarola, and a reproduction of Fra Bartolommeo's portrait of him, on which the description of Hieronymus is based, stood permanently on his desk. 'Hieronymus' and 'Girolamo' are of course the same name, and indeed the whole story might be said to be an ironic elaboration of the fact that the name of the Bavarian capital is derived from the Latin word for a monk.

These latent, almost explicit identifications reach their climax at the end of the story, where Hieronymus, ejected humiliatingly from the art shop, conjures up in his mind's eye a vengeful vision of the 'burning of the worldly vanities' (the notorious incident that took place on the Piazza della Signoria at Savonarola's behest) and himself quotes the imprecation from the Dominican's own *Compendium Revelationum*: 'May the sword of God come down upon this earth, swiftly and soon!' Mann's visit to Florence in 1901 had of course been for the purpose of further researching his historical hero, whom he was to celebrate more explicitly in *Fiorenza*. The core of this drama is the intellectual confrontation between Savonarola and the dying Lorenzo, seen by Mann as the supreme representative of Renaissance neo-paganism and aestheticism. Hieronymus-Girolamo's protest is against an unspiritual philosophy, an 'amoral' cult of form and beautiful physical externalities, against the kind of art that is not an analysis or criticism of life but a mindless glorification of it. But does the creation of beauty not depend upon sensuous inspiration? How, on the basis merely of the protesting (and indeed Protestant) critical intellect, is it possible to achieve a creativity that will be genuinely poetic (*dichterisch*) as distinct from merely literary (*schriftstellerisch*)? For years this problem preoccupied Mann – as a Nietzschean humanist, as a Naturalistic and would-be post-Naturalistic writer. The preoccupation continued in *Intellect and Art* and then in *Death in Venice*, to the hero of which the authorship of the unfinished aesthetic essay was appropriately transferred.

Nietzsche's destructive psychological theories about the basis of critical intellectuality and morality loom large behind *Gladius Dei* and *Fiorenza*. Savonarola's zeal is seen, in Nietzschean terms, as a disguised will to power; both he and Hieronymus represent the psychology of the 'ascetic priest', which Nietzsche analyses in *The Genealogy of Morals*. But the Schopenhauerian ingredient is also plainly detectable in Mann's conception. In both *Gladius Dei* and *Fiorenza* he gives, through the mouths of his protagonists, a definition of *genuine* (literary) art – a definition scarcely intelligible except in the light of Schopenhauer's metaphysics, and which amounts, oddly enough, to a kind of Schopenhauerian aesthetic of literary Naturalism. 'Art', declares Hieronymus at the peroration of his futile sermon in the art shop,

> is not a cynical deception, a seductive stimulus to confirm and strengthen the lusts of the flesh! Art is the sacred torch that must *shed its merciful light into all life's terrible depths, into every shameful and sorrowful abyss*; art is the divine flame that must set fire to the world, until *the world with all its infamy and anguish burns and melts away in redeeming compassion*

(italics mine). The visual arts are being attacked here because they are the wrong sort of art – because they are allied to immediate life, naïve vitality, unreflecting sensuality; and literature ('these luxurious volumes of love poetry') comes under the same condemnation in so far as it, too, is content to be a mere 'seductive stimulus', an 'insolent idolatry of the glistering surface of things'. Such art asserts and celebrates life at the merely empirical level, its subject-matter is no more than what Schopenhauer called 'the world as *Vorstellung*': his word has been rather misleadingly translated as 'idea' and as 'representation' but means something more like 'illusory show', that which is 'put in front' of one, the merely phenomenal ('shown') world which appears to the senses as the manifestation of the universal underlying life-will. For Schopenhauer the portrayal of this 'show' was of course primarily the function of the representational visual arts: music, by contrast, was something profounder, as an expression of pure emotion, the 'will itself'. (It then became possible to assign, as the young Nietzsche did in *The Birth of Tragedy*, an interesting intermediate position to literature.) But Schopenhauer had conceded that in all aesthetic experience, including that inspired by beautiful phenomena, there was that 'will-less' (passionless) contemplative element, by virtue of which the artist could be credited with some degree of asceticism, even described as being half-way between the ordinary man and the saint. When Mann puts into Hieronymus's mouth his rather improbably sophisticated speech on the nature of 'true' art, he seems intent on emphasizing this ascetic, as opposed to sensuous, element in the artist's vision and creative process. He also makes interesting use of Schopenhauer's central ethical concept of compassion –against which, since it entailed 'negation of the life-will', Nietzsche had chiefly polemicized. An apologia of 'compassion' is appropriate in the mouth of Hieronymus, as the representative of a mentality Nietzsche had attacked; but it is also not foreign to Mann, who tended to distance himself from Nietzsche's more ruthless theoretical positions. Hieronymus, in fact, is really talking about Mann's own art, the narrative fiction especially of his early period, in so far as Mann's fiction does indeed explore and illuminate the 'shameful and sorrowful abysses of life', and does so with the basic compassion of the realistic writer. Seen in this light, and in the light of his rather more Schopenhauerian than Christian peroration, Hieronymus's imaginary holocaust of books and pictures is not simply the prescient fantasy of a barbarous act but a vision – almost paralleling the close of Wagner's *Götterdämmerung* – of the redemption of sensuality, and thus of the world, in the 'fire of compassion' that must burn it away.

In *Tristan* Mann uses the same complex procedure as in *Gladius Dei*: its central figure, like Hieronymus, is presented in a parodistic, ironic light during most of the story, but has towards the end, like Hieronymus, a 'peroration' (in this case a letter) in which he comes into his own and reveals himself to be speaking with Mann's voice. In both stories an experimental *alter ego* is caricatured, explored as an extreme case of what he represents (religious fanaticism in the one case, *fin de siècle* aestheticism in the other). Of the writer Detlev Spinell, Mann later explained, in an essay published in 1906, that his intention had been to use this figure satirically, as a judgement on

an undesirable element *in myself*, that lifeless preciosity of the aesthete which I consider supremely dangerous. I gave this character the mask of a literary gentleman I knew, a man whose talent was exquisite but remote from life . . . For the rest, I made my writer an intellectual and a weakling, a fanatical devotee of beauty and a humanly impoverished person. I elevated him to a type, to a walking symbol, and made him suffer a miserable defeat in his confrontation with the comically healthy brutality of a Hanseatic businessman – the husband of the lady in the sanatorium with whom my author has been conducting a high-minded flirtation. It must not be overlooked that *in this character I was castigating myself*

(italics mine). The literary gentleman in question has not been identified with certainty, and Mann may have fictionally combined characteristics of more than one person. In any case, since he twice in this passage acknowledges that Spinell is an aspect of himself, the presentation of him in the story cannot be regarded as wholly negative.

It is interesting to note, as a technique of this carefully ambiguous presentation, Mann's use in *Tristan* of a shadowy narrator-figure with a viewpoint recognizably distinct from his own. This interposed narrator conducts the reader round the sanatorium which is the scene of the story, addressing him in reassuringly humorous tones and, so to speak, mediating between Mann's identification with the aesthete-protagonist and his identification with the normal world of common sense ('there is even a writer here, idling away his time – an eccentric fellow with a name reminiscent of some sort of mineral or precious stone'; '. . . it must be admitted that Herr Spinell's letter did give the impression of smooth spontaneity and vigour, notwithstanding its odd and dubious and often scarcely intelligible content'). Masquerading in the role of this narrator and commentator, Mann ironically affects to share the 'philistine' values of the other patients in the sanatorium and (by implication) of the reader; the comic protagonist thus appears to be further distanced from the author than he in fact is. A similar narrator-device was used in *The Road to the Churchyard* ('It is hard to explain these matters to happy people like yourselves . . . a ruinous liquid which we shall take the precaution of not identifying . . . We are reluctant to acquaint our readers with such matters . . .') though it is a less noticeable feature of *Gladius Dei* and is for good reasons absent from *Tonio Kröger* and *Death in Venice*. It remains, however, one of Mann's characteristic comic or ironic techniques and gains prominence in his increasingly self-conscious later novels.

Tristan is remarkable for its blend of rich farcical comedy with serious and touching elements. Writing to his brother Heinrich in 1901 about his early work on the story, he announced it as 'a burlesque' and commented on the piquancy of writing 'a burlesque with the title *Tristan*'. And although it contains two of Mann's most brilliantly realized comic characters and the great comic scene (comparable to anything in *The Buddenbrooks* or *Felix Krull*) of their final encounter, we should overlook neither the poignancy of their innocent victim, Gabriele (there is no comparable figure in *Gladius Dei* or the other stories), nor the basically serious element of identity between Spinell's values and Mann's. Spinell represents not only the snobbish and absurd affectations of the *l'art pour l'art* cult but also a pessimistic, sceptical, psychologically sophisticated intellectuality entirely characteristic of the young Thomas Mann, and which Mann in his description of this 'figure of satire' barely mentions. Spinell reveals this aspect of himself occasionally in his conversations with Gabriele (in the passage about his early rising for example) but chiefly in his letter to Klöterjahn – a letter which we must take seriously despite the ironic disclaimers deliberately put into the mouth of the narrator. Spinell here declares it to be his 'mission' to uncover uncomfortable truths and 'use intellect and the power of words' to destroy naïvety and disturb complacency. If this is Spinell's view of the function of literature, it may not seem to be borne out by his own novel (to judge by the way the narrator describes it); nevertheless, it is not essentially different from the view expounded by Hieronymus, and both are recognizable as an important aspect of Mann's own literary programme. Spinell and Hieronymus also resemble each other, and Mann, in their basic protest: that of Hieronymus against the vulgar commercialism of near-pornographic *bellezza*, that of Spinell (as of Hanno Buddenbrook before him) against the vulgar materialism of Wilhelmine Germany; that of both, against the mindless grossness of 'nature'.

Spinell sees 'life' as what Klöterjahn stands for and declares himself its mortal enemy – enviously no doubt, but with passionate conviction and in the name of a 'higher principle', as Mann himself later explained in a letter to a young reader. Spinell, he added, is meant to be a comic character but not totally contemptible. The same, of course, can be said of Klöterjahn, and the story brilliantly develops the complex contrast between these two polarized figures. Even their names are symbolic: Klöterjahn's is derived from a Low German dialect word meaning testicles (in High German it might be *Hodenhans*, in English Bollockjohn), whereas 'Spinell' suggests the inorganic sterility of 'some sort of mineral or precious stone' (and according to one perspicacious medical critic, he is in the sanatorium to be treated for impotence resulting from *dystrophia adiposogenitalis*). For Klöterjahn life is business success, buxom women and savoury meals; for Spinell, as for Villiers de l'Isle Adam, it is something that should be left to the servants. The beautiful, consumptive Gabriele is for him not 'Herr Klöterjahn's wife' but a sylph-like creature not of this world; accordingly, comic character or not, he plays the slightly sinister role of deliberately accelerating her death. But her health had been broken in the first place by her marriage to Klöterjahn and by bearing his gross child. In a sense they are both responsible for her death but also for the enhancement and fulfilment of her existence: Klöterjahn on the 'natural' level by making her a wife and mother, Spinell by enlarging her intellectual horizons and taking her, in a ceremony of Beauty and Death, into Tristan's 'magic kingdom of the night'.

Nowhere is the secret identification of Mann with Spinell more evident than in the scene in which this extraordinary Wagnerian seduction is carried out. The composer's name is nowhere mentioned, any more than Lübeck is named in *The Buddenbrooks* or *Tonio Kröger*, or Nietzsche in *Doctor Faustus*. To understand the central role of the *Tristan*-music in the story, we do not need to read this scene as a pastiche of Act 2 of the opera, or a satire on the Wagner cult, or even to know that Mann could have recently read D'Annunzio's *Il Trionfo della Morte* in the *Neue Rundschau*. The 'love duet' scene is an emotional climax to the story, a scene during which Mann's usual irony is almost completely suspended. Even the bored departure of Frau Spatz and the eerie intrusion of Pastorin Höhlenrauch are merely technical devices necessary to punctuate the transitions from the Prelude to the love duet and from the latter's interruption to the *Liebestod*. Mann's evocations of the music follow closely, even verbatim at times, his descriptions of the adolescent Hanno Buddenbrook's solitary pseudo-Wagnerian improvisations at his piano; in both cases he further underlines the erotic implications already evident in the sublime near-pornophony of

Wagner's score. Gabriele Klöterjahn, persuaded that 'the beauty that might come to life under her fingers' is more important than her mere survival, performs this canon of the high mass of nineteenth-century suicidal romanticism; Mann sees no need, moreover, to trivialize with further explanation or comment the mystery into which she is being initiated:

> . . . 'I am not always sure what it means, Herr Spinell . . . What is: *then – I myself am the world?* . . . He explained it to her, softly and briefly. . . . 'Yes, I see . . .'

It has been pointed out that *Tristan* is also linked to the *Jugendstil* or *art nouveau* taste of the period and has a pictorial as well as a musical centrepiece. A turning-point of Gabriele's life has been her first meeting with Klöterjahn on an occasion when she and several of her friends were sitting round a fountain in the garden of her father's house. She mentions this recollection in her first slightly more personal conversation with Spinell, so that in a sense it becomes his first 'meeting' with her too. He at once stylizes the scene in his imagination: with a little golden crown in her hair, the young queen and her six maidens sat round a fountain singing. This is pure *Jugendstil*, and Mann may even have had a particular drawing or painting in mind. In reality, according to Klöterjahn, they were not singing but knitting and discussing a potato recipe. Both versions are equally absurd, and each is true on another level. The garden scene is thus a focal point representing the contrasting aspects of Gabriele herself as the two men see her. The fountain itself seems to symbolize her destiny: its rising and falling jets are the waxing and waning of human life, the assertion and surrender of individuality. Lives perish, the flow of life continues, the great cycle of life and death is unbroken. *Tristan* is thus a story rich in symbolic implications, and this is one of the ways in which it may be said to anticipate *Death in Venice*, both technically and thematically.

Although *Tonio Kröger* was not finished until late in 1902, the germ of its conception goes back to September 1899, when Mann left Munich for a short holiday in Denmark, spending about a week at the little seaside resort of Aalsgaard on the Øresund. On the way there he had revisited his native Lübeck for the first time since leaving it five years earlier, and spent a few days there incognito. It was then, at the Hotel Stadt Hamburg, that the bizarre incident occurred in which, like Tonio Kröger, he was nearly arrested by mistake as some kind of adventurer from foreign parts. The story evidently first took shape in his mind during this journey, though it did not reach its final form until more than three years later. It was intended for inclusion in the *Tristan* volume, but even after the publication date of this had been deferred until March 1903, *Tonio Kröger* was still unfinished when the proofs of the other five stories in the volume were already to hand. In the event, it appeared in this second collection, as well as in the February issue of the *Neue Rundschau*.

Tonio Kröger had essentially been born of two interacting themes, one intellectual and one deeply personal (in this respect it resembles *Death in Venice*). The intellectual material was Mann's continuing argument with himself about the psychological origins and effects of literary talent: particularly, at this time, the question of whether an intellectually sophisticated kind of literary creativity, involving irony and detachment, did not dehumanize the artist, diminishing his capacity for compassion, driving him into a kind of emotional limbo, depriving him increasingly of his ability to feel. This was compounded by the already familiar Nietzschean problem of philosophical dyspepsia: knowledge and insight (*Erkenntnis*) that seemed inevitably to entail disillusionment, pessimism and ethical nihilism, to the point at which one rebels against it in what Tonio Kröger was to call *Erkenntnisekel*, the nausea of knowledge. The intellectual artist's necessary constant struggle against naïvety and cliché, both of style and thought, thus appears as a chilling and humanly alienating process. In this dilemma Mann was not helped by the reaction of many critics to his early stories, which were widely judged to be unpleasant and morbid in their themes and to betoken cynicism and heartlessness in their author. Mann continued to be particularly sensitive to the accusation that he lacked human warmth. Writing in August 1904 to his future wife, Katia Pringsheim, he complains of 'that old whining about my coldness of heart' and adds:

> Only four or five people in Germany know what irony is, and that it is not necessarily the product of a withered mind. One tries to write pointedly and to husband one's resources, and thereby proves that one

is a soulless conjuror. I am always surprised they have not declared Wagner to be an ice-cold *faiseur* because he puts the *Liebestod* at the end of the act.

The accusation cannot, however, have entirely surprised him, and it is clear that his main purpose, as he came to complete *Tonio Kröger*, was to perform with it a public recantation of his alleged cynicism, nihilism and inhumanity.

Privately, the young Thomas Mann was anything but unemotional. The other indispensable element in the story's genesis, which enabled him to use the 'Tonio Kröger' theme for the intended personal manifesto, was the complex of emotional experiences associated with his nostalgic journey of September 1899. The way this journey is elaborated in the closing chapters of the *Novelle* makes it clear that it is no mere episode but an inner event which the whole of the rest of the story prepares. The opening chapters, laying the foundations that make this closing sequence meaningful, describe the northern land of lost content to which Tonio Kröger will make his dreamlike, haunted return. As in *The Joker* and *The Buddenbrooks*, Mann here draws heavily on facts and memories of his early life. He had in fact disliked his Lübeck school as much as all three of these works suggest; he had despised the masters, earned bad reports, been happiest during the family's summer holidays by the sea at the old Kurhaus in Travemünde. But, as *A Sketch of My Life* also tells us, there had been an original of 'Hans Hansen': a 'beloved friend', Armin Martens, to whom he had written poems. The boy, in adult life, took to drink and came to a sad end in Africa. Later, there had been a 'dark girl with pigtails' whom he met at private dancing lessons conducted by a Herr Knoll from Hamburg; she became the 'blonde Ingeborg' of the story. A factor that Mann does not mention, however, was evidently more immediate and important for the story than either of these memories, namely his intensely emotional attachment to the young painter Paul Ehrenberg, one of two brothers with whom he became friendly in December 1899. Ehrenberg was three years younger than Mann, had some physical resemblance to Armin Martens, and must have taken over the latter's role, as well as perhaps that of Willri Timpe, another beloved schoolmate. The gestation period of *Tonio Kröger* largely coincided with the most intense phase of this friendship.

Mann married Katia Pringsheim in 1905, and the marriage, of which there were six children, was so far as we know happy enough. His posthumous private diaries however, published since only recently, confirm that he retained a homosexual orientation of feeling: in later life he could still, if only fleetingly, fall romantically in love with young men. Entries of 1935 and 1942, for instance, refer nostalgically to his passion for the seventeen-year-old Klaus Heuser whom he had met in 1927:

> . . . the last variation of a love that will probably never be kindled again. How strange: happy and requited at fifty – and there's an end to it. Goethe stayed the erotic course till he was over seventy-nine – 'always girls'. But in my case I suppose the inhibitions are stronger and one tires earlier, even apart from differences in vitality

(14 September 1935). In 1942 he records poring over 'old diaries' (which a few years later he destroyed):

> from the Klaus Heuser period, when I was a happy lover . . . Well, there it is – I have 'lived and loved'. Dark eyes that shed tears for me, beloved lips that I kissed – it all happened, to me too it was given, I shall be able to tell myself this as I die

(20 February 1942). Mann kept such diaries all his life but allowed no one to see them. In 1945 he burned them all except some written between 1918 and 1921 and those written after the beginning of his involuntary exile in 1933; those not destroyed were to be kept unpublished until twenty years after his death. The diaries of the Paul Ehrenberg period have therefore also disappeared.

Curiously, however, another contemporary document indirectly expresses the intensity of Mann's feelings in that case: namely, the still extant work notes for a novel about Munich society which he was planning in 1902 but later abandoned. It was to have been called *The Loved Ones* (*Die Geliebten*) and was apparently to have been largely about the relationship between a charming and rather flirtatious young violinist called Rudolf and a woman, Adelaide, who is infatuated with him over a period of years. She eventually murders him by shooting him in a tramcar after a concert (this incident was to be based on an exactly similar murder that had taken place in Dresden, probably in 1901). The biographical significance of the copious notes for this work, dating chiefly from 1902, lies in the way Mann refers to them in a diary of 1934, unpublished until 1977. In 1934 he was working on *Joseph in Egypt*, and in particular on the story of Potiphar's wife Mut-em-enet's fatal passion for the beautiful young Joseph. The entry (6 May) reads in part:

> I was looking through old notebooks for some verses of Elizabeth Barrett Browning and became engrossed in notes which I made at that time about my relations with P. E. in the context of the projected novel *The Loved Ones*. The passion and melancholy psychologizing emotion of those far-off days came through to me with a familiar ring of the sadness of life . . . I had already been quietly searching for my notations of passion from that period, as material for Mut-em-enet's infatuation, and I shall be able to make partial use of them in depicting her helpless stricken state.

Mann appears here to be referring to the work notes rather than to his personal diaries; we can only speculate on what further 'passionate' material for use in the Joseph story he may or might have found in the latter, but it is clear enough that the line between them and the work notes for *The Loved Ones* cannot be rigidly drawn, and that both must have recorded emotions which Mann was then himself experiencing. About ten years after the surviving 1934 diary entry. Mann finally made a more direct use of the Paul Ehrenberg material by incorporating it in *Doctor Faustus*: 'Rudolf' appears as the young violinist Rudi Schwertfeger who is shot in the tram by his infatuated former mistress, after having also formed a homosexual relationship with the composer-hero, who regards himself as secretly responsible for Rudolf's murder. The crisscrossing identifications here are material for further speculation on Mann's emotional life and working methods. In the same diary entry of 6 May 1934 Mann remarks of the Ehrenberg relationship that so 'overwhelming' and 'intoxicating' an experience had 'only happened – and quite rightly – once in my lifetime'. He adds that the earlier attachments to 'A. M. and W. T.' were childlike by comparison and refers to the 'youthful intensity of feeling, the careless rapture and deep shock of that central experience of my heart when I was twenty-five'.

Nevertheless, the memory of Armin and of the 'passion of innocence' he felt for him was also (according to a letter written to another old schoolfriend in the last year of his life) nostalgically cherished to the end 'like a treasure' (19 March 1955, to Hermann Lange).

The fact that in later life Mann so often declared *Tonio Kröger* to be his favourite among his works and even (which is not quite the same thing) his best work is partly to be explained by the story's close association with these youthful loves. The 'experiment' of the story was to give 'Tonio Kröger' the problem he himself had experienced, namely the dilemma of how to be human without losing the ability to write well, and to make his *alter ego* solve this problem by recovering his ability to feel, in the course of a nostalgic return to the scenes of his youth. The effect of nostalgia is chiefly brought about by Mann's use of leitmotivistic repetition, a technique which he did not invent but notably developed in various ways, especially in *Tristan*, *Tonio Kröger* and *Death in Venice*. The story is unified by a 'musical' nexus (as Mann liked to call it) of recurring phrases, descriptions, and even characters and situations. Thus as Tonio revisits Lübeck in Chapter 6, Hans Hansen is never mentioned by name but poignantly recalled by the exact repetition of words associated with him in Chapter 1; and in Aalsgaard the scene of the dancing class 'repeats itself' exactly, culminating in the 'recurrence', as it seems, of Hans and Inge themselves. The text makes it clear, on closer inspection, that they are not the 'real' Hans and Inge but representatives of the Nordic type which for Tonio Kröger has acquired symbolic value (it may also be that Mann intended a private allusion to the 'recurrence' of Armin Martens in Paul Ehrenberg). They represent innocence, immediacy, the unproblematic norm, 'life in its seductive banality', the very un-Nietzschean kind of Life that Tonio Kröger has declared himself able to love. The leitmotif closest to the story's central theme is the recurring statement about the hero that 'his heart was alive then' (in Lübeck) and its contrary 'his heart was dead' (in Munich); and the essence of the 'positive' ending is that in this case the experimental self is not repudiated, divided off from the author as what 'but for the grace of God' he might have been, but accepted into the more complex substance of the experimenter, welcomed so to speak into the joy of his creator. Tonio Kröger's function is to represent a conciliatory solution which Mann would have liked to find for the Intellect-Life problem: he is to reverse Spinell's declaration of hatred, repudiate aristocratic aestheticism and disclaim nihilism. Art and Intellect are to be no longer at open war with ordinary existence but sentimentally, unhappily of course and with 'just a touch of contempt', in love with it. Mann and Kröger are thus identified in the new position of still distanced but reconciled outsider. Their identity is signalized at the end by the repetition, as the last sentence of the story, of the statement made about the hero in the last sentence of Chapter 1: there it was made of him by the author, now he says it of himself.

So optimistic and programmatic a conclusion represents a considerable personal investment by Mann, and it is not surprising that *Tonio Kröger* was a work he came to value so highly. This is partly also to be explained by its immediate and continuing success with the critics. The recantation had worked, and it became a critical tradition simply to endorse Mann's judgement of the story. More recent commentators have been less sure, and even Mann seems to have had doubts at first, writing to a friend that *Tonio Kröger* contains 'a declaration of love for life which is almost inartistic in its clarity and directness. Is this declaration incredible? Is it mere rhetoric??' (to Kurt Martens, 28 March 1906). On his own showing (in Kröger's aesthetic theory as expounded to Lisaveta in Chapter 4), it could have been expected that a piece of writing so full of the author's own heart and hopes would not wholly avoid the pitfall of sentimentality. Many readers today, perhaps, will prefer the harder cutting edge of *Tristan* or *Gladius Dei*, both of which may also, after all, be read as repudiations of decadence. In addition, *Tristan* and *Gladius Dei* both point forward in interesting ways to *Death in Venice*: if *Tonio Kröger* did so, it was chiefly in a sobering negative sense. The Devil, notoriously, has most of the good tunes, and the new 'positive' *Tonio Kröger* position could not last: *Death in Venice* was to represent a reversion to the tragic view of the artist, while at the same time advancing into a new dimension of art.

During the eight years or so between the completion of *Tonio Kröger* and the writing of *Death in Venice* – a period which also included the first six years of his marriage – Mann produced no major work. *Fiorenza* is generally accounted a failure, and the short novel *Royal Highness* (1909), though it has interest and charm, cannot begin to compare in significance with *The Buddenbrooks* or *The Magic Mountain*, any more than the few *Novellen* written during those years can stand comparison with those of the breakthrough period at the turn of the century, 1897–1902, which must count as Mann's first mature creative phase. On the other hand, these relatively unproductive intermediate years saw a number of important beginnings and reorientations. Mann's reflections were now being influenced by his own increasing fame and by new ideas about art current in the generation that was following him. What were the special problems and vulnerabilities of being the kind of writer he was, in the years of maturity that lay ahead? Could he perhaps become a different kind of writer? Could not some intoxicating impulse be found, some *Rausch*, even if it were of diabolic origin, that would give his flagging creativity a new direction? It is no accident that in 1904 one of Mann's notebooks briefly records for future use the motif of an artist of genius who bargains with the Devil for special inspiration by deliberately contracting syphilis. It is the germ of *Doctor Faustus*, to be used forty years later; and one of the at first inconspicuous links between *Doctor Faustus* and *Death in Venice* is that the latter opens with Aschenbach, a mature but tired writer, unconsciously desiring just such a new and mysterious stimulus.

At the *Tonio Kröger* stage, the problem of *Geist*, of the critical intellect, had been that it combined with artistic creativity to threaten the writer with personal dehumanization. But *Geist* is now threatening his creativity itself, by binding it to a mode now outmoded. The coming generation seemed tired of analysis and introspection, of pathological themes, of naturalism and psychology. The appeal was increasingly to the other pole of the Nietzschean dialectic: *Leben*, regeneration, vitality, irrationalism, the Renaissance cult. The world of passion and beauty was now again intellectually fashionable. But Mann, although he had already taken sides with Savonarola against Lorenzo, had not yet resolved the personal Lorenzo-Savonarola conflict in himself, the conflict between passion and puritanism. It seems also to underlie his continuing interest in the Friedemann motif, that of the erotic visitation, the emotional invasion that changes a whole existence. He perceived the same conflict in Nietzsche and was fascinated by a perhaps apocryphal anecdote which he had read in the memoirs of one of Nietzsche's friends: the young Nietzsche, it reported, had as a shy and austere student unwittingly strayed into a brothel, fled from it in embarrassment, but returned later to seek out the beautiful prostitute he had encountered. Mann was to transfer this story to the Nietzsche-like hero of *Doctor Faustus*, combining it with the 1904 germ idea for his Devil's-bargain novel. It was a variant of the Friedemann theme, and a variant also of the theme of the creative artist's tragedy. A further modulation of the latter also appears in a 1905 notebook, as the tragedy of an *older* writer who destroys himself by ambitiously pursuing achievements that exceed his capacities. This version (also eventually reflected in the Aschenbach story) clearly had dramatic possibilities if combined with the Friedemann motif as well.

At some stage in these pre-*Death in Venice* years (we do not know the exact chronology) Mann came to consider a specific historical instance of an elderly and renowned writer who loses his dignity by falling in love: that of the seventy-four-year-old Goethe and his infatuation, while on holiday in Marienbad in 1823, with the seventeen-year-old Ulrike von Levetzow. (Goethe, in fact, came quickly to his senses, though not before going so far, almost incredibly, as to initiate a proposal of marriage with the girl.) It seems from Mann's own account that his plan to write a story on this subject which might be called *Goethe in Marienbad* dated from before 1911; in any case, it was not dropped until some years after the publication of *Death in Venice*, to which the proposed Goethe-*Novelle* would have been a tragi-comic parallel piece. The story in both cases was that of a highly disciplined but emotionally isolated and perhaps instinctually deprived man of mature years whose 'Olympian' existence is invaded by the dark inner forces of disorder. The *Novelle* Mann actually wrote, as we know, was this story with a difference. It was still a story about an artist's *loss of dignity* (*Entwürdigung*), and Mann afterwards frequently insisted that the essential theme was this, the capacity of 'passion' as such – any infatuation or obsessive love – to destroy dignity. In Mann's personal variant the passion becomes a homosexual one, although by his account this was not of the essence of the original conception. The reason for the change, we are not surprised to learn, was the final precipitating personal factor in the genesis of *Death in Venice*: a journey involving an emotional experience. The same had happened in the genesis of *Tonio Kröger*, but with the journey taking place at the beginning of the work's incubation period: in 1911 it came at the end.

In May of that year Mann travelled to the Adriatic for a short holiday with his wife and his brother Heinrich; they stayed first on the island of Brioni near Pola, where they read in the Austrian papers the news of the death of Gustav Mahler (whom Mann had recently met and whom he deeply admired). After about a week they crossed to Venice. Mann tells us in *A Sketch of My Life* that on this journey everything played into his hands, as indeed it had done in *Tonio Kröger*:

> Nothing is invented: the wanderer at the Northern Cemetery in Munich, the gloomy ship from Pola, the foppish old man, the suspect gondolier, Tadzio and his family, the departure prevented by a muddle with the luggage, the cholera, the honest clerk at the travel agency, the sinister singer . . .

He did in fact modify certain details (the cholera outbreak was in Palermo, not in Venice, the lost luggage was Heinrich's, etc.), but the essential point which he of course does not underline in the autobiographical essay, the inner event round which the rest of the story crystallized, was the 'passion' itself, his sudden intense, if brief, infatuation with the real 'Tadzio'. The Polish boy was identified in 1964 as Wladyslaw, the future Baron Moes, born on 17 November 1900, who was on holiday at the Lido in May 1911 with his mother and three sisters. Mann heard this attractive child addressed by diminutives of his name such as 'Wladzio' or 'Adzio' and, after taking advice, decided to stylize this as Tadzio (from Tadeusz). Baroness Moes's friend Mme Fudakowska was also there with her own son, Jan, the Jasio (vocative 'Jasiu') of the story who fights with Tadzio. Wtadystaw Moes learned twelve years later that a story had been written 'about him' and read it, but never identified himself to Mann; only some years after the latter's death did he give Mann's Polish translator an impeccable account, supported by photographs, of the details of that particular Venetian holiday (including 'an old man' looking at him on the beach and his quarrel with Fudakowski). Curiously, too, while Luchino Visconti was making his film of *Death in Venice* in the late 1960s, Jan Fudakowski also turned up, bearing a photograph of himself and Wladyslaw taken on the Lido in May 1911.

Mann no doubt somewhat dramatizes his feelings about this pre-adolescent boy, whose age he amended from ten and a half to fourteen.

Katia in her later recollections confirmed that her husband was 'fascinated' by him, though no to the point of following him all over Venice. But in this extrapolated self 'Aschenbach' (his age too is fictionalized to fifty-three, seventeen years older than Mann was in 1911) the experiment is clearly, on the personal level, an exploration of the possibilities of homosexual emotion, while on the intellectual and creative level it tries out in earnest those of a certain kind of post-naturalistic, post-decadent aesthetic theory and practice. Mann was here specifically influenced by the short-lived 'Neo-classical' reaction against naturalism, a movement represented by some of his minor contemporaries (Paul Ernst, Samuel Lublinski) to which for a time he felt drawn. We have to distinguish here (though the distinction is very fine) between what Aschenbach is represented as doing in writing his own works and what Mann himself does in writing *Death in Venice*. In the former, the emphasis falls strongly on the creation and exaltation of beauty, though this is not the neo-romantic, musical and decadent, introverted and life-negating aesthetic cult represented by Spinell (which Aschenbach has 'overcome') but a 'neo-classical' principle, with a strongly ethical, educative and humanistic colouring; Aschenbach stresses the 'moral' value of disciplined artistic form, as well as resolutely repudiating all introspective *Erkenntnisekel* and cynicism. Mann, too, in telling the story of Aschenbach, seeks to create and evoke a kind of visible, concrete, external but symbolic beauty, such as he has not aimed at before in his fiction; the basis, nevertheless, is still one of 'naturalism' in the sense of literary realism, and there is a continuing 'naturalistic' implication of compassionate psychological under-standing. He thus seems both to encapsulate the contemporary neo-classical tendency and to distance himself from it. The *Death in Venice* 'experiment' with the noble aesthetic moralist Aschenbach ends unsuccessfully, that is to say tragically, in Aschenbach's destruction; nevertheless, the story itself, transcending the traditional and prosaic modes in what was probably Mann's most important technical breakthrough, creates a noble stylistic synthesis worthy of its regretfully repudiated hero.

In achieving this striking fusion of realism and concrete symbolism, Mann was decisively assisted by the nature of the subject-matter and by the strange complex of real-life experiences on his Venetian journey,

this uncanny coming-together of seemingly significant and intercon-
nected events as if by some unwitting and magical authorial command.
A nexus of coincidences and chance impressions, none inexplicable but
many indefinably disturbing, is heightened in its meaningfulness by the
use of leitmotif: recurring phrases hint at the identity of recurring
figures, noticeable to the reader but apparently never to Aschenbach,
who thus moves ironically to his doom like a Greek hero only half aware
of what is happening. Strangers he 'happens' to meet or observe are on
another level messengers of death, incarnations of the wild god
Dionysus to whom his excessive Apolline discipline betrays him.
Lingering too long in the breakfast-room at the behest of his still half-
conscious passion (and one of the most remarkable features of the story is
the subtlety with which it portrays the *process* of falling in love), he
himself unwittingly causes the 'fateful' loss of his luggage. Sinister,
half-apprehended forces intrude into the naturalist-realist world as
externalizations of half-understood psychological developments.
Aschenbach's 'case' could have been presented merely as a medical-
psychological study (reaction against libidinal over-deprivation, a
'climacteric' episode at the age of fifty-three, as Mann himself pointed
out): instead, it is given a mythological dimension as well, as the drama
of a foredoomed initiate and the revenge of an insulted god. Venice,
too, as a setting both shabbily real and mythically mysterious, lent itself
to this double purpose. Even the cholera epidemic, invading Europe
from India, is on its other level the irruption of Dionysus, whose cult
swept into Greece from the east.

But the chief visible yet enigmatic, real yet symbolic element is of
course Tadzio himself. He is the meeting-point of the Apolline cult of
disciplined sculptured beauty and the dark destructive longing of Eros-
Dionysus. He is presented with extraordinary subtlety, mysteriously yet
very realistically poised somewhere between innocence and a certain
half-conscious sensuous coquetry. The remarkable descriptions of him
in the last three chapters rise above Mann's normal ironic tone to an
ecstatic seriousness, lyrically exalted yet saturated with sensuality and
emotion, in which the narrating author and the fictional contemplative
lover are unmistakably identified. Tadzio's 'sublime background', the
sun and the sea, are evoked in similar celebratory language, which
breaks from time to time into the rhythm of Homer's hexameters. These

central 'hymnic' passages (as Mann was to call them) resemble in some ways the unironic evocations of Wagner's music in the central scene of *Tristan*, but with a decisive difference. Ten years after *Tristan*, Mann is seeking to break both the Wagnerian spell and the naturalistic counterspell. His post-*Tonio Kröger* aesthetic programme has been a struggle to move from *Geist* to *Kunst*, from moralizing or demoralizing analysis to a more resolute and extroverted cult of beautiful form. But he now seems more clearly than before to be engaged in a corresponding personal struggle to achieve the kind of neo-pagan sensibility in which his sensuous impulses could be affirmed. The model for such a break-through was evidently the culture of ancient Greece, as Mann came to understand it at the time of writing *Death in Venice*.

The classical Greek element in the story is essential and central, and one of the ways in which Visconti seriously damaged his film version was by totally omitting it, preferring to identify his Aschenbach with the post-Wagnerian, neo-romantic atmosphere of Mahler's music (although, in fact, Mahler has virtually nothing to do with *Death in Venice* except that Mann had been moved by the news of his death and decided to give Aschenbach the composer's first name and physical appearance). But in treating a homosexual theme, it was natural that Mann should seek to associate it strongly with a pre-Christian world which looked upon homosexuality as normal; and his notebooks attest that while working on *Death in Venice* he not only refreshed his memories of Homer but, above all, immersed himself in the study of the Platonic theory of love. He read especially the *Symposium* and the *Phaedrus* and Plutarch's *Erotikos* – all of which he interestingly and perhaps knowingly misquotes in the text of the story. His understanding of the theory (for purposes of the Aschenbach project and as transmitted through Aschenbach) has a strongly monistic and paganizing, aesthetic and sensuous tendency; in fact it has been shown that Mann's use of the material seems to aim at a synthesis of Platonic doctrine with pagan mythological elements. He evidently understood Plato's perception of the profound continuity between 'Eros' and the 'higher' intellectual or spiritual faculties – a perception which of course amounts to a transfiguration of sexual love rather than a devaluation of it. Mann was familiar with Nietzsche's observation that human sexuality (*Geschlechtlichkeit*) branches upwards into the highest reaches of our intellectuality (*Geistigkeit*); and this observation may be said to reach back to Plato as well as forwards to Freud, if we understand Freud as integrative rather than reductive, and Plato as integrative rather than 'puritanical'. Mann's excerpts from Plato and Plutarch in his *Death in Venice* work notes, as well as the Platonizing passages in the story itself, suggest that he was aware of this. The Platonic Eros theory, with its 'positive' aspects thus emphasized, offered him the most appropriate cultural framework for an experience of love which was both sexual and visionary: it could become the classical philosophic endorsement for Aschenbach's passionate vision of Tadzio. Why then, we may ask, is Mann's view of this passion polarized rather than integrated? In other words, why does *Death in Venice* end tragically, rather than as a story of inner liberation? The answer seems to lie both in Mann's psychology and in his artistry, his instinct as a dramatic storyteller.

In Mann's presentation of Aschenbach's experience, the reader is constantly invited to take two opposite views simultaneously: one of them positive (because aesthetic, neo-pagan, imaginative and mythologizing) and the other negative (because naturalistic-moralistic). This *ambiguity* in the best sense of the word is of course an artistic enrichment, but it also seems to reflect a profound *ambivalence* (in the sense of emotional conflict) in Mann himself, such as we have already noticed in other contexts. *Death in Venice* is even plainer evidence than *Friedemann* or *Gladius Dei* that Mann's 'puritan' temperament conflicted at a deep psychological level with the passionate and sensuous elements in his nature, whether homosexual or otherwise. The inner drama of the story is sustained by this struggle, this schizoid cerebral dread of instinctual disorder, which we encounter again and again in Mann's works. In Aschenbach's case we have a man committed to order, who in his maturity has turned even beautiful form into moral affirmation and art itself into discipline and service, into respectability and dignity. But the compromise solution cannot hold, the element of sensuality in the vision of beauty cannot be accepted and integrated. Instead, it is rejected (in a quite un-Platonic way), and the opposites thus remain dramatically polarized. Mann projects into Aschenbach not only his homosexuality but also his puritan repudiation of it: Aschenbach's declaration of love to the absent Tadzio at the end of Chapter 4 is described as 'impossible, absurd, depraved and ludicrous' as

well as 'sacred nevertheless, still worthy of honour', and in his last
interior monologue of Chapter 5 he condemns it as 'horrifying criminal
emotion (*grauenhafter Gefühlsfrevel*)'. The absurdity of imagining such
strictures in the mouth of Plato or even of Socrates at once reveals
their modern, quite un-Greek and indeed idiosyncratic character.

Mann's own most far-reaching and interesting published statement
about *Death in Venice* is his letter of 4 July 1902 to Carl Maria Weber.
Weber was a young poet who had understandably formed the
impression that the story was an exercise in anti-homosexual propaganda (that the opposite impression was formed by some of its other
indignant readers is also understandable). He wrote anxiously to Mann
for clarification. Mann replies diplomatically that he respects homosexual feeling, that it is far from alien to his own experience, and that
he had no intention of negating or repudiating it in the story. He goes on
to analyse the conflicting underlying tendencies of *Death in Venice* as
he sees them:

> The *artistic* reason [for the misunderstanding] lies in the difference
> between the Dionysian spirit of lyric poetry as it individualistically and
> irresponsibly pours itself out, and the Apolline spirit of epic narrative
> with its objective commitment and its moral responsibilities to
> society. What I was trying to achieve was an equilibrium of sensuality
> and morality, such as I found ideally realized in [Goethe's novel] *The
> Elective Affinities*, which, if I remember rightly, I read five times while
> I was writing *Death in Venice*. But you cannot have failed to notice
> that the story in its innermost nucleus has a hymnic character, indeed
> that it is hymnic in origin. The painful process of objectivization
> which the necessities of my nature obliged me to carry out is described
> in the prologue to my otherwise quite unsuccessful poem *The Lay of
> the Little Child*:
>
> > 'Do you remember? A higher intoxication, amazing
> > Passionate feelings once visited you as well, and they cast you
> > Down, your brow in your hands. To hymnic impulse your spirit
> > Rose, amid tears your struggling mind pressed urgently upwards
> > Into song. But unhappily things stayed just as they had been:
> > For there began a process of sobering, cooling, and mastering –
> > See, what came of your *drunken song*? An *ethical fable*!'*

But the artistic occasion for misunderstanding is in fact only one among others, the purely intellectual reasons are even more important: for example, the *naturalistic* attitude of my generation, which is so alien to you younger writers: it forced me to see the 'case' as *also* pathological and to allow this motif (climacteric) to interweave iridescently with the symbolic theme (Tadzio as Hermes Psychopompos). An additional factor was something even more intellectual, because more personal: a fundamentally *not at all 'Greek'* but Protestant and puritanical ('bourgeois') nature, my own nature as well as that of the hero who undergoes the experience; in other words our *fundamentally mistrustful, fundamentally pessimistic view of passion as such and in general* . . . [italics here mine]. Passion that drives to distraction and destroys dignity = that was really the subject-matter of my tale.

Mann goes on to explain that he had not originally intended a homosexual theme but that of Goethe and Ulrike, and that what had changed his mind was 'a personal lyrical travel-experience which moved me to make it all still more pointed by introducing the motif of "forbidden love" '. The letter then continues at some length, but these extracts contain the essential points. Mann was evidently aware that neither he nor 'Aschenbach' had been 'Greek' enough for a real breakthrough into an integrated neo-pagan sensibility, much as he perhaps desired to achieve this. Nor, indeed, were they moralists enough either; certainly no whole-hearted moralist speaks in the letter to Weber, in one passage of which Mann also remarks that 'the moralist's standpoint [is] *of course one that can only be adopted ironically*' (italics mine). In *Death in Venice*, it seems, he had been nearly successful in achieving an affirmative view of the 'Aschenbach' experience, only to be defeated by the old self-punitive puritan tendency which comes so strongly to the fore in the last chapter of the story. How, under its pressure, was he to devise a more positive, balanced ending?

We should bear in mind that this whole last chapter belongs to the purely fictional stage of the 'experiment', when Aschenbach has been acting as Mann himself never did in reality. It is here that Aschenbach embarks on his final self-destructive course and (to use Mann's terms)

*Translation (which I have slightly altered) by T. J. Reed, in *Thomas Mann: The Uses of Tradition* (1974), p. 152. As Mr Reed points out, these lines taken in conjunction with Mann's remarks to Weber may mean that his original impulse was to write about the Venice experience in verse, probably in hexameters, rather than to turn it into a *Novelle*.

'loses his dignity', both in a quite ordinary sense (by following Tadzio about, resorting to cosmetics, letting his passion become noticeable to the boy's family) and more importantly in the deeper sense of losing that rational freedom of the will which moralists in the Kantian tradition would call the specific dignity (*Würde*) of man. Aschenbach becomes unable to do the rational, self-preservative and 'decent' thing, which is to warn the Polish family of the epidemic and leave Venice himself immediately. This failure (and not of course the homosexual infatuation as such) is his real 'fall', his *Entwürdigung* as Mann calls it – meaning 'degradation' in the strict sense of demotion from a higher rank to a lower, from dignity to indignity. In terms of Mann's psychology, we may interpret this self-damaging, 'degraded' behaviour of the experimental ego as a fictional development or extrapolation which Mann's own self-disapproval needed in order to corroborate and rationalize itself. There are, however, artistic as well as psychological reasons why the last chapter of *Death in Venice* should take this negative turn. Whatever may have been the degree of Mann's or Aschenbach's intolerance or tolerance of the emotional and behavioural extravagance portrayed by the story, *Death in Venice* was clearly intended as a *dramatization* of the Venice events in *Novelle* form, a dramatic *Novelle* which required a dramatic conclusion. It is structurally necessary that 'Ashenbach's' experience should be brought full cycle; rather as Goethe remarked of the tragic ending of his *Elective Affinities* that it was needed to restore the balance after 'sensuality' had triumphed. Mann knew that tragic implications were inherent from the start in such a love, as in any serious realistic treatment of an erotic theme, and they demanded to be represented in the story's structure.

This temperamentally and artistically necessary combination of contrasting elements in *Death in Venice* was seen by Mann himself, in the letter to Weber, not as a discrepancy or inconsistency but as an 'iridescent interweaving' (*changieren*; I have slightly expanded the translation of this word to bring out the clearly implied metaphor of *changierende Seide*, i.e. alternating or 'shot' silk, in which threads of contrasting colour are interwoven). This striking image is in fact the key to the structure of *Death in Venice*. It is not really necessary to postulate (as T. J. Reed did in the book already referred to and in his earlier annotated edition of the story*) any radical change of plan by Mann in the course of writing it, if by this is meant a simple linear development from an originally celebratory conception of the homosexual theme (possibly in verse) to a later more prosaic, critical and, at least ostensibly, moralizing treatment. It is more likely that a complexity of conflicting elements was fully present from the beginning. There may have been some shift of emphasis (as seems to be suggested by the last two lines of the passage from *The Lay of the Little Child* that Mann quotes to Weber), but we know too little about the process of the story's composition to be able to reconstruct it with certainty. The finished version is the only one extant and the only one we need. To detect an author's exact attitude to his fictional hero is always problematic, not least with an author of so ironic a disposition as Mann. The remarkable thing is that, notwithstanding any complexity of conception or underlying dramatic conflict in his sensibility, Mann has achieved in *Death in Venice* (as Mr Reed also points out) so near-perfect an artistic synthesis. The finished *Novelle* is, in fact, remarkably lucid and formally integrated; its *opposita* are paradoxically and realistically embraced in a convincing organic whole. Mann himself, after its completion, remarked that for once he seemed to have written something 'completely successful', something entirely self-consistent ('*es stimmt einmal alles*'), which he compared to a many-faceted and 'pure' crystal (letter to Philip Witkop, 12 March 1913). In his letters to his friends during the year it took him to write the story there are, not surprisingly, occasional complaints that he is finding it a difficult task, but the correspondence also, no less naturally, contains expressions of confidence in the progress of his work. Indeed the *Sketch of My Life*, looking back, recalls how the happy coincidences of the 'given' material filled him during the process of composition with a sense of being 'borne up with sovereign ease'. If he felt some indecision about how to end the story (as a letter of April 1912 to his brother suggests), we may guess that this may have been due to a sense that if Aschenbach's drama was to be brought to a not wholly negative, aesthetically satisfying (because balanced) full close, he would have to reach an accommodation with his past and take a step back from Homer and Plato towards naturalism –

*Thomas Mann, *Der Tod in Venedig* (with introduction and notes), Oxford University Press, 1971 (Clarendon German Series).

and perhaps also towards the kind of consummation he had celebrated ten years earlier in *Tristan*.

He did both these things in the two climaxes of the last chapter: the scene of Aschenbach's concluding reflections by the fountain in the depths of Venice, and the closing scene of his death on the beach. In the inner monologue by the fountain, both Mann and Aschenbach finally spell out their negative, disillusioned view not only of Aschenbach but of artistic creativity and 'classical' beauty in general, as well as of the neo-pagan, integrative interpretation of the Eros theory that Mann had tried and failed to embrace. Yet, even at this point, as the defeated and degraded hero collapses despairingly in the shabby, haunted little square, his dramatically necessary 'tragic fall' is mitigated for the sake of a more complex truth. His bitter recital of the ironies of his own situation ('There he sat, the master . . .') itself ironically recalls the 'forthright' moralism of his earlier stance, and this too-much-protesting moralism is thereby implicitly relativized. And Aschenbach's speech of final self-*Erkenntnis* has a sad, paradoxical dignity, the dignity of man's awareness and acceptance of his own destruction ('And now I shall go, Phaedrus . . .'). Contemplating the failure of his *alter ego* to achieve regeneration, Mann must himself revert to the psychological method of his own unregenerate days and to the all-embracing principle that 'understanding is forgiving'. Aschenbach, refusing unlike Mann to mix irony with morality, had repudiated this principle, which now is his only absolution. The 'moral' of Mann's unintended 'ethical fable' seems to be his sobering insight into the difficulty of radically changing, by sheer 'resolution', the kind of person and the kind of artist one is; his conclusion that a writer born into a 'decadent' generation is and remains a vulnerable type, since even the 'overcoming' of decadence may reveal itself as decadence in yet another form.

In the last short section of Chapter 5 that follows, the naturalistic and symbolic threads are again 'iridescently interwoven', and a double view is demanded. Aschenbach sits on the beach watching Tadzio for the last time as he wanders out to sea. Prosaically and factually, Aschenbach is now dying of cholera (in its milder form of rapid collapse into coma) and is in a state of 'menopausal' infatuation verging on delusion. Mythically and poetically, Tadzio's allurement has now become that of the death-god Hermes Psychopompos, the 'guide of souls' to the underworld. And whether or not Aschenbach merely imagines the boy's final gesture as it beckons him out to sea into 'an immensity rich with unutterable expectation', this last pursuit of his vision – of the finite god silhouetted against infinity – raises him paradoxically into a mysterious apotheosis, into that region of indefinable reconciliation in which true tragedy has always ended. In Plato's *Symposium*, the 'wise woman' Diotima explains to Socrates how the initiate of Eros, in the end, 'turns to the open sea of Beauty'; and it may be significant that Mann copied and underlined these words (in Kassner's rather neo-romantically elaborated translation) in his *Death in Venice* notebook. Equally it may be relevant here to notice the subject-matter of Mann's short essay written in May 1911 on the paper of the Hotel des Bains, which became the 'page and a half of exquisite prose' written by Aschenbach, at an earlier and central scene of the story, on the beach in Tadzio's presence. Mann's essay, in reality, was about Wagner; but we are not told that this was Aschenbach's topic, merely that he had been asked in a circular letter to contribute his views on 'a certain important cultural problem, a burning question of taste'. Transmuting the biographical reality, the text seems here to hint ('the theme was familiar to him, it was close to his experience') that the topic proposed to Aschenbach was the role of homosexuality in literature and the arts. In reality, again, Mann in this essay (originally published in 1911 as *A critical view of Richard Wagner*) was anti-Wagnerian as so often, calling for a post-Wagnerian 'neo-classical' culture. But there was perhaps a further transmutation when, about a year later, he wrote the carefully balanced scene of Aschenbach's death, the scene that has been called the '*Liebestod* ending' to this classical and classic tale of romantic passion. The city in which Aschenbach dies was profoundly associated with Wagner, the arch-romantic, who had composed much of *Tristan and Isolde* there and had died there; Aschenbach himself seemed to allude to him in his thoughts as he drifted along the canals in pursuit of Tadzio ('Venice . . . where composers have been inspired to lulling tones of somniferous eroticism'). If in the fictional death-scene's nexus of associations Diotima's words implicitly accompany the hero's last journey, so too perhaps does the final climax of what to Mann, even in 1912, was still music's ultimate statement: the mystic trance of Isolde as she contemplates the dead Tristan and breathes the murmur of waves, listens and drowns as the odour of music, 'the world-soul's vast breath', engulfs her consciousness.

So movingly retrogressive a 'full close' is of course immediately followed by the few lines prosaically narrating Aschenbach's physical collapse and death, rather as Goethe's *Werther* ends with chilling details of what happens after the hero has in final ecstasy shot himself. They are the necessary naturalistic postscript, by which the preceding passage is not so much contradicted as completed.

A double view also suggests itself when we consider the prose style of the story and Mann's comments on this aspect of it. In the lecture *On Myself* delivered in Princeton in 1940, he described *Death in Venice* as

> a strange sort of moral self-castigation by means of a book which itself, with intentional irony, displays in its manner and style that very stance of dignity and mastery which is denounced in it as spurious and foolish.

And quite soon after the story's publication, irritated by critics who read into the elevated prose a pompously implied authorial claim to magisterial status, he insisted that it was not his own style but Aschenbach's, that it was parody and mimicry, yet another way of exposing Aschenbach's pretensions (10 September 1915, to Paul Amann; 6 June 1919, to Joseph Ponten). But this self-interpretation, like some of Mann's remarks on Spinell, is again too one-sidedly negative: if it were the whole truth, the language of the story, as a deliberate *reductio ad absurdum*, would carry a faint aura of ridicule throughout. Instead, it remains a serious, heightened and noble language, 'parodistic' only if parody can also be filled with sadness, the sadness of leave-taking from a noble impossibility.

Death in Venice was written between July 1911 and July 1912, much of it in Mann's recently built summer villa in Bad Tölz, Upper Bavaria. It was published in two parts in the October and November numbers of the *Neue Rundschau* in 1912, then in Fischer's book edition in February 1913 (a special luxury edition of a hundred copies had also appeared in 1912 with another publisher). Fischer's first printing of eight thousand was sold out at once, sales of eighteen thousand were reached at the end of the year, thirty-three thousand by the end of the First World War, eighty thousand by 1930. During Mann's lifetime,

Death in Venice appeared in twenty countries and thirty-seven editions, being translated more than once into some of the languages. The first English translation was by Kenneth Burke (Knopf, 1925); in 1928 Secker and Warburg published the version by Helen Lowe-Porter, who remained for many decades, on both sides of the Atlantic, the exclusively copyrighted translator of nearly all the works of Thomas Mann. It is now increasingly recognized that Mrs Lowe-Porter's grasp of German was rather less than adequate and that a fresh attempt to translate Mann into English is overdue; the present volume is conceived as a step in that direction. It is embarrassing but necessary at this point to put on record some examples of the shortcomings of the hitherto accepted sole mediator of Mann's *oeuvre* to the English-reading public. They can be representatively illustrated even from a few of the stories, indeed from *Death in Venice* alone. The following brief catalogue of errors confines itself in the first instance to unwitting factual mis-representations of the meaning, due to obvious incomprehension of the German vocabulary or syntax; I am not here concerned with the kind of acceptable conscious inexactitudes which are within a translator's limited but legitimate area of freedom. The main list also excludes the more imponderable defects of style and taste which are matters less of fact than of judgement, though I refer later to a few of these; the reader may perhaps fairly infer their prevalence from that of the more palpable failures. The page-references below are to *Stories of Three Decades* (Secker and Warburg, 1936; I quote from the 1946 reprint). The English words in parentheses immediately following the quoted German material are correct translations or explanatory paraphrases; the English in quotation marks is Mrs Lowe-Porter's. In most cases I have then added a summary indication of the nature of the mistake.

From *Tonio Kröger*:

'quadratischer Liniennetz' (the squared-off network of LINES on the painter's canvas): 'a square LINEN mesh' (p. 100). (Confusion of *Linien* with *Leinen*.)

'ungeWÜRZT' (savourless): 'without ROOTS' (p. 103). (Confusion of *Würze* with *Wurzel*.)

'mich vor dem Frühling meines Künstlertums ein wenig zu schämen' (feel a little ashamed of my art when confronted with the spring): 'feel a little ashamed of the SPRINGTIME OF MY ART' (p. 103). (Misconstruction of the syntax.)

'heiligend' (sanctifying): 'healing' (p. 106). (Confusion with *heilend*.)

From *Tristan*:

'(ich kann) das *Empire* einfach NICHT ENTBEHREN' (cannot bear NOT to be surrounded by *Empire* furnishings): 'I cannot ENDURE *Empire*' (p. 141).

'(eine) unsäglich EMPÖRENDE Geschichte' (an unspeakably REVOLTING story): 'unspeakably TOUCHING story' (p. 158).

From *Death in Venice*:

'innigere Geistigkeit' (the more INWARD SPIRITUALITY of a clergyman among Aschenbach's ancestors): 'a LIVELIER MENTALITY' (p. 382).

'sinnlicheres Blut' (the more SENSUOUS blood of Aschenbach's mother): 'more PERCEPTIVE blood' (p. 382).

'Wertzeichen' (the foreign stamps on Aschenbach's mail): 'tributes' from abroad (p. 383).

'Er hatte dem Geiste gefrönt, mit der Erkenntnis Raubbau getrieben, Saatfrucht vermahlen, Geheimnisse preisgegeben, das Talent verdächtigt, die Kunst verraten' (he had BEEN ENSLAVED TO intellect, had exhausted the soil by excessive analysis, had ground up the seed-corn of growth, GIVEN AWAY SECRETS, made talent seem suspect, betrayed the truth about art): 'he had DONE HOMAGE to intellect . . . had TURNED HIS BACK ON THE "MYSTERIES" ' (p. 385).

'sich ein Schicksal erschleicht' (cheats his way into a destiny of sorts): 'manages to lead fate by the nose' (p. 386).

'Nichtswürdigkeiten begehen' (behave with contemptible baseness): 'trifle away the rest of his life' (p. 386).

'UNBEFANGENHEIT' (naïvety, single-mindedness): 'detachment' (p. 386, p. 435). (Thought and context misunderstood.)

'eine Vereinfachung, eine sittliche VEREINFÄLTIGUNG der Welt und der Seele' (a simplification, a morally simplistic and naïve view of the world and of human psychology): 'a dangerous simplification, a TENDENCY TO EQUATE the world and the human soul' (p. 386). (A wild guess that makes no sense.)

'WÜRDE' (dignity). In *Death in Venice* the theme of 'dignity' and its loss is central, and the word recurs in the story as a kind of technical term and continuing leitmotif. In defiance of this and of the contexts in which the word appears, Mrs Lowe-Porter translates it variously as 'HONOUR' (p. 385), 'UTILITY' (p. 386), 'WORTH' (pp. 387, 434), etc.

'die WÜRDE des Geistes ausdrucksvoll WAHRZUNEHMEN' (to be an expressive representative of the dignity of the intellect): 'RECOGNIZES his own WORTH' (p. 387). (*Wahrnehmen* here has the less common sense of *vertreten*.)

'von schon gestalteter Empfindung mühelos bewegt' (effortlessly moved by a passion already shaped into language): 'easily susceptible to a PRESCIENCE already shaped within him' (p. 391). (The allusion to August von Platen's sonnet has been missed, but the resulting version in any case makes no sense.)

'QUER über die Insel' (the avenue running straight across the elongated Isola del Lido from the steamship pier to the Hotel des Bains): 'across the island DIAGONALLY' (p. 395); cf. 'QUERstehende Hütten' (bathing huts at right angles to the main row): 'DIAGONAL row of cabins' (p. 401). (The correct sense in these two cases could have been ascertained from a map or by personal inspection.)

'Schönheit schaffende Ungerechtigkeit' (the injustice that creates beauty): 'THE BEAUTY THAT BREAKS HEARTS' (p. 397). (Syntax misconstrued.)

'seine BILDUNG geriet ins Wallen, sein Gedächtnis warf uralte, seiner Jugend überlieferte . . . Gedanken auf' (his mind's store of culture was in ferment, his memory threw up thoughts from ancient tradition which he had been taught as a boy): 'his whole MENTAL BACKGROUND [was] in a state of flux. Memory flung up in him the PRIMITIVE thoughts which are youth's inheritance' (p. 412). (Missing the specific and clearly implied theme of school or college education in the Greek classics.)

'als sei DER Eros, der sich seiner bemeistert, einem solchen Leben auf irgendeine Weise besonders gemäß und geneigt. Hatte er nicht bei den tapfersten Völkern vorzüglich in Ansehen gestanden' etc. (it seemed to him that THE KIND OF love that had taken possession of him [i.e. homosexual love] did, in a certain way, suit and befit such a life. Had it not been highly honoured by the most valiant of peoples, etc.): '[he wondered] if such a life might not be somehow specially PLEASING IN THE EYES OF THE GOD who had him in his power. For EROS had received most countenance among the most valiant nations' etc. (p. 422). This glosses over (for reasons of prudery perhaps) the specific point about Greek homosexuality as such.

'(der Flötenton lockte ihn) schamlos BEHARRLICH zum Feste' (the flute music was enticing him with shameless INSISTENCE to the feast): 'beguiling too it was to him who struggled [etc.] . . . shamelessly AWAITING the coming feast' (p. 431). (Vocabulary and syntax misunderstood.)

Some of these errors are of no great consequence, merely contributing to a cumulative effect of minor irritation; most are relatively serious distortions of the intended meaning of Thomas Mann's text. In addition, Mrs Lowe-Porter was in the habit (and this applies to her translations generally) of unnecessarily and often damagingly excising words, phrases, even whole sentences. I will mention here only two cases of such omission, the second very much more important than the first, from *Death in Venice*. In Chapter 3 Aschenbach is hurrying to catch his train and leave Venice, very much against his own secret wishes:

> Es ist sehr spät, er hat keinen Augenblick zu verlieren, wenn er den Zug erreichen will. Er will es und will es nicht. Aber die Zeit drängt . . .

In Mrs Lowe-Porter's version (p. 407) the reference to the train and the significant words 'er will es und will es nicht' (he both wants and does not want to catch it) have simply vanished without trace: she writes merely 'It was very late, he had not a moment to lose. Time pressed . . .' The more crucial and almost incredible case comes at the very end of the story, in the passage describing Aschenbach's final vision and death, to which I have referred earlier. Tadzio turns round to glance

at the dying Aschenbach at the moment of his collapse into unconsciousness, and we read:

> Ihm war aber, als ob der bleiche und liebliche Psychagog dort draußen
> ihm lächle, ihm winke; als ob er, die Hand aus der Hüfte lösend,
> hinausdeute, voranschwebe ins Verheißungsvoll-Ungeheure. UND
> WIE SO OFT, MACHTE ER SICH AUF, IHM ZU FOLGEN.

Mrs Lowe-Porter's version of this (p. 437) is so far as it goes
unexceptionable – indeed, her phrase 'an immensity of richest
expectation' is even a felicitous rendering of 'das Verheißungsvoll-
Ungeheure'; unaccountably, however, ending her whole paragraph at
'expectation', she omits altogether the final, dramatically indispensable
sentence 'And as so often, he set out to follow him.'

No one is incapable of oversight, and Mrs Lowe-Porter was clearly
working under great pressure of time to complete her immense task of
translating the many long volumes of Mann's work as each appeared;
more vigilant copy-editing might have improved the result. Regrettably,
none of the errors was corrected in later reprintings.

In my own versions, as well as trying to be more accurate, I have tried
to reflect, so far as is possible in English, the complexity of Mann's prose
generally and especially the enhanced, ceremonious prose which he
uses, for reasons already discussed, in *Death in Venice*. It is well known
that Mann's sentences tend to be long and elaborate (he himself parodies
this in the opening paragraph of *Doctor Faustus*). They are however
never ill-balanced or obscure, at least not in his best works of fiction.
Because of the inherent differences between the languages, a translator's
equivalent English sentences should not try to follow the structure of
Mann's German sentences too closely, or they will cease to be
equivalent; but they should be as complex as is consistent with what
sounds natural for a single sentence by English standards. Mrs Lowe-
Porter ignores this point; the most flagrant example is her cavalier
treatment of the deliberately complex opening sentence of Chapter 2 in
Death in Venice, where Mann inserts a catalogue of Aschenbach's most
important works into his bare statement of the place of his birth. Mrs
Lowe-Porter quite unnecessarily breaks this sentence up, shifting most
of it to a later point after four intervening sentences, so that the
paragraph's whole structure is rearranged and destroyed (in addition to

the already mentioned garbling of some of its details). Her version of *Death in Venice* in general also ignores the characteristic style of this story: its solemnity and just detectable preciosity, its preference for the unusual, elevated (*gehoben*), 'literary' word. She also ignores the passages in which Mann's prose, 'hymnically' celebrating Tadzio and his Homeric-Platonic background, breaks into hexameters, once or twice quoting actual lines from Homer; the most notable case of this occurs at the opening of Chapter 4, where dactylic rhythms are woven into the first paragraph, and Aschenbach's delight at being no longer in the gloomy Bavarian Alps is expressed in a clear sequence of almost three complete hexameter lines (Mann's adaptation of Erwin Rohde's translation of *The Odyssey* iv, 536ff): '. . . als sei er entrückt ins elysische Land, an die Grenzen der Erde, wo leichtestes Leben den Menschen beschert ist, wo nicht Schnee ist und Winter, noch Sturm und strömender Regen'. I have attempted to devise prosodic equivalents in this and the other cases.

I have preferred not to overburden this introductory essay with references and footnotes, but must gratefully acknowledge much indebtedness to my colleagues H. R. Vaget (specifically his *Kommentar* to the complete stories, Winkler-Verlag, 1984) and T. J. Reed (especially his valuable new edition, with much interpretative and auxiliary material, of *Death in Venice*, Hanser-Verlag, 1983); my debt to Proffesor Reed is not diminished by my disagreement with him in certain respects. Miscellaneous particular points are also attributable to other Thomas Mann scholars such as Erich Heller, the late Peter de Mendelssohn and the late Wolfdietrich Rasch. I am grateful to Professor Hans Wysling and Mr Gilbert Adair for additional information on Władysław Moes.

My versions of the first six stories in this selection were published as *Tonio Kröger and Other Stories* by Bantam Books (New York) in 1970, by which date the originals had come into the public domain under the current United States copyright law. This did not happen in the case of *Death in Venice* until 1987, when it became possible to re-issue the volume with a new translation of that story added (*Death in Venice and Other Stories*, Bantam Books, 1988; the earlier translations were here slightly revised and the introduction rewritten). For the present British edition further slight revisions have been made.

D. L.

Little Herr Friedemann

Der kleine Herr Friedemann

1897[*]

*The dates are those of first publication.

Little Herr Friedemann

1

It was the nurse's fault. In vain Frau Consul Friedemann, when the matter was first suspected, had solemnly urged her to relinquish so heinous a vice; in vain she had dispensed to her daily a glass of red wine in addition to her nourishing stout. It suddenly came to light that the girl had actually sunk so low as to drink the methylated spirits intended for the coffee-machine; and before a replacement for her had arrived, before she could be sent away, the accident had happened. One day, when little Johannes was about a month old, his mother and three adolescent sisters returned from a walk to find that he had fallen from the swaddling table and was lying on the floor making a horribly faint whimpering noise, with the nurse standing by looking stupidly down at him.

The doctor's face, as he carefully but firmly probed the limbs of the crooked, twitching little creature, wore an exceedingly serious expression; the three girls stood in a corner sobbing, and Frau Friedemann prayed aloud in her mortal anguish.

Even before the baby was born it had been the poor woman's lot to see her husband, the consul for the Netherlands, reft from her by an illness both sudden and acute, and she was still too broken in spirit to be even capable of hoping that the life of her little Johannes might be spared. Two days later, however, the doctor squeezed her hand encouragingly and pronounced that there was now absolutely no question of any immediate danger; above all, the slight concussion of the brain had completely cleared up. This, he explained, was obvious if one looked at the child's eyes; there had been a vacant stare in them at first which had now quite disappeared . . . 'Of course,' he added, 'we must wait and see how things go on – and we must hope for the best, you know, hope for the best . . .'

2

The grey gabled house in which Johannes Friedemann grew up was near the north gate of the old, scarcely middle-sized merchant city. Its front door opened on to a spacious stone-paved hall, from which a stair with white wooden banisters led to the upper floors. On the first was the living-room with its walls papered in a faded landscape pattern, and its heavy mahogany table draped in crimson plush, with high-backed chairs and settees standing stiffly round it.

Here, as a child, he would often sit by the window, where there was always a fine display of flowers; he would sit on a little stool at his mother's feet, listening perhaps as she told him some wonderful story, gazing at her smooth grey hair and her kind gentle face, and breathing in the slight fragrance of scent that always hung about her. Or perhaps he would get her to show him the portrait of his father, an amiable gentleman with grey side-whiskers. He was (said his mother) now living in heaven, waiting for them all to join him there.

Behind the house was a little garden, and during the summer they would spend a good deal of time in it, notwithstanding the almost perpetual sickly-sweet exhalations from a nearby sugar refinery. In the garden stood an old gnarled walnut tree, and in its shade little Johannes would often sit on a low wooden stool cracking nuts, while Frau Friedemann and her three daughters, now grown-up, sat together in a grey canvas tent. But Frau Friedemann would often raise her eyes from her needlework and glance tenderly and sadly across at her son.

Little Johannes was no beauty, with his pigeon chest, his steeply humped back and his disproportionately long skinny arms, and as he squatted there on his stool, nimbly and eagerly cracking his nuts, he was certainly a strange sight. But his hands and feet were small and neatly shaped, and he had great liquid brown eyes, a sensitive mouth and soft light brown hair. In fact, although his face sat so pitifully low down between his shoulders, it could nevertheless almost have been called beautiful.

3

When he was seven he was sent to school, and now the years passed uniformly and rapidly. Every day, walking past the gabled houses and shops with the quaintly solemn gait that deformed people often have, he made his way to the old schoolhouse with its Gothic vaulting; and at home, when he had done his homework, he would perhaps read some of his beautiful books with their brightly coloured illustrations, or potter about in the garden, while his sisters kept house for their ailing mother. The girls also went to parties, for the Friedemanns moved in the best local society; but unfortunately none of the three had yet married, for their family fortune was by no means large and they were distinctly plain.

Johannes, too, occasionally got an invitation from one or another of his contemporaries, but it was no great pleasure for him to associate with them. He was unable to join in their games, and since they always treated him with embarrassed reserve, it was impossible for any real companionship to develop.

Later there came a time when he would often hear them discuss certain matters in the school yard; wide-eyed and attentive, he would listen in silence as they talked of their passions for this little girl or that. Such experiences, he decided, obviously engrossing though they were for the others, belonged like gymnastics and ball games to the category of things for which he was not suited. This was at times a rather saddening thought; but after all, he had long been accustomed to going his own way and not sharing the interests of other people. .

It nevertheless came to pass – he was sixteen years old at the time – that he found himself suddenly enamoured of a girl of his own age. She was the sister of one of his classmates, a blonde, exuberant creature whom he had met at her brother's house. He felt a strange uneasiness in her company, and the studied self-conscious cordiality with which she too treated him saddened him profoundly.

One summer afternoon when he was taking a solitary walk along the promenade outside the old city wall, he heard whispered words being exchanged behind a jasmine bush. He cautiously peeped through the branches, and there on a seat sat this girl and a tall red-haired boy whom he knew very well by sight; the boy's arm was round her and he was pressing a kiss on her lips, which with much giggling she reciprocated. When Johannes had seen this he turned on his heel and walked softly away.

His head had sunk lower than ever between his shoulders, his hands were trembling and a sharp, biting pain rose from his chest and seemed to choke him. But he swallowed it down, and resolutely drew himself up as straight as he could. 'Very well,' he said to himself, 'that is over. I will never again concern myself with such things. To the others they mean joy and happiness, but to me they can only bring grief and suffering. I am done with it all. It is finished for me. Never again.'

The decision was a relief to him. He had made a renunciation, a renunciation for ever. He went home and took up a book or played the violin, which he had learned to do despite his deformity.

4

At seventeen he left school to go into business, like everyone else of his social standing, and became an apprentice in Herr Schlievogt's big timber firm down by the river. They treated him with special consideration, he for his part was amiable and cooperative, and the years passed by in a peaceful and well ordered manner. But in his twenty-first year his mother died after a long illness.

This was a great sorrow for Johannes Friedemann, and one that he long cherished. He savoured this sorrow, he surrendered himself to it as one surrenders oneself to a great happiness, he nourished it with innumerable memories from his childhood and made the most of it, as his first major experience.

Is not life in itself a thing of goodness, irrespective of whether the course it takes for us can be called a 'happy' one? Johannes Friedemann felt that this was so, and he loved life. He had renounced the greatest happiness it has to offer, but who shall say with what passionate care he cultivated those pleasures that were accessible to him? A walk in springtime through the parks outside the town, the scent of a flower, the song of a bird – surely these were things to be thankful for?

He also well understood that a capacity for the enjoyment of life presupposes education, indeed that education always adds at once to that capacity, and he took pains to educate himself. He loved music and attended any concerts that were given in the town. And although it was uncommonly odd to watch him play, he did himself become not a bad violinist and took pleasure in every beautiful and tender note he was able to draw from his instrument. And by dint of much reading he had in the course of time acquired a degree of literary taste which in that town was probably unique. He was versed in all the latest publications both in Germany and abroad, he knew how to savour the exquisite rhythms of a poem, he could appreciate the subtle atmosphere of a finely written short story . . . One might indeed almost say that he was an epicurean.

He came to see that there is nothing that cannot be enjoyed and that it is almost absurd to distinguish between happy and unhappy experiences. He accepted all his sensations and moods as they came to him, he welcomed and cultivated them, whether they were sad or glad: even his unfulfilled wishes, even his heart's longing. It was precious to him for its own sake, and he would tell himself that if it ever came to fulfilment the best part of the pleasure would be over. Is not the sweet pain of vague desires and hopes on a still spring evening richer in delight than any fulfilment the summer could bring? Ah yes, little Herr Friedemann was an epicurean and no mistake.

This was something of which the people who passed him in the street, greeting him with that mixture of cordiality and pity to which he had so long been accustomed, were doubtless unaware. They did not know that this unfortunate cripple, strutting so quaintly and solemnly along in his light grey overcoat and his shiny top hat (for oddly enough he was a little vain of his appearance) was a man to whom life was very sweet, this life of his that flowed so gently by, unmarked by any strong emotions but filled with a quiet and delicate happiness of which he had taught himself the secret.

5

But Herr Friedemann's chief and most absorbing passion was for the theatre. He had an uncommonly strong sense of drama and at moments of high theatrical effect or tragic catastrophe the whole of his little body would quiver with emotion. At the principal theatre of the town he had a seat permanently reserved for him in the front row, and he would go there regularly, sometimes accompanied by his three sisters. Since their mother's death they had lived on in the big house which they and their brother jointly owned, and did all the housekeeping for themselves and him.

They were, alas, still unmarried; but they had long reached an age at which one sets aside all such expectations, for the eldest of them, Friederike, was seventeen years older than Herr Friedemann. She and her sister Henriette were rather too tall and thin, whereas Pfiffi, the youngest, was regrettably short and plump. This youngest girl moreover had an odd habit of wriggling and wetting the corners of her mouth whenever she spoke.

Little Herr Friedemann did not pay much attention to the three girls, but they stuck loyally together and were always of the same opinion. In particular, whenever any engagement between persons of their acquaintance was announced, they would unanimously declare that this was *very* gratifying news.

Their brother went on living with them even after he had left Herr Schlievogt's timber firm and set up on his own by taking over some small business, some sort of agency which did not demand much exertion. He lived in a couple of rooms on the ground floor of the house, in order not to have to climb the stairs except at mealtimes, for he occasionally suffered from asthma.

On his thirtieth birthday, a fine warm June day, he was sitting after lunch in the grey tent in the garden, leaning against a new soft neck-rest which Henriette had made for him, with a good cigar in his mouth and a good book in his hand. Now and then he would put the book aside, listen to the contented twittering of the sparrows in the old walnut tree and look at the neat gravel drive that led up to the house and at the lawn with its bright flower-beds.

Little Herr Friedemann was clean-shaven, and his face had scarcely changed at all except for a slight sharpening of his features. He wore his soft light brown hair smoothly parted on one side.

Once, lowering the book right into his lap, he gazed up at the clear blue sky and said to himself: 'Well, that's thirty years gone. And now I

8

suppose there will be another ten or perhaps another twenty, God knows. They will come upon me silently and pass by without any commotion, as the others have done, and I look forward to them with peace of mind.'

6

It was in July of that year that the new military commandant for the district was appointed, a change of office that caused a considerable stir. The stout and jovial gentleman who had held the post for many years had been a great favourite with local society, and his departure was regretted. And now, for God knows what reason, it must needs be Herr von Rinnlingen who was sent from the capital to replace him.

It seemed, in fact, to be not a bad exchange, for the new lieutenant-colonel, who was married but had no children, rented a very spacious villa in the southern suburbs, from which it was concluded that he intended to keep house in some style. At all events the rumour that he was quite exceptionally rich found further confirmation in the fact that he brought with him four servants, five riding and carriage horses, a landau and a light hunting brake.

Shortly after their arrival he and his wife had been to pay calls on all the best families, and everyone was talking about them; the chief object of interest however was definitely not Herr von Rinnlingen himself, but his wife. The men were dumbfounded by her and did not at first know what to think; but the ladies most decidedly did not approve of Gerda von Rinnlingen's character and ways.

'Of course, one can tell at once that she comes from the capital,' observed Frau Hagenström, the lawyer's wife, in the course of conversation with Henriette Friedemann. 'One doesn't mind that, one doesn't mind her smoking and riding – naturally not! But her behaviour isn't merely free and easy, it's unrefined, and even that isn't quite the right word . . . She's by no means ugly, you know, some might even think her pretty – and yet she totally lacks feminine charm, her eyes and her laugh and her movements are simply not at all calculated to appeal to men. She is no flirt, and far be it from me to find fault with her for that, goodness knows – but can it be right for so young a woman, a woman of twenty-four, to show absolutely no sign of . . . a certain natural grace and attractiveness? My dear, I am not very good at expressing myself, but I know what I mean. The men still seem to be quite stunned, poor dears; mark my words, they will all be sick to death of her in a few weeks' time.'

'Well,' said Fräulein Friedemann, 'she has made a very good marriage, anyway.'

'Oh, as to her husband!' exclaimed Frau Hagenström. 'You should see how she treats him! You will see it soon enough! I am the last person to deny that up to a point a married woman should act towards the opposite sex with a certain reserve. But how does she behave to her own husband? She has a way of freezing him with her eyes and calling him *"mon cher ami"* in pitying tones, which I find quite outrageous! You have only to look at *him* – a fine upstanding first-class officer and gentleman of forty, well behaved and well mannered and very well preserved! They've been married for four years . . . My dear . . .'

7

The scene of little Herr Friedemann's first encounter with Frau von Rinnlingen was the main street of the town, a street lined almost entirely with shops and offices. He was vouchsafed this first sight of her at midday, just after leaving the Stock Exchange, where he had been making his modest contribution to the morning's business.

He was trudging along, a tiny and solemn figure, beside Herr Stephens, the wholesale merchant, who was an unusually large and solid man with round-trimmed side-whiskers and formidably bushy eyebrows. They were both wearing top hats, and had opened their overcoats as it was a very hot day. They were discussing politics, and their walking-sticks tapped the pavement in regular rhythm. But when they were about half-way down the street Herr Stephens suddenly remarked: 'Devil take me, here comes that Rinnlingen woman driving towards us.'

'Well, that's a lucky coincidence,' replied Herr Friedemann in his high-pitched, rather strident voice, and peered expectantly ahead. 'I've never yet set eyes on her, you know. Ah, so that is the yellow brake.'

And so indeed it was: Frau von Rinnlingen was using the light yellow hunting brake today, and she herself was driving the pair of thoroughbreds; the groom sat behind her with his arms folded. She wore a loose-fitting, very light-coloured coat, and her skirt was of a light colour as well. From under her little round straw hat with its brown leather band came her luxuriant auburn hair, well curled at the sides and thickly tressed at the back where it fell almost to her shoulders. The complexion of her oval face was pale, and there were blue shadows in the corners of her unusually close-set eyes. Across her short but finely shaped nose ran a very becoming little ridge of freckles; the beauty or otherwise of her mouth, however, was hard to judge, for she kept protruding and withdrawing her lower lip, chafing it continually against the other.

Herr Stephens greeted Frau von Rinnlingen with an exceedingly respectful salutation as her carriage drew abreast of them, and little Herr Friedemann also raised his hat and stared at her very attentively. She lowered her whip, inclined her head slightly and drove slowly past, glancing at the houses and shop-windows on either side.

A few paces further on Herr Stephens remarked: 'She's been out for a drive and now she's on her way home.'

Little Herr Friedemann made no reply but gazed down at the pavement in front of him. Then he suddenly looked up at Stephens and asked: 'What did you say?'

And Herr Stephens, the wholesale merchant, repeated his perspicacious observation.

8

Three days later, at noon, Johannes Friedemann returned home from his regular morning walk. Luncheon was served at half-past twelve, so there would be time for him to spend another half-hour in his 'office', which was just to the right of the front door. But as he was about to enter it the maid came up to him in the hall and said:

'There are visitors, Herr Friedemann.'

11

'In my room?' he asked.

'No, upstairs with the ladies, sir.'

'But who are they?'

'Lieutenant-Colonel and Frau von Rinnlingen.'

'Oh,' said Herr Friedemann, 'then of course I'll . . .'

And he climbed the stairs to the first floor and walked across the lobby towards the room with the landscape wallpaper. But with the handle of the tall white door already in his hand, he suddenly stopped, drew back a pace, turned and went slowly down again the way he had come. And although he was completely alone he said out loud to himself:

'No. Better not.'

He went into his 'office', sat down at his desk and took up a newspaper. But presently he let it drop again, and sat with his head turned to one side, looking out of the window. Thus he remained till the maid came and announced that luncheon was served: then he went upstairs to the dining-room where his sisters were already waiting for him, and seated himself on his chair on top of three volumes of music.

Henriette, ladling out the soup, said:

'Who do you think has been here, Johannes?'

'Well?' he asked.

'The new lieutenant-colonel with his wife.'

'Indeed? That is very kind of them.'

'Yes,' said Pfiffi, dribbling at the corners of her mouth, 'I think they are both very agreeable people.'

'Anyway,' said Friederike, 'we must return the call without delay. I suggest we go on Sunday, the day after tomorrow.'

'On Sunday,' said Henriette and Pfiffi.

'You'll come with us of course, Johannes?' asked Friederike.

'Naturally!' said Pfiffi, wriggling. Herr Friedemann had completely ignored the question and was swallowing his soup, silently and apprehensively. He seemed somehow to be listening, listening to some uncanny noise from nowhere.

9

The following evening there was a performance of *Lohengrin* at the city theatre, and all well-educated people were present. The small auditorium was packed from top to bottom and filled with the hum of voices, the smell of gas and a medley of scent. But every eyeglass, in the stalls and in the circles, was trained on box number thirteen, just to the right of the stage; for there, this evening, Herr and Frau von Rinnlingen had appeared for the first time, and now was the chance to give them a thorough inspection.

When little Herr Friedemann, in faultless evening dress with a glistening white pigeon-breasted shirt-front, entered his box – box thirteen – he stopped dead on the threshold: his hand rose to his brow and for a moment his nostrils dilated convulsively. But then he took his seat, the seat immediately to the left of Frau von Rinnlingen.

As he sat down she contemplated him attentively, protruding her lower lip; she then turned and exchanged a few words with her husband, who was standing behind her. He was a tall well-built man with upturned moustaches and a tanned, good-humoured face.

When the prelude began and Frau von Rinnlingen leaned forward over the balustrade, Herr Friedemann gave her a quick, furtive, sideways look. She was wearing a light-coloured evening gown and was even slightly *décolletée*, unlike any other woman present. Her sleeves were wide and ample and her white evening gloves came up to her elbows. Tonight there was something voluptuous about her figure which had not been noticeable the other day under her loose coat; her bosom rose and fell slowly and firmly, and her heavy auburn tresses hung low down behind her head.

Herr Friedemann was pale, much paler than usual, and below his smoothly parted brown hair little drops of sweat stood out on his forehead. Frau von Rinnlingen had removed her left glove and was resting her bare arm on the red plush balustrade: a round, pale arm, with pale blue veins running through it and through her hand, on which she wore no rings. This arm lay constantly just where he could see it; there was no help for that.

The violins sang, the trombones blared, Telramund was struck down, the orchestra sounded a general triumph and little Herr Friedemann sat motionless, pale and silent, with his head drooping right down between his shoulders, one forefinger propped against his mouth and the other hand thrust under his lapel.

As the curtain fell, Frau von Rinnlingen rose to leave the box with her husband. Herr Friedemann, without looking at them, saw them go; he drew his handkerchief across his brow, stood up suddenly, got as far as the door that led into the corridor, then turned back again, resumed his seat, and sat on without stirring in the same posture as before.

When the bell rang and his neighbours came back into the box, he sensed that Frau von Rinnlingen was looking at him, and involuntarily he raised his head and returned her gaze. When their eyes met, so far from turning hers away, she went on scrutinizing him without a trace of embarrassment until he himself felt humiliated and compelled to look down. His pallor increased, and a strange, bitter-sweet rage welled up inside him . . . The music began.

Towards the end of that act Frau von Rinnlingen happened to drop her fan and it fell to the ground beside Herr Friedemann. Both of them stooped simultaneously, but she reached it first and said with a mocking smile:

'Thank you.'

His head had been close to hers, and for a moment, unavoidably, he had caught the warm fragrance of her breast. His face was contorted, his whole body was convulsed and his heart throbbed with such appalling violence that he could not breathe. He sat for half a minute longer, then pushed back his chair, got up quietly and quietly left the box.

10

The clamour of the orchestra followed him as he crossed the corridor, reclaimed his top hat and light grey overcoat and stick from the cloakroom and went downstairs and out into the street.

It was a warm, still evening. In the gaslight the grey gabled houses stood silent against the sky, and the stars gleamed and glistened softly. Only a few people passed Herr Friedemann in the street, their steps re-echoing along the pavement. Someone greeted him but he did not notice; his head was bowed low and his misshapen chest shuddered as he gasped for breath. Now and then, scarcely audibly, he exclaimed to himself:

'Oh my God! my God!'

He examined his feelings with horrified apprehension, realizing that his so carefully cherished, prudently cultivated sensibility had now been uprooted, upchurned, stirred into wild upheaval. And suddenly, quite overcome by emotion, drunk with vertiginous desire, he leaned against a lamp-post and whispered in trembling anguish:

'Gerda!'

There was complete silence. Far and wide there was not a soul to be seen. Little Herr Friedemann pulled himself together and trudged on. He had reached the top of the street in which the theatre stood and which ran quite steeply down to the river, and now he was walking northwards along the main street towards his house . . .

How she had looked at him! Was it possible? She had forced him to look away! She had humbled him with her gaze! Was she not a woman and he a man? And had not her strange brown eyes positively quivered with pleasure as she had done so?

Again he felt that impotent, voluptuous hatred welling up inside him, but then he thought of the moment when her head had touched his, when he had breathed her fragrance – and once more he stopped, half straightened his deformed back, and again murmured helplessly, desperately, distractedly:

'Oh my God! my God!'

Then mechanically he resumed his slow advance along the empty, echoing streets, through the sultry evening air, and walked on till he reached his house. He paused for a moment in the hall to sniff its cool, dank atmosphere, then went into his 'office'.

He sat down at his desk beside the open window and stared straight in front of him at a big yellow rose which someone had put there for him in a glass of water. He took it and inhaled its fragrance with closed eyes; but then, with a sad, weary gesture, he put it aside. No, no! All that was over. What was that sweet smell to him now? What were any of them now, those things that had hitherto constituted his 'happiness'? . . .

He turned and looked out into the silent street. Now and then the sound of passing footsteps approached and faded. The stars glittered in the sky. How dead tired he was growing, how weak he felt! The thoughts seemed to drain from his head, and his despair began to dissolve into a great soft sadness. A few lines of poetry floated through his mind, he seemed to hear the music of *Lohengrin* again, to see again Frau von Rinnlingen sitting beside him, her white arm resting on the red plush. Then he fell into a heavy, feverish sleep.

11

Often he was on the point of waking up, yet dreaded to do so and sank back every time into unconsciousness. But when it was broad daylight he opened his eyes and gazed sorrowfully round. All that had happened was still vividly present to him; it was as if sleep had not interrupted his suffering at all.

His head was heavy and his eyes hot, but when he had washed and dabbed his forehead with eau-de-cologne he felt better, and quietly resumed his seat by the window, which was still open. It was still very early, about five o'clock in the morning. Occasionally a baker's boy passed, but there was no one else to be seen. In the house opposite all the blinds were still down. But the birds were twittering, and the sky was blue and radiant. It was an absolutely beautiful Sunday morning.

A feeling of well-being and confidence came over little Herr Friedemann. What was there to be afraid of? Had anything changed? Last night, admittedly, he had suffered a bad attack; very well, but that must be the last of it! It was still not too late, it was still possible to avert disaster! He would have to avoid everything that might occasion a renewal of the attack; he felt strong enough to do so. He felt strong enough to overcome this thing, to nip it completely in the bud . . .

When half-past seven struck, Friederike brought in his coffee and set it down on the round table in front of the leather sofa by the far wall.

'Good morning, Johannes,' she said, 'here is your breakfast.'

'Thank you,' said Herr Friedemann. Then he added: 'Friederike dear, I am sorry, but I am afraid you will have to pay that call without me. I don't feel well enough to come with you. I haven't slept well, I have a headache – in short, I must ask you to excuse me . . .'

Friederike replied:

'What a pity. I think you should certainly call on them another time. But it's true that you're not looking well. Shall I lend you my migraine pencil?'

'No, thank you,' said Herr Friedemann. 'It will pass.' And Friederike left the room.

Standing at the table, he slowly drank his coffee and ate a crescent-shaped roll. He was pleased with himself and proud of his strong-mindedness. When he had finished he took a cigar and sat down again at the window. Breakfast had done him good and he felt happy and hopeful. He took up a book, read, smoked and looked out from time to time into the dazzling sunlight.

The street had grown lively now; through his window he could hear the clatter of carriages, the sound of voices and the bells from the horse tramway. But the birds twittered through it all, and a soft warm breeze stirred in the shining blue sky.

At ten o'clock he heard his sisters crossing the hall and the front door creaking open, and presently he saw the three ladies walk past his window, but thought nothing much of it. An hour passed; he felt happier and happier.

A kind of elation began to fill him. How balmy the air was, and how the birds sang! Why should he not go for a short walk? And then suddenly, spontaneously, the sweet and terrifying thought simply surged up inside him: Why not call on her? Warning apprehensions followed the impulse, but with an almost muscular effort he suppressed them and added with exultant resolve: I will call on her!

And he put on his black Sunday suit, took his hat and stick and hurried, breathing rapidly, right across the town to the southern suburb. His head rose and fell busily with every step, but he saw no one, and remained absorbed in his exalted mood until he had reached the chestnut-lined avenue and the red villa that bore at its entrance the name 'Lieutenant-Colonel von Rinnlingen'.

12

At this point he began to tremble and his heart pounded convulsively against his ribs. But he crossed the outer hall and rang the doorbell. The die was cast now and there was no going back. Let it take its course, he thought. In him there was a sudden deathly stillness.

The door was thrown open, the manservant came across the hall towards him, received his card and carried it smartly up the red-carpeted stairs. Herr Friedemann stared motionlessly at the red carpet till the servant came back and declared that his mistress would be glad if Herr Friedemann would kindly come up.

On the first floor he placed his walking-stick outside the door of the drawing-room, and glanced at himself in the mirror. He was very pale, his eyes were red and above them the hair clung to his forehead; the hand in which he held his top hat was trembling uncontrollably.

The manservant opened the door and he went in. It was a fairly large, half-darkened room; the curtains were drawn. On the right stood a grand piano, and armchairs upholstered in brown silk were grouped about the round table in the centre. A landscape in a massive gilt frame hung on the wall to the left above the sofa. The wallpaper was also dark. Palm trees stood in the bay window at the far end.

A minute passed before Frau von Rinnlingen emerged from the curtained doorway on the right and advanced noiselessly towards him across the deep-pile brown carpet. She was wearing a quite simply cut dress with a red and black check pattern. From the bay window a shaft of light, full of dancing motes of dust, fell straight on to her heavy red hair, so that for a moment it flashed like gold. She was looking straight at him, studying him with her strange eyes, and protruding her lower lip as usual.

'Frau Commandant,' began Herr Friedemann, looking up at her, for his head reached only to her chest, 'my sisters have already paid you their respects and I should like to do so myself as well. When you honoured them with a call I was unfortunately not at home . . . to my great regret . . .'

He could think of absolutely no more to say, but she stood gazing implacably at him as if she meant to force him to continue speaking. The blood suddenly rushed to his head. 'She wants to torment me and mock me!' he thought, 'and she has guessed my feelings! Her eyes are simply quivering. . . !' Finally she said in a quite high, clear voice:

'It is very kind of you to have come. I was sorry, too, to miss you the other day. Won't you please take a seat?'

She sat down quite close to him and leaned back in her chair, laying her arms on the armrests. He sat leaning forward, holding his hat between his knees. She said:

'Do you know that your sisters were here only a quarter of an hour ago? They told me you were ill.'

'That is true,' replied Herr Friedemann. 'I did not feel well this morning. I thought I should not be able to go out. I must ask you to excuse my late arrival.'

'You still do not look quite well,' she remarked calmly, with her eyes fixed steadily on him. 'You are pale, and your eyes are inflamed. Perhaps your health is usually not very good?'

'Oh . . .' stammered Herr Friedemann, 'in general I cannot complain . . .'

'I am often ill too,' she went on, still not averting her gaze, 'but no one ever notices it. My nerves are bad and I have very odd moods sometimes.'

She paused, lowered her chin to her breast and looked up at him expectantly. But he made no answer. He sat on in silence looking at her, wide-eyed and thoughtful. How strangely she talked, and what an extraordinary effect her clear, cynical voice had on him! His heart was beating more quietly now; he felt as if he were dreaming. Frau von Rinnlingen spoke again:

'If I am not mistaken, you left the theatre last night before the end of the opera?'

'Yes, Frau Commandant.'

'I was sorry you did. You were a very appreciative neighbour, although it was not a good performance, or only a relatively good one. I suppose you are fond of music? Do you play the piano?'

'I play the violin a little,' said Herr Friedemann. 'That is to say – really hardly at all . . .'

'You play the violin?' she asked. Then she gazed past him for a moment and seemed to reflect.

'But then we could play together now and then,' she said suddenly. 'I can accompany a little. I should be glad to have found someone here who . . . Will you come?'

'I shall be delighted to place myself at your disposal,' he replied. He still had the feeling that he was in a dream. There was a pause. Then suddenly her face changed. He saw it twist into a scarcely perceptible expression of cruel mockery, and saw again, for the third time, that uncanny tremor in her eyes as they unswervingly scrutinized him. He blushed scarlet, and not knowing where to look, helpless, distraught, he let his head droop right down between his shoulders and stared in utter dismay at the carpet. But again, for a moment, that impotent, sweet, agonizing fury shuddered and trickled through him . . .

When with a desperate effort he raised his eyes again she was no longer looking at him, but gazing calmly over his head towards the door. He forced himself to utter a few words:

'And are you tolerably satisfied so far with your stay in our town, Frau Commandant?'

'Oh, yes,' said Frau von Rinnlingen indifferently, 'yes indeed. Why should I not be satisfied? Of course, I do feel somewhat constrained and conspicuous, but . . . By the way,' she added at once, 'before I forget: we are thinking of inviting some people round in a few days' time. Just a small informal party. We might play a little music and talk about this and that . . . Also we have rather a pretty garden behind the house; it goes right down to the river. In short, you and your ladies will of course be sent an invitation, but I should like to ask you here and now if we may have the pleasure of your company: shall we?'

Herr Friedemann had scarcely expressed his thanks and signified his acceptance when the door handle was pressed smartly down and the lieutenant-colonel entered. They both rose, and as Frau von Rinnlingen introduced the men to each other her husband bowed to her and to Herr Friedemann with equal courtesy. His tanned face was glistening in the heat.

As he removed his gloves he said something or other in his loud energetic voice to Herr Friedemann, who stared up at him with wide, vacant eyes, fully expecting to be slapped benevolently on the shoulder. Meanwhile the commandant turned to his wife. Standing with heels together and slightly bowing to her from the waist, he said in a noticeably softer voice:

'I hope you have asked Herr Friedemann if he will come to our little gathering, my dear? If you agree, I think we should arrange for it to take place a week today. I hope this weather will last and that we shall be able to use the garden as well.'

'As you think best,' replied Frau von Rinnlingen, gazing past him.

Two minutes later Herr Friedemann took his leave. As he bowed again at the door his eyes met hers, which were expressionlessly fixed on him.

13

He went on his way, not returning into town but involuntarily taking a side-road that led off the avenue towards the old fortified wall by the river, where there was a well-kept park with shady paths and seats.

He walked hurriedly, aimlessly, without raising his eyes. He was flushed with an unbearable heat, he could feel it licking up in him and subsiding like flames, and his weary head throbbed relentlessly . . .

Were those not her eyes still gazing into his? Not empty of expression as they had been when he left her, but with that earlier gaze, that quivering cruelty which had filled them the very moment after she had spoken to him so strangely and softly. Did she take delight in his helplessness, in driving him to distraction? And oh, if she did read his feelings, could she not at least feel some pity? . . .

Down by the river he had walked along the bank, beside the old city wall overgrown with green, and he sat down on a seat half encircled by jasmine bushes. The sweetish fragrance hung heavily in the air all round him. In front of him the sun brooded over the tremulous water.

How weary and worn-out he felt, and yet what an agonizing turmoil filled him! Surely the best thing to do would be to take one more look round him and then walk straight down into the silent water, where he would suffer for a few moments and then be free and rescued from existence and at peace! Oh, all he wanted was peace, peace! Yet not peace in an empty, unheeding nothingness, but a quiet place in gentle sunlight, where he might sit and think good, quiet thoughts.

At that instant all his deep love for life came back to him, piercing his heart with poignant nostalgia for his lost happiness. But then he looked about him, he looked at the mute, infinite tranquillity and indifference of nature, he saw the river wending its way in the sun, saw the grass waving and the flowers standing each in its place, just where it had bloomed, waiting to wither and be blown away: he saw all these things, all bowing in dumb submission to their existence – and suddenly he was overcome by that feeling of goodwill, of acceptance of necessity, which can in a certain sense lift us above all the adversities of fate.

He remembered that afternoon of his thirtieth birthday, when he had been happy in the possession of a quiet mind and had told himself that he could look forward, without fear or hope, to the remainder of his life. He had seen ahead of him neither brightness nor shadow, but a future bathed in gentle twilight, stretching away to a point where it merged almost imperceptibly into the dark; and with a calm and confident smile he had surveyed the years that were yet to come. How long ago had that day been?

Then this woman had come, she had had to come, it was his fate, she herself was his fate, she alone! Had he not sensed this from the very first moment? She had come, and he had tried to defend his peace of mind – but for her there had to be this rebellion within him of everything he had suppressed since his youth, because he had known instinctively that for him it meant misery and destruction. It had seized him with terrible, irresistible violence and it was destroying him!

It was destroying him, that he knew. But why go on with the vain agonizing struggle? Let it all take its course! Let him continue on his way, with his eyes closed to the gaping abyss beyond, obedient to fate, obedient to the invincible, sweetly tormenting power from which there is no escape.

The water gleamed, the jasmine breathed out its heavy pungent scent, the birds twittered in the branches all round him, and between the trees shone a dense velvet blue sky. But little hunchbacked Herr Friedemann did not stir from his seat. He sat on and on, leaning forward with his head bowed down into his hands.

14

Everyone agreed that the Rinnlingen party was a vast success. About thirty people sat round the long, tastefully decorated table which ran the length of the large dining-room; the butler and two hired waiters were already hurrying round serving ices, the room was filled with the clink and clatter of glasses and tableware and the warm aroma of food mingled with scent. The guests included a genial assemblage of men of business with their wives and daughters, almost the entire corps of officers from the garrison, an elderly doctor whom everyone liked, a few lawyers and other representatives of the best local society. Also present was a student of mathematics, a nephew of the commandant's who was here visiting his relatives; he was engaged in profound conversation with Fräulein Hagenström, who sat opposite Herr Friedemann.

The latter had been placed at the far end of the table, on a fine velvet cushion, next to the rather plain wife of the headmaster of the classical grammar school. He was not far from Frau von Rinnlingen, who had been escorted in to table by Consul Stephens. It was astonishing what a change had come over little Herr Friedemann in the last week. Perhaps it was partly the white gaslight in the dining-room that made his face look so alarmingly pale; but his cheeks were sunken, his eyes reddened, dark rings surrounded them, they shone with an unspeakable sadness; and he seemed more stunted and crippled than ever. He drank a lot of wine, and occasionally addressed a remark to his neighbour.

Frau von Rinnlingen had so far spoken not a word to Herr Friedemann at table; now she leaned forward a little and called across to him:

'I've been waiting in vain these last few days for you to pay me a visit with your fiddle.'

He gazed at her vacantly for a moment before answering. She was wearing a pale-coloured, light evening gown that left her white neck showing, and in her gleaming hair she had fastened a Maréchal Niel rose in full bloom. Her cheeks were slightly flushed this evening, but there were blue shadows, as always, in the corners of her eyes.

Herr Friedemann looked down at his place and stammered out some kind of reply; whereupon he also had to answer the headmaster's wife, who inquired whether he was fond of Beethoven. At this point however

Lieutenant-Colonel von Rinnlingen, at the head of the table, exchanged glances with his wife, tapped his glass and said:

'Ladies and gentlemen, I suggest we take our coffee in the other rooms. And it must be rather pleasant in the garden too, on an evening like this; if anyone cares to take a spot of air out there, I'll be very glad to do the same.'

Lieutenant von Deidesheim tactfully cracked a joke to break the silence which followed, and everyone rose from table amid peals of laughter. Herr Friedemann was one of the last to leave the dining-room with his partner; he escorted her, through the room decorated in medieval style in which the guests were already beginning to smoke, into the dimly lit luxurious drawing-room, and there took leave of her.

He was most carefully attired, in faultless evening dress with a dazzlingly white shirt and with patent leather shoes on his slender, neatly shaped feet. From time to time it could be observed that he was wearing red silk socks.

He looked out into the corridor and saw that quite large numbers of people were already going downstairs into the garden. But he sat down with his cigar and his coffee near the door of the medieval smoking-room, in which a few of the gentlemen were standing around talking, and from here he looked into the drawing-room.

At a table immediately to the right of the door a small circle had formed around the student, who was discoursing volubly. He had asserted that more than one parallel to a given straight line could be drawn through one and the same point; Dr Hagenström's wife had exclaimed, 'But that's impossible!' and he was now proving his proposition so cogently that everyone was pretending to have understood it.

But at the back of the room, on the divan, by the low lamp with the red shade, sat Gerda von Rinnlingen, in conversation with young Fräulein Stephens. She sat half reclined against the yellow silk cushion, with her legs crossed, and was smoking a cigarette in a leisurely manner, blowing the smoke out through her nose and protruding her lower lip. Fräulein Stephens sat facing her bolt-upright like a statue, answering her with a nervous smile.

No one noticed little Herr Friedemann, and no one noticed that his large eyes were fixed incessantly on Frau von Rinnlingen. He sat limply and gazed at her. There was no passion in his gaze, scarcely even any pain; only a dull, dead expression of senseless, powerless, will-less surrender.

About ten minutes passed in this manner; then Frau von Rinnlingen suddenly got up, and without looking at him, as if she had been secretly observing him all this time, she walked over and stopped in front of him. He rose to his feet, looked up at her and heard her say:

'Would you like to come into the garden with me, Herr Friedemann?'

He answered:

'With pleasure, Frau Commandant.'

15

'So you haven't yet seen our garden?' she asked him as they went downstairs. 'It's quite big. I hope there won't be too many people there already; I should like to get away from them all for a little. I got a headache during dinner; perhaps that red wine was too strong for me . . . This is our way out, through this door.' It was a glass door leading from the hall into a small cool passage, from which they went down a few steps into the open air.

It was a wonderfully warm clear starlit night, and all the flower-beds were pouring out their fragrance. The full moon was shining down on the garden, and along the gleaming white gravel paths the guests were strolling about, talking and smoking. One group had gathered round the fountain, where the elderly doctor whom everyone liked was causing general merriment by sailing paper boats.

Frau von Rinnlingen walked past them with a slight inclination of the head, and pointed into the distance where the elegant flower garden darkened into a park.

'Let's go down the centre avenue,' she said. At the head of it stood two short thick obelisks.

At the far end of the dead-straight chestnut-lined avenue they could see the greenish glint of the moonlit river. All round them it was dark and cool. Here and there a side-path branched off; these probably all curved down to the river as well. For a long time not a sound could be heard.

'There's a pretty place beside the water,' she said, 'where I've often been. We could sit there and talk for a few minutes. Look, now and then one can see a star glittering between the leaves.'

He made no answer, and stared at the green glimmering surface of the water as they approached it. The far bank was visible, where the public gardens were and the old city wall. At the end of the avenue, as they emerged on to the open grass that sloped down to the river, Frau von Rinnlingen said:

'Here is our spot, a little to the right; look, there's no one else there.'

The seat they sat down on had its back to the park, a few yards to one side of the avenue. It was warmer here than among the great trees. The crickets chirped in the grass, which at the very edge of the water ended in a thin line of reeds. The river gleamed palely in the moonlight.

They both sat in silence for a while, looking at the water. Then he listened with a sudden shock of emotion, for she was speaking again in that soft, gentle, pensive voice he had heard a week ago.

'How long have you had your disability, Herr Friedemann?' she asked. 'Were you born with it?'

He swallowed, for his throat felt constricted as if he were choking. Then he answered gently and politely:

'No, Frau Commandant. When I was a baby I was dropped on the floor, and that caused it.'

'How old are you now?' she went on.

'Thirty, Frau Commandant.'

'Thirty,' she repeated. 'So you have not been happy during these thirty years?'

Herr Friedemann shook his head, and his lips trembled. 'No,' he said. 'It was a lie and an illusion.'

'So you believed you were happy?' she asked.

'I tried to,' he said, and she replied:

'That was brave of you.'

A minute passed. Only the crickets chirped, and the tree behind them rustled softly.

Then she said: 'I have had some experience of unhappiness. These summer nights by the water are the best remedy for it.'

He made no reply to this, but gestured weakly, pointing across to the opposite bank, where all was peaceful and dark.

'I sat there the other day,' he said.

'Just after you had been to see me?' she asked.

He merely nodded.

Then suddenly, shuddering all over, he started to his feet, uttering a sobbing noise, a moan of sorrow which was somehow at the same time a cry of relief, and slowly sank to the ground in front of her. He had put his hand on hers, which had lain beside him on the seat; he clutched it now and seized the other as well; and as this little, totally deformed creature knelt there before her, quivering convulsively and burying his face in her lap, he stammered out in a hardly human, strangled voice:

'But you know! You know I . . . Let me . . . I can't go on . . . Oh my God . . . my God . . .'

She did not push him away, nor did she lower her head towards him. She sat erect, leaning back slightly, and her small close-set eyes, which seemed to mirror the liquid glint of the water, stared intently straight ahead, beyond him, into the distance.

And then, with a sudden violent movement, with a short, proud, scornful laugh, she had snatched her hands from his burning fingers, seized him by the arm, flung him sideways right on to the ground, leapt to her feet and vanished into the avenue.

He lay there with his face in the grass, stunned and desperate, with his body shuddering and twitching. He picked himself up, took two steps and collapsed again on to the grass. He was lying by the water's edge.

What was really his state of mind, his motive in what followed? Perhaps it was that same voluptuous hatred he had felt when she humbled him with her eyes; and now that he was lying here on the ground like a dog she had kicked, did this hatred perhaps degenerate into an insane fury which had to be translated into action, even if it was only action against himself – did it become an access of self-disgust, a craving to annihilate himself, to tear himself to pieces, to blot himself out . . . ?

He dragged himself on his stomach further down the slope, lifted the upper part of his body and let it drop into the water. He did not raise his head again; even his legs on the bank lay still.

The splash had silenced the crickets for a moment. Now they began their chirping as before, the park rustled softly and down the long avenue came the muted sound of laughter.

The Joker

Der Bajazzo

1897

The Joker

The end of it all, the upshot of life – of my life – is the disgust with which it fills me. A worthy ending indeed! Disgust with it all, disgust with the whole thing, this disgust that chokes me, goads me to frenzy and casts me down again into despair – sooner or later, no doubt, it will give me the necessary impetus to cut short the whole ridiculous, contemptible business and clear out for good. True enough, I may well hold out for a month or two yet; maybe for another three or six months I shall carry on eating, sleeping and passing the time – in the same mechanical, calm and well ordered fashion in which my life has outwardly gone by all this winter, contrasting so hideously with the vile process of my inner disintegration. One might almost suppose that a man's inner experiences become all the more violent and disturbing the more undisturbed and uncommitted and detached from the world his outward life is. There is no help for it: life has to be lived – and if one refuses to be a man of action and retires into the quiet of a hermit's solitude, even then the vicissitudes of existence will assault one inwardly, they will still be there to test one's character and to prove one a hero or a half-wit.

I have equipped myself with this neat notebook in order to write down my so-called 'story'. Why, I wonder? Perhaps just in order to have something to do? As an interesting psychological study perhaps, and to relish the thought that it was all in accordance with necessity? Necessity is so consoling! And perhaps even in order to enjoy an occasional sense of superiority over myself, an occasional moment of something like indifference? For I realize that indifference would be happiness of a kind.

31

1

It seems so far away and long ago, the little old town with its narrow angular streets and gabled houses, its Gothic churches and fountains, its industrious, respectable and simple inhabitants and the stately old grey patrician house in which I grew up.

The house stood in the centre of the town, and had outlasted four generations of rich and respected merchants. 'Ora et labora' was the motto over the front door. The great stone-paved entrance hall had a white wooden gallery running round it, and a wide stairway leading up to another spacious landing, after which one still had to walk along a dark little pillared lobby before passing through one of the tall white doors into the drawing-room where my mother sat playing the piano.

She sat in a dim light, for heavy dark red curtains hung across the windows; and the white gods and goddesses on the wallpaper seemed to stand out like real rounded figures from their blue background, and to be listening to the deep heavy opening notes of that Chopin nocturne, the piece she especially loved and always played very slowly as if to savour to the utmost the sadness of every chord. The grand piano was old and not as resonant as it had once been, but with the help of the soft pedal, which veiled the high notes so that they sounded like dull silver, the most unusual effects could be produced on it.

I would sit on the massive, straight-backed, damask sofa, listening to my mother and watching her. She was small and delicately built and usually wore a dress of soft, pale grey material. Her slender face was not beautiful, but under her parted, slightly wavy, unobtrusively blond hair it was like a peaceful, delicate, dreamy child's face, and as she sat at the piano with her head slightly to one side she resembled those small touching angelic figures often seen on old pictures, at the feet of the Madonna, playing on guitars.

When I was little she would often, in her gentle discreet voice, tell me tales of wonder such as no one else knew; or she would simply lay her hands on my head where it rested on her lap, and sit without speaking or stirring. I think those were the happiest and most contented hours of my life. Her hair did not turn grey, and she never seemed to me to grow any older; her figure merely became more and more fragile and her face slenderer, dreamier and more peaceful.

But my father was a tall stout gentleman in an elegant black coat and a white waistcoat, on which his gold pince-nez dangled. Between his short iron-grey side-whiskers his chin, clean-shaven like his upper lip, stood out roundly and firmly, and between his eyebrows there were always two deep vertical furrows. He was a man of considerable power and influence in public affairs; I have seen some men leave his presence with quickened breath and eyes aglow, others apparently broken and in utter despair. For it sometimes happened that I, and occasionally my mother and two elder sisters as well, were present at such scenes; perhaps because my father wanted to stimulate in me an ambition to rise as high in the world as he had done; or perhaps, as I suspect, because he needed an audience. Even as a child I was led to surmise this by the way he had of leaning back against his chair, with one hand thrust into his lapel, to watch the departure of his elated or discomfited visitor.

I would sit in a corner and observe my father and mother, rather as if I were choosing between the two of them and considering whether it was better to lead a life of dreamy meditation or one of action and power. And in the end it was on my mother's peaceful face that my eyes lingered.

2

One could not say that I resembled her in my outward behaviour, for the greater part of my occupations were by no means quiet and noiseless. I remember one to which I was passionately devoted: I preferred it to any association with companions of my own age and the kind of games they liked, and even now, when I am nearly thirty, the thought of it amuses and delights me.

What I am referring to was a large and well equipped puppet theatre: with this I would shut myself up all alone in my room and on its stage I would produce very remarkable music dramas. My room was on the second floor and contained gloomy portraits of two of our ancestors with pointed seventeenth-century beards. I would draw the curtains and stand a lamp near the theatre, for I considered that artificial lighting was necessary to heighten the effect. I seated myself immediately in front of the stage, for I was also the conductor, and I placed my left hand on a large round cardboard box which was the only visible orchestral instrument.

The performers now also arrived: I had drawn them myself with pen and ink, cut them out and fastened them to strips of wood so that they could stand. The men wore overcoats and top hats, and the women were very beautiful.

'Good evening, ladies and gentlemen!' I would say. 'I trust you are all in good health? I have arrived already, as there were still a few preparations to be made. But I think it is now time to proceed to the dressing-rooms.'

They proceeded to the dressing-rooms at the back of the stage, and presently returned completely transfigured into colourful theatrical characters. I had cut a peep-hole in the curtain through which they could look to see if the house was well filled; and so indeed it was. I rang the bell to warn myself that the performance was about to begin, then raised my baton and paused to savour the profound silence which this gesture imposed. But immediately, upon my next motion, the overture began with a deep premonitory roll of drums, executed by my left hand on the lid of the cardboard box; this was joined by the trumpets, clarinets and flutes, the timbre of which my mouth reproduced with incomparable fidelity; and thus the music continued until, at a mighty crescendo, the curtain swept up and revealed the dark forest or resplendent hall in which the opening scene of the drama was to take place.

The action had been roughly thought out in advance, but the details had to be improvised. The vocal strains, accompanied by the warbling of the clarinets and the drone of my cardboard drum, were sweet and passionate, and the text was strange and sonorous: verses full of bold and grandiose words, which occasionally rhymed but seldom made sense. The opera nevertheless took its course: with my left hand I drummed, with my mouth I sang and played, and with my right hand I conducted not only the performers on the stage but everyone else, with such diligent care that as each act ended enthusiastic applause broke out, the curtain had to rise again and again and the conductor was often obliged to turn round on his rostrum and express his thanks with a dignified but gratified bow to the auditorium.

34

And indeed, as I packed up my theatre after such a performance, flushed by my exertions, I would feel both exhausted and happy, as a great artist must feel at the triumphant completion of a work in which he has given of his best. This game remained my favourite occupation until I was thirteen or fourteen years old.

3

How in fact did they pass, my childhood and boyhood, in that great house with its ground-floor rooms where my father conducted his business, while my mother sat upstairs dreaming in an armchair or softly and pensively playing the piano, and my two sisters, who were two and three years older than me, busied themselves in the kitchen or with the household linen? I can remember so little about it all.

What is certain is that I was a prodigiously lively boy, and that I succeeded in making myself respected and liked by my schoolmates on account of my privileged background, my exemplary imitations of the masters, a large variety of histrionic feats and a rather superior manner of expressing myself. But in class I did badly, for I was far too preoccupied with studying the comic possibilities of the masters' movements and gestures to pay attention to anything else, and at home my head was so full of operatic plots, verses and a medley of other nonsense that any serious attempt to work was out of the question.

'Disgraceful!' my father would say, with the furrows deepening between his brows, when I had brought my school report into the drawing-room after luncheon and he had read it through, standing there with one hand in his lapel. 'You're a disappointment to me, I must say. Will you have the goodness to tell me what is to become of you? I can't see you ever making your way in life . . .'

That was depressing; but it did not prevent me from reading aloud to my parents and sisters, after dinner on that same day, a poem I had composed during the afternoon. My father laughed as I read, making his pince-nez bounce about all over his white waistcoat. 'What a pack of nonsense!' he kept exclaiming. But my mother drew me close to her, stroked my hair back from my forehead and said: 'It's not at all bad, my dear. I think there are one or two quite nice passages in it.'

Later, when I was a little older, I taught myself on my own initiative to play the piano after a fashion. I began by striking F-sharp major chords because I found the black notes particularly attractive; from this point I explored modulations into other keys and gradually, by dint of long hours at the instrument, acquired a certain facility in the art of harmonic variation and could produce a mystic wash of sound which had neither rhythm nor melody but was as expressive as I could make it.

My mother said: 'He has a very tasteful touch.' And she arranged for me to have piano lessons, which were kept up for six months; I really had no aptitude for learning the correct fingering and rhythm.

Well, the years went by and I grew up, enjoying myself enormously despite my troubles at school. I circulated among my acquaintances and relations, happy and popular, and I behaved adroitly and charmingly to them because I liked playing the charmer, though instinctively I was beginning to despise all these prosaic, unimaginative people.

4

One afternoon when I was about eighteen and on the point of entering the top classes at school, I overheard a short conversation between my parents, who were sitting together in the drawing-room at the round sofa table and did not know that I was next door in the dining-room, lying idly in the window-seat and contemplating the pale sky above the gabled roofs. When I heard my name mentioned I tiptoed to the white double door, which was standing ajar.

My father was leaning back in his chair with his legs crossed holding the Stock Exchange journal with one hand on his knee and slowly stroking his chin between his mutton-chop whiskers with the other. My mother was sitting on the sofa with her peaceful face bowed over some embroidery. The lamp stood between them.

My father said: 'In my view it's about time he was removed from school and entered for training with some large, well established firm.'

'Oh!' exclaimed my mother, looking up in dismay. 'Such a talented boy!'

My father was silent for a moment and carefully blew a speck of dust from his coat. Then he hunched his shoulders and spread out his arms, turning the palms of his hands towards my mother, and said:

'If you suppose, my dear, that to do well in business requires no talent, then let me tell you that you are mistaken. In any case I regret to say that it is becoming increasingly clear to me that the boy is getting absolutely nowhere at school. His talent, as you call it, is the talent of a kind of mimicking buffoon or joker – though let me hasten to add that I do not by any means underestimate such gifts. He can be charming when he wants to be, he knows how to handle people, how to amuse and flatter them; he has a need to please them and to be a success with them. Many a man with that sort of disposition has made his fortune by it; and in view of his indifference to everything else I would say that his qualifications for a fairly successful business career are relatively good.'

Having thus delivered himself my father leaned back with a satisfied air, took a cigarette from his cigarette-case and lit it with deliberation.

'I dare say you are right,' said my mother, and her eyes wandered unhappily round the room. 'It's just that I have often thought, and in a way hoped, that one day he might become an artist . . . It's true I suppose that his musical gifts have remained undeveloped and that we can't expect anything to come of them; but have you noticed that since he went to the little art exhibition recently he has been doing some drawing? And he draws not at all badly, I think.'

My father blew a puff of smoke, adjusted himself in his chair and said curtly:

'That's all clowning and hocus-pocus. Anyway we can, of course, as is only right, consult the boy's own wishes.'

My own wishes! And what might they be? But I found the prospect of a change in my outward circumstances distinctly cheering. I declared with a solemn face that I was willing to leave school and become a businessman; and I was duly apprenticed to Herr Schlievogt's big timber firm down by the river.

5

Needless to say, the change was purely external. My interest in Herr Schlievogt's big timber business was extremely slight, and I sat on my revolving stool under the gaslight in that dark narrow office feeling as much a stranger and as absent in spirit as I had felt in the schoolroom. I had fewer worries now; that was the only difference.

Herr Schlievogt, a corpulent, red-faced man with a stiff grey nautical beard, paid little attention to me, since he spent most of his time in the sawmill which was some distance from the timber yard and offices. His employees treated me with respect. I entertained friendly relations with only one of them, a gifted and self-satisfied young man of good family whose acquaintance I had already made at school and whose name was Schilling. Like myself he made fun of everyone and everything, but he none the less took a very lively interest in the timber trade and never let a day pass without declaring it to be his definite purpose to become, somehow or other, a rich man.

I for my part mechanically carried out my necessary duties and devoted the rest of the day to sauntering about the yard among the workmen and the stacks of timber, gazing through the high wooden fence at the river, where a freight train occasionally lumbered by, and as I sauntered and gazed I would be thinking about some theatrical performance or concert I had attended, or some book I had read.

I read a great deal, in fact I read everything I could lay my hands on, and I was exceedingly impressionable. I had an intuitive understanding of the personalities of authors, I seemed to see in each of them a reflection of myself, and I would go on thinking and feeling in the style of a particular book until a new one had influenced me in its turn. In my room, the room where I had once set up my puppet theatre, I now sat with a book on my knees, looking up at the portraits of my two ancestors, savouring the inflections of the writer to whom I had surrendered myself, and with an unproductive chaos of half-formed thoughts and fanciful images filling my mind . . .

My sisters had got married in quick succession, and when I was not at the office I often went down to the drawing-room, where my mother would now usually be sitting quite alone. She was slightly ailing and her face was growing more and more placid and childlike. When she had played me some Chopin and I had showed her some newly discovered trick of harmonic modulation, she would sometimes ask me whether I was contented in my work and happy . . . There was no doubt that I was happy.

I was not much more than twenty, my situation was a merely provisional one, and I not infrequently reflected that I was by no means obliged to spend my life working for Herr Schlievogt or for any other timber business, however prosperous. I told myself that I should one day be able to kick over the traces, leave this town and its gabled houses behind me and live somewhere or other doing exactly as I pleased: reading good, elegantly written novels, going to the theatre, playing the piano a little . . . Happy? But after all I ate extremely well, I wore the best clothes, and even when I was younger and still at school I had noticed how my poorer and shabbily dressed contemporaries habitually deferred to me and to others like me, treating us with a kind of flattering diffidence which indicated their willing acceptance of us as lords and leaders of fashion: and this had made me happily conscious of the fact that I belonged to the élite, to that class of rich and envied persons whose birthright it is to look down on the poor, the unlucky and the envious with benevolent contempt. Had I not every reason to be happy? I was content to let things take their course. For the time being it was very gratifying to live as a rather alien, effortlessly superior figure among these acquaintances and relations of mine whose limited outlook I found so amusing but to whom, because I liked to be liked, I behaved with adroit charm. I basked complacently in the respect which they all showed me; but it remained a puzzled respect, for they obscurely sensed something antagonistic and extravagant in my nature and character.

6

A change was beginning to come over my father. Every day when he joined us for dinner at four o'clock the furrows between his brows seemed to have grown deeper, and he no longer thrust his hand into his lapel with an imposing gesture, but looked depressed, nervous and diffident. One day he said to me:

'You are old enough by now to share with me the anxieties which are undermining my health. It is in any case my duty to acquaint you with them, in case you should be entertaining any false expectations with regard to your future position in life. As you know, the marriages of your sisters entailed considerable sacrifices. And recently the firm has suffered losses which have reduced the capital quite severely. I am an old man, I have lost heart, and I think it is too late now to expect any appreciable improvement in the situation. I must ask you to take note that you will be cast upon your own resources . . .'

He said this about two months before his death. One day he was found slumped in the armchair in his private office, pallid, paralysed and mumbling inarticulately. A week later the whole town attended his funeral.

My mother sat quietly on the sofa by the round table in the drawing-room; she looked frail and her eyes were nearly always closed. When my sisters and I attended to her needs, she would perhaps nod and smile, but then she would sit on in silence, motionless, with her hands folded on her lap and her strange sad wide-eyed gaze fixed on one of the gods in the wallpaper pattern. When the gentlemen in frock coats came to report on the liquidation of the firm, she would nod in the same way and close her eyes again.

She no longer played Chopin, and when now and then she gently stroked her hair, her pale, frail, tired hand would tremble. Hardly six months after my father's death she took to her bed and died without a murmur, letting her life go without a struggle . . .

So now all that was over. What was there to keep me in the place? The business had been wound up, for better or for worse, and it turned out that my inheritance was about a hundred thousand marks. That was enough to make me independent – completely independent, particularly as I had, for some reason or other which is of no consequence, been declared unfit for military service.

There were no longer any ties between me and these people among whom I had grown up, who looked at me now with an air of increasing estrangement and bewilderment, and whose outlook on life was far too narrow for me to have any wish to conform to it. True, they recognized me for what I was – an absolutely useless individual. Even I recognized this. But I was sufficiently sceptical and fatalistic to take a light-hearted view of what my father had called my 'talent of a buffoon or joker'. I was cheerfully determined to enjoy life in my own way, and thoroughly satisfied with myself.

I took possession of my small fortune and left my native town, almost without saying goodbye. I intended in the first instance to travel.

7

The three years that now followed, those years in which I surrendered myself with eager appetite to a host of new, changing, enriching impressions, have remained in my memory like an enchanting, faraway dream. How long is it since I spent that night with the monks up on the Simplon Pass, celebrating New Year's Eve amid ice and snow? How long since I strolled across the Piazza Erbe in Verona? since I stepped out for the first time from the Borgo Santo Spirito into the colonnade at Saint Peter's and let my eyes wander awestruck over that enormous square? since I stood on the Corso Vittorio Emmanuele looking down over the gleaming white buildings of Naples and saw the graceful silhouette of Capri far out to sea, just visible in the blue haze? . . . In actual fact it was all scarcely more than six years ago.

Oh, to be sure, I lived very prudently and in a manner befitting my situation: in simple private rooms, in cheap boarding-houses – but what with moving from place to place, and because I found it hard at first to do without the upper-middle-class comforts to which I was accustomed, I nevertheless could not help spending considerable sums of money. I had set aside fifteen thousand marks from my capital for my period of travelling; this sum, needless to say, was exceeded.

I felt at ease, however, among the people with whom my wanderings brought me in contact; often they were disinterested and very interesting acquaintances, and although I was of course not an object of respect to them as I had been in my previous environment, I at least had no need to fear that they would look at me askance or ask me questions.

Occasionally my particular social accomplishments made me genuinely popular with the clientele of boarding-houses at which I stayed. I remember especially a scene in the public room at the Pensione

Minelli in Palermo. Amid a circle of Frenchmen of various ages I had somehow begun to play the piano and to improvise a music drama 'by Richard Wagner', with much tragic grimacing, declamatory song and rolling harmony. I had just finished, to thunderous applause, when an old gentleman hastened up to me. He was almost totally bald, with scanty white mutton-chop whiskers drooping over his grey travelling coat. He seized both my hands and exclaimed with tears in his eyes:

'But that was fantastic! That was fantastic, my dear sir! I swear I have not been so delightfully entertained for the last thirty years! Pray, sir, allow me to thank you from the bottom of my heart! But you must, yes you must, become an actor or a musician!'

I confess that on such occasions I felt something of the pride of genius, such as a great painter must feel who has condescended to scribble an absurd yet brilliant caricature on the top of a table at which he is sitting among friends. After dinner however I returned alone to the sitting-room and passed a solitary and wistful hour coaxing the instrument into a series of sustained chords, expressive, as I thought, of the mood inspired in me by the sight of Palermo.

From Sicily I had paid a fleeting visit to Africa, then I had gone on to Spain; and it was there, in the country near Madrid, on a dreary wet winter afternoon, that I first became conscious of a wish to return to Germany – and realized, moreover, that it was now necessary for me to do so. For apart from the fact that I was beginning to long for a quiet, regular and settled existence, it was not hard to calculate that by the time I reached Germany, however much I economized, I should have spent twenty thousand marks.

I began my slow return journey through France without over-much delay, but lingered for some time in this town and that, so that it took nearly six months. I remember with nostalgic clarity the summer evening on which my train drew into the main station of the provincial capital in central Germany which I had already selected as my destination before setting out. And now I had reached it – a little wiser, the richer by some experiences, equipped with some items of know-ledge, and full of childlike delight at the prospect of establishing myself here in carefree independence, subject of course to the limits of my modest means, and settling down to a life of untroubled, contemplative leisure.

At that time I was twenty-five years old.

8

It was not a bad choice of place. The town is an important centre, still free of the excessive noise and bustle and ugly industrialization of a very large city, but containing some quite spacious old squares and streets which lack neither liveliness nor a certain elegance. On its outskirts there are a number of pleasant spots, but my favourite among them has always been the so-called Lerchenberg promenade, a tastefully laid-out avenue traversing the long narrow hill on the side of which most of the town is built and from which one has an extensive view over the houses and churches, across the gently meandering river and into the distance. At certain points, especially on fine summer afternoons when a military band is playing and carriages and pedestrians are circulating, it is reminiscent of the Pincio. But I shall have occasion to refer again to this promenade . . .

I had rented a fair-sized room, with a small adjoining bedroom, in a lively district near the centre of the town, and I took an incredibly elaborate pleasure in furnishing it. Most of my parents' furniture, to be sure, had passed into my sisters' possession, but enough of it had come my way to suffice for my needs: handsome, solid pieces, which now arrived together with my books and the two family portraits, and above all the old grand piano, which my mother had specially bequeathed to me.

And in fact, when everything had been set up in its place – when every wall, the heavy mahogany desk and the commodious chest of drawers, had been adorned with the photographs I had collected during my travels –when with my arrangements made and all secure I let myself sink into an armchair by the window and proceeded by turns to look out into the streets and to survey my new lodging – I felt an undoubted sense of well-being. Yet nevertheless (for it was a moment I have not forgotten) amid all my contentment and confidence there was something else softly stirring within me: some slight misgiving and uneasiness, some half-conscious impulse of revolt and rebellion against a power that menaced me . . . It was the faintly depressing thought that my situation, which had hitherto never been more than merely provisional, must now for the first time be regarded as definitive and permanent . . .

I will not deny that I occasionally felt a recurrence of this and similar sensations. But how, after all, can any of us hope to avoid certain late-afternoon moods: those moments in which we gaze out into the gathering dusk, perhaps into a drizzle of rain as well, and are assailed by twinges of foreboding? I could at all events be certain that my future was fully provided for. I had entrusted the round sum of eighty thousand marks to the city bank; the interest – these are poor times, heaven knows! – amounted to about six hundred marks a quarter, and this was enough to permit me to live decently, to buy books, to go to the theatre now and then – not excluding an occasional lighter diversion.

From that time on I really did pass my days in a manner conforming to the ideal to which I had always aspired – I got up at ten, had breakfast, spent part of the morning at the piano and the rest of it reading a literary periodical or a book. At midday I strolled down the street to the little restaurant which I regularly patronized, and had lunch there; then I would go for a fairly long walk along the streets, round a gallery, through the outskirts of the town, up to the Lerchenberg. On returning home I would resume my morning's occupations: reading, making music, sometimes even drawing, after a fashion, to amuse myself, or writing a carefully penned letter. In the evening, if I was not going to a play or a concert after dinner, I sat on at the café reading the papers till bedtime. And I would assess the day as a good one, as one that had contained some pleasure and happiness, if I had succeeded in producing at the piano some effect which struck me as new and beautiful, or if in reading a short story or looking at a picture I had experienced some emotion which had lasted for a while . . .

I will, however, not omit to mention that there was a certain idealistic purposefulness in my arrangements, that I made it my serious business to ensure that each of my days should 'contain' as much as possible. I ate modestly, I usually had only one suit, in short I carefully limited my bodily needs in order to be able to afford a good seat at the opera or an expensive concert ticket, and to be in a position to buy the latest literary publications or visit an occasional art exhibition . . .

But the days went by, and they turned into weeks and months – was I bored? I will concede that one does not always have a book that will yield hour after hour of memorable experience; moreover one's attempts to improvise at the piano have at times been complete failures, and one has sat by the window, smoking cigarettes, while gradually and irresistibly a feeling of distaste creeps over one, distaste for oneself and for everything else. Once again one is assailed by misgiving, by that unpleasantly familiar misgiving – and one jumps from one's chair, one leaves the house and walks along the streets, watching those others go by: the people with jobs, the people with professions, at whom one can cheerfully shrug one's shoulders, in happy contempt for the intellectual inferiority and material misfortune which deprives them of leisure and of the capacity to enjoy it

9

Is it possible for any man, at the age of twenty-seven, seriously to believe that his situation has been unalterably finalized, however depressingly probable this may in fact be? The twittering of a bird, a tiny gap of blue in the sky, some half-remembered dream when one wakes in the morning – all these are enough to flood one's heart with sudden vague hopes, to fill it with a festive expectation of some great unforeseen happiness . . . I drifted from one day to the next, meditatively, aimlessly, my mind busy with this or that trivial hope, even looking forward to such things as the next issue of an amusing periodical: I was filled with the resolute conviction that I was happy, but from time to time I felt the weariness of solitude.

If the truth were told, they were by no means rare, these moods of exasperation at the thought of my lack of friends and social intercourse; for this lack scarcely needs explaining. I had no connections with the best or even with the second-best local society; to get on a convivial footing with the *jeunesse dorée* I should have needed, God knows, a great deal more money than I possessed; and as for bohemian circles – why, damn it, I am a man of education, I wear clean linen and a decent suit: am I supposed to enjoy sitting with unkempt young men round tables sticky with absinthe, discussing anarchism? In brief: there was no specific social circle to which I obviously belonged, and such acquaintanceships as I happened in one way or another to make were few and far between, superficial and uncordial – this, I admit, was my own fault, for in these cases too I behaved with diffident reserve, disagreeably conscious of the fact that I was unable to tell even a down-at-heel painter, in brief clear words that would command his respect, who and what I actually was.

I had, of course, severed my ties with 'society' and renounced it, as soon as I had taken the liberty of going my own way instead of somehow making myself useful to it. Had I needed 'other people' in order to be happy? If so, then I was bound to ask myself whether I should not now have been busy enriching myself as a fairly successful entrepreneur, who would at the same time be serving the community and earning its envy and esteem.

Whereas – whereas! The fact remained that I was finding my philosophic isolation excessively vexing, and in the last resort quite inconsistent with my conception of 'happiness' – with my consciousness, my conviction, that I was happy. And that this conviction should be shaken was, of course, beyond any shadow of doubt quite out of the question. Not to be happy – to be unhappy – why, was this even thinkable? It was unthinkable. Thus I decided, and thus I disposed of the question – until the mood returned and I felt again that there was something wrong, something very far wrong, about my self-isolation, my retired seclusion, my outsider's life. And this thought put me most shockingly out of humour.

Is one 'out of humour' if one is happy? I remembered my earlier life in my native town, that restricted society in which I had moved, full of the gratifying consciousness of my artistic gifts and genius – sociable, charming, my eyes sparkling with high-spirited mockery and an air of benevolent superiority to everyone; people had thought me rather odd, but I had nevertheless been popular. I had been happy then, in spite of having to work in Herr Schlievogt's big timber firm. And what was I now?

But after all, an absolutely fascinating book has just been published, a new French novel which I have decided I can afford to buy and which I shall have leisure to enjoy, sitting comfortably in my armchair. Another three hundred pages, full of taste, *blague* and exquisite artistry! Come now, I have arranged my life the way I wanted it! Can I possibly not be happy? The question is ridiculous. The question is utterly absurd . . .

10

Another day has drawn to a close, a day which has undeniably, thank God, contained its quota of pleasure; darkness has fallen, I have drawn the curtains and lit the reading lamp; it is nearly midnight. I could go to bed; instead of which I sit on in my armchair, leaning right back with my hands folded on my lap, gazing at the ceiling, and attending submissively to the noiseless delving and gnawing of some scarcely identifiable distress which I have been unable to shake off.

Only a couple of hours ago I was allowing a great masterpiece to do its work on me – one of those monstrous, cruel masterpieces by an unprincipled dilettantistic genius, full of decadent splendours that shake and dumbfound the spectator, torture him to ecstasy and overwhelm him . . . My nerves are still quivering, my imagination has been violently stirred, strange moods are surging up and down within me, moods of passionate longing, of religious ardour, of exultation, of mystic peace – and mingled with all this is a craving, an impulse that constantly restimulates these moods, an impulse to work them out of my system: the need to express them, to communicate them, to 'make something of them' . . .

What if I really were an artist, capable of expressing myself in sound, or words, or visual images – or rather, as I should frankly prefer, in all three simultaneously? And yet it is true that I have all sorts of talents! For example, first and foremost, I can sit down at the piano and treat myself, in the intimacy of my own room, to a display of my beautiful feelings: surely that is enough? For if I needed 'other people' in order to be happy, then I – yes, well, all this I concede. But let us suppose that I did set some slight store by success, by fame, recognition, praise, envy, love? . . . Oh, God, if I so much as think of the scene at that inn in Palermo, I have to admit that it would be so indescribably encouraging and comforting if a similar incident were to happen now!

On careful reflection I feel bound to admit that there must be a distinction (sophistical and absurd though it seems) between internal and external happiness. 'External happiness'! What in fact is it? There is a certain class of human beings who seem to be the favourites of the gods, whose good fortune is their genius and whose genius is their good fortune: they are children of light, and with the sun's radiance mirrored in their eyes they move lightly, gracefully, charmingly, playfully through life, admiringly surrounded by everyone, praised and envied and loved by everyone, because even envy cannot bring itself to hate them. But they return the general gaze as rather spoiled children do, with a kind of whimsical irreverent mockery and unclouded goodwill, secure in their good fortune and in their genius, never for a moment entertaining the thought that things might be otherwise . . .

As for myself, I confess my weakness: I should dearly like to belong to that privileged category. And rightly or wrongly, I am still beset by the thought that once upon a time I did belong to it. Whether I am right or wrong in thinking so matters not a jot – for let us be candid: the important thing is what one thinks of oneself, the image one presents of oneself, the image of oneself that one has the confidence to present!

Perhaps in reality the situation is simply that I renounced this 'external happiness' by contracting out of the service of 'society' and arranging to live my life independently of 'other people'. But it goes without saying that I am content with such an arrangement: this is not for one moment to be doubted, it cannot be doubted, it must not be doubted. For let me repeat with desperate emphasis: I intend to be happy, and I must be happy! The conception of 'good fortune' as something meritorious, as a kind of genius, of aristocratic distinction, of special charm, and the contrary conception of 'misfortune' as something ugly, skulking, contemptible and in a word ridiculous, are both so deeply rooted in me that if I were unhappy I should inevitably lose my self-respect.

How could I possibly allow myself to be unhappy? What sort of a figure should I then cut in my own eyes? I should have to squat in outer darkness like some sort of bat or owl, blinking as I gazed enviously across the gulf at the happy, charming 'children of light'. I should have to hate them, with that hatred which is merely love turned sour – and I should have to despise myself!

'To squat in outer darkness'! Oh, it comes back to me now, all I have thought and felt, over and over again for many a month, about my 'outsider's life' and my 'philosophic isolation'! And the anxiety returns, that unpleasantly familiar anxiety! And that vague impulse of rebellion against some menacing power . . .

Needless to say, some consolation was to hand, some anodyne distraction, on this occasion and on the next, and again on the next. But the same reflections returned; all of them returned a thousand times in the course of the months and the years.

11

There are certain autumn days that are like a miracle. Summer is already over, the leaves began to turn yellow some time ago, and for days the wind has been whistling all round the streets and muddy water streaming down the gutters. One has resigned oneself to the change of season, one has so to speak taken one's seat by the fire, ready to submit to the coming of winter. But one morning one wakes up and cannot believe one's eyes: between the curtains a narrow strip of brilliant blue is shining into the room. In amazement one leaps out of bed and throws the window open: a flood of tremulous sunlight bursts over one, through all the street noise one can hear the birds happily twittering and chattering, and as one breathes in the light, fresh October air it seems to have exactly the aroma of the wind in May – so incomparably sweet, so incomparably full of promise. It is spring, quite obviously spring, despite the calendar; and one flings on one's clothes and hurries out into the streets, into the open, under this radiant sky . . .

About four months ago – we are now at the beginning of February – there was just such an unexpected and unusual day; and on that day I saw a quite remarkably pretty thing. I had set out in the morning before nine o'clock and was making my way towards the Lerchenberg, light of heart and high in spirits and full of a vague expectation that something or other was going to change, that something surprising and delightful was going to happen. I approached the hill from the right and walked all the way up it and along the top, keeping close to the edge of the main promenade, beside the low stone parapet: from here, for the whole length of the avenue – that is for something like half an hour's walk – I could have an unobstructed view across the town as it drops with a slightly terraced effect down the slope, and over the meandering links of the river as they gleamed in the sunlight, with the hills and greenery of the open countryside lost in a shimmering haze beyond them.

There was hardly anyone else up here yet. The seats on the far side of the promenade were empty, and here and there a statue looked out from among the trees, glittering white in the sun, although now and then a withered leaf would drift slowly down and settle on it. As I walked I watched the bright panorama to one side of me, and listened to the silence, which remained unbroken until I reached the end of the hill where the road begins to dip and is lined with old chestnut trees. But at this point I heard behind me the clatter of horses' hooves and wheels; a carriage was approaching at a brisk trot, and I had to make way for it about half-way down the hill. I stepped aside and paused to let it pass.

It was a small, quite light two-wheeled carriage, drawn by a pair of large, glossy, spirited, snorting bays. The reins were held by a young lady of about nineteen or twenty, and beside her sat an old gentleman of handsome and distinguished appearance, with white moustaches à la russe and bushy white eyebrows. The rear seat was occupied by a smart-looking groom in plain black and silver livery.

The horses had been reined back to a walk at the beginning of the descent, as one of them seemed nervous and refractory. It had pulled clear of the shaft right over to one side, holding its head against its chest, and its slender legs picked their way downhill in so restive and mettlesome a manner that the old gentleman was leaning forward rather anxiously, offering the young lady his elegantly gloved left hand to help her pull the reins tight. The driving seemed to have been entrusted to her only temporarily and only half in earnest: she appeared at any rate to be manoeuvring the vehicle with a mixture of childlike self-importance and inexperience. She was making a solemn, indignant little movement with her head as she tried to control the shying, stumbling animal.

She was dark and slender. Her hair was wound into a firm knot behind her neck but lay quite lightly and loosely over her forehead and temples, where an occasional light brown strand could be seen. On it was perched a round straw hat, dark in colour and decorated only with a modest arrangement of ribbons. For the rest, she was wearing a short dark blue jacket and a simple skirt of light grey material.

In her finely shaped oval face with its dark brown complexion slightly flushed in the morning air, the most attractive feature was undoubtedly her eyes: they were long and narrow, their scarcely visible irises were a glittering black, and the brows arched above them were extraordinarily even, as if traced with a pen. Her nose was perhaps a trifle long, and her mouth might well have been smaller, although her lips were clearly and finely cut. But at the moment it was looking particularly charming, for one could see her gleaming white, rather widely spaced teeth, and as she tugged at the horse the young lady pressed them hard on to her lower lip, giving a slight upward tilt to her almost childishly round chin.

It would be quite incorrect to say that this was a face of outstanding and admirable beauty. It had the charm of youth and freshness and high spirits, and this charm had so to speak been smoothed, refined and ennobled by easy affluence, gentle upbringing and luxurious care. There was no doubt that those narrow, sparkling eyes, which were now concentrated with fastidious petulance on the fractious horse, would in a minute or two resume an expression of secure happiness, of happiness taken for granted. The sleeves of her jacket, widely cut at the shoulders, fitted closely round her slender wrists, and I thought I had never seen anything so enchantingly, so exquisitely elegant as the way those tiny, pale, ungloved hands held the reins!

I stood quite unnoticed by the side of the road as the carriage passed, and walked slowly on as the horses quickened their pace again and rapidly drew out of sight. My feelings were, in the first instance, pleasure and admiration; but I simultaneously became conscious of a strange, burning pain, a bitter, insistent upsurge – of envy? of love? – I did not dare analyse it. Of self-contempt?

As I write, the image that occurs to me is that of a wretched beggar standing outside a jeweller's shop, staring at some precious glittering gem in the window. Such a man cannot let the desire to possess the jewel present itself clearly to his mind: for even the thought of such a desire would be an absurdity, an impossibility, a thought that would make him utterly ridiculous in his own eyes.

12

I will report that only a week later, by chance, I saw that young lady again: this time it was at the opera, at a performance of Gounod's *Faust*. I had just entered the brightly lit auditorium and was proceeding towards my seat in the stalls when I caught sight of her, sitting on the old gentleman's left, in a stage box at the other side of the house. I incidentally noticed, ludicrous though it seems, that this rather startled me and threw me into a kind of confusion, so that for some reason I at once averted my eyes and aimlessly surveyed the other boxes and rows of seats. Not until the overture began did I resolve to inspect the pair a little more closely.

The old gentleman, wearing a carefully fastened frock coat with a black silk necktie, was leaning back in his chair in a calm and dignified posture, resting one brown-gloved hand lightly on the plush balustrade of his box, and now and then slowly stroking his beard or his well trimmed grey hair with the other. But the young lady – who was no doubt his daughter – sat leaning forward with an air of lively interest; she had both hands on the balustrade and they were holding her fan. From time to time she made a slight movement with her head to toss back the loose, light brown hair from her forehead and temples.

She was wearing a very light pale silk blouse, with a posy of violets in the girdle; and in the bright lights her narrow eyes were gleaming still blacker than when I had seen her before. I also observed that the expression of her mouth which I had noticed a week ago was evidently a habit with her: not a moment passed but she pressed her lower lip with her little white regularly spaced teeth, and drew up her chin slightly. This innocent gesture in which there was not a trace of coquetry, those calmly yet gaily wandering eyes, that delicate white neck, which she wore uncovered except for a neatly fitting narrow silk ribbon the same colour as her bodice, and the way she turned now and then to draw the old gentleman's attention to something in the orchestra pit or some feature of the curtain or someone in another box – all this made an impression of ineffably subtle childlike charm which was at the same time entirely unsentimental and aroused no kind of 'compassionate' tenderness whatsoever. It was an aristocratic, measured childlikeness, coloured by the security and confidence that come of a refined and gracious way of living. Her evident happiness had nothing arrogant about it: it was the kind of quiet happiness that can be taken for granted.

Gounod's brilliant and tender music was, I thought, no bad accompaniment to this spectacle. As I listened to it I paid no attention to what was happening on the stage and became entirely absorbed in a reflective mood of gentle melancholy, which without this music would perhaps have been more acute. But in the very first interval, after Act I, a gentleman of, let us say, twenty-seven to thirty rose from his seat in the stalls, disappeared and immediately reappeared, with a deftly executed bow, in the box on which my eyes were fixed. The old man at once shook hands with him, and the young lady too, with a cordial inclination of the head, held out hers, which he gracefully raised to his lips; whereupon he was invited to take a seat.

I declare that I am willing to concede that this young man possessed the most incomparable shirt-front that I have ever in my life been privileged to see. It was a shirt-front completely exposed to view, for his waistcoat was no more than a narrow black band and his evening jacket, fastened by one button quite some way below his stomach, was cut out from the shoulders in an unusually sweeping curve. But the shirt-front – which ended in a tall, stiff, smartly turned down butterfly collar and a wide black bow-tie, and was fastened at regular intervals by two large square buttons, also black – was dazzlingly white, and although admirably starched it did not lack flexibility, for in the region of his stomach it formed a pleasing hollow, only to rise again, further up, to a satisfying and gleaming apex.

I need hardly say that it was this shirt that chiefly claimed one's attention; as for his head, however, which was completely spherical and covered with very blond hair cropped close to the skull, it was adorned with a pair of rimless and ribbonless eyeglasses, a none-too-thick blond moustache with slightly curled points, and a number of small duelling scars on one cheek, running right up to the temple. For the rest, this gentleman was of unexceptionable build and moved with an air of assurance.

In the course of the evening – for he remained in the box – I noticed two postures which seemed especially characteristic of him. On the one hand, if conversation with his companions flagged, he would lean comfortably back with his legs crossed and his opera-glasses on his lap, lower his head, energetically protrude the whole of his mouth and relapse into profound contemplation of both points of his moustache, evidently quite hypnotized by them, and slowly and silently turning his head to and fro. If on the other hand he was engaged in discourse with the young lady, he would respectfully modify the position of his legs, but lean back still further, grasping his chair with both hands; as he did so he would raise his head as high as possible and smile, opening his mouth rather wide, charmingly and a shade patronizingly down at his young neighbour. There could be no doubt that this gentleman rejoiced in a wonderfully happy conceit of himself . . .

I declare in all seriousness that these are characteristics which I fully appreciate. The nonchalance of his movements may have been a trifle daring, but not one of them gave rise to a moment's embarrassment; his self-confidence sustained him throughout. And why should it be otherwise? Here, clearly, was a man who while perhaps lacking any particular distinction had irreproachably made his way, and would pursue it to clear and profitable ends; who sheltered in the shade of agreement with all men, and basked in the sunshine of their general approval. And in the mean time there he sat in the box, chattering with a girl to whose pure and exquisite charm he was perhaps not unsusceptible, and whose hand, if this were so, he could with a good conscience request in marriage. Most assuredly, I have no wish to utter a single disrespectful word about this gentleman.

But what of myself? I sat on down here and was at liberty to observe from a distance, peering bitterly out of the darkness, that precious inaccessible creature as she chatted and joked with this contemptible wretch! Excluded, unheeded, unauthorized, a stranger, *hors ligne*, *déclassé*, a pariah, a pitiful object even in my own eyes . . .

I stayed till the end, and I met the trio again in the cloakroom, where they lingered a little as they donned their fur coats, exchanging a word here and there with some lady or some officer . . . The young gentleman accompanied the father and daughter as they left the theatre, and I followed them at a discreet interval across the foyer.

It was not raining, there were a few stars in the sky, and they did not take a carriage. They walked ahead of me at a leisurely pace, talking busily, and some way behind I timidly dogged their footsteps – crushed and tormented by a dreadful feeling of biting, mocking misery . . .

They had not far to walk; it was scarcely a street's length to where they stopped in front of the simple façade of an imposing-looking house, and a moment later the young lady and her father vanished into it after bidding a cordial good-night to their escort, who in turn quickened his pace and disappeared.

The heavy, carved front door of the house bore the title and name 'Justizrat Rainer'.

13

I am determined to complete this written record, despite the inner repugnance which constantly impels me to throw down my pen and rush out into the street. I have pondered this affair and brooded over it to the point of utter exhaustion! How sick to death, how nauseated I am by the whole thing! . . .

Not quite three months ago I learned from the papers that a 'bazaar' for charitable purposes had been arranged and would take place in the town hall; and that it would be attended by the best society. I read this announcement attentively and at once decided to go to the bazaar. She will be there, I thought, perhaps selling things at one of the stalls, and in that case there will be nothing to prevent my approaching her. When all is said and done I am a man of education and good family, and if I find this Fräulein Rainer attractive, then on an occasion of that sort I have as much right as the gentleman with the astonishing shirt-front to address her and exchange a few pleasantries with her . . .

It was a windy and rainy afternoon when I betook myself to the town hall; there was a throng of people and carriages in front of the entrance. I managed to penetrate into the building, paid the admission fee, deposited my coat and hat and made my way with some difficulty up the wide, crowded stair to the first floor and into the banqueting hall. The air in here was sultry and smelled heavily of wine, food, scent and pine needles, and there was a confused hubbub of laughter, conversation, music, vendors' cries and ringing gongs.

The vast hall with its enormously high ceiling was gaily festooned with flags and garlands of all colours, and there were vending stalls in the middle of the floor as well as all along the sides – open stalls and closed booths, with men in fantastic masks standing outside the latter and inviting custom at the tops of their voices. The ladies who were standing round selling flowers, needlework, tobacco and various refreshments were also wearing all kinds of costumes. The band was playing loudly at one end of the hall on a platform covered with potted plants; and a tightly packed procession of people was slowly advancing along the rather narrow passageway that had been left between the stalls.

Somewhat stunned by the noise of the music and by the high-spirited shouting from the booths and lottery tubs, I joined the general stream, and scarcely a minute has passed when I caught sight of the young lady I was looking for, a few paces to the left of the entrance. She was selling wine and lemonade at a little stall decorated with pine branches, and she had chosen an Italian costume: the brightly coloured skirt, the four-square white headdress and short bodice such as Albanese women wear, with the sleeves leaving her dainty arms bare to the elbow. She was leaning sideways against her serving-table, slightly flushed, toying with her colourful fan and chatting to a group of men who stood round the stall smoking. Among these I discerned at first glance the figure already familiar to me; he was standing close beside her, with four fingers of each hand in the side pockets of his jacket.

I pressed slowly past, resolving to approach her as soon as an opportunity should present itself, as soon as she was a little less busy. Now, by God, it would be seen whether I still had any remnant of happy self-possession, any pride and *savoir-faire* left in me, or whether my morose, half-desperate mood of the last few weeks had been justified! What on earth had been the matter with me? Why should the sight of this girl fill me with the agonizing miserable mixture of envy, love, shame and bitter resentment with which – I confess it – my cheeks were now once again burning? Single-mindedness! Charm! Lightness of heart, devil take it, and elegant self-complacency, as befits a gifted and fortunate man! And with nervous eagerness I rehearsed the jocular phrase, the *bon mot*, the Italian greeting with which I intended to address her . . .

It was some time before the crowd had clumsily squeezed its way round the room and brought me full circle – and sure enough, when I reached the little wine stall again, the group of gentlemen had dispersed, and only my familiar rival was still leaning against the table, in animated conversation with the young saleswoman. Well then, by his leave, I must take the liberty of interrupting this discussion . . . And with a brisk movement I disengaged myself from the stream and stepped up to the stall.

What happened? Why, nothing! Virtually nothing! The conversation broke off, my rival stepped aside, seized his rimless and ribbonless cyeglasses with all five fingers of one hand and inspected me through these fingers; while the young lady looked me calmly and critically up and down – she surveyed my suit and surveyed my boots. The suit was by no means a new one, and the boots were muddy; I was aware of that. In addition I was flushed, and I dare say it is quite possible that my hair was untidy. I was not cool, I was not at ease, I was not equal to the situation. I was overwhelmed by the feeling that I was intruding, that I was a stranger who had no rights here and did not belong and was making himself ridiculous. Insecurity, helplessness, hatred and pitiful mortification made it impossible for me to return her gaze – in a word, the upshot of my high-spirited intentions was that with darkly knitted brows and in a hoarse voice I said curtly and almost rudely:

'A glass of wine, please.'

It is not of the slightest consequence whether I was right or wrong in thinking that I noticed a fleeting exchange of derisive glances between the girl and her friend. None of us uttered a word as she handed me the wine, and without raising my eyes, red and distraught with rage and anguish, a wretched and ridiculous figure, I stood between the pair of them, gulped a mouthful or two, put the money down on the table, made a confused bow, left the hall and rushed out of the building.

Since that moment I have known that I am doomed; and it makes precious little difference to my story to add that a few days later I read the following notice in the papers:

'Justizrat Rainer has the honour to announce the engagement of his daughter Anna to Herr Assessor Dr Alfred Witznagel.'

14

Since that moment I have known that I am doomed. My last fugitive remnant of well-being and self-complacency has collapsed and dis-integrated. I can bear no more. Yes, I confess it now: I am unhappy, and I see myself as a pitiful and ridiculous figure. But this is unendurable! It will kill me! Today or tomorrow I shall blow my brains out!

My first impulse, my first instinct, was to try to dramatize the affair and cunningly cloak my contemptible wretchedness in the aesthetic garb of 'unhappy love'. A puerile stratagem, I need hardly say. One does not die of unhappy love. Unhappy love is a pose, and quite a comfortable one. Unhappy love can be a source of self-satisfaction. But what is destroying me is the knowledge that all the self-satisfaction I once possessed is now for ever at an end!

And was I really – let me face the question – was I really in love with this girl? It may be so . . . but in what way and why? Was this love not a product of my already wounded, already sick vanity, my vanity which had flared up agonizingly at the first sight of this precious jewel so far beyond my reach, and had filled me with feelings of envy, hatred and self-contempt for which love had then been no more than a cover, a refuge, a lifeline?

Yes, it has all been vanity! Did my father not long ago call me a buffoon and joker?

What right did I have, I of all people, to hold myself aloof from 'society' and to turn my back on it, I who am too vain to bear its scorn and disregard, I who cannot live without society and without its approval! And yet was it really a matter of what I had or had not the right to do? Was it not a matter of necessity? Could my useless buffooning ever have earned me any social position? No: it was this very thing, this joker's talent, that was bound in any case to destroy me.

I realize that indifference would be happiness of a kind . . . But I am unable to feel that indifference about myself, I am unable to view myself except through the eyes of 'other people' and I am being destroyed by a bad conscience – although I feel in no way to blame! Is even a bad conscience nothing more than festering vanity? .

There is only one real misfortune: to forfeit one's own good opinion of oneself. To have lost one's self-respect: that is what unhappiness is. Oh,

I have always known that so well! Everything else is part of the game, an enrichment of one's life; in every other form of suffering one can feel such extraordinary self-satisfaction, one can cut such a fine figure. Only when one has fallen out with oneself and no longer suffers with a good conscience, only in the throes of stricken vanity – only then does one become a pitiful and repulsive spectacle.

An old acquaintance appeared on the scene, a gentleman of the name of Schilling: long ago, as employees of Herr Schlievogt's big timber firm, we had worked together in the service of society. He was briefly visiting the town on business, and he came to see me – a 'sceptical fellow', with his hands in his trouser pockets, black-rimmed pince-nez and a realistic, tolerant shrug of the shoulders. He arrived one evening and said: 'I shall be here for a few days.' We went and sat in a tavern.

He treated me as if I were still the happy, self-satisfied man he had once known, and thinking in all good faith that he was only echoing my own blithe self-esteem, he said:

'By God, my dear fellow, you've arranged your life very pleasantly! Independent, what? Free! You're right of course, damn it! We only live once, don't we? What does anything else matter, after all? You're the wiser of the two of us, I must say. Of course, you were always a genius . . .' And he continued most cordially, as he had done long ago, to express his respect for me and pay me compliments, little dreaming that I for my part was anxiously dreading his disapproval.

I made desperate efforts to sustain the role in which he had cast me, to keep up the appearance of success, of happiness, of self-complacency. It was useless! There was no resilience left in me, no aplomb, no self-possession. I could respond to him only with crestfallen embarrassment and cringing diffidence – and he was incredibly quick to sense this! It was frightening to watch how this man who had at first been fully prepared to recognize and respect me as a fortunate and superior person began to see through me, to look at me in astonishment, to grow cool, then superior, then impatient and irritated, and finally to treat me with undisguised contempt. It was still early when he got up to go, and next day he sent me a brief note saying that he had been obliged to leave town after all.

The fact is that everyone is much too busily preoccupied with himself to be able to form a serious opinion about another person. The indolent world is all too ready to treat any man with whatever degree of respect corresponds to his own self-confidence. Be what you please, live as you please – but put a bold face on it, act with self-assurance and show no qualms, and no one will be moralist enough to point the finger of scorn at you. But once have the misfortune to forfeit your single-mindedness and lose your self-complacency, once betray your own self-contempt – and the world will unhesitatingly endorse it. As for me, I am past hope . . .

At this point I stop writing. I cast my pen aside – full of disgust, of disgust! Shall I make an end of it all? Surely that would be rather too heroic for a 'buffoon and joker'! I am afraid the upshot of the matter will be that I shall continue to live, to eat, to sleep, to dabble in this and dabble in that; and gradually, as my apathy increases, I shall get used to being a 'wretched and ridiculous figure'.

Oh, God, who would have supposed – who could have supposed – that to be born a joker was so disastrous a fate!

The Road to the Churchyard

Der Weg zum Friedhof

1900

The Road to the Churchyard

The road to the churchyard ran parallel to the main highway, and kept close beside it until it reached the place to which it led, namely the churchyard. On the other side of it there was, at first, a row of human habitations – new suburban houses, some of them still under construction; and then came fields. As for the highway, it was lined with trees, gnarled beech trees of respectable age; and only one half of it was paved, the other was not. But the road to the churchyard was lightly strewn with gravel, and for this reason it was really more like a pleasant footpath. The two roads were separated by a narrow dry ditch, full of grass and meadow flowers.

It was spring, indeed it was already nearly summer. The world was smiling. The Lord God's blue sky was full of little round compact lumps of cloud, quaint little snow-white tufts scattered gaily all over it. The birds were twittering in the beeches, and a gentle breeze was blowing across the fields.

On the highway, a cart from the next village was crawling towards the town, half of it on the paved part of the road and half on the unpaved part. The carter was letting his legs hang down on either side of the shaft, and whistling very much out of tune. But at the far end of the cart, with its back to him, sat a little yellow dog with a little pointed nose over which it was gazing, with an indescribably solemn and meditative expression, back along the way it had come. It was an exquisite and highly amusing little dog, worth its weight in gold; unfortunately however it is irrelevant in the present context, and we must therefore ignore it. A troop of soldiers was passing. They were from the nearby barracks and they marched along through their own sweaty exhalations, singing as they marched. A second cart, coming from the direction of the town, was crawling towards the next village. The driver was asleep, and there was no dog on this vehicle, which is therefore of no interest whatsoever. Two apprentices came by, one of them a hunchback and the other gigantically tall. They walked barefoot, because they were carrying their boots over their shoulders; they called out some merry quip or other to the sleeping carter and proceeded on their way. Such was the moderate traffic, and it pursued its course without any complications or incidents.

Only one man was walking along the road to the churchyard; he was walking slowly, with bowed head and leaning on a black stick. This man's name was Piepsam – Lobgott Piepsam, believe it or not, and I expressly mention it on account of his subsequent extremely odd behaviour.

He was dressed in black, for he was on his way to visit the graves of his loved ones. He wore a rough-surfaced curved top hat, a frock coat shiny with age, trousers which were both too narrow and too short and black kid gloves with all the surface worn off. His neck, a long skinny neck with a prominent Adam's apple, rose out of a turn-down collar which was beginning to fray – yes, this collar was already rather ravelled at the edges. But when the man raised his head, which from time to time he did to see how far he was from the churchyard, then his face became visible, and this was a rare sight; for undoubtedly it was a face one would not forget again in a hurry.

It was clean-shaven and pale. But from between the hollow cheeks a bulbous nose protruded, a nose thicker at its tip than at its base, glowing with a monstrous and unnatural redness and closely covered, for good measure, with little insalubrious excrescences which gave it an irregular and fantastic appearance. There was something improbable and picturesque about this deeply flushed nose which stood out so sharply against the dull pallor of the rest of the face; it looked as if it had been stuck on like a carnival nose, in melancholy jest. But it had not . . . His mouth was wide, with drooping corners, and he kept it tight shut; his eyebrows were black but speckled with white, and when he looked up he would arch them almost to the brim of his hat, exposing to full view his woefully inflamed, dark-ringed eyes. In a word, it was a face which could not fail in the end to inspire the liveliest compassion.

Lobgott Piepsam's appearance was far from cheerful, it ill became this delightful morning, and even for a man about to visit the graves of his loved ones it was excessively woebegone. A glimpse of his state of mind, however, would have been enough to satisfy anyone that there was good cause for this. He was, shall we say, in rather low spirits . . . It is hard to explain these matters to happy people like yourselves . . . But yes, he had his little troubles, you know, he was rather badly done by. Alas, if the truth be told, his troubles were by no means little, but grievous in the highest degree – in fact, his condition could fairly be described as absolutely wretched.

To begin with, he drank. Well, we shall have occasion to refer to this again. Secondly he was a widower and a bereaved father, forsaken by everyone; he had not a soul left on earth to whom he was dear. His wife, whose maiden name had been Lebzelt, had been snatched from him six months ago when she had borne him a child; it was their third child, and it had been born dead. The other two had also died, one of diphtheria, the other of nothing in particular, perhaps just of general deficiency. As if this were not enough, he had shortly afterwards lost his job, he had been shamefully dismissed from his employment and livelihood, and this had been in consequence of the above-mentioned ruling passion, which was a passion stronger than Piepsam.

In the old days he had been able to resist it up to a point, despite periodic bouts of immoderate indulgence. But when he had been bereft of wife and children and stood alone in the world without guidance or support, deprived of all dependants, the vice had become his master, and had increasingly broken his resistance and his spirit. He had had a position on the staff of an insurance company, as a kind of superior clerk earning ninety marks a month. But he had been guilty, when in a condition of irresponsibility, of various acts of gross negligence, and in the end his employers, after repeatedly reprimanding him, had dismissed him as hopelessly unreliable.

It need hardly be said that this had in no way improved Piepsam's moral character; on the contrary he had now gone completely to pieces. The fact is, dear readers, that misfortune destroys human dignity. (And yet it is just as well, you know, to have a certain insight into these

65

matters.) The truth in this case is strange and rather horrible. It is no use for a man to go on protesting his innocence to himself: he will usually despise himself simply for being unfortunate. But there is a dreadful reciprocal intimacy between self-contempt and vice – they nourish each other, they play into each other's hands in a way that is quite uncanny. And thus it was with Piepsam. He drank because he did not respect himself, and he respected himself less and less because his self-confidence was undermined by the ever-recurring collapse of all his good resolutions. At home in his wardrobe there stood a bottle of poisonous-looking yellow liquid, a ruinous liquid which we shall take the precaution of not identifying. In front of this wardrobe Lobgott Piepsam had before now literally fallen on his knees, with his clenched teeth nearly severing his tongue; and nevertheless he had finally succumbed to the temptation . . . We are reluctant to acquaint our readers with such matters; but they are after all very instructive. So now he was proceeding along the road to the churchyard, thrusting his black walking-stick before him. The gentle breeze played round his nose as it did round anyone else's, but he did not notice it. With eyebrows steeply arched he stared at the world with a hollow melancholy stare, like the lost wretched soul he was. Suddenly he heard behind him a sound that caught his attention: a soft whirr was approaching from a distance at high speed. He turned and stopped in his tracks . . . It was a bicycle: with its tyres crunching over the lightly gravelled surface, it was approaching at full tilt but presently slowed down, as Piepsam was standing in the middle of the road.

On the saddle sat a young man – a boy, a carefree tourist. He made no pretension to be counted among the great ones of this earth, oh dear me no! He was riding quite an inexpensive machine of no matter what make, a bicycle costing two hundred marks, just as it came. And on it he was out for a ride in the country, coming out of town for a bit of a spin, bowling along with his pedals glittering in the sunlight, into God's wide open spaces, hurrah! He was wearing a gaily coloured shirt with a grey jacket over it, sports gaiters and the sauciest little cap you ever saw – a joke of a cap, made of brown check material with a button at the top. But from under it came a thick tangled mop of blond hair, standing up round his forehead. His eyes were a gleaming blue. He sped towards Piepsam like Life itself, ringing his bicycle bell. But Piepsam did not budge an inch out of the way. He stood there and stared at Life, not a muscle of his face moving.

Life irritably returned his gaze and rode slowly past him, whereupon Piepsam likewise resumed his progress. But when Life was just in front of him he said slowly and with heavy emphasis:

'Number nine thousand seven hundred and seven.'

Then he pursed his lips and stared straight down at the road in front of him, aware that the eyes of Life were contemplating him in some perplexity.

Life had turned round, resting one hand on the back of the saddle and riding very slowly.

'What?' it asked . . .

'Number nine thousand seven hundred and seven,' repeated Piepsam. 'Oh, nothing. I shall report you.'

'Report me?' asked Life, turning round still further and pedalling still more slowly, which necessitated a strenuous balancing manoeuvre with the handlebars.

'Certainly,' replied Piepsam from a distance of five or six paces.

'What for?' asked Life, dismounting and standing still with an air of expectancy.

'You know perfectly well yourself.'

'No, I do not.'

'You must know.'

'But I do *not* know,' said Life, 'and what is more, I care even less!' Whereupon it prepared to remount its bicycle. Life was certainly not at a loss for words.

'I shall report you because you are riding here, not out there on the main road but here on the road to the churchyard,' said Piepsam.

'But my dear sir,' said Life with an exasperated impatient laugh, turning round again and stopping, 'you can see that there are bicycle tracks here all the way along . . . Everyone rides here . . .'

'That makes not the slightest difference to me,' answered Piepsam, 'I shall report you.'

'Oh well, then, do whatever you please!' exclaimed Life, and mounted its bicycle. It mounted well and truly, not disgracing itself by any fumbling of the operation, but with one thrust of the foot swung itself up into the saddle and there energetically prepared to resume its progress at the speed appropriate to its temperament.

'If you go on riding here on the road to the churchyard I shall most certainly report you,' said Piepsam, tremulously raising his voice. But Life paid precious little attention and simply rode on, gathering speed.

If you had seen Lobgott Piepsam's face at that moment you would have been profoundly startled. He compressed his lips so violently that his cheeks and even his fiery nose were pulled right out of shape; his brows were arched to a preternatural height, and under them his eyes stared insanely at the bicycle as it drew away from him. Suddenly he dashed forward. A short distance separated him from the vehicle; he covered it at a run, and seized the saddlebag. He clutched it with both hands, he positively clung to it: and, still pressing his lips together with superhuman force, speechless and wild-eyed, he tugged with all his strength at the unsteadily advancing machine. Anyone who had seen him might have wondered whether he maliciously intended to prevent the young man from riding on, or whether the fancy had suddenly taken him to be towed in the rider's wake, to mount up behind him and ride with him, bowling along with glittering pedals into God's wide open spaces, hurrah! . . . The bicycle could not support this monstrous load for long; it came to a stop, it tilted, it fell over.

But at this point Life lost its temper. It had ended up perching on one leg, and now, lunging out with its right arm, it fetched Herr Piepsam such a clout on the chest that he staggered back several paces. Then, with its voice rising in a threatening crescendo, it said:

'You must be drunk, man! You crazy old crackpot! Just you try once more to stop me and I'll knock your block off, do you understand? I give you fair warning, I'll break every bone in your body!' Thereupon it turned its back on Herr Piepsam, indignantly readjusted its little cap, and remounted the bicycle. Oh yes, it was certainly not lost for words. And it mounted just as skilfully and successfully as before. Just one thrust of the foot and it sat secure in the saddle and at once had the machine under control. Piepsam saw its back receding faster and faster into the distance.

There he stood, gasping, staring at Life as it left him behind . . . Life did not fall off, no accident occurred, no tyre burst, and there was no stone in its path; it sped resiliently away. And now Piepsam began to shriek and to curse – one might almost say to bellow: it was certainly no longer a human voice.

'Get off!' he yelled. 'Stop riding here! You are to ride out there on the main road and not on the road to the churchyard, do you hear me?! . . . Dismount! Dismount at once! Oh! Oh! I'll report you, I'll have you prosecuted! Oh, by God in heaven, why don't you fall, why don't you fall off, you riff-raff! I'd kick you! I'd trample your face in with my boot, you damned young puppy . . .'

Never had such a scene been witnessed! A man on the road to the churchyard screaming curses, a man swollen-faced and bellowing, a man dancing and capering in a frenzy of invective, flinging his arms and legs about, completely beside himself. The bicycle was away out of sight already, and Piepsam was still raging on the same spot.

'Stop him! Stop him! He's riding on the road to the churchyard! Pull him off his bicycle, the damned young monkey! Ah . . . ah . . . if I had you here, how I'd flay the hide off you, you brainless brute, you shallow hooligan, you clown, you ignorant fool! . . . Dismount! Dismount this instant! Will no one pull him down into the dust, the blackguard? . . . Ride your bicycle, will you? On the road to the churchyard, would you?! You scoundrel! You insolent lout! You damned popinjay! Bright blue eyes you have, haven't you! And what else? May the Devil claw them out of your head, you ignorant, ignorant, ignorant fool! . . .'

Piepsam now began to use expressions which cannot be repeated; he foamed at the mouth and hoarsely poured forth the vilest abuse, while his bodily movements became increasingly frenzied. A few children were walking along the main road with a basket and a pinscher dog: they came across, climbed the ditch, stood round the screaming man and gazed curiously at his distorted face. Some labourers, busy on the new building sites beyond him or just starting their lunch-break, now also took notice, and a number of them, accompanied by hod-women, advanced along the path towards the group. But Piepsam went on raving, in fact he got worse and worse. Blindly, wildly, he shook his fists at heaven and in all directions, kicked and thrashed with his legs, spun round and round, bent his knees and then jerked himself upright again, in a frantic effort to yell still louder. His flow of invective continued without pause, he scarcely left himself time to breathe, and his command of vocabulary was astonishing. His face was hideously swollen, his top hat had slid half-way down his neck and his shirt-front was hanging out from under his waistcoat. But he had long ago passed over into generalities and was uttering things which no longer had the remotest connection with the matter in hand. They included allusions to his life of vice, and religious intimations, all spluttered out in so very unsuitable a tone and disgracefully mingled with terms of abuse.

'Come hither, come here to me all of you!' he roared. 'Not you, not only you, but you others as well, you others with the caps and the bright blue eyes! I will shout truths into your ears that will make your flesh creep for ever and ever, you shallow *canaille*! . . . Do you grin? Do you shrug your shoulders? . . . I drink . . . yes, I drink! I even booze, if you want to know! What of that?! The end is not yet come! There shall be a day, you worthless vermin, when God shall weigh us all and find us wanting . . . Oh . . . Oh . . . the Son of Man shall come in the clouds of heaven, you innocent riff-raff, and his justice is not of this world! He shall cast you into outer darkness, you light-hearted rabble, and there shall be wailing and . . .'

He was now surrounded by a quite considerable assemblage of people. Some were laughing and some were staring at him with puckered brows. More labourers and hod-women had come up from the building sites. A driver had stopped his cart on the main road, dismounted, crossed the ditch and likewise approached, whip in hand. One man shook Piepsam by the arm, but this had no effect. A troop of soldiers craned their necks and laughed as they marched past him. The pinscher could contain itself no longer, braced its forepaws against the ground, wedged its tail between its hindquarters and howled up into his face.

Suddenly Lobgott Piepsam yelled once more at the top of his voice: 'Dismount, dismount at once, you ignorant puppy!' Then he described a wide semicircle with one arm, and collapsed. He lay there, abruptly silent, a black heap amid the curious crowd. His curved top hat had flown from his head, bounced once on the ground and then also lay still.

Two masons bent over the motionless Piepsam and discussed the case in the sensible straightforward language that working-men use. Then one of them set off at a run and disappeared. The remaining bystanders made a few further attempts to revive the senseless man. One of them sprinkled him with water from a pail, another took out a bottle of brandy, poured some of it into the hollow of his hand and rubbed Piepsam's temples with it. But these experiments proved unavailing.

Thus a short time elapsed. Then the sound of wheels was heard and a vehicle approached along the main road. It was an ambulance, and it stopped on the very spot. It was drawn by two neat little horses and had an enormous red cross painted on each side. Two men in smart uniforms got down from the driving seat, and while one of them went round to the back of the vehicle to open it and pull out the stretcher, the other crossed quickly to the road to the churchyard, pushed aside the staring onlookers and with the assistance of a labourer dragged Herr Piepsam to the ambulance. They loaded him on to the stretcher and slid him inside, like a loaf into an oven; whereupon the door clicked shut again and the two uniformed men remounted the box. The whole thing was done with great precision, with a few practised movements, swiftly and deftly, like something in a pantomime.

And then they drove Lobgott Piepsam away.

Gladius Dei

Gladius Dei

1902

Gladius Dei

1

Munich was resplendent. A shining vault of silky blue sky stood above the festive squares, the white colonnades, the classicistic monuments and baroque churches, the leaping fountains, palaces and parks of the capital city, and its broad bright vistas, tree-lined and beautifully proportioned, basked in the shimmering haze of a fine early June day.

Over every little street the chatter of birds, an air of secret exultation . . . And across the squares, and past the rows of houses, the droll unhurried life of this beautiful leisurely town dawdles and trundles and rumbles along. Tourists of all nationalities are driving about in the slow little cabs, gazing with unselective curiosity at the house-fronts to right and left of them, or walking up the steps into museums . . .

Many windows stand open, and through many of them music floats out into the streets – the sound of pianos or violins or cellos being practised, of earnest and well-meant amateur endeavours. But from the Odeon a number of grand pianos can be heard simultaneously, on which serious study is in progress.

Young men whistling the Nothung motif, the kind of young men who fill the gallery of the modern Schauspielhaus every night, are strolling in and out of the University and the State Library, with literary periodicals in their side pockets. In front of the Academy of Fine Arts, which spreads its white wings between the Türkenstrasse and the Siegestor, a court carriage has stopped. And at the top of the ramp, standing, sitting and lounging in colourful groups, are the models – picturesque old men, children and women in the costume of peasants from the Alban Hills.

In the northern quarter, all the long streets are full of indolent, unhurrying, sauntering people . . . This place is not exactly the home of feverish cutthroat commercial competition: its inhabitants devote themselves to more agreeable pursuits. Young artists with small round hats perched on the backs of their heads, loosely tied cravats and no walking-sticks – carefree young men who pay their rent with an occasional sketch – are out walking, seeking moods of inspiration in the bright blue morning sky and letting their eyes stray after the girls: those pretty, rather dumpy little girls with their dark hair plaited *en bandeaux*, their slightly too large feet, and their accommodating morals . . . One house in five, here, has studio windows that gleam in the sun. Often, in a row of dull solid buildings, some artistic edifice stands out, the work of some young and imaginative architect: wide-fronted, with shallow arches and bizarre decorative motifs, full of style and inventive wit. Or suddenly, in some very boring façade, one door is framed by a saucy improvisation of flowing lines and luminous colours, Bacchantes, water nymphs and rose-pink nudes . . .

It is always unfailingly delightful to linger in front of a cabinet-maker's window display, or those of the large stores which sell modern luxury articles of all kinds. What sybaritic imagination, what humour there is in the lines and outlines of all these things! There are little shops everywhere selling sculptures and frames and antiques, and through their windows the busts of Florentine ladies of the quattrocento sublimely and suggestively confront one's gaze. And the owner of even the smallest and most modest of these establishments will talk to one about Donatello and Mino da Fiesole for all the world as if they had personally given him sole reproduction rights . . .

But up there on the Odeonsplatz, near the massive loggia with the wide expanse of mosaic pavement in front of it, diagonally opposite the Prince Regent's palace, there are always people pressing round the wide windows and showcases of one large art shop: the elaborate beauty emporium of Herr M. Blüthenzweig. What a sumptuous array of delightful exhibits it offers! There are reproductions of masterpieces from every gallery on earth, presented in expensive frames which have been subtly tinted and decorated in a taste combining simplicity with preciosity. There are facsimiles of modern paintings, gay sensuous fantasies in which the world of antiquity seems to have been brought back to life with humorous realism; perfect casts of Renaissance sculpture; bronze nudes and fragile ornamental glassware; tall earthenware vases which have emerged from baths of metal vapour clad in iridescent colours; volumes in exquisite bindings, triumphs of fine modern book production, lavish luxury editions of the works of fashionable lyric poets. And among all this the portraits of artists, musicians, philosophers, actors and writers are displayed to gratify the inquisitive public's taste for personal details . . . On an easel in the first window, the one nearest the adjacent bookshop, there is a large picture which particularly attracts the crowd: an excellent sepia photograph in a massive old-gold frame. It is a rather sensational item – a copy of the chief attraction in this year's great international exhibition, the exhibition so effectively publicized by the quaintly printed placards which are to be seen on every poster-pillar, in concert programmes and even in artistic advertisements for toilet preparations.

Look about you, survey the windows of the bookshops! Your eyes will encounter such titles as *Interior Decoration Since the Renaissance, Colour Sense and How to Train It, The Renaissance in Modern Applied Art, The Book as a Work of Art, The Art of Decoration, The Hunger for Art.* Reflect, too, that these stimulating publications are bought and read by the thousand, and that the very same topics are lectured on every evening to packed halls . . .

With any luck, you will also personally encounter one of the famous women already familiar to you through the medium of art – one of those rich, beautiful ladies with dyed Titian-blonde hair and diamond necklaces, whose bewitching features have been immortalized by some portrait-painter of genius, and whose love-life is the talk of the town. At carnival time they preside as queens over the artists' revels: slightly rouged, slightly painted, sublimely suggestive, flirtatious and adorable. And look! there goes a great painter with his mistress, driving up the Ludwigstrasse. People point at the carriage, people stop and gaze after the pair. Many salute them. The policemen all but stand to attention.

Art is flourishing, art rules the day, art with its rose-entwined sceptre holds smiling sway over the city. That it should continue so to thrive is a matter of general and reverent concern; on all sides diligent work and propaganda are devoted to its service; everywhere there is a pious cult of line, of ornament, of form, of the senses, of beauty . . . Munich is resplendent.

2

A young man was walking along the Schellingstrasse. Surrounded by cyclists ringing their bells, he was striding down the middle of the woodblock paving towards the broad façade of the Ludwigskirche. When one looked at him, a shadow seemed to pass across the sun or a memory of dark hours across the soul. Did he dislike the sun that was bathing this lovely city in festive light? Why did he keep his eyes fixed on the ground as he walked, engrossed in his own thoughts and heedless of the world?

He was hatless, which was no matter for comment amid the sartorial freedom of this easygoing town; instead of a hat he had pulled the hood of his wide black cloak over his head, so that it shaded his low, bony protruding forehead, covered his ears and surrounded his gaunt visage. What torment of conscience, what scruples and what self-inflicted hardships could have so hollowed out those cheeks? Is it not horrible to see care written on a man's sunken face on so beautiful a day? His dark eyebrows thickened sharply at the narrow base of his long, aquiline, overprominent nose, and his lips were full and fleshy. Each time he raised his rather close-set brown eyes, wrinkles formed on his angular forehead. His gaze betokened knowledge, narrowness of spirit and suffering. Seen in profile, this face exactly resembled an old portrait once painted by a monk and now preserved in Florence in a hard narrow cloister cell, from which long ago there issued forth a terrible and overwhelming protest against life and its triumphs . . .

Hieronymus strode along the Schellingstrasse, slowly and firmly, holding his wide cloak together from inside with both hands. Two young girls, two of those pretty, dumpy creatures with plaited hair, rather too large feet and accommodating morals, were strolling along arm in arm, out for adventure; as they passed him they nudged each other and giggled at the sight of his hood and his face, indeed they bent double with laughter and had to break into a run. But he paid no heed to this. With head bowed, and looking neither right nor left, he crossed the Ludwigstrasse and mounted the steps of the church.

The great central portal was wide open. In the dim religious light of the interior, cool and musty and heavy with the scent of incense, a faint red glow was visible from somewhere far within. An old woman with bloodshot eyes got up from a prayer-stool and dragged herself on crutches between the columns. Otherwise the church was empty.

Hieronymus sprinkled his brow and breast from the stoup, genuflected before the high altar and then remained standing in the nave. Somehow he seemed to have grown in stature here. He stood erect and motionless, holding his head high; his great hooked nose jutted out over his full lips with a masterful expression, and his eyes were no longer fixed on the ground but gazed boldly straight ahead towards the crucifix on the distant high altar. Thus he paused for a while without stirring; then he genuflected again as he stepped back, and left the church.

He strode up the Ludwigstrasse, slowly and firmly, with head bowed, walking in the middle of the broad unpaved carriageway, towards the massive loggia and its statues. But on reaching the Odeonsplatz he raised his eyes, and wrinkles formed on his angular forehead: he came to a halt, his attention drawn by the crowd in front of the great art shop, in front of the elaborate beauty emporium of M. Blüthenzweig.

People were moving from window to window, pointing out to each other the treasures there displayed, exchanging views and peering over each other's shoulders. Hieronymus mingled with them, and he too began to survey the various objects, to inspect them all, one by one.

He saw the reproductions of masterpieces from every gallery on earth; the expensive, artlessly bizarre frames; the Renaissance sculpture, the bronze nudes and ornamental glassware, the iridescent vases, the luxurious bookbindings, the portraits of artists, musicians, philosophers, actors and writers; he looked at them all, devoting a moment to every object. Holding his cloak firmly together from inside with both hands, he turned his hooded head with slight, curt movements from one thing to another; his dark eyebrows, thickening sharply at the base of his nose, were raised, and from under them his eyes rested for a while on every item in the display with a puzzled, cold, astonished stare. And so in due course he came to the first window, the one behind which the rather sensational picture stood. For some minutes he looked over the shoulders of the people who were crowding round it; then he managed to get to the front, and stood close to the glass.

The big sepia photograph, framed most tastefully in old gold, had been placed on an easel in the centre of the window. It was a Madonna, painted in a wholly modern and entirely unconventional manner. The sacred figure was ravishingly feminine, naked and beautiful. Her great sultry eyes were rimmed with shadow, and her lips were half parted in a strange and delicate smile. Her slender fingers were grouped rather nervously and convulsively round the waist of the Child, a nude boy of aristocratic, almost archaic slimness, who was playing with her breast and simultaneously casting a knowing sidelong glance at the spectator.

Two other young men were standing next to Hieronymus discussing the picture. They had books under their arms which they had just fetched from the State Library or were taking back to it; they were young men of classical education, well versed in the arts and other learning.

'Devil take me, but he's a lucky young fellow!' said one of them.

'And he clearly intends to make us envy him,' replied the other . . . 'A woman of parts, to be sure.'

'A woman to go crazy for! She does make one a bit doubtful about the dogma of the Immaculate Conception . . .'

'Oh, indeed, she doesn't look exactly *intacta*. Have you seen the original?'

'Of course. I found it most perturbing. She's even more *provoquante* in colour . . . especially the eyes.'

'It's certainly a very outspoken likeness.'

'How do you mean?'

'Don't you know the model? Why, he used that little milliner of his. It's almost a portrait of her, but with the depraved flavour deliberately emphasized . . . The girl herself is more innocent-looking.'

'I should hope so. Life would be rather a strain if there were many of them like this *mater amata* . . .'

'The Pinakothek has bought it.'

'Really? Well, well! They know what they're doing, of course. The treatment of the flesh and the flowing lines of the garment are certainly quite outstanding.'

'Yes, he's a fantastically talented chap.'

'Do you know him?'

'Slightly. There's no doubt that he'll have a successful career. He's been to dinner with the Prince Regent twice already . . .'

During this last exchange they had been preparing to take leave of each other.

'Shall we see you tonight at the theatre?' asked one of them. 'The Drama Club is putting on Machiavelli's *Mandragola*.'

'Oh, good! That's certain to be amusing. I was meaning to go to the Artists' Variety, but I dare say I shall give preference to our friend Niccolò after all. *Au revoir* . . .'

They separated, left the window and went off in different directions. New spectators took their place and gazed at the successful work of art. But Hieronymus stood on motionless; he stood with his head thrust forward, and his hands, as he grasped his cloak with them from inside and held it together on his breast, were seen to tighten convulsively. His brows were no longer raised as before in that expression of cold, rather resentful astonishment. They were lowered and frowning darkly; his cheeks, half hidden by the black hood, seemed more deeply sunken than ever, and his full lips had turned very pale. Slowly his head dropped further and further down, until finally his eyes were staring fixedly upward at the picture from well below it. The nostrils of his great nose were quivering.

He remained in this posture for about a quarter of an hour. A succession of different people stood round the window beside him, but he did not stir from the spot. Finally he turned round slowly, very slowly, on the balls of his feet, and walked away.

3

But the picture of the Madonna went with him. Continually, even as he sat in his small hard narrow room or knelt in the cool churches, it stood before his outraged soul with its sultry, dark-rimmed eyes, with a mysterious smile on its lips, naked and beautiful. And no prayer could exorcise it.

But on the third night it came to pass that Hieronymus received a command and a summons from on high, bidding him take action and raise his voice in protest against frivolous profligacy and the insolent, pretentious cult of beauty. In vain he pleaded, like Moses, that he was slow of speech and heavy of tongue: God's will remained inflexible, his bidding loud and clear. Faint-hearted or no, Hieronymus must go forth on this sacrificial mission among his mocking enemies.

And so in the morning he rose up and betook himself, since God so willed it, to the art shop – to M. Blüthenzweig's great beauty emporium. He wore his hood over his head and held his cloak together from inside with both hands as he walked.

4

It had grown sultry; the sky was livid and a storm was imminent. Once again, quite a multitude was besieging the windows of the art shop, especially the one in which the Madonna was exhibited. Hieronymus gave it only a cursory glance, and then pressed down the handle of the glass door hung with posters and art magazines. 'It is God's will!' he said, and entered the shop.

A young girl, a pretty, dark creature with plaited hair and rather too large feet who had been sitting somewhere at a desk writing in a ledger, approached and inquired politely how she could be of service to him.

'Thank you,' said Hieronymus, looking her gravely in the eyes and wrinkling his angular forehead, 'it is not to you I wish to speak, but to the owner of the shop, Herr Blüthenzweig.'

She hesitated a little, then withdrew and resumed her occupation. He remained standing in the middle of the shop.

All the objects exhibited singly outside were piled up here by the score, in a lavish display – an abundance of colour, line and form, of style, wit, taste and beauty. Hieronymus gazed slowly to his right and to his left, then drew the folds of his black cloak more tightly about him.

There were several people in the shop. At one of the broad tables that ran across the room sat a gentleman in a yellow suit with a black goatee, looking at a portfolio of French drawings, to which he occasionally reacted with a bleating laugh. A young man, who looked as if he were underpaid and lived on a vegetarian diet, was serving him and kept dragging further portfolios across for him to inspect. Diagonally opposite the bleating gentleman an important-looking elderly lady was examining some modern art needlework, huge fantastic flowers embroidered in pale colours, standing vertically side by side on long straight stalks. She too was being attended to by one of the assistants. An Englishman was sitting nonchalantly at another table, with his travelling cap on and a pipe in his mouth; cold, clean-shaven, of uncertain age and wearing solid durable clothes. He was in the act of choosing between a number of bronzes that were being offered to him by Herr Blüthenzweig in person. One of them was a graceful nude statuette of a young girl with an immature figure and delicate limbs, her little hands chastely and coquettishly crossed on her breast; he was holding her by the head, rotating her slowly and inspecting her in detail.

Herr Blüthenzweig, a man with short brown side-whiskers and moustaches and glistening eyes of the same colour, was hovering round him, rubbing his hands and praising the little girl with every adjective he could lay his tongue to.

'A hundred and fifty marks, sir,' he said in English. 'An example of Munich art, sir. Certainly quite enchanting. Full of charm, you know. The very embodiment of grace, sir. Really extremely pretty, very dainty, an admirable piece.' He added as an afterthought: 'Most attractive and seductive,' and then began again from the beginning.

His nose lay rather flat on his upper lip, so that he was constantly breathing into his moustache with a slight snorting sound; he also kept approaching the customer in a stooping posture, as if he were sniffing him. When Hieronymus entered, Herr Blüthenzweig briefly investigated him in exactly the same manner, but then turned back at once to the Englishman.

The aristocratic old lady had made her choice and left the shop. A new customer entered. Herr Blüthenzweig gave him a quick sniff as if to assess his purchasing power, and then handed him over to the young woman with the ledger. This gentleman merely bought a faience bust of Piero de' Medici, son of Lorenzo the Magnificent, and then departed. The Englishman now also prepared to leave. He had taken possession of the little nude girl and was shown to the door by Herr Blüthenzweig with much bowing and scraping. The art dealer then turned to Hieronymus and came up to him.

'What can I do for you?' he asked with scant deference.

Hieronymus held his cloak together from inside with both hands and looked Herr Blüthenzweig in the face almost without moving a muscle. Then he slowly parted his thick lips and said:

'I have come to you about the picture in that window, the big photograph, the Madonna.' His voice was husky and expressionless.

'Ah yes, of course,' said Herr Blüthenzweig with interest and began rubbing his hands. 'Seventy marks including the frame, sir. Guaranteed durability . . . a first-class reproduction. Most attractive and charming.'

Hieronymus was silent. He bowed his hooded head and seemed to shrink slightly as the art dealer spoke. Then he drew himself upright again and said:

'I must tell you in advance that I am not in a position to buy anything from you, nor do I in any case wish to do so. I regret to have to disappoint your expectations. If this upsets you, I am sorry. But in the first place I am poor, and in the second place I do not like the things you are offering for sale. No, I cannot buy anything.'

'You cannot . . . Oh, quite so,' said Herr Blüthenzweig, snorting loudly. 'Well, may I ask . . .'

'If I judge you right,' continued Hieronymus, 'you despise me because I am not able to buy anything from you . . .'

'Hm . . . not at all!' said Herr Blüthenzweig. 'But . . .'

'Nevertheless I beg you to listen to me and to give due weight to my words.'

'Give due weight. Hm. May I ask . . .'

'You may ask,' said Hieronymus, 'and I will answer you. I have come to request you to remove that picture, the big photograph, the Madonna, from your window immediately and never to exhibit it again.'

Herr Blüthenzweig stared at Hieronymus for a while in silence, as if expecting him to be covered with confusion by his own extraordinary speech. Since however no such thing happened, he snorted violently and delivered himself as follows:

'Will you be so good as to inform me whether you are here in some official capacity which authorizes you to dictate to me, or what exactly your business here is? . . .'

'Oh, no,' replied Hieronymus, 'I have no office or position under the State. The power of this world is not on my side, sir. What brings me here is solely my conscience.'

Herr Blüthenzweig, at a loss for a reply, wagged his head to and fro, snorted violently into his moustache and struggled to find words. Finally he said:

'Your conscience . . . Then will you kindly allow me . . . to inform you . . . that so far as we are concerned . . . your conscience is a thing of no importance whatsoever!'

With that he turned on his heel, walked quickly to his desk at the back of the shop and began to write. The two male assistants laughed heartily. The pretty young bookkeeper also giggled. As for the gentleman in yellow with the black beard, it became apparent that he was a foreigner, for he had obviously not understood a word, but went on studying the French drawings, uttering his bleating laugh from time to time.

'Will you please deal with the gentleman,' said Herr Blüthenzweig over his shoulder to his assistant. Then he went on writing. The young man with the ill-paid vegetarian look came up to Hieronymus, doing his best not to laugh, and the other assistant approached as well.

'Is there anything else we can do for you?' asked the ill-paid assistant gently. Hieronymus kept his sorrowful, obtuse yet penetrating gaze steadily fixed on him.

'No,' he said, 'there is not. I beg you to remove the picture of the Madonna from the window at once, and for ever.'

'Oh . . . Why?'

'It is the holy Mother of God . . .' said Hieronymus in hushed tones.

'Of course . . . But you have heard for yourself that Herr Blüthenzweig is not prepared to do as you request.'

'We must remember that it is the holy Mother of God,' said Hieronymus, his head trembling.

'That is so. But what follows? Is it wrong to exhibit Madonnas? Is it wrong to paint them?'

'Not like that! Not like that!' said Hieronymus almost in a whisper, straightening himself and shaking his head vehemently several times. The angular forehead under his hood was lined all over with long, deep furrows. 'You know very well that what has been painted there is vice

85

itself, naked lust! I heard with my own ears two simple, unreflecting young men, as they looked at that picture, say that it made them doubt the dogma of the Immaculate Conception . . .'

'Oh, excuse me, that is quite beside the point,' said the young assistant with a superior smile. In his leisure hours he was writing a pamphlet on the modern movement in art, and was quite capable of conducting a cultured conversation. 'The picture is a work of art,' he continued, 'and as such it must be judged by the appropriate standards. It has been acclaimed by everyone. The State has bought it . . .'

'I know that the State has bought it,' said Hieronymus. 'I also know that the painter has dined twice with the Prince Regent. This is common talk among the people, and God knows what conclusions they draw from the fact that by a work of that sort a man can become famous! What does such a fact attest? It attests the blindness of the world, a blindness that is incomprehensible unless it is mere shameless hypocrisy. That picture was painted in sensual lust, and it is enjoyed in sensual lust . . . Is this true or not? Answer me! You too, Herr Blüthenzweig, answer me!'

A pause ensued. Hieronymus seemed in all seriousness to be expecting a reply, and his sorrowful penetrating brown eyes looked by turns at Herr Blüthenzweig's rounded back and at the two assistants, who stared at him with embarrassed curiosity. There was silence, broken only by the bleating laugh of the gentleman in yellow with the black beard as he pored over the French drawings.

'It *is* true!' continued Hieronymus, his husky voice trembling with profound indignation. 'You dare not deny it! But how then is it possible that the painter of that picture should be solemnly extolled as if he had contributed something to the spiritual enrichment of mankind? How is it possible to stand before that picture and enjoy the vile pleasure it gives, and to silence one's conscience with talk of beauty – indeed to persuade oneself in all seriousness that one is undergoing a noble and refined experience, an experience worthy of the dignity of man? Is this wicked ignorance or the basest hypocrisy? It passes my comprehension . . . the absurdity of this fact passes my comprehension! That a man can rise to high renown on this earth by a witless, brazen manifestation of his animal instincts! Beauty . . . What is beauty? What impulses beget beauty, and to what does it appeal? No one can possibly be ignorant of this, Herr Blüthenzweig! But how can one conceivably see through something in this way and yet not be filled with grief and revulsion at the thought of it! This exaltation and blasphemous idolatry of beauty is a crime, for it confirms and encourages the ignorance of shameless children, it strengthens them in their folly – the folly of impudence, the folly of the morally blind who know nothing of suffering and still less of the way to salvation! . . ."Who are you," you will ask me, "who see things so blackly?" I tell you, knowledge is the bitterest torment in this world; but it is the fire of purgatory, the purifying anguish without which no soul can be saved. It is not impudent naïvety or wicked heedlessness that will avail, Herr Blüthenzweig, but only understanding, that insight by which the passions of our loathsome flesh are consumed and extinguished.'

Silence. The gentleman in yellow with the black beard uttered a short bleat.

'It would really be better if you left now,' said the ill-paid assistant gently.

But Hieronymus showed no sign whatsoever of leaving. Erect in his hooded cloak, with his eyes burning, he stood there in the middle of the art shop, and in a harsh voice that seemed rusty with disuse his thick lips went on pouring forth words of condemnation . . .

'Art! they cry – pleasure! beauty! Wrap the world in a veil of beauty and set upon everything the noble imprint of style! . . . Enough of this infamy! Do you think gaudy colours can gloss over the misery of the world? Do you think loud orgies of luxurious good taste can drown the moans of the tortured earth? You are wrong, you shameless wretches! God is not mocked, and your insolent idolatry of the glistering surface of things is an abomination in His sight! . . . "Who are you," you will answer, "to be reviling Art?" You lie, I tell you; I am not reviling art! Art is not a cynical deception, a seductive stimulus to confirm and strengthen the lusts of the flesh! Art is the sacred torch that must shed its merciful light into all life's terrible depths, into every shameful and sorrowful abyss; art is the divine flame that must set fire to the world, until the world with all its infamy and anguish burns and melts way in redeeming compassion! . . . Remove it, Herr Blüthenzweig, remove that famous painter's work from your window – indeed, you would do well to burn it with hot fire and scatter its ashes to the winds, yes, to all four winds! . . .'

His unlovely voice broke off. He had taken a vehement step backwards, had snatched one arm from under the fold of his black cloak with a passionate movement and was holding it far outstretched; with a strangely contorted, convulsively trembling hand he pointed towards the window display, the showcase containing the sensational picture of the Madonna. He paused in this masterful posture. His great hooked nose seemed to jut out imperiously, his dark brows that thickened sharply at its base were arched so high that his angular forehead under the overshadowing hood was covered with broad furrows, and a hectic flush had spread over his sunken cheeks.

But at this point Herr Blüthenzweig turned round. Perhaps it was the fact of being called upon to burn a reproduction worth seventy marks that had so genuinely outraged him, or perhaps Hieronymus's speeches in general had finally exhausted his patience; at all events he was the very picture of righteous wrath. He gesticulated with his pen towards the door of the shop, snorted sharply several times into his moustache, struggled for words in his agitation and then declared with extreme emphasis:

'Now listen to me, you crazy fellow: unless you clear out of here this very instant, I'll get the packer to facilitate your exit, do you understand?!'

'Oh, no, you shall not intimidate me, you shall not drive me away, you shall not silence my voice!' cried Hieronymus, pulling his hood together above his chest with one clenched hand and fearlessly shaking his head. 'I know I am alone and powerless, and yet I will not have done until you hear me, Herr Blüthenzweig! Take that picture out of your window and burn it, this very day! Oh, burn not only it! Burn these statuettes and busts as well – the sight of them tempts men to sin! Burn these vases and ornaments, these shameless revivals of paganism! Burn these luxurious volumes of love poetry! Burn everything in your shop, Herr Blüthenzweig, for it is filth in the sight of God! Burn it, burn it, burn it!' he cried, quite beside himself, and making a wild, sweeping, circular gesture with his arm . . . 'The harvest is ripe for the reaper . . . The insolence of this age exceeds all bounds . . . But I say unto you . . .'

'Krauthuber!' shouted Herr Blüthenzweig, turning towards a door at the back of the shop and raising his voice, 'come in here at once!'

The response to this summons was the appearance on the scene of an enormous, overwhelming figure, a monstrous, swollen hulk of terrifyingly massive humanity with gross, teeming limbs thickly padded with flesh and all shapelessly merging into each other – a prodigious, gigantic presence, slowly and ponderously heaving itself across the floor and puffing heavily: a son of the people, malt-nourished, herculean and awe-inspiring! A fringe of walrus moustache was discernible on his face, a huge paste-smeared leather apron enveloped his body and yellow shirt-sleeves were rolled back from his heroic arms.

'Will you open the door for this gentleman, Krauthuber,' said Herr Blüthenzweig, 'and if he still cannot find his way to it, will you help him out into the street.'

'Huh?' said the man, shifting his little elephant eyes to and fro between Hieronymus and his enraged employer . . . It was a primitive grunt, expressing vast strength held laboriously in check. Then he strode, with steps that made everything round him tremble, to the door and opened it.

Hieronymus had turned very pale. 'Burn it –' he began to exclaim, but already a fearful superior force was upon him, and he felt himself being turned round: a bodily bulk against which there could be no conceivable resistance was slowly and inexorably thrusting him towards the door.

'I am weak,' he gasped . . . 'My flesh will not avail against force . . . it cannot stand firm . . . no! but what does that prove? Burn –'

He stopped short. He was outside the art shop. Herr Blüthenzweig's colossal henchman had released him with a slight shove and a final little flourish which had obliged him to collapse sideways on to the stone threshold, supporting himself on one hand. And the glass door was slammed shut behind him.

He rose to his feet. He stood upright, breathing heavily, pulling his hood together above his chest with one clenched hand and letting the other hang down inside the cloak. A grey pallor had gathered in his sunken cheeks; the nostrils of his great hooked nose twitched open and shut; his ugly lips were contorted into an expression of desperate hatred, and his eyes, aflame with a kind of mad ecstasy, roved to and fro across the beautiful square.

He did not see the bystanders who were looking at him with curiosity and amusement. Instead, on the mosaic paving in front of the great loggia, he saw the vanities of the world: the artists' carnival costumes, the ornaments, vases, jewellery and *objets d'art*, the naked statues, the busts of women, the painted revivals of paganism, the masterly portraits of famous beauties, the luxurious volumes of love poetry and the art publications – he saw them all piled up into a great pyramid, and saw the multitude, enthralled by his terrible words, consign them to crackling flames amid cries of jubilation . . . And there, against a yellow wall of cloud that had drifted across from the Theatinerstrasse with a soft roll of thunder, he saw the broad blade of a fiery sword, outstretched in the sulphurous sky above this light-hearted city . . .

'*Gladius Dei super terram*,' his thick lips whispered; and drawing himself to his full height in his hooded cloak, he shook his hanging, hidden fist convulsively and added in a quivering undertone: '*cito et velociter!*'

Tristan

Tristan

1903

Tristan

1

Here we are at 'Einfried', the well-known sanatorium! It is white and rectilinear, a long low-lying main building with a side wing, standing in a spacious garden delightfully adorned with grottoes, leafy arcades and little bark pavilions; and behind its slate roofs the massive pine-green mountains rear their softly outlined peaks and clefts into the sky.

The director of the establishment, as always, is Dr Leander. With his double-pointed black beard, curled as crisply as horse-hair stuffing, his thick flashing spectacles and his general air of one into whom science has instilled a certain coldness and hardness and silent tolerant pessimism, he holds sway in his abrupt and reserved manner over his patients – over all these people who are too weak to impose laws upon themselves and obey them, and who therefore lavish their fortunes on Dr Leander in return for the protection of his rigorous regime.

As for Fräulein von Osterloh, she manages all domestic matters here, and does so with tireless devotion. Dear me, what a whirl of activity! She hurries upstairs and downstairs and from one end of the institution to the other. She is mistress of the kitchen and store-rooms, she rummages about in the linen cupboards, she has the servants at her beck and call, she plans the clients' daily fare on principles of economy, hygiene, taste and elegance. She keeps house with fanatical thoroughness; and in her extreme efficiency there lies concealed a standing reproach to the entire male sex, not one member of which has ever taken it into his head to make her his wife. But in two round crimson spots on her cheeks there burns the inextinguishable hope that one day she will become Frau Dr Leander . . .

Ozone, and still, unstirring air . . . Einfried, whatever Dr Leander's envious detractors and rivals may say, is most warmly to be recommended for all tubercular cases. But not only consumptives reside here: there are patients of all kinds – ladies, gentlemen and even children; Dr Leander can boast of successes in the most varied fields. There are people with gastric disorders, such as Magistratsrätin Spatz, who is also hard of hearing; there are heart cases, paralytics, rheumatics and nervous sufferers of all sorts and conditions. There is a diabetic general, who grumbles continually as he consumes his pension. There are several gentlemen with lean, shrivelled faces, walking with that unruly dancing gait which is always a bad sign. There is a lady of fifty, Pastorin Höhlenrauch, who has had nineteen children and is now totally incapable of thought, despite which her mind is still not at peace: for a whole year now, driven by some restless nervous impulse, she has been wandering aimlessly all over the house – a staring, speechless, uncanny figure, leaning on the arm of her private attendant.

Occasionally a death occurs among the 'serious cases', those who are confined to their beds and do not appear at meals or in the drawing-room; and no one is ever aware of it, not even the patient next door. In the silence of night the waxen guest is removed, and Einfried pursues the even tenor of its way: the massage, the electrical treatment, the injections, douches, medicinal baths, gymnastics, exsudations and inhalations all continue, in premises equipped with every wonder of modern science . . .

Ah yes, this is a lively place. The establishment is flourishing. The porter at the entrance in the side wing sounds the great bell when new guests arrive, and all who leave are shown to the carriage with due formality by Dr Leander and Fräulein von Osterloh in person. Many an odd figure has lived under Einfried's hospitable roof. There is even a writer here, idling away his time – an eccentric fellow with a name reminiscent of some sort of mineral or precious stone . . .

Apart from Dr Leander there is, moreover, a second resident physician, who deals with those cases which are not serious at all and those which are hopeless. But his name is Müller and we need waste no time discussing him.

2

At the beginning of January Herr Klöterjahn the wholesale merchant, of the firm of A. C. Klöterjahn & Co., brought his wife to Einfried. The porter sounded the bell, and Fräulein von Osterloh came to greet the new arrivals after their long journey; she met them in the reception-room, which like almost all the rest of this elegant old house was furnished in remarkably pure *Empire* style. In a moment or two Dr Leander also appeared; he bowed, and an introductory, mutually informative conversation ensued.

Outside lay the wintry garden, its flower-beds covered with matting, its grottoes blocked with snow, its little temples isolated; and two porters were dragging in the new guests' luggage from the carriage which had stopped at the wrought-iron gate, for there was no drive up to the house.

'Take your time, Gabriele, take care, darling, and keep your mouth closed,' Herr Klöterjahn had said as he conducted his wife across the garden; and the moment one saw her one's heart trembled with such tender solicitude that one could not help inwardly echoing his words – though it must be admitted that Herr Klöterjahn's 'take care', which he had said in English, could equally well have been said in German.

The coachman who had driven the lady and gentleman from the station to the sanatorium was a plain, unsophisticated and unsentimental fellow; but he had positively bitten his tongue in an agony of helpless caution as the wholesale merchant assisted his wife down from the carriage. Indeed, even the two bay horses, as they stood steaming in the silent frosty air, had seemed to be rolling back their eyes and intently watching this anxious operation, full of concern for so much fragile grace and delicate charm.

The young lady had an ailment affecting her trachea, as was expressly stated in the letter which Herr Klöterjahn had dispatched from the shores of the Baltic to the medical director of Einfried, announcing their intended arrival; the trachea, and not, thank God, the lungs! And yet – even if it had been the lungs, this new patient could scarcely have looked more enchantingly remote, ethereal and insubstantial than she did now, as she sat by her burly husband, leaning softly and wearily back in her straight, white-lacquered armchair, listening to his conversation with the doctor.

Her beautiful pale hands, bare of jewellery except for a simple wedding ring, were resting in her lap among the folds of a dark, heavy cloth skirt, above which she wore a close-fitting silver-grey bodice with a stand-up collar and a pattern of cut velvet arabesques. But these warm and weighty materials made her ineffably delicate, sweet, languid little head look all the more touching, unearthly and lovely. Her light brown hair was brushed smoothly back and gathered in a knot low down on her neck; only one stray curl drooped towards her right temple, not far from the spot where a strange, sickly little pale blue vein branched out above one of her well marked eyebrows and across the clear, unblemished, almost translucent surface of her forehead. This little blue vein over one eye rather disturbingly dominated the whole of her delicate oval face. It stood out more strongly as soon as she began to speak, indeed as soon as she even smiled; and when this happened it gave her a strained look, an expression almost of anxiety, which filled the onlooker with obscure foreboding. And nevertheless she spoke, and she smiled. She spoke with candour and charm in her slightly husky voice, and smiled with her eyes, although she seemed to find it a little difficult to focus them, indeed they sometimes showed a slight uncontrollable unsteadiness. At their corners, on each side of her slender nose, there were deep shadows. She smiled with her mouth as well, which was wide and beautiful and seemed to shine despite its pallor, perhaps because the lips were so very sharply and clearly outlined. Often she would clear her throat a little. When she did so, she would put her handkerchief to her mouth and then look at it.

'Now, Gabriele, don't clear your throat,' said Herr Klöterjahn. 'You know Dr Hinzpeter at home particularly told you not to do that, darling, and it's merely a matter of pulling oneself together, my dear. As I said, it's the trachea,' he repeated. 'I really did think it was the lungs when it began; bless my soul, what a fright I got! But it's not the lungs – good God, no, we're not standing for any of that sort of thing, are we, Gabriele, what? Oh-ho, no!'

'Indubitably not,' said Dr Leander, flashing his spectacles at them.

Whereupon Herr Klöterjahn asked for coffee – coffee and buttered rolls; and the guttural northern way he pronounced 'coffee' and 'butter' was expressive enough to give anyone an appetite.

He was served with the desired refreshments, rooms were provided for him and his wife and they made themselves at home.

We should add that Dr Leander personally took charge of the case, without availing himself of the services of Dr Müller.

3

The personality of the new patient caused a considerable stir in Einfried; and Herr Klöterjahn, accustomed to such successes, accepted with satisfaction all the homage that was paid to her. The diabetic general stopped grumbling for a moment when he first caught sight of her; the gentlemen with the shrivelled faces, when they came anywhere near her, smiled and made a great effort to keep their legs under control; and Magistratsrätin Spatz immediately appointed herself her friend and chaperon. Ah yes, this lady who bore Herr Klöterjahn's name most certainly made an impression! A writer who had for a few weeks been passing his time in Einfried – an odd fish with a name reminiscent of some kind of precious stone – positively changed colour when she passed him in the corridor: he stopped short and was still standing as if rooted to the spot long after she had disappeared.

Not two days had passed before her story was known to every inmate of the sanatorium. She had been born in Bremen, a fact in any case attested by certain charming little peculiarities of her speech; and there, some two years since, she had consented to become the wedded wife of Herr Klöterjahn the wholesale merchant. She had gone with him to his native town up there on the Baltic coast, and about ten months ago she had borne him a child – an admirably lively and robust son and heir, born under quite extraordinarily difficult and dangerous circumstances. But since these terrible days she had never really recovered her strength, if indeed she had ever had any strength to recover. She had scarcely risen from her confinement, utterly exhausted, her vital powers utterly impoverished, when in a fit of coughing she had brought up a little blood – oh, not much, just an insignificant little drop; but it would of course have been better if there had been none at all. And the disturbing thing was that before long the same unpleasant little incident recurred. Well, this was a matter that could be dealt with, and Dr Hinzpeter, the family physician, took the appropriate measures. Complete rest was ordered, little pieces of ice were swallowed, morphine was prescribed to check the coughing and all possible steps were taken to tranquillize the heart. Nevertheless the patient's condition failed to improve; and whereas the child, that magnificent infant Anton Klöterjahn Jr, won and held his place in life with colossal energy and ruthlessness, his young mother seemed to be gently fading away, quietly burning herself out . . . It was, as we have mentioned, the trachea; and this word, when Dr Hinzpeter used it, had a remarkably soothing, reassuring, almost cheering effect upon all concerned. But even though it was not the lungs, the doctor had in the end strongly recommended a milder climate, and a period of residence in a sanatorium, to hasten the patient's recovery; and the reputation of Einfried and of its director had done the rest.

Thus matters stood; and Herr Klöterjahn himself would tell the whole story to anyone sufficiently interested to listen. He had a loud, slovenly, good-humoured way of talking, like a man whose digestion is as thoroughly sound as his finances. He spoke with extravagant movements of the lips, broadly yet fluently, as people from the north coast do; many of his words were spluttered out with a minor explosion in every syllable, and he would laugh at this as if at a successful joke.

He was of medium height, broad, strongly built, with short legs, a round red face, watery blue eyes, pale blond eyelashes, wide nostrils and moist lips. He wore English side-whiskers and a complete outfit of English clothes, and was delighted to encounter an English family at Einfried – father, mother and three attractive children with their nurse, who were here simply and solely because they could not think of anywhere else to live. Herr Klöterjahn ate an English breakfast with them every morning. He had a general predilection for eating and drinking plentifully and well; he displayed a real connoisseur's knowledge of food and wine, and would entertain the inmates of the sanatorium with highly stimulating accounts of dinners given by his friends at home, describing in particular certain choice dishes unknown in these southern parts. As he did so his eyes would narrow benevolently, while his speech became increasingly palatal and nasal and was accompanied by slight munching sounds at the back of his throat. He was also not altogether averse to certain other worldly pleasures, as was made evident one evening when one of the patients at

Einfried, a writer by profession, saw him flirting rather disgracefully with a chambermaid in the corridor – a trifling, humorous incident to which the writer in question reacted with a quite ludicrous grimace of disapproval.

As for Herr Klöterjahn's wife, it was plain for all to see that she was deeply attached to him. She watched his every movement and smiled at all he said. Her manner showed no trace of that patronizing indulgence with which many sick people treat those who are well; on the contrary she behaved as kindly and good-natured patients do, taking genuine pleasure in the hearty self-assurance of persons blessed with good health.

Herr Klöterjahn did not remain at Einfried for long. He had escorted his wife here; but after a week, having assured himself that she was well provided for and in good hands, he saw no reason to prolong his stay. Equally pressing duties – his flourishing child and his no less flourishing business – recalled him to his native town; they obliged him to depart, leaving his wife behind to enjoy the best of care.

4

The name of the writer who had been living in Einfried for several weeks was Spinell – Detlev Spinell; and his appearance was rather extraordinary.

Let us imagine a tall, well built man in his early thirties, with dark hair already beginning to turn distinctly grey about the temples, and a round, white, rather puffy face on which there was not the slightest sign of any growth of beard. It had not been shaved – that would have been noticeable; it was soft, indistinctly outlined and boyish, with nothing on it but an occasional little downy hair. And this really did look very odd. He had gentle, glistening, chestnut brown eyes and a thick, rather too fleshy nose. He also had an arched, porous, Roman-looking upper lip, large carious teeth and feet of remarkable dimensions. One of the gentlemen with the unruly legs, a cynic and would-be wit, had christened him behind his back 'the putrefied infant'; but this was malicious and wide of the mark. He dressed well and fashionably, in a long dark coat and a waistcoat with coloured spots.

He was unsociable and kept company with no one. Only occasionally was he seized by a mood of affability and exuberant friendliness, and this always happened when his aesthetic sensibilities were aroused – when the sight of something beautiful, a harmonious combination of colours, a vase of noble shape or the light of the setting sun on the mountains, transported him to articulate expressions of admiration. 'What beauty!' he would then exclaim, tilting his head to one side, raising his shoulders, spreading out his hands and curling back his nose and lips. 'Ah, dear me, pray observe, how beautiful that is!' And in the emotion of such moments Herr Spinell was capable of falling blindly upon the neck of no matter who might be at hand, whatever their status or sex . . .

On his desk, permanently on view to anyone who entered his room, lay the book he had written. It was a novel of moderate length with a completely baffling cover design, printed on the kind of paper one might use for filtering coffee, in elaborate typography with every letter looking like a Gothic cathedral. Fräulein von Osterloh had read it in an idle quarter of an hour and had declared it to be 'refined', which was her polite way of saying 'unconscionably tedious'. Its scenes were set in fashionable drawing-rooms and luxurious boudoirs full of exquisite *objets d'art*, full of Gobelin tapestries, very old furniture, priceless porcelain, rare materials and artistic treasures of every sort. They were all described at length and with loving devotion, and as one read one constantly seemed to see Herr Spinell curling back his nose and exclaiming: 'What beauty! Ah, dear me, pray observe, how beautiful that is!' It was, to be sure, rather surprising that he had not written any other books than this one, since his passion for writing was evidently extreme. He spent most of the time in his room doing so, and sent an extraordinary number of letters to the post, one or two almost every day – though the odd and amusing thing was that he himself very rarely received any . . .

5

Herr Spinell sat opposite Herr Klöterjahn's wife at table. On the occasion of the new guests' first appearance in the great dining-room on the ground floor of the side wing, he arrived a minute or two late, murmured a greeting to the company generally and took his seat, whereupon Dr Leander, without much ceremony, introduced him to the new arrivals. He bowed and began to eat, evidently a trifle embarrassed, and manoeuvring his knife and fork in a rather affected manner with his large, white, well formed hands which emerged from very narrow coat sleeves. Later he seemed less ill at ease and looked calmly by turns at Herr Klöterjahn and at his wife. Herr Klöterjahn too, in the course of the meal, addressed one or two questions and remarks to him about the topography and climate of Einfried; his wife also interspersed a few charming words, and Herr Spinell answered politely. His voice was soft and really quite agreeable, though he had a slightly impeded, dragging way of speaking, as if his teeth were getting in the way of his tongue.

After the meal, when the company had moved over to the drawing-room and Dr Leander was uttering the usual courtesies to the new guests in particular, Herr Klöterjahn's wife inquired about the gentleman who had sat opposite.

'What is his name?' she asked . . . 'Spinelli? I didn't quite catch it.'

'Spinell – not Spinelli, madam. No, he's not an Italian, merely a native of Lemberg, so far as I know . . .'

'Did you say he was a writer, or something like that?' asked Herr Klöterjahn. His hands were in the pockets of his easy-fitting English trousers; he tilted one ear towards the doctor, and opened his mouth to listen, as some people do.

'Yes, I don't know – he writes . . .' answered Dr Leander. 'He has published a book, I believe, some kind of novel; I really don't know . . .'

These repeated declarations of ignorance indicated that Dr Leander had no very high opinion of the writer and declined all responsibility for him.

'But that is extremely interesting!' said Herr Klöterjahn's wife. She had never yet met a writer face to face.

'Oh, yes,' replied Dr Leander obligingly. 'I am told he has a certain reputation . . .' After that no more was said about the writer.

But a little later, when the new guests had withdrawn and Dr Leander too was just about to leave the drawing-room, Herr Spinell detained him and made inquiries in his turn.

'What is the name of the couple?' he asked . . . 'I didn't catch it, of course.'

'Klöterjahn,' answered Dr Leander, already turning to go.

'*What* is his name?' asked Herr Spinell . . .

'Their name is *Klöterjahn*,' said Dr Leander, and walked away. He really had no very high opinion of the writer.

6

I think we had reached the point at which Herr Klöterjahn had returned home. Yes – he was back on the shores of the Baltic with his business and his baby, that ruthless vigorous little creature who had cost his mother so much suffering and a slight defect of the trachea. She herself, the young wife, remained behind at Einfried, and Magistratsrätin Spatz appointed herself as her friend and chaperon. This however did not prevent Herr Klöterjahn's wife from being on friendly terms with the other inmates of the sanatorium – for example, with Herr Spinell, who to everyone's astonishment (for hitherto he had kept company with no one) treated her from the outset in an extraordinarily devoted and courteous manner; and she for her part, during the few leisure hours permitted by her rigorous daily regime, seemed by no means averse to his conversation.

He would approach her with extreme circumspection and deference, and always talked to her in a carefully muted voice, so that Rätin Spatz, who was hard of hearing, usually did not catch a word of what he said. He would tiptoe on his great feet up to the armchair in which Herr Klöterjahn's wife reclined, fragile and smiling; at a distance of two paces he would stop, with one leg poised a little way behind the other and bowing from the waist; and in this posture he would talk to her in his rather impeded, dragging way, softly and intensely, but ready at any moment to withdraw and disappear as soon as her face should show the slightest sign of fatigue or annoyance. But she was not annoyed; she would invite him to sit down beside her and Frau Spatz; she would ask him some question or other and then listen to him with smiling curiosity, for often he said amusing and strange things such as no one had ever said to her before.

'Why actually are you at Einfried?' she asked. 'What treatment are you taking, Herr Spinell?'

'Treatment? . . . Oh, I am having a little electrical treatment. It's really nothing worth mentioning. I will tell you, dear madam, why I am here: it is on account of the style.'

'Ah?' said Herr Klöterjahn's wife, resting her chin on her hand and turning towards him with an exaggerated show of interest, as one does to children when they want to tell one something.

'Yes. Einfried is pure *Empire*; I am told it used to be a royal residence, a summer palace. This side wing of course is a later addition, but the main building is old and genuine. Now, there are times when I simply cannot do without *Empire*, times when it is absolutely necessary to me if I am to achieve even a modest degree of well-being. You will appreciate that one's state of mind when one is surrounded by voluptuously soft and luxurious furniture differs entirely from the mood inspired by the straight lines of these tables and chairs and draperies . . . This brightness and hardness, this cold, austere simplicity, this rigorous reserve imparts its composure and dignity to the beholder: prolonged contact with it has an inwardly purifying and restoring effect on me – there is no doubt that it raises my moral tone.'

'Really, how remarkable,' she said. 'And I think I can understand what you mean, if I make an effort.'

Whereupon he replied that what he meant was certainly not worth making an effort to understand, and they both laughed. Rätin Spatz also laughed and thought it remarkable; but she did not say that she understood what he meant.

The drawing-room was large and beautiful. A tall white double door, standing wide open, led to the adjacent billiard-room in which the gentlemen with the unruly legs and some others were playing. On the other side was a glass door through which one could see into the wide terrace and the garden. Near it stood a piano. There was a card-table with a green top at which the diabetic general and a few other gentlemen were playing whist. Ladies sat reading or doing needlework. The room was heated by an iron stove, but in front of the elegant fireplace with its pieces of imitation coal pasted over with glowing red paper, there were comfortable places to sit and talk.

'You are an early riser, Herr Spinell. I have already quite by chance seen you two or three times leaving the house at half-past seven in the morning.'

'An early riser? . . . Ah, only in a rather special sense, dear madam. The fact is that I rise early because I am really a late sleeper.'

'Now, that you must explain, Herr Spinell!' – Rätin Spatz also desired an explanation.

'Well . . . if one is an early riser, then it seems to me that one does not really need to get up so early. Conscience, dear lady – conscience is a terrible thing! I and my kind spend all our lives battling with it, and we have our hands full trying from time to time to deceive it and to satisfy it in cunning little ways. We are useless creatures, I and my kind, and apart from our few good hours we do nothing but chafe ourselves sore and sick against the knowledge of our own uselessness. We hate everything that is useful, we know that it is vulgar and ugly, and we defend this truth fanatically, as one only defends truths that are absolutely necessary to one's existence. And nevertheless our bad conscience so gnaws at us that it leaves not one spot on us unscathed. In addition, matters are made worse by the whole character of our inner life, by our outlook, our way of working – they are terribly unwholesome, they undermine us, they exhaust us. And so one has recourse to certain little palliatives, without which it would all be quite unendurable. For example, some of us feel the need for a well conducted outward existence, for a certain hygienic austerity in our habits. To get up early, cruelly early; to take a cold bath and a walk out into the snow . . . That makes us feel moderately satisfied with ourselves for perhaps an hour or so. If I were to act in accordance with my true nature, I should lie in bed until well into the afternoon, believe me. My early rising is really hypocrisy.'

'Why, not at all, Herr Spinell! I call it self-discipline . . . Don't you, Frau Rätin?' Rätin Spatz also called it self-discipline.

'Hypocrisy or self-discipline – whichever word you prefer! I have a melancholically honest disposition, and consequently . . .'

'That's just it. I am sure you are much too melancholic.'

'Yes, dear madam, I am melancholic.'

The fine weather continued. Everything was bright, hard and clean, windless and frosty; the house and garden, the surrounding countryside and the mountains, lay mantled in dazzling whiteness and pale blue shadows; and over it all stood a vaulted sky of delicate azure and utter purity, in which a myriad shimmering light particles and dazzling crystals seemed to be dancing. At this period Herr Klöterjahn's wife seemed to be in tolerably good health; she had no fever, scarcely coughed at all, and had not too bad an appetite. Often she would sit out on the terrace for hours in the frost and the sun, as her doctor had prescribed. She sat in the snow, warmly wrapped in blankets and furs, hopefully breathing in the pure icy air for the benefit of her trachea. Sometimes she would see Herr Spinell walking in the garden; he too was warmly dressed and wore fur boots which made his feet look absolutely enormous. He walked through the snow with a tentative gait and a careful, prim posture of the arms; when he reached the terrace he would greet her very respectfully and mount the steps to engage her in a little conversation.

'I saw a beautiful woman on my morning walk today . . . Ah, dear me, how beautiful she was!' he said, tilting his head to one side and spreading out his hands.

'Really, Herr Spinell? Do describe her to me!'

'No, that I cannot do. Or if I did, I should be giving you an incorrect picture of her. I only glanced fleetingly at the lady as I passed, I did not really see her. But that uncertain glimpse was sufficient to stir my imagination, and I received and took away with me a vision of beauty . . . ah, of what beauty!'

She laughed. 'Is that your way of looking at beautiful women, Herr Spinell?'

'Yes, dear madam; and it is a better way than if I were to stare them in the face with a crude appetite for reality, and imprint their actual imperfections on my mind . . .'

' "Appetite for reality" . . . what a strange phrase! That really is a phrase only a writer could have used. Herr Spinell! But I must confess that it impresses me. It suggests something to me that I partly understand, a certain feeling of independence and freedom, even a certain disrespect for reality – although I know that reality is more deserving of respect than anything else, indeed that it is the only truly respectable thing . . . And then I realize that there is something beyond what we can see and touch, something more delicate . . .'

'I know only one face,' he said suddenly, speaking with a strange exaltation, raising his clenched hands to his shoulders and showing his carious teeth in an ecstatic smile . . . 'I know only one face which even in reality is so noble and spiritual that any attempt by my imagination to improve upon it would be blasphemy – a face at which I could gaze, which I long to contemplate, not for minutes, not for hours, but for the whole of my life, for in it I should lose myself utterly and forget all earthly things . . .'

'Yes, quite, Herr Spinell. But Fräulein von Osterloh's ears stick out rather far, don't you think?'

He made no reply and bowed deeply. When he raised his eyes again, they rested with an expression of embarrassment and sadness on the strange, sickly little pale blue vein that branched out across the clear, almost translucent surface of her forehead.

7

A strange fellow, a really very odd fellow! Herr Klöterjahn's wife sometimes thought about him, for she had plenty of time for thinking. Perhaps the beneficial effect of the change of air had begun to wear off, or perhaps some positively harmful influence was at work upon her: at all events her state of health had deteriorated, the condition of her trachea seemed to leave much to be desired, she felt weak and weary, she had lost her appetite and was often feverish. Dr Leander had most emphatically urged her to rest, not to talk too much, to exercise the utmost care. And so, when she was allowed up at all, she would sit with Rätin Spatz, not talking too much, holding her needlework idly in her lap and thinking her thoughts as they came and went.

Yes, this curious Herr Spinell made her think and wonder; and the remarkable thing was that he made her think not so much about him as about herself; somehow he awakened in her a strange curiosity about her own nature, a kind of interest in it she had never felt before. One day, in the course of conversation, he had remarked:

'Yes, women are certainly very mysterious . . . the facts are nothing new, and yet they are a perpetual source of astonishment. One is confronted, let us say, with some wonderful creature – a sylph, a figure from a dream, a fairy's child. And what does she do? She goes off and marries some fairground Hercules, some butcher's apprentice. And there she comes, leaning on his arm, perhaps even with her head on his shoulder, and looking about her with a subtle smile as if to say: "Well, here's a phenomenon to make you all rack your brains!" And we rack them, we do indeed.'

This was a speech which Herr Klöterjahn's wife had repeatedly pondered.

On another occasion, to the astonishment of Rätin Spatz, the following dialogue took place between them.

'I am sure, dear madam, that it is very impertinent of me, but may I ask you what your name is – what it really is?'

'But my name is Klöterjahn, Herr Spinell, as you know!'

'Hm. Yes, that I know. Or rather: that I deny. I mean of course your own name, your maiden name. You must in all fairness concede, dear madam, that if anyone were to address you as "Frau Klöterjahn" he would deserve to be horsewhipped.'

She laughed so heartily that the little blue vein over her eyebrow stood out alarmingly clearly and gave her sweet delicate face a strained, anxious expression that was deeply disturbing.

'Why, good gracious, Herr Spinell! Horsewhipped? Do you find "Klöterjahn" so appalling?'

'Yes, dear madam, I have most profoundly detested that name ever since I first heard it. It is grotesque, it is unspeakably ugly; and to insist on social convention to the point of calling you by your husband's name is barbaric and outrageous.'

'Well, what about "Eckhof"? Is Eckhof any better? My father's name is Eckhof.'

'Ah, there now, you see! "Eckhof" is quite another matter! There was once even a great actor called Eckhof. Eckhof is appropriate. You only mentioned your father. Is your mother . . .'

'Yes; my mother died when I was little.'

'I see. Please tell me a little more about yourself; do you mind my asking? If it tires you, then do not do it. Just rest, and I will go on describing Paris to you, as I did the other day. But you could talk very softly, you know; you could even whisper, and it would make what you tell me all the more beautiful . . . You were born in Bremen?' He uttered this question almost voicelessly, with an expression of reverent awe, as if he were asking something momentous, as if Bremen were some city beyond compare, full of ineffable excitements and hidden beauties, and as if to have been born there conferred some kind of mysterious distinction.

'Yes, just fancy!' she said involuntarily. 'I was born in Bremen.'

'I was there once,' he remarked meditatively.

'Good gracious, you've been there, too? Why, Herr Spinell, I do believe you've seen everything there is to see between Tunis and Spitzbergen!'

'Yes, I was there once,' he repeated. 'For a few short hours, one evening. I remember an old, narrow street with gabled houses and the moon slanting strangely down on them. And then I was in a vaulted basement room that smelled of wine and decay. How vividly I recall it . . .'

'Really? I wonder where that was. Yes, I was born in a grey gabled house like that, an old patrician merchant's house with an echoing front hall and a white-painted gallery.'

'Then your father is a man of business?' he asked a little hesitantly.

'Yes. But in addition, or perhaps I should really say in the first place, he is an artist.'

'Ah! Ah! What kind of artist?'

'He plays the violin. But that is not saying much. It is *how* he plays it that matters, Herr Spinell! I have never been able to listen to certain notes without tears coming to my eyes – such strange, hot tears! No other experience has ever moved me like that. I dare say you will scarcely believe me . . .'

'I believe you! Oh, I believe you indeed! . . . Tell me, dear lady: surely your family is an old one? Surely, in that grey gabled house, many generations have already lived and laboured and been gathered to their forefathers?'

'Yes. But why do you ask?'

'Because it often happens that an old family, with traditions that are entirely practical, sober and bourgeois, undergoes in its declining days a kind of artistic transfiguration.'

'Is that so? Well, so far as my father is concerned he is certainly more of an artist than many a man who calls himself one and is famous for it. I only play the piano a little. Of course, now they have forbidden me to play; but I still did in those days, when I was at home. Father and I used to play together . . . Yes, all those years are a precious memory to me; especially the garden, our garden behind the house. It was terribly wild and overgrown, and the walls round it were crumbling and covered with moss; but that was just what gave it its great charm. It had a fountain in the middle, surrounded by a dense border of flag irises. In summer I used to sit there for hours with my friends. We would all sit on little garden chairs round the fountain . . .'

'What beauty!' said Herr Spinell, raising his shoulders. 'You sat round it singing?'

'No, we were usually crocheting.'

'Ah, nevertheless . . . nevertheless . . .'

'Yes, we crocheted and gossiped, my six friends and I . . .'

'What beauty! Ah, dear me, how beautiful that is!' cried Herr Spinell, with his face quite contorted.

'But what is so particularly beautiful about that, Herr Spinell?'

'Oh, the fact that there were six young ladies besides yourself, the fact that you were not one of their number, but stood out amongst them like a queen . . . You were singled out from your six friends. A little golden crown, quite inconspicuous yet full of significance, gleamed in your hair . . .'

'Oh, what nonsense, there was no such crown . . .'

'Ah, but there was: it gleamed there in secret. I should have seen it, I should have seen it in your hair quite plainly, if I had been standing unnoticed among the bushes on one of those occasions . . .'

'Heaven knows what you would have seen. But you were not standing there, on the contrary it was my husband, as he now is, who one day stepped out of the bushes with my father beside him. I'm afraid they had even been listening to a lot of our chatter . . .'

'So that, dear madam, was where you first met your husband?'

'Yes, that was where I met him!' Her voice was firm and happy, and as she smiled the little delicate blue vein stood out strangely and strenuously above her brow. 'He was visiting my father on business, you see. He came to dinner the following evening, and only three days later he asked for my hand.'

'Really! Did it all happen so very fast?'

'Yes . . . Or rather, from then on it went a little more slowly. You see, my father was not at all keen on the marriage, and insisted on our postponing it for quite a long time to think it over properly. It was partly that he would have preferred me to go on living with him, and he had other reservations about it as well. But . . .'

'But?'

'But *I* was quite determined,' she said with a smile, and once more the little pale blue vein overshadowed her sweet face with an anxious, sickly expression.

'Ah, you were determined.'

'Yes, and I made my wishes quite clear and stood my ground, as you see . . .'

'As I see. Yes.'

'. . . so that my father had to give his consent in the end.'

'And so you forsook him and his violin, you forsook the old house and the overgrown garden and the fountain and your six friends, and followed after Herr Klöterjahn.'

' "And followed after" . . . How strangely you put things, Herr Spinell! It sounds almost biblical! Yes, I left all that behind me, for after all, that is the law of nature.'

'Of nature, yes, I dare say it is.'

'And after all, my future happiness was at stake.'

'Of course. And you came to know that happiness . . .'

'I came to know it, Herr Spinell, when they first brought little Anton to me, our little Anton, and when I heard him crying so noisily with his healthy little lungs, the strong, healthy little creature . . .'

'I have heard you mention the good health of your little Anton before, dear lady. He must be a quite exceptionally healthy child?'

'Yes, he is. And he looks so absurdly like my husband!'

'Ah! I see. So that was how it happened. And now your name is no longer Eckhof, but something else, and you have your healthy little Anton and a slight defect of the trachea.'

'Yes. And as for *you*, Herr Spinell, you are a most mysterious person, I do assure you . . .'

'Yes, God bless my soul, so you are!' said Rätin Spatz, who was, after all, still there.

But this conversation too was one to which Herr Klöterjahn's wife afterwards frequently reverted in her thoughts. Insignificant though it had been, there had nevertheless been several things latent in it which gave her food for reflection about herself. Could *this* be the harmful influence that was affecting her? Her weakness increased, and her temperature often rose: she would lie in a quiet feverish glow, in a state of mild euphoria to which she surrendered herself pensively, fastidiously, complacently, with a faintly injured air. When she was not confined to her bed, Herr Spinell would approach her, tiptoeing up to her on his great feet with extreme circumspection, stopping at a distance of two paces with one leg poised a little way behind the other, and bowing from the waist: he would talk to her in a deferentially muted voice, as if he were raising her gently aloft with reverent awe, and laying her down on soft cushioning clouds where no strident noise nor earthly contact should reach her. At such moments she would remember Herr Klöterjahn's way of saying 'Careful, Gabriele, take care, darling, and keep your mouth closed!' in a voice as hard as a well-meant slap on the back. But then she would at once put this memory aside and lie back weakly and euphorically on the cloudy cushions which Herr Spinell so assiduously spread out beneath her.

One day, apropos of nothing at all, she suddenly reverted to the little conversation they had had about her background and earlier life.

'So it is really true, Herr Spinell,' she asked, 'that you would have seen the crown?'

And although it was already a fortnight since they had talked of this, he at once knew what she meant and ardently assured her that if he had been there then, as she sat with her six friends by the fountain, he would have seen the little golden crown gleaming – would have seen it secretly gleaming in her hair.

A few days later one of the patients politely inquired whether her little Anton at home was in good health. She exchanged a fleeting glance with Herr Spinell who was nearby, and answered with a slightly bored expression:

'Thank you, he is quite well; why should he not be? And so is my husband.'

8

One frosty day at the end of February, a day purer and more brilliant than any that had preceded it, high spirits prevailed at Einfried. The heart cases chattered away to each other with flushed cheeks, the diabetic general hummed and chirruped like a boy, and the gentlemen with the unruly legs were quite beside themselves with excitement. What was it all about? A communal outing had been planned, nothing less: an excursion into the mountains in several sleighs, with jingling bells and cracking whips. Dr Leander had decided upon this diversion for his patients.

Of course, the 'serious cases' would have to stay at home, poor things! With much meaningful nodding it was tacitly agreed that the entire project must be concealed from them, and the opportunity to exercise this degree of compassion and consideration filled everyone with a glow of self-righteousness. But even a few of those who might very well have taken part in the treat declined to do so. Fräulein von Osterloh was of course excused in any case. No one so overburdened with duties as herself could seriously contemplate going on sleigh excursions. The tasks of the household imperatively required her presence – and in short, at Einfried she remained. But there was general disappointment when Herr Klöterjahn's wife also declared her intention of staying at home. In vain Dr Leander urged upon her the benefits of the refreshing trip; she insisted that she was not in the mood, that she had a headache, that she felt tired; and so there was no more to be said. But the cynical would-be wit took occasion to observe:

'Mark my words, now the Putrefied Infant won't come either.'

And he was right, for Herr Spinell let it be known that he intended to spend the afternoon working – he was very fond of describing his dubious activity as 'work'. The prospect of his absence was in any case regretted by no one, and equally little dismay was caused by Rätin Spatz's decision to remain behind and keep her young friend company, since (as she said) sleigh-riding made her feel seasick.

There was an early lunch that day, at about noon, and immediately after it the sleighs drew up in front of Einfried. The patients, warmly wrapped up, made their way across the garden in animated groups, full of excitement and curiosity. The scene was watched by Herr

Klöterjahn's wife and Rätin Spatz from the glass door leading out to the terrace, and by Herr Spinell from the window of his room. There was a certain amount of playful and hilarious fighting about who should sit where; Fräulein von Osterloh, with a fur boa round her neck, darted from sleigh to sleigh pushing hampers of food under the seats; finally Dr Leander, wearing a fur cap above his flashing spectacles, sat down himself after a last look round, and gave the signal for departure . . . The horses drew away, a few ladies shrieked and fell over backwards, the bells jangled, the short-shafted whips cracked and their long lashes trailed across the snow beside the runners; and Fräulein von Osterloh stood at the garden gate waving her handkerchief until the vehicles slid out of sight round a bend in the road and the merry noise died away. Then she hurried back through the garden to set about her tasks again; the two ladies left the glass door, and almost simultaneously Herr Spinell retired from his vantage-point.

Silence prevailed in Einfried. The expedition was not expected back before evening. The 'serious cases' lay in their rooms and suffered. Herr Klöterjahn's wife and her companion took a short walk and then withdrew to their rooms. Herr Spinell, too, was in his room, occupied after his fashion. At about four o'clock half a litre of milk was brought to each of the ladies, and Herr Spinell was served with his usual weak tea. Shortly after this Herr Klöterjahn's wife tapped on the wall between her room and that of Magistratsrätin Spatz and said:

'Shall we go down to the drawing-room, Frau Rätin? I really can't think of anything else to do here.'

'Certainly, my dear, I'll come at once,' answered Frau Spatz. 'I'll just put on my boots, if you don't mind, because I've just been taking a bit of a rest, as a matter of fact.'

As might have been expected, the drawing-room was empty. The ladies sat down by the fireplace. Rätin Spatz was embroidering flowers on a piece of canvas; Herr Klöterjahn's wife, too, began a little needlework, but presently let it drop into her lap and gazed dreamily over the arm of her chair at nothing in particular. Finally she made a remark which was really not worth opening one's mouth to reply to. But Rätin Spatz nevertheless asked: 'What did you say?' so that to her humiliation she had to repeat the whole sentence. Rätin Spatz again asked: 'What?' But just at this moment they heard steps in the lobby, the door opened and Herr Spinell came into the room.

'Do I disturb you?' he asked softly, pausing on the threshold, looking only at Herr Klöterjahn's wife, and executing a kind of delicately hovering half-bow from the waist . . . She replied: 'Why, not at all, Herr Spinell! In the first place this room is supposed to be open to all comers, as you know, and in any case what is there to disturb? I have a very strong suspicion that I am boring Frau Spatz . . .'

He could think of no answer to this, but merely smiled, showing his carious teeth. The eyes of the two ladies followed him as with a certain air of embarrassment he walked to the glass door, where he stopped and stood looking out, rather ill-manneredly turning his back on them. Then he half turned towards them, but continued to gaze out into the garden as he said:

'The sun has disappeared. The sky has imperceptibly clouded over. It's beginning to get dark already.'

'Yes, indeed, there are shadows everywhere,' replied Herr Klöterjahn's wife. 'I should think it may well be snowing before our sleighing party gets back. Yesterday at this time it was still broad daylight, and now dusk is falling.'

'Oh,' he said, 'what a relief it is to the eyes! There has been too much brightness these last few weeks – too much of this sun which glares with such obtrusive clarity on everything, whether beautiful or vulgar . . . I am really thankful that it is hiding its face for a little at last.'

'Do you not like the sun, Herr Spinell?'

'Well, I am no painter, you know . . . When there is no sun one feels more spiritual. There is a thick, pale grey layer of cloud all over the sky. Perhaps it means there will be a thaw tomorrow. Incidentally I would not advise you, dear madam, to go on gazing at your needlework over there.'

'Oh, you need not worry, I've stopped it in any case. But what else is there to do?'

He had sat down on the revolving stool in front of the piano, leaning on the lid of the instrument with one arm.

'Music . . .' he said. 'If only there were a chance to hear a little music nowadays! Sometimes the English children sing little Negro songs, and that is all.'

'And yesterday afternoon Fräulein von Osterloh gave a high-speed rendering of "The Monastery Bells",' remarked Herr Klöterjahn's wife.

'But dear lady, you play, do you not?' he said pleadingly, and rose to his feet . . . 'There was a time when you used to make music every day with your father.'

'Yes, Herr Spinell, that was in the old days! The days of the fountain in the garden, you know . . .'

'Do it today!' he begged. 'Play a few bars just this once! If you knew how I craved to hear them . . .'

'Our family doctor and Dr Leander have both expressly forbidden me to play, Herr Spinell.'

'They are not here; neither of them is here! We are free . . . you are free, dear lady! A few trifling little chords . . .'

'No, Herr Spinell, it's no use your trying to persuade me. Heaven knows what sort of marvels you expect of me! And I have forgotten everything, I assure you. I can play scarcely a note by heart.'

'Oh, then play that! Play scarcely a note! Besides, there is some music here too – here it is, on the top of the piano. No, this is nothing. But here is some Chopin . . .'

'Chopin?'

'Yes, the nocturnes. And now all that remains is for us to light the candles . . .'

'Don't imagine that I am going to play, Herr Spinell! I must not play! What if it were to do me harm?'

He was silent. With his great feet, his long black coat, his grey hair and his beardless face with its indistinctly outlined features, he stood there in the light of the two piano candles, letting his hands hang down by his sides.

Finally he said in a soft voice: 'In that case I cannot ask it of you. If you are afraid it will do you harm, dear madam, then let the beauty that might come to life under your fingers remain dead and mute. You were not always so very prudent; not, at least, when you were asked to make the opposite decision and renounce beauty. You were not concerned about your bodily welfare then, you showed less hesitation and a stronger will when you left the fountain and took off the little golden crown . . . Listen!' he said after a pause, dropping his voice still lower. 'If you sit here now and play as you once did, when your father was still standing beside you and drawing those notes out of his violin that brought tears to your eyes – then perhaps it will be seen again, gleaming secretly in your hair, the little golden crown . . .'

'Really?' she said, with a smile. It somehow happened that her voice failed her on this word, which came out huskily and half in a whisper. She cleared her throat and asked:

'Are those really Chopin's nocturnes you have there?'

'Indeed they are. They are open and everything is ready.'

'Well, then, in God's name, I will play one of them,' she said. 'But only one, do you understand? In any case, after one you certainly won't want to hear any more.'

So saying she rose, put down her needlework and came across to the piano. She sat down on the revolving stool, on which two or three bound volumes of music lay; she adjusted the lights, and began turning over the pages of the Chopin album. Herr Spinell had drawn up a chair, and sat beside her like a music master.

She played the Nocturne in E-flat major, Opus 9, no. 2. If it was really true that she had forgotten anything of what she had once learned, then she must in those days have been a consummate artist. The piano was only a mediocre one, but after the very first notes she was able to handle it with perfect taste and control. She showed a fastidious ear for differences of timbre, and her enthusiastic command of rhythmic mobility verged on the fantastic. Her touch was both firm and gentle. Under her hands the melody sang forth its uttermost sweetness, and the figurations entwined themselves round it with diffident grace.

She was wearing the dress she had worn the day of her arrival, the one with the dark heavy bodice and the thick cut-velvet arabesques, which gave to her head and her hands a look of such unearthly delicacy. The expression of her face did not change as she played, but her lips seemed to grow more clear-cut than ever and the shadows seemed to deepen in the corners of her eyes. When she had finished she lowered her hands to her lap and went on gazing at the music. Herr Spinell sat on motionless, without saying a word.

She played another nocturne, she played a second and a third. Then she rose, but only to look for some more music on the top of the piano.

It occurred to Herr Spinell to examine the black bound albums on the piano stool. Suddenly he uttered an unintelligible sound, and his great white hands passionately fingered one of the neglected volumes.

'It's not possible! . . . It can't be true! . . . And yet there is no doubt of it! . . . Do you know what this is? . . . Do you realize what has been lying here – what I have in my hands? . . .'

'What is it?' she asked.

Speechlessly he pointed to the title page. He had turned quite pale; he lowered the volume and looked at her with trembling lips.

'Indeed? I wonder how that got here? Well, give it to me,' she said simply. She put it on the music stand, sat down, and after a moment's silence began to play the first page.

He sat beside her, leaning forward, with his hands between his knees and his head bowed. She played the opening at an extravagantly, tormentingly slow tempo, with a disturbingly long pause between each of the phrases. The *Sehnsucht* motif, a lonely wandering voice in the night, softly uttered its tremulous question. Silence followed, a silence of waiting. And then the answer: the same hesitant, lonely strain, but higher in pitch, more radiant and tender. Silence again. And then, with that wonderful muted sforzando which is like an upsurging, uprearing impulse of joy and passion, the love motif began: it rose, it climbed ecstatically to a mingling sweetness, reached its climax and fell away, while the deep song of the cellos came into prominence and continued the melody in grave, sorrowful rapture . . .

Despite the inferiority of her instrument the performer tried with some success to suggest the appropriate orchestral effects. She rendered with brilliant precision the violin scales in the great crescendo. She played with fastidious reverence, lingering faithfully over every significant detail of the structure, humbly and ceremoniously exhibiting it, like a priest elevating the sacred host. What story did the music tell? It told of two forces, two enraptured lovers reaching out towards each other in suffering and ecstasy and embracing in a convulsive mad desire for eternity, for the absolute . . . The prelude blazed to its consummation and died down. She stopped at the point where the curtain parts and continued to gaze silently at the music.

The boredom of Rätin Spatz had by this time reached that degree of intensity at which it causes protrusion of the eyes and a terrifying, corpse-like disfigurement of the human countenance. In addition this kind of music affected her stomach nerves, it threw her dyspeptic organism into a turmoil of anxiety, and Frau Spatz began to fear that she was about to have a fit.

'I'm afraid I must go to my room,' she said in a faint voice. 'Goodbye, I shall be back presently.'

And she departed. The evening dusk was already far advanced. Outside on the terrace, thick snow was silently falling. The two candles gave a close and flickering light.

'The second act,' he whispered; and she turned the pages and began playing the second act.

The sound of horns dying away in the distance . . . or was it the wind in the leaves? The soft murmuring of the stream? Already the night had flooded the grove with its stillness and hushed the castle halls, and no warning entreaty availed now to stem the tide of overmastering desire. The sacred mystery was enacted. The torch was extinguished; the descending notes of the death-motif spoke with a strange, suddenly clouded sonority; and in tumultuous impatience the white veil was passionately waved, signalling to the beloved as he approached with outspread arms through the darkness.

Oh boundless, oh unending exultation of this meeting in an eternal place beyond all visible things! Delivered from the tormenting illusion, set free from the bondage of space and time, self and not-self blissfully mingling, 'thine' and 'mine' mystically made one! The mocking falsehoods of day could divide them, but its pomp and show no longer had power to deceive them, for the magic potion had opened their eyes: it had made them initiates and visionaries of night. He who has gazed with love into the darkness of death and beheld its sweet mystery can long for one thing only while daylight still holds him in its delusive thrall: all his desire and yearning is for the sacred night which is eternal and true, and which unifies all that has been separated.

Oh sink down, night of love, upon them; give them that forgetfulness they long for, enfold them utterly in your joy and free them from the world of deception and division! 'See, the last lamp has been extinguished! Thought and the vanity of thinking have vanished in the holy twilight, the world-redeeming dusk outspread over all illusion and all woe. And then, as the shining phantasm fades and my eyes fail with passion: then this world from which the falsehood of day debarred me, which to my unquenchable torment it held out before me as the object of my desire – then I myself, oh wonder of wishes granted! then I *myself* am the world . . .' And there followed

Brangäne's warning call, with those rising violin phrases that pass all understanding.

'I am not always sure what it means, Herr Spinell; I can only guess at some of it. What is "then I myself am the world"?'

He explained it to her, softly and briefly.

'Yes, I see. But how can you understand it all so well, and yet not be able to play it?'

Strangely enough, this simple question quite overwhelmed him. He coloured, wrung his hands and seemed to sink into the floor, chair and all. Finally he answered in stricken tones:

'The two seldom go together. No, I cannot play. But please continue.'

And the drunken paeans of the mystery drama continued. 'Can love ever die? Tristan's love? The love of thy Isolde, of my Isolde? Oh, it is everlasting, death cannot assail it! What could perish by death but the powers that interfere, the pretences that part us, we who are two and one?' By the sweet word 'and' love bound them together – and if death should sunder that bond, how could death come to either of them and not bring with it the other's own life? . . . And thus they sang their mysterious duo, sang of their nameless hope, their death-in-love, their union unending, lost for ever in the embrace of night's magic kingdom. O sweet night, everlasting night of love! Land of blessedness whose frontiers are infinite! What visionary once has dreamed of you and does not dread to wake again into desolate day? O grace of death, cast out that dread! Set free these lovers utterly from the anguish of waking! Ah, this miraculous tempest of rhythms, this chromatic uprushing ecstasy, this metaphysical revelation! 'A rapture beyond knowing, beyond foregoing, far from the pangs of the light that parts us, a tender longing with no fear or feigning, a ceasing in beauty with no pain, an enchanted dreaming in immensity! Thou art Isolde, I am Isolde no longer; I am Tristan no longer, thou art Tristan –'

At this point there was a startling interruption. The pianist suddenly stopped playing and shaded her eyes with her hand to peer into the darkness; and Herr Spinell swung round on his chair. At the far side of the room the door that led into the passage had opened, and a shadowy figure entered, leaning on the arm of a second figure. It was one of the Einfried patients, one who had also been unable to join in the sleigh ride, but had chosen this evening hour for one of her pathetic instinctive tours round the institution: it was the lady who had had nineteen children and was no longer capable of thought – it was Pastorin Höhlenrauch on the arm of her attendant. She did not raise her eyes, but wandered with groping steps across the background of the room and disappeared through the opposite door, like a sleepwalker, dumb and staring and conscious of nothing. All was silent.

'That was Pastorin Höhlenrauch,' he said.

'Yes, that was poor Frau Höhlenrauch,' she replied. Then she turned the pages and played the closing passage of the whole work, the *Liebestod*, Isolde's death-song.

How pale and clear her lips were, and how the shadows deepened in the corners of her eyes! The little pale blue vein over one eyebrow, which gave her face such a disturbingly strained look, stood out more and more prominently on her translucent forehead. Under her rapidly moving hands the fantastic crescendo mounted to its climax, broken by that almost shameless, sudden pianissimo in which the ground seems to slide away under our feet and a sublime lust to engulf us in its depths. The triumph of a vast release, a tremendous fulfilment, a roaring tumult of immense delight, was heard and heard again, insatiably repeated, flooding back and reshaping itself; when it seemed on the point of ebbing away it once more wove the *Sehnsucht*-motif into its harmony, then breathed out its uttermost breath and died, faded into silence, floated into nothingness. A profound stillness reigned.

They both sat listening, tilting their heads to one side and listening.

'That's the sound of bells,' she said.

'It's the sleighs,' he said. 'I shall go.'

He rose and walked across the room. When he came to the door at the far end he stopped, turned round and stood for a moment, uneasily shifting his weight from one foot to the other. And then, fifteen or twenty paces from her, he suddenly sank down on his knees – down on both knees, without a word. His long black frock coat spread out round him on the floor. His hands were clasped across his mouth and his shoulders twitched convulsively.

She sat with her hands in her lap, leaning forward away from the piano, and looked at him. She was smiling with a strained, uncertain smile, and her eyes gazed pensively into the half-darkness, focusing themselves with difficulty, with a slight uncontrollable unsteadiness.

From some way off the jangle of sleigh-bells, the crack of whips and a babel of human voices could be heard approaching.

9

The sleigh excursion, which remained the chief topic of conversation for a considerable time, had taken place on the twenty-sixth of February. On the twenty-seventh a thaw set in, everything turned soft and slushy and dripped and dribbled, and on that day Herr Klöterjahn's wife was in excellent health. On the twenty-eighth she coughed up a little blood – oh, hardly any to speak of; but it was blood. At the same time she began to feel weaker than ever before, and took to her bed.

Dr Leander examined her, and his face as he did so was cold and hard. He then prescribed the remedies indicated by medical science: little pieces of ice, morphine, complete rest. It also happened that on the following day he declared himself unable to continue the treatment personally owing to pressure of work, and handed it over to Dr Müller, who meekly undertook it, as his contract required. He was a quiet, pale, insignificant, sad-looking man, whose modest and unapplauded function it was to care for those patients who were scarcely ill at all and for those whose cases were hopeless.

The opinion expressed by Dr Müller, first and foremost, was that the separation between Herr Klöterjahn and his wedded wife had now lasted rather a long time. It was, in his view, extremely desirable that Herr Klöterjahn – if, of course, his prosperous business could possibly spare him – should pay another visit to Einfried. One might write to him, one might even send him a little telegram . . . And it would, Dr Müller thought, undoubtedly cheer and strengthen the young mother if he were to bring little Anton with him – quite apart from the fact that it would be of considerable interest to the doctors to make the acquaintance of this very healthy little child.

And lo and behold, Herr Klöterjahn came. He had received Dr Müller's little telegram and had arrived from the Baltic coast. He dismounted from the carriage, ordered coffee and buttered rolls and looked extremely put out.

'Sir,' he said, 'what is the matter? Why have I been summoned to her?'

'Because it is desirable,' answered Dr Müller, 'that you should be near your wife at the present time.'

'Desirable . . . desirable . . .! But is it *necessary*? I have to consider my money, sir – times are bad and railway fares are high. Was this lengthy journey really indispensable? I'd say nothing if for example it were her lungs; but since, thank God, it's only her trachea . . .'

'Herr Klöterjahn,' said Dr Müller gently, 'in the first place the trachea is an important organ . . .' He said 'in the first place', although this was incorrect, since he did not then mention any second place.

But simultaneously with Herr Klöterjahn a buxom young woman appeared at Einfried, clad entirely in red and tartan and gold, and it was she who on one arm carried Anton Klöterjahn Jr, little healthy Anton. Yes – he was here, and no one could deny that he was in fact a prodigy of good health. Pink and white, cleanly and freshly clothed, fat and fragrant, he reposed heavily upon the bare red arm of his gold-braided nurse, devoured enormous quantities of milk and chopped meat, screamed and abandoned himself in all respects to his instincts.

From the window of his room, the writer Spinell had observed the arrival of the Klöterjahn child. Through half-closed eyes, with a strange yet penetrating scrutiny, he had watched him being lifted out of the carriage and conveyed into the house; and he had then stood on motionless for some time with his expression unchanged.

Thereafter, so far as was feasible, he avoided all contact with Anton Klöterjahn Jr.

10

Herr Spinell was sitting in his room 'working'.

It was a room like all the others in Einfried, furnished in a simple and elegant period style. The massive chest of drawers had metal lion's-head mountings; the tall pier-glass was not one smooth sheet, but composed of numerous small panes framed in lead; the gleaming floor was uncarpeted and the stiff legs of the furniture seemed to extend as light shadows into its bluish, varnished surface. A large writing-table stood near the window, across which the novelist had drawn a yellow curtain, presumably to make himself feel more spiritual.

In a yellowish twilight he was sitting bowed over the desk and writing – he was writing one of those numerous letters which he sent to the post every week and to which, comically enough, he usually received no reply. A large thick sheet of writing-paper lay before him, and in its top left-hand corner, under an intricately vignetted landscape, the name 'Detlev Spinell' was printed in letters of an entirely novel design. He was covering this sheet with tiny handwriting, with a neat and most carefully executed calligraphy.

'Sir!' he had written, 'I am addressing the following lines to you because I simply cannot help it – because my heart is so full of what I have to say to you that it aches and trembles, and the words come to me in such a rush that they would choke me if I could not unburden myself of them in this letter . . .'

To be strictly correct, this statement about the words coming to him in a rush was quite simply untrue, and God knows what foolish vanity induced Herr Spinell to make such an assertion. Rushing was the very last thing his words seemed to be doing; indeed, for one whose profession and social status it was to be a writer, he was making miserably slow progress, and no one could have watched him without reaching the conclusion that a writer is a man to whom writing comes harder than to anyone else.

Between two fingertips he held one of the strange little downy hairs that grew on his face and went on twirling it for periods of a quarter of an hour or more, at the same time staring into vacancy and adding not a line to his composition; he would then daintily pen a few words and come to a halt once more. On the other hand it must be admitted that what he finally produced did give the impression of smooth spontaneity and vigour, notwithstanding its odd and dubious and often scarcely intelligible content.

'I am', the letter continued, 'under an inescapable compulsion to make you see what I see, to make you share the inextinguishable vision that has haunted me for weeks, to make you see it with my eyes, illuminated by the language in which I myself would express what I inwardly behold. An imperative instinct bids me communicate my experiences to the world, to communicate them in unforgettable words each chosen and placed with burning accuracy; and this is an instinct which it is my habit to obey. I ask you, therefore, to hear me.

'I merely wish to tell you about something as it was and as it now is. It is a quite short and unspeakably outrageous story, and I shall tell it without comment, accusation or judgement, but in my own words. It is the story of Gabriele Eckhof, sir, the lady whom you call your wife . . . and please note: although the experience was yours, it is nevertheless I whose words will for the first time raise it for you to the level of a significant event.

'Do you remember the garden, sir, the old neglected garden behind the grey patrician house? Green moss grew in the crevices of the weather-beaten walls that surrounded this wild and dreaming place. And do you remember the fountain in the centre? Lilac-coloured sword-lilies drooped over its crumbling edge, and its silvery jet murmured mysteriously as it played upon the riven stonework. The summer day was drawing to its close.

'Seven maidens were sitting in a circle round the fountain; but in the hair of the seventh, the one and chiefest among them all, the sunset's rays seemed secretly to be weaving a glittering emblem of royal rank. Her eyes were like troubled dreams, and yet her bright lips were parted in a smile . . .

'They were singing. Lifting their slender faces they watched the leaping jet, they gazed up at the point where it wearily and nobly curved into its fall, and their soft clear voices hovered around its graceful dance. Their delicate hands, perhaps, were clasped about their knees as they sang . . .

'Do you remember this scene, sir? Did you even see it? No, you did not. It was not for your eyes, and yours were not the ears to hear the chaste sweetness of that melody. Had you seen it, you would not have dared to draw breath, and your heart would have checked its beat. You would have had to withdraw, go back into life, back to your own life, and preserve what you had beheld as something untouchable and inviolable, as a sacred treasure within your soul, to the end of your earthly days. But what did you do?

'That scene, sir, was the end of a tale. Why did you have to come and destroy it, why give the story so vulgar and ugly and painful a sequel? It had been a moving, tranquil apotheosis, immersed in the transfiguring sunset glow of decline and decay and extinction. An old family, already grown too weary and too noble for life and action, had reached the end of its history, and its last utterances were sounds of music: a few violin notes, full of the sad insight which is ripeness for death . . . Did you look into the eyes that were filled with tears by those notes? It may be that the souls of her six companions belonged to life – but not hers, the soul of their sister and queen: for on it beauty and death had set their mark.

'You saw it, that death-doomed beauty: you looked upon it to lust after it. No reverence, no awe touched your heart at the sight of something so moving and holy. You were not content to look upon it: you had to possess it, to exploit it, to desecrate it . . . What a subtle choice you made! You are a gourmet, sir, a plebeian gourmet, a peasant with taste.

'Please note that I have no wish whatever to offend you. What I have said is not abuse: I am merely stating the formula, the simple psychological formula of your simple, aesthetically quite uninteresting personality; and I am stating it solely because I feel the need to shed a little light for you on your own nature and behaviour – because it is my ineluctable vocation on this earth to call things by their names, to make them articulate, and to illuminate whatever is unconscious. The world is full of what I call "the unconscious type", and all these unconscious types are what I cannot bear! I cannot bear all this primitive, ignorant life, all this naïve activity, this world of infuriating intellectual blindness all round me! I am possessed by a tormenting irresistible impulse to analyse all these human lives in my vicinity, to do my utmost to give to each its correct definition and bring it to consciousness of itself – and I am unrestrained by consideration of the consequences of doing so, I care not whether my words help or hinder, whether they carry comfort and solace or inflict pain.

'You, sir, as I have said, are a plebeian gourmet, a peasant with taste. Although in fact your natural constitution is coarse and your position on the evolutionary scale extremely low, your wealth and your sedentary habits have enabled you to achieve a certain barbarian corruption of the nervous system, sudden and historically quite inappropriate, but lending a certain lascivious refinement to your appetites. I dare say your throat muscles began to contract automatically, as if stimulated by the prospect of swallowing some delicious soup or masticating some rare dish, when you decided to take possession of Gabriele Eckhof . . .

'And so indeed you did: interrupting her dream and imposing your misguided will upon hers, leading her out of the neglected garden into life and ugliness, giving her your vulgar name and making her a married woman, a housewife, a mother. You degraded that weary diffident beauty, which belonged to death and was blossoming in sublime uselessness, by harnessing it to the service of everyday triviality and of that mindless, gross and contemptible idol which is called "nature"; and your peasant conscience has never stirred with the slightest inkling of how profound an outrage you committed.

'Once again: what in fact has happened? She, with those eyes that are like troubled dreams, has borne you a child; to that creature, that mere continuation of its begetter's crude existence, she at the same time gave every particle of vitality and viability she possessed – and now she dies. She is dying, sir! And if nevertheless her departure is not vulgar and trivial, if at the very end she has risen from her degradation and perishes proudly and joyfully under the deadly kiss of beauty, then it is *I* who have made it my business to bring that about. You, I dare say, were in the mean time diverting yourself in quiet corridors with chambermaids.

'But her son, Gabriele Eckhof's son, is living and thriving and triumphant. Perhaps he will continue his father's career and become an active trading citizen, paying his taxes and eating well; perhaps he will be a soldier or an official, an unenlightened and efficient pillar of society; in any case he will be a normally functioning philistine type, unscrupulous and self-assured, strong and stupid.

'Let me confess to you, sir, that I hate you, you and your child, as I hate life itself – the vulgar, absurd and nevertheless triumphant life which you represent, and which is the eternal antithesis and arch-enemy of beauty. I cannot say that I despise you. I am unable to despise you. I honestly admit this. You are the stronger man. In our struggle I have only one thing to turn against you, the sublime avenging weapon of the weak: intellect and the power of words. Today I have used this weapon. For this letter – here too let me make an honest admission – is nothing but an act of revenge; and if it contains even a single phrase that is biting and brilliant and beautiful enough to strike home, to make you aware of an alien force, to shake your robust equanimity even for one moment, then I shall exult in that discomfiture. – DETLEV SPINELL.'

And Herr Spinell put this piece of writing in an envelope, added a stamp, daintily penned an address, and delivered it to the post.

11

Herr Klöterjahn knocked at the door of Herr Spinell's room; he held a large, neatly written sheet of paper in one hand, and wore the air of a man determined upon energetic measures. The post had done its duty, the letter had completed its curious journey from Einfried to Einfried and had duly reached its intended recipient. The time was four o'clock in the afternoon.

When Herr Klöterjahn entered, Herr Spinell was sitting on the sofa reading his own novel, the book with the baffling cover design. He rose to his feet with a surprised and interrogative glance at his visitor, while at the same time colouring perceptibly.

'Good afternoon,' said Herr Klöterjahn. 'Pardon my intrusion upon your occupations. But may I ask whether you wrote this?' So saying he held up the large, neatly written sheet in his left hand and struck it with the back of his right, making it crackle sharply. He then pushed his right hand into the pocket of his wide, easy-fitting trousers, tilted his head to one side and opened his mouth to listen, as some people do.

Oddly enough Herr Spinell smiled; with an obliging, rather confused and half-apologetic smile he raised one hand to his forehead as if he were trying to recollect what he had done, and said:

'Ah yes . . . that is so . . . I took the liberty . . .'

The fact was that on this particular day he had acted in accordance with his true nature and slept until noon. Consequently he was suffering from a bad conscience, his head was not clear, he felt nervous and his resistance was low. In addition there was now a touch of spring in the air, which he found fatiguing and deeply depressing. This must all be mentioned in extenuation of the pitifully silly figure he cut throughout the following scene.

'Did you indeed? Ah-ha! Very well!' Herr Klöterjahn, having got this

127

opening formality out of the way, thrust his chin down against his chest, raised his eyebrows, flexed his arms and gave various other indications that he was about to come mercilessly to the point. His exuberant self-satisfaction was such that he slightly overdid these preparatory antics, so that what eventually followed did not quite live up to the elaborate menace of the preliminary pantomime. But Herr Spinell had turned several shades paler.

'Very well, my dear sir!' repeated Herr Klöterjahn. 'Then I shall answer it by word of mouth, if you don't mind, having regard to the fact that I consider it idiotic to write letters several pages long to a person to whom one can speak at any hour of the day . . .'

'Well . . . idiotic perhaps . . .' said Herr Spinell with an apologetic, almost humble smile.

'Idiotic!' repeated Herr Klöterjahn, energetically shaking his head in token of the utter unassailability of his position. 'And I'd not be wasting words now on this scribbled piece of trash, frankly I'd not even have kept it to use for wrapping up sandwiches, but for the fact that it has opened my eyes and clarified certain matters which I had not understood, certain changes . . . however, that's no concern of yours and it's beside the point. I am a busy man, I have more important things to think about than your indistinguishable visions . . .'

'I wrote "inextinguishable vision",' said Herr Spinell, drawing himself up to his full height. During this whole scene it was the one moment in which he displayed a minimum of dignity.

'Inextinguishable . . . indistinguishable . . .!' retorted Herr Klöterjahn, glancing at the manuscript. 'Your handwriting's wretched, my dear sir; you'd not get a job in my office. At first sight it seems decent enough, but when you look at it closely it's full of gaps and all of a quiver. However, that's your affair and not mine. I came here to tell you that in the first place you are a fool and a clown – well, let's hope you're aware of that already. But in addition you are a damned coward, and I dare say I don't need to prove that to you in detail either. My wife once wrote to me that when you meet women you don't look them square in the face but just give them a sort of squint from the side, because you're afraid of reality and want to carry away a beautiful impression in your mind's eye. Later on unfortunately she stopped mentioning you in her letters, or I'd have heard some more fine stories about you. But that's the sort of man you are. It's 'beauty' and 'beauty' in every sentence you speak, but the basis of it all is cringing cowardice and envy, and I suppose that also explains your impudent allusion to "quiet corridors". I dare say that remark was intended to knock me absolutely flat, and all it did was to give me a good laugh. A damned good laugh! Well, now have I told you a few home truths? Have I – let me see – "shed a little light for you on your nature and behaviour", you miserable specimen? Not, of course, that it's my "indestructible vocation" to do so, heh, heh! . . .'

'I wrote "ineluctable vocation",' said Herr Spinell; but he let the point go. He stood there crestfallen and helpless, like a great pathetic grey haired scolded schoolboy.

'Indestructible . . . ineluctable . . . I tell you you are a contemptible cowardly cur. Every day you see me at table. You bow to me and smile, you pass me dishes and smile, you say the polite things and smile. And one fine day you fling this screed of abusive drivel into my face. Ho, yes, you're bold enough on paper! And this ridiculous letter's not the whole story. You've been intriguing against me behind my back, I see that now quite clearly . . . Although you needn't imagine you've had any success. If you flatter yourself that you've put any fancy notions into my wife's head, then you're barking up the wrong tree, my fine friend! My wife has too much common sense! Or if you should even be thinking that when I got here with the child her behaviour towards us was in any way different from what it used to be, then you're even more of a half-wit than I supposed! It's true she didn't kiss the little fellow, but that was a precaution, because just lately the suggestion's been made that the trouble isn't with her trachea but with her lungs, and if that's so one can't be too . . . but anyhow they're still a long way from proving their lung theory, and as for you and your "she is dying, sir" – why, you crazy ninny, you . . .!'

Here Herr Klöterjahn struggled a little to recover his breath. By now he had worked himself up into a passionate rage; he kept stabbing the air with his right forefinger and crumpling the manuscript with his left hand till it was scarcely fit to be seen. His face, between its blond English side-whiskers, had turned terribly red, and swollen veins ran like streaks of wrathful lightning across his clouded brow.

'You hate me,' he went on, 'and you would despise me if I were not the stronger man . . . Yes, and so I am, by God! My heart's in the right place; and where's yours? In your boots most of the time I suppose, and if it were not forbidden by law I'd knock you to pieces, with your "intellect and power of words" and all, you blithering snake in the grass! But that does not mean, my fine fellow, that I intend to put up with your insults lying down, and when I get back and show my lawyer that bit about my "vulgar name" – then we'll see whether you don't get the shock of your life. My name is good, sir, and it's my own hard work that made it good. Just you ask yourself whether anyone will lend you a brass farthing on yours, you idle tramp from God knows where! The law of the land is for dealing with people like you! You're a public danger! You drive people crazy! . . . But I'll have you know that you've not got away with your little tricks this time, my very smart friend! I'm not the man to let your sort get the better of me, oh no! My heart's in the right place . . .'

Herr Klöterjahn was now in a real fury. He was positively bellowing, and kept on repeating that his heart was in the right place.

' "They were singing". Full stop. They were doing nothing of the sort! They were knitting. What's more, from what I overheard, they were discussing a recipe for potato pancakes; and when I show this passage about "decline and decay" to my father-in-law, he'll take you to court too, you may be sure of that! . . . "Do you remember that scene, did you see it?" Of course I saw it, but what I don't see is why I should have held my breath at the sight and run away. I don't squint and leer at women from the side, I look them in the face, and if I like the look of them and they like me, I go ahead and get them. My heart's in the right pl . . .'

Someone was knocking. Knocking at the door of the room, nine or ten times in rapid succession, in an urgent, frantic little tattoo which stopped Herr Klöterjahn in mid-sentence; and a voice exclaimed, panic-stricken and stumbling with distress and haste:

'Herr Klöterjahn, Herr Klöterjahn – oh, is Herr Klöterjahn there?'

'Keep out!' said Herr Klöterjahn rudely. 'What's the matter? I'm busy here talking.'

'Herr Klöterjahn,' said the tremulous, gasping voice, 'you must come . . . the doctors are there too . . . oh, it's so dreadfully sad . . .'

He was at the door with one stride and snatched it open. Rätin Spatz was standing outside. She was holding her handkerchief to her mouth, and great long tears were rolling down into it from both her eyes.

'Herr Klöterjahn,' she managed to say, '. . . .it's so terribly sad . . .
She brought up so much blood, such a dreadful lot . . . She was sitting
up quite quietly in her bed humming a little snatch of music to herself,
and then it came – oh, God, there was such a lot, you never saw such a
lot . . .'

'Is she dead?' shrieked Herr Klöterjahn, seizing Frau Spatz by the arm
and dragging her to and fro on the threshold . . . 'No, not quite, what?
Not quite dead yet, she can still see me, can't she? Brought up a little
blood again, has she? From the lungs, was it? Maybe it does come from
the lungs, I admit that it may . . . Gabriele!' he cried suddenly, tears
starting to his eyes, and the warm, kindly, honest, human emotion that
welled up from within him was plain to see. 'Yes, I'm coming!' he said,
and with long strides he dragged Frau Spatz out of the room and away
along the corridor. From far in the distance his rapidly receding voice
could still be heard: 'Not quite, what? . . . From her lungs, you say?'

12

Herr Spinell went on standing exactly where he had stood throughout
Herr Klöterjahn's so abruptly terminated visit. He stared at the open
door; finally he advanced a few steps into the passage and listened. But in
the distance all was silent; and so he returned to his room, closing the
door behind him.

He contemplated himself in the mirror for several minutes, then went
to his desk, took a small flask and a glass from somewhere inside it and
swallowed a brandy – for which in the circumstances he could scarcely
be blamed. Then he lay down on the sofa and closed his eyes.

The window was open at the top. Outside in the garden of Einfried
the birds were twittering; and somehow the whole of spring was
expressed in those subtle, tender, penetrating, insolent little notes. At
one point Herr Spinell muttered the phrase 'indestructible vocation . . .!' to himself, and shook his head from side to side, sucking the
breath in between his teeth as if afflicted by acute nervous discomfort.

To regain calm and composure was out of the question. One's
constitution is really quite unsuited to these coarse experiences! By a

psychological process the analysis of which would carry us too far afield, Herr Spinell reached the decision to get up and take a little exercise, a short walk in the open air. Accordingly he picked up his hat and left his room.

As he stepped out of the house into the balmy, fragrant air he turned his head back towards the building and slowly raised his eyes until they reached a certain window, a window across which the curtains had been drawn: he gazed fixedly at it for a while, and his expression was grave and sombre. Then, with his hands on his back, he went on his way along the gravel path. He was deep in thought as he walked.

The flower-beds were still covered with matting, the trees and bushes were still bare; but the snow had gone, and there were only a few damp patches here and there on the paths. The spacious garden with its grottoes, leafy arcades and little pavilions was bathed in the splendid intense colours of late afternoon, full of strong shadows and a rich golden light, and intricate patterns of dark branches and twigs stood sharply and finely silhouetted against the bright sky.

It was the time of day at which the sun's outline becomes clear, when it is no longer a shapeless brilliant mass but a visibly sinking disc whose richer, milder glow the eye can bear to behold. Herr Spinell did not see the sun; he walked with his head bowed, humming a little snatch of music to himself, a brief phrase, a few anguished, plaintively rising notes: the *Sehnsucht*-motif . . . But suddenly, with a start, with a quick convulsive intake of breath, he stood still as if rooted to the spot and stared straight ahead of him, wide-eyed, with sharply contracted brows and an expression of horrified repugnance . . .

The path had turned; it now led straight towards the setting sun, which stood large and low in the sky, its surface intersected by two narrow wisps of gleaming cloud with gilded edges, its warm yellow radiance flooding the garden and setting the tree-tops on fire. And in the very midst of this golden transfiguration, erect on the path, with the sun's disc surrounding her head like a mightly halo, stood a buxom young woman clad entirely in red and gold and tartan. She was resting her right hand on her well-rounded hip, while with her left she lightly rocked a graceful little perambulator to and fro. But in front of her, in this perambulator, sat the child – sat Anton Klöterjahn Jr, Gabriele Eckhof's fat son!

There he sat among his cushions, in a white woolly jacket and a big white hat – chubby, magnificent and robust; and his eyes, unabashed and alive with merriment, looked straight into Herr Spinell's. The novelist was just on the point of pulling himself together; after all, he was a grown man, he would have had the strength to step right past this unexpected sight, this resplendent phenomenon, and continue his walk. But at that very moment the appalling thing happened: Anton Klöterjahn began to laugh – he screamed with laughter, he squealed, he crowed: it was inexplicable. It was positively uncanny.

God knows what had come over him, what had set him off into this wild hilarity: the sight of the black-clad figure in front of him perhaps, or some sudden spasm of sheer animal high spirits. He had a bone teething ring in one hand and a tin rattle in the other, and he held up these two objects triumphantly into the sunshine, brandishing them and banging them together, as if he were mockingly trying to scare someone off. His eyes were almost screwed shut with pleasure, and his mouth gaped open so wide that his entire pink palate was exposed. He even wagged his head to and fro in his exultation.

And Herr Spinell turned on his heel and walked back the way he had come. Pursued by the infant Klöterjahn's jubilant shrieks, he walked along the gravel path, holding his arms in a careful, prim posture; and something in his gait suggested that it cost him an effort to walk slowly – the effort of a man intent upon concealing the fact that he is inwardly running away.

Tonio Kröger

Tonio Kröger

1903

Tonio Kröger

1

The winter sun was no more than a feeble gleam, milky and wan behind layers of cloud above the narrow streets of the town. Down among the gabled houses it was damp and draughty, with occasional showers of a kind of soft hail that was neither ice nor snow.

School was over. The hosts of liberated pupils streamed across the cobbled yard and out through the wrought-iron gate, where they dispersed and hastened off in opposite directions. The older ones held their bundles of books in a dignified manner, high up against their left shoulders, and with their right arms to windward steered their course towards dinner; the little ones trotted merrily off with their feet splashing in the icy slush and the paraphernalia of learning rattling about in their sealskin satchels. But now and then they would one and all snatch off their caps with an air of pious awe as some senior master with the beard of Jove and the hat of Wotan strode solemnly by . . .

'Are you coming now, Hans?' said Tonio Kröger; he had been waiting in the street for some time. With a smile he approached his friend, who had just emerged from the gate, chattering to some other boys and about to move off with them . . . 'What?' he asked, looking at Tonio . . . 'Oh yes, of course! All right, let's walk a little.'

Tonio did not speak, and his eyes clouded over with sadness. Had Hans forgotten, had he only just remembered that they had arranged to walk home together this afternoon? And he himself, ever since Hans had promised to come, had been almost continuously looking forward to it!

'Well, so long, you fellows,' said Hans Hansen to his companions.

'I'm just going for a walk now with Kröger.' And the two of them turned to the left, while the others sauntered off to the right.

Hans and Tonio had time to take a walk after school, because they both came from families in which dinner was not served until four o'clock. Their fathers were important men of business, who held public office in the town and wielded considerable influence. The Hansens had for many generations owned the big timber yard down by the river, where powerful mechanical saws hissed and spat as they cut up the tree trunks. But Tonio was the son of Consul Kröger, whose sacks of grain could be seen any day being driven through the streets, with his firm's name stamped on them in great black letters; and his spacious old ancestral house was the grandest in the whole town . . . The two friends were constantly having to doff their caps to their numerous acquaintances; indeed, although they were only fourteen, many of those they met were the first to greet them . . .

Both had slung their satchels across their shoulders, and both were well and warmly dressed: Hans in a short reefer jacket with the broad blue collar of his sailor's suit hanging out over his back, and Tonio in a grey, belted overcoat. Hans wore a Danish sailor's cap with black ribbons, and a shock of his flaxen blond hair stood out from under it. He was extraordinarily good-looking and well built, broad in the shoulders and narrow in the hips, with keen, steely blue eyes set wide apart. But Tonio's complexion, under his round fur cap, was swarthy, his features were sharply cut and quite southern in character, and the look in his dark heavy-lidded eyes, ringed with delicate shadows, was dreamy and a little hesitant . . . The outlines of his mouth and chin were unusually soft. His gait was nonchalant and unsteady, whereas Hans's slender black-stockinged legs moved with a springy and rhythmic step . . .

Tonio was walking in silence. He was suffering. He had drawn his rather slanting brows together and rounded his lips as if to whistle, and was gazing into vacancy with his head tilted to one side. This attitude and facial expression were characteristic of him.

Suddenly Hans pushed his arm under Tonio's with a sidelong glance at him, for he understood very well what was the matter. And although Tonio still did not speak during the next few steps, he suddenly felt very moved.

'I hadn't forgotten, you know, Tonio,' said Hans, gazing down at the sidewalk, 'I just thought we probably wouldn't be having our walk after all today, because it's so wet and windy. But I don't mind the weather of course, and I think it's super of you to have waited for me all the same. I'd already decided you must have gone home, and I felt cross . . .'

Everything in Tonio began to dance with joy at these words.

'Well, then, let's go round along the promenade!' he said, in a voice full of emotion. 'Along the Mühlenwall and the Holstenwall, and that'll take us as far as your house, Hans . . . Oh, of course not, it doesn't matter, I don't mind walking home by myself afterwards; you can walk me home next time.'

In his heart he was not really convinced by what Hans had said, and sensed very clearly that his friend attached only half as much importance as he did to this tête-à-tête walk. But he perceived nevertheless that Hans was sorry for his forgetfulness and was going out of his way to conciliate him. And Tonio was very far from wishing to resist these conciliatory advances . . .

The fact was that Tonio loved Hans Hansen, and had already suffered a great deal on his account. Whoever loves the more is at a disadvantage and must suffer – life had already imparted this hard and simple truth to his fourteen-year-old soul; and his nature was such that when he learned something in this way he took careful note of it, inwardly writing it down, so to speak, and even taking a certain pleasure in it – though without, of course, modifying his own behaviour in the light of it or turning it to any practical account. He had, moreover, the kind of mind that found such lessons much more important and interesting than any of the knowledge that was forced on him at school; indeed, as he sat through the hours of instruction in the vaulted Gothic classrooms, he would chiefly be occupied in savouring these insights to their very depths and thinking out all their implications. And this pastime would give him just the same sort of satisfaction as he felt when he wandered round his own room with his violin (for he played the violin) and drew from it notes of such tenderness as only he could draw, notes which he mingled with the rippling sound of the fountain down in the garden as it leapt and danced under the branches of the old walnut tree . . .

The fountain, the old walnut tree, his violin and the sea in the distance, the Baltic Sea to whose summer reveries he could listen when he visited it in the holidays: these were the things he loved, the things which, so to speak, he arranged around himself and among which his inner life evolved – things with the names that may be employed in poetry to good effect, and which did indeed very frequently recur in the poems that Tonio Kröger from time to time composed.

The fact that he possessed a notebook full of poems written by himself had by his own fault become public knowledge, and it very adversely affected his reputation both with his schoolmates and with the masters. Consul Kröger's son on the one hand thought their disapproval stupid and contemptible, and consequently despised his fellow pupils as well as his teachers, whose ill-bred behaviour in any case repelled him and whose personal weaknesses had not escaped his uncommonly penetrating eye. But on the other hand he himself felt that there was something extravagant and really improper about writing poetry, and in a certain sense he could not help agreeing with all those who considered it a very odd occupation. Nevertheless this did not prevent him from continuing to write . . .

Since he frittered away his time at home and was lethargic and inattentive in class and out of favour with the masters, he continually brought back absolutely wretched reports, to the great annoyance and distress of his father, a tall, carefully dressed man with pensive blue eyes who always wore a wild flower in his buttonhole. To Tonio's mother, however – his beautiful dark-haired mother whose first name was Consuelo and who was in every way so unlike the other ladies of the city, his father having in days gone by fetched her up as his bride-to-be from somewhere right at the bottom of the map – to his mother these school reports did not matter in the least . . .

Tonio loved his dark, fiery mother, who played the piano and the mandolin so enchantingly, and he was glad that his dubious standing in human society did not grieve her. But on the other hand he felt that his father's anger was much more dignified and *comme il faut*, and though scolded by him he basically agreed with his father's view of the matter and found his mother's blithe unconcern slightly disreputable. Often his thoughts would run rather like this: 'It's bad enough that I am as I am, that I won't and can't change and am careless and stubborn and that my mind's full of things no one else thinks about. It's at least only right and proper that I should be seriously scolded and punished for it, instead of having it all passed over with kisses and music. After all, we're not gypsies in a green caravan, but respectable people – the Krögers, Consul Kröger's family . . .' And occasionally he would reflect: 'But why am I peculiar, why do I fight against everything, why am I in the masters' bad books and a stranger among the other boys? Just look at them, the good pupils and the solid mediocre ones! They don't find the masters ridiculous, they don't write poetry and they only think the kind of thoughts that one does and should think, the kind that can be spoken aloud. How decent they must feel, how at peace with everything and everyone! It must be good to be like that . . . But what is the matter with me, and what will come of it all?'

This way of thinking, this view of himself and of how he stood to life, was an important factor in Tonio's love for Hans Hansen. He loved him firstly because he was beautiful; but secondly because he saw him as his own counterpart and opposite in all respects. Hans Hansen was an outstanding pupil as well as being a fine fellow, a first-class rider and gymnast and swimmer who enjoyed universal popularity. The masters almost doted on him, called him by his first name and promoted his interests in every way; his schoolmates vied for his favour; ladies and gentlemen stopped him in the street, seized him by the shock of flaxen blond hair that stood out from under his Danish sailor's cap, and said: 'Good morning, Hans Hansen, with your nice head of hair! Still top of the class? That's a fine lad! Remember me to your father and mother . . .'

Such was Hans Hansen, and ever since they had first met the very sight of him had filled Tonio Kröger with longing, an envious longing which he could feel as a burning sensation in his chest. 'If only one could have blue eyes like yours,' he thought, 'if only one could live so normally and in such happy harmony with all the world as you do! You are always doing something suitable, something that everyone respects. When you have finished your school tasks you take riding lessons or work at things with your fretsaw, and even when you go down to the sea in the holidays you are busy rowing and sailing and swimming, while I lounge about forlornly on the sand, gazing at the mysterious changing expressions that fleet across the face of the sea. But that is why your eyes are so clear. If I could be like you . . .'

He made no attempt to become like Hans Hansen, indeed his wish to be like him was perhaps even hardly serious. But he did most painfully desire that Hans should love him for what he was; and so he sought his love, wooing him after his fashion – patiently and ardently and devotedly. It was a wooing full of anguish and sadness, and this sadness burned deeper and sharper than any impulsive passion such as might have been expected from someone of Tonio's exotic appearance.

And his wooing was not entirely in vain; for Hans, who in any case respected in Tonio a certain superiority, a certain gift of speech, a talent for expressing complicated things, sensed very clearly that he had roused in him an unusually strong and tender feeling. He was grateful for this, and responded in a way that gave Tonio much happiness – but also cost him many a pang of jealousy and disappointment in his frustrated efforts to establish intellectual companionship between them. For oddly enough, although Tonio envied Hans Hansen for being the kind of person he was, he constantly strove to entice him into being like Tonio; and the success of such attempts could at best be only momentary and even then only apparent . . .

'I've just been reading something wonderful, something quite splendid . . .' he was saying. They were walking along eating by turns out of a paper bag of fruit lozenges which they had purchased at Iwersen's store in the Mühlenstrasse for ten pfennigs. 'You must read it, Hans. It's *Don Carlos* by Schiller, actually . . . I'll lend it to you if you like . . .'

'Oh, no,' said Hans Hansen, 'don't bother, Tonio, that isn't my kind of thing. I'd rather stick to my horse books, you know. The illustrations in them are really super. Next time you're at my house I'll show you them. They're instantaneous photographs, so you can see the horses trotting and galloping and jumping, in all the positions – you can never see them like that in real life because they move so fast . . .'

'In all the positions?' asked Tonio politely. 'Yes, that must be nice. But *Don Carlos*, you know, it's quite unbelievable. There are passages in it, you'll find, they're so beautiful they give you a jolt, it's like a kind of explosion . . .'

'An explosion?' asked Hans Hansen . . . 'How do you mean?'

'For example, the passage where the king has wept because the marquis has betrayed him . . . but the marquis, you see, has only betrayed him to help the prince, he's sacrificing himself for the prince's sake. And then word is brought from the king's study into the ante-room that the king has wept. "Wept?" "The king wept?" All the courtiers are absolutely amazed, and it pierces you through and through, because he's a frightfully strict and stern king. But you can understand so well why he weeps, and actually I feel sorrier for him than for the prince and the marquis put together. He's always so very alone, and no one loves him, and then he thinks he has found someone, and that's the very man who betrays him . . .'

Hans Hansen glanced sideways at Tonio's face, and something in it must have aroused his interest in the subject, for he suddenly linked arms with him again and asked:

'Why, how does he betray him, Tonio?'

Tonio's heart leapt.

'Well, you see,' he began, 'all the dispatches for Brabant and Flanders . . .'

'Here comes Erwin Jimmerthal,' said Hans.

Tonio fell silent. If only, he thought, the earth would open and swallow that fellow Jimmerthal up! Why does he have to come and interrupt us? If only he doesn't join us and spend the whole walk talking about their riding lessons! For Erwin Jimmerthal took riding lessons too. He was the bank manager's son and lived out here beyond the city wall. He had already got rid of his satchel and was advancing towards them along the avenue with his bandy legs and slit-like eyes.

'Hullo, Jimmerthal,' said Hans. 'I'm going for a bit of a walk with Kröger . . .'

'I've got to go into town and get something,' said Jimmerthal. 'But I'll walk along with you for a little way . . . Are those fruit lozenges you've got there? Yes, thanks, I'll have a couple. It's our lesson again tomorrow, Hans.' He was referring to the riding lesson.

'Super!' said Hans. 'I'm going to be given my leather gaiters now, you know, because I was top in the essay the other day . . .'

'You don't take riding lessons, I suppose, Kröger?' asked Jimmerthal, and his eyes were just a pair of glinting slits . . .

'No . . .' replied Tonio in uncertain accents.

Hans Hansen remarked: 'You should ask your father to let you have lessons too, Kröger.'

'Yes . . .' said Tonio, hastily and without interest, his throat suddenly contracting because Hans had called him by his surname; Hans seemed to sense this and added by way of explanation:

'I call you Kröger because you've got such a crazy first name, you know; you mustn't mind my saying so, but I really can't stand it. Tonio . . . why, it isn't a name at all! Though of course it's not your fault, goodness me!'

'No, I suppose they called you that mainly because it sounds so foreign and special . . .' said Jimmerthal, with an air of trying to say something nice.

Tonio's mouth twitched. He pulled himself together and said:

'Yes, it's a silly name, God knows I'd rather it were Heinrich or Wilhelm, I can assure you. But it's all because I was christened after one of my mother's brothers whose name's Antonio; my mother comes from abroad, you know . . .'

Then he was silent and let the others talk on about horses and leather equipment. Hans had linked arms with Jimmerthal and was speaking with a fluent enthusiasm which *Don Carlos* could never have inspired in him . . . From time to time Tonio felt the tears welling up inside him, his nose tingled, and his chin kept trembling so that he could hardly control it . . .

Hans could not stand his name, and there was nothing to be done about it. His own name was Hans, and Jimmerthal's was Erwin – two good names which everyone recognized, to which no one could object. But 'Tonio' was something foreign and special. Yes, he was a special case in every way, whether he liked it or not; he was isolated, he did not belong among decent normal people – notwithstanding the fact that he was no gypsy in a green caravan, but Consul Kröger's son, a member of the Kröger family . . . But why did Hans always call him Tonio when they were alone together, if he felt ashamed of him as soon as anyone else appeared? Sometimes indeed there was a closeness between them, he was temporarily won over. 'Why, how does he betray him, Tonio?' he had asked, and had taken his arm. But the moment Jimmerthal had turned up he had breathed a sigh of relief nevertheless, he had dropped him and gratuitously criticized him for his foreign first name. How it hurt to have to understand all this so well! . . . He knew that in fact Hans Hansen did like him a little, when they were by themselves; but when anyone else was there he would feel ashamed and throw him over. And Tonio would be alone again. He thought of King Philip. The king wept . . .

'Oh, God,' said Erwin Jimmerthal, 'I really must go into town now.

Goodbye, you two – thanks for the fruit lozenges!' Whereupon he jumped on to a wooden seat at the side of the avenue, ran along it with his bandy legs and trotted away.

'I like Jimmerthal!' said Hans emphatically. Privileged as he was, he had a self-assured way of declaring his likes and dislikes, of graciously conferring them, so to speak . . . And then, having warmed to the theme, he went on talking about his riding lessons. In any case they were by now quite near the Hansens' house; it did not take long to reach it by the promenade along the old fortifications. They clutched their caps and bent their heads before the wind, the strong damp breeze that moaned and jurred among the leafless branches. And Hans Hansen talked, with Tonio merely interjecting an occasional insincere 'Ah!' or 'Oh, yes', and getting no pleasure from the fact that Hans, in the excitement of his discourse, had again linked arms with him; for it was merely a superficial and meaningless contact . . .

Presently, not far from the station, they turned off the promenade; they watched a train bustling and puffing past, counted the coaches just for fun, and as the last one went by, waved to the man who sat up there wrapped in his fur overcoat. Then they stopped in the Lindenplatz in front of the villa of Herr Hansen the wholesale timber merchant, and Hans demonstrated in detail what fun it was to stand on the bottom rail of the garden gate and swing oneself to and fro on its creaking hinges. But after that he took his leave.

'Well, I must go in now,' he said. 'Goodbye, Tonio. Next time I'll walk *you* home, I promise.'

'Goodbye, Hans,' said Tonio. 'It was a nice walk.'

Their hands, as they touched, were all wet and rusty from the garden gate. But when Hans glanced into Tonio's eyes he seemed to recollect himself, and a look of contrition came over his handsome face.

'And by the way, I'll read *Don Carlos* sometime soon,' he said quickly. 'That bit about the king in his study must be super!' Whereupon he hitched his satchel under his arm and ran off through the front garden. Before disappearing into the house he turned round and nodded once more.

And Tonio Kröger sped off homeward, joy lending him wings. The wind was behind him, but it was not only the wind that bore him so lightly along.

Hans was going to read *Don Carlos*, and then they would have something in common, something they could talk about, and neither Jimmerthal nor anyone else would be able to join in! How well they understood each other! Perhaps – who could say? – he would one day even be able to get him to write poetry, like Tonio himself . . . No, no, he didn't want that to happen. Hans must never become like Tonio, but stay as he was, with his strength and his sun-like happiness which made everyone love him, and Tonio most of all! But still, it would be no bad thing if he read *Don Carlos* . . . And Tonio walked under the low arch of the old gate, he walked along the quayside and up the steep, draughty, damp little street with its gabled buildings, till he reached his parents' house. His heart was alive in those days; in it there was longing, and sad envy, and just a touch of contempt, and a whole world of innocent delight.

2

Ingeborg Holm, the daughter of Dr Holm who lived in the market square with its tall pointed complicated Gothic fountain – the fair-haired Inge it was whom Tonio Kröger loved at the age of sixteen.

How did it come about? He had seen her hundreds of times; but one evening he saw her in a certain light. As she talked to a friend he saw how she had a certain way of tossing her head to one side with a saucy laugh, and a certain way of raising her hand – a hand by no means particularly tiny or delicately girlish – to smooth her hair at the back, letting her sleeve of fine white gauze slide away from her elbow. He heard her pronounce some word in a certain way, some quite insignificant word, but with a certain warm timbre in her voice. And his heart was seized by a rapture far more intense than the rapture he had sometimes felt at the sight of Hans Hansen, long ago, when he had still been a silly little boy.

That evening her image remained imprinted on his mind: her thick blond tresses, her rather narrowly cut laughing blue eyes, the delicate hint of freckles across the bridge of her nose. The timbre of her voice haunted him and he could not sleep; he tried softly to imitate the particular way she had pronounced that insignificant word, and a tremor ran through him as he did so. He knew from experience that this was love. And he knew only too well that love would cost him much pain, distress and humiliation; he knew also that it destroys the lover's peace of mind, flooding his heart with music and leaving him no time to form and shape his experience, to recollect it in tranquillity and forge it into a whole. Nevertheless he accepted this love with joy, abandoning himself to it utterly and nourishing it with all the strength of his spirit; for he knew that it would enrich him and make him more fully alive – and he longed to be enriched and more fully alive, rather than to recollect things in tranquillity and forge them into a whole . . .

It was thus that Tonio Kröger had lost his heart to blithe Inge Holm; and it had happened in Frau Consul Husteede's drawing-room, from which the furniture had been removed that evening, because it was the Frau Consul's turn to have the dancing class at her house. It was a private class, attended only by members of the best families, and the parents took turns in inviting all the young people together to receive their instruction in dancing and deportment. The dancing master, Herr Knaak, came once a week specially from Hamburg for this purpose.

François Knaak was his name, and what a character he was! '*J'ai l'honneur de me vous présenter,*' he would say, '*mon nom est Knaak* . . . And we say this not during our bow but after it, when we are standing up straight again. Quietly, but distinctly. It does not happen every day that we have to introduce ourselves in French, but if we can do it correctly and faultlessly in that language then we are all the more likely to get it right in German.' How magnificently his silky black tailcoat clung to his plump hips! His trousers fell in soft folds over his patent leather shoes with their wide satin bows, and his brown eyes gazed round with an air of wearily satisfied consciousness of their own beauty . . .

His self-assurance and urbanity were absolutely overwhelming. He would walk – and no one but he could walk with so rhythmic, so supple, so resilient, so royal a tread – up to the lady of the house, bow to her and wait for her to extend her hand. When she had done so he would murmur his thanks, step buoyantly back, turn on his left heel, smartly raise his right foot from the ground, pointing it outward and downward, and walk away with his hips swaying to and fro.

When one left a party one stepped backwards out of the door, with a bow; when one fetched a chair, one did not seize it by one leg and drag it across the floor, but carried it lightly by the back and set it down noiselessly. One did not stand with one's hands crossed on one's stomach and one's tongue in the corner of one's mouth; if anyone did do so, Herr Knaak had a way of imitating the posture that put one off it for the rest of one's life . . .

So much for deportment. As for dancing, Herr Knaak's mastery of that was possibly even more remarkable. The empty drawing-room was lit by a gas chandelier and by candles over the fireplace. Talcum powder had been strewn on the floor and the pupils stood round in a silent semicircle; and in the adjacent room, beyond the curtained doorways, their mothers and aunts sat on plush-covered chairs watching Herr Knaak through their lorgnettes, as with a forward inclination of the body, two fingers of each hand grasping his coat-tails, he capered elastically through a step-by-step demonstration of the mazurka. But when he wished to dumbfound his audience utterly, he would all of a sudden and for no good reason leap vertically off the floor, whirling his legs round each other in the air with bewildering rapidity as though he were executing a trill with them, and then return to terra firma with a discreet but earth-shaking thump . . .

'What a preposterous monkey!' thought Tonio Kröger to himself. But he could not fail to notice that Inge, blithe Inge Holm, would often watch Herr Knaak's every movement with rapt and smiling attention; and this was not the only reason why, in the last resort, he could not help feeling a certain grudging admiration for the dancing-master's impressively controlled physique. How calm and imperturbable was Herr Knaak's gaze! His eyes did not look deeply into things, they did not penetrate to the point at which life becomes complex and sad; all they knew was that they were beautiful brown eyes. But that was why he had such a proud bearing! Yes, it was necessary to be stupid in order to be able to walk like that; and then one was loved, for then people found one charming. How well he understood why Inge, sweet fair-haired Inge, gazed at Herr Knaak the way she did. But would no girl ever look that way at Tonio?

Oh yes, it did happen. There was the daughter, for instance, of Dr Vermehren the lawyer—Magdalena Vermehren, with her gentle mouth and her big, dark, glossy eyes so full of solemn enthusiasm. She often fell over when she danced. But when it was the ladies' turn to choose partners she always came to him; for she knew that he wrote poems, she had twice asked him to show them to her and she would often sit with her head drooping and gaze at him from a distance. But what good was that to Tonio? *He* loved Inge Holm, blithe, fair-haired Inge, who certainly despised him for his poetic scribblings . . . He watched her, he watched her narrow blue eyes so full of happiness and mockery; and an envious longing burned in his heart, a bitter insistent pain at the thought that to her he would always be an outsider and a stranger . . .

'First couple *en avant!*' said Herr Knaak, and words cannot describe how exquisitely he enunciated the nasal vowel. They were practising quadrilles, and to Tonio Kröger's profound alarm he was in the same set as Inge Holm. He avoided her as best he could, and yet constantly found himself near her; he forced his eyes not to look at her, and yet they constantly wandered in her direction . . . And now, hand-in-hand with the red-haired Ferdinand Matthiessen, she came gliding and running towards him, tossed her head back and stopped opposite him, recovering her breath. Herr Heinzelmann, the pianist, attacked the keyboard with his bony hands, Herr Knaak called out his instructions and the quadrille began.

She moved to and fro in front of him, stepping and turning, forwards and backwards; often he caught a fragrance from her hair or from the delicate white material of her dress, and his eyes clouded over with ever-increasing pain. 'I love you, dear, sweet Inge,' he said to himself, and the words contained all the anguish he felt as he saw her so eagerly and happily concentrating on the dance and paying no attention to him. A wonderful poem by Theodor Storm came into his mind: 'I long to sleep, to sleep, but you must dance.' What a torment, what a humiliating contradiction it was to have to dance when one's heart was heavy with love . . .

'First couple *en avant!*' said Herr Knaak; the next figure was beginning. '*Compliment! Moulinet des dames! Tour de main!*' And no words can do justice to his elegant muting of the *e* in '*de*'.

'Second couple *en avant!*' Tonio Kröger and his partner were the second couple. '*Compliment!*' And Tonio Kröger bowed. '*Moulinet des dames!*' And Tonio Kröger, with bent head and frowning brows, laid his hand on the hands of the four ladies, on Inge Holm's hand, and danced the *moulinet*.

All round him people began to titter and laugh. Herr Knaak struck a ballet-dancer's pose expressing stylized horror. 'Oh dear, oh dear!' he exclaimed. 'Stop, stop! Kröger has got mixed up with the ladies! *En arrière*, Miss Kröger, get back, *fi donc!* Everyone but you understands the steps by now. *Allons, vite!* Begone! *Retirez-vous!*' And he drew out his yellow silk handkerchief and flapped it at Tonio Kröger, chasing him back to his place.

Everyone laughed, the boys and the girls and the ladies in the next room, for Herr Knaak had turned the incident to such comical account; it was as entertaining as a play. Only Herr Heinzelmann, with a dry professional air, waited for the signal to go on playing; he was inured against Herr Knaak's devices.

And the quadrille continued. Then there was an interval. The parlourmaid entered with a tray of wine jellies in clinking glass cups, closely followed by the cook with a load of plum cake. But Tonio Kröger slipped unobtrusively out of the room into the corridor, and stood with his hands on his back gazing at a window, regardless of the fact that since the venetian blind was down one could see nothing and it was therefore absurd to stand in front of this window pretending to be looking out of it.

But it was inwards he was looking, inwards at his own grief and longing. Why, why was he here? Why was he not sitting at the window in his own room, reading Storm's *Immensee* and occasionally glancing out into the garden where it lay in the evening light, with the old walnut tree and its heavy creaking branches? That was where he should have been. Let the others dance and enjoy themselves and be good at it! . . . But no, no, this was his place nevertheless – here where he knew he was near Inge, even if all he could do was to stand by himself in the distance, listening to the hum and the clatter and the laughter and trying to pick out her voice from among it all, her voice so full of warmth and life. Dear, fair-haired Inge, with your narrow-cut, laughing blue eyes! Only people who do not read *Immensee* and never try to write anything like it can be as beautiful and light-hearted as you; that is the tragedy! . . .

Surely she would come! Surely she would notice that he had left the room, and feel what he was suffering, and slip out after him – even if it were only pity that brought her – and put her hand on his shoulder and say: 'Come back and join us, don't be sad, I love you!' And he listened to the voices behind him, waiting in senseless excitement for her to come. But she did not come. Such things did not happen on earth.

Had she laughed at him too, like all the others? Yes, she had, however much he would have liked to deny it for her sake and his. And yet he had only joined in the *moulinet des dames* because he had been so engrossed by her presence. And what did it matter anyway? One day perhaps they would stop laughing. Had he not recently had a poem accepted by a periodical – even if the periodical had gone out of business before the poem could appear? The day was coming when he would be famous and when everything he wrote would be printed; and then it would be seen whether that would not impress Inge Holm . . . No; it would *not* impress her; that was just the point. Magdalena Vermehren, the girl who was always falling over – yes, she would be impressed. But not Inge Holm, not blithe blue-eyed Inge, never. So what was the good of it all? . . .

Tonio Kröger's heart contracted in anguish at the thought. How it hurt to feel the upsurge of wonderful, sad, creative powers within one, and yet to know that they can mean nothing to those happy people at whom one gazes in love and longing across a gulf of inaccessibility! And yet – alone and excluded though he was, standing hopelessly with his distress in front of a drawn blind pretending to be looking through it – he was nevertheless happy. For his heart was alive in those days. Warmly and sorrowfully it throbbed for you, Ingeborg Holm, and in blissful self-forgetfulness his whole soul embraced your blond, radiant, exuberantly normal little personality.

More than once he stood thus by himself, with flushed cheeks, in out-of-the-way corners where the music, the scent of flowers and the clink of glasses could only faintly be heard, trying to pick out the timbre of your voice from among the other distant festive sounds; he stood there and pined for you, and was nevertheless happy. More than once it mortified him that he should be able to talk to Magdalena Vermehren, the girl who was always falling over – that she should understand him and laugh with him and be serious with him, whereas fair-haired Inge, even when he was sitting beside her, seemed distant and alien and embarrassed by him, for they did not speak the same language. And nevertheless he was happy. For happiness, he told himself, does not consist in being loved; that merely gratifies one's vanity and is mingled with repugnance. Happiness consists in loving – and perhaps snatching a few little moments of illusory nearness to the beloved. And he inwardly noted down this reflection, thought out all its implications and savoured it to its very depths.

'*Fidelity!*' thought Tonio Kröger. 'I will be faithful and love you, Ingeborg, for the rest of my life.' For he had a well-meaning nature. And nevertheless there was a sad whisper of misgiving within him, reminding him that he had, after all, quite forgotten Hans Hansen too, although he saw him daily. And the hateful, pitiable thing was that this soft, slightly mocking voice turned out to be right. Time went by, and the day came when Tonio Kröger was no longer so unreservedly ready as he had once been to lay down his life for blithe Inge; for he now felt within himself the desire and the power to achieve something of his own in this world, indeed to achieve in his own way much that would be remarkable.

And he hovered watchfully round the sacrificial altar on which his love burned like a pure, chaste flame; he knelt before it and did all he could to fan it and feed it and remain faithful. And he found that after a time, imperceptibly, silently and without fuss, the flame had nevertheless gone out.

But Tonio Kröger stood on for a while before the cold altar, full of astonishment and disillusionment as he realized that in this world fidelity is not possible. Then he shrugged his shoulders and went his way.

3

He went the way he had to go; rather nonchalantly and unsteadily, whistling to himself, gazing into vacancy with his head tilted to one side. And if it was the wrong way, then that was because for certain people no such thing as a right way exists. When he was asked what on earth he intended to do with his life, he would give various answers; for he would often remark (and had already written the observation down) that he carried within himself a thousand possible ways of life, although at the same time privately aware that none of them was possible at all . . .

Even before he left his native city and its narrow streets, the threads and bonds that held him to it had been quietly severed. The old Kröger family had gradually fallen into a state of decay and disintegration, and Tonio Kröger's own existence and nature were with good reason generally regarded as symptomatic of this decline. His father's mother, the family's senior and dominant member, had died; and his father, that tall, pensive, carefully dressed man with the wild flower in his buttonhole, had not been long in following her. The great Kröger mansion with all its venerable history was put up for sale and the firm was liquidated. But Tonio's mother, his beautiful fiery mother who played the piano and the mandolin so enchantingly and to whom nothing really mattered, got married again a year later – to a musician, a virtuoso with an Italian name, with whom she departed to live under far-off blue skies. Tonio Kröger thought this slightly disreputable; but who was he to set himself against it? He wrote poetry and could not even give an answer when asked what on earth he intended to do with his life . . .

So he left his home town with its gabled houses and the damp wind whistling round them; he left the fountain and the old walnut tree in the garden, those faithful companions of his youth; he left the sea too, his beloved sea, and left it all without a pang. For he was grown-up and enlightened now, he understood his situation and was full of contempt for the crude and primitive way of life that had enveloped him for so long.

He surrendered himself utterly to that power which he felt to be the sublimest power on earth, to the service of which he felt called and which promised him honour and renown: the power of intellect and words, a power that sits smilingly enthroned above mere inarticulate, unconscious life. He surrendered to it with youthful passion, and it rewarded him with all that it has to give, while inexorably exacting its full price in return.

It sharpened his perceptions and enabled him to see through the high-sounding phrases that swell the human breast, it unlocked for him the mysteries of the human mind and of his own, it made him clear-sighted, it showed him life from the inside and revealed to him the fundamental motives behind what men say and do. But what did he see? Absurdity and wretchedness – absurdity and wretchedness.

And with the torment and the pride of such insight came loneliness; for he could not feel at ease among the innocent, among the light of heart and dark of understanding, and they shrank from the sign on his brow. But at the same time he savoured ever more sweetly the delight of words and of form, for he would often remark (and had already written the observation down) that mere knowledge of human psychology would in itself infallibly make us despondent if we were not cheered and kept alert by the satisfaction of expressing it . . .

He lived in large cities in the south, for he felt that his art would ripen more lushly in the southern sun; and perhaps it was heredity on his mother's side that drew him there. But because his heart was dead and had no love in it, he fell into carnal adventures, far into the hot guilty depths of sensuality, although such experiences cost him intense suffering. Perhaps it was because of something inside him inherited from his father – from the tall, pensive, neatly dressed man with the wild flower in his buttonhole – that he suffered so much there: something that often stirred within him the faint nostalgic recollection of a more heartfelt joy he had once known and which now, amid these other pleasures, he could never recapture.

He was seized by revulsion, by a hatred of the senses, by a craving for purity and decency and peace of mind; and yet he was breathing the atmosphere of art, the mild, sweet, heavily fragrant air of a continual spring in which everything sprouts and burgeons and germinates in mysterious procreative delight. And so he could do no more than let himself be cast helplessly to and fro between gross extremes, between icy intellectuality on the one hand and devouring feverish lust on the other. The life he lived was exhausting, tormented by remorse, extravagant, dissipated and monstrous, and one which Tonio Kröger himself in his heart of hearts abhorred. 'How far astray I have gone!' he would sometimes think. 'How was it possible for me to become involved in all these eccentric adventures? After all, I wasn't born a gypsy in a green caravan . . .'

But as his health suffered, so his artistry grew more refined: it became fastidious, exquisite, rich, subtle, intolerant of banality and hyper-sensitive in matters of tact and taste. His first publication was received by the competent critics with considerable acclaim and appreciation, for it was a well-made piece of work, full of humour and the knowledge of suffering. And very soon his name – the same name that had once been shouted at him by angry schoolmasters, the name with which he had signed his first verses addressed to the sea and the walnut tree and the fountain, this mixture of southern and northern sounds, this respectable middle-class name with an exotic flavour – became a formula betokening excellence. For the profound painfulness of his experience of life was allied to a rare capacity for hard, ambitious, unremitting toil; and of this perseverance, joined in anguished combat with his fastidiously sensitive taste, works of quite unusual quality were born.

He worked, not like a man who works in order to live, but like one who has no desire but to work, because he sets no store by himself as a living human being, seeks recognition only as a creative artist, and spends the rest of his time in a grey incognito, like an actor with his make-up off, who has no identity when he is not performing. He worked in silence, in invisible privacy, for he utterly despised those minor hacks who treated their talent as a social ornament – who, whether they were poor or rich, whether they affected an unkempt and shabby appearance or sumptuous individualistic neckwear, aimed above all else at living happily, charmingly and artistically, little suspecting that good work is brought forth only under the pressure of a bad life, that living and working are incompatible and that one must have died if one is to be wholly a creator.

4

'Do I disturb you?' asked Tonio Kröger, pausing at the studio door. He had his hat in his hand and even bowed slightly, although Lisaveta Ivanovna was an intimate friend and he could talk to her about anything.

'For pity's sake, Tonio Kröger, come in and never mind the politeness,' she answered in her jerky accent. 'We all know that you were well brought up and taught how to behave.' So saying, she transferred her brush to the same hand as her palette, held out her right hand to him and gazed at him laughingly, shaking her head.

'Yes, but you're working,' he said. 'Let me see . . . Oh but you've made progress.' And he looked by turns at the colour sketches propped against chair-backs on either side of the easel, and at the big canvas marked off in squares and covered with a confused schematic charcoal sketch on which the first patches of colour were beginning to appear.

They were in Munich, in a rear apartment on Schellingstrasse, several floors up. Outside the wide north-facing window the sky was blue, the birds twittered and the sun shone; and the young sweet spring air, streaming in through an open pane, mingled in the large studio with the smell of fixative and oil paint. The bright golden afternoon light flooded unhindered all over the bare spacious room, frankly showing up the rather worn floor-boards, falling on the rough window-table covered with brushes and tubes and little bottles, and on the unframed studies that hung on the unpapered walls; it fell on the torn silk screen that enclosed a tastefully furnished little living corner near the door; it fell on the work that was gradually taking shape on the easel, and on the painter and the writer as they looked at it.

She was about the same age as himself, rather over thirty. In her dark blue paint-stained overall she sat on a low stool, propping her chin in her hand. Her brown hair was firmly set, greying a little at the sides already, and slightly waved over the temples; it framed a dark, very charming face of Slav cut, with a snub nose, prominent cheekbones and little shiny black eyes. Tensely, sceptically, with an air almost of irritation, she scrutinized her work from the side, with her eyes half-closed.

He stood beside her with his right hand on his hip and his left hand rapidly twirling his brown moustache. His slanting brows were frowning and working energetically, and he whistled softly to himself as usual. He was very carefully and punctiliously dressed, in a quiet grey suit of reserved cut. But his forehead, under the dark hair with its exceedingly correct and simple parting, twitched nervously, and his southern features were already sharp, clear-cut and traced as if with a hard chisel, although his mouth and chin were so gently and softly outlined . . . Presently he drew his hand across his forehead and eyes and turned away.

'I shouldn't have come,' he said.

'Why not, Tonio Kröger?'

'I've just been working, Lisaveta, and inside my head everything looks just as it does on this canvas. A skeleton, a faint sketch, a mess of corrections, and a few patches of colour, to be sure; and now I come here and see the same thing. And the same contradiction is here too,' he said, sniffing the air, 'the same conflict that was bothering me at home. It's odd. Once a thought has got hold of you, you find expressions of it everywhere, you even *smell* it in the wind, don't you? Fixative and the scent of spring! Art and – well, what is the opposite? Don't call it "nature", Lisaveta, "nature" isn't an adequate term. Oh, no, I dare say I ought to have gone for a walk instead, though it's doubtful whether that would have made me feel any better. Five minutes ago, quite near here, I met a colleague – Adalbert, the short-story writer. "God damn the spring!" he said in his aggressive way. "It is and always was the most abominable season of the year! Can you think a single thought that makes sense, Kröger? Have you peace of mind enough to work out any little thing, anything pointed and effective, with all this indecent itching in your blood and a whole swarm of irrelevant sensations pestering you, which turn out when you examine them to be absolutely trivial, unusable rubbish? As for me, I'm off to a café. It's neutral territory, you know, untouched by change of season; it so to speak symbolizes literature – that remote and sublime sphere in which one is incapable of grosser thoughts . . ." And off he went into the café; and perhaps I should have followed him.'

Lisaveta was amused.

'Very good, Tonio Kröger! "Indecent itching" – that's good. And he's not far wrong, because one really doesn't get much work done in spring. But now listen to me, I am now, in spite of the spring, going to do this little piece here – work out this pointed little effect, as Adalbert would say – and then we shall go into my "salon" and have some tea, and you shall tell me all; for I can see well enough that you have a lot on your mind today. Until then please arrange yourself somewhere – on that chest, for example, unless you think your aristocratic garments will be the worse for it . . .'

'Oh, stop going on at me about my clothes, Lisaveta Ivanovna! Would you like me to be running around in a torn velvet jacket or a red silk waistcoat? As an artist I'm already enough of an adventurer in my inner life. So far as outward appearances are concerned one should dress decently, damn it, and behave like a respectable citizen . . . No, I haven't got a lot on my mind,' he went on, watching her mix some colours on her palette. 'As I told you, I'm just preoccupied with a certain problem and contradiction, and it's been preventing me from working . . . What were we talking about just now? Yes: Adalbert, the short-story writer – he's a proud man and knows his own mind. "Spring is the most abominable season," he said, and went into a café. One must know what one wants, mustn't one? You see, I get nervous in spring too; I get distracted by the sweet trivial memories and feelings it revives in me. The difference is that I can't bring myself to put the blame on the spring and to despise it; for the fact is that the spring makes me feel ashamed. I am put to shame by its pure naturalness, its triumphant youthfulness. And I don't know whether to envy or despise Adalbert for not having any such reaction . . .

'One certainly does work badly in spring: and why? Because one's feelings are being stimulated. And only amateurs think that a creative artist can afford to have feelings. It's a naïve amateur illusion; any genuine honest artist will smile at it. Sadly, perhaps, but he will smile. Because, of course, *what* one says must never be one's main concern. It must merely be the raw material, quite indifferent in itself, out of which the work of art is made; and the act of making must be a game, aloof and detached, performed in tranquillity. If you attach too much importance to what you have to say, if it means too much to you emotionally, then you may be certain that your work will be a complete fiasco. You will become solemn, you will become sentimental, you will produce something clumsy, ponderous, pompous, ungainly, unironical, insipid, dreary and commonplace; it will be of no interest to anyone, and you yourself will end up disillusioned and miserable . . . For that is how it is, Lisaveta: emotion, warm, heartfelt emotion, is invariably commonplace and unserviceable – only the stimulation of our corrupt nervous system, its cold ecstasies and acrobatics, can bring forth art. One simply has to be something inhuman, something standing outside humanity, strangely remote and detached from its concerns, if one is to have the ability or indeed even the desire to play this game with it, to play with men's lives, to portray them effectively and tastefully. Our stylistic and formal talent, our gift of expression, itself presupposes this cold-blooded, fastidious attitude to mankind, indeed it presupposes a certain human impoverishment and stagnation. For the fact is: all healthy emotion, all strong emotion lacks taste. As soon as an artist becomes human and begins to feel, he is finished as an artist. Adalbert knew this, and that is why he retreated into a café, into the "remote sphere" – ah yes!'

'Well, God be with him, *batushka*,' said Lisaveta, washing her hands in a tin basin. 'After all, there's no need for you to follow him.'

'No, Lisaveta, I shall not follow him; and the only reason I shall not is that I am occasionally capable, when confronted with spring, of feeling slightly ashamed of being an artist. You know, I sometimes get letters from complete strangers, from appreciative and grateful readers, expressions of admiration from people whom my work has moved. I read these communications and am touched by the warm, clumsy emotions stirred up by my art – I am overcome by a kind of pity for the enthusiastic naïvety that speaks from every line, and I blush to think what a sobering effect it would have on the honest man who wrote such a letter if he could ever take a look behind the scenes, if his innocent mind could ever grasp the fact that the last thing any proper, healthy, decent human being ever does is to write or act or compose . . . Though needless to say all this does not stop me using his admiration for my genius as an enrichment and a stimulus; I still take it uncommonly seriously and ape the solemn airs of a great man . . . Oh, don't start contradicting me, Lisaveta! I tell you I am often sick to death of being a portrayer of humanity and having no share in human experience . . . Can one even say that an artist *is* a man? Let Woman answer that! I think we artists are all in rather the same situation as those artificial papal sopranos . . . Our voices are quite touchingly beautiful. But –'

'Be ashamed of yourself, Tonio Kröger. Come along and have tea. The water will be boiling in a minute, and here are some *papirosi*. Now, you stopped at the soprano singers; so please continue from that point. But you ought to be a little ashamed of what you are saying. If I did not know how passionately devoted to your profession and how proud of it you are . . .'

'Don't speak to me of my "profession", Lisaveta Ivanovna! Literature isn't a profession at all, I'll have you know – it's a curse. And when do we first discover that this curse has come upon us? At a terribly early age. An age when by rights one should still be living at peace and harmony with God and the world. You begin to feel that you are a marked man, mysteriously different from other people, from ordinary normal folk; a gulf of irony, of scepticism, of antagonism, of awareness, of sensibility, is fixed between you and your fellow men – it gets deeper and deeper, it isolates you from them, and in the end all communication with them becomes impossible. What a fate! Always supposing, of course, that you still have enough feeling, enough *love* left in your heart to know how appalling it is . . . You develop an exacerbated self-consciousness, because you are well aware of being marked out among thousands by a sign on your brow which no one fails to notice. I once knew an actor of genius who, as a man, had to struggle against a morbid instability and lack of confidence. This was how his overstimulated consciousness of himself affected him when he was not actually engaged in performing a part. He was a consummate artist and an impoverished human being . . . A real artist is not one who has taken up art as his profession, but a man predestined and foredoomed to it; and such an artist can be picked out from a crowd by anyone with the slightest perspicacity. You can read in his face that he is a man apart, a man who does not belong, who feels that he is recognized and is being watched; there is somehow an air of royalty about him and at the same time an air of embarrassment. A prince walking incognito among the people wears a rather similar expression. But the incognito doesn't work, Lisaveta! Disguise yourself, put on civilian costume, dress up like an attaché or a guards lieutenant on leave – you will hardly have raised your eyes and uttered a word before everyone will know that you are not a human being but something strange, something alien, something different . . .

'But what *is* an artist? I know of no other question to which human complacency and incuriosity has remained so impervious. "That sort of thing is a gift," say average decent folk humbly, when a work of art has produced its intended effect upon them; and because in the goodness of their hearts they assume that exhilarating and noble effects must necessarily have exhilarating and noble causes, it never enters their heads that the origins of this so-called "gift" may well be extremely dubious and extremely disreputable . . . It's well known that artists are easily offended; and it's also well known that this is not usually the case with people who have a good conscience and solidly grounded self-confidence . . . You see, Lisaveta, I harbour in my very soul a rooted suspicion of the artist as a type – I suspect him no less deeply, though in a more intellectual way, than every one of my honourable ancestors up there in that city of narrow streets would have suspected any sort of mountebank or performing adventurer who had strolled into his house. Listen to this. I know a banker, a middle-aged man of business, who has a talent for writing short stories. He exercises this talent in his spare time, and what he writes is often quite first-class. Despite – I call it "despite" – this admirable gift he is a man of not entirely blameless reputation: on the contrary he has already served quite a heavy prison sentence, and for good reason. In fact it was actually in gaol that he first became aware of his talents, and his experiences as a prisoner are the basic theme in all his work. One might draw the rather fanciful conclusion from this that it is necessary to have been in some kind of house of correction if one is to become a writer. But can one help suspecting that in its roots and origins his artistic tendency had less to do with his experiences in gaol than with *what got him sent there*? A banker who writes short stories: that's an oddity, isn't it? But a banker with no criminal record and no stain on his character who writes short stories – *there's no such phenomenon* . . . Yes, you may laugh, but I am half serious nevertheless. There's no problem on earth so tantalizing as the problem of what an artist is and what art does to human beings. Take the case of the most remarkable masterpiece of the most typical and therefore mightiest of all artists – take a morbid, profoundly equivocal work like *Tristan and Isolde*, and observe the effects of this work on a young, healthy listener of entirely normal sensibility. He will be filled with exaltation, animation, warm, honest enthusiasm, perhaps even inspired to "artistic" creative efforts of his own . . . Poor, decent dilettante! We artists have an inner life very different from what our "warm-hearted" admirers in their "genuine enthusiasm" imagine. I have seen artists with women and young men crowding round them, applauding and idolizing them, artists about whom *I knew the truth* . . . The sources and side-effects and preconditions of artistic talent are something about which one constantly makes the most curious discoveries . . .'

'Discoveries, Tonio Kröger – forgive my asking – about other artists? Or not only about others?'

He did not reply. He contracted his slanting brows in a frown and whistled to himself.

'Give me your cup, Tonio. The tea's not strong. And have another cigarette. And in any case you know very well that it is not necessary to take such a view of things as you are taking . . .'

'That's Horatio's answer, isn't it, my dear Lisaveta. " 'Twere to consider too curiously to consider so." '

'I mean, Tonio Kröger, that they can be considered just as curiously from another angle. I am only a stupid painting female, and if I can manage to make any reply to you, and offer some sort of defence of your own profession against you, I am sure there will be nothing new to you in what I say; I can only remind you of things you know very well yourself . . . Of the purifying, sanctifying effect of literature, for example; of the way our passions dissolve when they are grasped by insight and expressed in words; of literature as a path to understanding, to forgiveness and love. Think of the redeeming power of language, of the literary intellect as the sublimest manifestation of all human intellect, of the writer as supreme humanity, the writer as saint – to consider things so, is that not to consider them curiously enough?'

'You have a right to talk that way, Lisaveta Ivanovna, and it is conferred upon you by your national literature, by the sublime writers of Russia; their work I will willingly worship as the sacred literature of which you speak. But I have not left your objections out of account, on the contrary they too are part of what I have got on my mind today . . . Look at me. I don't look exactly bursting with high spirits, do I? Rather old and sharp-featured and weary, don't I? Well, to revert to the subject of "insight": can you not imagine someone with an innately unsceptical disposition, placid and well-meaning and a bit sentimental, being quite literally worn out and destroyed by psychological enlightenment? Not to let oneself be overwhelmed by the sadness of everything; to observe and study it all, to put even anguish into a category, and to remain in a good humour into the bargain, if only because of one's proud consciousness of moral superiority over the abominable invention of existence – oh, yes, indeed! But there are times, notwithstanding all the delights of expression, when the whole thing becomes a little too much for one. *"Tout comprendre, c'est tout pardonner"*? I'm not so sure. There is something that I call the nausea of knowledge, Lisaveta: a state of mind in which a man has no sooner seen through a thing than so far from feeling reconciled to it he is immediately sickened to death by it. This was how Hamlet felt, Hamlet the Dane, that typical literary artist. He knew what it was like to be called upon to bear a burden of knowledge for which one was not born. To be clear-sighted even through the mist of tears – even then to have to understand, to study, to observe and ironically discard what one has seen – even at moments when hands clasp and lips touch and eyes fail, blinded by emotion – it's infamous, Lisaveta, it's contemptible and outrageous . . . But what good does it do to feel outraged?

'Another equally charming aspect of the matter, of course, is the way one becomes sophisticated and indifferent to truth, blasé and weary of it all. It's well known that you'll never find such mute hopelessness as among a gathering of intellectuals, all of them thoroughly hagridden already. All insights are old and stale to them. Try telling them about some truth you have discovered, in the acquisition and possession of which you perhaps feel a certain youthful pride, and their response to your vulgar knowledgeableness will be a very brief expulsion of air through the nose . . . Oh yes, Lisaveta, literature wears people out! I assure you that in ordinary human society, by sheer scepticism and suspension of judgement, one can give the impression of being stupid, whereas in fact one is merely arrogant and lacking in courage . . . So much for "insight". As for "words", I wonder if they really redeem our passions: is it not rather that they refrigerate them and put them in cold storage? Don't you seriously think that there is a chilling, outrageous effrontery in the instant, facile process by which literary language eliminates emotion? What does one do when one's heart is too full, when some sweet or sublime experience has moved one too deeply? The answer is simple! Apply to a writer: the whole thing will be settled in a trice. He will analyse it all for you, formulate it, name it, express it and make it articulate, and so far as you are concerned the entire affair will be eliminated once and for all: he will have turned it for you into a matter of total indifference, and he'll not even expect you to thank him for doing so. But you will go home with your heart lightened, all warmth and all mystery dispelled, wondering why on earth you were distraught with such delicious excitement only a moment ago. Can we seriously defend this vain cold-hearted charlatan? Anything that has been expressed has thereby been eliminated – that is his creed. When the whole world has been expressed, it too will have been eliminated, redeemed, abolished . . . Très bien! But I am not a nihilist . . .'

'You are not a –' said Lisaveta . . . She was just about to take a sip of tea and stopped dead with the spoon near her mouth.

'Well, of course not . . . What's the matter with you, Lisaveta! I tell you I am not a nihilist inasmuch as I affirm the value of living emotion. Don't you see, what the literary artist basically fails to grasp is that life goes on, that it is not ashamed to go on living, even after it has been expressed and "eliminated". Lo and behold! Literature may redeem it as much as it pleases, it just carries on in its same old sinful way; for to the intellectual eye all activity is sinful . . .

'I'm nearly finished, Lisaveta. Listen to me. I love life – that is a confession. I present it to you for safe keeping; you are the first person to whom I have made it. It has been said, it has even been written and printed, that I hate or fear or despise or abominate life. I enjoy this suggestion, I have always felt flattered by it; but it is none the less false. I love life . . . You smile, Lisaveta, and I know why. But I implore you not to mistake what I am saying for mere literature! Do not think of Cesare Borgia or of any drunken philosophy that makes him its hero! This Cesare Borgia is nothing to me, I feel not a particle of respect for him, and I shall never be able to understand this idealization and cult of the extraordinary and the demonic. No: "life" confronts intellect and art as their eternal opposite – but not as a vision of bloodstained greatness and savage beauty. We who are exceptions do not see life as something exceptional; on the contrary! Normality, respectability, decency – these are our heart's desire, this to us is life, life in its seductive banality! No one, my dear, has a right to call himself an artist if his profoundest craving is for the refined, the eccentric and the satanic – if his heart knows no longing for innocence, simplicity and living warmth, for a little friendship and self-surrender and familiarity and human happiness – if he is not secretly devoured, Lisaveta, by this longing for the bliss of the commonplace! . . .

'A human friend! Will you believe me when I say that it would make me proud and happy to win the friendship of a human being? But until now all my friends have been demons, hobgoblins, phantoms struck dumb by the ghoulish profundity of their insight – in other words, men of letters.

'Sometimes I find myself on some public platform, facing a roomful of people who have come to listen to me. Do you know, it can happen on such occasions that I find myself surveying the audience, I catch myself secretly peering round the hall, and in my heart there is a question: Who are these who have come to me, whose is this grateful applause I hear, with whom have I achieved this spiritual union through my art? . . . I don't find what I am looking for, Lisaveta. I find my own flock, my familiar congregation, a sort of gathering of early Christians: people with clumsy bodies and refined souls, the kind of people, so to speak, who are always falling over when they dance, if you see what I mean; people to whom literature is a quiet way of taking their revenge on life – all of them sufferers, all repining and impoverished: never once is there one of the others among them, Lisaveta, one of the blue-eyed innocents who don't need intellect! . . .

'And after all it would be deplorably inconsistent, wouldn't it, to be glad if things were otherwise! It is absurd to love life and nevertheless to be trying with all the skill at one's command to entice it from its proper course, to interest it in our melancholy subtleties, in this whole sick aristocracy of literature. The kingdom of art is enlarging its frontiers in this world, and the realm of health and innocence is dwindling. What is left of it should be most carefully preserved: we have no right to try to seduce people into reading poetry when they would much rather be looking at books full of snapshots of horses!

'For when all's said and done, can you imagine a more pitiable spectacle than that of life attempting to be artistic! There is no one whom we artists so utterly despise as the dilettante, the living human being who thinks he can occasionally try his hand at being an artist as well. I assure you this particular kind of contempt is very familiar to me from personal experience. I am a guest, let us say, at a party, among members of the best society; we are eating and drinking and talking, and all getting on famously, and I am feeling glad and grateful to have escaped for a while into the company of simple, conventionally decent people who are treating me as an equal. And suddenly (this actually happened to me once) an officer rises to his feet, a lieutenant, a good-looking, fine, upstanding man whom I should never have believed capable of any conduct unbecoming his uniform, and asks in so many words for permission to recite to us a few lines of verse which he has composed. The permission is granted, with some smiling and raising of eyebrows, and he carries out his intention: he produces a piece of paper which he has hitherto been concealing in his coat-tail pocket, and he reads us his work. It was something or other about music and love, deeply felt and totally inept. I ask you: a lieutenant! A member of polite society! What need was there for him to do it, good heavens above! . . . Well, there was the predictable result: long faces, silence, a little polite applause and everyone feeling thoroughly uncomfortable. The first psychological effect upon myself of which I became aware was a feeling that I too, and not only this rash young man, was to blame for spoiling the party; and sure enough there were some mocking and unfriendly glances in my direction as well, for it was my trade he had bungled. But my second reaction was that this man, for whose character and way of life I had only a moment ago felt the sincerest respect, suddenly began to sink and sink and sink in my esteem . . . I felt sorry for him, I was filled with benevolent indulgence towards him. I and one or two other good-natured guests plucked up heart to approach him with a few encouraging words. "Congratulations, lieutenant!" I said. "What a charming talent you have! That was really very pretty!" And I very nearly patted him on the shoulder. But is indulgence a proper thing to feel towards a lieutenant? . . . It was his own fault! There he stood, in utter embarrassment, suffering the penalty of having supposed that one may pluck even a single leaf from the laurel tree of art and not pay for it with one's life. Oh, no! Give me my colleague, the banker with the criminal record . . . But don't you think, Lisaveta, that my eloquence today is worthy of Hamlet?'

'Have you finished now, Tonio Kröger?'

'No. But I shall say no more.'

'Well, you have certainly said enough. Are you expecting an answer?'

'Have you got one for me?'

'I certainly have. I have listened to you carefully, Tonio, from beginning to end, and I will now tell you what the answer is to everything you have said this afternoon, and what the solution is to the problem that has been worrying you so much. So! The solution is quite simply that you are, and always will be, a bourgeois.'

'Am I?' he asked, with a somewhat crestfallen air . . .

'That's a hard home truth for you, isn't it. And I don't wonder. So I don't mind modifying it a little, for it so happens that I can. You are a bourgeois who has taken the wrong turning, Tonio Kröger – a bourgeois *manqué.*'

There was silence. Then he got up resolutely and seized his hat and walking-stick.

'Thank you, Lisaveta Ivanovna; now I can go home with a good conscience. *I have been eliminated.*'

5

Near the end of the summer Tonio Kröger said to Lisaveta Ivanovna:

'Well, I'm leaving now, Lisaveta; I must have a change of air, a change of scene, I must get away from it all.'

'So, *batushka,* I suppose you will honour Italy with another visit?'

'Oh God, Lisaveta, don't talk to me of Italy! I am bored with Italy to the point of despising it! It's a long time since I thought I felt at home there. The land of art! Velvet-blue skies, heady wine and sweet sensuality . . . No thank you, that's not for me. I renounce it. All that *bellezza* gets on my nerves. And I can't stand all that dreadful southern vivacity, all those people with their black animal eyes. They've no conscience in their eyes, those Latin races . . . No, this time I'm going for a little trip to Denmark.'

'Denmark?'

'Yes. And I think I shall benefit from it. It so happens that I've never yet got round to going there, although I was so near the frontier during the whole of my youth, and yet it's a country I've always known about and loved. I suppose I must get this northern predilection from my father, for my mother really preferred the *bellezza,* you know, that is in so far as anything mattered to her at all. But think of the books they write up there in the north, Lisaveta, books of such depth and purity and humour – there's nothing like them, I love them. Think of the Scandinavian meals, those incomparable meals, only digestible in a strong salty air – in fact, I doubt if I shall be able to digest them at all now; I know them too from my childhood, the food's just like that even where I come from. And just think of the names, the names they christen people by up there – you'll find a lot of them in my part of the world as well: names like "Ingeborg", for instance – three syllables plucked on a harp of purest poetry. And then there's the sea – one is on the Baltic Sea up there! . . . Anyway, that's where I'm going, Lisaveta. I want to see the Baltic again, to hear those names again, to read those books in the country where they were written; and I want to stand on the battlements at Kronborg, where the "spirit"* came to Hamlet and brought anguish and death to the poor noble youth . . .'

'How shall you travel, Tonio, if I may ask? What route will you be taking?'

'The usual route,' he said, shrugging his shoulders and blushing visibly. 'Yes, I shall be passing through my – my point of departure, Lisaveta, after these thirteen years, and I dare say it may be a rather odd experience.'

She smiled.

'That's what I wanted to hear, Tonio Kröger. Well, be off with you, in God's name. And be sure you write to me, won't you? I'm looking forward to an eventful description of your journey to – Denmark . . .'

6

And Tonio Kröger travelled north. He travelled first-class (for he would often say that a man whose psychological problems are so much more difficult than those of other people has a right to a little external comfort) and he continued without a halt until the towers of his native town, that town of narrow streets, rose before him into the grey sky. There he made a brief and singular sojourn . . .

It was a dreary afternoon, already almost evening, when the train steamed into the little smoke-stained terminus which he remembered with such strange vividness; under its dirty glass roof the smoke was still rolling up into clouds or drifting to and fro in straggling wisps, just as it had done long ago when Tonio Kröger had left this place with nothing but mockery in his heart. He saw to his luggage, gave instructions that it was to be sent to his hotel and left the station.

*Mann here untranslatably plays upon two different meanings of the word 'Geist' ('intellect' and 'ghost'). (Translator's note.)

There stood the cabs, black and absurdly tall and wide, each drawn by a pair of horses, the cabs that had always been used in this town, waiting in a row outside the station! He did not take one; he merely looked at them, and he looked at everything else as well: the narrow gables and pointed towers that looked back at him over the nearby roofs, the fair-haired, easygoing unsophisticated people with their broad yet rapid way of talking – there they were, all round him, and laughter welled up within him, strangely hysterical laughter that was not far from tears. He went on foot, walking slowly, feeling the steady pressure of the damp wind on his face; he crossed the bridge, with its parapets decorated by mythological statues, and walked a little way along the quayside.

Great heavens, what a tiny, nookshotten place it all seemed! Had it been like this all these years, with these narrow gabled streets, climbing so steeply and quaintly up into the town? The ships' funnels and masts swayed gently in the dusk as the wind swept across the dull grey river. Should he walk up that street now, that street that led to the house he remembered so well? No, he would go tomorrow. He was feeling so sleepy now. The journey had made him drowsy, and his head was full of drifting nebulous thoughts.

Occasionally during these thirteen years, when suffering from indigestion, he had dreamed he was at home again in the old, echoing house on the slanting street, and that his father was there again too, indignantly upbraiding him for his degenerate way of life; and he had always felt that this was entirely as it should be. And he could in no way distinguish his present impressions from one of these delusive and compelling fabrications of the dreaming mind during which one asks oneself whether this is fantasy or reality and is driven firmly to the latter conclusion, only to end by waking up after all . . . He advanced through the half-empty, draughty streets, bending his head before the breeze, moving like a sleepwalker towards the hotel where he had decided to spend the night, the best hotel in the town. Ahead of him, a bow-legged man with a rolling nautical gait was carrying a pole with a little flame at the top, and lighting the gas-lamps with it.

What was he really feeling? Under the ashes of his weariness something was glowing, obscurely and painfully, not flickering up into a clear flame: what was it? Hush, he must not say it! He must not put it into words! He would have liked to stroll on indefinitely, in the wind and the dusk, along these familiar streets of his dreams. But it was all so close, so near together. One reached one's destination at once.

In the upper part of the town there were arc-lamps, and they were just coming alight. There was the hotel, and there were the two black lions couched in front of it; as a child he had always been afraid of them. They were still staring at each other, looking as if they were just about to sneeze; but they seemed to have grown much smaller now. Tonio Kröger walked between them into the hotel.

As a guest arriving on foot he was received without much ceremony. He encountered the inquiring gaze of the porter and of a very smartly dressed gentleman in black who was doing the honours, and who had a habit of constantly pushing his shirt-cuffs back into his coat-sleeves with his little fingers. They both looked him carefully up and down from head to foot, obviously trying hard to place him, to assign him an approximate position in the social hierarchy which would determine the degree of respect that was his due; they were unable, however, to reach a satisfactory conclusion on this point, and therefore decided in favour of a moderate show of politeness. A mild-mannered waiter with sandy side-whiskers, a frock coat shiny with age and rosettes on his noiseless shoes, conducted him two floors up to a neatly furnished, old-fashioned room. From its window, in the twilight, there was a picturesque medieval view of courtyards, gables and the bizarre massive outlines of the church near which the hotel was situated. Tonio Kröger stood for a while looking out of this window; then he sat with folded arms on the commodious sofa, frowning and whistling to himself.

Lights were brought, and his luggage arrived. At the same time the mild-mannered waiter laid the registration form on the table, and Tonio Kröger, with his head tilted to one side, scrawled something on it that would pass for his name and status and place of origin. He then ordered some supper and continued to stare into vacancy from the corner of his sofa. When the food had been placed before him he left it untouched for a long time, then finally ate a morsel or two and walked up and down in the room for another hour, occasionally stopping and closing his eyes. Then he slowly undressed and went to bed. He slept for a long time and had confused, strangely nostalgic dreams.

When he woke up his room was full of broad daylight. In some haste and confusion he recalled where he was, and got up to draw the curtains. The blue of the late-summer sky was already rather pale, and covered with wind-reft wisps of cloud; but the sun was shining over his native town.

He devoted more care than usual to his toilet, washed and shaved meticulously until he was as fresh and immaculate as if he were about to pay a call on a conventional, well bred family with whom he would have to look his best and be on his best behaviour; and as he went through the processes of dressing he listened to the anxious beating of his heart.

How bright it was outside! He would have felt better if the streets had been dusky like yesterday; but now he would have to walk through clear sunlight exposed to the public gaze. Would he meet people he knew, would they stop him and call him to account by asking him how he had spent the last thirteen years? No, thank God, no one knew him now, and anyone who remembered him would not recognize him, for he had indeed somewhat changed in the mean time. He inspected himself attentively in the mirror, and suddenly felt safer behind his mask, behind his face on which experience had laid its mark early, his face that was older than his years . . . He sent for breakfast, and then he left the hotel, crossing the front hall under the calculating gaze of the porter and the elegant gentleman in black, and passing out into the street between the two lions.

Where was he going? He scarcely knew. He had the same sensation as yesterday. No sooner was he surrounded again by this strangely dignified and long-familiar complex of gables, turrets, arcades and fountains – no sooner did he feel again on his face the pressure of the wind, this strong fresh wind full of the delicate sharp flavour of distant dreams – than a misty veil of fantasy benumbed his senses . . . The muscles of his face relaxed; and his eyes as he gazed at people and things had grown calm. Perhaps, at the next corner, just over there, he would wake up after all . . .

Where was he going? He had an impression that the route he chose was not unconnected with last night's sad and strangely rueful dreams . . . He walked to the market square, under the arcades of the town hall; here were the butchers, weighing their wares with blood-stained hands, and here on the square was the tall, pointed, complicated Gothic fountain. Here he paused in front of a certain house, a simple narrow house much like any of the others, with an ornamental pierced gable. He stood gazing at it, read the name on the plate by the door, and let his eyes rest for a little on each of the windows in turn. Then he turned slowly away.

Where was he going? He was going home. But he made a detour, he took a walk outside the old city walls, for he had plenty of time. He walked along the Mühlenwall and the Holstenwall, clutching his hat before the wind that rustled and jarred among the trees. Presently, not far from the station, he turned off the promenade, watched a train bustling and puffing past, counted the coaches just for fun and gazed after the man who sat up there on the last one as it went by. But in the Lindenplatz he stopped in front of one of its handsome villas, stared for a long time into the garden and up at the windows, and finally took to swinging the iron gate to and fro on its creaking hinges. He gazed for a few moments at his hands, cold now and stained with rust; then he went on his way, he walked under the low arch of the old gate, along the harbour and up the steep draughty little street to his parents' house.

There it stood, surrounded by the neighbouring buildings, its gable rising above them: it was as grey and solemn as it had been for the last three hundred years, and Tonio Kröger read the pious motto engraved over the doorway in letters now half obliterated. Then he took a deep breath and went in.

His heart was beating anxiously, for it would not have surprised him if his father had thrown open one of the doors on the ground floor as he passed them, emerging in his office coat and with his pen behind his ear to confront him and take him severely to task for his dissolute life; and Tonio would have felt that this was just as it should be. But he got past without being interfered with by anyone. The inner door of the porch was not closed, only left ajar, a fact which he noted with disapproval, although at the same time he had the sensation of being in one of those elated dreams in which obstacles dissolve before one of their own accord and one advances unimpeded, favoured by some miraculous good fortune . . . The wide entrance hall, paved with great square flagstones, re-echoed with the sound of his footsteps. Opposite the kitchen, which was silent now, the strange, clumsy but neatly painted wooden cubicles still projected from high up in the wall as they had always done: these had been the maids' rooms, only accessible from the hall by a kind of open flight of steps. But the great cupboards and the carved chest that had once stood here were gone . . . The son of the house began to climb the imposing main stairway, resting his hand on the white-painted openwork balustrade; with every step he took he raised it and gently let it fall again, as if he were diffidently trying to discover whether his former familiarity with this solid old handrail could be re-established . . . But on the landing he stopped. At the entrance to the intermediate floor was a white board with black lettering which said: 'Public Library'.

Public library? thought Tonio Kröger, for in his opinion this was no place either for the public or for literature. He knocked on the door . . . He was bidden to enter, and did so. Tense and frowning, he beheld before him a most unseemly transformation.

There were three rooms on this intermediate floor, and their communicating doors stood open. The walls were covered almost up to the ceiling with uniformly bound books, standing in long rows on dark shelves. In each of the rooms a seedy-looking man was sitting writing at a sort of counter. Two of them merely turned their heads towards Tonio Kröger, but the first rose hastily to his feet, placed both hands on the desk to support himself, thrust his head forwards, pursed his lips, raised his eyebrows and surveyed the visitor with rapidly blinking eyes . . .

'Excuse me,' said Tonio Kröger, still staring at the multitude of books. 'I am a stranger here, I am making a tour of the town. So this is the public library? Would you allow me to take a short look at your collection?'

'Certainly!' said the official, blinking more vigorously than ever . . . 'Certainly, anyone may do so. Please take a look round . . . Would you like a catalogue?'

'No, thank you,' answered Tonio Kröger. 'I shall find my way about quite easily.' And he began to walk slowly along the walls, pretending to be studying the titles of the books. Finally he took down a volume, opened it, and stationed himself with it at the window.

This had been the morning-room. They had always had breakfast here, not upstairs in the big dining-room, with its blue wallpaper boldly decorated with the white figures of Greek gods . . . The adjoining room had been used as a bedroom. His father's mother had died there, and her death-struggle had been terrible, old as she was, for she had been a woman of the world who enjoyed life and clung to it. And later in that same room his father too had breathed his last, the tall, correct, rather

sad and pensive gentleman with the wild flower in his buttonhole . . .
Tonio had sat at the foot of his deathbed, his eyes hot with tears, in
sincere and utter surrender to an inarticulate intense emotion of love
and grief. And his mother too had knelt by the bed, his beautiful fiery
mother, weeping her heart out; whereupon she had departed with that
artist from the south to live under far-off blue skies . . . But the third
room, the little one at the back, now fully stocked with books like the
other two, with a seedy-looking attendant to supervise them – this for
many years had been his own room. This was the room to which he had
returned from school, perhaps after just such a walk as he had taken just
now; there was the wall where his desk had stood, with its drawer where
he had kept his first heartfelt clumsy efforts at verse composition . . .
The walnut tree . . . He felt a sharp pang of grief. He glanced sideways
through the window. The garden was neglected and overgrown, but the
old walnut tree was still there, heavily creaking and rustling in the wind.
And Tonio Kröger let his eyes wander back to the book he was holding in
his hand, an outstanding work of literature which he knew well. He
looked down at the black lines of print and groups of sentences, followed
the elegant flow of the text for a little, observing its passionate
stylization, noting how effectively it rose to a climax and fell away from
it again . . .

Yes, that's well done, he said to himself; he replaced the work on the
shelf and turned away. And he noticed that the official was still on his
feet, still blinking hard, with a mingled expression of eager servility and
puzzled suspicion.

'I see you have an excellent collection,' said Tonio Kröger. 'I have
already formed a general impression of it. I am most grateful to you.
Good-day.' Whereupon he left the room; but it was not a very successful
exit, and he had the strong impression that the library attendant was so
disconcerted by his visit that he would still be standing there blinking
several minutes later.

He felt disinclined to explore further. He had visited his home. The
large rooms upstairs, beyond the pillared hall, were now obviously
occupied by strangers; for the staircase ended in a glass door which had
not previously been there, and there was some kind of name-plate beside
it. He turned away, walked downstairs and across the echoing entrance
hall and left the house of his fathers. He went to a restaurant and sat at a

corner table, deep in thought, eating a rich, heavy meal; then he returned to his hotel.

'I have finished my business,' he said to the elegant gentleman in black. 'I shall leave this afternoon.' And he asked for his bill, at the same time ordering a cab which would take him down to the harbour to board the steamer for Copenhagen. Then he went to his room and sat upright and in silence, resting his cheek on his hand and gazing down at the desk with unseeing eyes. Later he settled his bill and packed his luggage. At the appointed time the cab was announced and Tonio Kröger went downstairs, ready for his journey.

At the foot of the staircase the elegant gentleman in black was waiting for him.

'Excuse me!' he said, pushing his cuffs back into his sleeves with his little fingers . . . 'I beg your pardon, sir, but we must just detain you for one moment. Herr Seehaase – the proprietor of the hotel – would like to have a word with you. A mere formality . . . He's just over there . . . Would you be so kind as to come with me . . . It's *only* Herr Seehaase, the proprietor.'

And with polite gestures he ushered Tonio Kröger to the back of the hall. There, to be sure, stood Herr Seehaase. Tonio Kröger knew him by sight, from days gone by. He was short, plump and bow-legged. His clipped side-whiskers were white now; but he still wore a low-cut frock coat and a little velvet cap embroidered with green. He was, moreover, not alone. Beside him, at a small high desk fixed to the wall, stood a policeman with his helmet on and his gloved right hand resting on a complicated-looking document which lay before him on the desk. He was looking straight at Tonio Kröger with his honest soldierly eyes as if he expected him to sink right into the ground at the sight of him.

Tonio Kröger looked from one to the other and decided to await developments.

'You have come here from Munich?' asked the policeman eventually in a slow, good-natured voice.

Tonio Kröger answered this question in the affirmative.

'You are travelling to Copenhagen?'

'Yes, I am on my way to a Danish seaside resort.'

'Seaside resort? Well, you must let me see your papers,' said the policeman, uttering the last word with an air of special satisfaction.

'Papers . . .?' He had no papers. He took out his pocket-book and glanced at its contents; but apart from some money it contained only the proofs of a short story, which he intended to correct at his destination. He did not like dealing with officials, and had never yet had a passport issued to him . . .

'I am sorry,' he said, 'but I have no papers with me.'

'Indeed!' said the policeman . . . 'None at all? What is your name?'

Tonio Kröger answered him.

'Is that the truth?' asked the policeman, drawing himself up to his full height and suddenly opening his nostrils as wide as he could.

'Certainly,' replied Tonio Kröger.

'And what's your occupation, may I ask?'

Tonio Kröger swallowed and in a firm voice named his profession. Herr Seehaase raised his head and looked up at him with curiosity.

'Hm!' said the policeman. 'And you allege that you are not identical with an individial of the name of –' He said 'individial', and proceeded to spell out from the complicated document a highly intricate and romantic name which seemed to have been bizarrely compounded from the languages of various races; Tonio Kröger had no sooner heard it than he had forgotten it. 'An individial,' the policeman continued, 'of unknown parentage and dubious domicile, who is wanted by the Munich police in connection with various frauds and other offences and is probably trying to escape to Denmark?'

'I do not merely "allege" this,' said Tonio Kröger, with a nervous movement of his shoulders. That made a certain impression.

'What? Oh, quite, yes, of course!' said the policeman. 'But you can't identify yourself in any way, can you!'

Herr Seehaase attempted a conciliatory intervention.

'The whole thing is a formality,' he said, 'nothing more! You must realize that the officer is merely doing his duty. If you could show some kind of identification . . . some document . . .'

They all fell silent. Should he make an end of the matter by disclosing who he was, by informing Herr Seehaase that he was not an adventurer of dubious domicile, not born a gypsy in a green caravan, but the son of Consul Kröger, a member of the Kröger family? No, he had no wish to say anything of the sort. And were they not right, in a way, these representatives of bourgeois society? In a certain sense he entirely agreed with them . . . He shrugged his shoulders and said nothing.

'What have you got there?' asked the policeman. 'There, in your pocket-book?'

'Here? Nothing. Only a proof,' answered Tonio Kröger.

'Proof? Proof of what? Let's have a look.'

And Tonio Kröger handed him his work. The policeman spread it out on the desk and began to read it. Herr Seehaase, stepping closer, did the same. Tonio Kröger glanced over their shoulders to see what part of the text they had reached. It was a good passage, pointed and effective; he had taken pains with it and got it exactly right. He was pleased with himself.

'You see!' he said. 'There is my name. I wrote this, and now it is being published, you understand.'

'Well, that's good enough!' said Herr Seehaase decisively. He put the sheets together, folded them and returned them to their author. 'It must be good enough, Petersen,' he repeated curtly, surreptitiously closing his eyes and shaking his head to forestall any objections. 'We must not delay the gentleman any longer. His cab is waiting. I hope, sir, you will excuse this slight inconvenience. The officer was of course only doing his duty, though I told him at once that he was on the wrong track . . .'

'Did you, now?' thought Tonio Kröger.

The policeman did not seem entirely satisfied; he raised some further query about 'individial' and 'identification'. But Herr Seehaase conducted his guest back through the foyer, with repeated expressions of regret; he accompanied him out between the two lions to his cab and saw him into it, closing the door himself with a great display of respect. Whereupon the absurdly tall, broad vehicle, rumbling and stumbling, noisily and clumsily rolled down the steep narrow streets to the harbour . . .

And that was Tonio Kröger's curious visit to the city of his fathers.

7

Night was falling, and the moon was rising, its silver radiance floating up the sky, as Tonio Kröger's ship moved out into the open sea. He stood in the bows, warmly wrapped against the mounting wind, and gazed down at the dark restless wandering of the great smooth waves beneath him, watching them slithering round each other, dashing against each other, darting away from each other in unexpected directions with a sudden glitter of foam . . .

His heart was dancing with silent elation. The experience of being nearly arrested in his native town as a criminal adventurer had somewhat damped his spirits, to be sure – even although in a certain sense he had felt that this was just as it should be. But then he had come on board and stood, as he had sometimes done with his father as a boy, watching the freight being loaded on to the boat: its capacious hold had been stuffed with bales and crates, amid shouts in a mixture of Danish and Plattdeutsch, and even a polar bear and a Bengal tiger had been lowered into it in cages with strong iron bars; evidently they had been sent from Hamburg for delivery to some Danish menagerie. And all this had cheered him up. Later, as the steamer had slipped downstream between the flat embankments, he had completely forgotten his interrogation by Constable Petersen, and all his previous impressions had revived again in his mind: his sweet, sad, rueful dreams, his walk, the sight of the walnut tree. And now, as they passed out of the estuary, he saw in the distance the shore where as a boy he had listened to the sea's summer reveries, he saw the flash of the lighthouse and the lighted windows of the resort's principal hotel at which he and his parents had stayed . . . The Baltic Sea! He bent his head before the strong salt wind which was blowing now with full unimpeded force; it enveloped him, drowning all other sounds, making him feel slightly giddy, half numbed with a blissful lethargy which swallowed up all his unpleasant memories, all his sufferings and errors and efforts and struggles. And in the clashing, foaming, moaning uproar all round him he thought he heard the rustling and jarring of the old walnut tree, the creaking of a garden gate . . . The darkness was thickening.

'The sstars, my God, just look at the sstars!' said a voice suddenly. It spoke in a plaintively singsong northern accent and seemed to come from the interior of a large barrel. He had heard it already; it belonged to a sandy-haired, plainly dressed man with reddened eyelids and a chilled, damp look, as if he had just been bathing. He had sat next to

Tonio Kröger at dinner in the saloon and had consumed, in a modest and hesitant manner, astonishing quantities of lobster omelette. He was now standing beside him leaning against the rail, staring up at the sky and holding his chin between his thumb and forefinger. He was obviously in one of those exceptional, festive and contemplative moods in which the barriers between oneself and one's fellow men are lowered, one's heart is laid bare to strangers and one's tongue speaks of matters on which it would normally preserve an embarrassed silence . . .

'Look, sir, just look at the sstars! Twinkling away up there; by God, the whole sky's full of them. And when you look up at it all and consider that a lot of them are supposed to be a hundred times the size of the earth, well, I ask you, how does it make one feel! We men have invented the telegraph and the telephone and so many wonders of modern times, yes, so we have. But when we look up there we have to realize nevertheless that when all's said and done we are just worms, just miserable little worms and nothing more – am I right or am I wrong, sir? Yes,' he concluded, answering his own question, 'that's what we are: worms!' And he nodded towards the firmament in abject contrition.

Oh, Lord, thought Tonio Kröger. No, he's got no literature in his system. And at once he recalled something he had recently read by a famous French writer, an essay on the cosmological and the psychological world view; it had been quite a clever piece of verbiage.

He made some kind of reply to the young man's heartfelt observation, and they then continued to converse, leaning over the rail and gazing into the flickering, stormy dusk. It turned out that Tonio Kröger's travelling companion was a young businessman from Hamburg who was devoting his holiday to this excursion . . .

'I thought: why not take the ssteamer and pop up to Copenhagen?' he explained. 'So here I am, and so far so good, I must say. But those lobster omelettes were a misstake, sir, I can tell you, because there's going to be a gale tonight, the captain said so himself, and that's no joke with indigestible food like that in your sstomach . . .'

Tonio Kröger listened with a certain secret sympathy to these foolish familiar overtures.

'Yes,' he said, 'the food's generally too heavy up in these parts. It makes one sluggish and melancholy.'

'Melancholy?' repeated the young man, looking at him in some puzzlement, then suddenly added: 'You're a sstranger here, sir, I suppose?'

'Oh yes, I'm from a long way away!' answered Tonio Kröger with a vague and evasive gesture.

'But you're right,' said the young man. 'God knows, you're right about feeling melancholy! I'm nearly always melancholy, but especially on evenings like this when there are sstars in the sky.' And he rested his chin again on his thumb and forefinger.

He probably writes poetry, thought Tonio Kröger; deeply felt, honest, businessman's poetry . . .

It was getting late, and the wind was so high now that it made conversation impossible. So they decided to retire, and bade each other good-night.

Tonio Kröger lay down on the narrow bunk in his cabin, but could not sleep. The strong gale with its sharp tang had strangely excited him, and his heart beat anxiously, as if troubled by the expectation of some sweet experience. He also felt extremely seasick, for the ship was in violent motion, sliding down one steep wave after another with its propeller lifting right out of the water and whirring convulsively. He put on all his clothes again and returned to the deck.

Clouds were racing across the moon. The sea was dancing. The waves were not rounded and rolling in ordered succession, they were being lashed and torn and churned into frenzy as far as the eye could reach. In the pallid, flickering light they licked and leapt upwards like gigantic pointed tongues of flame: between foam-filled gulfs, jagged and incredible shapes were hurled on high: the sea seemed to be lifting mighty arms, tossing its spume into the air in wild, monstrous exhilaration. The ship was having a hard passage: pitching and rolling, thudding and groaning, it struggled on through the tumult, and from time to time the polar bear and the tiger could be heard roaring miserably from below decks. A man in an oilskin, with the hood over his head and a lantern strapped round his waist, was pacing the deck with straddled legs, keeping his balance with difficulty. But there in the stern, leaning far overboard, stood the young man from Hamburg, woefully afflicted.

'My God,' he remarked in hollow, unsteady tones when he caught sight of Tonio Kröger, 'just look at the uproar of the elements, sir!' But at this point he was interrupted and turned away hastily.

Tonio Kröger clutched the first taut piece of rope he could find and stood gazing out into all this mad, exuberant chaos. His spirits soared in an exultation that felt mighty enough to outshout the storm and the waves. Inwardly he began to sing a song of love, a paean of praise to the sea. Friend of my youth, ah wild sea weather, once more we meet, once more together . . . But there the poem ended. It was not a finished product, not an experience formed and shaped, recollected in tranquillity and forged into a whole. His heart was alive . . .

Thus he stood for a long time; then he lay down on a bench beside the deck-house and looked up at the sky with its glittering array of stars. He even dozed off for a while. And when the cold foam sprayed his face as he lay there half asleep, he felt it as a caress.

Vertical chalk cliffs loomed ghostly in the moonlight and drew nearer; it was the island of Møn. And again he dozed off, wakened from time to time by salt showers of spray which bit into his face and numbed his features . . . By the time he was fully awake it was already broad daylight, a fresh pale grey morning, and the green sea was calmer. At breakfast he again encountered the young businessman, who blushed scarlet, obviously ashamed of having said such discreditably poetical things under cover of darkness. He readjusted his small reddish moustache, stroking it upwards with all five fingers, barked out a brisk military 'Good morning!' to Tonio Kröger and then carefully steered clear of him.

And Tonio Kröger landed in Denmark. He arrived in Copenhagen, gave a tip to everyone who showed signs of expecting him to do so and then spent three days exploring the city from his hotel, holding his guidebook open in front of him and in general behaving like a well bred foreigner intent on improving his mind. He inspected Kongens Nytorv and the 'Horse' in its midst, glanced up respectfully at the columns of the Fruekirke, paused long before Thorwaldsen's noble and charming sculptures, climbed the Round Tower, visited various palaces and passed two colourful evenings at Tivoli. Yet all this was not really what he saw.

He saw houses which often exactly resembled those of his native town, houses with ornamental pierced gables, and the names by their front doors were names familiar to him from long ago, names symbolizing for him something tender and precious, and containing at the same time a kind of reproach, the sorrowful nostalgic reminder of something lost. And everywhere he went, slowly and pensively breathing in the damp sea air, he saw eyes just as blue, hair just as blond, faces just like those that had filled the strange sad rueful dreams of that night in his native town. As he walked these streets he would suddenly encounter a look, a vocal inflection, a peal of laughter, that pierced him to the heart . . .

The lively city did not hold him for long. He felt driven from it by a certain restlessness, by mingled memory and expectancy, and because he longed to be able to lie quietly somewhere on the sea-shore and not have to play the part of a busily circulating tourist. And so he embarked once more and sailed northwards, on a dull day, over an inky sea, up the coast of Zealand to Elsinore. From there he at once continued his journey for another few miles by coach along the main road, which also ran close to the sea, until he reached his final and true destination. It was a little white seaside hotel with green shutters, surrounded by a cluster of low-lying houses and looking out with its wooden-shingled tower across the sound towards the Swedish coast. Here he stopped, took possession of the bright sunny room they had reserved for him, filled its shelves and cupboards with his belongings and settled down to live here for a while.

8

It was late September already; there were not many visitors left in Aalsgaard. Meals were served in the big dining-room on the ground floor, which had a beamed ceiling and tall windows overlooking the glazed veranda and the sea; they were presided over by the proprietress, an elderly spinster with white hair, colourless eyes, faintly pink cheeks and a vague twittering voice, who always tried to arrange her reddened hands on the tablecloth in a manner that would display them to their best advantage. One of the guests was a short-necked old gentleman with a hoary sailor's beard and a dark bluish complexion; he was a fish dealer from the capital and could speak German. He seemed to be completely congested and inclined to apoplexy, for he breathed in short gasps and occasionally lifted a ringed index finger to his nose, pressed it against one nostril and blew hard through the other as if to clear it a little. Notwithstanding this he addressed himself continually to a bottle of aquavit which stood before him at breakfast, lunch and dinner. The only other members of the company were three tall American boys with their tutor or director of studies, who played football with them day in and day out and otherwise merely fidgeted with his spectacles and said nothing. The three youths had reddish fair hair parted in the middle, and elongated expressionless faces. 'Will you pass me some of that *Wurst*, please,' one of them would say in English. 'It's not *Wurst*, it's *Schinken*,' the other would reply; and that was the extent of their contribution to the conversation; for the rest of the time they and their tutor sat in silence drinking hot water.

Such were Tonio Kröger's neighbours at table, and they could not have been more to his liking. He was left in peace, and sat listening to the Danish glottal stops and front and back vowels in the speeches which the fish dealer and the proprietress now and then addressed to each other; with the former he would exchange an occasional simple remark about the state of the weather; he would then take his leave, pass through the veranda and walk down again to the beach, where he had already spent most of the morning.

Sometimes it was all summer stillness there. The sea lay idle and smooth, streaked with blue and bottle-green and pale red, and the light played over it in glittering silvery reflections. The seaweed withered like hay in the sun, and the stranded jellyfish shrivelled. There was a slight smell of decay, and a whiff of tar from the fishing boat against which Tonio Kröger leaned as he sat on the sand, facing away from the Swedish coast and towards the open horizon; but over it all swept the pure, fresh, gentle breath of the sea.

And then there would be grey, stormy days. The waves curved downwards like bulls lowering their horns for a charge, and dashed themselves furiously against the shore, which was strewn with shining wet sea-grass, mussel-shells and pieces of driftwood, for the water rushed far inland. Under the overcast sky the wave troughs were foaming green, like long valleys between ranges of watery hills; but where the sun shone down from beyond the clouds, the sea's surface shimmered like white velvet.

Tonio Kröger would stand there enveloped in the noise of the wind and the surf, immersed in this perpetual, ponderous, deafening roar he loved so much. When he turned and moved away, everything all round him suddenly seemed calm and warm. But he always knew that the sea was behind him, calling, luring, beckoning. And he would smile.

He would walk far inland, along solitary paths across meadows, and would soon find himself surrounded by the beech trees which covered most of the low, undulating coastland. He would sit on the mossy ground, leaning against a tree trunk, at a point from which a strip of the sea was still visible through the wood. Sometimes the clash of the surf, like wooden boards falling against each other in the distance, would be carried to him by the breeze. Crows cawed above the tree-tops, hoarse and desolate and forlorn . . . He would sit with a book on his knees, but reading not a word of it. He was experiencing a profound forgetfulness, floating as if disembodied above space and time, and only at certain moments did he feel his heart stricken by a pang of sorrow, a brief, piercing, nostalgic or remorseful emotion which in his lethargic trance he made no attempt to define or analyse.

Thus many days passed; he could not have told how many, and had no desire to know. But then came one on which something happened; when the sun was shining and many people were there, and Tonio Kröger did not even find it particularly surprising.

There was something festive and delightful about that day from its very beginning. Tonio Kröger woke unusually early and quite suddenly; he was gently and vaguely startled out of his sleep and at once confronted with an apparently magical spectacle, an elfin miracle of morning radiance. His room had a glass door and balcony facing out over the sound; it was divided into a sleeping and a living area by a white gauze curtain, and papered and furnished lightly in delicate pale shades, so that it always looked bright and cheerful. But now, before his sleep-dazed eyes, it had undergone an unearthly transfiguration and illumination, it was completely drenched in an indescribably lovely and fragrant rose-coloured light: the walls and furniture shone golden and the gauze curtain was a glowing pink . . . For some time Tonio Kröger could not understand what was happening. But when he stood by the glass door and looked out, he saw that the sun was rising.

It had been dull and rainy for several days on end, but now, over land and sea, the sky was like tight-stretched pale blue silk, bright and glistening; and the sun's disc, traversed and surrounded by resplendent red and gold clouds, was mounting in triumph above the shimmering, wrinkled water, which seemed to quiver and catch fire beneath it . . . Thus the day opened, and in joy and confusion Tonio Kröger threw on his clothes; he had breakfast down in the veranda before anyone else, then swam some way out into the sound from the little wooden bathing hut, then walked for an hour along the beach. When he got back to the hotel there were several horse-drawn omnibuses standing in front of it, and from the dining-room he could see that a large number of visitors had arrived: both in the adjoining parlour where the piano stood, and on the veranda and on the terrace in front of it, they were sitting at round tables consuming beer and sandwiches and talking excitedly. They were visitors in simple middle-class attire, whole families, young people and older people, even a few children.

At mid-morning lunch – the table was heavily laden with cold food, smoked and salted delicacies and pastries – Tonio Kröger inquired what was afoot.

'Day visitors!' declared the fish dealer. 'A party from Elsinore; they're having a dance here. Yes, God help us, we'll not sleep a wink tonight. There'll be dancing and music, and you can depend on it, they'll go on till all hours. It's some sort of subscription affair with various families taking part, an excursion in the country with a ball afterwards to make the most of the fine day. They came by boat and by road and now they're having lunch. Afterwards they'll go for another drive, but they'll be back in the evening, and then it'll be dancing and fun and games here in the dining-room. Yes, damn and confound it, we'll not shut an eye this night . . .'

'It makes an agreeable change,' said Tonio Kröger.

Whereupon silence was resumed. The proprietress sorted out her red fingers, the fish dealer snorted through his right nostril to clear it a little and the Americans drank hot water and made long faces.

Then suddenly it happened: *Hans Hansen and Ingeborg Holm walked through the dining-room.*

Tonio Kröger, pleasantly weary after his swim and his rapid walk, was leaning back in his chair eating smoked salmon on toast; he was facing the veranda and the sea. And suddenly the door opened and the two of them sauntered in, unhurried, hand-in-hand. Ingeborg, the fair-haired Inge, was wearing a light-coloured frock, just as she had done at Herr

Knaak's dancing lessons. It was made of thin material with a floral pattern, and reached down only to her ankles; round her shoulders was a broad white tulle collar cut well down in front and exposing her soft, supple neck. She had tied the ribbons of her hat together and slung it over one arm. She had perhaps grown up a little since he had last seen her, and her wonderful blonde tresses were wound round her head now; but Hans Hansen was just as he had always been. He was wearing his reefer jacket with the gold buttons and with the broad blue collar hanging out over his back; in his free hand he held his sailor's cap with its short ribbons, carelessly dangling it to and fro. Ingeborg kept her narrow-cut eyes averted, feeling perhaps a little shy under the gaze of the people sitting over their lunch. But Hans Hansen, as if in defiance of all and sundry, turned his head straight towards the table, and his steely blue eyes inspected each member of the company in turn, with a challenging and slightly contemptuous air; he even let go of Ingeborg's hand and swung his cap more vigorously to and fro, to show what a fine fellow he was. Thus the pair of them passed by before Tonio Kröger's eyes, against the background of the calm blue sea; they walked the length of the dining-room and disappeared through the door at the far end, into the parlour.

This happened at half-past eleven, and while the residents were still eating, the visiting party next door and on the veranda set out on their excursion; no one else came into the dining-room, they left the hotel by the side entrance. Outside, they could be heard getting into their omnibuses, amid much laughter and joking, and then there was the sound of one vehicle after another rumbling away . . .

'So they're coming back?' asked Tonio Kröger.

'They are indeed!' said the fish dealer. 'And God damn the whole thing, I say. They've engaged a band, and I sleep right over this room.'

'It makes an agreeable change,' said Tonio Kröger again. Then he got up and left.

He spent that day as he had spent the others, on the beach and in the woods, holding a book on his knee and blinking in the sunlight. There was only one thought in his mind: that they would be coming back and holding a dance in the dining-room as the fish dealer had predicted, and he did nothing all day but look forward to this, with a sweet apprehensive excitement such as he had not felt throughout all these long, dead years. Once, by some associative trick of thought, he fleetingly remembered a far-off acquaintance: Adalbert, the short-story writer, the man who knew what he wanted and had retreated into a café to escape the spring air. And he shrugged his shoulders at the thought of him . . .

Dinner was earlier than usual; supper was also served in advance of the normal time and in the parlour, because preparations for the dance were already being made in the dining-room: the whole normal programme was delightfully disarranged for so festive an occasion. Then, when it was already dark and Tonio Kröger was sitting in his room, there were signs of life again on the road and in the hotel. The party was returning; there were even new guests arriving from Elsinore by bicycle or by carriage, and already he could hear, down below, a violin being tuned and the nasal tones of a clarinet practising scales . . . There was every indication that it would be a magnificent ball.

And now the little orchestra began playing: a march in strict time, muted but clearly audible upstairs. The dancing began with a polonaise. Tonio Kröger sat on quietly for a while and listened. But when the march tempo changed to a waltz rhythm, he rose and slipped quietly out of his room.

From his corridor there was a subsidiary flight of stairs leading down to the side entrance of the hotel, and from there one could reach the glazed veranda without passing through any of the rooms. He went this way, walking softly and stealthily as if he had no business to be there, groping cautiously through the darkness, irresistibly drawn towards the foolish, happily lilting music; he could hear it now quite loudly and distinctly.

The veranda was empty and unlit, but in the dining-room the two large paraffin lamps with their polished reflectors were shining brightly, and the glass door stood open. He crept noiselessly up to it; here he could stand in the dark unobserved, watching the dancers in the lighted room, and this furtive pleasure made his skin tingle. Quickly and eagerly he glanced round for the pair he sought . . .

The festivity was already in full swing, although the dancing had begun less than half an hour ago; but the participants had of course been already warmed up and excited by the time they had got back here, having spent the whole day together in happy and carefree companionship. In the parlour, into which Tonio Kröger could see if he ventured forward a little, several older men had settled down to smoke and drink and play cards; others again were sitting with their wives on the plush-upholstered chairs in the foreground or along the walls of the dining-room, watching the dance. They sat resting their hands on their outspread knees, with prosperous puffed-out faces; the mothers, wearing bonnets high up on their parted hair, looked on at the whirl of young people, with their hands folded in their laps and their heads tilted sideways. A platform had been erected against one of the longer walls, and on it the musicians were doing their best. There was even a trumpeter among them, blowing on his instrument rather diffidently and cautiously – it seemed to be afraid of its own voice, which despite all efforts kept breaking and tripping over itself . . . The dancing couples circled round each other, swaying and gyrating, while others walked about the room hand-in-hand. The company was not properly dressed for a ball, merely for a summer Sunday outing in the country: the young beaux wore suits of provincial cut which they obviously used only at weekends, and the girls were in light pale frocks with bunches of wild flowers on their bosoms. There were even some children present, dancing with each other after their fashion, even when the band was not playing. The master of ceremonies appeared to be a long-legged man in a swallow-tailed coat, some kind of small-town dandy with a monocle and artificially curled hair, an assistant postmaster perhaps – a comic character straight out of a Danish novel. He devoted himself heart and soul to his task, positively perspiring with officiousness; he was everywhere at once, curvetting busily round the room with a mincing gait, setting his toes down first and artfully criss-crossing his feet, which were clad in shining pointed half-boots of military cut. He waved his arms, issued instructions, called for music and clapped his hands; as he moved, the ribbons of the gaily coloured bow which had been pinned to his shoulder in token of his office fluttered behind him, and from time to time he glanced lovingly round at it.

Yes, there they were, the pair who had walked past Tonio Kröger that morning in the sunlight: he saw them again, his heart suddenly leaping with joy as he caught sight of them almost simultaneously. There stood Hans Hansen, quite near him, not far from the door; with outspread legs and leaning forward slightly, he was slowly and carefully devouring a large slice of sponge cake, holding one hand cupped under his chin to catch the crumbs. And there by the wall sat Ingeborg Holm, the fair-haired Inge; at that very moment the assistant postmaster minced up to her and invited her to dance with a stilted bow, placing one hand on the small of his back and gracefully inserting the other into his bosom, but she shook her head and indicated that she was too much out of breath and must rest for a little, whereupon the assistant postmaster sat down beside her.

Tonio Kröger looked at them both, those two for whom long ago he had suffered love: Hans and Ingeborg. For that was who they were – not so much by virtue of particular details of their appearance or similarities of dress, but by affinity of race and type: they too had that radiant blondness, those steely blue eyes, that air of untroubled purity and lightness of heart, of proud simplicity and unapproachable reserve . . . He watched them, watched Hans Hansen standing there in his sailor suit, bold and handsome as ever, broad in the shoulders and narrow in the hips; he watched Ingeborg's way of tossing her head to one side with a saucy laugh, her way of raising her hand – a hand by no means particularly tiny or delicately girlish – to smooth her hair at the back, letting her light sleeve slide away from the elbow; and suddenly his heart was pierced by such an agony of homesickness that he instinctively shrank further back into the shadows to hide the twitching of his face.

'Had I forgotten you?' he asked. 'No, never! I never forgot you, Hans, nor you, sweet fair-haired Inge! It was for you I wrote my works, and when I heard applause I secretly looked round the room to see if you had joined in it . . . . Have you read *Don Carlos* yet, Hans Hansen, as you promised me at your garden gate? Don't read it! I no longer want you to. What has that lonely weeping king to do with you? You must not make your bright eyes cloudy and dreamy and dim by peering into poetry and sadness . . . If I could be like you! If only I could begin all over again and grow up like you, decent and happy and simple, normal and *comme il faut*, at peace with God and the world, loved by the innocent and light of heart – and marry you, Ingeborg Holm, and have a son like you, Hans Hansen! If only I could be freed from the curse of insight and the creative torment, and live and love and be thankful and blissfully commonplace! . . . Begin all over again? It would be no good. It would all turn out the same – all happen again just as it has happened. For certain people are bound to go astray because for them no such thing as a right way exists.'

The music had stopped; there was an interval, and refreshments were being handed round. The assistant postmaster in person was tripping about with a trayful of herring salad, offering it to the ladies; but before

Ingeborg Holm he even went down on one knee as he handed her the dish, and this made her blush with pleasure.

The spectator by the glass door of the dining-room was now beginning to attract attention after all, and from handsome flushed faces uncordial and inquiring looks were cast in his direction; but he stood his ground. Ingeborg and Hans glanced at him too, almost simultaneously, with that air of utter indifference so very like contempt. But suddenly he became conscious that a gaze from some other quarter had sought him out and was resting on him . . . He turned his head, and his eyes at once met those whose scrutiny he had sensed. Not far from him a girl was standing, a girl with a pale, slender delicate face whom he had noticed before. She had not been dancing much, the gentlemen had paid scant heed to her, and he had seen her sitting alone by the wall with tightly pursed lips. She was standing by herself now too. She wore a light-coloured frock like the other girls, but through its transparent gossamer-like material one could glimpse bare shoulders which were thin and pointed, and between these meagre shoulders her thin neck sat so low that this quiet girl almost gave the impression of being slightly deformed. She had thin short gloves on, and held her hands against her flat breasts with their fingers just touching. She had lowered her head and was gazing up at Tonio Kröger with dark, melting eyes. He turned away . . .

Here, quite near him, sat Hans and Ingeborg. Possibly they were brother and sister; Hans had sat down next to her, and surrounded by other young people with healthy pink complexions they were eating and drinking, chattering and enjoying themselves and exchanging pleasantries, and their bright clear voices and laughter rang through the air. Could he not perhaps approach them for a moment? Could he not speak to one or other of them, make whatever humorous remark occurred to him, and would they not at least have to answer with a smile? It would give him such pleasure; he longed for it to happen; he would go back to his room contented, in the knowledge of having established some slight contact with them both. He thought out something he might say to them; but he could not nerve himself to go forward and say it. After all, the situation was as it had always been: they would not understand, they would listen to his words in puzzled embarrassment. For they did not speak the same language.

The dancing, apparently, was on the point of beginning again. The assistant postmaster burst into ubiquitous activity. He hurried to and fro, urged everyone to choose a partner, helped the waiter to clear chairs and glasses out of the way, issued instructions to the musicians and pushed a few awkward uncomprehending dancers into place, steering them by the shoulders. What was about to happen? Squares were being formed, of four couples each . . . A dreadful memory made Tonio Kröger blush. They were going to dance quadrilles.

The music began; the couples bowed and advanced and interchanged. The assistant postmaster directed the dance; great heavens, he was actually directing it in French, and pronouncing the nasal vowels with incomparable distinction! Ingeborg Holm was dancing just in front of Tonio Kröger, in the set nearest to the glass door. She moved to and fro in front of him, stepping and turning, forwards and backwards; often he caught a fragrance from her hair or from the delicate white material of her dress, and he closed his eyes, filled with an emotion so long familiar to him: during all these last days he had been faintly aware of its sharp enchanting flavour, and now it was welling up once more inside him in all its sweet urgency. What was it? Desire, tenderness? envy? self-contempt? . . . *Moulinet des dames!* Did you laugh, fair-haired Inge, did you laugh at me on that occasion, when I danced the *moulinet* and made such a miserable fool of myself? And would you still laugh today, even now when I have become, in my own way, a famous man? Yes you would – and you would be a thousand times right to do so, and even if I, single-handed, had composed the Nine Symphonies and written *The World as Will and Idea* and painted the *Last Judgement* – you would still be right to laugh, eternally right . . . He looked at her, and remembered a line of poetry, a line he had long forgotten and which was nevertheless so close to his mind and heart: 'I long to sleep, to sleep, but you must dance.' He knew so well the melancholy northern mood it expressed, awkward and half-articulate and heartfelt. To sleep . . . To long to be able to live simply for one's feelings alone, to rest idly in sweet self-sufficient emotion, uncompelled to translate it into activity, unconstrained to dance – and to have to dance nevertheless, to have to be alert and nimble and perform the difficult, difficult and perilous sword-dance of art, and never to be able quite to forget the humiliating paradox of having to dance when one's heart is heavy with love . . .

Suddenly, all round him, a wild extravagant whirl of movement developed. The sets had broken up, and everyone was leaping and gliding about in all directions: the quadrille was finishing with a gallopade. The couples, keeping time to the music's frantic prestissimo, were darting past Tonio Kröger, *chassé*ing, racing, overtaking each other with little gasps of laughter. One of them, caught up and swept forward by the general rush, came spinning towards him. The girl had a delicate pale face and thin, hunched shoulders. And all at once, directly in front of him, there was a slipping and tripping and stumbling . . . The pale girl had fallen over. She fell so hard and heavily that it looked quite dangerous, and her partner collapsed with her. He had evidently hurt himself so badly that he completely forgot the lady and began in a half-upright posture to grimace with pain and rub his knee; the girl seemed quite dazed by her fall and was still lying on the floor. Whereupon Tonio Kröger stepped forward, took her gently by both arms and lifted her to her feet. She looked up at him, exhausted, bewildered and wretched, and suddenly a pink flush spread over her delicate face.

'*Tak! O, mange tak!*' she said, and looked up at him with dark melting eyes.

'You had better not dance again, Fräulein,' he said gently. Then he glanced round until once more he saw *them*, Hans and Ingeborg; and turned away. He left the veranda and the ball and went back up to his room.

He was elated by these festivities in which he had not shared, and wearied by jealousy. It had all been the same as before, so exactly the same! With flushed face he had stood in the darkness, his heart aching for you all, you the fair-haired, the happy, the truly alive; and then he had gone away, alone. Surely someone would come now! Surely Ingeborg would come now, surely she would notice that he had left, and slip out after him, put her hand on his shoulder and say: 'Come back and join us! Don't be sad! I love you!' But she did not come. Such things do not happen. Yes, it was all as it had been long ago, and he was happy as he had been long ago. For his heart was alive. But what of all those years he had spent in becoming what he now was? Paralysis; barrenness; ice; and intellect! and art! . . .

He undressed and got into bed and put out the light. He whispered two names into his pillow, whispered those few chaste northern syllables which symbolized his true and native way of loving and suffering and being happy – which to him meant life and simple heartfelt emotion and home. He looked back over the years that had passed between then and now. He remembered the dissolute adventures in which his senses, his nervous system and his mind had indulged; he saw himself corroded by irony and intellect, laid waste and paralysed by insight, almost exhausted by the fevers and chills of creation, helplessly and contritely tossed to and fro between gross extremes, between saintly austerity and lust – oversophisticated and impoverished, worn out by cold, rare, artificial ecstasies, lost, ravaged, racked and sick – and he sobbed with remorse and nostalgia.

Round about him there was silence and darkness. But lilting up to him from below came the faint music, the sweet trivial waltz rhythm of life.

9

Tonio Kröger sat in the north writing to his friend Lisaveta Ivanovna, as he had promised he would do.

'My dear Lisaveta down there in Arcadia,' he wrote, 'to which I hope soon to return: here is a letter of sorts, but I am afraid it may disappoint you, for I propose to write in rather general terms. Not that I have nothing to tell you, or have not, after my fashion, undergone one or two experiences. At home, in my native town, I was even nearly arrested . . . but of that you shall hear by word of mouth. I sometimes now have days on which I prefer to attempt a well formulated general statement, rather than narrate particular events.

'I wonder if you still remember, Lisaveta, once calling me a bourgeois *manqué*? You called me that on an occasion on which I had allowed myself to be enticed, by various indiscreet confessions I had already let slip, into avowing to you my love for what I call "life"; and I wonder if you realized how very right you were, and how truly my bourgeois nature and my love for "life" are one and the same. My journey here has made me think about this point . . .

'My father, as you know, was of a northern temperament: contemplative, thorough, puritanically correct, and inclined to melancholy. My mother was of a vaguely exotic extraction, beautiful, sensuous, naïve, both reckless and passionate, and given to impulsive, rather disreputable behaviour. There is no doubt that this mixed heredity contained extraordinary possibilities – and extraordinary dangers. Its result was a bourgeois who went astray into art, a bohemian homesick for his decent background, an artist with a bad conscience. For after all it is my bourgeois conscience that makes me see the whole business of being an artist, of being any kind of exception or genius, as something profoundly equivocal, profoundly dubious, profoundly suspect; and it too has made me fall so foolishly in love with simplicity and naïvety, with the delightfully normal, the respectable and mediocre.

'I stand between two worlds, I am at home in neither, and this makes things a little difficult for me. You artists call me a bourgeois, and the bourgeois feel they ought to arrest me . . . I don't know which of the two hurts me more bitterly. The bourgeois are fools; but you worshippers of beauty, you who say I am phlegmatic and have no longing in my soul, you should remember that there is a kind of artist so profoundly, so primordially fated to be an artist that no longing seems sweeter and more precious to him than his longing for the bliss of the commonplace.

'I admire those proud, cold spirits who venture out along the paths of grandiose, demonic beauty and despise "humanity" – but I do not envy them. For if there is anything that can turn a *littérateur* into a true writer, then it is this bourgeois love of mine for the human and the living and the ordinary. It is the source of all warmth, of all kind-heartedness and of all humour, and I am almost persuaded it is that very love without which, as we are told, one may speak with the tongues of men and of angels and yet be a sounding brass and a tinkling cymbal.

'What I have achieved so far is nothing, not much, as good as nothing. I shall improve on it, Lisaveta – this I promise you. As I write this, I can hear below me the roar of the sea, and I close my eyes. I gaze into an unborn, unembodied world that demands to be ordered and shaped, I see before me a host of shadowy human figures whose gestures implore me to cast upon them the spell that shall be their deliverance: tragic and comic figures, and some who are both at once – and to these I am strongly drawn. But my deepest and most secret love belongs to the fair-haired and the blue-eyed, the bright children of life, the happy, the charming and the ordinary.

'Do not disparage this love, Lisaveta; it is good and fruitful. In it there is longing, and sad envy, and just a touch of contempt, and a whole world of innocent delight.'

Death in Venice

Der Tod in Venedig

1912

Death in Venice

1

On a spring afternoon in 19—, the year in which for months on end so grave a threat seemed to hang over the peace of Europe, Gustav Aschenbach, or von Aschenbach as he had been officially known since his fiftieth birthday, had set out from his apartment on the Prinzregentenstrasse in Munich to take a walk of some length by himself. The morning's writing had overstimulated him: his work had now reached a difficult and dangerous point which demanded the utmost care and circumspection, the most insistent and precise effort of will, and the productive mechanism in his mind – that *motus animi continuus* which according to Cicero is the essence of eloquence – had so pursued its reverberating rhythm that he had been unable to halt it even after lunch, and had missed the refreshing daily siesta which was now so necessary for him as he became increasingly subject to fatigue. And so, soon after taking tea, he had left the house hoping that fresh air and movement would set him to rights and enable him to spend a profitable evening.

It was the beginning of May, and after a succession of cold, wet weeks a premature high summer had set in. The Englischer Garten, although still only in its first delicate leaf, had been as sultry as in August, and at its city end full of traffic and pedestrians. Having made his way to the Aumeister along less and less frequented paths, Aschenbach had briefly surveyed the lively scene at the popular open-air restaurant, around which a few cabs and private carriages were standing; then, as the sun sank, he had started homewards across the open meadow beyond the park, and since he was now tired and a storm seemed to be brewing over

Föhring, he had stopped by the Northern Cemetery to wait for the tram that would take him straight back to the city.

As it happened, there was not a soul to be seen at or near the tram-stop. Not one vehicle passed along the Föhringer Chaussee or the paved Ungererstrasse on which solitary gleaming tram-rails pointed towards Schwabing; nothing stirred behind the fencing of the stonemasons' yards, where crosses and memorial tablets and monuments, ready for sale, composed a second and untenanted burial-ground; across the street, the mortuary chapel with its Byzantine styling stood silent in the glow of the westering day. Its façade, adorned with Greek crosses and brightly painted hieratic motifs, is also inscribed with symmetrically arranged texts in gilt lettering, selected scriptural passages about the life to come, such as: 'They shall go in unto the dwelling-place of the Lord', or 'May light perpetual shine upon them'. The waiting Aschenbach had already been engaged for some minutes in the solemn pastime of deciphering the words and letting his mind wander in contemplation of the mystic meaning that suffused them, when he noticed something that brought him back to reality: in the portico of the chapel, above the two apocalyptic beasts that guard the steps leading up to it, a man was standing, a man whose slightly unusual appearance gave his thoughts an altogether different turn.

It was not entirely clear whether he had emerged through the bronze doors from inside the chapel or had suddenly appeared and mounted the steps from outside. Aschenbach, without unduly pondering the question, inclined to the former hypothesis. The man was moderately tall, thin, beardless and remarkably snub-nosed; he belonged to the red-haired type and had its characteristic milky, freckled complexion. He was quite evidently not of Bavarian origin; at all events he wore a straw hat with a broad straight brim which gave him an exotic air, as of someone who had come from distant parts. It is true that he also had the typical Bavarian rucksack strapped to his shoulders and wore a yellowish belted outfit of what looked like frieze, as well as carrying a grey rain-cape over his left forearm which was propped against his waist, and in his right hand an iron-pointed walking-stick which he had thrust slantwise into the ground, crossing his feet and leaning his hip against its handle. His head was held high, so that the Adam's apple stood out stark and bare on his lean neck where it rose from the open shirt; and there were two pronounced vertical furrows, rather strangely ill-matched to his turned-up nose, between the colourless red-lashed eyes with which he peered sharply into the distance. There was thus – and perhaps the raised point of vantage on which he stood contributed to this impression – an air of imperious survey, something bold or even wild about his posture; for whether it was because he was dazzled into a grimace by the setting sun or by reason of some permanent facial deformity, the fact was that his lips seemed to be too short and were completely retracted from his teeth, so that the latter showed white and long between them, bared to the gums.

Aschenbach's half absent-minded, half inquisitive scrutiny of the stranger had no doubt been a little less than polite, for he suddenly became aware that his gaze was being returned: the man was in fact staring at him so aggressively, so straight in the eye, with so evident an intention to make an issue of the matter and outstare him, that Aschenbach turned away in disagreeable embarrassment and began to stroll along the fence, casually resolving to take no further notice of the fellow. A minute later he had put him out of his mind. But whether his imagination had been stirred by the stranger's itinerant appearance, or whether some other physical or psychological influence was at work, he now became conscious, to his complete surprise, of an extraordinary expansion of his inner self, a kind of roving restlessness, a youthful craving for far-off places, a feeling so new or at least so long unaccustomed and forgotten that he stood as if rooted, with his hands clasped behind his back and his eyes to the ground, trying to ascertain the nature and purport of his emotion.

It was simply a desire to travel; but it had presented itself as nothing less than a seizure, with intensely passionate and indeed hallucinatory force, turning his craving into vision. His imagination, still not at rest from the morning's hours of work, shaped for itself a paradigm of all the wonders and terrors of the manifold earth, of all that it was now suddenly striving to envisage: he saw it, saw a landscape, a tropical swampland under a cloud-swollen sky, moist and lush and monstrous, a kind of primeval wilderness of islands, morasses and muddy alluvial channels; far and wide around him he saw hairy palm-trunks thrusting upwards from rank jungles of fern, from among thick fleshy plants in exuberant flower; saw strangely misshapen trees with roots that arched through the air before sinking into the ground or into stagnant, shadowy-green, glassy waters where milk-white blossoms floated as big as plates, and among them exotic birds with grotesque beaks stood hunched in the shallows, their heads tilted motionlessly sideways; saw between the knotted stems of the bamboo thicket the glinting eyes of a crouching tiger; and his heart throbbed with terror and mysterious longing. Then the vision faded; and with a shake of his head Aschenbach resumed his perambulation along the fencing of the gravestone yards.

His attitude to foreign travel, at least since he had had the means at his disposal to enjoy its advantages as often as he pleased, had always been that it was nothing more than a necessary health precaution, to be taken from time to time however disinclined to it one might be. Too preoccupied with the tasks imposed upon him by his own sensibility and by the collective European psyche, too heavily burdened with the compulsion to produce, too shy of distraction to have learned how to take leisure and pleasure in the colourful external world, he had been perfectly well satisfied to have no more detailed a view of the earth's surface than anyone can acquire without stirring far from home, and he had never even been tempted to venture outside Europe. This had been more especially the case since his life had begun its gradual decline and his artist's fear of not finishing his task – the apprehension that his time might run out before he had given the whole of himself by doing what he had it in him to do – was no longer something he could simply dismiss as an idle fancy; and during this time his outward existence had been almost entirely divided between the beautiful city which had become his home and the rustic mountain retreat he had set up for himself and where he passed his rainy summers.

And sure enough, the sudden and belated impulse that had just overwhelmed him very soon came under the moderating and corrective influence of common sense and of the self-discipline he had practised since his youth. It had been his intention that the book to which his life was at present dedicated should be advanced to a certain point before he moved to the country, and the idea of a jaunt in the wide world that would take him away from his work for months now seemed too casual, too upsetting to his plans to be considered seriously. Nevertheless, he knew the reason for the unexpected temptation only too well. This relaxation and forgetfulness – it had been, he was bound to admit, an

urge to escape, to run away from his writing, away from the humdrum
scene of his cold, inflexible, passionate duty. True, it was a duty he
loved, and by now he had almost even learned to love the enervating
daily struggle between his proud, tenacious, tried and tested will and
that growing weariness which no one must be allowed to suspect nor his
finished work betray by any tell-tale sign of debility or lassitude.
Nevertheless, it would be sensible, he decided, not to span the bow too
far and wilfully stifle a desire that had erupted in him with such vivid
force. He thought of his work, thought of the passage at which he had
again, today as yesterday, been forced to interrupt it – that stubborn
problem which neither patient care could solve nor a decisive *coup de
main* dispel. He reconsidered it, tried to break or dissolve the inhibition,
and, with a shudder of repugnance, abandoned the attempt. It was not a
case of very unusual difficulty, he was simply paralysed by a scruple of
distaste, manifesting itself as a perfectionistic fastidiousness which
nothing could satisfy. Perfectionism, of course, was something which
even as a young man he had come to see as the innermost essence of
talent, and for its sake he had curbed and cooled his feelings; for he knew
that feeling is apt to be content with high-spirited approximations and
with work that falls short of supreme excellence. Could it be that the
enslaved emotion was now avenging itself by deserting him, by refusing
from now on to bear up his art on its wings, by taking with it all his joy in
words, all his appetite for the beauty of form? Not that he was writing
badly: it was at least the advantage of his years to be master of his trade, a
mastery of which at any moment he could feel calmly confident. But
even as it brought him national honour he took no pleasure in it
himself, and it seemed to him that his work lacked that element of
sparkling and joyful improvisation, that quality which surpasses any
intellectual substance in its power to delight the receptive world. He
dreaded spending the summer in the country, alone in that little house
with the maid who prepared his meals and the servant who brought
them to him; dreaded the familiar profile of the mountain summits and
mountain walls which would once again surround his slow discontented
toil. So what did he need? An interlude, some impromptu living, some
dolce far niente, the invigoration of a distant climate, to make his
summer bearable and fruitful. Very well then – he would travel. Not all
that far, not quite to where the tigers were. A night in the wagon-lit and a

siesta of three or four weeks at some popular holiday resort in the charming south . . .

Such were his thoughts as the tram clattered towards him along the Ungererstrasse, and as he stepped into it he decided to devote that evening to the study of maps and timetables. On the platform it occurred to him to look round and see what had become of the man in the straw hat, his companion for the duration of this not inconsequential wait at a tram-stop. But the man's whereabouts remained a mystery, for he was no longer standing where he had stood, nor was he to be seen anywhere else at the stop or in the tramcar itself.

2

The author of the lucid and massive prose epic about the life of Frederic of Prussia; the patient artist who with long toil had woven the great tapestry of the novel called *Maya*, so rich in characters, gathering so many human destinies together under the shadow of one idea; the creator of that powerful tale entitled *A Study in Abjection*, which earned the gratitude of a whole younger generation by pointing to the possibility of moral resolution even for those who have plumbed the depths of knowledge; the author (lastly but not least in this summary enumeration of his maturer works) of that passionate treatise *Intellect and Art* which in its ordering energy and antithetical eloquence has led serious critics to place it immediately alongside Schiller's disquisition *On Naïve and Reflective Literature*: in a word, Gustav Aschenbach, was born in L—, an important city in the province of Silesia, as the son of a highly-placed legal official. His ancestors had been military officers, judges, government administrators; men who had spent their disciplined, decently austere life in the service of the King and the state. A more inward spirituality had shown itself in one of them who had been a preacher; a strain of livelier, more sensuous blood had entered the family in the previous generation with the writer's mother, the daughter of a director of music from Bohemia. Certain exotic racial characteristics in his external appearance had come to him from her. It was from this marriage between hard-working, sober conscientiousness and darker, more fiery impulses that an artist, and indeed this particular kind of artist, had come into being.

With his whole nature intent from the start upon fame, he had displayed not exactly precocity, but a certain decisiveness and personal trenchancy in his style of utterance, which at an early age made him ripe for a life in the public eye and well suited to it. He had made a name for himself at little more than school age. Ten years later he had learned to perform, at his writing desk, the social and administrative duties entailed by his reputation; he had learned to write letters which, however brief they had to be (for many claims beset the successful man who enjoys the confidence of the public), would always contain something kindly and pointed. By the age of forty he was obliged, wearied though he might be by the toils and vicissitudes of his real work, to deal with a daily correspondence that bore postage stamps from every part of the globe.

His talent, equally remote from the commonplace and from the eccentric, had a native capacity both to inspire confidence in the general public and to win admiration and encouragement from the discriminating connoisseur. Ever since his boyhood the duty to achieve – and to achieve exceptional things – had been imposed on him from all sides, and thus he had never known youth's idleness, its carefree negligent ways. When in his thirty-fifth year he fell ill in Vienna, a subtle observer remarked of him on a social occasion: 'You see, Aschenbach has always only lived like *this*' – and the speaker closed the fingers of his left hand tightly into a fist – 'and never like *this*' – and he let his open hand hang comfortably down along the back of the chair. It was a correct observation; and the morally courageous aspect of the matter was that Aschenbach's native constitution was by no means robust, that the constant harnessing of his energies was something to which he had been called, but not really born.

As a young boy, medical advice and care had made school attendance impossible and obliged him to have his education at home. He had grown up by himself, without companions, and had nevertheless had to recognize in good time that he belonged to a breed not seldom talented, yet seldom endowed with the physical basis which talent needs if it is to fulfil itself – a breed that usually gives of its best in youth, and in which the creative gift rarely survives into mature years. But he would 'stay the course' – it was his favourite motto, he saw his historical novel about Frederic the Great as nothing if not the apotheosis of this, the king's word of command, '*durchhalten!*', which to Aschenbach epitomized a manly ethos of suffering action. And he dearly longed to grow old, for it had always been his view that an artist's gift can only be called truly great and wide-ranging, or indeed truly admirable, if it has been fortunate enough to bear characteristic fruit at all the stages of human life.

They were not broad, the shoulders on which he thus carried the tasks laid upon him by his talent; and since his aims were high, he stood in great need of discipline – and discipline, after all, was fortunately his inborn heritage on his father's side. At the age of forty or fifty, and indeed during those younger years in which other men live prodigally and dilettantishly, happily procrastinating the execution of great plans, Aschenbach would begin his day early by dashing cold water over his chest and back, and then, with two tall wax candles in silver candlesticks placed at the head of his manuscript, he would offer up to art, for two or three ardently conscientious morning hours, the strength he had garnered during sleep. It was a pardonable error, indeed it was one that betokened as nothing else could the triumph of his moral will, that uninformed critics should mistake the great world of *Maya*, or the massive epic unfolding of Frederic's life, for the product of solid strength and long stamina, whereas in fact they had been built up to their impressive size from layer upon layer of daily opuscula, from a hundred or a thousand separate inspirations; and if they were indeed so excellent, wholly and in every detail, it was only because their creator, showing that same constancy of will and tenacity of purpose as had once conquered his native Silesia, had held out for years under the pressure of one and the same task, and had devoted to actual composition only his best and worthiest hours.

For a significant intellectual product to make a broad and deep immediate appeal, there must be a hidden affinity, indeed a congruence, between the personal destiny of the author and the wider destiny of his generation. The public does not know why it grants the accolade of fame to a work of art. Being in no sense connoisseurs, readers imagine they perceive a hundred good qualities in it which justify their admiration; but the real reason for their applause is something imponderable, a sense of sympathy. Hidden away among

Aschenbach's writings was a passage directly asserting that nearly all the great things that exist owe their existence to a defiant despite: it is despite grief and anguish, despite poverty, loneliness, bodily weakness, vice and passion and a thousand inhibitions, that they have come into being at all. But this was more than an observation, it was an experience, it was positively the formula of his life and his fame, the key to his work; is it surprising then that it was also the moral formula, the outward gesture, of his work's most characteristic figures?

The new hero-type favoured by Aschenbach, and recurring in his books in a multiplicity of individual variants, had already been remarked upon at an early stage by a shrewd commentator, who had described his conception as that of 'an intellectual and boyish manly virtue, that of a youth who clenches his teeth in proud shame and stands calmly on as the swords and spears pass through his body'. That was well put, perceptive and precisely true, for all its seemingly rather too passive emphasis. For composure under the blows of fate, grace in the midst of torment – this is not only endurance: it is an active achievement, a positive triumph, and the figure of Saint Sebastian is the most perfect symbol if not of art in general, then certainly of the kind of art here in question. What did one see if one looked in any depth into the world of this writer's fiction? Elegant self-control concealing from the world's eyes until the very last moment a state of inner disintegration and biological decay; sallow ugliness, sensuously marred and worsted, which nevertheless is able to fan its smouldering concupiscence to a pure flame, and even to exalt itself to mastery in the realm of beauty; pallid impotence, which from the glowing depths of the spirit draws strength to cast down a whole proud people at the foot of the Cross and set its own foot upon them as well; gracious poise and composure in the empty austere service of form; the false, dangerous life of the born deceiver, his ambition and his art which lead so soon to exhaustion – to contemplate all these destinies, and many others like them, was to doubt if there is any other heroism at all but the heroism of weakness. In any case, what other heroism could be more in keeping with the times? Gustav Aschenbach was the writer who spoke for all those who work on the brink of exhaustion, who labour and are heavy-laden, who are worn out already but still stand upright, all those moralists of achievement who are slight of stature and scanty of resources, but who yet, by some ecstasy of the will and by wise husbandry, manage at least for a time to force their work into a semblance of greatness. There are many such, they are the heroes of our age. And they all recognized themselves in his work, they found that it confirmed them and raised them on high and celebrated them; they were grateful for this, and they spread his name far and wide.

He had been young and raw with the times: ill advised by fashion, he had publicly stumbled, blundered, made himself look foolish, offended in speech and writing against tact and balanced civility. But he had achieved dignity, that goal towards which, as he declared, every great talent is innately driven and spurred; indeed it can be said that the conscious and defiant purpose of his entire development had been, leaving all the inhibitions of scepticism and irony behind him, an ascent to dignity.

Lively, clear-outlined, intellectually undemanding presentation is the delight of the great mass of the middle-class public, but passionate radical youth is interested only in problems: and Aschenbach had been as problematic and as radical as any young man ever was. He had been in thrall to intellect, had exhausted the soil by excessive analysis and ground up the seed-corn of growth; he had uncovered what is better kept hidden, made talent seem suspect, betrayed the truth about art – indeed, even as the sculptural vividness of his descriptions was giving pleasure to his more naïve devotees and lifting their minds and hearts, he, this same youthful artist, had fascinated twenty-year-olds with his breath-taking cynicisms about the questionable nature of art and of the artist himself.

But it seems that there is nothing to which a noble and active mind more quickly becomes inured than that pungent and bitter stimulus, the acquisition of knowledge; and it is very sure that even the most gloomily conscientious and radical sophistication of youth is shallow by comparison with Aschenbach's profound decision as a mature master to repudiate knowledge as such, to reject it, to step over it with head held high – in the recognition that knowledge can paralyse the will, paralyse and discourage action and emotion and even passion, and rob all these of their dignity. How else is the famous short story A *Study in Abjection* to be understood but as an outbreak of disgust against an age indecently undermined by psychology and represented by the figure of that spiritless, witless semi-scoundrel who cheats his way into a destiny of sorts when, motivated by his own ineptitude and depravity and ethical whimsicality, he drives his wife into the arms of a callow youth – convinced that his intellectual depths entitle him to behave with contemptible baseness? The forthright words of condemnation which here weighed vileness in the balance and found it wanting – they proclaimed their writer's renunciation of all moral scepticism, of every kind of sympathy with the abyss; they declared his repudiation of the laxity of that compassionate principle which holds that to understand all is to forgive all. And the development that was here being anticipated, indeed already taking place, was that 'miracle of reborn naïvety' to which, in a dialogue written a little later, the author himself had referred with a certain mysterious emphasis. How strange these associations! Was it an intellectual consequence of this 'rebirth', of this new dignity and rigour, that, at about the same time, his sense of beauty was observed to undergo an almost excessive resurgence, that his style took on the noble purity, simplicity and symmetry that were to set upon all his subsequent works that so evident and evidently intentional stamp of the classical master? And yet: moral resoluteness at the far side of knowledge, achieved in despite of all corrosive and inhibiting insight – does not this in its turn signify a simplification, a morally simplistic view of the world and of human psychology, and thus also a resurgence of energies that are evil, forbidden, morally impossible? And is form not two-faced? Is it not at one and the same time moral and immoral – moral as the product and expression of discipline, but immoral and even anti-moral inasmuch as it harbours within itself an innate moral indifference, and indeed essentially strives for nothing less than to bend morality under its proud and absolute sceptre?

Be that as it may! A development is a destiny; and one that is accompanied by the admiration and mass confidence of a wide public must inevitably differ in its course from one that takes place far from the limelight and from the commitments of fame. Only the eternal intellectual vagrant is bored and prompted to mockery when a great talent grows out of its libertinistic chrysalis-stage, becomes an expressive representative of the dignity of mind, takes on the courtly bearing of that solitude which has been full of hard, uncounselled, self-reliant sufferings and struggles, and has achieved power and honour among men. And what a game it is too, how much defiance there is in it and how much satisfaction, this self-formation of a talent! As time passed, Gustav Aschenbach's presentations took on something of an official air, of an educator's stance; his style in later years came to eschew direct audacities, new and subtle nuances, it developed towards the exemplary and definitive, the fastidiously conventional, the conservative and formal and even formulaic; and as tradition has it of Louis XIV, so Aschenbach as he grew older banned from his utterance every unrefined word. It was at this time that the education authority adopted selected pages from his works for inclusion in the prescribed school readers. And when a German ruler who had just come to the throne granted personal nobilitation to the author of *Frederic of Prussia* on his fiftieth birthday, he sensed the inner appropriateness of this honour and did not decline it.

After a few restless years of experimental living in different places, he soon chose Munich as his permanent home and lived there in the kind of upper-bourgeois status which is occasionally the lot of certain intellectuals. The marriage which he had contracted while still young with the daughter of an academic family had been ended by his wife's death after a short period of happiness. She had left him a daughter, now already married. He had never had a son.

Gustav von Aschenbach was of rather less than average height, dark and clean-shaven. His head seemed a little too large in proportion to his almost delicate stature. His brushed-back hair, thinning at the top, very thick and distinctly grey over the temples, framed a high, deeply lined, scarred-looking forehead. The bow of a pair of gold spectacles with rimless lenses cut into the base of his strong, nobly curved nose. His mouth was large, often relaxed, often suddenly narrow and tense; the cheeks were lean and furrowed, the well-formed chin slightly cleft. Grave visitations of fate seemed to have passed over this head, which usually inclined to one side with an air of suffering. And yet it was art that had here performed that fashioning of the physiognomy which is usually the work of a life full of action and stress. The flashing exchanges of the dialogue between Voltaire and the king on the subject of war had been born behind this brow; these eyes that looked so wearily and deeply through their glasses had seen the bloody inferno of the Seven Years War sick-bays. Even in a personal sense, after all, art is an intensified life. By art one is more deeply satisfied and more rapidly used up. It engraves on the countenance of its servant the traces of imaginary and intellectual adventures, and even if he has outwardly existed in cloistral tranquillity, it leads in the long term to overfastidiousness, over-refinement, nervous fatigue and overstimulation, such as can seldom result from a life full of the most extravagant passions and pleasures.

3

Mundane and literary business of various kinds delayed Aschenbach's eagerly awaited departure until about a fortnight after that walk in Munich. Finally he gave instructions that his country house was to be made ready for occupation in four weeks' time, and then, one day between the middle and end of May, he took the night train to Trieste, where he stayed only twenty-four hours, embarking on the following morning for Pola.

What he sought was something strange and random, but in a place easily reached, and accordingly he took up his abode on an Adriatic island which had been highly spoken of for some years: a little way off the Istrian coast, with colourful, ragged inhabitants speaking a wild unintelligible dialect, and picturesque fragmented cliffs overlooking the open sea. But rain and sultry air, a self-enclosed provincial Austrian hotel clientele, the lack of that restful intimate contact with the sea which can only be had on a gentle, sandy coast, filled him with vexation and with a feeling that he had not yet come to his journey's end. He was haunted by an inner impulse that still had no clear direction; he studied shipping timetables, looked up one place after another – and suddenly his surprising yet at the same time self-evident destination stared him in the face. If one wanted to travel overnight to somewhere incomparable, to a fantastic mutation of normal reality, where did one go? Why, the answer was obvious. What was he doing here? He had gone completely astray. *That* was where he had longed to travel. He at once gave notice of departure from his present, mischosen stopping-place. Ten days after his arrival on the island, in the early-morning mist, a rapid motor-launch carried him and his luggage back over the water to the naval base, and here he landed only to re-embark immediately, crossing the gangway on to the damp deck of a ship that was waiting under steam to leave for Venice.

It was an ancient Italian boat, out of date and dingy and black with soot. Aschenbach was no sooner aboard than a grubby hunchbacked seaman, grinning obsequiously, conducted him to an artificially lit cave-like cabin in the ship's interior. Here, behind a table, with his cap askew and a cigarette-end in the corner of his mouth, sat a goat-bearded man with the air of an old-fashioned circus director and a slick caricatured business manner, taking passengers' particulars and issuing their tickets. 'To Venice!' he exclaimed, echoing Aschenbach's request, and extending his arm he pushed his pen into some coagulated leftover ink in a tilted inkstand. 'One first class to Venice. Certainly, sir!' He scribbled elaborately, shook some blue sand from a box over the writing and ran it off into an earthenware dish, then folded the paper with his yellow bony fingers and wrote on it again. 'A very happily chosen destination!' he chattered as he did so. 'Ah, Venice! A splendid city! A city irresistibly attractive to the man of culture, by its history no less than by its present charms!' There was something hypnotic and distracting about the smooth facility of his movements and the glib empty talk with which he accompanied them, almost as if he were anxious that the traveller might have second thoughts about his decision to go to Venice. He hastily took Aschenbach's money and with the dexterity of a croupier dropped the change on the stained tablecloth. '*Buon divertimento, signore,*' he said, bowing histrionically. 'It is an honour to serve you . . . Next, please, gentlemen!' he exclaimed with a wave of the arm, as if he were doing a lively trade, although in fact there was no one else there to be dealt with. Aschenbach returned on deck.

Resting one elbow on the handrail, he watched the idle crowd hanging about the quayside to see the ship's departure, and watched the passengers who had come aboard. Those with second-class tickets were squatting, men and women together, on the forward deck, using boxes and bundles as seats. The company on the upper deck consisted of a group of young men, probably shop or office workers from Pola, a high-spirited party about to set off on an excursion to Italy. They were making a considerable exhibition of themselves and their enterprise, chattering, laughing, fatuously enjoying their own gesticulations, leaning overboard and shouting glibly derisive ribaldries at their friends in the harbour-side street, who were hurrying about their business with briefcases under their arms and waved their sticks peevishly at the holiday-makers. One of the party, who wore a light yellow summer suit of extravagant cut, a scarlet necktie and a rakishly tilted Panama hat, was the most conspicuous of them all in his shrill hilarity. But as soon as Aschenbach took a slightly closer look at him, he realized with a kind of horror that the man's youth was false. He was old, there was no mistaking it. There were wrinkles round his eyes and mouth. His cheeks' faint carmine was rouge, the brown hair under his straw hat with its coloured ribbon was a wig, his neck was flaccid and scrawny, his small stuck-on moustache and the little imperial on his chin were dyed, his yellowish full complement of teeth, displayed when he laughed, were a cheap artificial set, and his hands, with signet rings on both index fingers, were those of an old man. With a spasm of distaste Aschenbach watched him as he kept company with his young friends. Did they not know, did they not notice that he was old, that he had no right to be acting as if he were one of them? They seemed to be tolerating his presence among them as something habitual and to be taken for granted, they treated him as an equal, reciprocated without embarrassment when he teasingly poked them in the ribs. How was this possible? Aschenbach put his hand over his forehead and closed his eyes, which were hot from too little sleep. He had a feeling that something not quite usual was beginning to happen, that the world was undergoing a dreamlike alienation, becoming increasingly deranged and bizarre, and that perhaps this process might be arrested if he were to cover his face for a little and then take a fresh look at things. But at that moment he had the sensation of being afloat, and starting up in irrational alarm, he noticed that the dark heavy hulk of the steamer was slowly parting company with the stone quayside. Inch by inch, as the engine pounded and reversed, the width of the dirty glinting water between the hull and the quay increased, and after clumsy manoeuvrings the ship turned its bows towards the open sea. Aschenbach crossed to the starboard side, where the hunchback had set up a deck-chair for him and a steward in a grease-stained frock coat offered his services.

The sky was grey, the wind damp. The port and the islands had been left behind, and soon all land was lost to view in the misty panorama.

Flecks of sodden soot drifted down on the washed deck, which never seemed to get dry. After only an hour an awning was set up, as it was beginning to rain.

Wrapped in his overcoat, a book lying on his lap, the traveller rested, scarcely noticing the hours as they passed him by. It had stopped raining; the canvas shelter was removed. The horizon was complete. Under the turbid dome of the sky the desolate sea surrounded him in an enormous circle. But in empty, unarticulated space our mind loses its sense of time as well, and we enter the twilight of the immeasurable. As Aschenbach lay there, strange and shadowy figures, the foppish old man, the goat-bearded purser from the ship's interior, passed with uncertain gestures and confused dream-words through his mind, and he fell asleep.

At midday he was requested to come below for luncheon in the long, narrow dining-saloon, which ended in the doors to the sleeping-berths; here he ate at the head of the long table, at the other end of which the group of apprentices, with the old man among them, had been quaffing since ten o'clock with the good-humoured ship's captain. The meal was wretched and he finished it quickly. He needed to be back in the open air, to look at the sky: perhaps it would clear over Venice.

It had never occurred to him that this would not happen, for the city had always received him in its full glory. But the sky and the sea remained dull and leaden, from time to time misty rain fell, and he resigned himself to arriving by water in a different Venice, one he had never encountered on the landward approach. He stood by the foremast, gazing into the distance, waiting for the sight of land. He recalled that poet of plangent inspiration who long ago had seen the cupolas and bell-towers of his dream rise before him out of these same waters; inwardly he recited a few lines of the measured music that had been made from that reverence and joy and sadness, and effortlessly moved by a passion already shaped into language, he questioned his grave and weary heart, wondering whether some new inspiration and distraction, some late adventure of the emotions, might yet be in store for him on his leisured journey.

And now, on his right, the flat coastline rose above the horizon, the sea came alive with fishing vessels, the island resort appeared: the steamer left it on its port side, glided at half-speed through the narrow channel named after it, entered the lagoon, and presently, near some shabby miscellaneous buildings, came to a complete halt, as this was where the launch carrying the public health inspector must be awaited.

An hour passed before it appeared. One had arrived and yet not arrived; there was no hurry, and yet one was impelled by impatience. The young men from Pola had come on deck, no doubt also patriotically attracted by the military sound of bugle calls across the water from the direction of the Public Gardens; and elated by the Asti they had drunk, they began cheering the *bersaglieri* as they drilled there in the park. But the dandified old man, thanks to his spurious fraternization with the young, was now in a condition repugnant to behold. His old head could not carry the wine as his sturdy youthful companions had done, and he was lamentably drunk. Eyes glazed, a cigarette between his trembling fingers, he stood swaying, tilted to and fro by inebriation and barely keeping his balance. Since he would have fallen at his first step he did not dare move from the spot, and was nevertheless full of wretched exuberance, clutching at everyone who approached him, babbling, winking, sniggering, lifting his ringed and wrinkled forefinger as he uttered some bantering inanity, and licking the corners of his mouth with the tip of his tongue in a repellently suggestive way. Aschenbach watched him with frowning disapproval, and once more a sense of numbness came over him, a feeling that the world was somehow, slightly yet uncontrollably, sliding into some kind of bizarre and grotesque derangement. It was a feeling on which, to be sure, he was unable to brood further in present circumstances, for at this moment the thudding motion of the engine began again, and the ship, having stopped short so close to its destination, resumed its passage along the San Marco Canal.

Thus it was that he saw it once more, that most astonishing of all landing-places, that dazzling composition of fantastic architecture which the Republic presented to the admiring gaze of approaching seafarers: the unburdened splendour of the Ducal Palace, the Bridge of Sighs, the lion and the saint on their two columns at the water's edge, the magnificently projecting side wing of the fabulous basilica, the vista beyond it of the gate tower and the Giants' Clock; and as he contemplated it all he reflected that to arrive in Venice by land, at the station, was like entering a palace by a back door: that only as he was now doing, only by ship, over the high sea, should one come to this most extraordinary of cities.

The engine stopped, gondolas pressed alongside, the gangway was let down, customs officers came on board and perfunctorily discharged their duties; disembarkation could begin. Aschenbach indicated that he would like a gondola to take him and his luggage to the stopping-place of the small steamboats that ply between the city and the Lido, since he intended to stay in a hotel by the sea. His wishes were approved, his orders shouted down to water-level, where the gondoliers were quarrelling in Venetian dialect. He was still prevented from leaving the ship, held up by his trunk which at that moment was being laboriously dragged and manoeuvred down the ladder-like gangway; and thus, for a full minute or two, he could not avoid the importunate attentions of the dreadful old man, who on some obscure drunken impulse felt obliged to do this stranger the parting honours. 'We wish the signore a most enjoyable stay!' he bleated, bowing and scraping. 'We hope the signore will not forget us! Au revoir, excusez and bon jour, your Excellency!' He drooled, he screwed up his eyes, licked the corners of his mouth, and the dyed imperial on his senile underlip reared itself upward. 'Our compliments,' he drivelled, touching his lips with two fingers, 'our compliments to your sweetheart, to your most charming, beautiful sweetheart . . .' And suddenly the upper set of his false teeth dropped half out of his jaw. Aschenbach was able to escape. 'Your sweetheart, your pretty sweetheart!' he heard from behind his back, in gurgling, cavernous, encumbered tones, as he clung to the rope railing and descended the gangway.

Can there be anyone who has not had to overcome a fleeting sense of dread, a secret shudder of uneasiness, on stepping for the first time or after a long interval of years into a Venetian gondola? How strange a vehicle it is, coming down unchanged from times of old romance, and so characteristically black, the way no other thing is black except a coffin – a vehicle evoking lawless adventures in the plashing stillness of night, and still more strongly evoking death itself, the bier, the dark obsequies, the last silent journey! And has it been observed that the seat of such a boat, that armchair with its coffin-black lacquer and dull black upholstery, is the softest, the most voluptuous, most enervating seat in the world? Aschenbach became aware of this when he had settled down at the gondolier's feet, sitting opposite his luggage, which was neatly assembled at the prow. The oarsmen were still quarrelling; raucously, unintelligibly, with threatening gestures. But in the peculiar silence of this city of water their voices seemed to be softly absorbed, to become bodiless, dissipated above the sea. It was sultry here in the harbour. As the warm breath of the sirocco touched him, as he leaned back on cushions over the yielding element, the traveller closed his eyes in the enjoyment of this lassitude as sweet as it was unaccustomed. It will be a short ride, he thought; if only it could last for ever! In a gently swaying motion he felt himself gliding away from the crowd and the confusion of voices.

How still it was growing all round him! There was nothing to be heard except the plashing of the oar, the dull slap of the wave against the boat's prow where it rose up steep and black and armed at its tip like a halberd, and a third sound also: that of a voice speaking and murmuring – it was the gondolier, whispering and muttering to himself between his teeth, in intermittent grunts pressed out of him by the labour of his arms. Aschenbach looked up and noticed with some consternation that the lagoon was widening round him and that his gondola was heading out to sea. It was thus evident that he must not relax too completely, but give some attention to the proper execution of his instructions.

'Well! To the *vaporetto* stop!' he said, half turning round. The muttering ceased, but no answer came.

'I said to the *vaporetto* stop!' he repeated, turning round completely and looking up into the face of the gondolier, who was standing behind him on his raised deck, towering between him and the pale sky. He was a man of displeasing, indeed brutal appearance, wearing blue seaman's clothes, with a yellow scarf round his waist and a shapeless, already fraying straw hat tilted rakishly on his head. To judge by the cast of his face and the blond curling moustache under his snub nose, he was quite evidently not of Italian origin. Although rather slightly built, so that one would not have thought him particularly well suited to his job, he plied his oar with great energy, putting his whole body into every stroke. Occasionally the effort made him retract his lips and bare his white teeth. With his reddish eyebrows knitted, he stared right over his passenger's head as he answered peremptorily, almost insolently:

'You are going to the Lido.'

Aschenbach replied:

'Of course. But I only engaged this gondola to row me across to San Marco. I wish to take the *vaporetto*.'

'You cannot take the *vaporetto*, signore.'

'And why not?'

'Because the *vaporetto* does not carry luggage.'

That was correct, as Aschenbach now remembered. He was silent. But the man's abrupt, presumptuous manner, so uncharacteristic of the way foreigners were usually treated in this country, struck him as unacceptable. He said:

'That is my affair. I may wish to deposit my luggage. Will you kindly turn round.'

There was silence. The oar plashed, the dull slap of the water against the bow continued, and the talking and muttering began again: the gondolier was talking to himself between his teeth.

What was to be done? Alone on the sea with this strangely contumacious, uncannily resolute fellow, the traveller could see no way of compelling him to obey his instructions. And in any case, how luxurious a rest he might have here if he simply accepted the situation! Had he not wished the trip were longer, wished it to last for ever? It was wisest to let things take their course, and above all it was very agreeable to do so. A magic spell of indolence seemed to emanate from his seat, from this low black-upholstered armchair, so softly rocked by the oarstrokes of the high-handed gondolier behind him. The thought that he had perhaps fallen into the hands of a criminal floated dreamily across Aschenbach's mind – powerless to stir him to any active plan of self-defence. There was the more annoying possibility that the whole thing was simply a device for extorting money from him. A kind of pride or sense of duty, a recollection, so to speak, that there are precautions to be taken against such things, impelled him to make one further effort. He asked:

'What is your charge for the trip?'

And looking straight over his head, the gondolier answered:

'You will pay, signore.'

The prescribed retort to this was clear enough. Aschenbach answered mechanically:

'I shall pay nothing, absolutely nothing, if you take me where I do not want to go.'

'The signore wants to go to the Lido.'

'But not with you.'

'I can row you well.'

True enough, thought Aschenbach, relaxing. True enough, you will row me well. Even if you are after my cash and dispatch me to the house of Hades with a blow of your oar from behind, you will have rowed me well.

But nothing of the sort happened. He was even provided with company: a boat full of piratical musicians, men and women singing to the guitar or mandolin, importunately travelling hard alongside the gondola and for the foreigner's benefit filling the silence of the waters with mercenary song. Aschenbach threw some money into the outheld hat, whereupon they fell silent and moved off. And the gondolier's muttering became audible again, as in fits and starts he continued his self-colloquy.

And so in due course one arrived, bobbing about in the wake of a *vaporetto* bound for the city. Two police officers, with their hands on their backs, were pacing up and down the embankment and looking out over the lagoon. Aschenbach stepped from the gondola on to the gangway, assisted by the old man with a boat-hook who turns up for this purpose at every landing-stage in Venice; and having run out of small change, he walked across to the hotel opposite the pier, intending to change money and pay off the oarsman with some suitable gratuity. He was served at the hall desk, and returned to the landing-stage to find his luggage loaded on to a trolley on the embankment: the gondola and the gondolier had vanished.

'He cleared off,' said the old man with the boat-hook. 'A bad man, a man without a licence, signore. He is the only gondolier who has no licence. The others telephoned across to us. He saw the police waiting for him. So he cleared off quick.'

Aschenbach shrugged his shoulders.

'The signore has had a free trip,' said the old man, holding out his hat. Aschenbach threw coins into it. He directed that his luggage should be taken to the Hotel des Bains, and followed the trolley along the avenue, that white-blossoming avenue, bordered on either side by taverns and bazaars and guest-houses, which runs straight across the island to the beach.

He entered the spacious hotel from the garden terrace at the back, passing through the main hall and the vestibule to the reception office.

As his arrival had been notified in advance, he was received with obsequious obligingness. A manager, a soft-spoken, flatteringly courteous little man with a black moustache and a frock coat of French cut, accompanied him in the lift to the second floor and showed him to his room, an agreeable apartment with cherry-wood furniture, strongly scented flowers put out to greet him, and a view through tall windows to the open sea. He went and stood by one of them when the manager had withdrawn, and as his luggage was brought in behind him and installed in the room, he gazed out over the beach, uncrowded at this time of the afternoon, and over the sunless sea which was at high tide, its long low waves beating with a quiet regular rhythm on the shore.

The observations and encounters of a devotee of solitude and silence are at once less distinct and more penetrating than those of the sociable man; his thoughts are weightier, stranger, and never without a tinge of sadness. Images and perceptions which might otherwise be easily dispelled by a glance, a laugh, an exchange of comments, concern him unduly, they sink into mute depths, take on significance, become experiences, adventures, emotions. The fruit of solitude is originality, something daringly and disconcertingly beautiful, the poetic creation. But the fruit of solitude can also be the perverse, the disproportionate, the absurd and the forbidden. And thus the phenomena of his journey to this place, the horrible old made-up man with his maudlin babble about a sweetheart, the illicit gondolier who had been done out of his money, were still weighing on the traveller's mind. Without in any way being rationally inexplicable, without even really offering food for thought, they were nevertheless, as it seemed to him, essentially strange, and indeed it was no doubt this very paradox that made them disturbing. In the mean time he saluted the sea with his gaze and rejoiced in the knowledge that Venice was now so near and accessible. Finally he turned round, bathed his face, gave the room-maid certain instructions for the enhancement of his comfort, and then had himself conveyed by the green-uniformed Swiss lift-attendant to the ground floor.

He took tea on the front terrace, then went down to the esplanade and walked some way along it in the direction of the Hotel Excelsior. When he returned, it was already nearly time to be changing for dinner. He did so in his usual leisurely and precise manner, for it was his custom to work when performing his toilet; despite this, he arrived a little early in the foyer, where he found a considerable number of the hotel guests assembled, unacquainted with each other and affecting a studied mutual indifference, yet all united in expectancy by the prospect of their evening meal. He picked up a newspaper from the table, settled down in a leather armchair and took stock of the company, which differed very agreeably from what he had encountered at his previous hotel.

A large horizon opened up before him, tolerantly embracing many elements. Discreetly muted, the sounds of the major world languages mingled. Evening dress, that internationally accepted uniform of civilization, imparted a decent outward semblance of unity to the wide variations of mankind here represented. One saw the dry elongated visages of Americans, many-membered Russian families, English ladies, German children with French nurses. The Slav component seemed to predominate. In his immediate vicinity he could hear Polish being spoken.

It was a group of adolescent and barely adult young people, sitting round a cane table under the supervision of a governess or companion: three young girls, of fifteen to seventeen as it seemed, and a long-haired boy of perhaps fourteen. With astonishment Aschenbach noticed that the boy was entirely beautiful. His countenance, pale and gracefully reserved, was surrounded by ringlets of honey-coloured hair, and with its straight nose, its enchanting mouth, its expression of sweet and divine gravity, it recalled Greek sculpture of the noblest period; yet despite the purest formal perfection, it had such unique personal charm that he who now contemplated it felt he had never beheld, in nature or in art, anything so consummately successful. What also struck him was an obvious contrast of educational principles in the way the boy and his sisters were dressed and generally treated. The system adopted for the three girls, the eldest of whom could be considered to be grown-up, was austere and chaste to the point of disfigurement. They all wore exactly the same slate-coloured half-length dresses, sober and of a deliberately unbecoming cut, with white turnover collars as the only relieving feature, and any charm of figure they might have had was suppressed and negated from the outset by this cloistral uniform. Their hair, smoothed and stuck back firmly to their heads, gave their faces a nun-like emptiness and expressionlessness. A mother was clearly in charge here; and it had not even occurred to her to apply to the boy the same pedagogic strictness as she thought proper for the girls. In his life, softness and tenderness were evidently the rule. No one had ever dared to cut short his beautiful hair; like that of the *Boy Extracting a Thorn* it fell in curls over his forehead, over his ears, and still lower over his neck. The English sailor's suit, with its full sleeves tapering down to fit the fine wrists of his still childlike yet slender hands, and with its lanyards and bows and embroideries, enhanced his delicate shape with an air of richness and indulgence. He was sitting, in semi-profile to Aschenbach's gaze, with one foot in its patent leather shoe advanced in front of the other, with one elbow propped on the arm of his basket chair, with his cheek nestling against the closed hand, in a posture of relaxed dignity, without a trace of the almost servile stiffness to which his sisters seemed to have accustomed themselves. Was he in poor health? For his complexion was white as ivory against the dark gold of the surrounding curls. Or was he simply a pampered favourite child, borne up by the partiality of a capricious love? Aschenbach was inclined to think so. Inborn in almost every artistic nature is a luxuriant, tell-tale bias in favour of the injustice that creates beauty, a tendency to sympathize with aristocratic preference and pay it homage.

A waiter circulated and announced in English that dinner was served. Gradually the company disappeared through the glass door into the dining-room. Latecomers passed, emerging from the vestibule or the lifts. The service of dinner had already begun, but the young Poles were still waiting round their cane table, and Aschenbach, comfortably ensconced in his deep armchair, and additionally having the spectacle of beauty before his eyes, waited with them.

The governess, a corpulent and rather unladylike, red-faced little woman, finally gave the signal for them to rise. With arched brows she pushed back her chair and bowed as a tall lady, dressed in silvery grey and very richly adorned with pearls, entered the hall. This lady's attitude was cool and poised, her lightly powdered coiffure and the style of her dress both had that simplicity which is the governing principle of taste in circles where piety is regarded as one of the aristocratic values. In Germany she might have been the wife of a high official. The only thing that did give her appearance a fantastic and luxurious touch was her jewellery, which was indeed beyond price, consisting of earrings as well as a very long three-stranded necklace of gently shimmering pearls as big as cherries.

The brother and sisters had quickly risen to their feet. They bowed over their mother's hand to kiss it, while she, with a restrained smile on her well maintained but slightly weary and angular face, looked over their heads and addressed a few words in French to the governess. Then she walked towards the glass door. Her children followed her: the girls in order of age, after them the governess, finally the boy. For some reason or other he turned round before crossing the threshold, and as there was now no one else in the hall, his strangely twilight-grey eyes met those of Aschenbach, who with his paper in his lap, lost in contemplation, had been watching the group leave.

What he had seen had certainly not been remarkable in any particular. One does not go in to table before one's mother, they had waited for her, greeted her respectfully, and observed normal polite precedence in entering the dining-room. But this had all been carried out with such explicitness, with such a strongly accented air of discipline, obligation and self-respect, that Aschenbach felt strangely moved. He lingered for another few moments, then he too crossed into the dining-room and had himself shown to his table – which, as he noticed with a brief stirring of regret, was at some distance from that of the Polish family.

Tired and yet intellectually stimulated, he beguiled the long and tedious meal with abstract and indeed transcendental reflections. He meditated on the mysterious combination into which the canonical and the individual must enter for human beauty to come into being, proceeded from this point to general problems of form and art, and concluded in the end that his thoughts and findings resembled certain seemingly happy inspirations that come to us in dreams, only to be recognized by the sober senses as completely shallow and worthless. After dinner he lingered for a while, smoking and sitting and walking about, in the evening fragrance of the hotel garden, then retired early and passed the night in sleep which was sound and long, though dream images enlivened it from time to time.

Next day the weather did not seem to be improving. The wind was from landward. Under a pallid overcast sky the sea lay sluggishly still and shrunken-looking, with the horizon in prosaic proximity and the tide so far out that several rows of long sand-bars lay exposed. When Aschenbach opened his window, he thought he could smell the stagnant air of the lagoon.

Vexation overcame him. The thought of leaving occurred to him then and there. Once before, years ago, after fine spring weeks, this same weather had come on him here like a visitation, and so adversely affected his health that his departure from Venice had been like a precipitate escape. Were not the same symptoms now presenting themselves again, that unpleasant feverish sensation, the pressure in the temples, the heaviness in the eyelids? To move elsewhere yet again would be tiresome; but if the wind did not change, then there was no question of his staying here. As a precaution he did not unpack completely. At nine he breakfasted in the buffet between the hall and the main restaurant which was used for serving breakfast.

The kind of ceremonious silence prevailed here which a large hotel always aims to achieve. The serving waiters moved about noiselessly. A clink of crockery, a half-whispered word, were the only sounds audible. In one corner, obliquely opposite the door and two tables away from his own, Aschenbach noticed the Polish girls with their governess. Perched very upright, their ash-blond hair newly brushed and with reddened eyes, in stiff blue linen dresses with little white turnover collars and cuffs, they sat there passing each other a jar of preserves. They had almost finished their breakfast. The boy was missing.

Aschenbach smiled. Well, my little Phaeacian! he thought. You seem, unlike these young ladies, to enjoy the privilege of sleeping your fill. And with his spirits suddenly rising, he recited to himself the line: 'Varied garments to wear, warm baths and restful reposing.'

He breakfasted unhurriedly, received some forwarded mail from the porter who came into the breakfast-room with his braided cap in hand, and opened a few letters as he smoked a cigarette. Thus it happened that he was still present to witness the entry of the lie-abed they were waiting for across the room.

He came through the glass door and walked in the silence obliquely across the room to his sisters' table. His walk was extraordinarily graceful, in the carriage of his upper body, the motion of his knees, the placing of his white-shod foot; it was very light, both delicate and proud, and made still more beautiful by the childlike modesty with which he twice, turning his head towards the room, raised and lowered his eyes as he passed. With a smile and a murmured word in his soft liquescent language, he took his seat; and now especially, as his profile was exactly turned to the watching Aschenbach, the latter was again amazed, indeed startled, by the truly god-like beauty of this human creature. Today the boy was wearing a light casual suit of blue and white striped linen material with a red silk breast-knot, closing at the neck in a simple white stand-up collar. But on this collar – which did not even match the rest of the suit very elegantly – there, like a flower in bloom, his head was gracefully resting. It was the head of Eros, with the creamy lustre of Parian marble, the brows fine-drawn and serious, the temples and ear darkly and softly covered by the neat right-angled growth of the curling hair.

Good, good! thought Aschenbach, with that cool professional approval in which artists confronted by a masterpiece sometimes cloak their ecstasy, their rapture. And mentally he added: Truly, if the sea and the shore did not await me, I should stay here as long as you do! But as it was, he went, went through the hall accompanied by the courteous attentions of the hotel staff, went down over the wide terrace and straight along the wooden passageway to the enclosed beach reserved for hotel guests. Down there, a barefooted old man with linen trousers, sailor's jacket and straw hat functioned as bathing attendant: Aschenbach had himself conducted by him to his reserved beach cabin, had his table and chair set up on the sandy wooden platform in front of it, and made himself comfortable in the deck-chair which he had drawn further out towards the sea on to the wax-yellow sand.

The scene on the beach, the spectacle of civilization taking its carefree sensuous ease at the brink of the element, entertained and delighted him as much as ever. Already the grey, shallow sea was alive with children wading, with swimmers, with assorted figures lying on the sand-bars, their crossed arms under their heads. Others were rowing little keelless boats painted red and blue, and capsizing with shrieks of laughter. In front of the long row of *capanne*, with their platforms like little verandahs to sit on, there was animated play and leisurely sprawling repose, there was visiting and chattering, there was punctilious morning elegance as well as unabashed nakedness contentedly enjoying the liberal local conventions. Further out, on the moist firm sand, persons in white bathing-robes, in loose-fitting colourful shirt-wear, wandered to and fro. On the right, a complicated sandcastle built by children was bedecked by flags in all the national colours. Vendors of mussels, cakes and fruit knelt to display their wares. On the left, in front of one of the huts in the row that was set at right angles to the others and to the sea, forming a boundary to the beach at this end, a Russian family was encamped: men with beards and big teeth, overripe indolent women, a Baltic spinster sitting at an easel and painting the sea with exclamations of despair, two good-natured hideous children, an old nanny in a head-cloth who behaved in the caressingly deferential manner of the born serf. There they all were, gratefully enjoying their lives, tirelessly shouting the names of their disobediently romping children, mustering a few Italian words to joke at length with the amusing old man who sold them sweets, kissing each other on the cheeks and caring not a jot whether anyone was watching their scene of human solidarity.·

Well, I shall stay, thought Aschenbach. What better place could I find? And with his hands folded in his lap, he let his eyes wander in the sea's wide expanse, let his gaze glide away, dissolve and die in the monotonous haze of this desolate emptiness. There were profound reasons for his attachment to the sea: he loved it because as a hard-working artist he needed rest, needed to escape from the demanding complexity of phenomena and lie hidden on the bosom of the simple and tremendous; because of a forbidden longing deep within him that ran quite contrary to his life's task and was for that very reason seductive, a longing for the unarticulated and immeasurable, for eternity, for nothingness. To rest in the arms of perfection is the desire of any man intent upon creating excellence; and is not nothingness a form of perfection? But now, as he mused idly on such profound matters, the horizontal line of the sea-shore was suddenly intersected by a human figure, and when he had retrieved his gaze from limitless immensity and concentrated it again, he beheld the beautiful boy, coming from the left and walking past him across the sand. He walked barefoot, ready for wading, his slender legs naked to above the knees; his pace was leisured, but as light and proud as if he had long been used to going about without shoes. As he walked he looked round at the projecting row of huts: but scarcely had he noticed the Russian family, as it sat there in contented concord and going about its natural business, than a storm of angry contempt gathered over his face. He frowned darkly, his lips pouted, a bitter grimace pulled them to one side and distorted his cheek; his brows were contracted in so deep a scowl that his eyes seemed to have sunk right in under their pressure, glaring forth a black message of hatred. He looked down, looked back again menacingly, then made with one shoulder an emphatic gesture of rejection as he turned his back and left his enemies behind him.

A kind of delicacy or alarm, something like respect and embarrassment, moved Aschenbach to turn away as if he had seen nothing; for no serious person who witnesses a moment of passion by chance will wish to make any use, even privately, of what he has observed. But he was at one and the same time entertained and moved, that is to say he was filled with happiness. Such childish fanaticism, directed against so harmless a piece of good-natured living – it gave a human dimension to mute divinity, it made a statuesque masterpiece of nature, which had hitherto merely delighted the eyes, seem worthy of a profounder appreciation as well; and it placed the figure of this adolescent, remarkable already by his beauty, in a context which enabled one to take him seriously beyond his years.

With his head still averted, Aschenbach listened to the boy's voice, his high, not very strong voice, as he called out greetings to his playmates working at the sandcastle, announcing his arrival when he was still some way from them. They answered, repeatedly shouting his name or a diminutive of his name, and Aschenbach listened for this with a certain curiosity, unable to pick up anything more precise than two melodious syllables which sounded something like 'Adgio' or still oftener 'Adgiu', called out with a long u at the end. The sound pleased him, he found its euphony befitting to its object, repeated it quietly to himself and turned again with satisfaction to his letters and papers.

With his travelling writing-case on his knees, he took out his fountain pen and began to deal with this and that item of correspondence. But after no more than a quarter of an hour he felt that it was a great pity to turn his mind away like this from the present situation, this most enjoyable of all situations known to him, and to miss the experience of it for the sake of an insignificant activity. He threw his writing materials aside, he returned to the sea; and before long, his attention attracted by the youthful voices of the sandcastle builders, he turned his head comfortably to the right against the back of his chair, to investigate once more the whereabouts and doings of the excellent Adgio.

His first glance found him; the red breast-knot was unmistakable. He and some others were busy laying an old plank as a bridge across the damp moat of the sandcastle, and he was supervising this work, calling out instructions and motioning with his head. With him were about ten companions, both boys and girls, of his age and some of them younger, all chattering together in tongues, in Polish, in French and even in Balkan languages. But it was his name that was most often heard. It was obvious that he was sought after, wooed, admired. One boy in particular, a Pole like him, a sturdy youngster whom they called 'Yashu' or rather 'Jasiu', with glossy black hair and wearing a belted linen suit, seemed to be his particular vassal and friend. When the work on the sandcastle ended for the time being, they walked along the beach with their arms round each other, and the boy they called 'Jasiu' kissed his beautiful companion.

Aschenbach was tempted to shake his finger at him. 'But I counsel you, Critobulus,' he thought with a smile, 'to go travelling for a year! You will need that much time at least before you are cured.' And he then breakfasted on some large, fully ripe strawberries which he bought from a vendor. It had grown very warm, although the sun was unable to break through the sky's layer of cloud. Even as one's senses enjoyed the tremendous and dizzying spectacle of the sea's stillness, lassitude paralysed the mind. To the mature and serious Aschenbach it seemed an appropriate, fully satisfying task and occupation for him to guess or otherwise ascertain what name this could be that sounded approximately like 'Adgio'. And with the help of a few Polish recollections he established that what was meant must be 'Tadzio', the diminutive of 'Tadeusz' and changing in the vocative to 'Tadziu'.

Tadzio was bathing. Aschenbach, who had lost sight of him, identified his head and his flailing arm far out to sea; for the water was evidently still shallow a long way out. But already he seemed to be giving cause for alarm, already women's voices were calling out to him from the bathing huts, again shrieking this name which ruled the beach almost like a rallying-cry, and which with its soft consonants, its long drawn-out u-sound at the end, had both a sweetness and a wildness about it: 'Tadziu! Tadziu!' He returned, he came running, beating the resisting water to foam with his feet, his head thrown back, running through the waves. And to behold this living figure, lovely and austere in its early masculinity, with dripping locks and beautiful as a young god, approaching out of the depths of the sky and the sea, rising and escaping from the elements – this sight filled the mind with mythical images, it was like a poet's tale from a primitive age, a tale of the origins of form and of the birth of the gods. Aschenbach listened with closed eyes to this song as it began its music deep within him, and once again he reflected that it was good to be here and that here he would stay.

Later on, Tadzio lay in the sand resting from his bathe, wrapped in his white bathing-robe which he had drawn through under his right shoulder, and cradling his head on his naked arm; and even when Aschenbach was not watching him but reading a few pages of his book, he almost never forgot that the boy was lying there, and that he needed only to turn his head slightly to the right to have the admired vision again in view. It almost seemed to him that he was sitting here for the purpose of protecting the half-sleeping boy – busy with doings of his own and yet nevertheless constantly keeping watch over this noble human creature there on his right, only a little way from him. And his heart was filled and moved with a paternal fondness, the tender concern by which he who sacrifices himself to beget beauty in the spirit is drawn to him who possesses beauty.

After midday he left the beach, returned to the hotel and took the lift up to his room. Here he spent some time in front of the looking-glass studying his grey hair, his weary sharp-featured face. At that moment he thought of his fame, reflected that many people recognized him in the streets and would gaze at him respectfully, saluting the unerring and graceful power of his language – he recalled all the external successes he could think of that his talent had brought him, even calling to mind his elevation to the nobility. Then he went down to the restaurant and took lunch at his table. When he had finished and was entering the lift again, a group of young people who had also just been lunching crowded after him into the hovering cubicle, and Tadzio came with them. He stood quite near Aschenbach, so near that for the first time the latter was not seeing him as a distant image, but perceiving and taking precise cognizance of the details of his humanity. The boy was addressed by someone, and as he replied, with an indescribably charming smile, he was already leaving the lift again as it reached the first floor, stepping out backwards with downcast eyes. The beautiful are modest, thought

Aschenbach, and began to reflect very intensively on why this should be so. Nevertheless, he had noticed that Tadzio's teeth were not as attractive as they might have been: rather jagged and pale, lacking the lustre of health and having that peculiar brittle transparency which is sometimes found in cases of anaemia. 'He's very delicate, he's sickly,' thought Aschenbach, 'he'll probably not live to grow old.' And he made no attempt to explain to himself a certain feeling of satisfaction or relief that accompanied this thought.

He spent two hours in his room, and in mid-afternoon took the *vaporetto* across the stale-smelling lagoon to Venice. He got out at San Marco, took tea on the Piazza, and then, in accordance with the daily programme he had adopted for his stay here, set off on a walk through the streets. But it was this walk that brought about a complete change in his mood and intentions.

An unpleasant sultriness pervaded the narrow streets; the air was so thick that the exhalations from houses and shops and hot food stalls, the reek of oil, the smell of perfume and many other odours hung about in clouds instead of dispersing. Cigarette-smoke lingered and was slow to dissipate. The throng of people in the alleyways annoyed him as he walked instead of giving him pleasure. The further he went, the more overwhelmingly he was afflicted by that appalling condition sometimes caused by a combination of the sea air with the sirocco, a condition of simultaneous excitement and exhaustion. He began to sweat disagreeably. His eyes faltered, his chest felt constricted, he was feverish, the blood throbbed in his head. He fled from the crowded commercial thoroughfares, over bridges, into the poor quarters. There he was besieged by beggars, and the sickening stench from the canals made it difficult to breathe. In a silent square, one of those places in the depths of Venice that seem to have been forgotten and put under a spell, he rested on the edge of a fountain, wiped the sweat from his brow and realized that he would have to leave.

For the second time, and this time definitively, it had become evident that this city, in this state of the weather, was extremely injurious to him. To stay on wilfully would be contrary to good sense, the prospect of a change in the wind seemed quite uncertain. He must make up his mind at once. To return straight home was out of the question. Neither his summer nor his winter quarters were ready to receive him. But this was not the only place with the sea and a beach, and elsewhere they were to be had without the harmful additional ingredient of this lagoon with its mephitic vapours. He remembered a little coastal resort not far from Trieste which had been recommended to him. Why not go there? And he must do so without delay, if it was to be worth while changing to a different place yet again. He declared himself resolved and rose to his feet. At the next gondola stop he took a boat and had himself conveyed back to San Marco through the murky labyrinth of canals, under delicate marble balconies flanked with carved lions, round the slimy stone corners of buildings, past the mournful façades of *palazzi* on which boards bearing the names of commercial enterprises were mirrored in water where refuse bobbed up and down. He had some trouble getting to his destination, as the gondolier was in league with lace factories and glassworks and tried to land him at every place where he might view the wares and make a purchase; and whenever this bizarre journey through Venice might have cast its spell on him, he was effectively and irksomely disenchanted by the cutpurse mercantile spirit of the sunken queen of the Adriatic.

Back in the hotel, before he had even dined, he notified the office that unforeseen circumstances obliged him to leave on the following morning. Regret was expressed, his bill was settled. He took dinner and spent the warm evening reading newspapers in a rocking-chair on the back terrace. Before going to bed he packed completely for departure.

He slept fitfully, troubled by his impending further journey. When he opened his windows in the morning, the sky was still overcast, but the air seemed fresher, and – he began even now to regret his decision. Had he not given notice too impulsively, had it not been a mistake, an action prompted by a mere temporary indisposition? If only he had deferred it for a little, if only, without giving up so soon, he had taken a chance on acclimatizing himself to Venice or waiting for the wind to change, then he would now have before him not the hurry and flurry of a journey, but a morning on the beach like that of the previous day. Too late. What he had wanted yesterday he must go on wanting now. He got dressed and took the lift down to breakfast at eight o'clock.

When he entered the breakfast-room it was still empty of guests. A few came in as he was sitting waiting for what he had ordered. As he sipped his tea he saw the Polish girls arrive with their companion: strict and matutinal, with reddened eyes, they proceeded to their table in the window corner. Shortly after this the porter approached with cap in hand and reminded him that it was time to leave. The motor coach was standing ready to take him and other passengers to the Hotel Excelsior, from which point the motor-launch would convey the ladies and gentlemen through the company's private canal and across to the station. Time is pressing, signore. – In Aschenbach's opinion time was doing nothing of the sort. There was more than an hour till his train left. He found it extremely annoying that hotels should make a practice of getting their departing clients off the premises unnecessarily early, and indicated to the porter that he wished to have his breakfast in peace. The man hesitantly withdrew, only to reappear five minutes later. It was impossible, he said, for the automobile to wait any longer. Aschenbach retorted angrily that in that case it should leave, and take his trunk with it. He himself would take the public steamboat when it was time, and would they kindly leave it to him to deal with the problem of his own departure. The hotel servant bowed. Aschenbach, glad to have fended off these tiresome admonitions, finished his breakfast unhurriedly, and even got the waiter to hand him a newspaper. It was indeed getting very late by the time he rose. It so happened that at that same moment Tadzio entered through the glass door.

As he walked to his family's table his path crossed that of the departing guest. Meeting this grey-haired gentleman with the lofty brow, he modestly lowered his eyes, only to raise them again at once in his enchanting way, in a soft and full glance; and then he had passed. Goodbye, Tadzio! thought Aschenbach. How short our meeting was. And he added, actually shaping the thought with his lips and uttering it aloud to himself, as he normally never did: 'May God bless you!' – He then went through the routine of departure, distributed gratuities, received the parting courtesies of the soft-spoken little manager in the French frock coat, and left the hotel on foot as he had come, walking along the white-blossoming avenue with the hotel servant behind him carrying his hand luggage, straight across the island to the *vaporetto* landing-stage. He reached it, he took his seat on board – and what followed was a voyage of sorrow, a grievous passage that plumbed all the depths of regret.

It was the familiar trip across the lagoon, past San Marco, up the

Grand Canal. Aschenbach sat on the semicircular bench in the bows, one arm on the railing, shading his eyes with his hand. The Public Gardens fell away astern, the Piazzetta revealed itself once more in its princely elegance and was left behind, then came the great flight of the *palazzi*, with the splendid marble arch of the Rialto appearing as the waterway turned. The traveller contemplated it all, and his heart was rent with sorrow. The atmosphere of the city, this slightly mouldy smell of sea and swamp from which he had been so anxious to escape – he breathed it in now in deep, tenderly painful draughts. Was it possible that he had not known, had not considered how deeply his feelings were involved in all these things? What had been a mere qualm of compunction this morning, a slight stirring of doubt as to the wisdom of his behaviour, now became grief, became real suffering, an anguish of the soul, so bitter that several times it brought tears to his eyes, and which as he told himself he could not possibly have foreseen. What he found so hard to bear, what was indeed at times quite unendurable, was evidently the thought that he would never see Venice again, that this was a parting for ever. For since it had become clear a second time that this city made him ill, since he had been forced a second time to leave it precipitately, he must of course from now on regard it as an impossible and forbidden place to which he was not suited, and which it would be senseless to attempt to revisit. Indeed, he felt that if he left now, shame and pride must prevent him from ever setting eyes again on this beloved city which had twice physically defeated him; and this contention between his soul's desire and his physical capacities suddenly seemed to the ageing Aschenbach so grave and important, the bodily inadequacy so shameful, so necessary to overcome at all costs, that he could not understand the facile resignation with which he had decided yesterday, without any serious struggle, to tolerate that inadequacy and to acknowledge it.

In the mean time the *vaporetto* was approaching the station, and Aschenbach's distress and sense of helplessness increased to the point of distraction. In his torment he felt it to be impossible to leave and no less impossible to turn back. He entered the station torn by this acute inner conflict. It was very late, he had not a moment to lose if he was to catch his train. He both wanted to catch it and wanted to miss it. But time was pressing, lashing him on; he hurried to get his ticket, looking round in the crowded concourse for the hotel company's employee who would be on duty here. The man appeared and informed him that his large trunk had been sent off as registered baggage. Sent off already? Certainly – to Como. To Como? And from hasty comings and goings, from angry questions and embarrassed replies, it came to light that the trunk, before even leaving the luggage room in the Hotel Excelsior, had been put with some quite different baggage and dispatched to a totally incorrect address.

Aschenbach had some difficulty preserving the facial expression that would be the only comprehensible one in these circumstances. A wild joy, an unbelievable feeling of hilarity, shook him almost convulsively from the depths of his heart. The hotel employee rushed to see if it was still possible to stop the trunk, and needless to say returned without having had any success. Aschenbach accordingly declared that he was not prepared to travel without his luggage, that he had decided to go back and wait at the Hotel des Bains for the missing article to turn up again. Was the company's motor-launch still at the station? The man assured him that it was waiting immediately outside. With Italian eloquence he prevailed upon the official at the booking office to take back Aschenbach's already purchased ticket. He swore that telegrams would be sent, that nothing would be left undone and no effort spared to get the trunk back in no time at all – and thus it most strangely came about that the traveller, twenty minutes after arriving at the station, found himself on the Grand Canal again and on his way back to the Lido.

How unbelievably strange an experience it was, how shaming, how like a dream in its bizarre comedy: to be returning, by a quirk of fate, to places from which one has just taken leave for ever with the deepest sorrow – to be sent back and to be seeing them again within the hour! With spray tossing before its bows, deftly and entertainingly tacking to and fro between gondolas and *vaporetti*, the rapid little boat darted towards its destination, while its only passenger sat concealing under a mask of resigned annoyance the anxiously exuberant excitement of a truant schoolboy. From time to time he still inwardly shook with laughter at this mishap, telling himself that even a man born under a lucky star could not have had a more welcome piece of ill luck. There would be explanations to be given, surprised faces to be confronted –

and then, as he told himself, everything would be well again, a disaster would have been averted, a grievous mistake corrected, and everything he thought he had turned his back on for good would lie open again for him to enjoy, would be his for as long as he liked . . . And what was more, did the rapid movement of the motor-launch deceive him, or was there really now, to crown all else, a breeze blowing from the sea?

The bow waves dashed against the concrete walls of the narrow canal that cuts across the island to the Hotel Excelsior. There a motor omnibus was waiting for the returning guest and conveyed him along the road above the rippling sea straight to the Hotel des Bains. The little manager with the moustache and the fancily cut frock coat came down the flight of steps to welcome him.

In softly flattering tones he expressed regret for the incident, described it as highly embarrassing for himself and for the company, but emphatically endorsed Aschenbach's decision to wait here for his luggage. His room, to be sure, had been relet, but another, no less comfortable, was immediately at his disposal. *'Pas de chance, monsieur!'* said the Swiss lift-attendant as they glided up. And thus the fugitive was once more installed in a room situated and furnished almost exactly like the first.

Exhausted and numbed by the confusion of this strange morning, he had no sooner distributed the contents of his hand-luggage about the room than he collapsed into a reclining chair at the open window. The sea had turned pale green, the air seemed clearer and purer, the beach with its bathing cabins and boats more colourful, although the sky was still grey. Aschenbach gazed out, his hands folded in his lap, pleased to be here again but shaking his head with displeasure at his irresolution, his ignorance of his own wishes. Thus he sat for about an hour, resting and idly daydreaming. At midday he caught sight of Tadzio in his striped linen suit with the red breast-knot, coming from the sea, through the beach barrier and along the boarded walks back to the hotel. From up here at his window Aschenbach recognized him at once, before he had even looked at him properly, and some such thought came to him as: Why, Tadzio, there you are again too! But at the same instant he felt that casual greeting die on his lips, stricken dumb by the truth in his heart – he felt the rapturous kindling of his blood, the joy and the anguish of his soul, and realized that it was because of Tadzio that it had been so hard for him to leave.

He sat quite still, quite unseen at his high vantage-point, and began to search his feelings. His features were alert, his eyebrows rose, an attentive, intelligently inquisitive smile parted his lips. Then he raised his head, and with his arms hanging limply down along the back of his chair, described with both of them a slowly rotating and lifting motion, the palms of his hands turning forward, as if to sketch an opening and outspreading of the arms. It was a gesture that gladly bade welcome, a gesture of calm acceptance.

4

Now day after day the god with the burning cheeks soared naked, driving his four fire-breathing steeds through the spaces of heaven, and now, too, his yellow-gold locks fluttered wide in the outstorming east wind. Silk-white radiance gleamed on the slow-swelling deep's vast waters. The sand glowed. Under the silvery quivering blue of the ether, rust-coloured awnings were spread out in front of the beach cabins, and one spent the morning hours on the sharply defined patch of shade they provided. But exquisite, too, was the evening, when the plants in the park gave off a balmy fragrance, and the stars on high moved through their dance, and the softly audible murmur of the night-surrounded sea worked its magic on the soul. Such an evening carried with it the delightful promise of a new sunlit day of leisure easily ordered, and adorned with countless close-knit possibilities of charming chance encounter.

The guest whom so convenient a mishap had detained here was very far from seeing the recovery of his property as a reason for yet another departure. For a couple of days he had had to put up with some privations and appear in the main dining-room in his travelling clothes. Then, when finally the errant load was once more set down in his room, he unpacked completely and filled the cupboards and drawers with his possessions, resolving for the present to set no time-limit on his stay; he was glad now to be able to pass his hours on the beach in a tussore suit and to present himself again in seemly evening attire at the dinner-table.

The lulling rhythm of this existence had already cast its spell on him;

he had been quickly enchanted by the indulgent softness and splendour of this way of life. What a place this was indeed, combining the charms of a cultivated seaside resort in the south with the familiar ever-ready proximity of the strange and wonderful city! Aschenbach did not enjoy enjoying himself. Whenever and wherever he had to stop work, have a breathing-space, take things easily, he would soon find himself driven by restlessness and dissatisfaction – and this had been so in his youth above all – back to his lofty travail, to his stern and sacred daily routine. Only this place bewitched him, relaxed his will, gave him happiness. Often in the forenoon, under the awning of his hut, gazing dreamily at the blue of the southern sea, or on a mild night perhaps, reclining under a star-strewn sky on the cushions of a gondola that carried him back to the Lido from the Piazza where he had long lingered – and as the bright lights, the melting sounds of the serenade dropped away behind him – often he recalled his country house in the mountains, the scene of his summer labours, where the low clouds would drift through his garden, violent evening thunderstorms would put out all the lights, and the ravens he fed would take refuge in the tops of the pine trees. Then indeed he would feel he had been snatched away now to the Elysian land, to the ends of the earth, where lightest of living is granted to mortals, where no snow is nor winter, no storms and no rain down-streaming, but where Oceanus ever causes a gentle cooling breeze to ascend, and the days flow past in blessed idleness, with no labour or strife, for to the sun alone and its feasts they are all given over.

Aschenbach saw much of the boy Tadzio, he saw him almost constantly; in a confined environment, with a common daily pro-gramme, it was natural for the beautiful creature to be near him all day, with only brief interruptions. He saw him and met him everywhere: in the ground-floor rooms of the hotel, on their cooling journeys by water to the city and back, in the sumptuous Piazza itself, and often elsewhere from time to time, in alleys and byways, when chance had played a part. But it was during the mornings on the beach above all, and with the happiest regularity, that he could devote hours at a time to the contemplation and study of this exquisite phenomenon. Indeed, it was precisely this ordered routine of happiness, this equal daily repetition of favourable circumstances, that so filled him with contentment and zest for life, that made this place so precious to him, that allowed one sunlit day to follow another in such obligingly endless succession.

He rose early, as he would normally have done under the insistent compulsion of work, and was down at the beach before most of the other guests, when the sun's heat was still gentle and the sea lay dazzling white in its morning dreams. He greeted the barrier attendant affably, exchanged familiar greetings also with the barefooted, white-bearded old man who had prepared his place for him, spread the brown awning and shifted the cabin furniture out to the platform where Aschenbach would settle down. Three hours or four were then his, hours in which the sun would rise to its zenith and to terrible power, hours in which the sea would turn a deeper and deeper blue, hours in which he might watch Tadzio.

He saw him coming, walking along from the left by the water's edge, saw him from behind as he emerged between the cabins, or indeed would sometimes look up and discover, gladdened and startled, that he had missed his arrival and that the boy was already there, already in the blue and white bathing costume which now on the beach was his sole attire. There he would be, already busy with his customary activities in the sun and the sand – this charmingly trivial, idle yet ever-active life that was both play and repose, a life of sauntering, wading, digging, snatching, lying about and swimming, under the watchful eyes and at the constant call of the women on their platform, who with their high-pitched voices would cry out his name: 'Tadziu! Tadziu!' and to whom he would come running with eager gesticulation, to tell them what he had experienced, to show them what he had found, what he had caught: jellyfish, little sea-horses, and mussels, and crabs that go sideways. Aschenbach understood not a word of what he said, and commonplace though it might be, it was liquid melody in his ears. Thus the foreign sound of the boy's speech exalted it to music, the sun in its triumph shed lavish brightness all over him, and the sublime perspective of the sea was the constant contrasting background against which he appeared.

Soon the contemplative beholder knew every line and pose of that noble, so freely displayed body, he saluted again with joy each already familiar perfection, and there was no end to his wonder, to the delicate delight of his senses. The boy would be summoned to greet a guest who was making a polite call on the ladies in their cabin; he would run up, still wet perhaps from the sea, throw back his curls, and as he held out his hand, poised on one leg with the other on tiptoe, he had an enchanting way of turning and twisting his body, gracefully expectant, charmingly shamefaced, seeking to please because good breeding required him to do so. Or he would be lying full-length, his bathing-robe wrapped round his chest, his finely chiselled arm propped on the sand, his hand cupping his chin; the boy they called 'Jasiu' would squat beside him caressing him, and nothing could be more bewitching than the way the favoured Tadzio, smiling with his eyes and lips, would look up at this lesser and servile mortal. Or he would be standing at the edge of the sea, alone, some way from his family, quite near Aschenbach, standing upright with his hands clasped behind his neck, slowly rocking to and fro on the balls of his feet and dreamily gazing into the blue distance, while little waves ran up and bathed his toes. His honey-coloured hair nestled in ringlets at his temples and at the back of his neck, the sun gleamed in the down on his upper spine, the subtle outlining of his ribs and the symmetry of his breast stood out through the scanty covering of his torso, his armpits were still as smooth as those of a statue, the hollows of his knees glistened and their bluish veins made his body seem composed of some more translucent material. What discipline, what precision of thought was expressed in that outstretched, youthfully perfect physique! And yet the austere pure will that had here been darkly active, that had succeeded in bringing this divine sculptured shape to light – was it not well known and familiar to Aschenbach as an artist? Was it not also active in him, in the sober passion that filled him as he set free from the marble mass of language that slender form he had beheld in the spirit, and which he was presenting to mankind as a mirror and sculptured image of intellectual beauty?

A mirror and sculptured image! His eyes embraced that noble figure at the blue water's edge, and in rising ecstasy he felt he was gazing on Beauty itself, on Form as a thought of God, on the one and pure perfection that dwells in the spirit and of which a human similitude and likeness had here been lightly and graciously set up for him to worship. Such was his emotional intoxication; and the ageing artist welcomed it unhesitatingly, even greedily. His mind was in labour, its store of culture was in ferment, his memory threw up thoughts from ancient tradition which he had been taught as a boy, but which had never yet come alive in his own fire. Had he not read that the sun turns our attention from spiritual things to the things of the senses? He had read that it so numbs and bewitches our intelligence and memory that the soul, in its joy, quite forgets its proper state and clings with astonished admiration to that most beautiful of all the things the sun shines upon: yes, that only with the help of a bodily form is the soul then still able to exalt itself to a higher vision. That Cupid, indeed, does as mathematicians do, when they show dull-witted children tangible images of the pure Forms: so too the Love-god, in order to make spiritual things visible, loves to use the shapes and colours of young men, turning them into instruments of Recollection by adorning them with all the reflected splendour of Beauty, so that the sight of them truly sets us on fire with pain and hope.

Such were the thoughts the god inspired in his enthusiast, such were the emotions of which he grew capable. And a delightful vision came to him, spun from the sea's murmur and the glittering sunlight. It was the old plane tree not far from the walls of Athens – that place of sacred shade, fragrant with chaste-tree blossoms, adorned with votive statues and pious gifts in honour of the nymphs and of Acheloüs. The stream trickled crystal-clear over smooth pebbles at the foot of the great spreading tree; the crickets made their music. But on the grass, which sloped down gently so that one could hold up one's head as one lay, there reclined two men, sheltered here from the heat of the noonday: one elderly and one young, one ugly and one beautiful, the wise beside the desirable. And Socrates, wooing him with witty compliments and jests, was instructing Phaedrus on desire and virtue. He spoke to him of the burning tremor of fear which the lover will suffer when his eye perceives a likeness of eternal Beauty; spoke to him of the lusts of the profane and base who cannot turn their eyes to Beauty when they behold its image and are not capable of reverence; spoke of the sacred terror that visits the noble soul when a god-like countenance, a perfect body appears to him – of how he trembles then and is beside himself and hardly dares look at the possessor of beauty, and reveres him and would even sacrifice to him as to a graven image, if he did not fear to seem foolish in the eyes of men. For Beauty, dear Phaedrus, only Beauty is at one and the same time divinely desirable and visible: it is, mark well, the only form of the spiritual that we can receive with our senses and endure with our senses. For what would become of us if other divine things, if Reason and Virtue and Truth were to appear to us sensuously? Should we not perish in a conflagration of love, as once upon a time Semele did before Zeus? Thus Beauty is the lover's path to the spirit – only the path, only a means, little Phaedrus . . . And then he uttered the subtlest thing of all, that sly wooer: he who loves, he said, is more divine than the beloved, because the god is in the former, but not in the latter – this, the tenderest perhaps and the most mocking thought ever formulated, a thought alive with all the mischievousness and most secret voluptuousness of the heart.

The writer's joy is the thought that can become emotion, the emotion that can wholly become a thought. At that time the solitary Aschenbach took possession and control of just such a pulsating thought, just such a precise emotion: namely, that Nature trembles with rapture when the spirit bows in homage before Beauty. He suddenly desired to write. Eros indeed, we are told, loves idleness and is born only for the idle. But at this point of Aschenbach's crisis and visitation his excitement was driving him to produce. The occasion was almost a matter of indifference. An inquiry, an invitation to express a personal opinion on a certain important cultural problem, a burning question of taste, had been circulated to the intellectual world and had been forwarded to him on his travels. The theme was familiar to him, it was close to his experience; the desire to illuminate it in his own words was suddenly irresistible. And what he craved, indeed, was to work on it in Tadzio's presence, to take the boy's physique for a model as he wrote, to let his style follow the lineaments of this body which he saw as divine, and to carry its beauty on high into the spiritual world, as the eagle once carried the Trojan shepherd boy up into the ether. Never had he felt the joy of the word more sweetly, never had he known so clearly that Eros dwells in language, as during those perilously precious hours in which, seated at his rough table under the awning, in full view of his idol and with the music of his voice in his ears, he shaped upon Tadzio's beauty his brief essay – that page and a half of exquisite prose which with its limpid nobility and vibrant controlled passion was soon to win the admiration of many. It is as well that the world knows only a fine piece of work and not also its origins, the conditions under which it came into being; for knowledge of the sources of an artist's inspiration would often confuse readers and shock them, and the excellence of the writing would be of no avail. How strange those hours were! How strangely exhausting that labour! How mysterious this act of intercourse and begetting between a mind and a body! When Aschenbach put away his work and left the beach, he felt worn out, even broken, and his conscience seemed to be reproaching him as if after some kind of debauch.

On the following morning, just as he was leaving the hotel, he noticed from the steps that Tadzio, already on his way to the sea – and alone – was just approaching the beach barrier. The wish to use this opportunity, the mere thought of doing so, and thereby lightly, light-heartedly, making the acquaintance of one who had unknowingly so exalted and moved him: the thought of speaking to him, of enjoying his answer and his glance – all this seemed natural, it was the irresistibly obvious thing to do. The beautiful boy was walking in a leisurely fashion, he could be overtaken, and Aschenbach quickened his pace. He reached him on the boarded way behind the bathing cabins, he was just about to lay his hand on his head or his shoulder, and some phrase or other, some friendly words in French were on the tip of his tongue – when he felt his heart, perhaps partly because he had been walking fast, hammering wildly inside him, felt so breathless that he would only have been able to speak in a strangled and trembling voice. He hesitated, struggled to control himself, then was suddenly afraid that he had already been walking too long close behind the beautiful boy, afraid that Tadzio would notice this, that he would turn and look at him questioningly; he made one more attempt, failed, gave up, and hurried past with his head bowed.

Too late! he thought at that moment. Too late! But was it too late? This step he had failed to take would very possibly have been all to the good, it might have had a lightening and gladdening effect, led perhaps to a wholesome disenchantment. But the fact now seemed to be that the ageing lover no longer wished to be disenchanted, that the intoxication was too precious to him. Who shall unravel the mystery of an artist's nature and character! Who shall explain the profound instinctual fusion of discipline and licence on which it rests! For not to be able to desire wholesome disenchantment is to be licentious. Aschenbach was no longer disposed to self-criticism; taste, the intellectual mould of his years, self-respect, maturity and late simplicity all disinclined him to analyse his motives and decide whether what had prevented him from carrying out his intention had been a prompting of conscience or a disreputable weakness. He was confused, he was afraid that someone, even if only the bathing attendant, might have witnessed his haste and his defeat; he was very much afraid of exposure to ridicule. For the rest, he could not help inwardly smiling at his comic-sacred terror. 'Crestfallen,' he thought, 'spirits dashed, like a frightened cock hanging its wings in a fight! Truly this is the god who at the sight of the desired beauty so breaks our courage and dashes our pride so utterly to the ground . . .' He toyed with the theme, gave rein to his enthusiasm, plunged into emotions he was too proud to fear.

He was no longer keeping any tally of the leisure time he had allowed himself; the thought of returning home did not even occur to him. He had arranged for ample funds to be made available to him here. His one anxiety was that the Polish family might leave; but he had surreptitiously learned, by a casual question to the hotel barber, that these guests had begun their stay here only very shortly before his own arrival. The sun was browning his face and hands, the stimulating salty breeze heightened his capacity for feeling, and whereas formerly, when sleep or food or contact with nature had given him any refreshment, he would always have expended it completely on his writing, he now, with high-hearted prodigality, allowed all the daily revitalization he was receiving from the sun and leisure and sea air to burn itself up in intoxicating emotion.

He slept fleetingly; the days of precious monotony were punctuated by brief, happily restless nights. To be sure, he would retire early, for at nine o'clock, when Tadzio had disappeared from the scene, he judged his day to be over. But at the first glint of dawn a pang of tenderness would startle him awake, his heart would remember its adventure, he could bear his pillows no longer, he would get up, and lightly wrapped against the early-morning chill he would sit down at the open window to wait for the sunrise. His soul, still fresh with the solemnity of sleep, was filled with awe by this wonderful event. The sky, the earth and the sea still wore the glassy paleness of ghostly twilight; a dying star still floated in the void. But a murmur came, a winged message from dwelling-places no mortal may approach, that Eos was rising from her husband's side; and now it appeared, that first sweet blush at the furthest horizon of the sky and sea, which heralds the sensuous disclosure of creation. The goddess approached, that ravisher of youth, who carried off Cleitus and

Cephalus and defied the envy of all the Olympians to enjoy the love of the beautiful Orion. A scattering of roses began, there at the edge of the world, an ineffably lovely shining and blossoming; childlike clouds, transfigured and transparent with light, hovered like serving *amoretti* in the vermilion and violet haze; crimson light fell across the waves, which seemed to be washing it landwards; golden spears darted from below into the heights of heaven, the gleam became a conflagration, noiselessly and with overwhelming divine power the glow and the fire and the blazing flames reared upwards, and the sacred steeds of the goddess's brother Helios, tucking their hooves, leapt above the earth's round surface. With the splendour of the god irradiating him, the lone watcher sat; he closed his eyes and let the glory kiss his eyelids. Feelings he had had long ago, early and precious dolours of the heart, which had died out in his life's austere service and were now, so strangely transformed, returning to him – he recognized them with a confused and astonished smile. He meditated, he dreamed, slowly a name shaped itself on his lips, and still smiling, with upturned face, his hands folded in his lap, he fell asleep in his chair once more.

With such fiery ceremony the day began, but the rest of it, too, was strangely exalted and mythically transformed. Where did it come from, what was its origin, this sudden breeze that played so gently and speakingly around his temples and ears, like some higher insufflation? Innumerable white fleecy clouds covered the sky, like the grazing flocks of the gods. A stronger wind rose, and the horses of Poseidon reared and ran; his bulls too, the bulls of the blue-haired sea-god, roared and charged with lowered horns. But among the rocks and stones of the more distant beach the waves danced like leaping goats. A sacred deranged world, full of Panic life, enclosed the enchanted watcher, and his heart dreamed tender tales. Sometimes, as the sun was sinking behind Venice, he would sit on a bench in the hotel park to watch Tadzio, dressed in white with a colourful sash, at play on the rolled-gravel tennis court; and in his mind's eye he was watching Hyacinthus, doomed to perish because two gods loved him. He could even feel Zephyr's grievous envy of his rival, who had forgotten his oracle and his bow and his zither to be forever playing with the beautiful youth; he saw the discus, steered by cruel jealousy, strike the lovely head; he himself, turning pale too, caught the broken body in his arms, and the flower that sprang from that sweet blood bore the inscription of his undying lament.

Nothing is stranger, more delicate, than the relationship between people who know each other only by sight – who encounter and observe each other daily, even hourly, and yet are compelled by the constraint of convention or by their own temperament to keep up the pretence of being indifferent strangers, neither greeting nor speaking to each other. Between them is uneasiness and overstimulated curiosity, the nervous excitement of an unsatisfied, unnaturally suppressed need to know and to communicate; and above all, too, a kind of strained respect. For man loves and respects his fellow man for as long as he is not yet in a position to evaluate him, and desire is born of defective knowledge.

It was inevitable that some kind of relationship and acquaintance should develop between Aschenbach and the young Tadzio, and with a surge of joy the older man became aware that his interest and attention were not wholly unreciprocated. Why, for example, when the beautiful creature appeared in the morning on the beach, did he now never use the boarded walk behind the bathing cabins, but always take the front way, through the sand, passing Aschenbach's abode and often passing unnecessarily close to him, almost touching his table or his chair, as he sauntered towards the cabin where his family sat? Was this the attraction, the fascination exercised by a superior feeling on its tender and thoughtless object? Aschenbach waited daily for Tadzio to make his appearance and sometimes pretended to be busy when he did so, letting the boy pass him seemingly unnoticed. But sometimes, too, he would look up, and their eyes would meet. They would both be deeply serious when this happened. In the cultured and dignified countenance of the older man, nothing betrayed an inner emotion; but in Tadzio's eyes there was an inquiry, a thoughtful questioning, his walk became hesitant, he looked at the ground, looked sweetly up again, and when he had passed, something in his bearing seemed to suggest that only good breeding restrained him from turning to look back.

But once, one evening, it was different. The Poles and their governess had been absent from dinner in the main restaurant – Aschenbach had noticed this with concern. After dinner, very uneasy about where they might be, he was walking in evening dress and a straw hat in front of the hotel, at the foot of the terrace, when suddenly he saw the nun-like sisters appearing with their companion, in the light of the arc-lamps, and four paces behind them was Tadzio. Obviously they had come from the *vaporetto* pier, having for some reason dined in the city. The crossing had been chilly perhaps; Tadzio was wearing a dark blue reefer jacket with gold buttons and a naval cap to match. The sun and sea air never burned his skin, it was marble-pale as always; but today he seemed paler than usual, either because of the cool weather or in the blanching moonlight of the lamps. His symmetrical eyebrows stood out more sharply, his eyes seemed much darker. He was more beautiful than words can express, and Aschenbach felt, as so often already, the painful awareness that language can only praise sensuous beauty, but not reproduce it.

He had not been prepared for the beloved encounter, it came unexpectedly, he had not had time to put on an expression of calm and dignity. Joy no doubt, surprise, admiration, were openly displayed on his face when his eyes met those of the returning absentee – and in that instant it happened that Tadzio smiled: smiled at him, speakingly, familiarly, enchantingly and quite unabashed, with his lips parting slowly as the smile was formed. It was the smile of Narcissus as he bows his head over the mirroring water, that profound, fascinated, protracted smile with which he reaches out his arms towards the reflection of his own beauty – a very slightly contorted smile, contorted by the hopelessness of his attempt to kiss the sweet lips of his shadow; a smile that was provocative, curious and imperceptibly troubled, bewitched and bewitching.

He who had received this smile carried it quickly away with him like a fateful gift. He was so deeply shaken that he was forced to flee the lighted terrace and the front garden and hurry into the darkness of the park at the rear. Words struggled from his lips, strangely indignant and tender reproaches: 'You mustn't smile like that! One mustn't, do you hear, mustn't smile like that at anyone!' He sank down on one of the seats, deliriously breathing the nocturnal fragrance of the flowers and trees. And leaning back, his arms hanging down, overwhelmed, trembling, shuddering all over, he whispered the standing formula of the heart's desire – impossible here, absurd, depraved, ludicrous and sacred nevertheless, still worthy of honour even here: 'I love you!'

5

During the fourth week of his stay at the Lido Gustav von Aschenbach began to notice certain uncanny developments in the outside world. In the first place it struck him that as the height of the season approached, the number of guests at his hotel was diminishing rather than increasing, and in particular that the German language seemed to be dying away into silence all round him, so that in the end only foreign sounds fell on his ear at table and on the beach. Then one day the hotel barber, whom he visited frequently now, let slip in conversation a remark that aroused his suspicions. The man had mentioned a German family who had just left after only a brief stay, and in his chattering, flattering manner he added: 'But you are staying on, signore; you are not afraid of the sickness.' Aschenbach looked at him. 'The sickness?' he repeated. The fellow stopped his talk, pretended to be busy, had not heard the question. And when it was put to him again more sharply, he declared that he knew nothing and tried with embarrassed loquacity to change the subject.

That was at midday. In the afternoon, with the sea dead calm and the sun burning, Aschenbach crossed to Venice, for he was now driven by a mad compulsion to follow the Polish boy and his sisters, having seen them set off towards the pier with their companion. He did not find his idol at San Marco. But at tea, sitting at his round wrought-iron table on the shady side of the Piazza, he suddenly scented in the air a peculiar aroma, one which it now seemed to him he had been noticing for days without really being conscious of it – a sweetish, medicinal smell that suggested squalor and wounds and suspect cleanliness. He scrutinized it, pondered and identified it, finished his tea and left the Piazza at the far end opposite the basilica. In the narrow streets the smell was stronger. At corners, printed notices had been pasted up in which the civic authorities, with fatherly concern, gave warning to the local population that since certain ailments of the gastric system were normal in this weather, they should refrain from eating oysters and mussels and indeed from using water from the canals. The euphemistic character of the announcement was obvious. Groups of people were standing about silently on bridges or in squares, and the stranger stood among them, brooding and scenting the truth.

He found a shopkeeper leaning against his vaulted doorway, surrounded by coral necklaces and trinkets made of imitation amethyst, and asked him about the unpleasant smell. The man looked him over with heavy eyes, and hastily gathered his wits. 'A precautionary measure, signore,' he answered, gesticulating. 'The police have laid down regulations, and quite right too, it must be said. This weather is oppressive, the sirocco is not very wholesome. In short, the signore will understand – an exaggerated precaution no doubt . . .' Aschenbach thanked him and walked on. Even on the *vaporetto* taking him back to the Lido he now noticed the smell of the bactericide.

Back at the hotel, he went at once to the table in the hall where the newspapers were kept, and carried out some research. In the foreign papers he found nothing. Those in his own language mentioned rumours, quoted contradictory statistics, reported official denials and questioned their veracity. This explained the withdrawal of the German and Austrian clientele. Visitors of other nationalities evidently knew nothing, suspected nothing, still had no apprehensions. 'They want it kept quiet!' thought Aschenbach in some agitation, throwing the newspapers back on the table. 'They're hushing this up!' But at the same time his heart filled with elation at the thought of the adventure in which the outside world was about to be involved. For to passion, as to crime, the assured everyday order and stability of things is not opportune, and any weakening of the civil structure, any chaos and disaster afflicting the world, must be welcome to it, as offering a vague hope of turning such circumstances to its advantage. Thus Aschenbach felt an obscure sense of satisfaction at what was going on in the dirty alleyways of Venice, cloaked in official secrecy – this guilty secret of the city, which merged with his own innermost secret and which it was also so much in his own interests to protect. For in his enamoured state his one anxiety was that Tadzio might leave, and he realized with a kind of horror that he would not be able to go on living if that were to happen.

Lately he had not been content to owe the sight and proximity of the beautiful boy merely) to daily routine and chance: he had begun pursuing him, following him obtrusively. On Sunday, for example, the Poles never appeared on the beach; he rightly guessed that they were attending mass in San Marco, and hastened to the church himself. There, stepping from the fiery heat of the Piazza into the golden twilight of the sanctuary, he would find him whom he had missed, bowed over a prie-dieu and performing his devotions. Then he would stand in the background, on the cracked mosaic floor, amid a throng of people kneeling, murmuring and crossing themselves, and the massive magnificence of the oriental temple would weigh sumptuously on his senses. At the front, the ornately vested priest walked to and fro, doing his business and chanting. Incense billowed up, clouding the feeble flames of the altar candles, and with its heavy, sweet sacrificial odour another seemed to mingle: the smell of the sick city. But through the vaporous dimness and the flickering lights Aschenbach saw the boy, up there at the front, turn his head and seek him with his eyes until he found him.

Then, when the great doors were opened and the crowd streamed out into the shining Piazza swarming with pigeons, the beguiled lover would hide in the antebasilica, he would lurk and lie in wait. He would see the Poles leave the church, see the brother and sisters take ceremonious leave of their mother, who would then set off home, turning towards the Piazzetta; he would observe the boy, the cloistral sisters and the governess turn right and walk through the clock-tower gateway into the Merceria, and after letting them get a little way ahead he would follow them – follow them furtively on their walk through Venice. He had to stop when they lingered, had to take refuge in hot food stalls and courtyards to let them pass when they turned round; he would lose them, search for them frantically and exhaustingly, rushing over bridges and along filthy culs-de-sac, and would then have to endure minutes of mortal embarrassment when he suddenly saw them coming towards him in a narrow passageway where no escape was possible. And yet one cannot say that he suffered. His head and his heart were drunk, and his steps followed the dictates of that dark god whose pleasure it is to trample man's reason and dignity underfoot.

Presently, somewhere or other, Tadzio and his family would take a gondola, and while they were getting into it Aschenbach, hiding behind a fountain or the projecting part of a building, would wait till they were a little way from the shore and then do the same. Speaking hurriedly and in an undertone, he would instruct the oarsman, promising him a large tip, to follow that gondola ahead of them that was just turning the corner, to follow it at a discreet distance; and a shiver would run down his spine when the fellow, with the roguish compliance of a pander, would answer him in the same tone, assuring him that he was at his service, entirely at his service.

Thus he glided and swayed gently along, reclining on soft black cushions, shadowing that other black, beaked craft, chained to its pursuit by his infatuation. Sometimes he would lose sight of it and become distressed and anxious, but his steersman, who seemed to be well practised in commissions of this kind, would always know some cunning manoeuvre, some side-canal or short cut that would again bring Aschenbach in sight of what he craved. The air was stagnant and malodorous, the sun burned oppressively through the haze that had turned the sky to the colour of slate. Water lapped against wood and stone. The gondolier's call, half warning and half greeting, was answered from a distance out of the silent labyrinth, in accordance with some strange convention. Out of little overhead gardens umbelliferous blossoms spilled over and hung down the crumbling masonry, white and purple and almond-scented. Moorish windows were mirrored in the murky water. The marble steps of a church dipped below the surface; a beggar squatted on them, protesting his misery, holding out his hat and showing the whites of his eyes as if he were blind; an antique dealer beckoned to them with crawling obsequiousness as they passed his den, inviting them to stop and be swindled. This was Venice, the flattering and suspect beauty – this city, half fairy-tale and half tourist trap, in whose insalubrious air the arts once rankly and voluptuously blossomed, where composers have been inspired to lulling tones of somniferous eroticism. Gripped by his adventure, the traveller felt his eyes drinking in this sumptuousness, his ears wooed by these melodies; he remembered, too, that the city was stricken with sickness and concealing it for reasons of cupidity, and he peered around still more wildly in search of the gondola that hovered ahead.

So it was that in his state of distraction he could no longer think of anything or want anything except this ceaseless pursuit of the object that so inflamed him: nothing but to follow him, to dream of him when he was not there, and after the fashion of lovers to address tender words to his mere shadow. Solitariness, the foreign environment, and the joy of an intoxication of feeling that had come to him so late and affected him so profoundly – all this encouraged and persuaded him to indulge himself in the most astonishing ways: as when it had happened that late one evening, returning from Venice and reaching the first floor of the hotel, he had paused outside the boy's bedroom door, leaning his head against the door-frame in a complete drunken ecstasy, and had for a long time been unable to move from the spot, at the risk of being surprised and discovered in this insane situation.

Nevertheless, there were moments at which he paused and half came to his senses. Where is this leading me! he would reflect in consternation at such moments. Where was it leading him! Like any man whose natural merits move him to take an aristocratic interest in his origins, Aschenbach habitually let the achievements and successes of his life remind him of his ancestors, for in imagination he could then feel sure of their approval, of their satisfaction, of the respect they could not have withheld. And he thought of them even here and now, entangled as he was in so impermissible an experience, involved in such exotic extravagances of feeling; he thought, with a sad smile, of their dignified austerity, their decent manliness of character. What would they say? But for that matter, what would they have said about his entire life, a life that had deviated from theirs to the point of degeneracy, this life of his in the compulsive service of art, this life about which he himself, adopting the civic values of his forefathers, had once let fall such mocking observations – and which nevertheless had essentially been so much like theirs! He too had served, he too had been a soldier and a warrior, like many of them: for art was a war, an exhausting struggle, it was hard these days to remain fit for it for long. A life of self-conquest and defiant resolve, an astringent, steadfast and frugal life which he had turned into the symbol of that heroism for delicate constitutions, that heroism so much in keeping with the times – surely he might call this manly, might call it courageous? And it seemed to him that the kind of love that had taken possession of him did, in a certain way, suit and befit such a life. Had it not been highly honoured by the most valiant of peoples, indeed had he not read that in their cities it had flourished by inspiring valorous deeds? Numerous warrior-heroes of olden times had willingly borne its yoke, for there was no kind of abasement that could be reckoned as such if the god had imposed it; and actions that would have been castigated as signs of cowardice had their motives been different, such as falling to the ground in supplication, desperate pleas and slavish demeanour – these were accounted no disgrace to a lover, but rather won him still greater praise.

Such were the thoughts with which love beguiled him, and thus he sought to sustain himself, to preserve his dignity. But at the same time he kept turning his attention, inquisitively and persistently, to the disreputable events that were evolving in the depths of Venice, to that adventure of the outside world which darkly mingled with the adventure of his heart, and which nourished his passion with vague and lawless hopes. Obstinately determined to obtain new and reliable information about the status and progress of the malady, he would sit in the city's coffee-houses searching through the German newspapers, which several days ago had disappeared from the reading desk in the hotel foyer. They carried assertions and retractions by turns. The number of cases, the number of deaths, was said to be twenty, or forty, or a hundred and more, such reports being immediately followed by statements flatly denying the outbreak of an epidemic, or at least reducing it to a few quite isolated cases brought in from outside the city. Scattered here and there were warning admonitions, or protests against the dangerous policy being pursued by the Italian authorities. There was no certainty to be had.

The solitary traveller was nevertheless conscious of having a special claim to participation in this secret, and although excluded from it, he took a perverse pleasure in putting embarrassing questions to those in possession of the facts, and thus, since they were pledged to silence, forcing them to lie to him directly. One day, at luncheon in the main dining-room, he interrogated the hotel manager in this fashion, the soft-footed little man in the French frock coat who was moving around among the tables supervising the meal and greeting the clients, and who also stopped at Aschenbach's table for a few words of converstion. Why, in fact, asked his guest in a casual and nonchalant way, why on earth had they begun recently to disinfect Venice? – 'It is merely a police measure, sir,' answered the trickster, 'taken in good time, as a safeguard against various disagreeable public health problems that might otherwise arise from this sultry and exceptionally warm weather – a precautionary measure which it is their duty to take.' – 'Very praiseworthy of the police,' replied Aschenbach; and after exchanging a few meteorological observations with him the manager took his leave.

On the very same day, in the evening after dinner, it happened that a small group of street singers from the city gave a performance in the front garden of the hotel. They stood by one of the iron arc-lamp standards, two men and two women, their faces glinting white in the glare, looking up at the spacious terrace where the hotel guests sat over their coffee and cooling drinks, resigned to watching this exhibition of folk culture. The hotel staff, the lift-boys, waiters, office employees, had come out to listen in the hall doorways. The Russian family, eager to savour every pleasure, had had cane chairs put out for them down in the garden in order to be nearer the performers and were contentedly sitting there in a semicircle. Behind her master and mistress, in a turban like head cloth, stood their aged serf.

The beggar virtuosi were playing a mandolin, a guitar, a harmonica and a squeaking fiddle. Instrumental developments alternated with vocal numbers, as when the younger of the women, shrill and squawky of voice, joined the tenor with his sweet falsetto notes in an ardent love duet. But the real talent and leader of the ensemble was quite evidently the other man, the one who had the guitar and was a kind of buffo-baritone in character, with hardly any voice but with a mimic gift and remarkable comic verve. Often he would detach himself from the rest of the group and come forward, playing his large instrument and gesticulating, towards the terrace, where his pranks were rewarded with encouraging laughter. The Russians in their parterre seats took special delight in all this southern vivacity, and their plaudits and admiring shouts led him on to ever further and bolder extravagances.

Aschenbach sat by the balustrade, cooling his lips from time to time with the mixture of pomegranate juice and soda water that sparkled ruby-red in the glass before him. His nervous system greedily drank in the jangling tones, for passion paralyses discrimination and responds in all seriousness to stimuli which the sober senses would either treat with humorous tolerance or impatiently reject. The antics of the mountebank had distorted his features into a rictus-like smile which he was already finding painful. He sat on with a casual air, but inwardly he was utterly engrossed; for six paces from him Tadzio was leaning against the stone parapet.

There he stood, in the white, belted suit he occasionally put on for dinner, in a posture of innate and inevitable grace, his left forearm on the parapet, his feet crossed, his right hand on the supporting hip: and he looked down at the entertainers with an expression that was scarcely a smile, merely one of remote curiosity, a polite observation of the spectacle. Sometimes he straightened himself, stretching his chest, and with an elegant movement of both arms drew his white tunic down through his leather belt. But sometimes, too, and the older man noticed it with a mind-dizzying sense of triumph as well as with terror, he would turn his head hesitantly and cautiously, or even quickly and suddenly as if to gain the advantage of surprise, and look over his left shoulder to where his lover was sitting. Their eyes did not meet, for an ignominious apprehension was forcing the stricken man to keep his looks anxiously in check. Behind them on the terrace sat the women who watched over Tadzio, and at the point things had now reached, the enamoured Aschenbach had reason to fear that he had attracted attention and aroused suspicion. Indeed, he had several times, on the beach, in the hotel foyer and on the Piazza San Marco, been frozen with alarm to notice that Tadzio was being called away if he was near him, that they were taking care to keep them apart – and although his pride writhed in torments it had never known under the appalling insult that this implied, he could not in conscience deny its justice.

In the mean time the guitarist had begun a solo to his own accompaniment, a song in many stanzas which was then a popular hit all over Italy, and which he managed to perform in a graphic and dramatic manner, with the rest of his troupe joining regularly in the refrain. He was a lean fellow, thin and cadaverous in the face as well, standing there on the gravel detached from his companions, with a shabby felt hat on the back of his head and a quiff of his red hair bulging out under the brim, in a posture of insolent bravado; strumming and thrumming on his instrument, he tossed his pleasantries up to the terrace in a vivid *parlando*, enacting it all so strenuously that the veins swelled on his forehead. He was quite evidently not of Venetian origin, but rather of the Neapolitan comic type, half pimp, half actor, brutal and bold-faced, dangerous and entertaining. The actual words of his song were merely foolish, but in his presentation, with his grimaces and bodily movements, his way of winking suggestively and lasciviously licking the corner of his mouth, it had something indecent and vaguely offensive about it. Though otherwise dressed in urban fashion he wore a sports shirt, out of the soft collar of which his skinny neck projected, displaying a remarkably large and naked Adam's apple. His pallid snub-nosed face, the features of which gave little clue to his age, seemed to be lined with contortions and vice, and the grinning of his mobile mouth was rather strangely ill-matched to the two deep furrows that stood defiantly, imperiously, almost savagely, between his reddish brows. But what really fixed the solitary Aschenbach's deep attention on him was his observation that this suspect figure seemed to be carrying his own suspect atmosphere about with him as well. For every time the refrain was repeated the singer would perform, with much grimacing and wagging of his hand as if in greeting, a grotesque march round the scene, which brought him immediately below where Aschenbach sat; and every time this happened a stench of carbolic from his clothes or his body drifted up to the terrace.

Having completed his ballad he began to collect money. He started with the Russians, who were seen to give generously, and then came up the steps. Saucy as his performance had been, up here he was humility itself. Bowing and scraping, he crept from table to table, and a sly obsequious grin bared his prominent teeth, although the two furrows still stood threateningly between his red eyebrows. The spectacle of this alien being gathering in his livelihood was viewed with curiosity and not a little distaste; one threw coins with the tips of one's fingers into the hat, which one took care not to touch. Removal of the physical distance between the entertainer and decent folk always causes, however great one's pleasure has been, a certain embarrassment. He sensed this, and sought to make amends by cringing. He approached Aschenbach, and with him came the smell, which no one else in the company appeared to have noticed.

'Listen to me!' said the solitary traveller in an undertone and almost mechanically. 'Venice is being disinfected. Why?' – The comedian answered hoarsely: 'Because of the police! It's the regulations, signore, when it's so hot and when there's sirocco. The sirocco is oppressive. It's not good for the health . . .' He spoke in a tone of surprise that such a question could be asked, and demonstrated with his outspread hand how oppressive the sirocco was. – 'So there is no sickness in Venice?' asked Aschenbach very softly and between his teeth. – The clown's muscular features collapsed into a grimace of comic helplessness. 'A sickness? But what sickness? Is the sirocco a sickness? Is our police a sickness perhaps? The signore is having his little joke! A sickness! Certainly not, signore! A preventive measure, you must understand, a police precaution against the effects of the oppressive weather . . .' He gesticulated. 'Very well,' said Aschenbach briefly, still without raising his voice, and quickly dropped an unduly large coin into the fellow's hat. Then he motioned him with his eyes to clear off. The man obeyed, grinning and bowing low. But he had not even reached the steps when two hotel servants bore down on him, and with their faces close to his subjected him to a whispered cross-examination. He shrugged, gave assurances, swore that he had been discreet; it was obvious. Released, he returned to the garden, and after a brief consultation with his colleagues under the arc-lamp he came forward once more, to express his thanks in a parting number.

It was a song that Aschenbach could not remember ever having heard before; a bold hit in an unintelligible dialect, and having a laughing refrain in which the rest of the band regularly and loudly joined. At this point both the words and the instrumental accompaniment stopped, and nothing remained except a burst of laughter, to some extent rhythmically ordered but treated with a high degree of naturalism, the soloist in particular showing great talent in his life-like rendering of it. With artistic distance restored between himself and the spectators, he had recovered all his impudence, and the simulated laughter which he shamelessly directed at the terrace was a laughter of mockery. Even before the end of the articulated part of each stanza he would pretend to be struggling with an irresistible impulse of hilarity. He would sob, his voice would waver, he would press his hand against his mouth and hunch his shoulders, till at the proper moment the laughter would burst out of him, exploding in a wild howl, with such authenticity that it was infectious and communicated itself to the audience, so that a wave of objectless and merely self-propagating merriment swept over the terrace as well. And precisely this seemed to redouble the singer's exuberance. He bent his knees, slapped his thighs, held his sides, he nearly burst with what was now no longer laughing but shrieking; he pointed his finger up at the guests, as if that laughing company above him were itself the most comical thing in the world, and in the end they were all laughing, everyone in the garden and on the verandah, the waiters and the lift-boys and the house servants in the doorways.

Aschenbach reclined in his chair no longer, he was sitting bolt upright as if trying to fend off an attack or flee from it. But the laughter, the hospital smell drifting towards him, and the nearness of the beautiful boy, all mingled for him into an immobilizing nightmare, an unbreakable and inescapable spell that held his mind and senses captive. In the general commotion and distraction he ventured to steal a glance at Tadzio, and as he did so he became aware that the boy, returning his glance, had remained no less serious than himself, just as if he were regulating his attitude and expression by those of the older man, and as if the general mood had no power over him while Aschenbach kept aloof from it. There was something so disarming and overwhelmingly moving about this childlike submissiveness, so rich in meaning, that the grey-haired lover could only with difficulty restrain himself from burying his face in his hands. He had also had the impression that the way Tadzio from time to time drew himself up with an intake of breath was like a kind of sighing, as if from a constriction of the chest. 'He's sickly, he'll probably not live long,' he thought again, with that sober objectivity into which the drunken ecstasy of desire sometimes strangely escapes; and his heart was filled at one and the same time with pure concern on the boy's behalf and with a certain wild satisfaction.

In the mean time the troupe of Venetians had finished their performance and were leaving. Applause accompanied them, and their leader took care to embellish even his exit with comical pranks. His bowing and scraping and hand-kissing amused the company, and so he redoubled them. When his companions were already outside, he put on yet another act of running backwards and painfully colliding with a lamp-post, then hobbling to the gate apparently doubled up in agony. When he got there, however, he suddenly discarded the mask of comic underdog, uncoiled like a spring to his full height, insolently stuck out his tongue at the hotel guests on the terrace and slipped away into the darkness. The company was dispersing; Tadzio had left the balustrade some time ago. But the solitary Aschenbach, to the annoyance of the waiters, sat on and on at his little table over his unfinished pomegranate drink. The night was advancing, time was ebbing away. In his parents' house, many years ago, there had been an hourglass – he suddenly saw that fragile symbolic little instrument as clearly as if it were standing before him. Silently, subtly, the rust-red sand trickled through the narrow glass aperture, dwindling away out of the upper vessel, in which a little whirling vortex had formed.

On the very next day, in the afternoon, Aschenbach took a further step in his persistent probing of the outside world, and this time his success was complete. What he did was to enter the British travel agency just off the Piazza San Marco, and after changing some money at the cash desk, he put on the look of a suspicious foreigner and addressed his embarrassing question to the clerk who had served him. The clerk was a tweed-clad Englishman, still young, with his hair parted in the middle, his eyes close-set, and having that sober, honest demeanour which makes so unusual and striking an impression amid the glib knaveries of the south. 'No cause for concern, sir,' he began. 'An administrative measure, nothing serious. They often issue directives of this kind, as a precaution against the unhealthy effects of the heat and the sirocco . . .' But raising his blue eyes he met those of the stranger, which were looking wearily and rather sadly at his lips, with an expression of slight contempt. At this the Englishman coloured. 'That is,' he continued in an undertone and with some feeling, 'the official explanation, which the authorities here see fit to stick to. I can tell you that there is rather more to it than that.' And then, in his straightforward comfortable language, he told Aschenbach the truth.

For several years now, Asiatic cholera had been showing an increased tendency to spread and migrate. Originating in the sultry morasses of the Ganges delta, rising with the mephitic exhalations of that wilderness of rank useless luxuriance, that primitive island jungle shunned by man, where tigers crouch in the bamboo thickets, the pestilence had raged with unusual and prolonged virulence all over northern India; it had struck eastward into China, westward into Afghanistan and Persia, and following the main caravan routes it had borne its terrors to Astrakhan and even to Moscow. But while Europe trembled with apprehension that from there the spectre might advance and arrive by land, it had been brought by Syrian traders over the sea; it had appeared almost simultaneously in several Mediterranean ports, raising its head in Toulon and Malaga, showing its face repeatedly in Palermo and Naples, and taking a seemingly permanent hold all over Calabria and Apulia. The northern half of the peninsula had still been spared. But in the middle of May this year, in Venice, the dreadful comma bacilli had been found on one and the same day in the emaciated and blackened corpses of a ship's hand and of a woman who sold greengroceries. The two cases were hushed up. But a week later there were ten, there were twenty and then thirty, and they occurred in different quarters of the city. A man from a small provincial town in Austria who had been taking a few days' holiday in Venice died with unmistakable symptoms after returning home, and that was why the first rumours of a Venetian outbreak had appeared in German newspapers. The city authorities replied with a statement that the public health situation in Venice had never been better, and at the same time adopted the most necessary preventive measures. But the taint had probably now passed into foodstuffs, into vegetables or meat or milk; for despite every denial and concealment, the mortal sickness went on eating its way through the narrow little streets, and with the premature summer heat warming the water in the canals, conditions for the spread of infection were particularly favourable. It even seemed as if the pestilence had undergone a renewal of its energy, as if the tenacity and fertility of its pathogens had redoubled. Cases of recovery were rare; eighty per cent of the victims died, and they died in a horrible manner, for the sickness presented itself in an extremely acute form and was frequently of the so-called 'dry' type, which is the most dangerous of all. In this condition the body could not even evacuate the massive fluid lost from the blood-vessels. Within a few hours the patient would become dehydrated, his blood would thicken like pitch and he would suffocate with convulsions and hoarse cries. He was lucky if, as sometimes happened, the disease took the form of a slight malaise followed by a deep coma from which one never, or scarcely at all, regained consciousness. By the beginning of June the isolation wards in the Ospedale Civile were quietly filling, the two orphanages were running out of accommodation, and there was a gruesomely brisk traffic between the quayside of the Fondamente Nuove and the cemetery island of San Michele. But fear of general detriment to the city, concern for the recently opened art exhibition in the Public Gardens, consideration of the appalling losses which panic and disrepute would inflict on the hotels, on the shops, on the whole nexus of the tourist trade, proved stronger in Venice than respect for the truth and for international agreements; it was for this reason that the city authorities obstinately adhered to their policy of concealment and denial. The city's chief medical officer, a man of high repute, had resigned from his post in indignation and had been quietly replaced by a more pliable personality. This had become public knowledge; and such corruption in high places, combined with the prevailing insecurity, the state of crisis into which the city had been plunged by the death that walked its streets, led at the lower social levels to a certain breakdown of moral standards, to an activation of the dark and antisocial forces, which manifested itself in intemperance, shameless licence and growing criminality. Drunkenness in the evenings became noticeably more frequent; thieves and ruffians, it was said, were making the streets unsafe at night; there were repeated robberies and even murders, for it had already twice come to light that persons alleged to have died of the plague had in fact been poisoned by their own relatives; and commercial vice was now taking obtrusive and extravagant forms hitherto unknown in this area and indigenous only to southern Italy or oriental countries.

The Englishman's narrative conveyed the substance of all this to Aschenbach. 'You would be well advised, sir,' he concluded, 'to leave today rather than tomorrow. The imposition of quarantine can be expected any day now.' – 'Thank you,' said Aschenbach, and left the office.

The Piazza was sunless and sultry. Unsuspecting foreigners were sitting at the cafés, or standing in front of the church with pigeons completely enveloping them, watching the birds swarm and beat their wings and push each other out of the way as they snatched with their beaks at the hollow hands offering them grains of maize. Feverish with excitement, triumphant in his possession of the truth, yet with a taste of disgust on his tongue and a fantastic horror in his heart, the solitary traveller paced up and down the flagstones of the magnificent precinct. He was considering a decent action which would cleanse his conscience. Tonight, after dinner, he might approach the lady in the pearls and address her with words which he now mentally rehearsed: 'Madam, allow me as a complete stranger to do you a service, to warn you of something which is being concealed from you for reasons of self-interest. Leave here at once with Tadzio and your daughters! Cholera has broken out in Venice.' He might then lay his hand in farewell on the head of a mocking deity's instrument, turn away and flee from this quagmire. But at the same time he sensed an infinite distance between himself and any serious resolve to take such a step. It would lead him back to where he had been, give him back to himself again; but to one who is beside himself, no prospect is so distasteful as that of self-recovery. He remembered a white building adorned with inscriptions that glinted in the evening light, suffused with mystic meaning in which his mind had wandered; remembered then that strange itinerant figure who had wakened in him, in his middle age, a young man's longing to rove to far-off and strange places; and the thought of returning home, of level-headedness and sobriety, of toil and mastery, filled him with such repugnance that his face twisted into an expression of physical nausea. 'They want it kept quiet!' he whispered vehemently. And: 'I shall say nothing!' The consciousness of his complicity in the secret, of his share in the guilt, intoxicated him as small quantities of wine intoxicate a weary brain. The image of the stricken and disordered city, hovering wildly before his mind's eye, inflamed him with hopes that were beyond comprehension, beyond reason and full of monstrous sweetness. What, compared with such expectations, was that tender happiness of which he had briefly dreamed a few moments ago? What could art and virtue mean to him now, when he might reap the advantages of chaos? He said nothing, and stayed on.

That night he had a terrible dream, if dream is the right word for a bodily and mental experience which did indeed overtake him during deepest sleep, in complete independence of his will and with complete sensuous vividness, but with no perception of himself as present and moving about in any space external to the events themselves; rather, the scene of the events was his own soul, and they irrupted into it from outside, violently defeating his resistance – a profound, intellectual resistance – as they passed through him, and leaving his whole being, the culture of a lifetime, devastated and destroyed.

It began with fear, fear and joy and a horrified curiosity about what was to come. It was night, and his senses were alert; for from far off a hubbub was approaching, an uproar, a compendium of noise, a clangour and blare and dull thundering, yells of exultation and a particular howl with a long-drawn-out *u* at the end – all of it permeated and dominated by a terrible sweet sound of flute music: by deep-warbling, infamously persistent, shamelessly clinging tones that bewitched the innermost heart. Yet he was aware of a word, an obscure word, but one that gave a name to what was coming: '*the stranger-god!*' There was a glow of smoky fire: in it he could see a mountain landscape, like the mountains round his summer home. And in fragmented light from wooded heights, between tree trunks and mossy boulders, it came tumbling and whirling down: a human and animal swarm, a raging rout, flooding the slope with bodies, with flames, with tumult and frenzied dancing. Women, stumbling on the hide garments that fell too far about them from the waist, held up tambourines and moaned as they shook them above their thrown-back heads; they swung blazing torches, scattering the sparks, and brandished naked daggers; they carried snakes with flickering tongues which they had seized in the middle of the body, or they bore up their own breasts in both hands, shrieking as they did so. Men with horns over their brows, hairy-skinned and girdled with pelts, bowed their necks and threw up their arms and thighs, clanging brazen cymbals and beating a furious tattoo on drums, while smooth-skinned boys prodded goats with leafy staves, clinging to their horns and yelling with delight as the leaping beasts dragged them along. And the god's enthusiasts howled out the cry with the soft consonants and long-drawn-out final *u*, sweet and wild both at once, like no cry that was ever heard: here it was raised, belled out into the air as by rutting stags, and there they threw it back with many voices, in ribald triumph, urging each other on with it to dancing and tossing of limbs, and never did it cease. But the deep, enticing flute music mingled irresistibly with everything. Was it not also enticing him, the dreamer who experienced all this while struggling not to, enticing him with shameless insistence to the feast and frenzy of the uttermost surrender? Great was his loathing, great his fear, honourable his effort of will to defend to the last what was his and protect it against the Stranger, against the enemy of the composed and dignified intellect. But the noise, the howling grew louder, with the echoing cliffs reiterating it: it increased beyond measure, swelled up to an enrapturing madness. Odours besieged the mind, the pungent reek of the goats, the scent of panting bodies and an exhalation as of staling waters, with another smell, too, that was familiar: that of wounds and wandering disease. His heart throbbed to the drumbeats, his brain whirled, a fury seized him, a blindness, a dizzying lust, and his soul craved to join the round-dance of the god. The obscene symbol, wooden and gigantic, was uncovered and raised aloft: and still more unbridled grew the howling of the rallying-cry. With foaming mouths they raged, they roused each other with lewd gestures and licentious hands, laughing and moaning they thrust the prods into each other's flesh and licked the blood from each other's limbs. But the dreamer now was with them and in them, he belonged to the stranger-god. Yes, they were himself as they flung themselves, tearing and slaying, on the animals and devoured steaming gobbets of flesh, they were himself as an orgy of limitless coupling, in homage to the god, began on the trampled, mossy ground. And his very soul savoured the lascivious delirium of annihilation.

Out of this dream the stricken man woke unnerved, shattered and powerlessly enslaved to the daemon-god. He no longer feared the observant eyes of other people, whether he was exposing himself to their suspicions he no longer cared. In any case they were running away, leaving Venice; many of the bathing cabins were empty now, there were great gaps in the clientele at dinner, and in the city one scarcely saw any foreigners. The truth seemed to have leaked out, and however tightly the interested parties closed ranks, panic could no longer be stemmed. But the lady in the pearls stayed on with her family, either because the rumours were not reaching her or because she was too proud and fearless to heed them. Tadzio stayed on; and to Aschenbach, in his beleaguered state, it sometimes seemed that all these unwanted people all round him might flee from the place or die, that every living being might disappear and leave him alone on this island with the beautiful boy – indeed, as he sat every morning by the sea with his gaze resting heavily, recklessly, incessantly on the object of his desire, or as he continued his undignified pursuit of him in the evenings along streets in which the disgusting mortal malady wound its underground way, then indeed monstrous things seemed full of promise to him, and the moral law no longer valid.

Like any other lover, he desired to please and bitterly dreaded that he might fail to do so. He added brightening and rejuvenating touches to his clothes, he wore jewellery and used scent, he devoted long sessions to his toilet several times a day, arriving at table elaborately attired and full of excited expectation. As he beheld the sweet youthful creature who had so entranced him he felt disgust at his own ageing body, the sight of his grey hair and sharp features filled him with a sense of shame and hopelessness. He felt a compulsive need to refresh and restore himself physically; he paid frequent visits to the hotel barber.

Cloaked in a hairdressing gown, leaning back in the chair as the chatterer's hands tended him, he stared in dismay at his reflection in the looking-glass.

'Grey,' he remarked with a wry grimace.

'A little,' the man replied. 'And the reason? A slight neglect, a slight lack of interest in outward appearances, very understandable in persons of distinction, but not altogether to be commended, especially as one would expect those very persons to be free from prejudice about such matters as the natural and the artificial. If certain people who profess moral disapproval of cosmetics were to be logical enough to extend such rigorous principles to their teeth, the result would be rather disgusting. After all, we are only as old as we feel in our minds and hearts, and sometimes grey hair is actually further from the truth than the despised corrective would be. In your case, signore, one has a right to the natural colour of one's hair. Will you permit me simply to give your colour back to you?'

'How so?' asked Aschenbach.

Whereupon the eloquent tempter washed his client's hair in two kinds of water, one clear and one dark; and his hair was as black as when he had been young. Then he folded it into soft waves with the curling-tongs, stepped back and surveyed his handiwork.

'Now the only other thing,' he said, 'would be just to freshen up the signore's complexion a little.'

And like a craftsman unable to finish, unable to satisfy himself, he passed busily and indefatigably from one procedure to another. Aschenbach, reclining comfortably, incapable of resistance, filled rather with exciting hopes by what was happening, gazed at the glass and saw his eyebrows arched more clearly and evenly, the shape of his eyes lengthened, their brightness enhanced by a slight underlining of the lids; saw below them a delicate carmine come to life as it was softly applied to skin that had been brown and leathery; saw his lips that had just been so pallid now burgeoning cherry-red; saw the furrows on his cheeks, round his mouth, the wrinkles by his eyes, all vanishing under face cream and an aura of youth – with beating heart he saw himself as a young man in earliest bloom. The cosmetician finally declared himself satisfied, with the grovelling politeness usual in such people, by profusely thanking the client he had served. 'An insignificant adjustment, signore,' he said as he gave a final helping hand to Aschenbach's outward appearance. 'Now the signore can fall in love as soon as he pleases.' And the spellbound lover departed, confused and timorous but happy as in a dream. His necktie was scarlet, his broad-brimmed straw hat encircled with a many-coloured ribbon.

A warm gale had blown up; it rained little and lightly, but the air was humid and thick and filled with smells of decay. The ear was beset with fluttering, flapping and whistling noises, and to the fevered devotee, sweating under his make-up, it seemed that a vile race of wind-demons was disporting itself in the sky, malignant sea-birds that churn up and gnaw and befoul a condemned man's food. For the sultry weather was taking away his appetite, and he could not put aside the thought that what he ate might be tainted with infection.

One afternoon, dogging Tadzio's footsteps, Aschenbach had plunged into the confused network of streets in the depths of the sick city. Quite losing his bearings in this labyrinth of alleys, narrow waterways, bridges and little squares that all looked so much like each other, not sure now even of the points of the compass, he was intent above all on not losing sight of the vision he so passionately pursued. Ignominious caution forced him to flatten himself against walls and hide behind the backs of people walking in front of him; and for a long time he was not conscious of the weariness, the exhaustion that emotion and constant tension had inflicted on his body and mind. Tadzio walked behind his family; he usually gave precedence in narrow passages to his attendant and his nun-like sisters, and as he strolled along by himself he sometimes turned his head and glanced over his shoulder with his strange twilight-grey eyes, to ascertain that his lover was still following him. He saw him, and did not give him away. Drunk with excitement as he realized this, lured onward by those eyes, helpless in the leading strings of his mad desire, the infatuated Aschenbach stole upon the trail of his unseemly hope – only to find it vanish from his sight in the end. The Poles had crossed a little humpback bridge; the height of the arch hid them from their pursuer, and when in his turn he reached the top of it, they were no longer to be seen. He looked frantically for them in three directions, straight ahead and to left and right along the narrow, dirty canalside, but in vain. Unnerved and weakened, he was compelled to abandon his search.

His head was burning, his body was covered with sticky sweat, his neck quivered, a no longer endurable thirst tormented him; he looked round for something, no matter what, that would instantly relieve it. At a little greengrocer's shop he bought some fruit, some overripe soft strawberries, and ate some of them as he walked. A little square, one that seemed to have been abandoned, to have been put under a spell, opened up in front of him: he recognized it, he had been here, it was where he had made that vain decision weeks ago to leave Venice. On the steps of the well in its centre he sank down and leaned his head against the stone rim. The place was silent, grass grew between the cobblestones, garbage was lying about. Among the dilapidated houses of uneven height all round him was one that looked like a *palazzo*, with Gothic windows that now had nothing behind them, and little lion balconies. On the ground floor of another was a chemist's shop. From time to time warm gusts of wind blew the stench of carbolic across to him.

There he sat, the master, the artist who had achieved dignity, the author of A *Study in Abjection*, he who in such paradigmatically pure form had repudiated intellectual vagrancy and the murky depths, who had proclaimed his renunciation of all sympathy with the abyss, who had weighed vileness in the balance and found it wanting; he who had risen so high, who had set his face against his own sophistication, grown out of all his irony, and taken on the commitments of one whom the public trusted; he, whose fame was official, whose name had been ennobled, and on whose style young boys were taught to model their own – there he sat, with his eyelids closed, with only an occasional mocking and rueful sideways glance from under them which he hid again at once; and his drooping, cosmetically brightened lips shaped an occasional word of the discourse his brain was delivering, his half-asleep brain with its tissue of strange dream-logic.

'For Beauty, Phaedrus, mark well! only Beauty is at one and the same time divine and visible, and so it is indeed the sensuous lover's path, little Phaedrus, it is the artist's path to the spirit. But do you believe, dear boy, that the man whose path to the spiritual passes through the senses can ever achieve wisdom and true manly dignity? Or do you think rather (I leave it to you to decide) that this is a path of dangerous charm, very much an errant and sinful path which must of necessity lead us astray? For I must tell you that we artists cannot tread the path of Beauty without

Eros keeping company with us and appointing himself as our guide; yes, though we may be heroes in our fashion and disciplined warriors, yet we are like women, for it is passion that exalts us, and the longing of our soul must remain the longing of a lover – that is our joy and our shame. Do you see now perhaps why we writers can be neither wise nor dignified? That we necessarily go astray, necessarily remain dissolute emotional adventurers? The magisterial poise of our style is a lie and a farce, our fame and social position are an absurdity, the public's faith in us is altogether ridiculous, the use of art to educate the nation and its youth is a reprehensible undertaking which should be forbidden by law. For how can one be fit to be an educator when one has been born with an incorrigible and natural tendency towards the abyss? We try to achieve dignity by repudiating that abyss, but whichever way we turn we are subject to its allurement. We renounce, let us say, the corrosive process of knowledge – for knowledge, Phaedrus, has neither dignity nor rigour: it is all insight and understanding and tolerance, uncontrolled and formless; it sympathizes with the abyss, it *is* the abyss. And so we reject it resolutely, and henceforth our pursuit is of Beauty alone, of Beauty which is simplicity, which is grandeur and a new kind of rigour and a second naïvety, of Beauty which is Form. But form and naïvety, Phaedrus, lead to intoxication and lust; they may lead a noble mind into terrible criminal emotions, which his own fine rigour condemns as infamous; they lead, they too lead, to the abyss. I tell you, that is where they lead us writers; for we are not capable of self-exaltation, we are merely capable of self-debauchery. And now I shall go, Phaedrus, and you shall stay here; and leave this place only when you no longer see me.'

A few days later Gustav von Aschenbach, who had been feeling unwell, left the Hotel des Bains at a later morning hour than usual. He was being attacked by waves of dizziness, only half physical, and with them went an increasing sense of dread, a feeling of hopelessness and pointlessness, though he could not decide whether this referred to the external world or to his personal existence. In the foyer he saw a large quantity of luggage standing ready for dispatch, asked one of the doormen which guests were leaving, and was given in reply the aristocratic Polish name which he had inwardly been expecting to hear. As he received the information there was no change in his ravaged features, only that slight lift of the head with which one casually notes something one did not need to know. He merely added the question: 'When?' and was told: 'After lunch.' He nodded and went down to the sea.

It was a bleak spectacle there. Tremors gusted outwards across the water between the beach and the first long sand-bar, wrinkling its wide flat surface. An autumnal, out-of-season air seemed to hang over the once so colourful and populous resort, now almost deserted, with litter left lying about on the sand. An apparently abandoned camera stood on its tripod at the edge of the sea, and the black cloth over it fluttered and flapped in the freshening breeze.

Tadzio, with the three or four playmates he still had, was walking about on the right in front of his family's bathing cabin; and reclining in his deck-chair with a rug over his knees, about midway between the sea and the row of cabins, Aschenbach once more sat watching him. The boys' play was unsupervised, as the women were probably busy with travel preparations; it seemed to be unruly and degenerating into roughness. The sturdy boy he had noticed before, the one in the belted suit and with glossy black hair whom they called 'Jasiu', had been angered and blinded by some sand thrown into his face: he forced Tadzio to a wrestling match, which soon ended in the downfall of the less muscular beauty. But as if in this hour of leave-taking the submissiveness of the lesser partner had been transformed into cruel brutality, as if he were now bent on revenge for his long servitude, the victor did not release his defeated friend even then, but knelt on his back and pressed his face into the sand so hard and so long that Tadzio, breathless from the fight in any case, seemed to be on the point of suffocation. His attempts to shake off the weight of his tormentor were convulsive; they stopped altogether for moments on end and became a mere repeated twitching. Appalled, Aschenbach was about to spring to the rescue when the bully finally released his victim. Tadzio, very pale, sat up and went on sitting motionless for some minutes, propped on one arm, his hair tousled and his eyes darkening. Then he stood right up and walked slowly away. His friends called to him, laughingly at first, then anxiously and pleadingly; he took no notice. The dark-haired boy, who had no doubt been seized at once by remorse at having gone so far, ran after him and tried to make up the quarrel. A jerk of Tadzio's shoulder rejected him. Tadzio walked on at an angle down to the water. He was barefooted and wearing his striped linen costume with the red bow.

At the edge of the sea he lingered, head bowed, drawing figures in the wet sand with the point of one foot, then walked into the shallow high water, which at its deepest point did not even wet his knees; he waded through it, advancing easily, and reached the sand-bar. There he stood for a moment looking out into the distance and then, moving left, began slowly to pace the length of this narrow strip of unsubmerged land. Divided from the shore by a width of water, divided from his companions by proud caprice, he walked, a quite isolated and unrelated apparition, walked with floating hair out there in the sea, in the wind, in front of the nebulous vastness. Once more he stopped to survey the scene. And suddenly, as if prompted by a memory, by an impulse, he turned at the waist, one hand on his hip, with an enchanting twist of the body, and looked back over his shoulder at the beach. There the watcher sat, as he had sat once before when those twilight-grey eyes, looking back at him then from that other threshold, had for the first time met his. Resting his head on the back of his chair, he had slowly turned it to follow the movements of the walking figure in the distance; now he lifted it towards this last look, then it sank down on his breast, so that his eyes stared up from below, while his face wore the inert, deep-sunken expression of profound slumber. But to him it was as if the pale and lovely soul-summoner out there were smiling to him, beckoning to him; as if he loosed his hand from his hip and pointed outwards, hovering ahead and onwards, into an immensity rich with unutterable expectation. And as so often, he set out to follow him.

Minutes passed, after he had collapsed sideways in his chair, before anyone hurried to his assistance. He was carried to his room. And later that same day the world was respectfully shocked to receive the news of his death.

Death in Venice

The film adaptation of *Death in Venice* was directed by Luchino Visconti and was released in 1971. It stars Dirk Bogarde, Mark Burns and Björn Andrésen.

While the protagonist, Aschenbach, is an author in Thomas Mann's novel, Visconti chose to make him a composer for the film adaptation. Bogarde reportedly based his character's appearance on that of composer Gustav Mahler, whose music is used prominently in the film.

Warner Bros. initially wanted to write off the project for fear it would be banned in the US due to its subject matter. They changed their minds after the London premiere was attended by Queen Elizabeth II and Princess Anne. The event was also a fundraiser for the preservation of the city of Venice.

The film won four BAFTA Awards, including Best Art Direction and Best Cinematography, and four Nastro D'Argento Awards, including Best Director, and the Palme D'Or at the Cannes Film Festival.

Certificate: 12A
Running Time: 130 minutes

www.vintage-books.co.uk

Christopher Hope was born in Johannesburg in 1944. He published his first book of poems, *Cape Drives*, in 1974 for which he later received the Cholmondeley Award. His first novel *A Separate Development*, banned for a period shortly after publication in South Africa in 1980, received the David Higham Prize for Fiction in 1981. A collection of short stories, *Private Parts & Other Tales*, published in 1982, won the International P.E.N. Silver Pen Award for that year. As well as a second collection of poems entitled *In the Country of the Black Pig* he has written a children's book, *The King, The Cat and the Fiddle*. A regular contributor to various journals and reviews, Christopher Hope has lived in London since 1976. In 1982 he was awarded an Arts Council Bursary.

'Hope has given South African literature a new injection of life. KRUGER'S ALP is more than a satirical fantasy, it is the story of a summit in self-deception . . . an iconoclast's delight'

Johannesburg Star

Christopher Hope

KRUGER'S ALP

First published in Great Britain by
William Heinemann Ltd 1984
Published in Abacus by
Sphere Books Ltd 1985
30–32 Gray's Inn Road, London WC1X 8JL
Copyright © Christopher Hope 1984

The quotation by President Kruger (page 72) is taken from *The Memoirs of Paul Kruger* (Negro University Press, New York, 1969)

Printed and bound in Great Britain by
Cox & Wyman Ltd, Reading

For Mike Kirkwood
Who showed me a few gaps in the laager

Pray, did you never hear what happened to a man some time ago of this town (whose name was Christian) that went on a Pilgrimage up towards the higher regions?

> John Bunyan
> *Pilgrim's Progress*

They took the hill (Whose hill? What for?)
But what a climb they left to do!
Out of that bungled, unwise war
An alp of unforgiveness grew.

> William Plomer
> 'The Boer War'

We knew nothing of the theatrical element which is part of all revolutionary movements in France, and we believed sincerely in all we heard.

> A. Herzen
> *Childhood, Youth and Exile*

CHAPTER 1

As I walked through the wilderness of what remained of the world of Father Lynch and his 'little guild', I saw much to disturb me. Here was the last vestige of the parish garden where the bulldozers, earth-movers, grabbers and cranes had frozen into that peculiar menacing immobility giant machines assume when switched off; left as if stunned, open-mouthed, gaping at the human foolishness of wishing to stop work when they are strong and willing to continue. They stood silent, it being Sunday, resting from their merciless preparation of this new site for one of the enormous hostels of the huge University of National Christian Education, widely declared to be the largest in the southern hemisphere. I looked around me and found the work nearly complete. However, the machines had stopped eating for the moment; ours is a holy land and even the destruction of redundant churches halts on the Sabbath.

The advance of the university over the years had been slow but inexorable; at first, parcels of the extensive grounds of St Jude's had gone and, wisely, Lynch had not fought against this but had preserved his energies for guarding the church itself and his garden. His community of priests and lay brothers had been whittled away one by one. Bishop Blashford had conducted negotiations with the university so as to safeguard what he called 'an orderly withdrawal', with a skill which had won him the admiration of municipal councils across the country – and the commendation of the Papal Nuncio, Agnelli.

I stood in the destroyed church with the gaping roof. All religious ornaments had been removed, the sentimental paintings of lambs in emerald meadows, the wooden stations of the cross, the stained-glass windows of obscure martyrs, the baptismal font, the giant crucifix which had swung above the altar, the doors of the confessionals torn off so that now the little chambers gaped like disused lavatories. All gone – the golden tabernacle, the candles, the altar stone, the plaster Virgin in her sky-blue drapery and her brass circlet of stars, the wooden St Joseph with his surprising paunch, his bluff good looks and his blue sea-captain's eyes; all the gaudy, inappropriate prints of Italianate saints, all gone; the ruby

1

glass altar lamps in which the tiny flame glowed perpetually, the wooden altar rail at which Blanchaille had stood with his boat boy, Mickey the Poet, beside him, fumigating the first few rows of the congregation with pungent incense, the sacred cardboard hosts that stuck to the roof of the mouth for half an hour after Communion, the chalices, the sweet and rather yeasty smell of the cheap Jewish wine Lynch favoured for the Mass, the ciborium, the copes and chasubles stiff with gold thread, all the intoxicating plumage by which ordinary, irritable, balding men transformed themselves into birds of paradise and paraded to the strangely comforting sound of brass bells; all the absurdly delightful foreign paraphernalia with which a diminishing band of Catholics in a not very notable parish chimed, chanted, blessed and perfumed the start of each bright indifferent African morning. Only the pews remained now, the dark, polished mahogany pews, on the last two of which, at the rear of the church, I could make out still, small oblong patches of lighter wood where the brass plates had been; they were marked RESERVED, thus delicately designating the seats for the handful of black servants who used this church until Father Lynch had the plates removed, in the face of considerable opposition, in the days when these things were regarded as perfectly normal and fully in accord with the will of God and the customs of the country.

I saw that only Father Lynch's favourite tree, from beneath which the dying master of altar boys once conducted his famous picnics, was still standing. The Tree of Heaven, we called it, or *Ailanthus altissima* Father Lynch taught with desperate pedantry. Like Buddha, beneath the sacred Bo tree, Father Lynch sat – though there had been nothing Eastern about Father Lynch, who was small, thin and elfish and who told his boys that the name of the tree was highly misleading since its male flowers smelt pretty damn awful and its roots were a threat to the foundations of the church. It was beneath this Tree of Heaven that I lay down around noon and slept. And while I slept I dreamed.

In my dream I saw Theodore Blanchaille and he was not particularly well-dressed. But then he'd always been rather a sloppy character, old Blanchie, or Father Theodore Blanchaille as we learnt to refer to him, or Father Theo of the Camps, as he was known in the old days, or plain Mr Blanchaille as we must refer to him now, I suppose. He was wearing an old pair of khaki shorts, baggy, creased and much too big for him, and a weird kind of sailor's top of jagged dark blue stripes, squared at the neck. He was barefoot and sat in an

2

empty room on a plastic chair. He was a big fellow carrying too much weight, but then he'd always been heavy, and I could see his belly pushing at the thin cotton shirt, and the plastic bands of the garden chair he sat in pressed against his lower back and made rolls of flesh protrude, meaty and tubular, stacked one above the other like bales of cloth. He was leaning forward with his elbows on his knees and reading a paper which was on the floor in front of him and turning the pages with his bare toes. He was holding a can of beans and occasionally he'd spoon a few of these into his mouth. No ordinary spoon this, but a square-tongued sugar spoon, silver-plated and made for the last visit of their Royal Majesties, King George VI and Queen Elizabeth, whose crowned heads in blue enamel tilted lovingly together above their coat of arms. As he read he wept and the tears landed on his knees and ran down the thick hair of his legs and stained the newspaper.

This struck me as extraordinary. A fellow who had been educated by the Margaret Brethren did not weep easily. But he was crying. Great shuddering sobs made the sailor shirt ripple and the tears glittered upon the thick hairs of his legs. His rather pear-shaped face wore a crumpled hopeless look, the big forehead creased. He bent his chin closer to his knees and with his free hand he clutched his hair which was dark and full of curls and strongly suggested his French blood given him by a Mauritian sailor father who left home shortly after his birth and never returned.

I saw the headline of the paper he held: FISCAL OFFICIAL IN MYSTERY SLAYING.

I knew he was reading about the death of Tony Ferreira who had been his friend in the old days when they were altar boys together under Father Lynch. This was to say in the time before Ferreira showed the signs of mathematical and financial abilities which were to carry him into the Civil Service and then to a high position in the Auditor General's office. It was extraordinary, given the advanced political education these boys received from Father Lynch, that any of them should ever go to work for the Regime, and yet two of them had done so. This boy whom Father Lynch in one of his wild prophesies had seen as a future visionary. Instead he became a Government accountant, of a very special and rarefied sort, but an accountant all the same. Someone had once asked Ferreira how he found it in him to go and work for the Regime and he simply shrugged and replied that he followed figures wherever they led. Figures were value free, they kept him out of politics and he found that a tremendous relief. Naturally his answer was received with

3

considerable disgust by those who knew him in the old days. Of course this was before an even more shocking betrayal when Trevor Van Vuuren joined the police.

The altar boys of Father Lynch were Theodore Blanchaille, Tony Ferreira, Trevor Van Vuuren, Roberto Giuseppe Zandrotti, Ronald Kipsel and little Michael Yates, afterwards Mickey the Poet. And I saw in my dream how in the old days they would occupy this very garden while Father Lynch sat beneath the Tree of Heaven; beside him on the picnic blanket two black boys, Gabriel and his brother Looksmart, the children of Grace Dladla, his housekeeper. I saw how Father Lynch reclined on an elbow and sipped a drink from a flask while he and the two black boys watched the white boys slaving in the sun, pulling up weeds, cutting back the bushes, raking, watering and desnailing Father Lynch's impossible parish garden. Gabriel and Looksmart Dladla were given bottles of fizzy orange to drink while Father Lynch leaned at his leisure, sipping iced cocktails from an aquamarine thermos flask. It did black boys good to sit in the shade and watch white boys work. It did white boys good to be watched. The mutual educational advantages of the experience should not be underestimated. This was among the many principles enunciated at Father Lynch's famous picnics.

Another was that it was given to each of us to discover the secrets of our own particular universe – but we should expect to be punished for it.

Another, that President Paul Kruger when he fled into exile at the end of the Boer War had taken large amounts of money with him – the missing Kruger millions. A glimpse of the purpose to which he had put these millions would be like a view of paradise – or at least as close to it as we were ever likely to get.

Another, that the Regime was corrupt, weak and dying from within – this at a time when our country was regarded as being as powerful as either Israel or Taiwan, had invaded almost every country along our border and even a number across the sea, some several times, always with crushing military victories.

Another, that destruction threatened everyone – this at a time when President Adolph Gerhardus Bubé had just returned from his extensive foreign tour of European capitals and initiated a new diplomatic policy of open relations with foreign countries which was said to have gained us many friends abroad and continued support in the world at large.

Father Ignatius Lynch, transplanted Irish hothead who never

understood Africa, or perhaps understood it too well, had been sent into this wilderness, he would say, indicating with a gesture of his small shapely hand the entire southern sub-continent of Africa, by error, misdirected by his boneheaded supervisors in Eire. A man with his gifts for the analysis of power, and the disguises which it took on, should have been retained at home as one who would recognise and appreciate the close bonds between clergy and rulers in his own country, or should have been posted to some superior European Catholic parish in Spain, or Portugal, or even to Rome, where his gifts might have been acknowledged. Being deprived of an adult, mature European culture where even babes and sucklings understood that the desirability of morality could never replace the necessities of power, and despite the realisation that Africa was not going to live up to his expectations, he worked hard at giving his boys a lively political sense.

Then, too, Father Lynch had alarming gifts for prophecy; he prophesied often, with tremendous conviction, of the future which lay ahead for his boys; prophecies truly imaginative, but magnificently inaccurate.

There was, too, this strange addiction to South African history, or at least to one of its distant and probably mythical sub-themes, the question of the missing Kruger millions, the great pile of gold which according to some legends Paul Kruger, President of the Transvaal Republic and leader of the Boer nation in the great war of freedom against the British imperialists at the turn of the century, had taken with him when he fled into exile as the victorious English *Rooineks* marched into the capital. This must have begun as a faint interest, a hobby perhaps, back in the mists of time, but what had been once a gentle historical investigation into a legend, which was very widely discounted by authorities, academic and political, became a passionate investigation into something which would supply the answer to the mystery of 'life as we know it', and was absolutely vital to their salvation, he told his boys – 'at least in so far as salvation could be defined or hoped for in this God-forsaken Calvinist African wilderness'. Father Lynch would express his belief with great finality, reclining on his elbow and sipping from his iced thermos beneath the Tree of Heaven as he watched his boys dragging at the leathery weeds.

I saw in my dream how Blanchaille sat in an empty room, with its bare parquet flooring and a few bad pieces of orange Rhodesian copper hanging on the walls, kudu drinking at a waterhole, and similar trifles, weeping as he read of the death of Ferreira, shaking his head and muttering. From somewhere outside the house, perhaps in the garden, I could hear angry voices raised, baying as if demanding to be let in and in my dream I saw who these angry ones were – they were Blanchaille's parishioners demonstrating against their priest.

Clearly unable to contain himself any longer, Blanchaille burst out with a choked cry: 'What shall I do? What the hell shall I do?'

And I saw in my dream four lines in small smudgy newsprint from the Press Association which reported that Dr Anthony Ferreira had been found dead in his ranch-style home in the Northern Suburbs. Police were investigating. Dr Ferreira had been his country's representative with various international monetary organisations abroad. Certain messages had been found written on the wall near the body.

It was possible to date this newspaper to the final days before the Onslaught because on the opposite page was a huge photograph of a darkened car window in which could be glimpsed the white blur of a man's face, and I knew at once that this was the picture of our President (our ex-President as he became), Adolph Gerhardus Bubé, on his celebrated foreign tour, the one which opened a new chapter in our international relations with the outside world. Ten countries in six days. It had been hailed at the time as a diplomatic triumph as well as a speed record. Photographs had appeared in the press: a man shielding his face outside the Louvre; an elderly gentleman in a hat on a' bridge in Berne, a shadowy figure, back turned, feeding the pigeons in Trafalgar Square; a dim white face peering from the darkened windows of a black limousine speeding past the Colosseum . . . proofs of a triumph. It was the first time a president had been abroad since President Kruger fled to Switzerland in 1902. But Bubé's tour, alas, did not open the new chapter in foreign relations which the Government promised. He came home and we began digging in for the long siege. The Total Onslaught had begun.

Blanchaille had heard from Ferreira very shortly before his death. Of course his line had been tapped. The call had come out of the blue, but he knew instantly the familiar flat vowels and the unemotional voice: 'I'm sending you some money, Blanchie.'

'I don't need your money.'

'Oh, come on, of course you need money. I don't care what you use it for. Say some masses for my soul if you like, but I'm off. I'm

6

through. Lynch was right, Blanchie. Something has been going on all these years. I've seen the books.'

Blanchaille did not wish to talk to Ferreira. He didn't like Ferreira. Ferreira had gone to work for the other side. He'd represented the country at the International Monetary Fund, he'd been co-opted into the office of the Auditor General. His speciality was currency movements, exchange control and foreign banking.

'You'll need this money, you'll need it to get where you're going. Don't be stubborn, Blanchie.'

'I'm not going anywhere.'

The eavesdroppers bugging the call handled their appliances in the customarily inept way. So many telephones, so many listeners needed. It was rumoured they took on students wishing to earn cash in their vacations. An unpleasant hum increasing in pitch and volume covered their piping exchanges. Ferreira's voice shrilled tinnily through the growing fog of interference. He was probably yelling his head off. 'I've had a revelation, Blanchie! I've found it – I've found the City of God!'

'Of what?' Blanchaille shrieked.

It was hopeless, the humming noise made the ear quiver. He knew then that the line had not merely been tapped, their conversation had been jammed.

The money came. There were hundreds, thousands perhaps. He hadn't counted it, wrapped in plastic film, crisp notes held tight with rubber bands. He hid it in a great tub of ice-cream in the freezer, scooping out the middle and sealing it with a plug of the peppermint chip and pistachio. It was the only food left in the house since Joyce had left, not counting the beans.

Now Ferreira was dead. The item itself in the paper was small, it might have been lost amongst the lists of divorces and the spreading columns of troop casualties on the Borders. The news of the Ferreira killing might not have been much but the stories surrounding it made clear the interest that it aroused. The young Secretary of the new Department of Communications, or Depcom, dynamic Miss Trudy Yssel, put out a statement deploring speculation about price falls on the Exchange and pointing out that the press must take a more responsible attitude and that this wasn't, after all, the Bubbles Schroeder murder case. This last a reference to one of the most celebrated murders in the country in which a pretty young whore named Bubbles Schroeder, who had slept with a number of people of note, was found lying in a grove of trees one morning with

7

a lump of limestone thrust into her mouth. And Yssel's boss, Minister for Parallel Equilibriums and Ethnic Autonomy, the formidable Augustus 'Gus' Kuiker who held, besides, the important portfolio of Cultural Communications, the Government's propaganda arm, took the opportunity to warn the press once again that the Government's patience was not limitless, that freedom was a privilege to be earned, not a licence for personal or political rumour-mongering. A further story reported the deaths of three brokers, Kranz, Lundquist and Skellum, and quoted the Chairman of the Exchange, Dov Solomon, as saying that an investigation had shown that these unfortunate accidents had no connection with one another, or with any other event. Blanchaille paid no attention to these attendant stories. It is probable that he detected no connection – but I saw in my dream that he would remember them later, when his investigative talents flowered as of course Father Lynch had prophesied they would.

Ah, the prophecies of Father Lynch! What is one to make of them?

Father Lynch had prophesied that Tony Ferreira was a natural visionary. Consequently he received the news of his interest in accountancy with what seemed like astonishing composure. He had taken to figures, he told Blanchaille once, because it kept his mind off his bruises. Now that was fair enough. Ferreira had been beaten since he was a baby. Indeed one of Blanchaille's earliest memories was seeing Ferreira arrive to serve early morning Mass with two eyes so swollen, so bruised, he could hardly see where he walked and had to take Blanchaille's arm as they made their way from the sacristy into the church, along the altar rail, through the gate and up the five grey marble steps leading to the altar. He could remember counting, 'here's one, now two coming up, here is three . . .' then they crossed the flat grey granite expanse and knelt together on the top altar step where Ferreira remained for the rest of the Mass too blind to move.

His father had been a bricklayer. Big head and a jutting lower lip. He drove a powder blue Pontiac with a pink plastic butterfly on the bonnet. Mrs Ferreira was white-faced, plain as a gate-post, cracked and peeling, whom Mr Ferreira carried everywhere with him like a club and used with terrible effect on his son when his own arm tired. Looking at them in their pew, the Ferreiras senior, he with pale hair on his sun-tanned arms and she solid, straight, wooden, with a blankness in their eyes as the Mass progressed, like two strangers who have darted out of the rain into church only to find they have

8

strayed into some foreign funeral service and must now patiently wait it out, masking their incomprehension in a slumberous passivity intended to suggest the appropriate demeanour. Hard to imagine them flinging themselves fist and boot on their only son. But Tony bore the marks.

Hemmed in on both sides his only escape was upward. Tony grew tall and elegant as if to repudiate his father's squat energy and outstrip it. With his father's thick pale hair and his mother's immobile features he was delicate, sensitive, smart. A war of attrition began as Tony set out deliberately to bait his father into extending himself by making plain his open contempt for his bricklaying business. Mr Ferreira responded, fighting back by opening branches, getting draughtsmen into his office; soon he denied he was a bricklayer and described himself as a quantity surveyor. He went on to employ other quantity surveyors and his picture even appeared in the papers as a man on the move in 'our thrusting, dynamic economy'. Father Lynch remarked on Ferreira's father's success, at which Tony nodded pleasantly: 'Yes, he's fully extended on all fronts now. His order books are bursting and he has substantial credit lines. The banks are falling over each other to lend him money.' When the big crash came Tony explained the reasons for it with gentle composure. 'It happens every day. He'd stretched himself to breaking point. Simply couldn't service his debts. Nailed by his own ambition. Crucified by his own success.' And then the final twist of the knife, elegant and terrible, Tony attended his father's bankruptcy hearing wearing a rich red tie and a glossy, heavily scented rose in his buttonhole and listened with rapt attention as the quantity surveyor's empire was dismantled brick by brick and thrown to his creditors.

Even Lynch heard of the crash.

'It seems your dad has been under fire, Tony.'

'Yes, Father. I'd say he's taken a good knock.'

'Snapped his head back, did it?'

'Decapitating.'

But why had Lynch described Ferreira as a visionary? The priest explained: 'They will tell you, the people who run this country, that they built the New Jerusalem in this brown, dry, prickly land. To see the lie behind the boast requires the eyes of the seer.'

Again: 'They will proffer the moral principles on which their empire is built, the keepers of the uneasy peace. Refuse their invitation. Ask instead to see the books.'

And: 'We are dealing here with questions of faith,' a favourite

9

opening, 'which in the neo-Calvinism followed by the Regime is in fact a matter of money. There's been no question of faith since Kruger left and his heirs forsook morality for power. We know this to be true. The difficulty will be in proving it.'

Father Lynch always had a line, a view. Mad he was, but reliable. I saw how desperately Blanchaille needed to consult the old priest long forsaken by his altar boys who not unnaturally believed they had outgrown him. The man I saw in my dream was cracking up. He wept and raved. Things were closing in. He sat in the empty house. Waiting, or hoping? His bags had never been unpacked since he arrived to take up his incumbency as parish priest in the new suburb of Merrievale. They waited for him now, by the door, three heavy tartan suitcases reinforced with leather straps. He had packed them when he left the camp and went to the priests' home in the mountains for rest and recuperation. He had carried them to his new post as parish priest in Merrievale. They contained clerical suits he never wore; books he did not read; boots, brushes, toiletries he no longer used; they were in effect the relics of a life he no longer led. Now and then he bought a new toothbrush, a pair of shoes, a couple of shirts whenever he needed them and left them behind when he moved on. But the cases he carried with him. Heavy, useless, but all he had to remind him of what, and to some extent where, he had been. He hadn't lasted long in Merrievale. His tenure as parish priest could be measured in three sermons and a siege. Outside his window his parishioners bayed for his blood. They waved banners and shook their fists, led by big-knuckled Tertius Makapan, the brick salesman. Word had it that Father Lynch was dying, but then Lynch had been dying ever since he'd met him. He'd made a profession of dying. 'I'm not long for this world, my boys!' he would shout from the shade of the Tree of Heaven. 'Get a move on!'

Lynch's love of easeful death wasn't quite what it seemed; it was rather as if he saw in it the chance of the transfer the Church had always denied him. Death might be the far country from whence no traveller returned – and if so he was all for it. Anywhere must be better than this. Hence the constant warnings: 'Hurry, my boys, I am not much longer for this life . . .' and 'Listen to these words of wisdom from a departing soul – the idealism of the Boer freedom fighters died with Kruger's flight into exile. What followed was not a success for Calvinist nationalism but a policy of "get what you can and keep it" – only remember to call it God's work.'

10

This urge to depart was more to be pitied than feared. Lynch knew that short of a miracle, or his own defection (and that meant air tickets and where was he to find the money?), he was condemned for life to this wild African place.

He suffered from dreams of money. Perhaps a rich relative would die and leave him a legacy? No, he was a practical man. But then again perhaps one of his altar boys would one day be rich enough to make a present to his old priest and mentor – enough to enable him to escape to what he called some serious country.

Perhaps this was the source of his fascination with the last days of the old Boer leader of the Transvaal Republic, Stephanus Johannes Paulus Kruger. Father Lynch knew the *Memoirs* very well, and he owned also what he claimed was the last surviving copy of *Further Memoirs of a Boer President*; a fat, red leather-bound book of reminiscences and prophecies apparently dictated by the exiled president to his faithful valet Happé in the old man's few remaining months of life in his rented house by the lake in Clarens, Switzerland, as the desolate, near-blind old lion mused over the future of his country and his people, broken by war and scattered in defeat to St Helena and Patagonia, Ceylon, Malaya, Madagascar, Mozambique, Angola and Tanganyika – a diaspora of Boers, the African Israelites, blown by history around the globe.

> . . . And I shall use the short remaining time the Lord has been pleased to grant me to labour mightily, though conscious of my frailty and infirmity, to bring His people home to Him [Kruger promised in *Further Memoirs*], and since He has entrusted to my care the means whereby His will shall be accomplished I shall not rest until I find that place, 'the land', as the Lord said to Moses, 'which I have given unto the children of Israel' . . .

Father Lynch would interpret this for his altar boys, saying that by that 'place' Kruger undoubtedly meant a physical location, a home for dispossessed and faithful Boers who would not return to serve under the hated English, and by 'the means' Kruger certainly meant the treasure which had accompanied him into exile, the famed Kruger hoard, the gold millions of legend (taken in the form of ingots, bullion-bars or dust, who could say?) – from the inexhaustible mines of the Reef and smuggled out when the President fled.

This obsession with the millions came to outweigh all of Lynch's religious duties and the *Further Memoirs* became his daily office, his

11

'familiar bible' he called it, though it was widely believed among the altar boys he had written it himself.

It was precisely these unexpected ideas, combined with a complete lack of any religious scruple, which attracted to Father Lynch the boys from the nearby boarding hostel who were to form his little group of altar servers.

That Father Lynch was in disgrace with all the orthodox clergy appealed enormously to the wayward boys, handed by their parents into the care of Father Cradley, rector of the hostel: Ferreira, Blanchaille, Van Vuuren, Zandrotti, little Michael Yates, and, for a brief period, even Ronald Kipsel (afterwards the infamous Kipsel), these were the altar servers in Lynch's little guild. The boys detested the Church and yet were drawn to Father Lynch, for, after all, did the Church not hate Father Lynch? Wasn't it Father Lynch who insisted on integrating the two dozen black servants, washerwomen and gardeners who knelt in the two final pews on either side of the nave, into the white congregation? Until ordered by Bishop Blashford to restore segregation immediately, because, desirable though a certain mixing might be in an ideal world and certain though it was that such things would one day happen – though not in our lifetime – the move was premature.

And was it not Father Lynch some years later who refused to introduce the new form of the Mass with its responses in English and its furtive handshakes and blushing kisses of peace, saying that although he understood the move was designed to counter dwindling congregations by giving the laity the idea that they were a vital part of the service, a move which he understood was known among theatre people as 'audience participation', he and his congregation were too old to change and he would continue to say Mass in the old Latin rite? Threats were made. They were ignored. And eventually the point was not pursued. After all, Lynch was an old man ministering to an elderly and diminishing congregation served by a little band of altar boys so bound by loyalty to the obstinate priest that they were probably beyond salvation.

And of course it was Lynch who, some years later still, when Blashford announced the Church's discovery of its new mission to Africa which meant reaching out to embrace its black brothers and sisters in Christ, retorted that having been ordered by his bishop to reverse his own attempt at integration some years before, he was not prepared to shame and humiliate his remaining black parishioners by ordering them back into the white pews from which they had been barred for so long. 'It is the nature of all power structures, whether armed or not, to present changes, however contradictory or cruel, as necessary progress towards the light,' Father Lynch, Parish Priest of St Jude's, taught his boys beneath the Tree of Heaven.

The church of St Jude, gloomy Catholic stronghold built of rough-hewn local stone with a wide-eaved heavy roof of grey slate, was set right next door to the young and rampantly spreading Calvinist university, a rock in a Rome-devouring sea, Lynch declared. It was from the nearby hostel for homeless boys that Father Lynch recruited his altar servers, for whom he promised many surprises in the years ahead, terrible surprises for his little guild. This was Father Lynch's way of dignifying his unpromising rag-bag of altar servers.

The hostel was presided over by another import, Father Benjamin Cradley, who came from England. He was soft, pink and mildly mannered and had come to them, as he so often said, from the Oratory. Of course they hadn't the faintest idea where that was. Some deep note in the resonant openness of the vowels suggested to Blanchaille a giant orifice, echoing cave or great clanging iron canal down which ships were launched. The Oratory! What a round, empty ring it had, that Oratory which had sent Benjamin Cradley to this wild hostel full of discarded boys in ill-mannered Africa. When you saw how little he understood of it all you realised how much the early white missionaries must have mystified and terrified the natives. What crusading ignorance was there! He sat up at high table, this fat man, happy to be on top of his little heap, this hostel for the children of the destitute, dead, divorced, distant and decamped families. It was a magnificently incongruous appointment. Cradley was not interested in where he was, or who these boys were, but gazed out into the middle distance through narrowed eyes, faint watery blue, continually screwed up against the cigarettes he chain-smoked, a few wisps of hair greased over the big forehead, the brass crucifix behind the belt moulded into the big belly pushed out before him, meditating not upon God but on the meal to come.

He wandered down the gleaming corridors of the hostel with a curiously beatific smile on his face, scattering cigarette ash and dreaming of dinner time. His large fleshy head with its neat sleek hair seemed too heavy for his shoulders and he always carried it cocked a little to the left, the heavily veined lids lowered over the eyes. This gave him a slightly oriental, half-devious look, underlined by an idiot simper quite at odds with that meaty, pink English

13

face. When angered he flushed from the chin up and one could watch the blood pressure rising rosily like alcohol mounting in a thermometer. He was waited on hand and foot by two little nuns from some obscure Austrian order, the name of which Blanchaille could not remember – the White Sisters of the Virgin's Milk, or something exotic like that. Had it been? Anyway, they served and worshipped. Sister Gert, who was little and ugly, gnarled and nutty brown, looking not unlike Adolf Eichmann, and by her side the tall, plump, pretty Sister Isle, who spoke no English whatsoever but cooked, scrubbed, sewed and served with love and reverence verging on idolatory. Both of them called him 'Milord', and he spoke to them as one would to a pair of budgies: 'Who's a clever cook then?' and 'Father wants his pudding now – quick, quick!' And they tittered and curtsied and obeyed. They fussed about him at the head of the table, heaping his plate with fried potatoes and bending to flick away the ash which had lodged in the broad creases his belly made in his dusty black soutane. These two sisters in their white cotton habits and their short workmanlike veils, with their tremulous lips and their soft downy moustaches, and the way they chirped and flapped about their solitary, beaming, bovine master reminded him of tick birds attending to some old, solid bull. One day he remembered being delegated to clear the dishes at the head table and he stood close up watching Father Cradley digging plump fingers into a mound of Black Forest cake rather as a gardener drills the soil to take his seedlings, and then Blanchaille thought he understood why the Boers had gone to war against the English. He told Father Lynch.

'That is a misapprehension, boy. The English are capable of being lean, hard-faced killers just as the Boers are capable of running to fat. We should not judge things as they seem to be, or people as they look. If we all looked what we were the jails would be full.'

'The jails are full.'

'That's because we are in Africa. The jails here are built to be full. That doesn't remove from us responsibility for trying to get underneath the layer of illusion. Why is it, for instance, that although everyone here knows they're finished they appear not to have made contingency plans? You *do* all know you're finished? That you're on the way out? Your small white garrison can never hold out against the forces ranged against it. The end of your world is at hand.'

'It always has been,' said Blanchaille. 'We got in before you. We had that thought before you arrived.'

'Yes, but yours is a nightmare. I'm telling you the truth.'

Even then, young and ignorant, he felt the presumption of an Irish priest talking of apocalypse in this knowing way. What had this old leprechaun with his thousands of years of history, still green and damp from the bogs of Ireland, to tell an African child about the end of the world? You were born with the sense you'd been perched on the edge of the African continent for about two-and-a-half minutes and in that time you'd discovered that you were white and blacks didn't like you; that you were English and so the Dutch Africans known as Afrikaners didn't like you; that you were Catholics and not even the English liked you.

No, there was nothing about the apocalypse which Lynch could teach him. Power was another matter. Proper Europeans, you learnt from history, had a sense and experience of power, of killing and being killed on a wide and effective scale which was quite foreign to Africa. Efficient slaughter they understood. Proper wars. Even Cradley understood that and responded to it. You saw it in his appointment of Van Vuuren to be head boy of the hostel, to keep order among steel lockers and wooden beds in the dormitories. Van Vuuren with his strong square jaw, jet-black hair combed crisply up to a great wave and sleeked back behind his ears, his hard pointed chin and his bright blue eyes, the amazing muscles and the ability to hit and talk at the same time. All this recommended him to Father Cradley as having an aura of moral leadership as a result of which 'we have decided to elect him to this position of authority.'

'We have elected him? Jesus! It's as if the early Christians elected one of their lions as Pope,' said Zandrotti.

Van Vuuren administered fair-minded, fair-fisted power. It was difficult to bear him any resentment. There were certain rules and he saw to it that all the others observed them. He enforced order with a terrifying cordiality while continuing himself to flaunt every rule and regulation. He was really a law unto himself. He smoked, he drank, he slipped away with girls, drove a car without a licence, slunk off to the movies with a half jack of vodka sticking out of his back pocket and sprayed large grey streaks into his black sideburns. And this apparent contradiction never drew any criticism from any of his victims since he rested so securely on what must have seemed to him a God-given assignment to do what came best to him, drinking and whoring on the one hand, and enforcing hostel authority on the other. Father Lynch had prophesied that Trevor Van Vuuren was heading straight for the priesthood.

15

A few years later he joined the police, a move which did nothing to deter Father Lynch's faith in his own prophecies, and if asked about Van Vuuren he would say that he was engaged upon taking holy orders, that he was a man who had dedicated his life to truth. 'His hands,' Father Lynch maintained, despite the fact that all who knew him never thought of him as having hands but fists, 'his hands will one day baptise children, bless young brides and succour the dying . . .'

It was Blanchaille who had become a priest, but Lynch would have none of it. He was at police college, he maintained, and when Blanchaille called on him in a dog-collar he declared that he thought it was a wonderful disguise.

Of Zandrotti he was rather more vague: 'An angel of sorts though of course without angelic qualities. But a go-between, a messenger, an interpreter moving between the old world and the new.' Angel? He was too ugly, a glance showed you that. Zandrotti was the son of a crooked builder with a great raw salami face, who wore creamy, shiny suits, had a great round head and a round body tapering to tiny pigeon-toes. The father Zandrotti came once a month to the hostel in some great American car to abuse his skinny little son, Roberto, with his long white face thick with freckles and his wild, spiky black hair.

Everyone lived in the suburban Catholic ghetto which occupied no more than perhaps a couple of square miles and included Father Lynch's parish of St Jude, the hostel for displaced boys, the Catholic School of St Wilgefortis run by the Margaret Brethren across the way, the bishop's house, home of the unspeakable Blashford, with its large lawns, its vineyards and its chapel which backed on to the mansion occupied by the Papal Nuncio, Agnelli, to whom Father Gabriel Dladla later served as secretary, while also serving as chaplain to Bishop Blashford. Around this ghetto reached the long arms of the new National University, claws they were, embracing it in a pincer movement. Father Lynch used to take the boys up to the bell tower and show them how the Calvinist enemy was surrounding them, 'Truly a cancerous growth, note the classic crab formation. It will consume us utterly one of these days.'

And then I saw in my dream how Blanchaille remembered himself and the other altar boys in the dark sacristy of St Jude where the altar boys robed for early morning Mass, for Benediction and weekly Wednesday Novena. Cramped like the crew's quarters of some old schooner, smelling of wax candles, of paraffin, of white Cobra floor polish, of altar wine, incense, rank tobacco, of the pungent lemon and lime after-shave lotion which came off Father Lynch in waves as Mass wore on and he began sweating beneath his heavy vestments, and the terrifically strong brandy fumes from the old drunken sacristan, Brother Zacharias, of the socks and sweat of countless frantic altar boys dragging from the cheap boxwood cupboards their black cassocks, limp laced and always begrimed surplices, with a noisy clash of the frail, round shouldered wire hangers against the splintered plywood partitions. While from the robing room next door, so close you could hear the rumblings of his stomach knowing as it did that Mass still lay between it and breakfast, there came the smooth unceasing polished tirade of Father Lynch's invective as he briskly cursed the scrambling altar boys next door for the dirty-fingered, incompetent and unpunctual little poltroons they were. 'Oh, I shall die of hunger, or boredom, or both, at the hands of you little devils, far from home in this strange hot land, to be done to death by boredom and waiting . . .' Knock-knock went his black hairy knuckles on his biretta, 'Come along! Come along! What are you waiting for – the Last Judgement?' Those were the weekday Masses, early morning, low and swift.

In theory Brother Zacharias was there to assist the robing of Father Lynch. In reality he lay slumped in the chair most mornings nursing the hangover he'd got the previous evening from a colossal consumption of altar wine, cheap sweet stuff which came in thick-necked bottles with the Star of David stamped on the label, supplied by the firm of Fattis and Monis. Mass began a race between Father Lynch and his altar boys, as next door he struggled into his stole, maniple, chasuble, picked up the gold and bejewelled chalice, dropped onto his head with the finality of a man closing a manhole his four-winged biretta so that it rested on his jug ears and, swinging the key of the tabernacle on its long silver chain, he pounded on the plywood partition: 'Where is that damn server this morning?' And the server in question, frantically buttoning up his high collar and smoothing the lace that hung in tatters from the sleeves of his surplice, swooped out in front of him and led him down, out of the sacristy through the Gothic arch of the side chapel and on to the altar: *Introibo ad altarem Dei* . . . 'I will go to the altar of God . . . to God who gives joy to my youth . . .'

'– and employment to his priests,' Father Lynch liked to add.

On Sundays, in the olden times, when Father Lynch still had priests beneath him, before his clash with Blashford over his wish to integrate the pews, he had revolutionary dreams: 'Black and white, one Church in Christ,' Lynch said.

'More like a recipe for bloody disaster,' Blashford responded. 'Your parishioners will shoot you.'

These were the days before 'African renewal' or 'the mission to the townships', or 'the solidarity with our black brothers and sisters in Christ', with which Blashford was so closely associated in later years – it was before, in short, as Lynch said, 'the powers-that-be had looked closely at the figures'.

In those days then, on Sundays, there was in Lynch's church an occasional High Mass with enough priests to go around and of course Van Vuuren would dominate the altar as Master of Ceremonies, adroit, self-possessed; taller than most of the priests before the tabernacle, this smoothly assured MC moved, bowed, dispensed and disposed with expert precision. His command of the most technical details of the High Mass, the air of brooding concentration with which he overlooked the three concelebrating priests, his grave air of commanding authority and his expert choreography, moving between epistle and gospel sides of the altar, between chalice and the water and wine, between tabernacle and communicants, between incense bearers and bell boys, between altar and rail, was a marvel to see. His hands joined before his chest, the fingers curving in an elegant cathedral nave so that the tips almost touched his straight nose. The professional hauteur of it, the utter oiled assurance with which Van Vuuren managed such matters, always struck Blanchaille as a wonder and as being utterly at odds with the way he used his fists back in the dormitory in the hostel when he was about Father Cradley's business.

Thick creamy aromatic smoke rose from the bed of glowing charcoal on which they scattered the incense seeds, the smoke entered the nostrils like pincers, pierced the sinus passages and burst in a fragrant spray of bells somewhere deep inside the cranium. You never coughed, you learnt not to cough. Only the new ones coughed in the holy smoke. The new ones like little Michael Yates, who was Blanchaille's boat boy and was afterwards to become Mickey the Poet, martyr and victim of the traitor Kipsel, so tiny then that he came up to Blanchaille's hip and stood beside him holding the incense boat, the silver canoe with the hinged lid which closed with a snap upon the spoon at the flick of a finger. Father Lynch spooned incense from the incense boat, spreading it on the glowing charcoal in the thurifer where it crackled and spat and smoked. Van Vuuren, standing directly behind Lynch, sighted down his perfectly touching forefingers during the ladling of the incense and then with a contained nod, satisfied, dismissed Blanchaille and his boat boy. Both backed away slowly and bowed. Then Blanchaille adjusted the thurifer, lowering its perforated sugar-shaker cap down through the billowing incense, adjusting its closing with the complicated triple-chain pulley and then returned with little Yates to his place, swinging his smoking cargo before him slowly in a long lazy curve over his toe-caps. The fat puff of incense to left and right marked the furthest reaches of the swing. Van Vuuren wearing his elegant, economical, sober black and white cassock and surplice seemed in his plain costume almost a rebuke to the priests in their gaudy emerald-green vestments who lifted their arms to show the pearl-grey silk of their maniples, and turned their backs on their congregations to show the sacred markings, the great jewel-encrusted P slashed by the silver and oyster emphasis of the magic X. Van Vuuren carried more authority than all of them and it was about him, around the strong fixed point, that the other holy flamboyancies revolved like roman candles in the thickening aromatic fog of incense. Lynch had something of the truth in his prophecy about Van Vuuren because when you looked at Van Vuuren you knew, you said, he could have been a priest already. It was, Blanchaille supposed later, the air of authority that impressed, the sense of knowing what to do and when you had grown up among flounderers, it was an impressive sight.

All Father Lynch's boys, with the exception of Ferreira, lived in the hostel across the road from the Catholic High School of St Wilgefortis, a curious saint much celebrated in Flanders and generally depicted with a moustache and beard which God in his grace had granted to her to repulse the advances of would-be suitors. The school was run by the Margaret Brethren, a Flemish teaching order of brothers who, for reasons never known, took as their model of life the example of their medieval patroness, the formidable St Margaret of Cortona, who after a dissolute early life repented of her sins and began whipping into saintliness her flesh and the flesh of her flesh, her illegitimate son, the fruit of her seduction by a knight of Montepulciano.

Frequent and savage beatings she no doubt felt were deserved by this walking reproach to her saintly aspirations. At the same time she went about calling on the citizens of Cortona to repent, and given the lady's determination it was a call that would not be denied. As Margaret in the thirteenth century so did her Brethren in the twentieth, they beat the devil out of their boys with tireless piety and unstinting love for their souls and if this sometimes resulted in certain injuries, a simple fracture or bleeding from the ear, why

19

then the Brothers laid on the strap or stick once more, happy in their hearts they were drawing close to their beloved patroness.

Education was not their aim but salvation. Their job was to unveil the plots and stratagems by which unsuspecting boys were led into mortal sin, to sudden death and to eternal damnation. Improper thoughts, loose companions, tight underwear, non-Catholic girl-friends, political controversy, these were the several baits which sprung the trap of sudden death and broke the neck of Christian hope. Yet they could be beaten, they were beaten, daily.

The boys of the Catholic school endured their years under the whip with sullen obedience. Like some small unruly, barbarian state crushed by an occupying army, they paid lip service. They bided their time. They worshipped the gods of their conquerors in public, and spat on them in private; sat, knelt or stood stonily through the obligatory daily prayers and Masses with heads bowed only to return to the worship of their own horrid deities the moment the school gates closed behind them. The gods of their underground church were genuinely worthy of worship. They were lust, loose-living, idleness, tobacco, Elvis Presley, liberalism, science, the paradise called Overseas, as well as those bawdy spirits whom some held were hiding in girls' brassières and between their legs and of which strange exhilarating legends circulated among the hidden faithful in the bicycle sheds, the changing rooms and lavatories. And of course what made these native gods more powerful, more adorable than any other, was the fact that they so clearly haunted and terrified the Margaret Brethren. The Margaret Brethren taught the knowledge of death, they cultivated the more advanced understanding of dying, of judgement, of hell and heaven. Education for them was the pursuit of a reign of terror. The dirty little secrets of the native gods which promised fun, excitement, escape, horrified them and they fought them tooth and nail.

If this strengthened the boys' sense of coming doom, of impending Armageddon, that was because they were so naturally adapted to it. They grew up with it, it came as no surprise to learn that the end of the world was at hand, though there was no way they could have explained this to the uncomprehending Flemish immigrants who simply couldn't understand how it was possible to be hated by anybody, except perhaps the French. The Margaret Brethren taught lonely, sudden violent death as the Wages of Sin. But white children of a certain sort, born in South Africa, then as now, knew of a wider and more general catastrophe, that the world was very likely to end in violence and sooner rather than later. One noted at one's mother's knee that the end of the world very probably was at hand and it was only a question of time before the avenging hordes swept down from the north.

Whether this was true or not didn't matter. It was believed. It was an article of faith.

And then there was the deep loathing which the Margaret Brethren instinctively felt for the wayward and disreputable Father Lynch, another of the highly impressive qualities about him that attracted to him his altar servers.

Blanchaille was among the first. Blanchaille's mother lived three thousand miles away and sent him to the hostel when he was seven. She had been destitute and so the hostel, and the Margaret Brethren across the road, waived their fees and took him in in the name of Catholic charity. Blanchaille's father, a Mauritian sailor, had deserted his mother when she fell pregnant and never returned and yet she kept his name and passport, drew one for her son later which she renewed religiously, placing her faith in the French connection, clearly determined that her son would one day return to his motherland in triumph, like Napoleon. This foreign document embarrassed Blanchaille and he hid the passport for years. No one else had one. It looked strange and besides he wasn't going anywhere. No one was going anywhere. The others teased him about it, calling him Frenchie. But after he'd hidden it they forgot about it and began calling him Blanchie instead, a name that stuck. Trevor Van Vuuren appeared to have no parents but he had an elder brother who worked on the whalers and drove a bottle-green MG sports, which was all terrifically exciting. Zandrotti's father was a crooked businessman, a building contractor handling large commissions in the Government road programme. He made it his business to add rather too much sand to his cement and eventually catastrophe overtook him when bridges began collapsing across the country. A huge hulking man, he'd arrive in his blood-red Hudson Hornet to visit his skinny knock-kneed little son with his spiky hair and his ghostly pallor. Zandrotti Senior made these visits specifically for the purpose of abusing and ridiculing young Roberto. This so impressed the Margaret Brethren that they presented Zandrotti Senior with his very own scapular of the Third Order of St Francis, a devotional association to which they were vaguely attached for reasons never made clear except that Margaret of Cortona had been fond of it. His father, as Roberto later explained, had absolutely no culture and repaid the honour by making his mistress dance naked on a table for a visiting delegation of Portuguese Chianti merchants

21

wearing the scapular as a G-string. This story so delighted Father Lynch that he suggested that since the scapular had bounced up and down on what he called 'the lady's important point of entry', they should return it in the same wrapper to the Margaret Brethren challenging them to touch it to their nostrils and try to identify the fragrance, providing the helpful clue that they inhaled that very perfume which had so excited the saint's knightly seducer back in the bad old days when she was plain Margaret, just another unmarried mother of Cortona.

This love of the blasphemous jest was one of Father Lynch's appealing characteristics. Another was the conviction that he was dying and hence everything must be done in a hurry, a conviction repeated often but without any apparent sign of alarm since haste did not preclude style.

Kipsel seldom came to Mass and never to the picnics. Perversely as ever, Lynch praised his loyalty and predicted that Kipsel would go far in life.

Last in the group but first in martyrdom, poor Michael Yates, later Mickey the Poet. If there was any epitaph for him it was that he never knew what was going on. It might have been inscribed above his lost gravestone – 'He never had the faintest idea.' He was only to write one short poem, four lines of doggerel, which led Lynch to call him Mickey the Poet, and the name stuck. Lynch went on to discern in him, in that wild prophetic way, 'some gymnastic ability'.

Now I saw in my dream how Blanchaille grieved at the death of Ferreira. I saw him shaking his head and muttering to himself repeatedly: 'What shall I do? What shall I do? First Mickey the Poet, then Miranda, now Ferreira.'

Naturally he detected in these violent deaths real signs that the end was near, this fuelled his anxiety, deepened his general feeling of doom, of approaching extinction. It is common enough at the best of times in beleaguered minorities in Africa, this feeling of looming apocalypse. Blanchaille's people, a despised sub-group within a detested minority waited for the long-expected wrath to fall on them and destroy them. They didn't say so, of course. They didn't say anything unless drunk or tired or very pushed – and then they would say, 'Actually, we're all finished.' Or ruined, some of them said, or washed-up, or words a lot worse.

This was what in my dream I heard Blanchaille say again and again as he stared into his occupied garden. He knew, as I know, that as the years have passed more and more people have felt this and they knew it to be true and the greater their perception of truth so greater became the efforts to disbelieve it, to push it to the back of their minds, to discredit it until at last, at the time of the Total Onslaught, it became a punishable offence to admit to the possibility. You could be punished, arrested, beaten up, imprisoned for defeatism in the face of the enemy, for after all there was by then a war going on. In my dream I saw Blanchaille place his hands on the window-sill and bow his head, his whole body bent as if something heavy pressed down on his back and he leaned forward rolling his forehead against the window-pane and staring into the garden, the very picture of a man oppressed, weighed down. He thought only of ways of escape. But from what and in which direction remained dark to him.

CHAPTER 2

And when in my dream I saw how Blanchaille stood at his window looking out across the garden towards the small knot of angry folk outside the front gate, I knew them to be his parishioners. They were the stony ground on which his seed had fallen. He had preached, he had warned, but the lambs would not hear, instead they banded together and drove their shepherd out. Tertius Makapan, in a mustard suit and luminous magenta tie, leaning against his dusty Toyota. A colossal man, a brick salesman, responsible for co-ordinating the attack on him; there were, too, his storm-troopers, Duggie and Maureen Kreta, Makapan's willing creatures, formerly the treasurer and secretary of the Parish Council (before the Council was reconstituted into the Parochial Consensus Committee, the consensus being that Blanchaille must go); and poor Mary Muldoon, mad Mary, who knew no better, or at least he had thought so until she had tricked him out of his key to the church and so allowed the Committee to lock and bar the place against him; and there, hanging back, his black housekeeper, Joyce, who had joined them quite suddenly one night. Simply abandoned the dinner she was cooking for him and left his steak smoking on the stove and went over to his enemies. Maureen and Duggie Kreta carried a large banner: PINK PRIEST MUST GO! They waved the poles and flapped the banner at him when they saw him at the window.

PINK PRIEST MUST GO! *Priest*? The use of the singular case annoyed him. Not that it was intentional, but merely echoed the Kretas' way of speaking. Maureen, round and determined with thick, rather greasy dark hair, and Duggie, some years younger, sharp face, thin mouth and full, blond hair. They rode everywhere on an ancient Puch autocycle wearing white peaked crash helmets and dark blue macs. They spoke to him as if he were a not very intelligent puppy. Thus Maureen: 'Father want to watch out for some of the guys in this parish who don't give a button on Sunday, look at the plate like it was something the dog brought in. In fact some of 'em only look in it at all like they're wondering what they can pull out. Father got to watch 'em like a hawk.' And Duggie, parish treasurer's briefings about lack of funds: 'Not two cents to

24

rub together most times. You have to raise some funds. The father before Father was a hot shot at raising funds. Charity walks. Charity runs. That was Rischa. Running priest.'

PINK PRIEST MUST GO!

Blanchaille wished to pull down the window and shout at them: 'Yes, pink priest going! White priest come, pink priest go. Green priest yes, black priest no!' It was like living in a bloody nursery. Well, he was going to oblige. With pleasure.

He was getting out just as fast as he could.

The need to escape had become for Blanchaille an obsession: if he asked himself what it was he wanted, he answered – rest, peace. Now at the time of the Total Onslaught this feeling was naturally strong, as it always is at the time of killing and much blood, among people of all colour and political persuasions, sad to say. The dead were to some extent envied. They were out of it at least. Those who had disappeared were considered to be fortunate also. Nobody knew where they had disappeared to and no one cared. It was whispered by some that those who had vanished were perhaps also dead but this was widely discounted – they were said to have 'gone pilgrim', meaning they were believed to be travelling overseas, thus distinguishing them from the truly dead soldiers who were said to have 'joined the big battalion'. In war time, said Father Lynch, morphine for the wounded, euphemisms for the survivors. So people bravely pointed out that in war time casualties must be expected and it was best not to question too deeply. It was devoutly to be hoped that the dead and those who had disappeared had gone to some happier place where they would at least be at peace. Now, when asked where this place was, some would have replied vaguely that it was somewhere overseas, others would have given a religious answer and pointed to the sky; a few very brave souls would have whispered quietly that perhaps they'd gone to 'that shining city on the hill' or to 'that colony of the blessed'; or to that 'rest-home for disconsolate souls', which legend held President Paul Kruger established for his homeless countrymen somewhere in Switzerland early this century. Despite threats of imprisonment issued regularly by the Regime, the legend of Kruger's heritage persisted, a holy refuge, a haven, funded with the golden millions he had taken with him when he fled into exile. The Regime scoffed at these primitive, childish beliefs and punished their public expression with prison terms. They were joined by the academic historians who regularly issued bulletins exploding the 'myth of the Kruger millions'. People you met were similarly dismissive, in fact it was not unusual to begin a conversation by remarking, apropos of nothing at all, 'Naturally I don't believe a word about the gold Kruger stole from the mines. Not a bloody word of it.' But everyone, people, historians, perhaps even the Regime itself, continued to trust in and hope for the existence of that much dreamed of distant, better place. Some became obsessed and fled. So it was with Blanchaille.

When he could stand it no longer Blanchaille applied for a long leave of absence. The Church of course, through a number of unhappy experiences, knew the signs. Bishop Blashford sent Gabriel Dladla to find out the reason.

'Is there a girl, we wondered?' Gabriel asked gently.

'There was a girl. But not here.'

'Yes, we thought there was a girl. Somewhere.'

The ease with which Gabriel followed him into the past tense chilled Blanchaille.

'There was a girl, a nursing sister, a Canadian. Miranda was her name. I met her years ago soon after I went to work in the camps or what she called the new growth industries, the growing heaps of unwanted people springing up everywhere in the backveld.'

'I would hardly call that an industry,' said Gabriel with a gently disapproving frown. 'The camps are a scandal, an affront to human dignity. A sin. The Church condemns the camps and the policy of racial Hitlerism which creates them.'

'It was one of her jokes,' said Blanchaille. 'She had a distinctive brand of humour. She had what she called a traditional job, a nursing sister in the township. She refused to dramatise the job. "I could be doing something similar in Manitoba," she would say, "It's nothing special." The difference between us, she insisted, was that I was doing something important but she was just doing a job. "Don't build it up. I'm not giving a performance," she said. She said I was at the forefront of things in the camps, learning how to process the people who had been thrown away; "Soon the whole country will run on this human garbage," she said. It was another of her jokes.'

'I don't see the joke,' Gabriel replied tightly.

'Nor in a sense did I. "That's your problem, Blanchie, you don't see the joke," she said.'

'The camps are an obscenity. Your work has been crucial in showing that,' Gabriel persisted.

'What about the townships?'

He shrugged. 'They're institutions. At least they're peaceful now. But the camps. . . !'

26

'And yet the Church goes in and supports them, cleans them, strengthens their existence.'

'Supports the people in them. An enormous difference. The camps are there. They're real. We have to work in the real world.'

'Look Gabriel, once there were no camps and that was the real world, and the Church lived in it; then there were camps and that was the real world and the Church lived in it. One day, please God, there will be no camps again and that will be the real world and the Church will live in it. No wonder they call the Church eternal.'

'I think it might be better if we left the Church out of this and talked of carnal matters.' Gabriel's tone was mild.

'What about the girl?'

'She seduced me.'

Gabriel smiled, 'Now, now, you mustn't try to shock me.'

'We made love several times in her car, an old Morris Minor, in the township after dark. It was rather like a tickbird mating with a crow, she in her white starched uniform and I in my cassock. Or like being locked in a room full of curtains fighting towards the light. After several experiments we discovered that the best way was to remove her underwear and lift her skirt to her chin and then I settled myself on her first lifting my cassock to my waist and dropping it gently so it floated around us, covering us, and we made love as it were in this warm, black tent, within the more intense darkness of the African night. It was a very private affair. Anyone walking past the car and shining a bright light on us would have seen nothing but a kind of Siamese twin, black and white and contracting strangely.'

Gabriel held up a hand. 'What ended it?'

'She was murdered.' Now he had the satisfaction of seeing the astonishment crease Gabriel's smooth face. 'She was pulled from her car in the township one morning as she drove to her clinic, and stoned. It seems mainly large pebbles were thrown. There were some half bricks as well, I believe. I went to identify the body. They pulled the big tray out of the fridge, and it wasn't her. The skull was crushed, you see, or perhaps you don't – unless you've examined head injuries on that scale. The features had shifted, slipped to the side like a floppy rubber mask. The face hung. It was so covered with blood, so smashed, she was unrecognisable. I remember thinking it was almost as if the mob that stoned her had wanted especially to destroy the head. The rest of the body carried very large bruises. I couldn't identify her in the strict sense but I knew, as one would know. And then the point began to get to me. You see, I realised that, Jesus! there must have been some of her patients in the crowd who stoned her. People whom she had nursed, saved their children maybe, and this was what they had done to her! And all around me I could hear the outrage beginning. Here was this woman who'd given her life to these bastards and here's what she got in return. Then a funny thing happened. I laughed. I faintly got the point. Miranda might have expected this official reaction. This predictable outrage. And I knew – she would have opposed it. In her book nurses died, like everyone else. Sometimes they got murdered, not merely here but in New York, or Blantyre, or Tokyo, and yes it was tragic but it was not special, it didn't happen for mystical reasons. But we wouldn't believe that. In our superiority, Miranda's death had to be notable. It had to mean something really nasty. In fact Miranda was too important to be allowed to suffer her individual death, she wouldn't be allowed to die, she had to live, for the sake of the propaganda we fed ourselves to enable us to go on saying that this sort of thing should not, ought not, *must* not happen. In our war of words Miranda's death was a big event. But in terms of her own spilt blood, hell, it didn't matter a damn. What mattered were the detonator words, "should," "must", "ought", which we can use to blow up the enemy. The enemy wants us little, ordinary, human, while we want to be big and important. We care about our position relative to the audience. We want to put on a good show. Everything depends on how things are looking on the stage. Making a performance. . . .'

'It's a pity in the way there is no woman – any longer,' Gabriel said. 'The Bishop is sympathetically disposed, in the new enlightenment which prevails after Vatican II. The sexual problems of his priests deserve loving consideration. Perhaps you read his piece in *The Cross*? However, in your case you might be better advised to apply for a transfer.'

'Right! I apply for a transfer – to the world next-door. Kindly inform His Grace.'

PINK PRIEST MUST GO!

Blanchaille did not consider himself particularly pink and he certainly no longer thought of himself as a priest, but he was in full agreement with the sentiment expressed in the crudely lettered banner the Kretas waved so enthusiastically – he was fully prepared, indeed he most devoutly wished, to go.

Gabriel Dladla had returned with the Bishop's reply soon after the siege began.

'I'm afraid it can't be done, Blanchie. This is your place now.'

'I'm finished here.'

28

'Finished? For heaven's sake, you've barely started.'

Gabriel had arrived wearing what he called his second hat. This wasn't a hat at all but referred to the car he was driving, a sleek black Chrysler belonging to the Papal Nuncio, Agnelli, whose secretary he was, as well as serving as Bishop Blashford's chaplain, choice appointments both indicating to a sceptical world that the Roman Church in Southern Africa took to its heart its black followers, indeed did more than that, set them soaring into the firmament, rising stars. Gabriel had come a very long way from the picnic basket in Father Lynch's garden when the two brothers, Gabriel and Looksmart, sat flanking the little priest. 'My two negro princes', he called them, as they sat watching the altar boys struggle with the weeds. Gabriel's was the only entry into the priesthood which had been approved. His brother Looksmart's attempt had failed when the new black theology took hold of him and he burnt the Bible on the steps of the seminary as 'the white man's manual of exploitation' and joined the political underground. Blanchaille's vocation had been derided and ignored. Only Gabriel's decision to become a priest had been applauded.

'He is only doing what any intelligent boy would do who wishes to rise. His behaviour would be entirely logical in Spain, or Portugal or Ireland. May we skip any tiresome talk of faith or morals? Gabriel intends to get ahead.'

Father Gabriel Dladla in his beautifully tailored dark suit and its pristine dog-collar, in his soft black fedora which he did not remove in the course of their interview, his chunky gold watch which he consulted with elegant economy in an unmistakable signal that the interview was nearing its end, with his whole air of intelligent, assured concentration with which he listened to Blanchaille but which did not suppress the faint air of impatience of a busy man with other, more important things on his mind. This was once the barefoot boy on the blanket translated in what seemed like a wink of time into a personage of weight and responsibility in the Church hierarchy. And it was with a wink surely that Blanchaille could move him back again to the blanket in the garden. He tried and failed. His eyelid fluttered. Gabriel remained the elegant, deft, important young person he was.

'Now I'm sorry Blanchie but I must be off. I have a party of visiting Italians to collect from the airport, guests of the Papal Nuncio. They're flying in from Rome. Do you know Rome at all? I adore Rome. Quite apart from the obvious connections in our case, it is the most surprising, rejuvenating of cities.'

'Gabriel, I cannot stay here. There must be another parish . . .'

'If you ever go, I recommend to you the Piazza Navona, a square which should be everyone's first glimpse of Rome, not even the tourists can ruin its perfect proportions . . .'

'Another appointment –'

'Another appointment? But this is your appointment and I am here to let you know that Bishop Blashford confirms you in this appointment. There is nowhere for you to be but here. Nowhere to go but back, back to Pennyheaven, this time for an indefinite stay.'

Blanchaille watched him walking down the garden path. The protesting parishioners cheered when he approached. Gabriel doffed his hat, waved cheerily to them and was gone.

Blanchaille phoned Lynch. The old priest cackled at the news of the visit. The electronic eavesdroppers chirruped and squawked along with him.

'Speak up, Blanchie, and keep it short. The line's heavily and ineptly tapped. The bastards never worked out how to use the equipment they import in such quantities from America.'

'I'm thinking of moving on.'

'Good. Knew you would come to your senses one day. Perhaps we should have a few words. Where are you?'

Blanchaille told him.

'My God, right in the sticks. What's that noise? I can hear people shouting.'

'Those are my parishioners. I'm under siege.'

Lynch's laughter was drowned in a shriek of static.

And I saw in my dream how Blanchaille's stay in the new peri-urban suburb of Merrievale as parish priest of the spanking-new church of St Peter-in-the-Wild had come to end in undignified confusion after just one month. The defection of his black housekeeper Joyce upset him particularly. She'd never got used to his arrival or the loss of the man he had replaced. How dreadfully unfavourably he must have compared with his predecessor, the youthful, energetic Syrian, Father Rischa. The Parish Consensus Committee had got to Joyce. They told her that Blanchaille was on his way out, they'd shown her the fatal mark of blood upon his lintel imprinted there by the Angel of Death who had passed that way and she'd shot off like a rabbit, an absolute winner in the Petrine stakes, in the thrice-crowing cock awards. Traitress. To hell with her!

St Peter-in-theWild was Blanchaille's first parish and his last. He hadn't been there two minutes when the complaints began.

'And what is the nature of your complaint, Mr Makapan?'

'History,' came the simple if unexpected reply from the brick salesman. 'Not only your own particular history, but your lack of understanding of the historical process in general and of our parts in it.'

Blanchaille's particular history – what was it? Unremarkable, really. A hostel boy, one-time altar server who had gone up to the seminary to become a priest. Why a priest? Because he wished to be like Father Lynch who understood the system of the Regime and sought to expose it. 'You are not priestly material,' Father Lynch had cautioned. 'You are raised with the puritan, primitive, moralising web of the system and cannot destroy it, but what you can do is to hunt down the guilty men and bring them to book. That is your real vocation. Blanchaille, the police college waits for you – answer the call!'

For once Lynch and the Bishop were in agreement. Blashford opposed his entry into the seminary and when the time came for Blanchaille's ordination, continued to oppose it, avoiding the duty to perform the ceremony by being indisposed. Instead Blanchaille was ordained by a visiting Hungarian archbishop who was deported soon after the event for gross interference in the domestic affairs of the country. Blanchaille had long suspected Blashford's hand behind the expulsion. Newly ordained, his first visit to Lynch had been disastrous. Lynch had stood him up in the pulpit and introduced him to the congregation as 'the boy you might remember having served at this altar for many a year, and is now a policeman engaged in important undercover work in the country, hence his disguise . . .'

Blanchaille had done no parish work. After six years of moral theology mixed with intense sexual agonies in the seminary, applying the purity paddle (a miniature ping-pong bat without the usual rubber facings) with a short, downward slap morning and night, whenever his errant member stiffened beneath his soutane, he went to work in the transit camps, the garbage heaps where the human rubbish, the superfluous appendages were thrown away; the huge shanty towns in the remote and barren veld set aside by the Regime as temporary homes for a variety of black people: there were in the camps the dependants, wives, children, grandparents of black workers in the cities; there were illegal immigrants who had taken work in the cities without proper papers; there were the aged, infirm and unemployable who had failed to fulfil the requirements of their contracts; there were shattered black communities which had been living, either by historical accident or with illegal intent, in areas designated as being for other ethnic groups, tribes, races, clans, formations laid down according to the principles of Ethnic Autonomy.

When Blanchaille went to the camps no one had heard of them, or of him. Soon everyone had heard of him. 'Father Theo of the Camps' the newspapers called him. Bishop Blashford warned him to avoid political involvement. Later Blashford was to call on Catholics to 'embrace the suffering Christ of the camps' and the Church moved in with force. But by that time Blanchaille had gone, had written his notorious letter to *The Cross* with its ringing phrase 'Charity Kills', in which he called for the camps to be bulldozed. As a result he had been transferred for 'rest and recuperation' in a spirit of 'loving brotherly concern', and under heavy guard, to the place called Pennyheaven.

Pennyheaven was an imposing country mansion of tall white fluted columns and heavy sash windows, red polished verandas, great oak floorboards a foot across, balding peacocks, an empty dry and cracked swimming pool, a conservatory where lizards basked, pressed against the bleary Victorian stained-glass windows. It had belonged once to Sam Giltstein, an old drinking buddy of Barney Barnato's. An individual, this Giltstein. When many of the Jewish mining magnates went over to Christianity early in the century, Gilstein, perverse as ever, resisted the movement into the Anglican faith and opted instead for the Church of Rome. When he died he left his inaccessible summer place in the high remote mountains thirty miles north of the capital, to the Church as a 'home for homeless clergy'. Many miles from the nearest village and halfway up the rocky mountainside at the end of an almost inaccessible dirt road, Pennyheaven had remained as remote and as distant from human habitation as Giltstein had intended it to be. No one visited Pennyheaven. To go there you had to be sent. To leave you had to be fetched.

Blanchaille was six weeks there waiting for his new posting. To Pennyheaven came priests for whom no other place could be found: priests not bad enough to expel, not mad enough to confine; ancient clerics awaiting transfer to geriatric homes, little trembling creatures sitting out on the veranda from dawn to sunset, trembling and dribbling, leaning over their sticks and turning weak eyes on the shimmering blue peaks; dipsomaniacs and men with strange cravings for little girls.

Blanchaille met there Father Wüli, a huge Swiss who described himself as the last of the great African travellers, who had come 'to rest in Pennyheaven between voyages of exploration'. What this in fact meant, Blanchaille discovered, was that Wüli was an inveterate escapee. He would stride miles across the mountains in his tough boots, his Swiss sense of direction carrying him to the outskirts of some town and there he would lurk among the rocks and kranses, leaping out to expose himself to terrified picnickers on the remote hillsides, his unerring compass on these prodigious treks, the needle that pointed him onward, leaping massively from his unzipped flies. Father Wüli would return from his distant journeys in a police landrover, blanketed against sudden display, looking very fit and quite unabashed.

He met there, too, Brother Khourrie, a little Lebanese who'd once been sacristan in a church by the seaside and who had led a blameless life until he was granted a vision of the Redeemer. Khourrie and Blanchaille sat on the veranda of the big house staring across the baking, shimmering country which ran away into the blue mountains: huge boulders stood stark among the thick burly vegetation. The nearby hills appeared to be made almost entirely of rocks, some split from the main mass, seamed, pitted, cleft, the colour of sand, lying among the thorn trees where they had rolled thousands of years before. Christ was a boy of about eighteen, Khourrie confided, in ragged shorts, carrying the T-piece of his cross slung across his shoulders, his arms outstretched and hanging over the beams to steady it. He was tall with blond hair worn rather long, and his skin was golden. He must have been lying down shortly before Khourrie saw him because sand had covered his back and stuck in the oil with which he had rubbed himself. He was gleaming and encrusted with sand and oil and sunlight. A shining man. Very gently and diffidently Blanchaille suggested it might have been a surfer he saw, but Khourrie was firm – to those with eyes to see he was plainly the Messiah. He had proof. The proof he produced was novel. He explained to Blanchaille that the Jews too had identified the Boy Messiah. That was why they had bought flats along the beach front and why they continued to do so in such numbers. Nearly all the flats which followed the curve of the sea shore were owned by Jews. The Jews always knew, said Khourrie. Naturally he'd reported the matter to the Church. Their response had been unforgivable. They had dispatched him to Pennyheaven. The reasons he was quite clear about, the Church and the Jews were in league. Neither wished it to be known that the Messiah had returned to earth.

After Pennyheaven, Blanchaille had been appointed to St Peter-in-the-Wild. The church was so new it still smelt of cement and the walls and ceiling were painted sky blue. The whole place was severely angular with pews of pale natural pine and a baptismal font at the back made of stainless steel, deeply shining, rather like the wash-basins found on trains. In a pulpit of steel and smoked glass with its directional microphone Blanchaille talked of Malanskop, his first camp. It had been, he said, a most terrible garden full of deadly melodies, a music of wonderful names: kwashiorkor and pellagra, enteritis, lekkerkrap and rickets. How they rolled off the tongue! How lovely they sounded! Children in particular found the music irresistible. They listened and died. Every day ended with perfunctory funerals. No less euphonious afflictions decimated the adults: tuberculosis, cystitis, scabies and salpingitis, cholera, typhoid . . . The red burial mounds grew up overnight beyond the pit latrines as if an army of moles had passed that way. Later the little graves were piled with stones to keep the jackals off and finally came the clumsy wooden crosses tied with string, the names burnt into the wood in a charred scrawl, dates recording the months, weeks, days, hours, in the brief lives of 'Beauty' and 'Edgar', 'Sampson', 'Nicodemus' and 'Precious'.

The Church half emptied after this first sermon. Blanchaille began to feel rather better about his new appointment. At the second sermon he tried to encourage the congregation remaining to recite after him the names of the camps and perhaps to clap the beat: 'Kraaifontein, Witziesbek, Verneuk, Bittereind, Mooiplaats . . .' The microphone gave a hard dry sound as he clapped his way through the litany. No one joined him. 'I want to suggest that in the foyer of the church we build models of these camps, of the shoe-box shantytowns, the tent villages, that we show their corrugated iron roofs, the towns built of paraffin tins, the three stand-pipes on which thousands of people relied for their water, the solitary borehole and of course the spreading graveyards. Everywhere the graveyards. We might use papier mâché.'

At his third sermon the congregation had shrunk to those few who he later realised constituted the Consensus Committee: Makapan, the two Kretas, and Mary Muldoon. Mary wore a hat with bright red cherries. Her flower arrangements, he noticed, had not been changed since his first sermon. Before the altar the hyacinths were dying in their waterless brass vases.

'I wish to remember today, dear brethren, my third and final camp, Dolorosa, that tin and cardboard slum in the middle of nowhere which has since become so famous. In my day, the mortality rate for dysentery was a national record, the illness carried off three-quarters of the newborn in the first month after the camp was set up. People in their tin hovels with their sack doors died of despair, if they were lucky, before the more regular infections removed them. Dolorosa, as you know, is important because it caught the imagination of the country and the Church. It was called, in one of those detestable phrases, "a challenge to the conscience of the nation." Individuals arrived there in their private cars with loads of medicines and milk. Rotary Clubs collected blankets and bread. This charitable effort grew and teams of doctors and nurses, engineers and teachers made their way to Dolorosa. But more than anything else Dolorosa became the camp which the Church took up. It became, in the words of Bishop Blashford's episcopal letter, "the burning focal point of the charitable energies of the Catholic Church. . . ." A hospital was opened. Then a school. And a fine new church in the beehive style, this being judged as reflecting best the tribal architecture of the local people, was erected and dedicated. What was sought . . . What *was* sought? Oh yes, I remember, what was sought was "a living, long-term commitment" – they actually said that! Farsighted superiors in distant seminaries saw the potential. Could not such a place, these wise men asked themselves, provide a training ground for their priestlings? Give their chaps a taste of real poverty, they said, by billeting them on me for short periods. The spiritual directors of these seminaries took to visiting me by bus and helicopter. They brought tales of increasing interest among their novices. Inspired by the new direction the Church had found, these young men wished to live, for short periods, a sympathetic mirror existence with their brother outcasts, to embrace Mother Africa. A small pilot scheme was begun and proved to be extremely popular. It was likened to young doctors doing a year of housemanship. Parcels of young priests arrived simply crackling with a desire to do good and discover for themselves the vision of the suffering Christ of the camps. Well, of course, the word got round and before long other sympathisers and wellwishers asked if they too could take part in this scheme in a more practical way. It was one thing to drive down every weekend with a load of powdered milk in the back of the Datsun – but that was no substitute for actually "living in" . . . And if the priests were doing it, then why not the laity? The Church, keen to involve the faithful, agreed. Rather than to drive down to Dolorosa once a week with a fresh supply of saline drip, maybe people should get a taste of dysentery for themselves? A conference of bishops recognized the desire evident among the laity, and in their famous resolution called on them to "make living witness of their deep Christian concern for their dispossessed brethren by going among them, even as Our Lord did. . ." Well, you can imagine what happened. The accommodation problem at Dolorosa, and I believe at other camps, became suddenly very acute. Sociologists, writers, journalists, health workers, students, nuns, priests, all began crowding in. I found I had to ration the shanties, the lean-to's and huts. I had to open a waiting list. Soon we were doubling up on our volunteer workers, five or six to a hovel, three or four to a tent, up to half-a-dozen in the mobile homes donated by the Society of St Vincent de Paul on the proceeds gathered from a number of sponsored walks. Even so it wasn't enough. It became increasingly difficult to separate the races as the laws of the Regime required that we do, and harder still to keep the sexes apart, as morality demanded. Who hasn't heard of the tragic case of the Redemptorist Brother accused of raping an African girl behind the soup kitchen run by the Sisters of Mercy? Of the nurse who died of dysentery? Of the Dominican novice taken to hospital suffering from mal-nutrition? Of the infestation of head lice among a party of visiting Canadian clergy? For a while it seemed as if the whole project of "embracing the poor" was in serious doubt since the faithful seemed unable to resist the very diseases they came to relieve. As a temporary measure all inhabitants, both victims and volunteers, had to be moved into tents miles away from the infected zone while the entire shantytown was fumigated by volunteers from the Knights of Columbus wearing breathing apparatus supplied free of charge by a local firm. At the time the problem seemed insur-mountable but with that particular genius which has triumphed through the ages, the Church found a solution. The answer, as we now know, was the careful demarcation of areas of infection. This was achieved by driving sanitary corridors between the healthy volunteer forces on the outside and the infected slum people within; these were the so-called "fire breaks against infection", a kind of Hadrian's Wall of Defensive Medicine buttressed at strategic intervals by the SST's, camp jargon for the scour and shower ablutions, obligatory for all personnel passing between secure areas and infected zones. It was, according to the Bishop's Conference, a pioneering effort in disease control, a highly imaginative protective health measure sufficiently flexible to take into account the varying degrees of resistance (or lack of it) existing among the ethnic plurality of groups which made up the rich diversity of Southern African peoples . . .'

Blanchaille gripped the edge of the pulpit. His words no longer seemed to carry through the church. He tapped the microphone. Dead. The bastards had cut his mike. He peered at Mary Muldoon, the red cherries on her hat pulsed in the gloom. The rest of the parishioners stared back at him sullenly. 'It was at this time that I composed my letter to *The Cross*,' Blanchaille yelled. 'Perhaps you've heard of it? In it I said that if the people in the camps prayed for anything they should pray for the bulldozer. Enough of these smooth and resonant phrases, of plump churchmen talking of people living in a manner consonant with human dignity. Disease kills but so does charity, more slowly but just as surely. Flatten the camps, that is freedom! Release their inhabitants to a decent beggary, let them wander the countryside pleading for alms, calling on us to remember what we have done to them!'

It was his last sermon. After that the siege began.

And Makapan's second and general objection?

'You don't understand our role in history. We are not simply crude racialists of the sort you think – may I say perhaps even hope – that we are. We don't hate, despise, spit upon black people, not any longer. We recognise our failings. We reach out to embrace them.' He reached out his big, dusty hands towards Blanchaille's neck, he flexed the knuckles with the sound of distant rifle fire. 'You want to condemn us, but the prisoner has left the dock. The old charges against white South Africans have no force anywhere. Everywhere there is change. We are changing.'

Blanchaille shook his head. 'We are ruined. It's too late to change. It is time we left, got out.'

'Got out? But Father Blanchaille we have nowhere to go.'

'There are numbers of places – abroad.'

'Lies.'

'And stories of people who have disappeared.'

'Filthy slanders.'

'There is even talk of the formation of a government in exile.'

Makapan's hands descended on his shoulders. 'No more. Only your dog-collar protects you. There is no other place, no better place this side of the grave, than our country here. I will die for that belief.'

The thumbs, kneading his throat now, suggested that he would kill for that belief too. But Blanchaille was past caring. 'That is quite probable, Mr Makapan.'

Then in my dream I saw Blanchaille open the window and fix his eye on the figure in white; long white flowing robes like a nun, and a nursing sister's head-dress. Try as she might to hide herself behind the others she could not evade his eyes. This was his former black housekeeper, Joyce Nkwenzi. She had served Blanchaille's predecessor, the muscular Father Rischa, long and loyally, but she'd lasted with Blanchaille only until trouble struck and then left him, abruptly one evening.

Father Rischa had been popular. He had also been extremely fit. He'd left Blanchaille in possession of a house, empty but for a couple of pieces of very bad Rhodesian copperware and a larder full of inedible food: bean sprouts, soya-based products, nuts, grains, seaweed and porridge. It turned out he'd spent a lot of time organising footraces and sponsored walks and testing country runs along the rutted veld tracks from Uncle Vigo's Roadhouse to the African location several miles away.

'At first we looked at Rischa a little skew, if you know what I mean. We could hardly help it. When he was appointed here he seemed to spend hours in his tiny blue running shorts, his big thigh muscles sticking out, pounding up and down the sanitary lanes behind the houses. Thick black hair he had, and well oiled, the way they wear it, you know? He got a few stares in passing I can tell you, at least to begin with, but he was a good sport.'

The brick salesman's hands were big, square and yellow and he had a habit of knocking them together when speaking, perhaps developed over years of handling the samples stacked on his back seat, knocking off the brick dust. He evidently expected Blanchaille to be something of a good sport . . . 'When he left, he preached a sermon saying that he was happy to be going to the townships because he was going to search for those Africans who hadn't been ruined yet by the white man's diet of Coca-Cola and white bread and he was going to turn them into runners, he said. Look at the Kenyans, he said. Look at the Ethiopians. Aren't they excellent long-distance men? Well is there any reason why our tough boys in the bush shouldn't do just as well? He was going to organise camps for training them right there in the bush.'

'Why not? The bush is full of camps, Mr Makapan.'

'He was a fighter, was Father Rischa. He stuck up for his

country.'

'And the camps are full of starving people.'

'You don't have to tell me about the camps. I've done the weekly run like everyone else. The milk run, the medicine run. We know all about the camps.'

And then I saw the embattled priest, Blanchaille, glaring at the demonstrators at the bottom of his garden and he raised his hand pointing at the black woman: 'God sees you, Joyce Nkwenzi! You cannot hide.'

At the garden fence, Maureen and Duggie Kreta rattled their big banner. 'Shame! Leave her alone!'

'God sees you have deserted his minister!' roared Blanchaille. 'He will send you to hell, Joyce Nkwenzi.'

The girl's nerve broke and she threw herself down on her knees lifting clasped hands beseechingly towards her accuser in the window.

'There you will fry, faithless servant, like a fish in boiling oil – forever!'

With a shriek Joyce pitched forward on her face in the dust.

Blanchaille returned to his chair.

It was nearly midnight when Lynch arrived, slipping by the pickets at the gate with ease. Blanchaille embraced him, weeping a little. Lynch produced a flask and two glasses. 'Brandy. Stop that flood or you'll water the booze.'

'I'm leaving,' said Blanchaille.

'Not a moment too soon,' said Lynch. 'You've heard about Ferreira? Well, now they want you.' He took from his pocket a note typed on a sheet of cheap paper. He read out: 'Tell B. to get going. They're gunning for him.'

'Who sent that?'

'Van Vuuren.'

'Why should Van Vuuren care? He works for the Regime.'

'Don't see him that way. He's kept faith.'

Lynch wore a black coat and an old black beret. Blanchaille recognised the beret. He'd worn it when he'd taken his altar boys on a tour of the Air Force base near the school. The reasons for this odd Gallic touch had soon become clear.

On the windy airstrip, all those years before, he had made a speech: 'Every lad should get a view of his country's armaments. My beret is applicable since what we're going to look at is the new French jet. The French have supported our Government for many years. The Air Force is very proud of their new plane. It's a form of confidence building, they say. Between ourselves I suspect this display of weapons is similar to the impulse that makes some men expose themselves to little girls in public parks.' They trailed round behind him inspecting the sleek fighter. 'It is called a Mirage. Wonderfully appropriate,' Lynch said. 'It replaces the Sabre, which is obsolete. Not swords into ploughshares, you understand? But Sabres into Mirages . . .'

Blanchaille tried to remember how long it was since he'd last seen Lynch. Ten years? The black hair beneath the beret was peppered with grey and the face thinner, the chin more pointed, but for the rest he was the same, the beautifully flared nostrils, the prominent jug ears, the hard bright green eyes. 'I live alone now, since Brother Zacharias died of the cheap wine,' he said. 'The university encroaches, it swallows up more and more ground each day and you know that Blashford has sold my entire parish to the university? He says the money will be used to establish a new seminary somewhere in the country for black priests. He was advised by his banker to sell my church. Our old church. Has it ever occurred to you, Theodore, that the banks are at the forefront of innovation here? Remember how the banks introduced the new scheme for appointing black managers in their township branches? There was a lot of opposition to it from the white managers but head office decreed and head office was looking further ahead than the people here. Well you know how a little later the Church discovered its mission to the townships, the Church reaffirmed its historic role in Africa, acting, once again, on instructions from head office. In this case, Rome. It is interesting to see from where the power flows. It would be fascinating to talk more of this, but we can't. Ferreira is dead and you are suspected of being a connection in the case.'

'Why me?'

'He telephoned you. That's enough.'

'He was raving. He talked of the City of God.'

Lynch laughed and poured himself more brandy. 'Not God. It was a bad line, Blanchie. You had a lot of interference. What he said was not God but *gold*!'

'You're well informed.'

'I've heard the tapes, a friend of mine obliged.'

'Who killed him?'

Lynch shook his head. 'There are two possibilities which the police are following up. There was something painted in the room where he was found, scrawled low down on the wall. Three letters:

ASK followed by what might have been part of a *B*, or perhaps the number 3. The obvious organisations spring to mind. The Azanian Strike Kommando No. 3, the hit squad, I believe connected with the Azanian Liberation Front. The choice of the word Kommando being a deliberate gibe, a taking in vain of the name of the mobile fighting unit venerated by the Boers.'

'Well, it makes a kind of sense, I suppose. Tony was in the Government.'

'Not exactly. He was a Civil Servant. And besides, if you're going to assassinate someone why pick on an accountant?'

'Well, who then?'

'There is another lot, home based, with the same initials – the Afrika Straf Kaffir Brigade. Both are mysterious outfits – the Strike Kommando claims to have infiltrated the country to carry out executions of enemies of the people. The Straf Kaffir Brigade is a group of right-wing maniacs who claim to protect the white man's way of life, motherhood and freedom – whether all of those, or you take your pick, I don't know. Despite their name it is not actually blacks they're after, it's white men who they believe are destroying the soul of the Afrikaner. The Regime, needless to say, denies the existence of both groups. The Brigade has claimed responsibility for shooting up the houses of liberal lawyers, painting swastikas on the houses of selected targets like the local rabbi, which incensed him no end as it turned out he is a fervent supporter of the Regime. They go about generally making a nuisance of themselves.'

'I remember seeing the name,' Blanchaille said. 'Didn't they release syphilis-infected mice in several of these new casinos these entrepreneurs are opening in all the Bantu homelands, in the hopes of spreading the pox among white gamblers?'

'The same. They are demented. But why should even a bunch of madmen who ostensibly at least support the Regime, assassinate one of its officials? Equally, why should the Azanian lot murder Ferreira? He was no big noise, no minister, no target. It seems to me that the question we ought to ask is not which of these groups carried out the killing but why they should bother to' remove a remote financial official who spent his time locked away with the ledgers poring over the figures?'

Blanchaille knew the old priest had to some extent at least answered his own questions. He suspected, as anyone would who knew Ferreira, that the answer lay in those figures.

'Do you believe in these organisations?'

'Believe? Of course I do! Whether they exist or not is another

41

question. But certainly I believe, just as I believe in the Kruger millions.'

'And the city of gold?'

'Naturally. It is a question of faith which I cling to with Augustinian ferocity. May God help you with your unbelief, poor Blanchie. Sadly I do not have time to explain my allusion.' He walked to the window and beckoned Blanchaille. 'Those lights over there – the flashing red and yellow neon, do you see? That's the Airport Palace Hotel. Ask to see the manager when you arrive. He'll handle things. Leave here as soon as you can.'

'What, now?'

'Certainly. The very instant your watchers settle down for the night.'

'But I'm not ready – not right now, anyway.'

'What? Not ready? Your sainted mother gave you your wonderful French passport. Your dead friend has supplied you with funds. Your bags are packed, I take it?'

Blanchaille nodded and pointed to the three tartan suitcases.

'What more do you want?'

He thought hard. 'I have no air ticket.'

Lynch tapped his nose and winked. 'Faith, my son.' He drained his brandy and rose. 'It will be taken care of. Now I'm on my way.'

'But you haven't said yet who you think killed Ferreira. Straf Kaffir Brigade, or Azanian Strike Kommando?'

Lynch regarded him unblinkingly. What he said next made Blanchaille's head spin: 'Or both?' he said.

Blanchaille went over to his chair, the same blue plastic garden chair on which he must have sat many a night and on which he was sitting when I first saw him in my dream.

'I am as much in the dark as you are,' Lynch said with a complete lack of sincerity. 'Now I must go. I'm not long for this world.'

'So you've said,' Blanchaille remarked sceptically.

'Can't be said often enough. Only this time I say it in hope. This time before the shades come down I see a gleam of something that may be –'

'Light?' Blanchaille put in helpfully.

'Gold!' said Lynch, 'and the deliriously exciting perception that history, or what passes for such in this dust-bin, may just be about to repeat itself. Remember, Theodore, red and yellow neon, Airport Palace – don't delay.' And with a grin the little priest stepped out into the darkness.

CHAPTER 3

Now in my dream I saw Blanchaille set off early in one of those typical highveld dawns, a sky of light blue plated steel arcing overhead. He wore old grey flannels and a white cotton jacket, grunting beneath the weight of his three bulky tartan suitcases well strapped, belted around their fat middles in thick-tongued fraying leather. He slipped quietly out of the house and set off down the dirt road. But Joyce, who was sleeping rolled in a blanket by the embers of the night fire, had sharp ears and shouted after him. This woke Makapan who was dozing behind the wheel of his motor car. Both came running after Blanchaille: 'What's this? Where are you going?'

'Somewhere where you won't be able to bother me.'

'But are you going for good?'

'For good.'

'You're running away then?' There was a jeering note in Makapan's voice. His eyelashes were crusted with sleep.

Blanchaille nodded. 'As fast as I can.'

Joyce said; 'Father won't get very far, those cases are too heavy. He'll have to walk slowly.'

'I expected you to stand and fight at least,' said Makapan.

'Where are you going?' Joyce asked.

'I don't know yet.'

Joyce became rather excited. Grasping one of the heavy suitcases Blanchaille held she tried to help him, half hobbling and half running alongside him. 'Are you going overseas?'

Blanchaille nodded. 'Perhaps.'

Makapan lumbered up. 'That's nonsense, man. You're starting to talk politics again. We're not that badly off. We're not finished. Even the Americans think there's life in us yet. I saw only yesterday in the paper how their Secretary for State for Political Affairs came all this way to tell us that it will come right in the end, that we're getting better all the time, that we will give political rights to other groups when the time is right, that we will be saved. There is no threat, not outside nor in, that our armed forces cannot handle. Even at the time of the Total Onslaught we hold our own. I assure you myself, and I am a captain in the Signals Corps. You do your military duty – even if it does sometimes harm your career prospects. My fight with you is religious, not political . . .'

Blanchaille understood this qualification.

In the time of the Total Onslaught of course everyone was in the armed services. For many years a quarter of a million young men capable of bearing arms were on active service or on reserve or in training. All immigrants were called up. However, the Regime decided this base was not sufficient and announced a plan to push this figure to one million men, by drafting individuals, old and young, who for various reasons had been overlooked in the years of the huge defence build-up. In a total white population of little over five million, this force represented a great army, at least on paper, able surely to withstand the Total Onslaught. However, it was also a considerable drain on the available workforce. The army had an insatiable appetite for more men because even the best strategic planners could not predict where the attack would come from next. The chief problem lay in guarding the borders which were thousands of miles long and growing longer all the time. There were, besides the national borders, the borders around the new Homelands, the former reserves in the rural areas which the Government declared independent and sovereign, and guaranteed that sovereignty by fencing them off. New countries meant new borders. New borders meant new fences. Entire battalions spent their period of military service banging in fence poles. Of course the Total Onslaught might also show itself from within, and as a result the huge black townships had to be encircled with wire and the resettlement camps fortified with foot patrols and armoured cars. Then there were Government buildings, the railheads, the power stations, the factories. Since these were frequently the targets of incendiary bombs and limpet mines, they required the strictest protection and the young men on active training might spend months on end sweating in desolate railway sidings or freezing by night outside the oil refineries waiting for something to happen. It seldom did, but then Total Onslaught required total preparedness.

The sons of the middle classes managed to defer their call up by going into university. Some emigrated, a few deserted and a tiny number pleaded conscientious objection and went to jail. But the great majority of young men went into the services and found the tedium quite lethal. Deaths from drink and drugs rose steadily; motor car accidents became more and more frequent and the number of deaths through careless, one might say carefree,

44

handling of fire-arms, a form of suicide traditionally associated with the police in the old days, grew so alarmingly that the annual mortality rates actually overtook those inflicted by the Total Onslaught. In a notorious case, a young man named Gussie Lamprecht, a draftee lance-corporal in a coastal barracks, was enterprising enough to draw attention to this problem by telephoning a local newspaper, giving his name, rank and number, and promising that if their crime reporter would come to the beach he would see 'something very interesting'. As the reporter walked along the pier, he related at the inquest, he saw before him a figure on the beach, whom he now knew to be the deceased, lift a pistol to his temple and fire. He remembered that the incident had terrified an Indian fisherman catching shad nearby. He had taken a picture which his newspaper was refused permission to publish, photographs of Defence Force property being forbidden, and young Gussie Lamprecht though deceased was still regarded as Defence Force property. The case caused an outcry, worried mothers of draftees demanded that the Government take action. The Regime responded by forbidding publication of any further figures relating to accidental death caused by firearms and a delegation of mothers thanked the Minister concerned from the depths of their hearts.

A problem more intractable was the increasing shortage of manpower. To ameliorate the imbalance caused by the giant call-up, the Regime suggested a new deal, a kind of leaseback of uniformed labour at army prices. The army would liaise with various businesses and industries and Government bodies which would state their requirements which would then be assessed in terms of manpower available and then where possible specialised labour would be leased back to organisations in need. Contingents of soldiers were deployed whose training in civilian life approximated to the skills required. The word 'approximated' covered a wide range and so cooks and engineers might find themselves spending the period of their military training working through files in the Department of Inland Revenue and young accountants could spend years knocking in fence posts to take the electrified wire surrounding the Independent Homelands in which the ethnic identity of each black tribe was so fiercely protected.

'Is it true, in that place called Overseas, that white people and black people can meet as they please? You come and go when you like? No one tells you what to do? Everybody is equal?' Joyce asked.

'I have never been there, but I believe so,' said Blanchaille.

'Stop and consider, Blanchaille,' Makapan was pleading with him now, 'We haven't got on well, I know that. But if you stayed maybe we could work something out.'

'What do you fear, Father?' Joyce demanded.

Blanchaille's answer was intended to be brutally direct: 'Destruction.'

He saw the shadow shift across her eyes like a bird dipping across still water, felt her dissatisfaction at his answer, for it told her nothing, or rather it told her what she already knew, what everyone knew. What he had been expected to say was in which scenario he anticipated that destruction. There were three main scenarios with which every South African was by that time so familiar that they referred to them by numbers, rather as Americans will talk of 'taking the Fifth', meaning the Fifth Amendment, or university students will say they're hoping for a 'good second', South Africans would commonly talk of 'going for One', which translated meant that they favoured the first scenario for the end of things; this envisaged black hordes from the North sweeping down, joining the local Africans and obliterating the whites. While this view was still accorded some respect by traditionalists, being the most ancient of the nightmares, it was widely discounted. More people believed in the Second, in which the hordes would still sweep down, the local population would revolt but the whites would resist, fight them to a standstill and some sort of uneasy truce would prevail – until the next eruption. A minority of daring dreamers contemplated what they called No.3, which imagined the unimaginable, a defeat for the white forces who would retreat to the sea burning all behind them and die on the beaches, shooting their women and children first. It was this scenario which appealed so directly to the Azanian Liberation Front that their so-called Strike Kommando added No.3 to their designation. More recently another vision of the future conflict had begun to circulate in whispers and rumours and this scenario was doubly terrifying since it gave credence to No.3 while seeking to reassure the population that the white nation had found a defence against its possible defeat. Known as the 'Fourth Option' or more colloquially as 'the Smash', it suggested that nuclear weapons were being secretly prepared and if the worst came to the worst would be deployed, destroying the entire Southern Continent in an instant. Whispers of the Fourth Option had first begun to circulate at the last congress of the ruling National Party at which President Adolph Bubé had declared in his characteristic throaty growl: 'We wish to live in peace – but if attacked we will resist and we shall never surrender. We will never leave this Africa we love but if by some misfortune we are forced to go, rest assured we shall not go alone . . . This is not a threat but a promise!' The promise was met with wild applause from the party faithful and the newspapers interpreted the speech in the usual imaginative fashion with headlines ranging from PRESIDENT PLEADS FOR PEACE! to BUBÉ TALKS TOUGH! 'WE'LL TAKE YOU WITH US' WARNS PRESIDENT, to SOUTH AFRICA HAS NO NUCLEAR STRATEGY – OFFICIAL! This last referring to an off-the-record meeting between Bubé and various reporters after the speech in which he categorically denied that the Republic possessed nuclear weapons, or intended to manufacture any. The fact that he pronounced the first and the last *b* in bomb was regarded as highly significant and analysed at some length. Some papers suggesting that by putting peculiar emphasis on the word 'bomb' the President was signalling to hostile states to the north that they shouldn't take his denial too seriously, while still others argued against attaching too much importance to peculiarities of pronunciation pointing out that Bubé had been talking English, which was not his first language, and he had, in any event, an emphatic, guttural way of speaking. Subtle observers reported that the fact that he had used English showed that he intended his warning to carry as far as possible. He had closed the meeting by consulting with a flourish his gold hunter, a time-piece of great beauty and fabled accuracy manufactured in Cologne, closing the case with a decisive snap which left no one in any doubt of his determination to protect the country's security at any cost.

Blanchaille's second answer to Joyce and Makapan at their dawn meeting was more specific. 'I am retiring.'

'Father is weak now. Joyce must carry his bags.'

Blanchaille was aghast. 'You want to come with me? When things got tough you went over to this man here. Now you've thought better of that and you return to me. What sort of behaviour is that?'

Joyce was not in the least abashed. 'I didn't know Father was going overseas.'

Makapan turned round and stalked off shouting: 'Overseas! What the hell do you know of overseas? No good can come of this. And you Joyce – don't make a fool of yourself. Stay with us. We will look after you. This man is mad. Don't listen to him. Don't go with him.'

But Joyce had now actually wrested one of Blanchaille's cases from him and was carrying it down the road. She took no notice of Makapan.

And so I saw how Blanchaille and the woman went on together. And in my dream I heard Joyce question Blanchaille, saying: 'Mr Makapan is a good man, but he is thick. He is thick in his head. He said Joyce must come to his side. If Joyce comes to his side then Father Rischa will come back and we will be happy again. Every night I sleep out in the cold waiting. I am tired of waiting. Why is Father going overseas?'

'I believe I will find a better place there.'

'And who told you of the better place?'

'It is written in a book.'

'Ah,' Joyce seemed pleased. 'In the book of the Lord?'

'No, it is in the book of the President.'

'Of the President Bubé?'

'No, of another President, of old President Kruger.'

'Has he also been overseas?'

'Yes. He was the only President who had been overseas until President Bubé went.'

'I have heard something of him. And the words in this book – are they true?'

Blanchaille hesitated. 'I cannot say if they are true, indeed it is said by some that this book does not exist. But if they are not true, these words, then they are interesting.'

'And what do they speak of, these promises in the book?'

'It is written that there is a place for hopeless souls who are tired of too much wandering. Good souls, African souls, who seek rest will find it in this special place.'

Joyce seized his elbow with such a powerful grip that he gasped. 'And what else?'

'There all people will be equal, there will be no segregation, no pass laws, no black and white skins, no separate lavatories, no servants' quarters, no resettlement camps. In that place friends who have disappeared will be found again and even some we thought were dead will greet us. There will be no police stations, no torture, no barbed wire, no guns, no soldiers and no bombs.'

'And in this place,' Joyce yipped excitedly catching the spirit of his peroration, and relying no doubt on her Bible reading, 'will we wear white clothes and golden crowns?'

'White clothes, certainly,' Blanchaille replied with all the conviction he could muster, 'but I cannot say about the crowns.'

'Yes. Golden crowns!' Joyce insisted with an expectant smile as if she were feeding clues to a not very bright child. She tapped her head. 'But not for *wearing*, maybe.'

48

At last he understood her. 'You mean *coins*. Golden coins! Krugerrands?'

Joyce nodded, satisfied to hear the words. 'That is what I remember of that old President, golden coins,' and she skipped before him like a child down the dirt road, despite the heavy suitcase she carried. 'Come on then. Let's go, my Father.'

My Father? Her temerity enraged him. First she had attached herself to Father Rischa, the sprinting Syrian, entranced by his popularity, then she left Blanchaille for his lack of it; she went over to the Parish Consensus Committee and now without a blink she had deserted them and returned to her original master in the mistaken belief that after all perhaps he offered the better deal. Look how she skipped ahead of him! Why she even lifted the suitcase onto her head in the way women carry water from the well and with it wonderfully balanced there she danced and jigged! It would do no good to talk to her of the difficulties of leaving without permission, without a ticket or passport. This was scarcely the time for discussion. But there were other ways perhaps. He had no intention of leaving before paying a few last calls, to Bishop Blashford in particular, perhaps to Gabriel. Ecclesiastical authority might do to Joyce what he could not. A momentary access of charity afflicted him at this point and he thought that he might have misjudged her, that perhaps she was a poor weak creature, easily swayed; but commonsense reasserted itself to tell him that this was nonsense, she was a ferocious woman determined on escape and mere legal detail would not deter her; that she had no permission or papers was no obstacle, for while she was with him, he was her permission, her passport, and her ticket. Her heavy body shook under her white skirt and blouse. Her head-dress was beautifully ironed. She endeavoured to look like a nun of the old sort, from the days before nuns began dressing like traffic wardens. If ever the situation changed and revolutionary firing squads roamed the streets executing their enemies, Joyce would be there, praying as the bodies hit the ground: 'He let me down, but forgive him, if you can.'

CHAPTER 4

And now I saw in my dream how the road which Blanchaille and Joyce followed took them past a great township on the edge of the city. Perhaps this was the township in which Blanchaille's friend Miranda had died, but if so he gave no indication of it. And outside this township, beside the usual scrolls of barbed wire so ornate they took on the look of some lean and spiky sculpture, the priest and his housekeeper saw police vans and Saracen armoured cars crowded in at the gates and armed policemen in positions on the roofs of the houses and in trees and on any high vantage point, training their guns on the township.

And then I saw a short, stocky man with a sub-machine gun under his arm step forward and introduce himself to the two travellers as Colonel Schlagter. This Schlagter was a burly capable-looking man, but that he was under some strain was clearly apparent from the tight grip he kept on the black machine gun, jabbing it at them and demanding to know their business.

'We are on a journey,' Blanchaille explained, indicating the suitcases.

Schlagter jerked his thumb at Joyce. 'Does this girl have a permit to be here? No one is allowed without a permit. Why is she outside? Why is she not inside with the others?'

'She's with me. She's my servant,' Blanchaille explained.

'O.K., in that case she can help you.' Schlagter turned to Joyce. 'I hope you got strong arms, my girl. There's lots of work for you here. Now both of you listen to me. This is the position. I'm commandeering you in terms of the State of Emergency, which gives me the right under the regulations to commandeer any civilians who in the opinion of the military commander or senior police officer on the scene may contribute to the safety of the State.'

'But what has happened? There's been trouble here, hasn't there?' Blanchaille demanded. 'I thought the townships were peaceful.'

Now this was a telling point because one of the proudest boasts of the Regime at that time was of the peace to be found in the townships. Full-page advertisements appeared in international newspapers: they showed happy scenes, a group of children playing

50

soccer; a roomful of smiling women taking sewing lessons; a crowded beer hall full of happy customers, and over the photographs the headline: YOU ARE LOOKING AT A RIOT IN A SOUTH AFRICAN TOWNSHIP. Trudy Yssel's Department of Communications ran this campaign with great success.

'The townships are peaceful. Don't you bother about that,' Schlagter snapped. 'Come along with me please.'

He led them into the township where before the huge and fortified police station a bleak sight met their eyes. In the dust there lay scores of people, very still, with just an edge of clothing, a corner of a dress, the tip of a headscarf lifting in the gentle breeze which carried on it the unmistakable heavy smell of meat and blood. Joyce put down the suitcase and drew close to Blanchaille, seizing his wrist in her terrible grip.

'Where have you brought Joyce? I believed in Father and where has he brought me?'

'We must do as he says,' Blanchaille whispered.

'We are caught here. Stuck forever,' Joyce replied.

'Less talk, more work my girl.' Schlagter indicated the fallen people in a matter-of-fact way, lifting his arms and drawing with his two forefingers an imaginary circle around them. 'The people you see here are guilty of attacking the police. Believing themselves to be in great danger my men, after several warnings, returned fire. Just in time, I can tell you. The Saracens held their fire. They were not called or the damage would have been far greater, particularly to peaceful people in their houses. I'm proud to say these officers contained the charge with rifle fire and well-directed barrages from their sub-machine guns, even though this is a comparatively new weapon, extremely light and portable but inclined to jam when fired in haste due to the palm-release mechanism which must be squeezed simultaneously with the trigger. It takes some time to get the knack of it. But it's no more than a teething problem, I can assure you. Now these casualties must be removed. You have a free hand. You and the girl will be covered throughout the operation so there's no cause for alarm' – this last was directed at Joyce who had begun sobbing. 'To your right you will see the front stoep of the police station which at the time of the murderous attack was occupied by only four black constables. Lay out the people there in orderly rows to facilitate counting and identification. Any problems, call on me.'

Priest and servant wandered among the fallen people, men, women and children tumbled into heaps or sprawled alone.

51

Blanchaille noticed the remnants of clothing, several old shoes, a petticoat and even an old kitchen chair scattered about. Most of the people had been shot recently for they were warm still and bled profusely. He'd never realised how much blood the human body could contain and how the violent perforations of heavy, close-range fire will make the blood gush and spread. And then, stranger still, there were others who showed no signs of blood, or wounds, not even a single puncture. But there was blood enough, soaking into the dust, making a pungent sticky mud which Blanchaille and Joyce stirred up still further with their feet, though they tried to be as careful as possible. The policemen from their vantage points sighted down their rifles.

'If we pick them up together that will be easier,' Blanchaille said.

'Do your own work yourself,' Joyce retorted.

Blanchaille began lifting the body of a young man, seizing his left arm and his right leg and carrying him across the stoep, hearing the blood drip as he shuffled across the open space. The man was a terrible weight. 'I cannot do it myself, nor can you. We must help one another.'

Joyce didn't even bother to look at him. She grabbed hold of the ankle of a plump woman with a gaping wound in her chest and simply dragged her across the ground in a slew of pebbles and dust. Blanchaille heard the woman's head bang on the edge of the wooden stoep as she hauled her on to the bare boards.

'Heads all the same way!' Schlagter yelled.

After that Blanchaille followed Joyce's example, seized a leg or an arm and turning his head away hauled the body to the stoep. Only the children he carried.

It was backbreaking labour and eventually Blanchaille could stand it no longer and went to Schlagter. 'There are so many, this is going to take a long time.

'Well, get on with it then.'

'Perhaps we could have some help?' Desperation made Blanchaille bold.

Schlagter shook his head. 'My men are on watch.'

'Watching for what? These people are dead,' Blanchaille said.

The Colonel smiled. 'When you've been in the police force as long as I have, you'll learn to be very careful before jumping to conclusions. These people may look like they're dead, I grant you that, but how do we know that some of them aren't pretending? Lying low? They're a sly lot these township people, I can tell you that from the years of working with them. What happens if some of them are just waiting until I order my men to put their guns down and go and start carrying the bodies? Then they jump up and attack! No man, I'm not taking any bloody chances.'

'These people are dead,' Blanchaille insisted.

'Says you! I'm in charge here and I'll decide who's dead or not.' Blanchaille went back to work.

'We will never escape,' Joyce snapped at him bitterly.

'Why should they want to hold us? Once this is finished we'll be out of here.'

'You think there aren't other townships, other bodies? They'll take us with them. Or perhaps they'll shoot us.'

She spat, a globule of moisture in the dust. What an odd collection of belongings littered the killing ground: there were quantities of shoes in different sizes and colours, some matching pairs as well as abandoned single shoes; there was a baby's push-chair, rusted, in blue leather, but still usable; there was, besides, a petticoat touchingly embroidered with pink lace, pink lace finely worked; a pair of spectacles with one lens smashed; a set of dentures, the teeth clicked shut, a bizarre solitary expression of naked obstinacy, the teeth presented an air of invulnerability which reminded him of that unyielding almost jaunty bravado that skeletons wear; and then, somehow most touchingly of all, there was the up-ended kitchen chair lying on its side as if someone had leapt from it only minutes before and left in a hurry. These small domestic details were more sad, and somehow more vocal, than the torn, shapeless bodies. The work was very hard. Joyce continued to drag the bodies to the stoep. He lifted some of them despite the strain and his aching muscles but he was now moving very slowly. Things changed when he came across a mother and child killed by a single bullet. The child was strapped to its mother's back in a red and blue blanket, tightly knotted. Their combined weight was too much for him to lift and he was forced, reluctantly, to try and separate the bodies but their blood had soaked the blanket and the knots would not budge. His hands slipped and reddened. With a snort of impatience Joyce came over and seized the mother's hands. He took her feet and between them they carried the bodies to the stoep. Joyce would have laid the mother out, face down, with the baby above but Blanchaille was revolted by the unnaturalness of this and gently turned the woman on her side so it looked as if mother and child were curled up asleep.

Perhaps this sign of gentleness softened Joyce, for she took up the next body with a brisk nod at Blanchaille, indicating that from now on they would clear the field together. Hoping this was the beginning of better relations, Blanchaille set the chair back on its feet, as if it would preside, become a witness, over their business. Joyce seemed to understand and approve of this gesture for there is always some comfort in extreme situations in the restoration of an even temporary normality. In the course of his work Blanchaille learnt something of bullet wounds. Learnt how the entry point may be smooth, how the speeding bullet may draw threads of clothing with it into the wound and the bullet, often encountering no obstacle on its passage through the body, burst out with ugly force from shoulder or neck. Or it might take a wildly eccentric course through the inner organs rebounding off bone to emerge in unexpected places, anything up to a foot above or below the point of entry. Head wounds could be particularly severe, seen from behind.

He went to Colonel Schlagter. 'You said that these people had been attacking your men.'

Schlagter eyed him warily, 'Well?'

'A lot of them have been shot in the back.'

'Christ man, what's that got to do with it?'

'Well it looks like they were running away.'

Schlagter shook his head. He laughed grimly. 'Front, sides, back – what the hell does it matter? Look, you've never been under attack. Let me tell you that when you're being attacked you don't stop to ask what direction the people are running in. Anyway, like I told you, they're a crafty lot. I mean for all you know some of them turned round and were running at us backwards. Have you thought of that?'

Blanchaille admitted that he had not.

When at last all the corpses were laid out on the long wooden veranda in front of the police station and an armed guard posted, 'just in case', Schlagter came over and thanked them for their work. 'You have been an indispensable help. You have served your country. All these people you see lying here will now be counted and photographed and their relatives will be brought to identify them, and afterwards they will be allowed to reclaim the members of their families. This is a strict procedure because the enemies of our country like nothing better than to inflate the figures of those killed and to claim that all sorts of people have been killed when they know this is a lie and a slander.'

The armed police were stood down and relaxed visibly. The Saracens left. Schlagter directed Blanchaille and Joyce to a stand-tap behind the police station building and asked them if they'd like to wash their hands.

Joyce washed first, holding her feet under the tap and then scrubbing ferociously at the blood stains on her white dress, folding handfuls of gravel into the material and rubbing it harshly, catching the water in a great scoop of her skirt like a prospector panning for gold and in this way she managed to reduce the vividness of the blood marks, but the stains remained.

Dust to dust, ashes to ashes, so the story went, Blanchaille reflected. Only it wasn't like that, not here. It was blood to dust and dust to mud and mud to water and away down the ditch with it. He watched as Joyce scrubbed at the blood which had caught in the cracks of her nails using the wet hem of her dress.

'I think they're going to let us go now.'

'You? Think! This is the new life you promised me. When I see how it starts, God knows how it will end!'

Blanchaille stepped up to the tap conscious of her rage, of her eyes boring into his back. He cleaned his face and his hands as best he could and rubbed rather hopelessly at the blood stains on his clothes but only succeeded in darkening and spreading them. When he turned again, Joyce was gone. He was not surprised and doubted whether anyone would have tried to stop her. Well, she would have a great deal to tell Makapan when she returned.

He walked to the front of the police station and, as he had expected, no one took any notice. He picked up his suitcases, one in each hand and one, bulky and uncomfortable, underneath his arm and began moving towards the front gate. Away to his right a group of policemen in shirt sleeves were playing a game of touch rugby using a water-bottle as a ball. The kitchen chair stood where he had left it, surveying the killing ground. He barely got out of the front gate before he collapsed, exhausted. He sat down in the dust on his suitcase beside the road.

And then I saw in my dream that a man driving a yellow Datsun estate stopped and offered him a lift. A short and balding man with a pleasant smile whose name was Derek Breslau. A commercial traveller for Lever Brothers dealing in ladies' shampoos. The inside of his car was so heavily perfumed it made Blanchaille swoon and he could barely find the words to thank him for his kindness.

'Don't mention it. Couldn't leave a guy sitting by the side of the road outside a bloody township. Normally I put my foot down and go like hell when I pass a township. You never know what's going on inside. Gee, you took a risk!' He examined Blanchaille's blood-stained, muddied clothes with interest.

'My bags are heavy and I can't go very far at a stretch.'

'Well, keep away from the townships.'

'It's a funny thing,' said Blanchaille, 'but I always believed that the townships were peaceful now.'

Breslau nodded. 'Well it depends on what you mean. If you mean the townships are peaceful except when there are riots, then I suppose that's correct. So I suppose you could say the townships are peaceful between riots. And I must say they're pretty peaceful after riots. If we need to go to the townships that's usually when we go. They have a period of mourning then, you see, and you got time to get in, do the job and get out again.'

'I suppose then you could also say that townships are peaceful before riots,' said Blanchaille, trying to be helpful.

Breslau thought this over and nodded approvingly. 'Yes, I suppose that's right. I never thought of it that way. But leaving all this aside, the truth is you can never be sure when the townships are going to be peaceful. You can drive into a township, and I have no option since I do business there, and find yourself in the middle of a riot. You can find yourself humping dead bodies or driving wounded to hospital. You can find yourself dispensing aid and comfort.'

'Aid and comfort?'

'Sure! That comes after the riots, usually, when they've laid out the victims and the relatives come along to claim them. It's an emotional time, as you can imagine. What they usually do these days is to get the priest up from the church and he gives each relative a blessing. Well one day I arrived just as the blessings had started. They didn't seem to be comforting people very much so the police officer in charge commandeered me and my vehicle and all my samples and he suggested that each relative should also get a sample of my shampoo, plus a blessing. Of course they weren't my samples to give, but on occasions like this you don't argue. Well, I stood next to the priest and he gave the blessing and I handed out the sample. Of course there was no question of matching hair types. I mean you can't stop the grieving relatives and ask them whether they suffer from dry, greasy or normal hair. I mean that's not exactly the time and place to start getting finicky. Can I drop you somewhere in town?'

Blanchaille mentioned the suburb where Bishop Blashford lived.

'Sure. Happy to help.'

'What disturbs the peace in the townships?'

Breslau shrugged. 'Everything – and nothing. Of course the

trouble is not having what they want, and then getting what they want. Like I mean first of all they don't have any sewage so the cry goes up for piped sewage and they get it. Then there's no electricity, so a consortium of businessmen organised by Himmelfarber and his Consolidated Holdings put in a private scheme of electrification. Then a football pitch is asked for. And given. And after each of these improvements there's a riot. It's interesting, that.'

'It's almost as if the trouble with the townships is the townships,' Blanchaille suggested.

'You can't not have townships or you wouldn't have any of this,' the salesman gestured out of the window at the blank and featureless veld on either side of the road. 'Cities have townships the way people have shadows. It's in the nature of things.'

'But we haven't always had townships.'

'Of course we have. Look, a township is just a reservoir. A pool. A depot for labour. I mean you look back to how it was when the first white settlers came here. You look at Van Riebeeck who came in – when was it – in 1652? And he arrives at the Cape of Good Hope what a name when you think how things turned out! A bloody long time ago, right? What does Van Riebeeck find when he arrives in this big open place? He finds he's got to build himself a fort. He finds the place occupied, there are all these damn Hottentots swanning around. Anyway he sees all these black guys wandering around and he thinks to himself – Jesus! This is Christmas! What I'm going to do is sit in my fort, grow lots of vegetables and sell them to passing ships. And all these black Hottentots I see wandering around here, they're going to work for me. If they don't work for me they get zapped. So he sits there at the Cape and the black guys work for him. Afterwards he gets to be so famous they put his face on all the money. It's been like that ever since.'

'But he didn't have a township.'

'What d'you mean, he didn't have a township? The whole damn country was his township.'

Ever cautious Blanchaille got Breslau to drop him not outside Blashford's house, but at the foot of the hill on which the Bishop lived. The salesman drove off with a cheerful wave, 'Keep your head down.'

Blanchaille picked up his cases and began the slow painful ascent of the hill.

Puzzled by this conversation, in my dream I took up the matter with Breslau.

'Surely things aren't that bad? That's a very simplistic analysis of history that you offered him.'

'Right, but then it's a very simplistic situation. There is the view that we're all stuffed. We can fight all we like but we're finished. The catch is that if anyone takes that line they get shot or locked up or whipped. Or all of those things. That's how it was. That's how it is. Nothing's changed since the first Dutchman arrived, opened a police station and started handing out passes to the servants.'

'Can nothing be done to improve conditions in the townships?' I persisted.

Breslau laughed and slapped the steering wheel. 'Sure. As I told the traveller. Lots can be done. Lots is done. Ever since the long-haired vegetable grower arrived from Holland, people have been battling to improve the townships. But after the beer halls and the soccer pitches, the electric lights, the social clubs, the sports stadiums, the literacy classes and the best will in the world, the townships are still townships. And townships are trouble.'

'Even when they're peaceful?' I asked.

'Especially when they're peaceful,' said Breslau.

CHAPTER 5

They walked in the Bishop's official garden. Ceres, Bishop Blashford's ample black housekeeper, had allowed him to leave his suitcases in the hall and sent him out to join His Grace with the warning that he would be allowed no more than ten minutes before His Grace took tea.

Blashford, the unspeakable Blashford, his open face ringed by soft pale curls, had in his younger days played first-class golf: no doubt clouded the sports-writers' prediction that he would have gone on to international competition had the Church not selected him first. He was that rare hierarch, an authentic indigenous bishop, born and educated in the country. By choosing a sportsman for this important appointment the Vatican had shown that it understood where the springs of religious fervour truly lay. Now his neatly shod feet pressed the grass. He was wearing what he called his gardening clothes, a fawn suit and panama hat, by which Blanchaille understood him to mean not those clothes in which he worked in his garden but walked there before tea, a trim, elegant figure with a fair complexion which reddened easily in the sun. His black, heavily armoured toe caps glistened, the double knots of his laces showed like chunky black seaweed as his shoes broke free from the bunched wave of his flannels. There was a brief gleam of polished leather with each assured step he planted on the smooth unwrinkled surface of his beautiful lawn. The end of the official garden was bound by a line of apple and peach trees and behind them a thick pyracantha hedge showed its spikes. Heads held high, wagtails sprinted through the splashes of sunlight beneath the fruit trees, their equilibrium secured by the rocking balance of their long tails. They shared Blashford's dainty-footed confidence.

'Well, Blanchaille?'

'I'm leaving.'

'What?'

'Parish, priesthood, country. The lot. I'm in a position of a bride whose marriage has not been consummated. My ministry is null and void. In short, I'm off.'

'I've been expecting you to call. The volume of complaints from your parishioners in Merrievale these past weeks has reached an absolute crescendo. Complaints had been laid with the police about political speeches from the pulpit. It was only with the greatest difficulty that I managed to persuade the authorities to allow the Church to deal with this in its own way.'

'You needn't have bothered. I also have friends in the police.'

'We all have friends in the police, Father. The question is will yours do what you ask them?'

He could feel the heat the Bishop gave off as he became angrier. He was vibrating like a cooking stove. He hissed from a corner of his mouth: 'It's not like leaving a party, you know. Or getting off a bus. Father Lynch is behind this I'm sure.'

'Father Lynch has never regarded me as a priest. He sees me as a policeman. I'm beginning to realise he knew what he was talking about. My relationship to the Church is that of a partner in an invalid marriage. The thing is null. I wanted to attack the Regime so I followed the only model I had – Father Lynch. I took holy orders. I would have done better learning to shoot.'

'Father Lynch is old, ill and not a little cracked. He flips about that decaying church of his like an ancient bat. He says masses in Latin to a band of parishioners as ill and decrepit as himself. He does so without permission. He keeps up the pretence of serving a parish where none exists. The building is scheduled for demolition. We are finding our way back into the world.'

Ah yes, the world. Blashford had been Bishop for as long as anyone could remember. Years ago he had been concerned with safeguarding the Church against the Calvinist aggressor, those who saw it as 'the Roman danger'. Then came Vatican II, and Blashford discovered 'the world'.

'Father Lynch always predicted that the day was coming when the Church hierarchy would be picked for their salesmanship.'

Blashford scowled. 'The church has been sold because it's redundant. Not only is the fabric beyond repair and the garden ruined, but only a handful of parishioners remain. There is no more room for all-white parishes, holy Mother Church embraces its South African responsibilities, she embraces her black brethren. Father Lynch, as I recall, refuses the embrace.'

The embrace. How long ago Lynch had foreseen that.

'Sitting in his garden long years ago, propped up on one arm with Gabriel and Looksmart Dladla on either side of him, he told us that the Church was ours now, we had better prepare ourselves for the embrace. Then he gathered us around him and he showed us the financial pages of the newspapers which were full of the new black appointments being made by foreign banks. Against fierce resistance from their white managers the head offices decreed that black managers be appointed to township banks. "Very soon now," he said, "we can expect the Church to follow suit. We have always taken our lead from the banks."'

Bishop Blashford joined his fingers together at the bridge of his nose in a prayerful gesture and spoke with a nasal twang into the tepee of his fingers. 'Lynch was headstrong, provocative, premature. Race relations in those days were primitive, it was only on sufferance that we allowed any blacks in our churches at all! You certainly didn't go round making a show of it, not unless you were looking for trouble. But then Lynch was always looking for trouble and you boys he gathered around him were gullible. He was an Irishman who never understood Africa, obsessed by myths and conspiracies. This madness over the Kruger millions, these holidays in fancy dress, these charades. Did you know that he continues to say Mass in Latin? Even though you boys are grown up and gone? Despite all my instructions?'

'He used to tell us that power was in love with secrecy but showed its public face in policies which arose quite arbitrarily or in reaction to outside forces, but were always presented to people as the result of due and deliberate consideration by wise minds. It's unlikely that Lynch would have seen the changes of the Vatican as anything more than panic-stricken measures taken in reaction to shrinking congregations. It was a case of swinging the stage around where they could keep an eye on the audience and getting them to sing along whenever possible. What is presented as the will of God is very often a response to a deteriorating market position, he said.'

'And where did it get you, this adulation of Lynch? You boys who surrounded him with your fancy dress revivals of the old Boer days and your talk of Uncle Paul Kruger? Where it got you was jail, exile, disgrace, death. That's what you got for listening to him.'

'But we never listened to him, that was the trouble. Ferreira was supposed to see visions. Van Vuuren was supposed to be a priest. I was scheduled to become a policeman. But maybe it's not too late. Maybe now he should be taken seriously.'

The Bishop stopped abruptly, he lowered his head, straightened his wrists and shook an imaginary putter, and then with utmost concentration he stroked an imaginary golf ball along the smooth surface of the lawn. This reversion to his old sporting ways suggested a certain tension. This was borne out when the Bishop at length straightened and said: 'There's blood on your shoes,' he looked more closely, 'and on your clothes,' he took Blanchaille's hand, 'and here, more on your hands, under the fingernails.'

'I was passing the township outside the city when I was ordered by the police officer in charge to help to remove the bodies of people shot during the riot.'

'There are no riots in the townships.'

Blanchaille held up his hands with their blood-stained fingernails.

'And what did he predict for Gabriel Dladla?' Blashford suddenly demanded.

'He never prophesied for the black boys. He said they were free agents, outside his range of understanding. Work with materials you know, he said. He would lie under the Tree of Heaven flanked by Gabriel and Looksmart Dladla, looking rather like those porcelain slave boys. You know the kind in turbans carrying bowls of fruit you sometimes see in old pictures? Look at what wins and know why, Lynch always told us. Be sure you select a winner you know, where you're connected. We weren't connected to the structures of Government power, we had no input there, but by the grace of God we had an example a whole lot closer, we had holy Mother Church herself! That would do, he said, as an analogue. All power institutions could be expected to adapt in similar ways. Their trick was to forbid individual alterations to the *status quo* while presenting their own changes as a genuine response to popular demands and altered circumstances, at the same time ensuring that such changes, as and when they were permitted to occur, safe-guarded their sole reason for being, that is to say, the retention of power. The capacity to praise today what you executed people for yesterday, and of course vice versa, always vice versa, and with complete sincerity is essential for the maintenance of power. He invited us to observe that the changes transforming the Catholic Church were undertaken by the very authorities who had forbidden those changes in previous times, to notice the vocabularies used, words like "renewal" and "reaffirmation" and "renaissance", and he invited us to apply what we learnt to the understanding of the way the Regime worked. The keywords for the Regime were "adaption", "evolution", "self-determination". What the words actually said were – O.K. Carruthers let the fuzzies out of the pens but shoot if they stampede. We saw the parallels. Church and Regime believed themselves divinely inspired, both regarded themselves as authoritative and both maintained that they held the secret of salvation. The parallels weren't exact but they were the best we had, he said. We would have to make do with them. And we did. The trouble was –'

Blashford interrupted angrily, 'The trouble was Lynch was mad and he never understood.'

Blanchaille shook his head. 'No, the trouble was we thought it was a game. Spot the connections. We enjoyed it but we didn't believe in it.'

The Bishop paused before a large and blowsy rose. Very deliberately he took the head in his hands and shook the petals so that they fluttered and drifted in the wind.

'This is a lovely garden. I remember it well,' Blanchaille said.

'You know my garden?' Blashford clearly deplored this news.

'I knew the other one better. The one behind the hedge.'

'I never knew I had another garden.'

The Bishop's official garden was very beautiful. The roses, large and blowsy, opened up their heavy red hearts and did not care where their petals drifted. Their perfume was heavy, meaty. Their bruised beefy solidity would have looked well on a butcher's slab. Sweetpeas thronged against the further trellis, the bougainvillaea foamed and dripped and six clipped lemon trees showed bright yellow fruit among darkly gleaming leaves.

But of course it was in the Bishop's other garden that the altar servers had grown up, the wilderness beyond the spiny hedge on the far side of the fruit trees, the neglected vineyard with its harsh, sour grapes, its choked lily pond, its loquat trees, its old disused well, its blackjacks and weeds. They met and smoked cheap American cigarettes, taking as their model the expertise of Van Vuuren who smoked with quite wonderful style and aplomb and adult poise. He was expert in making deep, lengthy inhalations which hollowed his cheeks and they watched fascinated as the jets of grey smoke expelled from his nostrils met and mixed with the single thick gust from his lips. They drank from quarter-bottles of brandy and vodka and dropped the empties down the well, too deep to hear the crash.

And they took girls there. He took Isobel Turner, first and foremost, not particularly highly rated it was true, in Ferreira's opinion 'no great shakes', but the only girl to show an interest. He walked her home from Wednesday Novena, coming to the Bishop's garden meant a lengthy detour but she didn't complain. A stocky twelve-year-old strutting by his side, her little heels clicking on the road, dark curls, large calves, short white socks, a very boyish, broad girl built like a little pony. She was known far and wide as Izzie for short, not a name to do anything for her femininity.

Somehow he summoned the courage to lead her into the garden, taking her hand and leading her beneath the trees and she following obediently with her little clip-clop. Once inside, the sharp rattle of undergrowth at their ankles and the moon high overhead, bright, severe and obtrusive like a naked light bulb in a small room, left him at a loss as to how to continue. He drew her beneath the trees where the shadows were and put his arm around her shoulders. They were so broad! He hadn't expected that. He took her hand instead and held it for long minutes, very tightly, and soon their palms were running with sweat. He was at a loss to know how to continue and in despair he said that perhaps they ought to be getting along. There was enough moonlight even under the trees to show her shoulders move in an indifferent shrug and he was conscious of having fallen below expectations. She pulled an apple down from the tree and crunched it right down to the core, ate that, then with a sigh which was more like a neigh, wheeled around and at a fast trot led the way home.

He went to the Bishop's other garden on a later occasion with Magdalena. The Magdalena who gave, the Magdalena who took up with the traitor Kipsel, who afterwards fled to London and was referred to in the papers as Red Magda, but at that time was no more than the amazing Magdalena who gave. Like crazy, without qualm, Ferreira had said. Like wow, Van Vuuren confirmed – his favourite expression of approval at the time. Blanchaille could remember him making the same response after Father Lynch had recounted the harrowing life of the great Italian composer, Gesualdo. Lynch's eyes had closed and a spasm of pain passed over his face.

'Wow? Van Vuuren. What is *wow*! It's hardly a reaction that answers the scale of the human tragedy I've unfolded, you young devil. One makes the mistake of talking about things European to you boys. One makes the mistake of thinking because you are white you must be European. In fact you are African boys. No, not boys but bombs, and in place of minds you have drawersful of high explosives on a short fuse. Not young boys, young bombs, that's what you are. Not listening, not learning, just sitting there waiting, fizzling, until the day you blow up and shower everyone with moral outrage.'

But with Magdalena, *wow*! seemed just about to cover it. He had invited her to Bishop Blashford's vineyard, his other garden, and she had nodded with complete enthusiasm. She had streaked blonde hair. Her face ended in a pointed chin. Her eyes were blue-grey.

He led her through the darkness with a churning stomach feeling rather like a young man who has come into a large fortune and has no idea how to begin spending it. She looked like a model, Van Vuuren had promised. So this was how a model looked! Clearly there could be no holding hands this time. He would grapple her to him. Kiss her. Remove her bra and fondle her breasts, maybe take them in his mouth. Why not? He was fifteen, it was about time. They would lie on the grass afterwards. It happened to be raining softly so perhaps they wouldn't, but if it stopped raining they could lie on her mac. That she wore a mac was evidence of her practicality and added to her charm. Would he try and take off her pants? He doubted it – but nothing was ruled out. They stood beneath the dripping trees and Magdalena drew him towards her and said: 'You're a pretty boy.' Her thin plastic raincoat crackled as she pressed him against her. There was something so practised in the kiss she gave him. Her lips were wet. With a stab of despair he noticed that the buttons on her mac were large and stuffed tightly through their buttonholes. This presented a smooth and shining armoured front. But she was well ahead of him and had no similar problems. Her hand reached up behind him under his shirt pressing into the small of his back. The other hand expertly opened his fly – smooth, fast, deft movements, and then she had his penis in her damp fingers and was lifting it over the elastic band of his underpants which slid painfully upwards to trap his testicles. But then she rubbed and rubbed and soon things grew warm and better. Then he groaned and spurted and all at once she laughed delightedly. 'But you're quick! The quickest I've ever met.' Not quite scorn in the laugh, but tones of someone pleased at their own handiwork and still willing to continue. He knew the matter wasn't closed as far as she was concerned. He also knew he'd come before he'd even kissed Magdalena. There might be more if he liked, he could feel it. It was up to him, he could feel that too. But of course it wasn't. What was to come had been and gone. The elastic cut more cruelly into his testicles. 'You're really nice,' Magdalena said, 'we'll do this again.' His own incompetence baffled and enraged him. Afterwards he picked a small bunch of the Bishop's grapes. Magdalena declined saying they were too sour, but he finished them anyway, sour or not, punishing himself. The perfectly ordinary, reasonable and agreeable reactions of human beings seemed closed to him. A few, like Magdalena, dwelt happily among them. And there was that girl he'd met when he was very much younger, somebody's big sister, whose he couldn't remember. He went to play with her, at her invitation. They played in the empty garage. Postman's knock and spin the bottle.

'How do you play?'

'If your number comes up you pay forfeits.'

'What forfeits?'

'Well, for instance, kisses or feelings, if you like. Otherwise hair-pulls and toe-stamps.'

He won a lot and took hair-pulls and toe-stamps and it was very many years later that it occurred to him what was being offered and why there was that strange, softly appealing note in her voice.

There was no possibility of normal, natural, obvious behaviour for him.

Instead he had, as Lynch said, moral crusades.

'You on our side believe in the multi-racial paradise in which Boer and Zulu lie down together like lambs. There are no longer any Kaffirs, coolies, Jew-boys, coloured bastards, hairies, rock spiders, Dutchmen, all the rich store of invective so vital to political debate – I mention too Rednecks and English swine – and no one notices what colour you are. You believe God is behind you in this. They, on the other side, believe that everyone has their own identity. Everyone deserves separate lavatories and if the crunch comes they will fight to the death, to the last man who will blow his brains out on the last beach, preferring death to dishonour and will go to heaven where there will also be parallel toilet facilities. We are all superior people, on both sides.'

Lynch spat on these dreams, sat beneath the Tree of Heaven spitting with amazing accuracy also into an old brass spittoon. Kruger had spat, with embarrassing frequency, he said, and he enjoyed learning how to do so. 'This society is one of deep criminality, its ministers have a tough job laying down the law, that's why if you want to be a priest, join the police force.'

The Bishop's other garden had been closed to Lynch's altar boys without warning. Three strands of barbed wire slanting inwards were fixed above the hedge and a great new lock appeared on the gate. Gabriel was given the key. The Garden of Eden had been closed, Father Lynch said, and the sinners ejected therefrom. The Archangel barred the way.

'We don't care a damn,' Van Vuuren said, 'he'll have to clear up our mess.'

'He'll have to pick up the french letters, the old cigarettes and clear the well of about a hundred vodka and brandy bottles.'

'He's ending up as just another garden boy,' Blanchaille said.

Father Lynch had listened to all of this with a faint smile. 'But he's in the Bishop's employ, isn't he? At his age and already an episcopal appointment! You keep an eye on Gabriel. That boy will go far.'

Bishop Blashford yawned and stretched. The interview was over.

'Perhaps Gabriel is around? I thought I might say goodbye,' Blanchaille said.

Bishop Blashford beat a retreat to the house where Ceres was waiting at the french windows. She held them open as he approached and once he'd slipped inside she quickly closed them to all but a few inches. Obviously Blanchaille was not invited to tea. 'You go up and see Gabriel,' Blashford shouted through the crack. 'He's our legal eagle. He'll get you whatever papers you need to make the application. There's no more I can do for you. Be it on your own head. Now, if you'll excuse me, I must go and wash my hands.'

'Your bags are outside by the front gate,' Ceres said and closed the french windows with considerable dignity.

CHAPTER 6

Blanchaille walked down the hill struggling with the heavy cases. He regretted vaguely having brought them. Books, socks, clerical suits he had never worn; the blue barathea blazer he was wearing when he entered the seminary, big lapels and double vents – quite out of fashion now . . . the weeds of yesteryear.

The sky above the crest of the hill was dark grey and becoming blacker with every moment. There was something huge and flamboyant about a highveld storm, an occasion of relentless melodrama. The sky grew heavy and crowded in over you. As the storm built, the air became more highly charged. The trees shook themselves. Birds would swoop and flee. The hush would begin to weigh. Occasionally a small wind would drift a few leaves past your ankles or slide past the eyebrows carrying a faint watery scent. The first flash would come, white as a slash of chalk across a blackboard and a crash that split the ear-drums. But it did not necessarily mean rain, something might happen in the atmosphere and the storm would wheel and miss you leaving you only with prodigious explosions, blackness and vivid fractures of light. All show, impressive but empty bluster, truncheon weather, crash, bash, wallop. Your hair stood on end but you didn't get wet. Yet you felt the threat, looked with respect at the towering darkness above. Not for nothing did the Regime sometimes broadcast important policy statements on radio and television during electrical storms, the words interspersed by static and thunder. When it did rain, the relief was palpable.

A large black car came bowling down the hill and stopped beside him with a shriek of brakes. The window descended with smooth electrical precision, and there was Gabriel. The interior of the car smelt of its blue vinyl coverings and the refrigerated whisper of its air conditioning. Gabriel didn't switch off the engine. The car waited, hissing faintly. Gabriel massaged his jaw, smooth, golden, smiling, a model of casual elegance.

'What's this, Blanchie? You'll be soaked if it comes down. You're a long way from home.'

Blanchaille nodded. Maybe he should ask his question now?

'I'd give you a lift but I'm meeting the Rome plane. Vatican bigwigs. Visiting firemen. Ah well – no rest for the wicked.'

'No.'

'Never be a bishop's chaplain.'

'No,' said Blanchaille, 'I won't.'

Blanchaille watched the big black car go purring down the hill. He hadn't asked his question. It was this: Looksmart Dladla had been warned to get out of the country by his brother. Fair enough. So then, if Gabriel told Looksmart the cops wanted him in connection with the Kipsel business, who told Gabriel?

As he reached the bottom of the hill the first drops fell but he was lucky enough to find a bus stop and gratefully took shelter beneath the corrugated iron roof, swung his cases up on the bench and himself up beside them while the rain sheeted down and ran rivers of red mud and gravel beneath the spindly metal legs of the shelter. Highveld rain was like no other, the drops were large and would sting the hand and batter the head, drilling into the earth, beating and upbraiding it. The highveld rain had weight and made each drop count, was a battering of the country, brief but overwhelming. The earth, so dry, was soon saturated in great pools everywhere, joining up into streams carrying off the top soil, rough brown surges hurtling down the gutters and thundering in the storm-water drains, and everything which had been settled was fluid and running. It never lasted of course. After the deluge the sun would come out and everything dried away to sticky mud and then to dust. But while it lasted the world ran free, and the mind with it.

Now in my dream, as the storm began tapering off, a figure stepped out of the rain and sat beside him on the bench. 'God Almighty, Blanchie! Did I not direct you to the Airport Palace?' Father Lynch's black raincoat was a sheen of wet cloth; rain gathered in the brim of his hat; when he spoke a hundred droplets exploded in the air before his mouth. 'You delayed. And now you may find the going harder. Bubé is gone!'

'So?'

'What do you mean – so? This is the most extraordinary news. At last the truth is beginning to emerge. Bubé has gone. Of course this affects your travel plans.'

'Why should it?'

'Why? Because the roads will be full of police. Theodore, for the first time since Paul Kruger's departure, a president has fled! Adolph Gerhardus Bubé has fled!'

Adolph Gerhardus Bubé, father of the nation. An intellectual who studied in his youth in universities in Holland, Germany and Belgium. One of the original founders of the old policy of ethnic parities, as it was then called, with his thesis 'Racial Separation with Justice', which became the Ur-text, the philosophical underpinning of the racial policy of equal freedoms or concomitant responsibilities, the vision of 'ethnic heartlands' each reflecting its distinctive tribal rhythm, each tribe breeding to its heart's content. It was from this thesis that many of the crucial ideas of modern South Africa originated, regarded as revolutionary once but now outmoded, its once striking maxims absorbed into everyday language, sentiments such as: 'There's no such place as South Africa', or as Pik Honneger, his most distinguished disciple put it, 'What's ours is ours, and what's theirs is what we are prepared to give them.'

Bubé's thesis had been required reading on Father Lynch's picnics. It was Lynch who pointed out how profoundly influenced Bubé had been throughout his career, as a young MP, as a distinguished Economics Minister and as President – by the birthrate. Bubé in his formal suits, with his paunch, his watch chain, his benign manner made speech after speech pointing to the burgeoning black population and he would appeal to his followers to remember the old Boer wife in the days of the Great Trek, during the wars of freedom and the oppression of the Boers by the British Empire. The old Boer wife, he said, had been a breeding machine, her womb was a weapon more potent than the Mauser, a holy factory in which there was renewed each month a new army, the white man's hope of a secure future in South Africa where he could thrive and prosper and protect his traditional way of life, his culture and his Christian God. But now the white birth-rate was spiralling down to zero growth while the black man was rearming in the belly of his wives. Tirelessly the President expounded his theme: 'White women, remember your duty!' HAVE A BABY FOR BUBÉ! the headlines ran. His supporters took up the slogan and ran through the streets chanting it, breaking into chemist shops, puncturing contraceptive sheaths and flushing birth control pills down the toilet and assaulting non-white persons for allegedly failing to respect pregnant white women. It was Bubé who funded the sterilisation campaign in the countryside, the secret radiation trucks, the so-called 'Nagasaki ambulances' which so terrified the rural population.

Lynch often expatiated upon the role of President Bubé, as he rested beneath the Tree of Heaven. 'It was our Adolph who reminded us that an earlier and better name for the Boer War was the Gold War. It was a war between Gold Bugs, who understood the importance of the metal, and the Boers who had still to learn this. The British Army came in on the side of the Gold Bugs – people like Werner and Beit, Himmelfarber etc. Let's not believe the story put out by men in an advanced state of dementia such as Cecil Rhodes, or Alfred Milner that they were defending the Anglo-Saxon race of which the English, God forgive poor Rhodes, were regarded as the most perfect flower, "the best, the most human, the most honourable race the world possesses . . ." This I quote to you from his *Confession of Faith*. Have you ever heard such rubbish? Reasons, you see – *reasons*. We must have reasons before the killing can begin. The Boers on their side under Kruger were fighting, they said, for the right to be free, for Calvinist Afrikanerdom, for the little man against the big, for independence, for truth. All lies, all lies. Gold it was and gold it has always been, the dream, the rumour, the hope and despair of the conquerors and of the conquerors before them, Arabs and Portuguese both. Stories of magical gilded cities, of Solomon's mines, of Monomatapa and Vigiti Magna lured them here. The Portuguese, the Dutch, the British and finally even the Boers, they all wanted it. Rhodes and all his fellow Bugs had the gold but Kruger owned the sacred soil from which it was mined. They thought that the Boers didn't want the gold. How absurd! It was the miners they hated. They saw them as the sub-life that crawled beneath the stone, so they averted their eyes, usually upward to God their Father and kept to the veld, content with their horses, their guns, a herd or two, the horizon endlessly receding, a host of servants and a wife in the back room breeding like a machine, claiming always simply that they wished to be left alone. The Boers were the Greta Garbos of history. The Boers didn't want the gold only so long as no one else had it. But they soon found the stuff had its uses. Before the war they were already building up their funds by illicitly buying gold stocks and amalgam from shady sellers. There were organised Government theft departments, that's what it amounted to. Contemporary observers were lost in admiration for the bribery, greed, corruption, the whole quality of the unblushing venality with which those involved enriched themselves in the Boer Republics. The lot of them. All those wily Hollanders surrounding Kruger, were rotten from the toes up. The Transvaal Government was supported by secret funds administered from secret accounts and with this stash fund the Krugerites bought votes, nobbled opponents, paid off old scores and enriched family and friends. When the war broke out they no longer had to buy their gold under the table, because they'd taken over the gold mines. They could take it straight out of the ground and put it into their vaults. So when they went to war with the British they said they were fighting for God and freedom and independence. But by then they knew that whoever got the gold had God and freedom thrown in buckshee. Even so, as Bubé points out in his thesis, men like Kruger and Rhodes were of the old century. Nineteenth-century men. And the quality of their hypocrisy and the nature of their corruption was a Victorian thing. The gold was a means, the way you paid for your dreams, financed them. The difference with us, the New Men, Bubé says, is that gold came first, the dreams later. You can see this change taking place at the end of the Boer War when even the most Christian fighting generals became bank robbers literally overnight. As the British marched into the capital, General Smuts was holding up the Standard Bank and the Mint and making off with a cool half-million in gold. Kruger saw it coming. His *Memoirs* make it clear that the discovery of gold was a catastrophe. It would 'soak the country in blood'.

The rain had stopped. Sheets of muddy water rushed past the two priests in the bus shelter. They could hear it thundering deep down in the storm-water drains.

'With Bubé's flight history comes full circle. It's the Kruger departure all over again. Heaven be praised!' Lynch's jug ears waggled in delight. Blanchaille noticed that the old man appeared to have lost more of his teeth. He grinned like an ancient baby. 'You're still planning to travel?'

Blanchaille nodded, 'Yes Father.'

'Oh you call me Father all right, but I'm not, you know. *Of course* you know! I'm more like an uncle to you boys. I like you, that makes me really different, close. Yes, I like you and mind you I'm probably the only one who does – and I nourish hopes for you all yet, though I look dark into your futures. But Father you call me! And what do you call your old President, the President Kruger? Why man, you call him Uncle, Uncle Paul! But that's all wrong. Sure it is. He's not your uncle, I am. He's your father, father of the nation, father of misfortune. Follow Kruger, find the truth. That's the line, Blanchie. Stick to it like glue as you're pitched into an uncertain future. Be sure and look out for your old Uncle Lynch because he'll be looking out for you. Take this. Trust me.' Lynch gave him a brown envelope on which an address was scrawled. 'You'll need cash.' The envelope smelt faintly of pistachio.

'You've taken Ferreira's money!' Blanchaille was outraged.

'I've simply returned the funds Ferreira bequeathed to you and which you unwisely left behind when you fled. I give it to you, after making suitable deductions. You can take a bus from here. At this address a friend is waiting. It's nine stages, and then you hop.'

Blanchaille counted the nine stages because he hoped against hope he might end up at an address different to that given on the envelope. It did no good. Nine stages brought him to the centre of the town, to the tall skyscraper known as Balthazar Buildings which housed the Security Police, the Special Branch and the organisation, so secret no one could be certain of its existence, known as the Bureau, under its phantom chief, Colonel Terblanche.

CHAPTER 7

Balthazar Buildings on Jan Smuts Square in the centre of the city –
notorious headquarters of the Security Police, scene of violent
incidents beyond number. Together with the usual offices it
comprised several hundred cells, interrogation rooms, as well as
offices of the Bureau for Public Safety, or, more briefly, the Bureau.
So mysterious that a Government committee found itself unable to
confirm its existence, despite the fact that a number of the
committee members were rumoured to be officers of the Bureau, or
Bureaucrats, as the knowing called them. Balthazar Buildings also
housed *Die Kring*, or the Ring, a secret society formed, according to
legend, at the turn of the century, at the time of Kruger's flight into
Swiss exile and dedicated to the preservation of the Calvinist ideal,
and the continuance, protection and furtherance of the Boer
nation. On the further fringes of the political spectrum, Blanchaille
remembered, there had been speculation that the Bureau and the
Ring were one and the same. Perhaps. There were many such secret
societies, all-male, dominated by devoted followers of the Regime,
dedicated to racial purity and in love with uniforms – the Phantom
Kommando; the Afrika Straf Kaffir Brigade; the Night Riders; the
Sons of Freedom; the Ox-Wagon Patriots – but the Ring, it was
said, controlled and dominated them all.

It had been claimed that the Ring was a fascist secret society.
Bubé had denied this, as had every president before him – all of
whom were members of the Ring. 'The English have their Rotary
Clubs, the Catholics have the Jesuits, the Bantu have their burial
societies – and we have the Ring. It is not a society, it is more like a
family gathering.'

It was with considerable trepidation that Blanchaille surveyed the
stone steps leading up to the great steel doors of Balthazar Buildings
and only by considerable effort of will did he tell himself that if this
was the place to which Lynch had directed him then he must have
his reasons. Across the road a boy was selling papers. PRESIDENT FOR
TREATMENT OVERSEAS? the posters ran. So Lynch had got hold of the
right story, at any rate. Blanchaille pushed the bell. Few who came
to Balthazar Buildings ever emerged unless they were led away to
waiting police vans, to court, to jail, to the gallows. Others left

briefly in flights from high windows, or tripped down staircases, or were found hanging from their cell bars by their belts or pyjama cords. This fortress housed the Russian spy Popov. Two TV cameras swivelled above his head and examined him silently.

The young constable who let him in was of the type Blanchaille knew well from school rugby matches against just such long-limbed, rangey sorts, full-grown men at twelve with moustaches to prove it. They smelt of sweat and onions and stomped you unmercifully whenever you went down with the ball. He gave his name. There he was in Balthazar Buildings along with the likes of Popov. He hoped Lynch knew what he was doing.

The story of Popov was widely known and loved and taught in school. Once a cipher clerk named Steenkamp was sitting at his desk in Balthazar Buildings on Sunday afternoon, hot and bored. He had just decided, by his own admission, that his job as a security policeman was at an end. The codes were beyond him and the amount of application required was simply too much for a simple man. And a simple man he was, this Steenkamp, the fifth son of a large and impoverished Karoo family, regarded by his superiors as a good policeman but unimaginative and perhaps a trifle slow. There was no hint then of the blaze of glory with which his career was to be crowned and was to make his photograph a familiar sight in every house in the country. Blanchaille had seen the photograph, everyone had seen the photograph. The mild empty eyes, the bored and unlined forehead which gave him the look of a man a decade younger than his forty years, the strong curling hair and the protuberant ears, the penalty of playing lock-forward for many years for the police team without wearing a scrum cap. It was this Steenkamp who one hot afternoon happened to look out of his window and see down below in the street a man taking photographs of him. He might have been picking his nose or yawning and there was this stranger in the street below taking pictures! He was down the stairs two at a time and he collared the impudent photographer who turned out to be Nikita Popov, a genuine, real, live Russian spy, and a full colonel in the KGB. It was a considerable coup and the President, wearing his other hat as Police Minister, went on television and thanked the Security Services for their watchfulness and said, 'Let this be a lesson to any other hostile countries who may have thought of infiltrating agents. The Security Forces are ready and waiting for them and will do their utmost to defend the country's integrity against the orchestrators of the Total Onslaught.' A police spokesman in turn thanked the Minister for thanking the police and the session ended in an orgy of mutual gratitude.

An anti-Regime paper caused a stir by suggesting the arrest was a fluke. The police issued a statement asserting that Steenkamp had known immediately that something deeply suspicious was going on since photographing police property was forbidden, along with army property, railway stations, harbours, electric pylons, atomic research centres and at least three hundred and sixty-three other items, from the servants of ministers to radio stations, which fell within the so-called 'Sensitive Subject Catalogue', regularly up-dated in the *Government Gazette*. As a general rule of thumb photographers should stick to photographing one another, unless one of them happened to be a banned person or a named Communist, in which case such photographs were also against the law. A few voices were raised inquiring how it was that a Russian colonel in the KGB should have entered the country in the first place and why he should spend his afternoons photographing police stations? But in a fiery parliamentary speech the Minister for Defence, the former army chief General Greaterman declared that the Russians were a devious and stealthy people and that such queries were clearly designed to denigrate the police and should cease immediately, or else. As for Steenkamp, he was sent to lecture at various police colleges and became a kind of saint for the new, young recruits who prayed that they too might one day strike such a blow for their country.

A photograph of Popov appeared which was to become 'the photograph': it showed a round, rather soft, boyish face with just a trace of a slant to the dark eyes, a sleepy, not unintelligent look, and, if you peered at it very closely, a gleam of utter astonishment in those eyes. Here was a living rebuke to those who accused the Regime of seeking Reds under the beds. Well, now the secret was out, they were in the streets taking photographs. The interest in Popov was enormous. It was presumed that he would be thoroughly interrogated, and then executed. A group of nurseryschool teachers canvassed the idea that the method of his execution should be one which would least disfigure his person. They argued that coming across Popov like this was rather like being given a giant panda, a rarity which should be preserved, perhaps put on display in a public place in a glass case where groups of school children could be taken to be shown the true reality of the Russian menace. 'Cut out his *derms*, stuff him and mount him!' sang the children in kindergarten as they drew pictures of the spy, Popov.

Blanchaille waited in the lobby, a bare place with a desk and a few chairs. On the walls were the TV monitors for the closed-circuit cameras. Could the screams of the detained be heard from here? He strained his ears. Silence. There were two portraits on the wall. One showed President Bubé in tribal dress. Chief for the afternoon of some forsaken tribe upon which the Regime had visited the dubious distinction of independence and the President had gone along in ceremonial tribal finery to cut the umbilical cord. He wore a bulky fur hat, perhaps torn from a meerkat, and its tail curled about his neck. Over his shoulders hung a pelt, monkey probably, and beneath that another spotted skin, leopard perhaps. Various herbs and amulets dangled from his shoulders and sleeves and he carried a short stabbing spear and a cowhide shield. Even beneath this exotic head-dress his round owlish face in its heavy spectacles peered out almost piteously. Beneath the animal skins he could be seen to be wearing a dark morning suit and tie. He looked as if he were about to burst into tears. He would have made a speech to the gathered tribe standing upon a chair beneath a thorn tree.

> 'Dear Friends, it is nice to be here with you. I am from the Government and the Government's attitude is that we have to help people like you to have a better life in this beautiful country of ours. With that I will say goodbye and may you stay well.'

A similar speech was given by ministers visiting resettlement camps. But there it was followed by a hymn from the people – usually a lament.

On the opposite wall was the famous Kruger portrait. Blanchaille knew it well for Lynch always had a copy on his wall. Uncle Paul wore a top hat and his beard was thick and white with holes in it like a hedge that has been eaten away. Around his barrel chest was a broad green sash and on the right shoulder was a silver epaulette to take the sash – this epaulette was thickly fringed in tufty gold thread hanging in rich fronds. The old man's beard, so untidy, yellowly white, had the look of a fake. It seemed theatrical, stuck on, as if a powerful hand reaching below the ear lobe might with a sudden tug strip it from the powerful jaw with a medicinal screech. Perhaps the same might be done with the cotton wool eyebrows. 'Look to the past,' Kruger had written to his people as he lay dying in exile,

Lynch had taught, the African Moses warning his unruly people that if they forgot their God then they would perish and never find the Promised Land. 'The old Israelites built a golden calf,' Lynch said, 'these new ones build a stock exchange, they build a share portfolio, they build an army, they build themselves. They look to the future.'

The officer who entered was instantly familiar, the thick black hair glossed over the ears, the square powerful hands, the solid square jaw and his manner somewhere between that of some distinguished visiting specialist in the house of a dangerous case and a powerful athlete, a weight-lifter with a muscle-bound body unused to moving in a suit, and that strange, well-remembered faintly menacing mixture of formality and muscle power. But the smile was the same: open, pleasant, appealing. An utter contradiction stretching back to hostel days when he would half kill a boy for stepping out of line, then break every rule with affable, serene good nature and never a qualm.

'Hello Blanchie, long time no see.'

How long? At least ten, fifteen, years since Father Lynch, Van Vuuren, Ferreira, Zandrotti, little Mickey and Kipsel set off on holiday. They rode in an old Studebaker which Lynch had borrowed from somewhere, towing a caravan. It had been a Sprite, he remembered that, he could still see the flighty 'Caravans International' logo. The caravan was not for sleeping in, they had tents for that. Instead the vehicle was packed with large black boxes tied up with string. It had been a last holiday for Father Lynch and his altar boys. They were suspicious of the term 'holiday', knowing what Lynch had done to 'picnics'. It was all very mysterious but Lynch would say no more. All in good time. Officially it was put about that they were going to the Game Reserve. They would be exploring the flora and fauna of the Eastern Transvaal.

The Eastern Transvaal was a countryside vividly beautiful, of tangled greenery, plunging waters, thronging banks of azaleas which grew ever thicker as they approached the water; and then the crouching, tousled, tawny veld with its stinging sibilance where the thorn trees held up their fierce yellow heads in the hottest of suns. And it *was* hot. At noon the tall choked grass began ticking like a clock. The day wore on, wore out, and with the evening coming on the sky would turn a flushed pink, the colour of an electric bar-heater and the glow caught the undersides of the clouds and showed them pink and gold. The day didn't die but burnt away, faded suddenly with the last light in a smell of wood-smoke and the first crickets shrieking among the lengthening shadows.

Lynch had taken them to the Kruger Game Reserve, advising them to enjoy it while it lasted for soon work would start. They saw some lion, several buck, a couple of giraffe and then an extraordinary aged buffalo. This beast was indelibly printed on Blanchaille's memory; it was a buffalo seemingly determined to shatter its reputation as the most dangerous animal alive, terrifying when angered, capable of moving at amazing speed. When they drove up beside it, it stood there with its shuffling lop-sided bulk and its expression of weary but disconcertingly kind intelligence. The horns were a marvel, razor sharp, ready to kill, but seemed more homely than dangerous, appropriate, even graceful. They looked like the stiffened plaits on a little girl, they traced the outlines of a Dutch cap beginning in two thick round plaits clamped to the top of the skull, sweeping down and up in beautifully symmetrical curves into whittled points. Looked at another way they gave the impression of a frozen hairstyle, a stylised wig. The buffalo's forehead was broad, deeply lined and strangely white, perhaps this was where he showed his age. It was, if one could conceive of such a thing, a thinker's forehead. The eyes were not impressive, being small, bleared, brown beneath their heavy lids. A single stem of broken grass hung head downwards from the buffalo's mouth. If anything looked dangerous and menacing about the buffalo it was the ears, which were busy, angry, muscular. 'People will not believe it when you tell them you were frightened by a buffalo's ears,' Lynch warned.

The Elands River Falls gave its name to two villages, one beneath the waterfall and appropriately called Waterval Onder, and the one above called Waterval Boven. It was to Waterval Onder that Father Lynch came with his boys and his caravan on that one and only holiday and just outside town the camp was set up. The mysterious cardboard boxes were unpacked and were found to contain the uniforms of Boer soldiers, leather trousers you wrapped around yourself called *klapbroek*, bandoliers, muskets and hats. The boys became Boers and the caravan became a railway saloon and Father Lynch, in yellow straggly beard and cotton wool eyebrows became, of course, President Kruger. For it was here at Waterval Onder that the Boers had their last glimpse of their leader, of the Old Lion, before the railway line carried him out of the country forever. Lynch pointed out that the building of this line had long been Kruger's dream. He wanted a rail link which ran from his capital through the Eastern Transvaal and into Portuguese East Africa and the friendly port of Lourenço Marques, a line which avoided the hated dependency on the ports in the rest of the country held by the British. As it happened, he proved to be the most valuable piece of freight it ever carried. Outside Waterval Boven, President Kruger old and ill (Lynch in the part) sat once again, watched by Denys Reitz and his brother Hjalmar (Blanchaille and Van Vuuren), reading his Bible in the railway saloon (played by the Sprite caravan), 'a lonely, tired man' Reitz observed.

Lynch made them walk the distance between Waterval Onder and Waterval Boven which, although only some eight kilometres in distance, was virtually straight uphill and Lynch pointed out to them the one and only stretch of railway still to be seen there, built by the South African Railway Company in 1883. He took them to the tunnel cut through the rock beside the pretty Elands River Falls to help reduce the gradient and he pointed out the old stone bridge with its graceful arches along which the trains had trundled as they crossed the aptly named Get-Lost-Hill stream. How much had been lost crossing that stream! The presidential train had strained up the steep gradient of one in twenty, crossed the border and steamed into the port of Lourenço Marques where the Dutch cruiser, the *Gelderland*, lay riding at anchor in the blue swell of the Indian Ocean. And the gold went with him on 21 October 1900.

In bullion or minted coins, in gold dust or in bars? And in what guise? And how much? Father Lynch stood on the quayside in Lourenço Marques and stroked his fake beard, and wondered aloud. His boys in their slouch hats and their crossed bandoliers sweated beside him in the moth-eaten uniforms, the stage property of some defunct theatrical company which Lynch had raided for these old khaki cast-offs, *velskoens* and reproduction muzzle loaders. And did the millions really go at all? Or was it another story? They wanted to ask but dared not. Lynch stood there comfortably enough in top hat and fake beard but his boys were deeply embarrassed by the looks they were given by the black Portuguese who giggled behind their hands and pointed.

'Jesus, what a bunch of tits we must look!' he remembered Ferreira fumed.

Blanchaille answered Van Vuuren, 'How long? Not since we were living history.'

'Living history! We were dying of embarrassment,' Van Vuuren said. 'He claimed he was trying to make us understand the roles we played.'

Blanchaille remembered how they had shuffled and glowered and banged their rifle butts on the ground. 'I never felt a bit like a Boer.'

'Lynch never cared about our feelings. He made us pretend because he knew that's what we did best. Lynch wanted us to understand that our lives were all play-acting. There was nothing real about them. He wanted us to see that all we lived for was to pretend to be what we weren't. Your role, Blanchie, has always reminded me of St Paul. You remember the trouble with St Paul, don't you? He spent all those years persecuting Christians for being Christian and then he got converted and spent the rest of his life persecuting them for not being Christian enough. And for that he was canonised by his grateful victims. God's policeman, old Paul was. And you're another. Why do you think Lynch always insisted that you'd gone to police college and refused to accept that you were in the Seminary? The dogmatic, policeman-like qualities in you, were what he saw. Look at your life! You went into the camps and you gave the Regime hell for treating people like garbage. You attacked the Church, your own church, at every turn for failing in its responsibility. Then you took to touring the country like a wandering madman demanding that the camps be bulldozed. Then you were given a church and you stood up in the pulpit and addressed your parishioners like the investigating officer. You stood up there to unmask the villain, like the tiny Flemish tax inspector or the seemingly genial ex-nun in the detective yarn unmasking the totally unsuspected killer. You expected them to stand up and confess. Instead, like Makapan, they lost their tempers and besieged your house. Well, what did you expect? You've lived the investigating life, you've taken the high moral ground, you've gone after the culprits, the criminals. Your vocation is to bring the guilty ones to book, you're the holy detective, the righteous sleuth. And where's it got you? Nowhere. It's done nothing for you – except to ruin you. You've taken the drugs this country offers – moral outrage, angry condemnation – and they've wrecked you. You're on your last legs and you're going down, you're going out.'

'And you? I suppose you know better,' Blanchaille said angrily.

'I joined the police because I believed I would find out what was really going on. You know what it's like. Under the Regime everything important is called a police matter, history is a police matter. All presidents as far back as Babbelas and Breker have also held the portfolio of Minister of Police. You know the argument –

the State is an instrument of God. Its security is a matter of divine concern. The police are the mediators between the Almighty and the citizen. I believed it. We all believed it.'

'Of course.'

'But Blanchie, what if it isn't true?'

'You mean it isn't true?'

'Not entirely. That's the thing. Nothing is entirely true. Or entirely anything. I began to learn that as a rookie cop when they put me on surveillance in a department called "foreign friends". Now that alone was an eye-opener. I thought we didn't have any foreign friends. Or need them. Or want them. We were the Albania of the South. Our foreign policy was to tell everyone to go and get stuffed. But that's wrong! We've got loads of foreign friends. That's why President Bubé went on his whirlwind foreign tour. He wasn't foisting himself on his hosts in the capitals of Europe. He was returning calls! We do have foreign friends. Lots. And I was detailed to watch over them. Once they came singly: businessmen, politicians – here to collect their bribes to arrange shipments of materials we needed like planes or football teams. But soon we had so many foreign friends they took block bookings and came on chartered flights calling themselves the Patagonian Hockey Team and were taken away in buses with darkened windows. I got assigned to one of these teams. The papers usually got the story after the new arrivals had been spirited away and ran headlines like: VICTORY FOR GOVERNMENT SPORTS POLICY: PATAGONIANS TO TOUR! This led to world-wide protests and the Patagonians would flatly deny that any of their teams was playing in South Africa. By then the 'team' had disappeared. I looked after a team who wore baseball caps the wrong way round, with the peaks down their necks. Or yarmulkas. And they'd get drunk with the township girls and cause us a lot of trouble. They worked in a camp in the mountains outside the capital. It turned out that the language they were speaking was Hebrew and they were scientists of some sort. I went to my superiors and said, "Look there's a colony of Jewish scientists working in the mountains." "Nonsense," my superiors said. "They're not Jews, they're Israelis. And this conversation did not take place." I was sent to another camp about five miles away. This one was a very different kettle of fish. It was full of Chinese. Now wasn't that strange? I mean we don't even have Chinese laundries and here is a colony of Chinese working in a strange factory. I went to my supervisors. "Look here," I said, "what are all these Chinese doing? I thought we didn't like Chinese. I thought the

Regime had taken a vow of No More Coolies! Ever since their bad experience with the indentured labourers on the gold mines early this century." "There are no Chinese," said my superiors, "only Taiwanese and this conversation did not take place." Then I was taken off people and put on to things. I was posted to security on the atomic research station out there in the mountains. I missed the voluble scientists and the quiet, hardworking technicians but you go where you're sent. The atomic research station was getting large shipments of equipment. I happened to see the inventories. They took delivery of something called the Cyber 750-170 which is an interesting computer. Because its main strength is multi-channel analysis, it's used for sorting through the hundreds of cables collecting data from a test-blast site. Other shipments to the research centre included vibration equipment and ballistic re-entry vehicles. Oh, I almost forgot, there were supplies of some gas too, Helium 3 it was. I thought about this. You put together the scientists, the technicians and the equipment and you come up with something that explodes.'

Blanchaille began to understand. He knew the rumours, the unmentionable stories.

Van Vuuren's blue eyes widened. 'Go on, Blanchie, take a guess.'

'A bomb! The bastards are building a bomb. Now the question is – are we working on a large dirty weapons system, or small, relatively clean devices? Neutron bombs, say? Or field launching systems. Yes, tactical battlefield weapons. Or both? That would give flexibility. Large bombs against hostile forces on our borders, or on the capital of an enemy, or on the capitals of states supporting that enemy. Then the smaller, cleaner, weapons for specific jobs, say the 155 millimeter cannon, capable of lobbing nuclear shells. But what's the gas for? This Helium 3?'

'It's used to make Tritium. That's a form of hydrogen used in thermo-nuclear weapons.'

'What a lot you know about this sort of thing,' Blanchaille said.

'I remember hearing about it first years ago from Kipsel, Silberstein and Zandrotti and the others in their bomb-making days. No, I did not interrogate them, that affair was before my appointment to Interrogation, or Twenty Questions, as they call it here. But I read the report of Kipsel's confessions. Even though all they were planning to demolish were a few pylons, Kipsel was never one to do anything by halves. He got Silberstein to swot up on everything from fireworks to weapons in the megaton range.'

Blanchaille nodded. 'Lawyers read.'

Van Vuuren looked cagey. 'They were young. They confused yearning with faith. They really believed the revolution had started. Zandrotti was convinced.' Again the odd look, almost embarrassment. 'Poor old Zandrotti.'

'We were all young and we all believed. What else could we do?'

'Sure, sure.' Van Vuuren regarded him steadily. 'From what I've told you, then, you conclude that we're building a bomb, or rather the Taiwanese are building us a bomb designed by the Israelis who are selling it to us wholesale?'

'Seems like it.'

'You know of course that the Regime deny that we possess any nuclear weapons – and when mysterious explosions occurred in the southern hemisphere the Regime rejected American claims that we were testing nuclear weapons. They said it was atmospheric disturbance, or the American instruments were faulty. Then they said a meteorite landed in the Namib Desert. So what do we surmise from that?'

'That they were lying.'

Van Vuuren's blue eyes widened still further. 'Certainly not. We agree that there was no explosion. From there we go on to state categorically that we have no nuclear weapons.'

Now it was Blanchaille's turn to stare. 'But you said –'

'No. I didn't.'

'But I heard you.'

'You couldn't have done. This conversation never took place.' Van Vuuren took a photograph from a desk drawer and fanned himself with it absently. 'What is the official policy towards the Russians, Blanchie?'

'The Russians are our enemies. They are after our gold, our diamonds, our minerals, our strategic positions, our sea-lanes. We do not talk to the Russians, have never talked to them, will never talk to them.'

'Excellent answer. Now have a look at this.' Van Vuuren handed him a small black and white photograph, rather grainy and blurred, as if taken from a distance. In the foreground two men were walking together, behind them a busy street with trams. 'Paradeplatz in Zurich where the banks sell gold like hot rolls in a baker's window. Do you recognise the men?'

Blanchaille studied the grainy photograph. The two men were deep in conversation. The older man wore a black Homburg. The other looked younger, was bare-headed, fair-haired.

84

'Never seen either before.'

'The man on the left in the hat is a Russian. The official, accredited roving representative of the Bank of Foreign Trade in Moscow, on secondment to the Wozchod Handelsbank in Zurich. The other man is Bennie Craddock, an executive of Consolidated Holdings and the nephew of its Chairman, Curtis Christian Himmelfarber. Here is another photograph of Craddock, this time in Moscow. Notice anything?'

The photograph showed Craddock standing in a snowy Red Square surrounded by what appeared to be curious bystanders.

'Yes,' said Blanchaille, 'he seems to be crying.'

'Odd, isn't it? Why go all the way to Moscow for a cry? It's as odd as the spy Popov's behaviour when he was arrested outside this very building. He was reported to be very, very angry. It puzzled me. That he was upset I can understand, even anguished, but *angry*? No, I can't make sense of that. And I can't clear up the mystery by asking anyone. What strikes me about this investigation is that there are more and more mysteries and fewer and fewer people to question. I've had the urge, increasingly hard to resist, to call off the whole damn investigation and start praying. It starts with Ferreira. Somebody has been telling stories about Ferreira. He dies. Shares fall on the Exchange. People disappear leaving behind only the stories we go on telling about them. Craddock has not been seen since the photograph was taken. And his uncle, Himmelfarber, is abroad. So many people are overseas. Have you noticed? Minister Gus Kuiker and his Secretary of Communications are out of the country. The President is said to be travelling overseas for medical treatment. Even you will soon be gone.'

'You could ask Popov yourself, you've got him here. "Why the rage Nikita?" you could say.'

'I heard why – from Himmelfarber. Popov's gone. He was spirited away by the Bureau and now he, like it, may or may not exist. You see how isolated I am, Blanchie? Even those who assigned me to investigate the murder of Tony Ferreira have gone. I had no shortage of instructions. First to put me on the case was the President himself. It's his prerogative when he wears his other hat as Minister of Police so I went to it with a will. President Bubé implied that Minister Kuiker might have had some involvement. As I knew that Gus Kuiker is a rising star in the Regime, tipped to succeed Bubé one day, or even replace him, I put this down to professional jealousy. After all Kuiker took over Bubé's baby platform. The President went around the country encouraging white women voters to breed; but Kuiker took positive steps to reduce the opposition birth-rate and he used science. He made it his aim to reduce the non-white breeding potential by one half and he got the boffins involved. All Bubé did was to encourage white women to have more babies. Whereas Kuiker hit the enemy where he lived –in the womb. He got the reputation of a modern whizz-kid. Bubé never forgave him. But Kuiker didn't care.'

Of course Kuiker did not care. Augustus Carel Kuiker, Minister for Parallel Equilibriums, Ethnic Autonomy and Cultural Communication, cared only for success. Kuiker with the thick, ridged, almost stepped hairstyle, a rugged jaw and heavy, surprisingly sensuous lips. He looked like a rather thuggish Charles Laughton. Blanchaille recalled Kuiker's speeches, how he tirelessly stomped the country reeling off figures. The total population was already over twenty-seven million, it could rise to thirty-eight million or more by the year 2000. The number of whites was dropping. Zero population growth might be all very well for the rest of the world but for the Europeans of the southern sub-continent it was suicide. The percentage, now about sixteen, would fall to eleven after the turn of the millennium. The Government, he announced, might have to introduce a programme. It would not shrink from introducing a programme. This programme might well involve penalising certain groups if they had too many children as well as offering sterilisation and abortion on demand. He felt sure that many black people would welcome abortion on demand, and even, he hinted with that famous frown wrinkling across his forehead, also by command. He was not afraid to speak plainly, if non-whites were not able to limit their own fertility, then the Government might have to step in to find a way to help them do it. This was not a threat but a promise. The Regime might also have to remind white women where their duty lay. Requests were not enough (this was a clear jibe at Bubé). Despite countless fertility crusades, tax incentives for larger families among whites, the ratio of black people to white people in the country was still five or six to one, and rising. The Government looked with new hope to the extraordinary advances in embryology and fertility drugs, much of which was due to the pioneering work of the brilliant young doctor, Wim Wonderluk. There were those who were clearly breeding for victory, who planned to bury the Boer. Well the Government would not stand by idly and see this happen. If offers of television sets and free operations did not work, then other measures must be taken. Soon rumours reached the capital that vasectomy platoons were stalking the countryside, that officials in Landrovers were rounding up herds of young black matrons and giving them the single shot, three-monthly contraceptive jabs. There were stories of secret radiation trucks known as scan vans, far superior to the old Nagasaki ambulances Bubé had sponsored, raiding the townships and tribal villages and the officials in these vans were armed with demographic studies and at the first sign of a birth bulge would visit those potential centres of population growth after dark and give them a burst of radiation, enough, the theory was, to impair fertility. A kind of human crop-spraying technique. People said it couldn't be true until they remembered that anything you could think about could very easily be true. Kuiker was as forthright in his address to white women, 'our breeders of the future' he called them and he talked of introductory programmes of fertility drugs for all who wanted or needed them. Teams of researchers were working with selected females of child-bearing age on Government sponsored programmes to increase the white birth-rate without excluding the possibility, difficult though it might be, of obligatory implantation of fertilised ova in the selfish white wombs of women who had put golf and pleasure before their duty to the country. Pregnancy was good for the nation. He compared it with the military training which all young men had to undergo and pointed out that nine months' service was not too much to ask of a woman. Gus Kuiker was clearly going places. He caught the public eye. He didn't look to the past, he looked to the future which could be won if allied to technology. 'Breed or bleed' had been his rallying cry and he asked the eminent embryologist, Professor Wim Wonderluk, to prepare a working document encompassing his plans for the new future. Yes, Blanchaille knew all about Kuiker. Knew more than enough to be going on with.

'Why have you got me here? I was heading out under my own steam. It would have been easier, cleaner.' Blanchaille stood up knowing the policeman was not ready to release him.

'Two reasons. Mine and Lynch's. I wanted to make you take another look at things you thought you knew all about. I don't want to be left alone with my mysteries. You're going out. Fine. So maybe you'll be able to use some of what I show you to get some answers out there in the outside world. That's my reason. Lynch's was more practical. He knew you'd never get out without my help.'

'Why not? How many have gone already?'

Van Vuuren's look was cold. 'Not all those who disappeared have left the country. Getting out is not what it was. It has become a police matter. Things got difficult when Bubé and Kuiker issued instructions that disappearances were becoming too frequent and a close watch was to be kept on ports and airports.'

'Then disappeared themselves.'

'Yes, but the orders are still in force,' Van Vuuren said.

Blanchaille sat down again. 'O.K. What else do you want to tell me?' he asked warily.

'Turn around,' Van Vuuren ordered, 'and watch the screen.'

On a television monitor behind him there appeared a group of men sitting at a long table, six to a side, all wearing earphones.

'A delegation from the Ring are meeting a delegation from an Italian secret society known as the *Manus Virginis*, the Hand of the Virgin. The Hand is some sort of expression of the Church Fiscal. This lot arrived in the country claiming to be a male voice choir and they all have names like Monteverdi and Gabrielli and Frescobaldi. The Hand appears very interested in investment. Each chapter or cell of the Hand is called a Finger and takes a different part of the world for its investment which is done through their own bank called the Banco Angelicus. On the other side of the table is the finance committee of the Ring. They read from left to right: Brother Hyslop – Chairman; Brother van Straaten – he's their political commissar; Brother Wilhelm – Treasurer; Brother Maisels – transport arrangements. Don't laugh. Getting here in style and doing it in secret is very important to them. Brother Snyman – catering and hospitality. Since the Brothers regard themselves as hosts they put themselves out for these meetings, they bring along wine, a good pâté, a selection of cheeses. Headphones are for simultaneous translation.'

'But why are you monitoring the Ring? All the major figures in the Regime are members of the Ring, so why get you to spy on it?'

'Because though all members of the Government are in the Ring, not all members of the Ring are in the Government.'

Blanchaille looked at the heavy men on both sides of the table with their earphones clamped around their heads like Alice-bands which had slipped, and thought how alike they looked with their big gold signet rings, hairy knuckles, gold tie-pins, three-piece suits, their burly assurance. Here were devoted Calvinist Afrikaners who spat on Catholics as a form of morning prayers, sitting down with a bunch of not only Catholics, but Roman *wops*! To talk about – what?

'Money,' said Van Vuuren. 'Highly technical chat about investments, exchange controls, off-shore banks, letters of credit, brokers, money moving backwards and forwards. But how are such meetings arranged and, more importantly, *why*?'

'Ferreira would have understood,' said Blanchaille. 'But I don't. What is the connection?'

'I think,' said Van Vuuren, 'that the connection isn't as odd as it seems. The philosophical ideas behind the Ring are not too dissimilar to those practised by Pope Pius X. He fired off salvos at the way we live. He attacked the ideas about humans improving themselves. He pissed on perfectability. He lambasted modern science and slack-kneed liberal ideas. So does the Ring. They have more in common than we think. Perhaps we do too.'

Blanchaille stared at the men on the screen. 'I still can't believe what I'm seeing.'

The picture faded into blackness. 'You haven't seen anything,' said Van Vuuren. 'Now come along and look at what we have in the holding cells.'

CHAPTER 8

The holding cells were below ground, arranged in tiers rather in the manner of an underground parking garage, Van Vuuren explained in what to Blanchaille was an inappropriate and chilling comparison. And why 'holding' cells? Van Vuuren was also quick to counter the notion that this was intended to distinguish them from 'hanging' cells, or 'jumping' cells. The policeman seemed, surprisingly, to regard this suspicion as being in bad taste.

Van Vuuren led him into a long concrete corridor: air-conditioning vents breathed coldly, a thin, flat hair-cord carpet on the floor, abrasive white walls, overhead fluorescent light-strips pallid and unforgiving. Down one side of the corridor were steel cell doors. At the far end of the corridor, in front of a cell, stood a group of uniformed officers. Senior men they must have been for Blanchaille caught the gleam of gold on caps and epaulettes. They seemed nervous, slapping their swagger-sticks against their thighs. One carried a clipboard and he was tapping his pencil nervously against his teeth.

'We'll wait here and watch,' said Van Vuuren.

Then I saw in my dream, marching around the corner, two more policemen and between them their prisoner, a powerful man in grey flannels and white shirt, at least a half a head taller than his captors. As they approached the cell door the policeman with the clipboard stepped forward and held up his hand. 'We are happy to inform you, Dr Strydom, that you are free to go. There is no further need to hold you. Your name has been removed from my list.'

The reaction of the prisoner to this information was sudden and violent. He gave the clipboard carrier an enormous blow to the head. The two men guarding him fell on him and tried to wrestle him to the ground, but he was too big, too strong. The uniformed policemen with the swagger-sticks joined in and a wild scrum of battling men seethed in the corridor. The prisoner laid about him with a will and reaching his objective, the cell door, opened it, rearing and lashing out with his feet, kicking backwards like a stallion at the policemen clawing at him. 'Now write down my name in your book,' he roared at the unfortunate clipboard carrier who was leaning shakily against the wall and then leapt into the cell, slamming the heavy door behind him.

Glumly the policemen gathered themselves together and wiped the blood from their faces. From behind the cell door Blanchaille could hear the prisoner's voice raised in the National Anthem:

'On your call we may not waver, so we pledge from near and far;
So to live, or so to perish – yes we come, South Africa-a-a-r!'

'That's quite a patriot you've got there,' Blanchaille said. He couldn't help smiling, 'Balthazar Buildings is a place from which generations of doomed prisoners have tried to escape. I think I've just seen a man fighting to get in. The world is suddenly stood on its head.'

'That man is Wessels Strydom, once a leading light in the Ring which he left claiming it had been undermined by the Communists. Strydom said that the Regime was going soft on the old enemies, Reds, liberals, Jews, internationalists, terrorists. He expressed the feeling that control was slipping away from God's people. With a group of like-thinking supporters he formed what they called the *Nuwe Orde*. This organisation aims to expose betrayals of the Boer nation, by direct action. The military wing of the *Nuwe Orde* is the Afrika Straf Kaffir Brigade. You've heard of their punishment squads who deal with people they see as threatening or sullying the old idea of purity? Their ideas of punishment are juvenile but no less painful for that, mind you. They'll hang about a house where they know blacks and whites are holding a party and slash tyres; a little while ago they devised a plan of releasing thousands of syphilis-infected white mice in one of the multi-racial casinos; they're not above kidnapping the children of social workers or trade unionists who they feel are betraying the Afrikaner nation; or breaking into cinemas and destroying films they disapprove of; or shooting up the houses of lawyers (Piatikus Lenski, the liberal defence lawyer was a favourite target); or preparing to mate with their wives in front of the Memorial to the Second Mauritian Invasion in response to the falling white birth-rate, a huge breed-in of hundreds of naked male members of the *Nuwe Orde* and their carefully positioned wives all preparing for insemination at a given signal. They want a homeland for the Boer nation and eventual independence. In this new homeland only white people will be admitted. The idea is to remove all dependence on black labour. They'll do their own housework, sweep their streets, run their own factories, deliver their own letters, mow their lawns. They'll be safe, separate, independent. They've bought a tract of land down on the

South Coast. The sea is important to them as a symbol, it's something that they have to have their backs to.'

'Would they be capable of killing?'

Van Vuuren shrugged. 'You're thinking of the writing on Ferreira's wall, aren't you? So were we. That's why we hauled this Strydom in. Frankly it was a terrible mistake. I'm not saying that the A.S.K. couldn't have killed him but Ferreira was dealing in highly complex matters concerning the movement of funds through very complicated channels which none of us understood. Certainly not this Strydom. He could barely read his own bank account. And he doesn't care about those things, he cares about race, about history, about being right. Arresting him has proved to be a terrible mistake. We can't get rid of him. We don't need him any more, we don't want to hold him, there's nothing he can tell us, but he won't go! And it suits the *Nuwe Orde* to have him here. It makes it look like the Regime is really taking them seriously, locking him up like any black radical. You can see how determined Strydom is. He literally fights his way in back into his holding cell. The thing to remember about the *Nuwe Orde* is that it is actually a very old order.'

Now I saw in my dream how Blanchaille and the policeman Van Vuuren moved to another cell and peered through the thick glass spyhole in the door and Blanchaille recoiled at what he saw. For there, lying on the bunk, was Roberto Giuseppe Zandrotti, the anarchist. He recognised immediately the spiky black hair, the long, thin chin, the freckled, ghostly white face. 'I don't believe this. He's in London.'

Van Vuuren shook his head. 'We had known he was planning to return secretly to the country. We knew when he would arrive and, most importantly, what he would be wearing. The information was top-grade. So accurate Zandrotti never stood a chance. Blanchie, he came back disguised as a nun, of the Loretto Order, to be precise. Imagine it if you will. There's this double-decker bus trundling through a green and leafy suburb, all the passengers peering out of the window and paying very little attention to what some of them afterwards thought of as perhaps rather 'swarthy' a sister who sat there on her seat keeping her eyes demurely downcast and most of her face hidden behind her large wimple. Imagine their surprise when three large men in hairy green sportscoats and thick rubber-soled brown shoes jump aboard the bus and begin attacking this nun. Apparently the conductor went to her assistance and was struck down with a blow to the temple. He lay sprawled in the aisle, bleeding, and all the coins from his ticket machine went rolling beneath the bus seats.'

Blanchaille imagined it. He saw it. He heard the jingling flutter as the coins spun and settled beneath the seats.

'Anyway, these three guys wrestled with the nun who hoofs them repeatedly in the nuts until they pick her up and carry her down the aisle head first. The other passengers see that this nun isn't what they thought because the headdress has been torn off and they look at the hair and the freckles and the beard and fall over themselves with amazement – this is a man! There was no end of trouble afterwards stopping them talking to the papers, and the conductor, he was well into negotiations to sell his story to something called *Flick*, a flashy picture magazine, when he was stopped at the last moment.'

Of course escaping from jail in clerical dress had a long history. There had been Magdalena who got out disguised as a nun. A less appropriate garb could not be imagined. From that day nuns leaving the country were abused by Customs officers still smarting over the one who got away. Then there had been Kramer and Lipshitz who bribed their way out of their cells dressed as Cistercian monks. But for a wanted man to return to the country in clerical dress, to certain arrest, that was beyond comprehension. The exit permit on which Zandrotti had left the country on his release from jail specified arrest should he return.

'Unless, of course, he wanted to be caught,' suggested Blanchaille.

'It makes no sense. But you know Roberto, and you know his way of thinking. Jesus, he must have wanted to be caught! There is no other explanation. He let it be known in London, in certain quarters, that he was going home – knowing the details would get back to us. They did. We even knew his seat number on the aircraft.' Van Vuuren unlocked the door and drew Blanchaille into the cell.

Zandrotti had always gone his own way, opposed not merely to the Regime but to every authority he encountered. His schemes for that opposition were novel, intriguing, entirely characteristic, quirkish, outrageous, quite impractical and wonderfully diverting. Zandrotti's plan for immediate revolution was a message, passed by word of mouth to all those opposed to the Regime, that on a particular day at a particular time each man, woman and child would fetch a stone, the biggest and heaviest that could be carried, and place it in the middle of the road and then go home and wait for the country to grind to a halt. Zandrotti's grand coup at school had been the occasion when he broke into the cadet armoury and stole a supply of .303 rifles and full sets of uniforms, khaki shorts and shirts, boots and puttees and caps, with which he dressed and armed a platoon of black school cleaners and drilled them on the school playground for all the world to see. The sight of black men marching with rifles caused panic in the neighbourhood. Zandrotti was expelled from the Hostel and they remembered how he was driven away in Father Cradley's grey DKW, sitting in the back fervently making the Sign of the Cross. The rector was a notoriously bad driver and they watched Zandrotti's mock gibbers of terror, helpless with laughter.

His star appearance was in the dock at the Kipsel trial. The trial of the so-called Fanatical Five. It wasn't Five for long. Looksmart Dladla had fled, mysteriously warned a few days previously by an unknown source. That left just four: Kipsel, Mickey the Poet, Magdalena and Zandrotti.

The number was further reduced when Mickey the Poet hanged himself in his cell. What a miracle of athletic agility that had been, what a wonder of tenacity! Michael Yates, little Mickey the Poet, short, blond, barrel-chested, the build of a youthful welter-weight with powerful forearms and lengthy reach (which perhaps helped in the miracle of his death). But Mickey wasn't a boxer, he was a poet, not by practice but by acclamation. He was known for four quite hopeless lines: *Bourgeois, bourgeois, bourgeois fool/ Little capitalistic tool/ What you ask, will end white rule?/ Ask the children in the school!* With these few lines of thudding doggerel Mickey acquired the sobriquet 'the Poet', and met his end. For not very long after that came the township disturbances when the school-children rioted and Mickey's words seemed amazingly prophetic, if not a straight case of incitement, and his little poem was printed in an anthology of revolutionary verse and was much quoted abroad. And then there was the photograph of Mickey with the 'Liberation Committee', as the leaders of what later became the Azanian Liberation Front were known. A famous photograph showing Mickey standing between Athol Ngogi and Horatio Vilakaze, and with Achmed Witbooi, Oscar Amandla and Ramsamy Gopak, all raising clenched fists and singing. Mickey said he had gone to the meeting by mistake, someone had told him it was a jazz concert, that he never knew. *He never knew*. Another brief epitaph for his gravestone. He never knew when he was approached by Kipsel for a lift what it was that Kipsel carried in the brown leather briefcase. Mickey's ignorance was invincible and nothing that the State Prosecutor, Natie Kirschbaum, said could pierce it. With wonderful simplicity Mickey informed the judge that since he hadn't the first idea of why he had been arrested but since the prosecution seemed to have a number of explanations, he planned to call the entire prosecution team as witnesses for the defence and to cross-examine them carefully on all aspects of his case. The surprised judge adjourned the hearing to consider the application and promised a decision the following day. It caused a sensation. POET TAKES ON PROSECUTION! the headlines read.

The next day never came for Mickey the Poet. Some time during the following twenty-four hours Mickey had attached a strip of towel to his bedstead and the other around his neck and strangled himself. The incredulity with which this was greeted stopped the trial while evidence was heard of Mickey's last hours. The shock of his death was only surpassed by the wonder of its achievement. The defence lawyers produced a statement in which Mickey complained of electric shocks, beatings, and frequent threats that he would be thrown from a high window in Balthazar Buildings. Mickey, it seemed, had demanded to see, as was his right, the Inspector of Detainees, but this had not happened. He had then, it was alleged, gone to bed, tied the towel around his neck and choked himself. Sergeant Betty Paine was called to the witness box to explain why the Inspector had not called. Sergeant Paine's job was to take down statements from prisoners when they complained that they had been tortured and, as she added charmingly with a little flick of her blonde head, to hand this to the interrogator so that he might determine whether indeed there was a case for reporting the complaint to the Inspector of Detainees. However, when the Inspector arrived he was told by Sergeant Paine that the prisoner, Michael Yates, was 'out'. The judge was puzzled by this and asked for the meaning of the word 'out'. Did Sergeant Paine mean 'out' as in 'out for the count,' or 'out for lunch', or 'out of order'? Or perhaps 'out like a light'? Presumably she did not mean 'out to tea' or 'out on the town'. There was laughter in court at this and the judge threatened to clear the galleries.

Sergeant Paine replied that political prisoners were the responsibility of the Security Police who were interrogating them. The police held the keys to the cell and entrance was by permission only, one could not simply go barging into a detainee's cell unannounced or uninvited at any old hour of the night, and although it was true that the officer in charge had given permission for the Inspector of Detainees to call on Yates, as it happened she did not have the keys that night and there was nothing she could do. Rather than hurt the Inspector's feelings she had told him that Yates was 'out'. Sergeant Paine told the court that she dreaded such requests and did her best to please, she even kept a sign on her desk which read: 'Please don't ask to see the prisoners as a refusal may offend . . .' Well, the judge enquired, if the Inspector of Detainees had not seen the prisoner, then presumably Paine had done so, since she had taken down his statement on her Brother electric typewriter. Did he strike her as someone who had been assaulted by interrogating officers? She gave a rather flustered glance desperately towards what were known as the choir stalls, the front benches of the court where the prosecution witnesses from the police sat. A security branch man was shaking his head vigorously at her. The defence counsel protested, claiming that the witness was being prompted from the wings. Sergeant Paine shrilly denied the charge and burst into tears and the judge cautioned the defence for hectoring the witness and permitted her to step down.

And that was the end of the inquiry into the strange death of Mickey the Poet.

The next day Kipsel turned state witness and gave his evidence in a hoarse whisper. He took all the blame on himself: he had persuaded Mickey the Poet to drive him, it was his uncle who ran the compound where the explosive store was situated, it was he who persuaded Looksmart to draw the map of the township and it was through her love for him that Magdalena had allowed herself to be persuaded to take part in the operation. And Zandrotti? Why, he hadn't really been involved at all, he'd merely winked, smiled and sang a couple of verses of the National Anthem.

Kipsel was given a suspended sentence and discharged.

· While he was giving evidence to a hushed courtroom, Magdalena turned her back on him and Zandrotti shouted angrily that he should keep his explanations to himself, better a bungling saboteur than a traitor. For this he was removed to the cells beneath the court room.

He received five years.

Magdalena was given three.

A few weeks later, after apparently bribing a wardress, and disguised as a nun, Magdalena escaped from jail and fled across the border. The disguise she affected led to a tremendous row between Church and State. President Bubé in a warmly received speech to his Party Congress warned that the Roman danger was growing, and called on the Pope's men and women to put their house in order. He hinted at Church connivance in Magdalena's escape and its tacit support of terrorist groups. Bishop Blashford, speaking for the Church, responded by ordering a central register of all working nuns, 'genuine sisters' as he called them and disclaimed any connection between the renegade Magdalena and the true Brides of Christ who, he said angrily, dedicated their lives to serving God and their fellow men and took no part in politics. At the same time he warned that violent opposition to the Regime would continue while they maintained their hideous racial policies. He took the occasion for attacking as well their authoritarian methods of birth control, the dumping of unwanted people in remote camps in the veld, and the crass folly and blatant inhumanity of the Regime's political arrangements. He drew parallels with Nazi Germany and went so far as to compare President Bubé with Hitler, a time-honoured insult and much appreciated throughout the country where Blashford earned enthusiastic praise from the anti-Regime opposition but equally delighted President Bubé's followers, so much so that in the traditional response he publicly thanked the good Bishop for the compliment, since after all Hitler had been a strong man, proud of his people and his country. Both men came out of the confrontation with their public prestige much enhanced and behind the scenes it was said they were both good friends and often went fishing together.

The anarchist's eyes were red-flecked milky pools surrounding pupils dark and hard as stones. And I saw in my dream how hesitantly Blanchaille approached him, not knowing what his reception was likely to be at the hands of his old friend not seen for so long, so cruelly used, for after that terrible trial it had been Zandrotti alone who faced the assaults of his jailers, cruelties not refined but oafish, coarse, persistently callous, and above all, juvenile. The young warders had waged a campaign of humiliation against him, Blanchaille heard on his weekly visits to the prison; they would apple-pie his bed, piss on his cigarettes replacing them limp and wet in the pack, tear pages from the books he was reading and allocate him cells from which he could hear the singing of the condemned men on death row. Lovely singing it was too, Zandrotti told him, day and night, right up to the last moment, this male voice choir of killers waiting for the end. They would sing special requests, the warders joked with Zandrotti. It had been his idea of hell, Zandrotti told Blanchaille afterwards when he was free, to be locked in a small room with the intellectual equivalent of the police rugby team. Beside that horror the fires of conventional Roman hell cooled to an inviting glow.

Blanchaille drove him to the airport after his release, the anarchist clutching a few clothes, a little cash and an exit visa which ensured he would depart from the country forever within forty-eight hours. 'They opened a little gate in the big prison gate and pushed me out clutching my money, in this badly fitting blue suit, carrying my passport and an exit permit and told me, God bless, old fellow. God bless! Can you believe that?' All he wanted on the road to the airport was news. He had none in the years inside. He greeted the news that Magdalena was regarded as dangerous by the Regime with a whistle of appreciation. But he was amazed to learn that Kipsel was still alive, had not done the expected and hanged himself, or shot himself.

Apparently Magdalena had helped Zandrotti when he reached London. Blanchaille had no idea of his situation there except for one report that showed his old perverse sense of humour operated still. He read of the anarchist being hauled before an English court for persistently photographing everyone who entered or left the South African embassy because, as he explained to the magistrate, this was a custom in his own country where everyone expected to be photographed on street corners by agents of the Regime not once but many times during their lives and he wished to continue this ancient custom in exile.

Now he lay in a bunk in the cells of Balthazar Buildings, strangely quiet, supine, and yet with a gleam of defiance which contrasted oddly with his air of defeat.

'Ask him why he's here,' Van Vuuren said.

'What brought you back, Roberto? And looking so holy, too. The flying nun. Mother Zandrotti of the Townships . . .'

The prisoner favoured him with a fleeting smile. 'I met Tony Ferreira in London. He was staying at this hotel and we went down to the bar. He was in London on the last leg of a world tour. He got very drunk in the bar, kept falling to his knees and reciting bits of the Litany. You will remember the sort of thing – "Bower of Roses, Tower of Ivory, Hope of Sinners", and so on. You know the lyrics, I'm sure you could sing it yourself. But in a bar in London surrounded by English Protestants, it can be rather alarming. Anyway the barman, thank God, ordered him to stop or leave . . .'

'But why did Ferreira want you back here?'

'He didn't. That was the last thing he wanted. The bastard slandered his country!'

'Slandered his country! God almighty, Roberto! What sort of rubbish is that? Where did he want you to go?'

'To the other place. To Geneva. Oh hell, you know, Uncle Paul's place.'

'What else did he say?'

'I don't remember.' The anarchist's eyes swam on their veined pools. 'Ask him yourself.'

'Ferreira is dead. Murdered.'

The anarchist shrugged. 'So they say. Well, not before time. I would have killed him myself.'

Blanchaille tried to control his astonishment. 'What did he do to you?'

'He tried to destroy everything I've ever believed in, hoped in. He pissed on it! He crapped on it! Rubbed my nose in it, between invocations to the Queen of Heaven . . . '

'But what did he say?'

'Don't remember.'

Van Vuuren interposed. 'That's all you'll get from him, the forgetfulness is strategic.'

They withdrew. The prisoner showed little sign of recognizing their going until they reached the door when Blanchaille said, 'Goodbye then, Roberto, and I'm sorry to meet you in this place.'

The anarchist sat upright and waved his fist in fury. 'I'm sorry for you, yes, because if you're going where I think you're going, then you're going to die of sorrow! Don't be sorry for me, Blanchie, save it for yourself. I'm still here.'

Outside in the corridor Blanchaille asked Van Vuuren: 'What does he mean – he's still here?'

'Just what he says. Here, in jail, he is Zandrotti, known as such, wanted by the police and dangerous enough to apprehend, torture, perhaps kill. These threats confirm his existence, his importance, not least to himself. Here and perhaps only here he is Zandrotti still. We are the police, this is the infamous prison, Balthazar Buildings. Everything is what it is expected to be. I don't know what Ferreira told him in London but clearly it made him so desperate that prison seems infinitely preferable to all other alternatives . . . But let's get something clear, we don't want him. We're not holding the anarchist Zandrotti, despite what the papers say overseas and the silent vigils in front of our embassy demanding the brave soul's release. No, he is clinging to us. It is he who won't let us go . . . '

Blanchaille was becoming more weary and confused by the mysteries which though they had a certain bizarre interest were not getting him very far along the road to the Airport Palace Hotel and his flight to freedom and he respectfully requested to be allowed to continue his journey.

'One last port of call,' Van Vuuren promised, 'and then you can go.' He paused outside a cell door and lifted the steel cover from the spyhole and invited Blanchaille to look inside. 'Recognise him?'

'Naturally.' How could he not do so? The large fine head, the grizzled steel-grey curls, the powerful dignified bearing of the man who had done more than anyone else to advance the cause of liberation in Southern Africa, Horatio Vilakaze, arrested soon after the fateful picture had appeared showing Mickey the Poet apparently in attendance on the liberation leaders, back in those exciting days before death, dispersal, imprisonment, exile, house arrest and age had split and destroyed the original organising committee of the Black Justice Campaign. How long ago? Years, years and years. It did no good to count them.

'Vilakaze is perhaps the saddest of all our cases,' Van Vuuren said. 'We don't have to go into the cell, we can listen to his speech from out here,' he flicked a switch and the old man's powerful voice reverberated along the chill, empty corridor.

'Brothers and sisters, comrades, freedom will be ours!' He held up his arms as if to still the cheering crowds and when the applause which must have rung between his ears like brass bands had died away he rallied the faithful thousands only he could see and hear. 'Within the country our forces are massing, our fighters are brave, the Regime shrinks from them. On the borders the armies of our allies gather like locusts to sweep on our enemy and defeat him. Together we will overcome, we will drive the oppressor into the sea, God is with us!'

Van Vuuren killed the vibrant, echoing words. 'Too sad to hear. That was his last great speech before he was arrested. He was speaking to thirty thousand supporters, and he can't forget it. It preys on his mind, he reruns the speech a dozen times a day. That was before the young men took over. He is a great man.'

'It didn't stop you arresting him.'

'Yes. We did arrest him, but only after we had been approached by a number of his friends anxious to spare him the humiliation of ejection from the movement he had helped to found. So yes, you can say we arrested him, but really we took him in.'

Took him in? *Took him in!* What a terrible thing to say. As if this place had been a home for strays, a dogs' home. Or an orphanage. There was in this something he could not accept. Something so awful it didn't bear thinking about.

'You're saying that it was an act of charity?' He could hear the incredulous ring in his voice.

'Something like that. And a mistake, too. Once in custody there was no releasing him. We tried once, sent him back to his people who wouldn't have him. They're hard-nosed, young, efficient elements who want power, who want to succeed at any cost even if it means some weird, subtle deal with the Regime, and to them old Vilakaze with his talk of armies and locusts is an embarrassment . . . they're happy to use his name, to keep the Free Vilakaze committees going all over the world, the silent vigils, the marches, the petitions calling for his release but what they won't stand for is for us to let him go. We've been warned – put him back on the street and he's a dead man,'

Back in the reception area with its portraits of the presidents, Blanchaille said, 'I think I begin to understand what you're up against. Once the police were there to arrest people they considered a danger to the State. This was our world. Ugly, perhaps cruel. But dependable. Things have changed. These people, Strydom, Zandrotti, Vilakaze, they don't know where they are anymore. Except when they're in here. What you've got here are specimens from another age. This isn't a prison, it's a museum.'

Van Vuuren reflected. 'And a hospital. They pose no threat to the State. The only people they're a danger to are themselves. These people shouldn't be here. They're not criminals. They're failures. They shouldn't be in jail. They should be sent somewhere for treatment. Some special hospital for incurable failures.'

'I believe there is,' said Blanchaille.

Van Vuuren joined his hands together in a pious gesture of the altar server of long ago. 'Let's hope so.'

CHAPTER 9

Van Vuuren loaded Blanchaille's cases into a small, powder-blue Volkswagen Golf. There wasn't room for the cases in the boot and he put them on the back seat. 'Don't worry about the car, just leave it at the airport. Its owner, I'm afraid, has no further use for it. It comes from our pool.'

'Goodbye,' Blanchaille said dazed by all he had learnt.

'Good luck,' Van Vuuren replied. 'I take it you see things a little differently now?'

Blanchaille felt embarrassed. Van Vuuren had made himself difficult to dislike. 'Why do you stay on?'

Van Vuuren looked uncomfortable. He shrugged. 'Duty, perhaps.'

'Duty? To what? To whom?'

Again Van Vuuren was silent but he gave Blanchaille an odd, rather mocking glance and waved him away. 'You're under police protection. It's about as good as being anointed.'

In order to reach the airport one takes the national highway, a great curving road much of it a long, gentle climb. It was getting dark. A stony, glittering moon rose swiftly, glared briefly and was gone. Just as he cleared the city it began to rain. Rounding a bend he found his way blocked when three men in orange oilskins stepped into the road and flagged him down. His bright lights reflected back off the brilliant orange plastic and dazzled him so that he had to shield his eyes. The men stepped up to the window: 'Theodore Blanchaille?'

'What do you want?'

'Please get out of the car,' said the first policeman.

'We're giving you something,' said the second policeman.

'Please take off your clothes,' said the third policeman.

The door was opened and Blanchaille was helped out. A large green and red golf umbrella was unfurled and held over his head. The first policeman reached into the car and dragged out Blanchaille's three cases.

'What are you doing with those?'

'We're relieving you of them.'

'But it's all my stuff.'

102

'You won't be needing it where you're going. Now in return we have three things to give you. A change of clothes, good advice and proper papers.'

The first policeman went over to his car and returned with a large cardboard box. This he unpacked carefully and took from it a white suit. There in the pouring rain, standing beneath the umbrella, Blanchaille was forced to remove his clothes and don the new white suit. There was a red woollen tie to go with it, silk shirt, a crimson spotted handkerchief for the breast pocket and slim, pale, pointed Italian shoes with cream silk socks.

The rain stopped, the wild moon reappeared. Blanchaille gleamed coldly in its light.

'That's better,' said the first policeman. 'Now you look like somebody.'

'I am to give you some advice,' said the second policeman. 'You're going out, you're leaving, you're going to visit the outside world, you will need to be prepared. Remember things aren't quite so simple there, people worry about different things, about inflation and unemployment. They worry about whether to have their children vaccinated against whooping cough. They argue about the environment and the rights of women and they fear the extinction of the world by atomic explosion.'

And then the third policeman stepped closer to the now resplendent priest looking like a plump, prosperous riverboat gambler in his white suit and after checking his passport, handed him his exit permit. 'Although we all know you are leaving, the point of this permit is to ensure that you take a one-way trip. There is no return.' Then stepping even closer he whispered in the fugitive's ear in a voice so low I could not catch them, the directions he was to take once he arrived safely at his final destination.

They put him back in his car, they stepped away from it in unison and they waved him on, three wet policemen, shining in the fierce moonlight.

I saw in my dream how Blanchaille went very little further that night but pulled over onto the side of the road and with his head swimming with all that had happened to him that day, and having first carefully folded his new jacket and put it on the back seat, he slept.

In the first light of the new day he started the car and set out to complete his drive to the airport. This gently rising country he knew well, here it was where the huge army camps were situated with their big red notices warning of electrified fencing and the regular watch towers. And on the other side of the road lay the military cemeteries, entered by way of giant bronze gates cast in the form of wagon wheels through the spokes of which he could glimpse the orange crosses on the graves. Orange crosses were a particular feature of the military graveyard. No other colour was suitable. White, brown, pink, black, yellow and even red, all carried racial or political connotations which were judged to be undesirable. After all, since the Total Onslaught began it had not been only Europeans who gave their lives for the mother country. People of many colours including large contingents of black storm-troopers, Indian cooks, coloured drivers, Bushmen trackers, served in the armed forces. So it was orange, the dominant colour of the national flag, colour of the original Free State, the substantial feature of the African sunset, that was found in military memorials.

Here was the Air Force base which they had visited as boys with Father Lynch, when the priest had worn his beret as a mark of cordiality to celebrate the French connection, 'an entirely appropriate symbol, I think, and a gesture of esteem for one of our most faithful arms suppliers, the old Sabre Jets are gone and the new French fighters are in.'

'Not swords into ploughshares, Sabres into Mirages . . .' Blanchaille muttered.

Along these perimeter fences he saw the early morning Alsatian patrols, the dogs held in a U-shaped metal lead with their trainers running behind them. It was rather reminiscent of guide dogs leading the blind. Here were endless miles of military suburbs named Shangri-La, Valhalla, El Dorado, Happy Valley.

The first of the great national monuments was the burly granite sarcophagus raised to the memory of the early Trekkers, grey and powerful on a low green hill and looking like nothing so much as an old-fashioned wireless, a giant Art-Deco piece, a great circular window intersected by deep parallel grooves where the loudspeaker would have been, hidden behind its wire and wicker screen. The monument sat in its massive bulk on the hill, forever.

Next, the monument to the dead of the concentration camps which the British ran in the Boer War, a huge, weeping, gilded Boer mother dipping her poke bonnet over her starving children who buried their faces in her ample lap.

Next, the monument to the first invasion of Angola, the bronze soldier posed behind a captured Russian artillery-piece mounted on a lorry, everything precise in all its details, the 122-millimetre rocket launcher, the famous 'Stalin organ', capable of firing salvos of forty rockets at a burst. The soldier and artillery-piece and lorry were on a raised grassy bank surrounded by a mass of flowers, a kind of floral gunpit, banks of white madonna lilies bloodily speckled here and there with clumps of red hot pokers.

Here was the monument to the dead of the abortive Mauritian landings, perhaps the first military invasion organised by private enterprise, the money having been put up by the large mining companies which had found themselves under fire for lack of patriotism and wished to provide assurances of good faith to the Regime. It had been a monumental error, the soldiers had come ashore from their landing craft under the most terrible mis-apprehension that the way was clear and that a coup would simultaneously topple the Government. Came ashore at the wrong time on the wrong day, and under the very guns of a section of the army out on manoeuvres who had observed the seaborne invasion with incredulity from their fortified emplacements and then opened fire with gusto laying the invaders face down on the beach in a grotesque and bloody mimicry of holiday sunbathers. The dead were remembered by a towering block of marble. The early morning sun hit the golden orange lettering in which their names were incised, row upon row.

And here were the military camps which stretched as far as the eye could see. Huge townships in the veld. Once the country had had a civilian army, when people left their jobs and served time in the forces. Now at the time of the Total Onslaught the length of military service was indefinite and people took off their uniforms for brief periods and served time in their old offices, in their firms and factories.

All this great military complex spread before Blanchaille was an expression of unshakable faith, an affirmation of survival, a substantiation of the vow that white men would survive in Southern Africa whatever the odds. It affirmed the covenant between God and his people that they would serve him and he would preserve the nation. The country was run by the national party in the national interest, the national borders were safeguarded against the national enemy, the arms the people carried were the arms of God. This was the war-music of the Republic. This was the song of the mourning Boer mother, it was the message broadcast from the granite wireless, it was the symphony played on the Stalin organ.

Blanchaille was within sight of the airport. He could see the hangars, he could see the planes on the tarmac, he passed the

Holiday Inn, he slowed down and looked about him for the Airport Palace. Two black men appeared running towards him holding up their hands and shouting. He slowed and rolled down the window. The men seized the window-frame panting, their eyes rolling, 'Sir, you must go back. Everybody must go back. There are soldiers in the airport. Crazy men. They have guns, they're shooting. Turn back, turn back!'

But Blanchaille knew he'd come too far to turn back, whatever the danger. 'Do you know the Airport Palace Hotel?'

'Yes, yes, we know it.'

'Can I walk there from here?'

'You can walk, but you must pass through the soldiers. And they're shooting. They are crazy and roaring like lions.'

Blanchaille got out of the car. He gave the keys to the men. 'You go back, but I have to tell you it's no safer behind me. Go. Take the car. I won't need it any more.'

They told him to keep walking down the road and he would find the hotel, he would hear the shooting and he would know he was there. And the roaring, he would hear that too.

Blanchaille set off. As the men had predicted he heard the firing first but quickened his pace. It meant the hotel was close.

The Airport Palace was built of steel and green glass. It was surrounded by a brick wall and outside this wall were the soldiers. He knew at once who they were. They weren't regular troops, they wore an unusual uniform, black three-cornered hats, bottle-green tunics with gold buttons, grey riding breeches and knee-high boots and they ran here and there, firing their rifles, shouting, weeping and groaning. It was these groans the fleeing men had taken for roars. They carried the traditional Boer muzzle loader and their firing, though noisy, was wild and inaccurate. They fired into the air and they fired into walls and they had to stop to reload each time, to prime the guns and to fire again. This was the ceremonial President's guard who accompanied Adolph Bubé on all official occasions. Their uniform was modelled on the guard of honour which had greeted the President on his celebrated visit to General Stroessner in Paraguay. He had gone home and designed the uniforms himself. Blanchaille remembered the headlines at the time: BUBÉ VISITS STROESSNER! A few years later the visit was returned: STROESSNER VISITS BUBÉ! Stroessner and Bubé presented each other with medals: PRESIDENT BUBÉ HONOURED BY REPUBLIC OF PARAGUAY – FREEDOM MEDAL FOR BUBÉ. AFRICA STAR FOR STROESSNER!

The soldiers ran here and there, wild-eyed and sweating in their heavy uniforms. They reminded Blanchaille of marionettes. They seemed out of control, demented with fear. There was a cast-iron gate in the wall. Blanchaille banged on the gate and called for someone to let him in. The soldiers ignored him, charging about in their stiff-legged tin-man way.

An elderly man limped to the gate, drying his hands on a tea towel.

'Name?'

'Blanchaille. I think I'm expected.'

'You used to be called Father Theo of the Settlements?'

'Of the Camps, but now it's plain Blanchaille.'

'What kept you?'

'It's a long story. I'd like to come inside. Are those real bullets those guys are firing?'

'Oh no. The President's guard were never provided with live ammo. In case they got tempted, see? No, they're just shouting and shooting and running around like chickens who've had their heads cut off. They've lost their President, you see. They're supposed to guard Bubé and Bubé's gone, and it has sent them round the bend. They're like deserted robots. The man who used to wind them up has gone away. Come inside. Come inside and meet the girls.'

CHAPTER 10

Now I saw in my dream the reception of the plump renegade Blanchaille by the ancient porter of the Airport Palace Hotel, a certain Visser, once a colonel in a tank corps fighting Rommel's troops in the desert war Up North. Something of a trace of military bearing remained about the doddering fellow who worked now unbeknown to the world as concierge, doorkeeper, porter, cleaner and barman at the Palace. He promised his guest 'interesting stories'.

To Visser there attached a tale no less tragic than the hundreds he had heard across the bar of the Airport Palace Hotel from sad pilgrims about to quit the country. Except Visser would never leave, he said. If he did he would shrivel up and die he claimed, not realising he had been as good as dead for years. For it was Visser who had started the once-famous Brigades of Light when he returned from the war and found enemy sympathisers poised to take power. From the stage of the Sir Benjamin D'Urban Memorial Hall on the South Coast with the Indian Ocean seething outside the windows, he told his audience of ex-servicemen that they had been betrayed. While they'd been fighting Up North the new Regime had been blowing up bridges and knitting woolly socks to send to Hitler's troops. Was it for this that young men had risked their lives in the desert war? He called on them to go home and set a lighted candle in the window to burn for liberty. And thus the Brigades of Light had been born. The name conjured up dedicated fighters for freedom. It turned out to be a group of newly demobbed, enthusiastic young men who went about at night in large cheerful rather drunken groups and stuck pictures of flaming candles on letter boxes and gates. It was good fun while it lasted but the raids, as they were called, soon deteriorated into nightly gallops and drunken binges. At Christmas their flaming taper was confused with that of the Carols by Candlelight organisation which collected for a host of deserving charities. After this discipline deteriorated. The exuberant ex-soldiers threw stones on corrugated iron roofs, rang the bells and ran away, or peered at young women undressing in their bedrooms. It was hardly the liberation force Colonel Visser had hoped for. For a while he managed to rally his troops. Duty platoons went to election meetings and fought with supporters of the Regime, collecting black eyes and bloody noses and feeling that at least they were doing something, though they knew in their hearts that the Regime was unstoppable. The wilder souls dreamt of burying rifles on the lonely beaches, there was even talk of secession but it didn't last. The young men went to work as accountants, got married, took up Sunday rugby. Colonel Visser issued increasingly desperate orders from Brigade headquarters but it was useless. He disappeared from public view and there were rumours that he had been hideously disfigured in a car crash and was hiding in some obscure Cape resort attended only by a faithful black servant; there was talk that he had emigrated to England where he entered a closed community of Anglican brothers; but instead he had come here, to the Airport Palace Hotel, despite its name an obscure hostelry for souls on their way out – and to be found in no hotel directory.

That Blanchaille should have been welcomed by an elderly military man who promised him a selection of tales not without historical interest to be told by a collection of 'rather special' ladies, might have surprised Blanchaille had his experience in the holding cells not destroyed his remaining reserves of surprise.

Visser talked to Blanchaille of the old connection between the Regime and the Nazi movement as he conducted him to his room and from there to the bar. 'Why did they support Hitler? On the basis that my enemy's enemy is my friend. Tradition played a part as well. The Kaiser had supported Paul Kruger against the British in the old days and that was a pretty good precedent for his descendants to do the same. There had been German support for the Boer fighters for freedom. *Ergo* – the later liaison between the Austrian housepainter and the hairy little rockspiders who run our country. A marriage of true minds.'

The hotel was huge and empty, built of steel and glass and filled with the hiss of the air-conditioning. The tinted windows did not open. Brown chocolate carpet climbed the walls. Visser stood behind the bar, a great polished bank of teak surrounded by a brass rail, and I saw in my dream how he summoned the first of the four girls whom he described as hostesses dedicated to the refreshment of guests at the Palace 'with a selection of stories and even an exhibition or two', he said. The first of the storytellers was Freia.

Freia was blonde, she wore denim shorts, Visser described her as 'our conductor'. She did not look like it. Her hair was scraped back and held in place by a blue Alice-band, she was crumpled and yawning and had obviously been sleeping. Across the front of her tee-shirt was the map of Switzerland cunningly placed so that there rose up from it the twin alps of her breasts. She ordered 'the usual' from Visser, a green cocktail in a frosty glass and licking the sugar from the rim with a sharp pink tongue, she began in a voice dreamy and lilting as if she recalled something recent and strange, but which Blanchaille soon understood from the expert timing and sardonic emphases of her delivery to be a story often told.

'I used to be a tour conductor. I worked in the townships in the days when we still ran tours. I was in Gus Kuiker's department – you know Gus Kuiker? Augustus Kuiker, the Minister? My job was to show tourists around, the official tourists who get invited out here, ageing film stars, American senators, elderly prima donnas, industrialists, pop-singers, tennis players, members of Anglican investigative commissions.' Freia laughed, drained her glass and held it out for a refill. 'I remember my last tour. Eighteen English footballers and one of their big men from British television, Cliff Irving, a pointy fellow with a sparse beard, balding, small bright black eyes, hands like soup-plates. They'd been bribed, of course. They're all bribed. When they come out here the townships are on every itinerary. Obligatory. There were, besides, a few Japanese businessmen, good loyal friends. It's the pig-iron they come for, or did, years ago. We'd stopped looking on them as little yellow devils with funny eyes and saw them as honorary white men. Loaded with cameras, of course. And a batch of Israelis in funny hats. We weren't supposed to know they were Israelis. They were described as a Chilean judo team. A smattering of Germans, industrialists or bankers, came too. The soccer tourists from Britain were ageing hacks for the most part, best years behind them, anxious to make more money in three weeks than they'd ever made before in their lives. Nice enough fellows, but forever making speeches. At the drop of a hat they'd tell you that they were really interested in pushing back the barriers of racial segregation, playing township teams, coaching barefoot piccaninnies, and so on. They climbed aboard loaded with coolbags full of beer because they'd just been to the brewery which sponsored their visit and put them on show. They were ticking nicely by the time they got to us and the famous TV sports journalist had trouble calming them down. First stop was the 200-megawatt generator which could supply millions of kilowatt hours, all the Japanese taking notes, very impressed to learn we were supplying electricity not only to our own industries but to big power stations hundreds and hundreds of miles away in independent countries to the north. Everybody needs our power. We told these countries. "Look, you deal with us. Or nothing. You either pay or you shut up." My tourists always glazed over when I hit them with pig-iron and electric power figures. But they had to get the sell. Not easy for me, with everyone gazing dutifully out of the windows at the cooling towers, except the Japanese. Pretty boring stuff I have to admit. Someone always asked why the power station was surrounded by barbed wire, fields of lean, cruel, spindly stuff like some dangerous crop. Well, you explained that it had to be there otherwise these guys came in and blew it up. You had to have the wire and the dogs and the night patrols, and so on. Then we drove through the town proper, I mean what can you say? Thousands upon thousands upon thousands of tiny brick and tin houses. There it is, staring you in the face, it lies there in the veld and the tourists stare at it for a while like they can't believe what they're seeing, and I remember one of the footballers said it was worse than bloody Manchester. So at this point we were trained to talk about murder. You sat back in your uniform and your perky cap in your seat next to the driver and turned the mike up and hit them with the murder rate. More people killed hourly in our townships than in New York on a good hot summer's night, more than in Guatemala! That was always good for a bit of a sharp intake of breath. They always believe that Guatemala is really the killing ground of the world. Down the dusty streets we trundled with the barefoot kids charging after us. The soccer players would get into the spirit of things and we'd open a window or two and encourage them to throw coins out to the kids, and perhaps a few sweets. Or they'd throw signed photographs of themselves. We passed the Umdombala Cash Store and the Dutch Reformed Church. Usual thing, polished blond wood, glass, with that thin skinny little black metal chicken on the steeple that's supposed to serve as a weather vane. One of those horrible little buildings that they put up, all sharp angles and shiny edges and you're supposed to get the feeling of upward thrust of flight, but the base is so broad and heavy it's like a fat space rocket that can't take off. And then we'd stop at the local cash store and we'd let them buy brightly coloured kaffir blankets. They had an absolute fascination for these sorts of native goods. They liked blankets and beads and wire work. We didn't hide things. We took them past the police station, they were always interested in that, and you know the police stations in the townships are always barred, with enormous gates and acres of barbed wire, with the armoured cars drawn up in front of the charge office and the parade ground with the flagpole and ornamental cannons. They all noticed the sportsfields and we'd make the point that the police would often invite neighbouring children to come and play with them, kids from the township, and if they were tough, well they had to be, that they were really not as bad as they had been painted, after all they were policing one of the murder capitals of the world. You'd get people who simply wouldn't let the murder rate drop, who'd say, "I still believe it's Guatemala that's the murder capital", and you'd say, "Look, maybe thirty or fifty people a night die in Guatemala, whereas here we're way ahead of anything like that, we're in a different league here". Then, to redress the balance as it were, we'd stop at the kindergarten run by a buxom little nun, Sister Edith. Sister Edith's crèche was a very popular tourist stop. She'd call the kids out and they'd sit on their little wooden benches in their blue smocks and their large yellow sashes and they'd sing for the tourists, beautiful singing, wonderful intonation, and you could tell that Sister Edith spent a lot of time polishing up these tiny choirs of hers. They used to sing laments usually. They seemed to be awfully good at laments those little kids. I remember one – it went "My mother has gone to Egoli . . . my father comes no more . . ."' Freia sang softly to herself, a mournful, achingly despairing little air echoing around the bar. 'We'd have to tear ourselves away from Sister Edith's singing kindergarten and I would generally drive them past the big hospital where the stab cases were recuperating, lying out on the big old stoep, paralysed from the waist down after being attacked by local hoodlums with sharpened bicycle spokes lunging at the spinal cord. And these young cripples would wave and smile as we drove by and show that they still had a lot of spirit. Next stop, millionaire's row, places like Mr Masinga's mansion and we'd make the point: look, no matter what you've read about starvation and so on in the townships, you will see that these people are actually thriving, that they are actually getting on bloody well. That men like Mr Masinga could have bought anybody on that bus, German, Japanese or Israeli, five times over. But remember, this isn't

112

Clacton or Bremerhaven, this is Africa! With that, off to the beer hall where the municipal authorities brewed their own beer, tremendously popular and fantastically healthy for the workers who absolutely lapped it up at a few cents for a great big plastic bucket of the stuff. Occasionally we saw a fight and I'd let them sit through it. Why hide the unpleasant side of life? After all they're adults. People fight all over the world when they've had too much to drink, not just our blacks. Then on to the pride of the township, the sports centre with its football pitch and its cycling track and the footballers would get excited because they would be playing there, or at least they expected to, but these bandit tours were often cancelled in mid-course when the centre-forward was arrested in a black brothel, or the sponsor got cold feet, so there was always an air of unease in the first glimpse of the soccer stadium. We'd watch a black cyclist in full gear making a circuit of the track in his Coca-Cola cap and his Barclays Bank shorts and his Raleigh bike. Finally we drove past the funeral parlour with all the coffin prices clearly displayed and the Christmas Club where you pay off so much a month to make sure that you get buried. So much for a funeral with car, without a car, and priced according to mourners, just like a roadhouse. The tourists were always fascinated and would ask questions like, why are these people sitting with bundles of blankets on their laps? And then of course it gradually dawned on the innocents that what looked like bundles of blankets were in fact dead babies. You should have seen their faces! I couldn't help smiling. Suddenly they realised that they were in Africa! I mean I don't have to tell you this, Father Theo of the Camps – but this was the place where you got babies dying like flies because of these epidemics sweeping through the new-born of the townships like Herod's soldiers. And then you'd get one of these Japanese – you know how it is, they'd photograph anything! – and one of them would pull out a camera and ask if he could take a shot and we'd say, look, you know, *look*, if you don't intrude on a mother's grief then it's okay. If you've got a telephoto lens then go ahead, but no going up close and snapping right in their faces, have some respect for the dead, this is Africa and Africa is cruel but we want to maintain civilised standards if at all possible . . . But why am I telling you this? You're Father Theo of the Camps –' Freia widened her big green eyes in mock astonishment.

'Was,' Blanchaille contradicted her. 'Was once.'

'Well, anyway, why tell you? You've seen more of infant mortality than I ever will. But that's my piece and you're welcome to it. Now it's Happy's turn. She'll give you a different view of things.'

Happy, tall, black, appeared with Visser leaning gratefully on her arm. She took a seat between Freia and Blanchaille and ordered a highball. Her hair was drawn up in a great dark crown and seeded with what looked like pearls. Her fingernails were painted pink. Her manner was strident, even aggressive and Blanchaille shifted uneasily. Freia caught his eye and winked. 'Takes all sorts,' she whispered sympathetically, 'that's the trouble.' Happy glared. Freia fell silent. Blanchaille sighed and turned to Happy. He was being punished with parables.

'I worked in the house of my Minister from about the age of fourteen onwards. Because my Minister was powerful I learnt things and because I learnt things I went places. My Minister's department decided that it was no good dealing with our northern black neighbours as we'd done in the old colonial times with the white men lording it over blacks. In the new age black must speak to black and so I became a negotiator, that's to say I dealt with heads of state and political officials in the enemy states to the north. Since as you may know, they buy the works from us – power, food, transport, arms, everything from nappies to canned fruit – I used to say to them, look, this is our price, take it or leave it. Sometimes I'd get a lot of opposition. Some big hero of the African revolution, chest clinking with medals, would meet me at the National Redeemer Airport and say: "Jesus Christ! You're black, Happy, you're one of us, how can you help them to bleed us to death?" And I'd say, "Man – we take forty thousand mine workers a year from you, and if you don't like the arrangement and the price per head we're quoting then fine – don't send them. Or maybe you'd prefer that instead of remitting their salaries to you *in toto*, direct, we might consider paying the poor bastards individually and in that case half your national income goes out the window . . ." Allow me to present you with a photograph of my Minister.'

Before he could refuse Happy thrust a photograph in his hands. Involuntarily he glanced at it: 'Kuiker, of course.'

This delighted his audience who clapped their hands and echoed him: 'Kuiker, of course.'

The face of a pugilist, of an all-in wrestler. The flesh kneaded into thick ridges around the jaw-line, eyebrows and lips; nose flat and wide, a bony spur run askew and bedded down in thick flat flesh. The full lips in their charateristic sneer, even when compressed.

MINISTER KUIKER WEARING HIS SARDONIC SMILE, the papers said. Thick dark hair combed back from the forehead in stiff, oiled ridges running over his ears and down the back of his neck. He had a taste for shiny suits and bright ties and a paradoxical reputation for unyielding conservatism combined with modern pragmatism. He was solid, powerful and dangerous, this man, the marbled eyes, the petrified hair, the enormous capacity for Scotch, the truculent ties and the cheap fashion jewellery, gold tie-pins with their diamond chips, the skull rings with red-glass bloodshot eyes he affected on both hands. Gus Kuiker was widely tipped to succeed President Bubé when the old man went. His only rival, young 'Bomber Vollenhoven', was seen as too inexperienced and too liberal. Kuiker was the mastermind behind President Bubé's lightning foreign tours and the man responsible for plucking a young statistical clerk by name of Trudy Yssel from a lowly job in the President's Department for Applied Ethnic Embryology and appointing her to the post of Secretary to the Department of Communications: YSSEL NEW SUPREMO AT DEPCOM, the papers said. KUIKER'S PROPAGANDA OFFENSIVE!

In the picture Kuiker gazed belligerently ahead. It might have been a police mug shot.

'Where was this taken?'

'Here.'

His eyes must have held the question which of course there was no need to ask, and his hosts were too tactful to answer. There was only one reason why anyone stopped at the Airport Palace Hotel. Blanchaille felt conscious once again of his naïvety. Well, he could not help that. He had been raised to believe such things were impossible. Only Lynch had disagreed. But then Lynch had been mad. Now it seemed increasingly that Lynch's madness was being borne out. It also, and this was ironic, seemed to bear out the charge of the Old Guard within the Regime, that the New Men, of whom Kuiker was a leading representative, would cut and run when things got tough.

The Old Guard believed in shooting. The New Men believed in certain adjustments. 'I was one of these adjustments he had in mind,' said Happy, 'when he talked about necessary adjustments to racial policies. He talked of ethnic autonomy, of equalised freedoms, of positive tribalism, of the thousand subtle easements of policy which, my Minister Gus Kuiker would say, were necessary to relax the corset of rigid white centralism and to allow us to reach and embrace the future, as we must if we were to survive. Did the

115

white man think – our Minister would ask – that he had a right in Africa because he had been there for three hundred years? Nonsense! The Portuguese had been in Africa for five hundred years, and where were they now? They were back in Lisbon on the dole. Therefore, in answer to the question – what shall we do to be saved? – the Old Guard would have replied, shoot to kill. But ask the New Men and they would tell you, do anything necessary. What kills them is to be condemned for acting for reasons of expediency when they believe as much as their predecessors, the Old Guard, that they act out of divine necessity. Watch out for Minister Kuiker, in whatever guise you find him. He has been abused by his own people and that has made him crazy.'

Now I saw in my dream that a pretty Indian arrived and took her place at the bar. She wore an apricot silk sari. Petite and teetotal, she drank only orange juice and announced herself to be a Moslem and a Marxist. Her name was Fatima. She spoke so softly Blanchaille had to strain to hear the words. Soon he wished he hadn't.

'I hope to replace the present Regime with a people's democracy,' Fatima said mildly. 'And as a result of my beliefs I was placed in preventive detention. My interrogators, who were all men, at first found themselves unwilling to inflict pain. That is to say, they didn't like to beat me since it flew in the face of beliefs deeply instilled into them that large men do not go around hitting women, and perhaps because of the fact that I am particularly small boned, they were actually unable to raise their fists to me. However, after a certain time they stripped me, secured my hands and legs, and attempted to torture me by introducing various objects – pen tops, broom handles and finally fingers – into my vagina and anus. The reasons why they did this were complicated. I presume that since they weren't attempting to extract any information from me, they must be trying to humiliate me, I being a slender girl and they being large and muscular white men and I suspect that they had read that Asian girls were naturally reticent and modest. But I wasn't prepared to allow myself to be humiliated and this put them in a difficult position. I also pointed out to the men assaulting me that without exception they had large erections which were quite discernible beneath their blue serge trousers. Perhaps for this reason I was returned to my cell and later discharged. It seemed to me that sexual excitement had begun to replace serious political discussion. This was some time ago. By now these interrogators have probably done away with prisoners and replaced them with perverse solitary sexual

116

acts. Not only did the revolution I envisaged seem impossible, but it had become impossible to even pose the question or the threat. I came here where at least I can help people to leave this world behind them.'

Blanchaille did not enjoy hearing his course of action so described but did not feel it was time to say so. Instead he babbled inanely to his hostesses of their extraordinary lives.

Freia shrugged. 'Characteristic.'

Blanchaille persisted. 'No, no. Wild – and awful.'

'That's their characteristic,' said Happy.

'If you wish to hear an extraordinary story we'll call Babybel,' said Fatima.

Babybel was by far the most beautiful of the four girls. Hair rich and auburn, the tiny lobes of her ears so delicate they were almost translucent; she wore a pale blue towelling robe which set off quite beautifully the soft, smooth milkiness of her skin. She'd been swimming, or at least relaxing by the pool, she said, until the sun became too much for her. With her fair skin she couldn't take too much sun and, besides, the noise of the President's demented guard firing away had driven her inside. She ordered champagne. 'She always drinks champagne,' said Freia.

'Nothing but the best for Babybel,' said Fatima.

'Tell Blanchaille your story,' said Happy.

'Despite appearances to the contrary, I am coloured. You may not believe this but you would see it immediately if you were to meet my brother, Calvin. When we were small we were at school together until one day they came and looked at Calvin. Inspected his brown skin and curly hair and said – Calvin must go! Go to the school up the road, a school for coloured children, for Capey children. I cried, I clung to him. Calvin did nothing. He went. But he whispered to me before he went, "My time will come." As I grew older and people noticed my looks Calvin evolved his plan, built it out of his very pure and uncompromising hatred for what had been done to him. "You will be my white poodle, Babybel," he said to me, "I will manicure, powder, preen you and I shall take you for walks through the suburbs where rich men will stop to stroke you and then, on an order from me, you will sink your teeth into their hands." It began when I left school and under Calvin's direction I made myself available to certain men, powerful in the Government. "You are jailbait, pure jailbait, my little Babybel," Calvin said to me. As I lay with these big *meneers* in bed, Calvin would reveal the truth. At first, in his boyish enthusiasm, he might hide in the cupboard and

117

jump out shouting – "I am the fruit of your union. I am the child you are making!" But as time went on he grew more subtle, he worked with letters, photographs, video tapes and he drove these powerful men, my lovers, to distraction, to suicide, to ruin. I was quite happy with my role as the flesh with which he baited his hook for I believed in the incorruptible anger, let me say the immaculate hatred, buried in Calvin's heart, I considered it as something commendable, noble even. Alas, Calvin became too subtle. "Equipment *costs*," he told me. He went to the banks. Worse, he went to the Bureau. He was funded by those who ruined his life. What begins as pure revenge ends as investment, in our country. Calvin began to rule. He had become one of the big *meneers*.'

The ladies around the bar were in complete agreement and called on Visser for fresh drinks and even Fatima gave a bleak little smile as if only Babybel's story approached her own in revealing the cruel and rich lunacy of everyday life among ordinary people in the days of the Total Onslaught.

'And so I came to the Palace, to this home for homeless girls.' Here she fluttered her delightful eyelashes at Blanchaille who understood what a potent lure she must have been to the big Government men she seduced.

'But explain one thing to me,' Blanchaille begged. 'Who brought you here?'

'We'll explain that, and a whole lot more to you in your all too brief stay with us,' Fatima said. 'But that question is to be explored with delicacy, so let's say that to a certain friend we were virgins pretending to be whores. It is he we have to thank for revealing this to Freia, Happy, Babybel and me. He sent us here, where we would be useful to those on their way out.'

'But that's enough of us,' said Babybel. 'tell us your story now.'

And Blanchaille told them how he had left his parish of Merrievale and passed through the township which was called peaceful. He told them of his call on Blashford and Gabriel and of his time with Van Vuuren in Balthazar Buildings, and of the meetings between the strange Italians and the members of the Ring. He told them of his visit to the holding cells and of seeing the man Strydom; of his sorrow and bewilderment at meeting his friend Zandrotti, now paralysed by some terrible knowledge obtained from Ferreira in London. Ferreira! who knew nothing but figures; of poor Vilakaze, condemned to make the same old speech to an audience who had long ago deserted him.

And they marvelled at his tale – except for Happy, that is, who

118

laughed a trifle harshly.

And this talk went on far into the night and of those details I can recall there was in particular the explanation of the secret Italian organisation Blanchaille had seen at work in Balthazar Buildings.

The *Manus Virginis* had been founded in Portugal in 1924 by a reprobate Lisbon cleric, a dissolute, lustful man, who'd more or less abandoned all his priestly duties, stolen the gold and silver from his church, and taken to pursuing women. His name was Juan Porres and he lived as if he believed, he once flagrantly said, that 'salvation lies in the laps of women'. Then one night as he lay sleeping beside his latest mistress, a short hairy creature of stupefying ugliness named Puta (or Petra) who was said later to be related distantly to the dictator Salazar, the Virgin Mary appeared to him and demanded that he mend his ways. She declared that from that moment on he would no longer be Porres the defiler of women, but the protector of their honour, and in particular the honour of the Virgin Mother. She advised him to invest his ill-gotten money in the Portuguese Marconi Company and devote the profits to the 'honour of the mother'. The Virgin afforded him several visions, in one of which she appeared with her hand extended over the globe of the world with her fingers resting on what Juan called in his memoirs 'troubled and vexed spots'. The next morning he put aside his ugly mistress and went into the street where he met a banker whom he converted to his cause. From this small beginning Juan Porres formed his association of militant groups of priests and laymen divided into sections, which spread with amazing rapidity throughout the world. Their aim was personal sanctity combined with financial integrity. From the late twenties these 'fingers', as they came to be called, grew from a mere dozen to sixty or seventy and their influence could now be felt all around the world. The 'honour of the mother' was later to be interpreted as referring not merely to the sanctity of women, but to the general safety of Holy Mother Church. Membership to the *Manus Virginis* was open to anyone, men, women, priests and laymen, but membership was strictly secret and the organisation had considerable autonomy within the Church, its controlling bishop had his headquarters in Rome and reported directly to the Pope. The organisation had changed little over the years. Members still practised various forms of mortification of the flesh. They used the hair shirt, the whip and the bracelet, a steel chain placed around the leg or upper arm and tightened daily. The *Manus Virginis* continued to have interests in cert in a pects of the welfare of women, in particular the preparation of anti-abortion literature, homes for unmarried mothers, and in marriage guidance counselling, but the emphasis over the past thirty years had really been in the field of finance. The *Manus* was to money what the Jesuits had been to education, the fiscal troops, the militant accountants, the sanctified economists. The *Manus Virginis* claimed to have reconciled the age-old contradiction between money and religion, God and Mammon. They invested quite simply for God and the greater honour of the Church. Strategic charity it was sometimes called, or tactical philanthropy. God repaid their investment with high returns and 'the divine portfolio', as the investment plan was known, had made the Hand grow extremely rich. The appeal of the Hand was that it allowed ordinary men and women everywhere to lead secret lives of heroic self-sacrifice and obedience, and to experience the effects of grace with which God rewarded his followers in a form which they could recognise, called 'divine funding', namely cash. The beautiful simplicity of the doctrine had made the attraction of the Hand extremely potent. The tactical charitable investment of the organisation was seen by its members as a form of holy warfare which was directed from its secret headquarters in Rome. Of course there were links with other secret societies, with various Masonic Lodges in Italy, with the Mafia and with other sympathetic organisations. It was an interesting fact to be noted, said Happy, that while secret societies turned inwards and away from the general public their mutual interest in power often enabled them to overcome the animosity they might feel for other clandestine groups. The Hand of the Virgin had its own bank, the Banco Angelicus, from which its investment policy was co-ordinated throughout the world. The Bank provided a useful receptacle for funds which did not seek public attention. It was said to play banker to various secret organisations including the South African Ring, and even, it was said, to the Vatican itself. It was a policy of the Hand of the Virgin that tactical investments should be made in regimes broadly sympathetic to the beliefs of western Christian civilisation. Funds were often used to stabilise regimes, and even large companies which, in the opinion of the *Manus Virginis*, deserved divine support. Where the funds for investment came from was no longer important once the money had passed into the bank, for in the Banco Angelicus there was no such thing as tainted money. All was for the greater glory of God. The Banco Angelicus manipulated its extensive investments through a series of offshore companies in Panama and Bermuda, and had especially close links with many South American dictatorships and was increasingly involved in Third World countries where growing Catholic communities were established.

'Naturally the Church claims to know nothing of the activities of the *Manus*, much as our Regime claims to be unconnected with the Ring. But how else would Church and Regime talk except through such organisations?' Fatima enquired, with eyes modestly lowered.

'There are other conversations which go on in Balthazar Buildings,' said Happy. 'It's probably just as well you didn't witness in any of them. There are, for instance, the talks between the Regime and Agnelli, the Papal Nuncio.'

Blanchaille nodded dully. Of course . . . why not? First they spoke through proxies. Those were the talks he'd witnessed between the Italians and the rough guys from the Ring. No doubt talks followed between the principals involved. He realised the girls had not offered him a drink. Now he knew why. They were plying him with information more potent than any booze. He felt as high as a kite.

'Of course, you see the Church has a great deal to teach the Regime about change. The Regime is now in the position not unlike that of the Church some years ago. Both are preaching to a shrinking audience, changes are to be made if that audience is to be kept. Some of the old slogans must be abandoned, slogans like "death before adaption", "separation is liberation", "tribalism is the future!". These had to be revalued, reassessed, reappraised and reviewed. Just as the Church's ringing affirmation of its mission to the townships and its irresistible embrace of its black brethren was not unrelated to a good hard look at the market. The Regime realised that if it was going to survive it was going to have to start allowing black people into white parks and removing discriminatory signs and stress the positive side of ethnic identity and equal freedoms. Those in power liked to present this as conscious choice, as liberalisation, but in fact it's a form of desperate accountancy.'

Blanchaille nodded. 'I do remember now how it was some years ago when you could go to a Catholic church and study in a Catholic school, recover in a Catholic hospital and never hear a single query raised about whether Jesus lived in the big house or in the servants' quarters, and to blurt out the question was to be threatened with divine punishment and beaten with a strap loaded with halfpennies and cast into the outer darkness. Then suddenly one day you found a whole lot of people were shouting at you for not applauding the

Church's eternal commitment to the liberation of Africa, and you were so deafened that it took a while to realise that you were being shouted at by the very people who beat you in the first place.'

'That's right,' Happy said. 'It's the figures again, you see. In the middle of this century the number of Catholics in the white West, in Europe and North America was over half the world total, but before much longer European Catholics will be a minority – the majority will be found in places like Asia and Africa. Not surprisingly, certain conclusions have been drawn . . .'

And so that night passed with talking and stories, rather too much drink and too little sleep, and the next day as well. Conversation and information was exchanged between the fleeing ex-priest and the kind hostesses of the secret travellers' rest known to lost souls as the Airport Palace Hotel, and their mentor, the man they referred to affectionately as their 'Commanding Officer', the elderly barman, Colonel Visser, who had founded with such great hopes the Brigades of Light.

Fatima spoke to him of recent travellers who had stopped at the Palace Hotel *en route* for some long-desired home in the faraway mountains, and mentioned startling names such as Ezra Savage the novelist, Claude Peterkin the radio producer, and Gus Kuiker and the Secretary of the Department of Communications, Trudy Yssel. Blanchaille had great difficulty in believing it, not knowing where truth ended and wishful thinking began.

He asked them how they had come to the Airport Palace Hotel and each described an encounter with the mysterious stranger who revealed to them that they were virgins pretending to be whores; this stranger had various names, Jack, or Fergus, or simply 'our friend'. Well before he heard that he spoke with an Irish accent Blanchaille knew who their saviour had been. Even before they had shown him in their little 'museum of mementoes' (in reality the ladies' cloakroom) an old black beret which he instantly recognized as the one Lynch had worn to the airbase. The implications only struck him later.

He was also given directions to his final destination. Geneva was the starting point and then old Kruger's house by the lakeside in Clarens, near Montreux. But this, it was stressed, was only the beginning. From the official Kruger house he must climb to 'the place itself'. Happy showed him grainy black and white photographs of what she called 'the place itself' and bad though the shots were, he recognised the wild turrets of mad King Ludwig's castle Hohenschwanstein, but said nothing, being loath to injure such simple, shining faith in the former Government negotiator. Having examined, in one of Lynch's living history classes, both Paul Kruger's official former residences and found them no more than a large bungalow and a simple farm respectively, it was impossible to credit that the old President's tastes would have run to anything so fanciful. 'Paul Kruger belonged to the Dopper sect of especially puritanical Calvinists, we can expect his last refuge to reflect his didactic, moralising spirit,' Father Lynch had explained. 'It is comical to reflect how his enemies might have played on this in the Boer War; consider – the British might have brought the war to an early end if they could have convinced the old man that the sight of white men shooting each other gave unalloyed pleasure to the natives . . .'

Fatima's directions were as unpersuasive: 'Above the lake and to the left,' she said. 'Start at Clarens. Where Kruger finished.'

So they made him ready for the journey. Babybel insisted on pressing his white shirt, because, she said, if a man was leaving for parts unknown with literally nothing but the clothes he stood up in, he would want to put his best foot forward. Visser agreed, saying that Blanchaille faced an ordeal ahead, a battle, a formidable enemy. When one entered the Garden of Eden, he explained somewhat mysteriously, one faced not merely the snake, but the apple, and there were circumstances in which apples were more subtle than serpents.

It was Freia who injected a note of realism into these conversations by revealing that Eden was hardly Blanchaille's destination. He was going to England. Indispensable Freia! Owing perhaps to her training as a township tour guide she had checked his ticket and revealed that he was flying to London with a thirty-six-hour stopover before his flight to Geneva. Why not a direct flight? Blanchaille protested, but there was nothing to be done. Besides, said Visser, the police themselves had booked his ticket and must have known what they were doing. *Only* the police knew what they were doing. They comprised the holy circle. Since the police in this instance were personified by Van Vuuren, whose status as a policeman was increasingly mysterious, Blanchaille hoped he still fell within the holy circle referred to by Visser. Blanchaille hoped he knew what he was doing.

As if to console him, Babybel gave him a necklace of golden Krugerrands, pierced and threaded on a string which she told him to wear at all times and promised him that it was a key, the use of which he would know when the time came.

And then, in the evening, I saw how they personally escorted him from the hotel to the airport, stepping over the bodies of the Presidential Guard which lay scattered on the streets and pavements like soldiers from a child's toy box. Whether dead or drunk, simply asleep or resting, he could not tell. Then I saw with what tears the girls fell upon his neck and kissed him goodbye. On the plane he was given a window seat beside an Indian gentleman. At ten o'clock the plane took off. Peering towards the bright lights of the airport as they began to taxi, the sight of Visser and his four girls waving from the roof of the building was the last he saw of Africa.

CHAPTER 11

On the non-stop flight to London Blanchaille sat beside Mr Mal who explained that he was a fleeing Asian. Blanchaille said he thought that Asians had stopped fleeing Africa, but Mr Mal replied that Africa was still full of fleeing Asians, if only you looked around you. Mr Mal had fled from Uganda to Tanzania, from Tanzania to South Africa, and he was now fleeing to Bradford. He spoke of Bradford in the terms of wonder American immigrants must once have used about California. In his opinion the Asians were the Jews of Africa. It was amazing, Blanchaille thought, just how many people claimed to be the Jews of Africa. President Bubé in a celebrated speech claimed that distinction for the Afrikaner; Bishop Blashford was not above claiming it for harassed Catholics in the days when they were often persecuted by the Calvinists as 'the Roman danger'. President Bubé issued a statement declaring that the Catholics could pretend to be Jews or Methodists or Scientologists for all he cared, but while subversives threatened the country under the cloak of religion, he would show no mercy . . . (this a reference to the flight of Magdalena dressed as a nun). Let them go around in prayer shawls and yarmulkas if they liked, the security forces would root them out. Newspapers discussed this animatedly. CAMPS FOR CATHOLICS? the headlines wondered excitedly, and BUBÉ PLANS POGROM? What did the real Jews of Africa call themselves – with so many people competing for the title?

There was a large party of deaf-mutes travelling on the plane, pleasant young people who seemed quite unaffected by their disability. Blanchaille watched a young man in blue jeans and a red shirt carrying out an animated conversation with his girlfriend. He was a walking picture show. He held his nose, pulled his ears and seemed able to rub his stomach and pat his head simultaneously. He also did impressions: a boxing referee counting his man out, the drunk in the bar thumping his chest angrily, he opened bottles, he snatched a hundred invisible midges out of the air, hitched a ride, sent semaphore signals across the cabin. His fingers, his hands, his busy silent tongue that lapped against his open lips were altogether an eloquent and loquacious display. His hands and fingers flew, pecked and parroted, swam in the air, signalled, sang, played the

125

old game of scissors, paper and stone. They were an excited aviary those flying hands, moving hieroglyphics, they signalled the meanings which words, if they had tongues of their own, would picture to themselves. His girl appeared to listen to him with her nose. Frequently her eyes applauded. He almost envied them their ability to talk so openly without fear of being overheard. He wished he knew why he had been routed through London. Beside him Mr Mal dozed, and cried out in his sleep of the pleasures of exotic Bradford.

Nothing prepared Blanchaille for the shock of finding her waiting at the barrier.

She took his trolley from him despite his protests and led him through the automatic glass doors into the thin uncertain sunshine of the English spring. He gazed at her, the thick blonde hair was pulled behind the pretty ears and expensively waved. Her perfume enveloped him in waves of warm musk. Magdalena looked chic and well cared for. He watched her small, square, capable, deft hands on the steering wheel. He couldn't believe he was sitting beside her again.

'This is kind, Magdalena. But not necessary, really.'

'Not kind or necessary. Blanchie, it is absolutely essential!'

He sat back in the car and watched the huge clouds passing low overhead like enormous aircraft showing their massive bellies. The sky in England seemed very low. That was his only observation to date. Magdalena had hugged him mightily and noted his weight increase. 'Too much beer,' she said affectionately.

In the old days Father Lynch had remarked on the abundance of Magdalena's affections. She resembled her biblical namesake, he said, and much would be forgiven her for she loved much, or more accurately she loved many. That was true. The altar boys had heard of Magdalena's powers as one hears of a wonderful cave of diamonds from which everyone is free to help themselves; of a hill of cash; a love goddess one dreamed of, panted after and never expected to get and who suddenly announced she was giving away the lot, for the asking.

Van Vuuren had announced the miracle: 'There's a girl called Magdalena. She gives.'

'How much?'

'Everything.'

It seemed inconceivable, a colossal lie. One could not accept the alarming hugeness of this claim. How much did she give? And what

126

exactly did that wild generalisation mean? Did she pet? Did she French kiss? Did she allow her bra to be removed? Was it possible to go any, well, further?

'Piss off,' said Van Vuuren. 'You're an unbelieving lot. I said the lot. I mean the lot. Everything.'

'How do you know?'

'How do you think?'

'You didn't? Just like that.'

'We don't believe you.'

'I don't care. But you can try for yourselves.'

And they did. Zandrotti first, followed by Ferreira and both returned glowing from the encounter, enchanted and absolutely converted, aflame with new faith and zeal. In her arms they had passed from uncertainty to deep belief. She was a miracle, a blessing! Kipsel confirmed, and Van Vuuren looked knowing, the veteran. Blanchaille held out in his scepticism. His unbelief was of Augustinian proportions and he prayed that it be strengthened with each fresh report of his friends' success, with Zandrotti's tears, always emotional, in recalling how amazingly easy it had been, *she* had been. She had just opened up and took him in and there he was, doing it like he'd been doing it all his life.

'What – without precautions?'

'Sure. When are you going to do it, Blanchie?'

'Soon.'

'How soon?'

'Just soon.'

'You're chicken.'

'No, I'm not. Look, all right, it happened with you but it doesn't necessarily follow that it will happen with *me*.'

And it did seem to him too fast and too far. Too implausible. Sexual intercourse was something that clearly required longterm planning, something worked up towards, a large project studied in the old *Chambers's Encyclopedia* of 1931 which he found in the hostel library and which dwelt in detail on the fertility rites of remote tribes in New Guinea. Not something you nipped in for on a Saturday afternoon. But it was for Saturday afternoon that it had been arranged and he was to be driven there by Van Vuuren, Zandrotti, Kipsel and Ferreira, in Van Vuuren's brother's bottle-green MG. It occurred to him that they feared that unless they took him there themselves he might not go, he might just say he'd been . . . He denied it vehemently but knew it could well have been true.

To Blanchaille's horror Magdalena's parents were at home,

something which deterred his grinning sponsors who began a swift retreat and left him with the miracle herself, a broad-shouldered, solid, commanding, shapely girl with a mature manner and a shrewd assessing look in her blue-grey eyes. Backing out with embarrassed grins his friends mumbled shamelessly about 'getting home', probably regarding the afternoon as lost. Suddenly the parents also left, claiming with what Blanchaille considered false sincerity that they'd remembered an urgent appointment at the bowls club. Blanchaille was contorted with shame and rage; could the parents of the easiest girl in town play bowls? Surely they knew why he was there and were not going to allow it? Could they remain slumped in deck chairs over their brandies after playing a couple of taxing lengths on the green without a care in the world about what their daughter was doing with her young friend?

Obviously they could.

Magdalena had sized him up with a practised eye. Blanchaille thrust his hands into the pockets of his grey raincoat which he had worn, not against the weather, but simply because it hid the frightful khaki shorts all the hostel boys were made to wear. What happened next was a blur. She did not ask him to sit down (speed was always her strength), she crossed the room, kissed him hard, so hard she lifted him off his heels. In his confusion he thanked her but she did not seem to require thanks. Indeed, seeming to regard all conversational niceties as superfluous she pushed him down onto the sofa and attempted to spread him out. The fear of her parents returned. His own unpreparedness plus some foolish juvenile desire to preserve at least a vestige of the romantic formality made Blanchaille resist her advance, bracing his legs, refusing to straighten the knees. Magdalena left off pushing and went to the heart of the matter by loosening his belt, lifting his shirt, easing him, fingering him, making him ready. All this with the one hand while the other, on his chest, pinned him firmly to the sofa and then directing his hands beneath her skirt, obliging him to lower her pants, wriggling expertly as she sloughed them off and planted herself upon him. Blanchaille attempted to say something but his tongue had thickened in his mouth and all that came out was a low gurgle. He thought afterwards that perhaps what he'd meant to say was something like: 'Shouldn't we at least close the curtains?' But the moment was gone, passed before he knew it. She moved once, twice, three times and Blanchaille was afloat in that warm sea he'd just entered.

And just as suddenly cast ashore. Someone who has invested so much reading time in such concepts as 'ejaculation' cannot but expect far more. But to have come and gone before one knew it! Brief and involuntary. Behind almost before it began. Like a hiccup. 'We might have been shaking hands.'

'Hell, Blanchie, you're a born romantic,' Kipsel said.

And then some time later, once again, in Blashford's other, unofficial garden.

What could one say of Magdalena? Everybody's girlfriend once, twice, and then she took off like a rocket into the political firmament, out of reach of mere altar servers, numbering among her lovers such heavy figures as Buffy Lestrade the Hegelian radical lecturer, and no more contact was made until Kipsel rediscovered her and carried her off to blow up pylons in the veld. Afterwards the trial, the betrayal, and the extraordinary escape. Magdalena, the saboteur turned demure nun in her audacious dash for freedom from beneath the very nose of the Regime, became a legend.

Once in London she came to be rated amongst the six most dangerous enemies beyond the borders. Connected with the Azanian Liberation Front, romantically linked for a time with one of its leaders, Kaiser Zulu, she was branded a convinced and radical believer in the violent overthrow of the Regime. Rumours and legends constantly appeared in the press. Red Magda they called her. He remembered Magdalena's mother had made an attempt to save her. She announced that she would go abroad and talk to her daughter, call on her to repent. Various well-wishers raised money. Her local bowling club of course, a building society, and several newspapers ran the campaign to raise money to send this brave mother to save her daughter from the clutches of a terror movement, notorious for its cruel atrocities throughout the southern sub-continent. The usual photographs of flyblown and swollen corpses of murdered nuns, frozen in typically blind poses of hopeless entreaty, were shown, the pathetic stumps of what had been arms and legs pushing against the concrete air. Those shockingly familiar pictures the newspapers so loved, of decaying remains pictured against the dusty landscape of Africa which seemed in a strange way to lend a curiously gentle, eerily inoffensive aspect to the once-human husk, as if the horror melted away amid these vast indifferent surroundings and the bones, the hide, the carcass spread-eagled in the veld like a lion kill, or a drought victim, was another of the necessary sights of Africa. Except these were holy remains. The papers said so. Sacred clay. Relics. Powerful muti. As those who killed them and those who photographed them knew, in Africa the only good nun was a dead nun.

Magdalena's mother's visit of redemption went badly wrong. She got on famously with Kaiser Zulu, who, she said, reminded her of her old cookboy, and she was pictured singing choruses of 'Down at the Old Bull and Bush' in some tourist nightspot and told reporters, on her return, that her daughter wasn't as black as she had been painted. Angry letters filled the newspapers from readers demanding their money back.

RED MAGDA'S MOTHER DUPED! the headlines yelled.

The sunshine lay shyly on the grey-green fields beside the motorway. Blanchaille's first glimpse of England showed it to be small and tightly woven. The fields fenced everything within view. Nothing out of eyeshot, everywhere contained, ordered, bounded. The jumble of houses to left and right, three small factories, a smudge of development eating away the green and then the countryside spluttering out in a last fling of parks and trees as the houses began in earnest, but still, even to Blanchaille's untrained eye, recognisably houses, double storeys, detached, heavily planted in muddy yards, in the strange green smallness of the countryside.

Magdalena drove well, fast, her small, pretty hands in speckled yellow gloves calm on the wheel. The road swept upwards and ran as an elevated motorway into the solid, metalled city with its row upon row of semi-detached dwellings. It struck the stranger, the sandy tongued foreigner, blinking with lack of sleep, this sudden mass of building. It asserted itself, this solid, glued immobility of London, everywhere packed, joined, touching, far fewer single houses now and these were bulge-fronted, pebble-dashed, red tiled roofs. And then blocks of them, stuck solid, identical, joined irretrievably and running on for streets seemingly without end. He shivered. Magdalena must have seen this for she smiled.

'You thin-blooded African creatures, travelling north without coats. You could freeze to death here. Even in summer.'

'I brought nothing, nothing except what I stand up in.'

'You're unprepared then, in many ways. I'm glad to see you, Blanchie. But I have to tell you I really don't know what you're doing here. Your clerical career was both wild and original. You upset the Church, your friends, the Regime and you did it damn well. We all depended on you, watching from here. You were useful there. I'm afraid you may be at a bit of a loss here.' She lit a cigarette, the grey smoke blurred and clung to the furry coat she wore. She smiled, perhaps to soften the force of her remarks and showed sharp white teeth, but when he protested he had not come 'here' in any sense but was merely passing through he was cut short by a growl of displeasure.

'This place is hell. I can't tell you what I've been through. People told me I was lucky to have missed the balance of payments crisis. They say that was worse. The English are a strange race, obsessed with economics and they seldom bath. You've no idea how I suffered when I first arrived. When I came the country was governed by a series of pressure groups who went around shrieking at one another about incomprehensible causes. The daily obsession of the country was the value of the pound. "Pound up a penny" the headlines screamed, day after day. "Pound down a half penny!" Nothing else counted. Nowhere else featured. Wild rumours swept the land. I remember going to the opera when suddenly through the stalls and around the banks of boxes ran the whisper: "Pound lost three points against the dollar!" Pandemonium! Strong men tore their hair, women swooned. And given the lack of washing facilities, to which I've already referred, you can imagine what a malodorous demoralised crowd they were. Like an elderly woman with a guilty past they are beset by their desire to confess, on the one hand, and deny it all, on the other. They regret, repent and deplore all they've been, never realising that it's only their past that makes them worth knowing.'

She lived in Sealion Mansions off Old Marylebone Road. A squat, solid, peeling green-painted block smelling of wax, dust and the sea. From the fishmonger's opposite there drifted an aroma, a cocktail of brine, shell and sand wafting across the street. A corridor of fragrance crossed the road between fishmonger's and entrance foyer along which the sea tang drifted from the boxes of silver fish, wide-eyed in their beds of crushed ice.

Also staring up at the flat were two men in raincoats. The sky was clear.

Magdalena's flat was luxurious but small. A little entrance hall, a sitting-room, a bathroom, bedroom and kitchen. The bedroom was done in apricot silk.

'You're looking for a shining city on a hill, a sort of heaven, but you won't find it, Blanchie. Not here, at any rate.'

'I'm not looking here.'

'Then why stop over?'

'I tell you, I don't know.'

He admired her bedroom. She seemed pleased. It was her lair, she said. An odd term. Above the circular bed hung a large painting in which two opposing forces shaped like tattered kites clashed violently. Red and black, two antagonistic whirlpools, fighting cocks, shredded and bloody, whirling and tearing at each other. Or perhaps two circular saws meeting tooth-on and the very sounds of their grinding collision were reflected in the shards of green and yellow paint with which the outer edges of the canvas were pierced.

She made him scrambled eggs and she ordered him to sleep in the large circular bed. He awoke in the late afternoon with the soft grey light in the room and found her above him, straddling him, naked. Her hand on his chest pinned him on the bed.

'Stay. Don't go on.'

Stay where? What did she mean? Sleepily he asked for an explanation but she drew him up into her and then fell to work from above, deftly rolling him from side to side and so their love-making began. Or not love-making really, but a struggle of sorts, without words, hot and desperate. She darting her head down to kiss him, his temple, foot, hand, sharp stinging kisses and he responding, no not responding but retaliating, giving little nips to lobes and elbows so that she squealed when she came, her hands gripping his buttocks and ramming herself home again and again, long after it was over. And still she would not release him and it was to be done again, their pubic bones jarred like shunting engines. He was bruised now. How hard she was down there, how rough! But she forced him over and over until he came at last, briefly, again, hopelessly, quite exhausted now, lying with his face in her neck and beginning to feel the pain in his back. She must have scratched him, the sweat ran into the score marks her nails had made and stung, but still she did not let up and since he was now past any sort of movement, slid from him, came out sideways, sliding, lubricated with sweat and turned him over now, mounted, reared up, placing precisely the lip of her vagina against his coccyx, rubbed herself there, scouring, grinding herself until she came to her climax, her breath hoarse in his ear.

He did not hear her leave. Perhaps he slept, briefly, or even passed out, but when he at last left the bed to look for her she'd gone.

He sat in the bathroom, his penis still achingly firm, throbbing to his heartbeat. The cool porcelain of the bath edge cooled him and he tried to relax, to clear his mind, to will the thing to fall and droop, an old seminary trick this. It had been an attack, a series of attacks. But why should she attack him? She had always had rough and ready ways, he remembered this from as far back as their first love-making. But this was an attack. Mounted attack, yes. There had been something angry, desperate, despairing in their encounter. And there was the speed with which it had happened. Almost a rush.

He tried to clear his mind. In the seminary there were tricks taught by the Monitor for Moral Instruction, Father Pauw. He had yellow teeth and green eyes and what he called a prodigious working knowledge of the fleshly ills. His lecture 'The young priest and the early morning erection – some observations', was a classic of its kind. 'You will find it,' he said, 'a common complaint amongst young men, particularly in the early days of their ministry, that the member has a mind of its own. You rise in the morning to find it's risen before you, a curse, a weapon which it cannot use against others and so often seeks to stab its owner. To treat this, first evacuate the bladder, then pray. If unsuccessful, reach for the paddle, the purity paddle.' This instrument was a piece of polished wood, rather like a miniature ping-pong bat. It was to be used often. It was indispensable. Seven sharp slaps put the flesh in its place, disarmed the enemy within.

He sat on the bath and took his red and angry throbbing weapon in his hand; his heart thumped in unison. Damn Magdalena! What the hell was she playing at?

He ran the bath and lay in the warm water. Threads of blood drifted by, fine ribbons and spirals floated in the water. The blood was real enough. How had she known he was coming? Why had she fallen on him so savagely? Where was she now?

When darkness fell and she had still not returned he dressed and went downstairs and across the road to the fishmongers where the two men in raincoats stared up at the building, waiting for him.

CHAPTER 12

Now I saw in my dream the truth of the supposition widespread in émigré circles amongst the refugees who have fled from the Regime, though this continues to be officially denied, that there are paid agents abroad who shadow, observe, report on, harass, hinder and even silence those individuals they fear.

Across the road from Magdalena's flat, outside the now empty, Arctic spaces of the fishmonger's window, the two men, one tall, one tiny, stood in the shadows. As he crossed the road towards them Blanchaille knew as soon as he set eyes on their raincoats, on their stiff and unyielding moustaches and heard their flat accents, that here were countrymen.

They stepped close to him and pressing him on either side said: 'Theodore Blanchaille, if you know what's good for you, go back.'

'Who are you?' Blanchaille asked.

'We are unwilling agents of the Regime,' came the prompt reply. 'Poor men who a long time ago booked on what was then known as a Pink Pussycat Tour of the Fun Capitals of Europe, and we looked forward to enjoying ourselves in Montparnasse and on the fabulous Reeperbahn. We were promised the time of our lives in the strip joints of Soho and the canalside brothels of Amsterdam. Here, look –' and he took from his pocket an old, creased, much thumbed and garish brochure showing a naked girl straddling a large pink cat which had orange whiskers and wore a monocle: 'Hiya fellas! Get out on the tiles! Just wear your smile. . . !' The naked girl pictured wore a tight, strained smile. Blanchaille looked at the ridiculous cat, blushed at the noisy old-fashioned dated enthusiasm of the invitation. It was all tremendously sad.

The large one folded the tissue-thin brochure with reverence and returned it gently to his pocket.

'We were ordinary blokes,' said the little one. 'Out for a good time. I was a butcher.'

'And I was a school inspector,' said the large one. 'And we saved long and hard, I can tell you. I mean, hell, it's no small thing, getting at our stage of life the promise of a really good time. We were in a button-popping hurry to inseminate the entire continent of Europe. Well, would you do otherwise? We planned for months, we scrimped, we bought Hawaiian shirts with orange suns and canary yellow sweaters to wear, just like Minister Kuiker who set the tone around that time, being the only person of note to venture outside the country publicly.'

'We dreamt of Dutch *vrouws* and silk beds. We saved every cent and when the big day came we kissed our wives goodbye and stepped onto the Boeing with hope in our hearts.'

'And stiffening pricks.'

The little one looked up at Blanchaille, unabashed, shrugged his shoulders and gave a bitter smile. 'Off to sleep with coloured girls.'

'Off to smoke dagga.'

'To go fishing on Sundays.'

'Get drunk on religious holidays.'

'Watch dirty movies and gamble into the small hours.'

The big one sighed wearily. 'But what we got was duty. We're stuck here, in the shadows.'

'This is hell,' said the little one. 'I thought a Free State Sunday was hell, but this is hell.'

'Who are you?' Blanchaille demanded.

'We're called Apple Two,' the big one explained, looking embarrassed, 'so-called because it stands for both of us.' He raised two fingers.

'But who is Apple One?'

The watchers shrugged. 'Don't ask us.'

'What sort of a name is that?'

'It's a code name. We can't give you our real names. Our orders were to stand out here and watch the flat until further notice.' The little one looked apologetic.

'Who gave the order?'

'Apple One. We were to watch the flat until you left,' said the big man.

'And then we were to tell you to go to the Embassy. Don't be hard on us, we don't like this job. We didn't ask for it,' said the little one, clutching Blanchaille's sleeve. 'We stepped off the plane in London and the Embassy car was waiting. We thought, Christ but this is odd! Why should our Government come and meet us? Anyway we took it as a gesture. We told ourselves they were just being hospitable. Little did we know. We were driven into town, chatting happily like any group of tourists in London the first time, lightheaded with that sense of freedom that comes to all South Africans who discover that the outside world really does exist, and we pulled up in Trafalgar Square at the sign of the golden springbuck and I remember turning before we were hustled through the swing doors, I remember seeing the fountains, the pigeons, the tourists mooning about, Nelson up on his column . . . my last glimpse of freedom.'

'What happened?' Blanchaille asked.

The two watchers in the shadows sighed and drew their coats around them. 'We were commissioned, into the security forces. It was explained to us that we should put duty above pleasure. Our air tickets would be refunded, they said. Our families had been notified that we were heroically responding to the call of our country abroad. With manpower shortages in security, as in all other industries, we were to be given the chance of serving our motherland by helping in the surveillance of suspected persons abroad.'

'Do you know what's happened to Magdalena?' Blanchaille asked.

'She left some time ago,' the large one said.

'Better not ask where she was going,' said the little one.

'Where was she going?' Blanchaille persisted doggedly.

'To the Embassy.'

'Where is the Embassy? How do I get there?'

'Go to Trafalgar Square. Look for the sign of the golden springbuck,' said the little one.

'Blanchaille,' said the large one, 'don't be a fool. Get out. Go back to our country. There's nothing for you here. Believe us, we know. This is hell. It's a small, rather dingy, gloomy northern country. Everything is dead, the only signs of life are to be detected in the police, the army and the monarchy. Go back to where there are real issues to fight for.'

'I wasn't thinking of staying here. I'm in transit.' Blanchaille replied. 'I'm only here for forty-eight hours, and believe me, that's not my idea. I'm heading for Europe. There are certain mysteries I wish to solve.'

'That's worse,' said the little one. 'That is the dark continent, Europe. It's littered with the bones of Africans searching for the answers to certain mysteries.'

'Then I'll follow the bones,' said Blanchaille. 'See what they tell me.'

The watchers shrugged. 'Rather you than us,' they said. 'Don't say we didn't warn you.'

And I saw in my dream how Blanchaille, having exchanged some of his money into British currency with the watchers, who gave him a good rate 'just for a feel of home', and having been pointed to the nearest tube, made his way down into the earth.

He was not prepared for life below ground. The elevator taking him down was very old and shook and its revolving belts squealed and cried like a man in agony. A hot wind carried on it the smell of metallic dust that blew from the yawning black holes at each end of the platform. A few desultory late-night passengers moped disconsolately in the shadows. Advertisements lined the sides of the tunnel. Most seemed to be taken up with lingerie and the delights of early retirement.

Blanchaille heard a terrible noise, a shouting, a screaming and howling as if troops of banshees were approaching, their cries emphasised by the hollowness of the deep underground. The waiting passengers seemed to know what was happening because he saw them scurrying for the far dark corners of the platform. With a great burst of shouting, singing, clapping, a strange army of young men arrived. They wore scarves and big boots, waved rattles and flags. The posse of policemen guarding them had trouble keeping them under control. Red seemed to be their colour, red bobble caps and scarves and shirts and socks, streamers and pennants.

They were marched to the far end of the platform, laughing and threatening to push each other onto the rails and terrorising the passengers. No sooner were they in place when the second army was ushered on to the platform and marched down towards the opposite end of the station, also with whistles and klaxons, hooters, cheering and whistles. Their colour seemed to be yellow: yellow hats and yellow flags. When the Reds caught sight of the Yellows pandemonium broke loose. Individuals broke free from both sides and hurled themselves at each other, kicking and clawing at one another and police and dogs struggled to keep them apart. Clearly the Reds and the Yellows were sworn enemies. The Reds shouting out, 'Niggers, niggers, niggers!' and the Yellows replied, 'Yids, yids, yids!' Blanchaille was reminded of the tremendous battles which took place between Fascists and Jews on the anniversary of Hitler's birthday on the pavement outside the beer cellars in the capital. The hatred they clearly felt for one another was so reminiscent of the life he had left, that for a moment he was overwhelmed with feelings of homesickness, even a kind of strange nostalgia. A train arrived and the Reds were allowed aboard. The Yellows were held back on the platform. No doubt they had their separate train.

As Blanchaille arrived at Trafalgar Square station I saw how a succession of young girls came up to him. 'Business, business,' they said repeatedly. This puzzled Blanchaille who could not imagine

137

what girls so young could be doing in such a place, so late at night.

The crowds pressing around him as the escalator rose slowly towards the light wore ecclesiastical costumes as if got up to resemble old religious pictures. He saw a bishop, a scattering of cardinals, a bevy of virgins in blue veils. It was only when he peered closely that he saw their stubbled chins and realised they were all men. They clustered behind Blanchaille on the escalator whispering, perhaps to each other, perhaps to themselves, perhaps it wasn't even they who spoke but only voices inside his head, but from wherever the words came they scandalised him. Their talk was of organs and orifices, of anal chic, of comings and goings, of tongues, testicles, of ruptures, lesions and sphincters, of AIDS, herpes and hepatitis, of pancake make-up and the versatility of latex, of leather and the ethics of climactic simulation and of the lover of some unfortunate creature who had lost her life, head smashed with a heavy hammer when it was discovered that she was not he pretending, coiffed and beguiling, but the very her she had been pretending to be. 'Come over to our side ducks and get the feel of life!' These ribald remarks caused a great deal of mirth among the knot of purpled cardinals whose faces, he saw, were painted dead white with large black eyes so that they looked like Japanese actors. The long staircase creaked its way upwards to the dirty patch of light above. Of course it was all too likely that these scenes took place only in his imagination and the crowds around him were perfectly ordinary people returning from walks in the country, and scout outings and the girls so desperate for business were collecting for charity. But that his imagination should run in these channels at such a time worried him deeply.

And then he was up in the Square. He saw the column with Nelson on top of it. He saw the fountains, he saw buildings which reminded him very much of the campus of the Christian National University with its predilection for the neo-Grecian temple style and then directly across the road he saw the sign of the golden springbuck. (You must note here, if you will, how typical were Blanchaille's feelings of excitement and ignorance, the feelings of an innocent abroad. Had he known it, the dangers he imagined in the underground were as nothing compared with the perils which now faced him.) He gazed up at the large corner building, the Embassy squat and solid, that old box of ashes and bones as it was called by that celebrated dissident, the Methodist missionary Ernest Wickham (and he should have known, since he was widely credited with having burgled the Embassy and taken away sensitive papers which were later passed to the Azanian Liberation Front). A daring triumph, but shortlived, for a little while later Wickham received a parcel from a favourite Methodist mission in the Kalahari, where much of his fieldwork had taken place. Wickham made the mistake of opening the parcel and was blown into smaller bits than would fill a small plastic bag, given that hair, teeth, bones and odd gobbits of flesh were dutifully collected notwithstanding. The bomb, it was suggested, might have come from the Pen Pals Division of the Bureau which had long exploited the exiles' weakness for welcoming parcels from home. (It should be noted here that the Regime had since commemorated the work of Pen Pals Division of the Bureau with the issue of a special stamp showing on an aquamarine background a large plain parcel wrapped in brown paper and neatly tied up with string. In the lefthand corner the keen-eyed observer will spot the tiny letters 'PP', which, he will now know, do not stand for postage paid.)

Sitting in a high window of the Embassy was Dirk Heiden, the so-called South African super-spy, a sobriquet well earned. This formidable man worked himself into the top job of the Students Advisory Bureau, a Swiss-based organisation promoting the aims of radical students abroad, particularly exiled students from the South African townships, a post which he held for some eighteen months in which time he took part in freedom marches in Lagos against the racism of the Regime and was photographed taking a sleigh ride in the Moscow snow. From his office in Geneva he monitored the activities of resistance groups, anti-war objectors and other dissidents abroad, tailing them, taping them, photocopying documents and insinuating himself into the clandestine councils of various radicals abroad who seemed as free with their secrets as they were with their brandy. As a result of his reports many at home were beaten, imprisoned, stripped, manacled and tortured. Heiden had returned home to the kind of triumphant reception normally accorded only to rugby teams or visiting pop-singers who had defied the international ban against appearances likely to benefit the Regime. But his hour of glory over, he fell prey to the boredom which so often affects those who have lived too long abroad. He grew fat and listless, developed a drink problem, was arrested for firing his pistol at passers-by, pined for his tie-maker and his old sophisticated life, and so his superiors returned him to an overseas post, a chair in the window of an upstairs room in the Embassy where he peered through the glass searching the Square for familiar faces.

Heiden sat in a chair by the window, so still he might have been dead. His weight had continued to increase, his facial skin was stretched tight and shining over the bones, it had the texture of rubber on a beach ball blown up to bursting point. He stared out of the window because it was his job to look at people who visit the Square below, look for faces he might recognise, for it is a well-known fact that South Africans abroad will come and stand silently outside their Embassy, prompted perhaps by the same impulses that bring early morning observers to wait outside the walls of a prison where a hanging is to take place, or crowds to stand outside the palace walls when the monarch is dying.

In another window on the same floor sat the Reverend Pabst, 'the holy hit man' they called him once, but a shambling wreck now, surrounded by empty cane spirit bottles and scraps of food. His career had been simple and brutal. God had instructed the Regime that His enemies should be identified and exterminated. Pabst went to work. A fine shot and a quick and efficient killer using his bare hands and no more than a length of fishing line, he had a considerable tally of victims to his credit. Sadly, unknown to himself, he had also killed, besides enemies of the Regime, certain members of the Regime, quite possibly tricked into doing so by other members of the Regime. He could no longer be allowed to roam loose. He sat in a chair with a small sub-machine gun in his lap. He would cradle it beneath his chin and sometimes even suck the snout-like barrel, pressing gently on the palm-release trigger. The gun was not loaded of course, and the door behind him was locked and bolted. Sometimes he would hurl himself at the window, mowing down imaginary hordes with his wicked little gun only to fall back in his chair with a streaming nose or broken tooth. The windows were thickly armour-plated. The old man would dribble and grin, dreaming of past assassinations.

Blanchaille passed by these dangers quite unknowing. It is not surprising. He was not known and would not have known the watchers in the windows. And besides, I saw in my dream that he had eyes for only one thing, a man on the other side of the busy street. He knew him instantly, despite the grey clerical suit, the dog-collar. His old clothes!

Blanchaille called his name, hopping from foot to foot on the edge of the Square while a steady stream of traffic surged between them. At first the man appeared not to hear. Blanchaille called again, and then, because the man appeared to be about to escape, without thinking he charged into the traffic. A large tourist bus narrowly missed him. He stumbled and almost fell beneath the wheels of a taxi, the driver squealing to a halt and cursing him. But he reached the other side and seized the coat of the man now hurrying down the Strand, seized him almost at the same instant as the watchers in the windows above saw him and positively identified his quarry (with what consequences I dread to think!) as Trevor Van Vuuren.

CHAPTER 13

Now that the absconding priest, Theodore Blanchaille, met and talked with the policeman, Trevor Van Vuuren, is not in doubt. Where opinions differ concerns the motives which brought Van Vuuren to London and the fate he suffered there. The official version put out by the Regime is well-known and straightforward. Van Vuuren visited London in pursuit of the renegade cleric, Blanchaille, because he believed the man had information which might throw light on the murder of Anthony Ferreira. His quarry, realising that the law was closing in, lured the policeman into a trap.

That is why there are still those who talk of Van Vuuren 'The Martyr'.

I saw things differently in my dream. I saw Blanchaille and Van Vuuren, arm in arm, making their way down the Strand. An odd picture they were, closer than ever to Lynch's predictions, for Blanchaille resembled a ruined Southern gambler in crumpled white suit and heavy stubble with his strange seal-like shuffle, the feet thrown out in a wide flipper shove, and Van Vuuren was the muscular priest beside him. They proceeded slowly down the street, the weightlifter and the punchbag. And so the short night passed.

They passed a bank which looked like a church and opposite it a station which looked to him like a palace and beside it a cinema showing a pornographic movie. Blanchaille had never seen a pornographic movie, he'd never seen a cinema advertise pornographic films. This one was called *Convent Girls*, and showed three naked blondes in nun's wimples running across a green field. 'Hellfire passions behind the convent walls!' How he envied the potential of European Catholicism! No wonder Lynch had felt cheated in Africa. Blanchaille remembered the convent girls of his youth, shy creatures in sky-blue dresses, white panamas and short white ankle socks, shepherded by swathed and nimble-booted nuns patched in black and white, nipping at their heels like sheep-dogs. Van Vuuren was dressed in his friend's old cast-off clerical suit, rather dirty charcoal with ash-grey V-necked vest and dog-collar far too large for him so that it hung below his adam's apple like one of those loops one tosses over a coconut in a fairground. He had not shaved and the black stubble gleamed on his chin in the early light, that pale English dawn light which comes on rather like a wan bureaucrat to give notice that the day ahead will once again be one of low horizons and modest expectations.

I heard their conversation which I record as accurately as possible.

'Thanks for waiting.'

'After seeing you plunge into the traffic in that suicidal manner I had to wait. If only to see if you made it.'

'I had to make a run for it because I saw the look on your face when you spotted me. I thought you were going to bolt.'

'I was. You don't want to be involved with me. I'm bad news, Blanchie.'

'Why are you here?'

'Because my people sent for me.'

'I couldn't believe it when I saw you. I said to myself, that's Trevor, but it can't be. He's at home.'

'This is home for me, Blanchie.'

'Who are your people?'

'The Azanian Liberation Front.'

'The ALF – your people? Since when?'

'From as far back as I can remember. I went with the Communion wafer still sticking to my palate, straight from my last Corpus Christi procession, and told them I wanted to enlist. I had a meeting with old Vilakaze, he was still boss in those days. I must have been the first, perhaps the only, white schoolboy member of the Azanian Liberation Front. When I was ready to leave school the Front said to me, go back and work for the Government. Join the police. Fall asleep in the arms of the Regime. We will wake you when you're needed.'

'What? All this time, Trevor, an agent for the Front?'

'All this time. A special sort of policeman, just as Lynch predicted. I kept the faith, like I told you. In my own way. Then, a couple of days ago, soon after I had seen you in Balthazar Buildings I got a message from London. My job was over. I could come home. I took the plane. When I arrived at the airport there was another message waiting for me. I was to go to the Embassy. It seemed strange. The Embassy is one of those places I would have expected to avoid. But then I'm a soldier. I take orders. The Front says go and I go. Even so, I was surprised no one met me at Heathrow. I didn't expect a band and streamers, but I thought someone might have shown up. So I came here, expecting someone familiar. But not a

143

sign of anyone, until you came along. Don't take this amiss, Blanchie, but you were hardly what I expected.'

'Why do you say you're bad news?'

'Well, I should have been met, you see. Something's very wrong.'

'I was met.'

And Blanchaille told him about Magdalena, about their meeting at the airport, about her flat, omitting the details of her extraordinary attack on him, about the watchers outside the fishmonger's.

'Apple Two,' said Van Vuuren and laughed. 'Who do you think Apple One is?'

Van Vuuren was pale in the early morning light. Blanchaille was put in mind neither of the policeman he had been nor the priest he now resembled. Blanchaille could smell the fear on him. He was sweating though it was still cool in the dawn, breathing heavily, lifting his face, the nostrils flaring and sniffing deeply as if by the couple of inches this gave him he might find pure air easier to breathe. Blanchaille was reminded of a buffalo he'd once seen looking for water, plunging into a swamp and drinking and drinking until he moved in too far and could not pull himself out. Half-submerged, with his curved horns pointed above the water line, the beast struggled to free himself only to sink all the more securely into the mud until only the line of his back and the flashing horns were visible and the long wet muzzle with just the nostrils clear, sucking at the air, taking in a little water each time with a rivelled hiss. A little more water each time and the brown eyes blinked and bulged helplessly as the animal slipped deeper. It fought for each breath, a gurgling hiss of air and water passing into the nostrils. Then the buffalo gave a convulsive jerk, let its body sink and angled its head up in the air fighting the nostrils clear; he heard the clogged snuffle, more laboured, more lengthy, the watery intake and then, suddenly, nothing – just an ear and the horns and the silence. Why did Van Vuuren make him think of that?

'Who sent for you?'

'Kaiser himself.'

Blanchaille didn't pursue the subject.

'I can still remember my last Corpus Christi procession,' said Van Vuuren. 'I see us all gathered outside the railway station getting ready for the march to the Cathedral. The Children of Mary in blue cloaks and white veils; a platoon from the Society of St Vincent de Paul, male pillars of the Church in their grey flannel suits and their neat side partings; nuns running excitedly to and fro with their veils fluttering in their faces, all freshly scrubbed and shining with anticipation of the treat to come; young men and women of the various religious sodalities, very pink and pious and most disturbingly calm about it all. Contingents, squads, whole battalions of priests forming up beneath the banners. A small group of White Fathers appeared in that strange outfit they wore that gave them a slightly sporting look, like female bowlers; and of course Franciscans with their bunching brown robes, tightly roped around the waist; and throngs of tiny boys and girls who'd made their first Communion that morning, girls in bridal flounces with flowers in their hair and little boys in bow ties all carrying baskets of flowers with which to strew the streets. We were all formed up in a procession and at the head was the Bishop, the unspeakable Blashford, decked out in gold vestments and flanked by assistant priests and served by an army of altar boys, incense bearers, boat boys, bell ringers and acolytes, all attending His Grace who was bearing aloft the gold and silver monstrance with its small circular glass window behind which you glimpsed the sacred host, the white and sacred heart of the golden sun, the rays of which were suggested in the jagged, spiky ruby-tipped petals of the monstrance, a sight to dazzle and astound the faithful. Behind the ranks of altar boys, the great crowd of assistant priests in white surplices. I remember how the onlookers began to form, how they used to crowd the streets which were usually very empty on Sunday and watched with blank incomprehension as the Corpus Christi procession in all its gaudy Roman glory snaked forward, chanted, sang, knelt, shuffled up from its knees and staggered on again. Fluttering above the Bishop and the monstrance was the silken canopy supported on four poles by members of the Knights of De Gama wearing broad sashes and white gloves. The crowds gawped. The white people looked stern and unimpressed; behind them the blacks giggled and pointed and shook their heads at this fantastic spectacle of mad pilgrims in curious costumes following their gorgeous leader beneath his wind-rippled canopy. The white spectators put their hands in their pockets and struck attitudes of contempt. The Africans gave little outbreaks of spontaneous applause, as if they were watching a varsity rag procession and admiring the different floats. I remember they saved their best applause for the little band of black Christians who traditionally brought up the rear of the procession, usually wearing religious costumes of their own design, long white flowing albs, shimmering chains of holy medals clinking on coloured ribbons worn around the neck, roughly cut wooden staffs in their hands. These wild prophets received a special police escort. Occasionally there were fights as a group of white bystanders isolated and assaulted some chosen black spectator, raining blows and kicks upon the victim for reasons you never understood – I mean you could hardly stop and ask. And the police moved in and rescued the fallen man with the customary arrest. Every so often, you remember, we stopped and knelt. I can still smell the hot tar. The old hands spread a handkerchief. Sometimes horses had passed that way and you could smell the dung. There were oil stains right there in the middle of the road. There we knelt in the middle of the city, on a bright Sunday morning, the whole great procession reciting the rosary, a vast murmur rising and falling. Do you remember how the spectators often shrieked if the holy water sprinkled by the priests accidentally touched them? And they would wave away the fog of incense with their newspapers. You remember how they used to cough and give artificial little explosions of irritation to show how much they disapproved of it all? And you remember how embarrassed we were? I was anyway. I knelt there and prayed that the buildings would topple and cover me. We had to endure *hours* of it! pretending that nothing strange or bizarre was happening, that this was what you did every Sunday morning, you got dressed up in crazy clothes and went out and knelt in the middle of the road while the traffic policemen kept the cars away. You remember the traffic policemen? They stood at the intersections and wore those black jodhpurs, black tunic, grey shirt, the sunglasses, and the black peak cap. They said the uniform was modelled on that of the SS. I knelt there and prayed for the earth to open or the sky to fall, or for bolts of lightning to obliterate the entire procession in an instant, or for bombs to go off, or for a madman armed with a sten gun to burst upon the scene and mow down every living soul. I prayed for a message: "Lord, tell me what to do." And the message came back: "Join the ALF, my son. It is the only act of faith left to you. You kneel here on the hot tarmac, foolish, exposed, embarrassed. You are that comical thing -- a white man in Africa. Repent whilst there is still time, join the Front . . ." It was a religious conversion. The Front ordered me into the police force. I knew my friends would see it as an act of treachery, but I could live with that. Let my friends think of me as the traitor-policeman. Let them spit at me. I could take it. For the Cause. For the Front! Actually, at the time I think I was suffering from a kind of religious mania. Luckily it had no outward sign. I mean it didn't issue in fainting fits or speaking in tongues or stigmata or levitation or uncontrolled miracles. All of that would have been rather inappropriate in a police officer, as you can imagine. And there was a short period when I experimented with flagellation, making a small branched whip with half a dozen tails securely attached to a short wooden stock and I beat myself with this whip but there were immediate difficulties. Probably few people know it, but it's not possible to direct the whip so as to avoid marking oneself on the neck or wrist, and these are places where the weals might show and so arouse suspicion. And then I had myself a hairshirt made of horsehair and wool and wore it next to the skin for over a week. Not very practical either. It was hot, you see. I'd sweat. And the sweat would saturate the hair on the shirt and the shirt clung to me underneath my tunic and gave me a very odd shape. One or two of my colleagues asked if I was putting on weight. It was a very odd time for me.'

Now I saw in my dream how Blanchaille and Van Vuuren, though unaware of it, talked and walked their way up the Strand, around Covent Garden and by degrees into Soho. And it was in Soho that they first noticed the black cab trailing along behind them and saw that it carried none other than their old mentor, Father Ignatius Lynch.

And Blanchaille remembered the famous black beret in the Airport Palace, and knew why it was there before him.

Stories abound concerning the conversation Blanchaille and Van Vuuren had with their old master at that strange meeting in Soho, once they had recovered from their astonishment. How they noted his tremendous excitement as well as his weariness. (This is hardly surprising when you consider the old man had achieved a lifetime's dream in escaping from Africa, helped no doubt by the pistachio-flavoured banknotes he had borrowed from the money poor Ferreira had left Blanchaille.) Yet having made good his escape from Africa at last, why come looking for them? Lynch cut short such enquiries. In fact, as I saw in my dream, he did most of the talking, telling them for the last time that his time was short and he was not much longer for this world and as if to emphasise it, he kept the taxi waiting, meter ticking over. Indeed, he implied that they might not be much longer for this world either. He reminded them that they were babes abroad, that neither had ever been out of the country before except for their living history lessons he'd provided years before. He said they wouldn't ever have known that they were now in Soho had he not told them, and grave dangers awaited them.

All his talk was of death, while the meter ticked. And for once it seemed true, this expectation of his own end. He was smaller, thinner, more frail than they had ever seen him before. It was by a fragile, grinning, big-eared wraith that they were addressed in a Soho street.

He told them about the strange suicides of the brokers Lundquist, Kranz and Skellum, which he described as the most extraordinary acts of self-destruction since Mickey the Poet strangled himself with his own hands.

'The broker Kranz died by hanging himself during a lunch given by the Woolgrowers' Association of which, for obscure family reasons that need not detain us, he was a director. It had been a very good lunch apparently and they got down to coffee and liqueurs when Kranz himself was, in the words of one witness, "as merry as hell". Setting off to the bathroom his last words were – again I have this from the family, "Keep the bottle coming around – I'm off for a splash", and then walking, or rather weaving, happily from the room, a large brandy in hand, he disappeared. The glass of brandy, now drained, was found in a basin in the men's lavatory and suspended from the window directly above the toilet, hanging by his own belt, was the unfortunate Kranz. It seems there were a number of puzzling bruises and contusions on the body for which no explanation could be found. Certainly it seems unlikely that Kranz could have injured himself like that, but the inquest finally decided that Kranz in his drunken state had probably clambered up on the seat of the lavatory and then onto the cistern itself, attaching the belt to a steel window frame. However, being drunk, he was clumsy and hadn't tied the knots correctly and he fell, or so the story goes, perhaps he fell several times only to clamber up again, stubborn fellow that he was, and try again. Everyone agreed that he had shown quite remarkable determination.

'Lundquist showed the same intensity of purpose as his colleague Kranz. For we must believe that this small man lifted his heavy executive chair, weighing half as much as he did, and using it as a kind of battering ram smashed a hole in the window large enough to pass through and so plunged to his death one hundred and fifty feet below. A wonderfully neat worker, too, this Lundquist. For although the body was badly broken, as you would expect after such a fall, it seems he had not been cut once by the wall of glass through which he had smashed in his feverish desire for extinction.

'Of Skellum, the third suicide, it must be said that we have an act

148

of self-destruction which deserves the palm. Here we had a man with a brilliant military record who was invalided out of the service suffering from shellshock. This was caused by a terrifying experience when the patrol he was leading was ambushed and lay under continual mortar fire for a full day and Skellum saw his companions killed beside him one by one. Not surprisingly this experience left him with an uncontrollable fear of sudden and violent explosions, a backfire, a slammed door, a firework, even a loud cough would reduce him to a state of gibbering terror. Yet this man so overcame his fear as to bounce into his office one morning bright and early, close the door, put a .38 pistol to his temple and blow his brains out, falling forward onto his desk, thereby unintentionally summoning his secretary who came in with her notebook thinking that her boss wanted to dictate some letters.

'Now these dead brokers might have been remembered for nothing more than their suicides,' Father Lynch concluded, 'had it not been for the fact that each had seen Ferreira shortly before his death. Ferreira had revealed to them that their dealings in gold and industrial shares for ostensibly reputable clients, were really deals on behalf of dummy companies set up by the Ring. Kranz, Lundquist and Skellum had been dealing for the Ring. And it in turn had been dealing for the Hand of the Virgin, you will know that organisation of devout Catholic freemasons. Unfortunately the Ring felt entitled to a decent commission. And they forgot to mention it to the Hand.

'The Bank of the Angels called in the accounts, checked them over – and had a convulsion. But the real culprits, the Ring, slipped out of reach of the Fingers by the simplest and time-honoured expedient in these matters, it blamed the brokers who had handled the deals. If there was money missing, the Italians were informed, then Kranz, Lundquist and Skellum were the guilty men. The Hand reached out. It reached for necks.

'It was now that Ferreira called in the brokers. The only way the brokers could save themselves, Ferreira told them, was to co-operate with his enquiry. Give him details of the shares purchased, sums remitted, names of contacts. And naturally the brokers fell over themselves to comply with this request. They firmed up Ferreira's case so tight you could have built battleships with the steel in it. And then Ferreira goes and gets murdered. Maybe the Azanian Kommando did it, maybe the Afrika Brigade – what did it matter to Kranz, Lundquist and Skellum? Did it matter what the writing on the wall really meant? To them its message was clear enough. It said "You next". So they panicked. Who wouldn't? They began off-loading shares, too many, too fast. Maybe they planned to skip? Or buy their way out of trouble – who knows? The market turned downwards. And there followed the sensational suicides. Truly, the only miracle left in our country these days is the wonderful and mysterious ways which men find to take their own lives. Of this, poor Mickey the Poet is the patron saint and initiating martyr. We can but pray that they find peace at last in another place, as we pray we all may do one day.'

'And may we pray that the Regime, the Ring and the Hand one day roast in hell?' demanded Van Vuuren, angrily.

'Certainly we may pray for no such thing,' came the prompt reply, 'but we can always hope.'

And then Blanchaille asked him this question: 'Father Lynch, you've cleared up one of the mysteries in this business. We know why share prices fell. But tell us – who killed Ferreira?'

'Read the writing on the wall,' replied the little priest. 'You're the policeman, remember, work it out.'

'But we read the writing on the wall and it told us that either the Straf Kaffir Brigade got him – or the black radicals, the Azanian Strike Kommando No. 3. But a lot of other people could have had a motive. Like Bubé, or Minister Kuiker and Trudy Yssel, or the Israelis, or the Taiwanese, or the Ring, or the Hand or just about anybody who believed Ferreira knew enough to sink them *and* he intended to publish it . . .'

Lynch inclined his head. 'Certainly, or it could have been the Papal Nuncio, or Himmelfarber, or the Bureau or the *Nuwe Orde*. So many suspects, so many motives. No good to go down that road. Perhaps the answer to at least part of the mystery is staring us in the face, providing we read the writing on the wall, providing we know how to read the writing. For has it not occurred to you that the letters ASK 3 might not have been left there by any of the persons or groups we have mentioned?'

'I'm sorry,' said Van Vuuren. 'I don't understand. If they didn't write the letters, who did?'

'Why Ferreira himself, of course,' said Father Lynch.

Well you can imagine the impact of this revelation. They fell to whistling and clicking their tongues in admiration and Van Vuuren sufficiently forgot himself to utter a few choice oaths, of which 'Well, I'll be fucked', is the only one I recall, and followed this with an apology.

And Lynch accepted their compliments with that curious little

150

smile which made his jug-ears lift and the corners of his mouth twitch as they always did when he was pleased. 'No, no! Merely part of the training of one who has read deeply in the history of the Church's relations with the State, where murder cannot always be allowed to blight an otherwise intelligent, well-meaning policy. It is possible for martyrs, poets, inquisitors, poisoners, canon lawyers, bankers, cardinals to connive, plot, campaign to arrive at a mystery which will thrill the devout and balance the books. Well in this case, never mind the devout, and as I've told you before – examine the books. Have the courage to face what stares you in the face.'

Then Lynch read to them from his favourite book, withdrawing it from an inside pocket of his cassock with a fluid movement, *Further Memoirs of a Boer President*, the familiar bible, the mysterious tome edged with gold in a red leather cover.

> In the mountains above and somewhat to the left of the town of Montreux we found the place we sought and kneeling down with my valet, Happé, supporting me, I gave thanks when I saw it; dead though its chambers now lie, still its voice, it shall live again when our people come, as over the years they shall assuredly come, sick for home, to this home from home . . .

Then Lynch warned them again that his time was short, and so was theirs. They were marked men and one of them, he could not say which, would not see another sunrise. And when they protested that he could not possibly know this for sure, he said nothing, just stepped back into his taxi and tapped on the glass and told the cabbie to drive on. When they ran after the cab as it gathered speed demanding to know how anyone would find them in London, he rolled down the window and asked them how they thought he had found them so easily. It would be no trouble to their enemies, they could find them whenever they liked simply by looking in the right place, just as one found characters in a book, simply by looking them up.

CHAPTER 14

Blanchaille looked at Soho with big eyes. Van Vuuren looked hardly at all, turning his gaze inward, as if he knew what was to come.

So they went, the priest and the policeman, the egg and spoon, through the little streets, this once great mixing place of European peoples, now all gone, leaving behind them only their tourists and their restaurants and a profusion of continental erotica. He looked at it with professional eyes, Blanchaille told himself, trying perhaps to explain his interest, as a centre dedicated to sin. It looked to him, Van Vuuren replied, like a dump – over-rated, over-priced, dull, tawdry and sad. Blanchaille stared at the hawkers, the barrow-boys, the suitcase salesmen. A fat man with one sleeve rolled up offering gold watches strapped to his arm like chain mail flashing in the sun, was trumpeting the bargains of a lifetime and waving the highly coloured guarantees like flags. Arab men with pot bellies and tight, flared tailored trousers walked around with their hands in their pockets, staring boldly at single women; a girl winked at him from a balcony; in the dull entrances of crumbling buildings he saw the name-plates of cheap cardboard inscribed in shaky ballpoint – MYRA, MODEL, WALK RIGHT UP. He peered through the bead curtains across the doorways of the 'adult film parlours' which gave them an oddly oriental look. A striptease club displayed pale cracked photographs, faded by infrequent suns, showing a female chorus line presenting their buttocks to a delirious audience. Blanchaille was ashamed to find himself hesitating fractionally, drawn as it were, downwards.

THE BARE PIT – SIX LOVELY LADIES IN FANTASTIC COMBINATIONS/DAY-NITE NUDES NON-STOP!!! Some had pound notes tacked to their pubic mounds. One carried a whip. Another was wearing nothing but an iron cross. Two oiled female wrestlers grappled in a miniature ring. A largish and very pale redhead was immersed, for some mysterious reason, in what looked like a giant goldfish bowl. But it was an empty black leather chair in the centre of the stage which looked truly obscene.

A burly and very black man blocked their path and invited them to step below and see for themselves the loveliest things in the universe, at the same time introducing himself to them as Minto, their guide to the pleasures of The Bare Pit. Van Vuuren attempted to brush him off but Minto was persistent and took his arm in what was clearly a very persuasive grip and, as Blanchaille realised when he saw pain succeed annoyance on the square handsome features, one that succeeded in its intentions.

'Run, Blanchie, run!' said Van Vuuren.

But there was another man, taller, very wiry, who declared himself to be Dudley from Malta, with a little black moustache and no less fierce a grip.

Of course Van Vuuren would have flattened them both, one, two, bang, bang, in his former life. Perhaps the clerical garb restrained him because he put up no struggle as they were marched downstairs.

It was dimly lit below stairs, a bar at one end and a stage at the other, the twenty or so rows of seats between furnished in red plush, redolent of ancient excitements of old men: of tobacco, sweat, aged underpants, hair oil, disappointed hope, stale beer, old socks, bitter anger, and various unidentifiable, recent stains. In the front row sat several large gentlemen.

Blanchaille remembered what he had read of such places, of the old men who came down here to watch women strip and masturbate beneath their plastic raincoats. One had read of such accounts since childhood, they were a part of the contemporary portrait of Britain, where all the people not on strike were on the dole, or on pension; where child murder was widely practised; few people bathed; income tax was 19/6d in the pound and nobody ate meat any longer. The Regime taught this in its schools. His French mother confirmed at least the last: 'The roast beefs,' as she used to call the English contemptuously, 'have no roast beef any longer.' Blanchaille's mother had never been to England, but then that hardly mattered. England was a repository, a store of rumours of decline from which the world could draw at will for stories to frighten children. It had no other use but to remind one, horribly, of what your country might become if the Total Onslaught succeeded.

Minto and Dudley from Malta introduced Blanchaille to the proprietor, a small and stout individual with black hair gleaming lushly in the concealed lighting around the bar. He was called Momzie. Without hesitation he poured Blanchaille a Scotch and soda and patted the bar stool beside him. 'May as well make yourself comfortable while those gentlemen over there have their little conversation with your friend.'

Minto and Dudley marched Van Vuuren up on to the stage. The props the girls used in their show were still there, the black leather chair, the wicked whip of grey rhino hide, the giant goldfish bowl of rather milky water, the wrestling ring. Van Vuuren was roped to the black leather chair.

'I think these people intend to injure my friend,' said Blanchaille.

'I hire out this place when we're not busy,' Momzie said. 'People want somewhere where they can have a quiet chat. It's money up front and I don't care who uses it as long as they watch their hours. I've got a show to run here and sometimes they're inclined to overshoot.'

The men in the front row weren't wearing plastic raincoats. They were young. They wore a variety of costume, sports jackets, tweeds and safari suits. One of them was a black man wearing a pale blue suit. They looked at Van Vuuren with special interest. From his seat on the stage he gazed defiantly back, but the footlights must have made it difficult to identify them at first.

'I see it now,' he said, 'a deputation from my old Department; Brandt from Signals, Kritzinger from Interrogation, Breda from Surveillance, Kramer from Accounts – well, hell's bells Jack! I never dreamt you were operational, or did you get promotion, or did they send you over to see the strippers for a Christmas treat, or something?'

'You fucked out on us, Trev,' said the man called Kramer from Accounts, 'and now you're tootling around England tricked out as a poncey priest. It's not right, Trev.'

Now Van Vuuren noticed the black man in the pale blue suit. Even from where he sat at the bar between Minto and Dudley from Malta, his drink untouched, Blanchaille saw the horror on his face.

'Oscar! What in Christ's name are you doing here?'

The man in the blue suit stood up. 'Things are complex,' he said. 'I could ask you the same question.'

'But you guys sent for me. I've come home, Oscar. Tell them! Why didn't you meet me at the airport?'

'We didn't expect you, Trevor.'

'But damn it to hell, Oscar, I *work* for you.'

'No, you work for us,' said the shaven-headed man called Kritzinger from Interrogation.

Van Vuuren was straining at the ropes now. 'What the hell is going on? Oscar what is someone from the ALF doing in this hole with these vultures from my Department? These guys shoot people like you, Oscar. Where is Kaiser? Does he know you're here?'

Oscar nodded. 'He sent me. He said to tell you hello –'

'And goodbye,' said Brandt from Signals.

The front row laughed heartily.

'I want to see Kaiser,' Van Vuuren demanded.

Oscar shook his head sorrowfully. 'Kaiser isn't in any condition to see you. He's suffered a major set-back, has Kaiser. He won't be dealing any more. From now on I'll be dealing.'

'And that means sitting down with these people?'

'Like I said, Trevor, things are complex. I don't expect you to understand because you don't see the whole story. But on certain issues the Azanian Liberation Front and the Regime have common interests that override the struggle.'

'Such as?'

'The disappearance of Bubé, the strange disappearance of Gus Kuiker and Trudy Yssel, the murder of Ferreira.'

'– the defection of security policemen,' said Kramer from Accounts. 'We're going to piss on you, Trev, I promise you.'

'The growing habit of certain people to whizz around the world like they owned the place. This threatens to destroy a delicate network of discussions, talks, negotiations, painfully achieved agreements between those who have the health of our country close to their hearts,' said Brandt from Signals.

'You fucked out on us, Trev,' repeated Kramer from Accounts.

The big men in the row of seats laughed loudly.

'The British have a great sense of humour,' said Momzie.

'Those people aren't British,' Blanchaille said. 'They're from my country, they're South Africans.'

Momzie ignored him. 'They like especially men dressed as women making jokes about foreigners. Speaking as a whole.'

'It is true,' said Dudley from Malta, 'speaking as a whole, and speaking of the English now, the English love to laugh at all sorts. It is one of their greatest gifts. They laugh even at themselves.'

'Yes,' agreed Minto, 'but what they don't like is other people laughing at them.'

'Even more hilarious do the English find than drag artists,' said Dudley from Malta, incoherent with excitement, 'speaking very much as a whole, are drag artists who make jokes about foreigners, Japs, frogs and whatnot.'

'There is something the English find even funnier than that,' said Minto defiantly.

'No,' said Momzie with heavy menace. 'There is nothing they find funnier than that.'

155

'Yes, yes,' Minto persisted. 'Yes there is and I know what it is!'

'What is it?' Momzie demanded. 'And this better be good.'

Minto beamed. 'They like even more than men dressed as women making jokes about foreigners, men dressed as women making jokes –'

'For God's sake get on with it!' Dudley groaned.

'Making jokes about foreigners . . . in *lavatories*!' crowed Minto triumphantly.

They seemed to recognise the justice of this, but Momzie was not giving up yet. 'Oh yes, how do you know?'

'Saw it on TV.'

That clinched it. They all nodded. Clearly there was no further argument.

'We watch a lot of television,' said Momzie. 'Ours is the best television service in the world.'

'Have you watched any of our television?' Minto asked.

But Blanchaille was watching Van Vuuren. 'Please,' he said, 'those guys are going to hurt my friend.'

'Balls,' said Momzie. 'We're here, aren't we. We're here to see fair play.'

Van Vuuren had stopped struggling against the ropes. 'I can't believe I'm hearing this.'

'You aren't,' the man called Oscar said bluntly. 'This conversation never took place.'

Kramer came over the Momzie. 'Do you have somewhere more private where we can continue our discussion. A cellar maybe?'

'This is a cellar,' said Momzie.

'There's the liquor store,' said Dudley from Malta.

'There's not much room in there,' said Minto.

'Going to cost you extra,' said Momzie.

The front row stood now, picked up the black leather chair and, in a procession which had a triumphant air about it, carried the prisoner from the stage. Blanchaille tried to intervene but Momzie produced an ugly little pistol from beneath the bar and hit him across the mouth. After that Blanchaille made no attempt to move but sat there watching the blood from his mouth dripping into his untouched whisky.

'This place of mine is in heavy demand, being an easy walk from your Embassy,' said Momzie proudly. He went on to tell the story of how he had recruited Minto and Dudley.

'I met these guys when we were on a tour through the regions, or at least they were. They were walking a troop. What's walking a troop? I hear you ask. It's like taking a show on the road. You march a bunch of slags around the place from hotel to hotel and you nail a customer or two. He's out there for a few days in the sun and isn't with his wife and wishes he was, or is and wishes he wasn't. It's hard work and pretty thankless. You get girls who fuck around just for the hell of it. And some of them won't keep accounts and they really begin to believe they are on holiday. They shoot off here and there and you spend half the day running after them like a fucking collie dog chasing sheep. I suppose you can't blame them, the holiday atmosphere gets to the girls. I can tell you there's nothing worse than a whore on holiday. These guys got so tired chasing after their pigeons they tried to lay it on me. Lay it on Momzie, shit that's a joke! I read them like a book. I told them – look get out of the provinces, I mean regions, as we got to call them now, and come up to town. I need a bit of knuckle on the door, I said, and you want a bit of peace and quiet after years of pushing fanny around the place. So here we are, as happy as sandboys in The Bare Pit.'

'This is the land of opportunity,' said Dudley from Malta.

'I'm proud to be British,' said Minto.

One would like to draw a veil over subsequent proceedings. Alas, in dreams veils cannot be drawn.

And so I saw them carry the prisoner into the cellar, in the chair, like some mutant pope, and there they beat him, stamped on him, stabbed him. Though whether he died when they stabbed him or was dead when the knives went in, I cannot say. Also they pissed on him, as Kramer had sworn they would do, showing that he had not been speaking metaphorically. They actually, together or singly, urinated on him as he lay in his blood among the broken whisky bottles the fumes of which were suffocating in the small room and the air soon became fetid – which I agree is not really surprising when you remember that there were several strong men taking violent exercise in a small space; a crude, enthusiastic, messy, bludgeoning assault of boots, fists, bottles. It resembled nothing so much as the violence which passes for pleasure in the lower divisions of the rugby league. Even in this instance they reverted to type. They whooped, stamped, yelled. It was foul play. It was the foulest play imaginable. But it was damn good sport! Those who speak of rugby as a game believe they are making a joke. I can tell them they've seen neither the game or the joke – for neither is involved. What we are talking about are matters of life and death, not of who should live, or who should die, but who should decide! We are

157

talking of sacred matters.

All this I saw through Blanchaille's eyes. He watched the men come out of the liquor store, smelt the spirits on them and imagined in his naïvety that they had been drinking and this accounted for their strained, pale faces, their laboured breathing, the slightly giddy looks, and the stains on Oscar's blue suit. He watched as the money was paid 'for the hire of the hall', as Momzie called it. A handful of small gold coins on the bar counter.

'Who else but these guys pays in Krugerrands?' he asked proudly, scooping up the hoard. 'But then again, who better? Ain't they got the market cornered?'

It was only when Dudley from Malta complained about the heat that they realised something had happened.

Minto went over and tried the handle.

The explosion blew off the door of the liquor store and carried away Minto, still attached to the handle. Momzie and Dudley from Malta screamed as they tried to beat back the flames with their jackets. The bottles of booze shattering like brilliant bombs. The body on the floor glowed like a lamp, and exploded, lighting up its own disfigurements, the smashed face, the knife wounds. A hot gust of alcohol, sweat and, yes, urine, hit them. And Blanchaille, finding himself unattended, took the dead man's earlier advice and ran.

CHAPTER 15

And so it was that I saw Blanchaille retrace his steps and I saw how despite his terrifying experience, once back in Magdalena's flat he cooked eggs. In the midst of tragedy, of bereavement, scorched by the fiery vision of Van Vuuren's pricked and broken body, he had not expected to feel suddenly, ravenously, hungry. But there it was. The fleshly appetites were unrelenting, the Margaret Brethren had warned their boys, which if not constantly beaten into submission would command the frail human creature and bend him to their will.

Now we know that the stories of how Van Vuuren met his end were eventually to differ widely. The Regime acted quickly to claim him for their own. He became the faithful detective murdered by agents for the Azanian Liberation Front. The Front further complicated matters by admitting responsibility for the 'execution', declaring that the police-spy's fate was a warning to any other agents of the Regime who attempted to subvert the forces of liberation. The Regime in turn announced that brilliant undercover work by Captain Van Vuuren had revealed a deep split within the Azanian terror group resulting in the demotion of its president, Kaiser Zulu. The Front in a statement called this a typical lie of fascist adventurers and claimed that President Zulu was enjoying a well-deserved retirement in a home for high state officials 'in the country of a friendly ally', somewhere on the Caspian Sea. The Regime then posthumously awarded to Van Vuuren its premier decoration, the Cross of the Golden Eland with Star, an honour previously accorded only to visiting Heads of State, that is to say, to General Stroessner of Paraguay, the only Head of State to pass that way in living memory. The national poet composed an ode in honour of the dead policeman. This was the former radical poet, Pik Groenewald, who after years of self-imposed exile in Mexico City plotting the destruction of the Regime had a vision one night of a lion attacked by army ants and returned home immediately and joined the tank-corps where besides valiant service in the operational areas he composed a series of laments upon his previous treachery which he dedicated, with apologies, to President Adolph Bubé. Groene-

159

wald's 'Ode to an Assassinated Security Branch Officer' played cleverly on the flammable connotations of Van Vuuren's name, in the celebrated line *Flame to the fire they fed him/Blade to the vein they bled him* . . . And it was quoted in Parliament to spontaneous applause.

Blanchaille of course, as I saw, knew the true story, knew that by some peculiar chain of logic both the Regime and the Front derived profit from the death of Van Vuuren. That this knowledge did not drive him to anger or despair but left him ravenous is testimony to the toughness of human nature or to the growing self-awareness of the fat ex-priest from the camps that nothing was what it seemed.

What a place this England was! Blanchaille stared at the English eggs, they were not like African eggs, they were pallid, waterish little things by comparison with the garish orange, cholesterol-packed bombs from the hot South. But he cooked three or four, even so, and a mound of bacon and ate without stopping, shovelling the food into his mouth and plugging it there with chunks of thin white bread, running a very fine line between sustenance and suffocation. In the cupboard beneath the sink he found half a bottle of Chianti and finished it off directly. It was as if there were spaces inside him he must fill, not simply hungry spaces but vulnerable sections which he must protect.

Afterwards he lay in the great white tub, soaking there beneath the benign gaze of the Duke of Wellington upon the wall, beneath Magdalena's stockings, hanging above him from a cunning arrangement of lines, and looking, through the steam, like skinny vultures perched upon telephone wires. Magdalena's depilatories, her soaps, her shampoos, some sort of nobbled glove affair, presumably meant for rubbing dry skin from the body, her back brush and sponge and bubble bath, all waited with the air of things that know their owner will not be returning. He lay in the bath and let the grime of the past hours float from him and begin to form a brown ring around the bath. Strangely comforting, this evidence of life, human dirt.

As he sat on the side of the bath drying his hair the doorbell rang.

Beside the door hung a photograph. It showed Magdalena in Moscow. She wore a white fur hat and a white fur coat. Beside her were the onion towers of the Kremlin. She was smiling radiantly. The photograph was a trophy. It showed how far and how successfully Magdalena had gone in the service of her cause. The picture was unassailable proof of her credentials as a radical, as a leading member of the Front, as one of the prime enemies of the Regime in exile. It insisted upon this achievement. And yet there were certain matters unexplained, certain questions he wanted to ask Magdalena which could not be answered by that photograph. 'I have been to Moscow', the photograph trumpeted. 'Few of you have been further than Durban!' True. But not enough.

It took him a few moments to recognise the man at the door. The hair was still as unruly as ever, growing now even more thickly above the ears. The eyebrows were more bushy than he remembered but the lips were the same. Oh yes, they were the same rather bulbous lips, wet from continuous nervous licking, the nose broad, the eyes soft waterish brown, and there it was, the characteristic pout with the lips pushed outwards into a little 'o', surrounded by soft white down. A fish pout. Kipsel!

'Hello Blanchie, long time no see.'

That was that. No apology, no cringing and fumbling explanation, no sign of regret or mortification. Merely – 'Hello Blanchie, long time no see.' Blanchaille stood back from the door and let Kipsel enter. And there he was in the room, that same Kipsel who had grievously betrayed everyone he knew, had fled the country in utter despair, the man who had had the gall to go on existing after the treachery, which even those who benefited from it had condemned. Why had he not done the only decent thing and slashed his wrists or hanged himself from a stout beam? Instead Kipsel had gone out and got a job, in a northern university, and taught sociology. Of all things, *sociology*, that quasi-religious subject with its faintly moralistic ring. Perhaps more than anything the choice of the subject he taught had scandalised friend and enemy alike.

'Why have you come?'

'Because there was a question I wanted to ask Magdalena. I've turned it over in my mind for so many years now but I can't come up with an answer. There is something I don't understand. I'm not sure she's got the answer. Or if she'd tell me if she knew. Or if I want to hear it. But I know I want to ask the question.'

'You can ask me if you like.'

'That's kind. But in the first place I didn't expect to see you. And secondly, you won't do.'

'I'm all you've got. Magdalena isn't here. I don't know where she is. She met me at the airport yesterday morning. She brought me here and then she disappeared.'

'What are you doing here?'

161

'Just passing through. My ticket gave me an unrequested stopover in London and I fly out tonight. Is that your question?'

Kipsel shook his head. His eyes were large and liquid. 'No, that was plain curiosity. The real question goes back much further. To the days I spent in jail, and before that to my interrogation in Balthazar Buildings, after the business of the pylons. The official story is that I gave the police information about everybody connected with the explosions. I told them everything. In exchange I got a deal, I got immunity from prosecution. Only I didn't! Do you hear, Blanchie? And for one bloody good reason. I didn't have to tell them. They knew! They knew already! About me, Mickey, Magdalena, Dladla – everyone! For God's sake, they even knew what brand of petrol we used, they had copies of the maps, recordings of our phone conversations . . . You name it, they had them. So I changed tack. I accepted everything – except where it concerned Magdalena. I confirmed everything they had was right – and dammit, it was! – except for the girl. She had known nothing of our plan, of the bombs, of the Azanian Liberation Front. She had been duped. She came along for the ride. She was only there because she loved me. That's what I told them. I tried to save Magdalena. I am *not* Kipsel the traitor. But if not me, then who?'

Blanchaille looked at the pale, trembling creature before him. The round, downy cheeks quivered. Kipsel's extraordinarily thick eyelashes rose and fell rapidly and his round mouth shone as his tongue licked the blubber lips. His hands flapped. He looked more like a fish than ever. A fish drowning in air.

'I understand your question. If you didn't tell the police, who did?'

Then the two friends flung their arms around each others' necks and embraced. Lost in the world, how they rejoiced in each other's company. Blanchaille told Kipsel of his arrival in London, of his meeting with Magdalena, of the visit to the Embassy, of the encounter with Father Lynch in a Soho street, of his warning and of Van Vuuren's brave death in a Soho cellar. At this news Kipsel broke down and wept unashamedly. I heard, too, how Blanchaille told his friend of the two watchers outside the fishmonger's and their strange name: Apple Two.

'I also have a question,' said Blanchaille. 'Who is Apple One?'

And Kipsel replied. 'Perhaps when we answer mine, we will answer yours.'

CHAPTER 16

Blanchaille knew the man at the airport bar as a fellow countryman from his accent. But he could also identify him from a picture he had just seen which showed him strolling along a Paris street. It had been printed in the English newspaper he bought on arriving at the airport. He was relieved to see that he drank brandy.

Is not the choice of strong drink one of the easiest, not to say one of the most pleasant ways of rising painlessly on the social scale, of impressing friends and confounding enemies? Or for that matter, of refuting the notion, lamentably widespread even in this day and age, that South Africans are only interested in beer and shooting kaffirs, and in either order. There is even a calumny, sadly current still, that a famous South African lager I must not name (suffice it to say that the beer in question is a product of a brewery owned by the Himmelfarber empire) is supposed to have run an advertising campaign with the slogan SHOOTING KAFFIRS IS THIRSTY WORK. Now the truth is not (as some Government apologists maintain) that the campaign in question was run many years ago and is now thoroughly discredited. Nor that Curtis Christian Himmelfarber himself led the campaign to deface the posters, altering the wording to something less likely to incite racial hostility and with his own hand struck down the forgotten manager who first coined the infamous slogan, although it is a satisfying tale. Misunderstandings abound. There is even argument about the precise wording of the slogan. There are some who maintain that what it really said was : Is SHOOTING THIRSTY KAFFIRS' WORK? Whilst others say it read: THIRSTY KAFFIRS IS SHOOTING WORK. Whereas in fact the truth is that the original slogan read simply: SHOOTING IS THIRSTY WORK, but unseen enemy hands across the land at a pre-arranged signal added the offending words, either with the intention of discrediting our country in the eyes of the world, or of embarrassing C.C. Himmelfarber who with his giant enterprise, Consolidated Holdings, had always been a stalwart champion of the progressive forces for political change in the country, or both. None the less the malicious legend lingers on and so when you come across a South African drinking not beer but brandy in a bar at Heathrow airport, as Blanchaille and Kipsel did as they waited to be called for their flight to Geneva, even if one does not particularly wish to meet another fellow South African at the time, a feeling of patriotic pride and relief suffuses the frame.

The so-called 'kaffir beer' scandal was a typical example of the concerted campaign waged by overseas dissidents, hostile forces and illegal organisations such as the Azanian Liberation Front, against the honest efforts of the Regime to offer justice to all its population groups. Such black propaganda was in turn just another adjunct of the universal campaign to destroy the white man in Southern Africa, which came to be known as the Total Onslaught.

It was to counter this campaign that the new minister of Ethnic Autonomy and Parallel Equilibriums, Augustus Kuiker, vowed to devote himself when he was appointed Deputy Leader of the Party by the President, Adolph Bubé. It had been Kuiker who replaced Hans Job when that decent man was driven from office by a scurrilous whispering campaign soon after he had succeeded the flamboyant but ailing merino millionaire, J.J. Vokker, when sudden ill health forced him to step down. This change had been the subject of a very cruel joke. 'Who will replace a Vokker?' went the question. 'Only a Hansjob!' came the reply and the whole country doubled up with ribald laughter. Even those who should have known better held their sides. It was then that the formidable Kuiker was appointed and the laughing had to stop. 'Our Gus', people called him, and shivered. The face of granite, the lips of a cement-mixer. It was Kuiker who had appointed Trudy Yssel to the newly formed Department of Communications with the brief to put our country's case abroad with all the punch she could muster. It was regarded as a brave move.

It was a very curious combination; Kuiker the granite man at home, but curiously, even distinctively, colourful abroad, with his taste for bright Hawaiian shirts aglow with orange sunsets and rampant palms, and the new Secretary to the Department of Communications, Trudy Yssel, young, pretty, tough as hell, shrewd and decidedly modern. There was always something stubbornly old-fashioned about Gus Kuiker. He was large, lumpish even. Trudy was svelte and auburn. He looked like a prize fighter, with a big bone-plated forehead, cauliflower ears, a doughy nose, fleshy and rather sensuous lips. But they were a formidable team, it was widely agreed, and of their determination to change the face of internal and foreign propaganda there could be no doubt. As far as Gus Kuiker was concerned, Trudy Yssel could simply do no wrong. What's more she was funded to the hilt. She seemed unstoppable.

As Blanchaille and Kipsel arrived at Heathrow Airport the newspapers they bought told a very strange story. DEPCOM MYSTERY DEEPENS. WHERE IS TRUDY?

Kipsel studied the paper. The Kuiker/Yssel affair was now making international news. The English papers printed an account of an interview given by a spokesman in Kuiker's Department.

Reporter: Can you give us any idea about the location of Trudy Yssel?

Spokesman: It is not in the public interest to disclose any further information.

Reporter: Would you comment on rumours that she has left the country?

Spokesman: The rumour is without foundation.

A few days later, after Trudy Yssel had been sighted in Philadelphia, another news conference was given.

Reporter: Will you confirm that Miss Yssel is now in Philadelphia?

Spokesman: I cannot confirm or deny that report.

Reporter: Do you admit that she is abroad?

Spokesman: I have not said that she is abroad.

Reporter: But she's in Philadelphia. Therefore she must be abroad.

Spokesman: You should learn a little more about your own country before leaping to conclusions. There are other Philadelphias nearer home.

Reporter: Whichever Philadelphia she may be in, what is she doing there?

Spokesman: I will not be cross-examined like this.

Well, of course, the invitation was impossible to resist and a search was immediately launched and indeed another Philadelphia was found, closer to hand, in the Cape province, a small town consisting of no more than the usual bank and church and a few hundred puzzled inhabitants who lined and cheered when the reporters from the nation's press arrived in their Japanese estate cars and their big Mercedes to interview everyone from the mayor to the town's oldest inhabitant, Granny Ryneveldt, aged 103, who declared that she hadn't seen such excitement since Dominee Vasbythoven ran off with his gardener and joined the gay community in the Maluti mountains. However, there was no trace of

Trudy. Everybody had heard of her, of course. But nobody had seen her.

It didn't matter. The Regime made capital out of the reporters' double discomfiture. Journalists, they said, should get to know their own country better and not always look overseas for glamorous stories. Various sanctions were hinted at if the newspapers did not take up this suggestion. Then ministers of the Dutch Reformed Church expressed their outrage that the affair of the renegade minister, Vasbythoven, had been dragged up once more. For their part, several liberal English clerics preached sermons against the hounding of the unfortunate minister, reminding their congregations that homosexual practice between consenting adults was widely regarded as acceptable in the outside world and they lauded Dominee Vasbythoven who had shown his bravery not only by taking as a lover one of his own sex but someone of another race which showed him to be not only sexually liberated but racially balanced and they pointed out that this was no small feat for a man whose great-great uncle had been Judge-President of the Orange Free State, when it had still been a Boer Republic. Here again the Regime waded in with warnings to the opposition press against attempts to slander the memory of the Boer Republics when, led by Uncle Paul Kruger, the Boer Nation with God's help had fought for its freedom against the wicked imperialist colonialist oppression of the British. Anti-Government papers were warned for the last time to put their house in order.

The English papers overseas, beyond the reach of the Regime, agreed that Minister Kuiker and his protégée Trudy Yssel had disappeared. They also agreed that large sums of Government money appeared to have gone missing with them. They printed a photograph which showed the missing pair in a Paris street. She carried several shopping bags and smiled vivaciously. He covered his face with one hand, but was instantly recognisable. Behind them walked two men in dark suits. One of these men now sat drinking at the bar.

The only other drinkers were a small group of oriental businessmen who drank from globular tankards foaming pink cocktails garnished with sprigs of mint and cherries, leaning forward above the liquid and tasting it with tongues and fingertips, giving excited little barks of encouragement. A small girl carrying an enormous soft green cat with wild eyes and a forest of woolly whiskers wandered around the footrail with tear-stained face obviously searching for her parents. All around was the teeming flux of anonymous travellers departing for a hundred destinations.

The drinker who aroused this rhapsody of patriotic memories in Blanchaille was painfully thin, his sports jacket hung on him, a loud tweed of blues and greens with an ugly stiffening of the bristles which had the effect of making the colours of the cloth shimmer, a sickly rainbow effect. His complexion too was strange, a light grey translucency tinged with pink. He'd been drinking for some time, Blanchaille judged, and despite the flush that warmed the bony face, it was the air of desiccation that struck him, as if a kind of internal emaciation had taken place, an interior drought, a profound dryness which no amount of watering could end. He had crisp, slightly oiled sandy hair through which the scalp gleamed bleakly. Altogether he had the look of St John of Capistrano, formidable Inquisitor-General of Vienna, a portrait of whom had hung in Blanchaille's class-room many years before.

His message to Kipsel was succinct: 'Cop.'

Kipsel did not thank him. 'I warn you Blanchie, when shown a South African security man competing urges threaten me.'

'Which?'

'Do I hit out, or throw up?'

At the bar the oriental businessmen had replenished their tankards and were lapping away happily at the pink stuff. The little girl had been given a bowl of crisps by the barman and sat eating steadily, gazing out into the seething concourse with tearful eyes. Blanchaille introduced his friend and himself to the solitary drinker.

'Jesus!' said the drinker, 'Not Kipsel the traitor?'

'No,' Kipsel said firmly. 'Not Kipsel the traitor.'

'Ernest Nokkles,' said the drinker, 'passing on to Geneva.'

'So are we.'

'Let me get you a drink,' said Blanchaille.

'Brandy,' said Nokkles. 'A large one if you will. The bloody English tot is about as much as a nun pees with her knees crossed. And Coke with it. I always have it with Coke. The bastards here drink it neat, y'know.'

'How are things at home?' Kipsel asked.

'Do you mean militarily or economically?'

'I didn't know there was a difference.'

'They're linked, but they're different. Militarily we're all right. Hell, there's nobody who's going to touch us. Frankly I think we're in more danger from the drought. But if you consider the Total Onslaught, then there's no doubt about its having an effect. Slow but cumulative. We might crack one day. But despite that, the Big

167

Seven reckon we're doing O.K., financially.'

The Big Seven were those groups which between them controlled almost every area of life and dominated the Stock Exchange. The gold mining companies of course and various major industries – armaments, insurance, drink and tobacco together with the Government control boards that regulated everything from transport to citrus. Seven was a mystical number. The Big Seven represented the aggregate of national interests.

The profile which emerged of your average South African was a dedicated smoker who took to booze in a big way, kept himself armed to the teeth but was sensible enough to insure against the risk that either cigarettes or drink or terrorists might blow him away, and paid for this lifestyle with gold bullion. For the rest he did as the Regime told him, travelled as the Government directed him and died when and where the State demanded it. This handful of huge conglomerates owned everything and they also owned slices of each other and were all held, in turn, in the capacious lap of the Regime which allowed and even encouraged these cliques, cartels, monopolies to operate and indeed took a very close interest in them to the extent of inviting their directors to sit on various Government boards, boards of arms companies and the rural development agencies. Private business responded by asking Government ministers to take up seats on the boards of the gold mining companies, army officers were invited to join insurance companies, tobacco groups and breweries. Complicated interlocking deals were set up between the State and the great conglomerates, a famous instance of which was the Life Saving Bond which allowed families of soldiers to purchase a special insurance policy on the life of their loved one for a small monthly premium. 'In the event of deprivation', as the preamble to the policy put it, the next of kin received a 'Life Saving Bond' certificate which showed the value of all their contributions to date. The premiums which had accrued were then 'sent forward', which meant the sum was invested in 'armaments and/or other industries vital to the war effort', thereby giving all soldiers a second chance to serve by helping to ensure that the country's weaponry was the best possible. The casualties joined what the field padres called the army invisible, or simply the Big Battalion, known familiarly as the BB. 'Oh, he's serving with the BB' became a common way of skirting around a tragedy and won for those who spoke the words a new respect. The Regime encouraged positive thinking and inspectors ensured that the attractive blue and white Bond Certificates were prominently displayed in the home. Every month a draw took place and the family with the lucky bond number won for themselves a tour of the forward operational areas, plus a visit to the site of some celebrated victory (combat conditions permitting) and invariably returned strengthened and resolute. The newspapers and television followed these visits with great interest and press stories appeared and television reports showing pictures of Dick and Eugenia and their children, Marta and Kobus, proudly wearing combat helmets they'd been given, trundling through the veld in an armoured troop carrier. 'My Day in the Operational Areas' was an increasingly popular title in school examination papers.

'The English,' said Nokkles, 'are bloody awful snobs. And racialists. They also have their kaffirs, you know. It's just that you can't tell them apart. Being English they all look alike. But they have them. Oh yes, they have them.'

He swallowed his brandy with relish, clicking his tongue. But no amount of drinking would irrigate that consuming desert within Ernie Nokkles.

A man in a dark green anorak and a big woman in a pixie cap, its straps pulled down hard over her ears and knotted cruelly beneath her chin, both of them buttoned everywhere, plumply encased, walked up to the little girl and removed her from the counter. 'We've been calling you on the loudspeaker,' the woman said between clenched teeth. And then bending over the little girl she administered several stinging slaps, saying at the same time and in rhythm to her blows: '*Why didn't you listen?*'

'And child beaters, too,' Nokkles said. 'What do you think?'

'We think that you must be Trudy's detective,' Blanchaille said.

'That,' said Nokkles with a contemptuous downward twitch of the lips and a sideways flick of the head, so sudden Blanchaille thought for the moment he might have spat on the floor, 'is a newspaper lie. I am not a policeman. In fact my function is quite vague. I fall within the remit of a number of officials – there's Pieter Weerhaan, Dominee Lippetaal, as well as Mr Glip, and then of course there is Ernest Tweegat and Dr Enigiets. Actually I work for all these people, and of course for Miss Yssel. This for me was a fairly recent move. By training I'm a population movement man. I came from the PRP, the Population Resettlement Programme. I only got this Yssel job because someone went sick and I was shoved in. Believe it or not, I began working as a rookie years ago in Old

Ma Dubbeltong's Department, as it then was, of Entry and Egress; that was the original outfit, that was the egg which this new-fangled Department for Population Settlements came from. The PRP is really just old wine in new bottles. Anyway when I was there it was a damn sight tougher than anything today. God! My boss was old Harry Waterman, my hell what a tartar! Screaming Harry we called him. Well, say what you like, credit where credit's due, he was largely instrumental, along with Ma, in formulating policy for what we now call population settlement. Screaming Harry was a blunt official, no fanciness about him. Nothing elegant. A straight guy, a removalist of the old school. Look, he'd say, you've got all these blackies wandering around the country or slipping into the towns or setting up camps wherever they feel like it and squatting here and there, and they've got to be moved. Right? They've got to be put down in some place of their own and made to stay there. Now you never beg or threaten when you're running a removal. It doesn't matter if you're endorsing out – because that's what we called it then, endorsing out – some old bastard who doesn't have a pass, or an entire fucking tribe. First, you notify deadline for removal, then you get your paper-work right, you double check that the trucks are ordered up – and then you move them. As I say, old Harry Waterman was a plain removalist. None of these fancy titles for him, like Resettlement Officer or Relocation Adviser, as they like to call themselves now, these clever dicks from Varsity. No, everything was straight talking for Harry. As the trucks come out of the camp which you're removing, Harry said, you put the bulldozers in and flatten the place. End of story. It's quick, clean, efficient. You know something?' Nokkles gazed earnestly at Blanchaille and Kipsel. 'I don't know if it's not a lot kinder than the boards of enquiry and appeal and so on which dominate the resettlement field today. After all we all know in the end, after all the talking's done, they're going to have to get out. So why lead them on? The only talent you need to be a removalist, old Harry was fond of saying, is eyes in the back of your head. Front eyes watch the trucks moving out, those in the back watch the bulldozers moving in. A great guy, old Harry. Dead now. But he never understood the new scheme of things. I believe you have to move with the times. So when the call came, I was ready. Fate spoke. "Ernie Nokkles," it said, "will you or will you not accept secondment to this new Department of Communications run by this hot lady said to be going places under the aegis of Minister Gus Kuiker?" And like a shot I answered back, "Damn sure!" But I am not, and never was, Trudy's detective.'

170

'What were you then?' asked Kipsel.

'Her aide, confidante and loyal member of her Department,' said Nokkles proudly. 'What I wanted was to help her and the Minister in their great task.'

'Great task,' Kipsel repeated scathingly. 'Trudy Yssel tried to carry the propaganda war to the enemy abroad, she wanted to coax, buy, bend overseas opinion about the true nature of the Regime. It was her task to show them as being not simply a gang of wooden headed, rock-brained farmers terrified that their grandfathers might have slept with their cooks – no – they were to become human ethnologists determined to allow all ethnic groups to blossom according to their cultural traditions within the natural parameters recognised by God, biology and history.'

'I don't know what you mean,' said Nokkles. 'But if you're saying she wanted to save us, I say *yes*. She and the Minister wanted to lead us out of the past, back into the world, into the future. And that's what I wanted too.'

'And what do you want now?' Blanchaille asked gently.

Nokkles looked around quickly. He dropped his voice. 'I wish I was back in old Ma Dubbeltong's department again. But that can't be. Look, you guys are going to Switzerland and I am going to Switzerland. We're countrymen abroad. So why don't we travel together? I mean we don't have to agree politically, just to keep company a bit – not so?'

'Sure, we'll go along with you, but you might not like where we're going,' said Blanchaille.

'We're heading for Uncle Paul's place,' said Kipsel.

The change in Nokkles was dramatic. He stood up and drained his glass. He picked up his bag. 'God help you then. That old dream's not for me.'

They watched him walk away, blindly shouldering his way through the crowds. They're ruined, these people, Blanchaille thought. They don't know who they are or where they're going. Once nothing would stop them doing their duty as they saw it and that was to defend their people and their way of life. And they were hated for it. Good, they accepted that hate. But then the new ideas took over, they got wise, got modern, took on the world. Once upon a time nothing would make them give up the principle that the tribe would survive because God wished it so – now there's nothing they won't do just to hang on a little longer. Uncle Paul's other place is a bad dream, it takes them back to the *velskoen* years, the days of biltong and boere biscuits, of muzzle loaders, Bibles, of creeping

171

backward slowly like an armour-plated ox, out of range of the future. Some no doubt wished to go back, as Nokkles did, wanted to go back to Old Ma Dubbeltong's department, back to the old dream of a country fit for farmers, where a man was free to ride his acres, shoot his game, father his children, lash his slaves, free from drought, English, Jews, missionaries, rinderpest, blacks, coolies and tax-collectors. But back there waited the hateful legend, the impossible story, the triumphant British, the defeated people, the exiled president, the store of gold, the secret heaven somewhere in Switzerland, the last refuge of a broken tribe.

'What do you think?' Kipsel asked.

'I think he's Trudy's detective and he's lost Trudy. All he's left with is what she taught him. He's dead. He's spinning out of control. He's like a space probe gone loco. Nothing can save him unless he finds another mother-ship to lock onto, or another planet to land on. He's spinning into space. And space is cold and big and blacker than Africa.'

On the plane service was polite but cool and they didn't get a drink until they asked the stewardess. 'It's a short flight, we prefer passengers to ask,' she told them. 'Except in first class.'

At one point the curtains closing off the first class cabin opened to reveal Nokkles sprawled across two seats. He was drinking champagne and his hand rested on the neck of the bottle in a protective yet rather showy manner. In the way that a man might rest his hand on the neck of an expensive girl whom he wishes to show off to the world. It was a gesture of desperate pride. It turned its back on Boers and shooting kaffirs and beer. It looked outward. It was confident, modern, worldly. Much had been invested in it.

CHAPTER 17

Of their arrival at Geneva Airport there is to be noted only that Ernest Nokkles was swept into the arms of that growing number of castaway agents abroad, all now increasingly anxious about the disappearances of their various chiefs and determined to reattach themselves to centres of influence or persons of importance whenever they appeared.

My dream showed me Nokkles, awash in good champagne, immediately claimed as he left the Customs area by three men who introduced themselves as Chris Dieweld, Emil Moolah and Koos Spahr. Two members of this burly trio claimed to have been recently attached to the office of the President, had travelled with him as far as London in search of medical treatment and there he had given them the slip. And I saw how these big men shivered and trembled at their loss.

Chris Dieweld, Emil Moolah and Koos Spahr surrounded Trudy's detective demanding to know what news he had brought. Dieweld was big and blond with a great cows-lick combed back from his forehead like a frozen wave, Moolah thin and springy with a mouth full of gold teeth and Spahr, bespectacled, with a round expressionless face and astonishingly bright blue eyes, gave no clue to his expertise with the parcel bomb. Nokkles knew Spahr as one of the men on Kuiker's security staff. The others he thought he knew vaguely from photographs of the President in foreign parts. Dieweld, he vaguely remembered, had disgraced himself by fainting when a demented maize farmer had attempted to shoot the President at the official opening of the Monument to Heroes of the Mauritian Invasion.

Nokkles' first question was about Bubé. The President was in Geneva, he had it on the best authority. Trace the President and surely the others could not be far away?

The security men looked glum. They too had heard of the President's visit to London. They had heard he was on his way to Geneva. They had met every plane. But the old fox must have disguised himself because he eluded them.

'Remember,' said Moolah, 'the President visited most of the European capitals during his celebrated tour and was never once recognised. What chance did we stand?'

As for Blanchaille and Kipsel, they stood on the moving pavement carrying them towards passport control and Customs, gazing with fascination at the advertisements for watches sculpted from coins, or carved from ingots, the offer of hotels so efficient they operated without manpower and the multitude of advertisements in cunningly illuminated panels alongside the moving pavement showing deep blue lakes and icing sugar alps. Most of all they stared at the multitudinous shapes and forms of gold to be purchased, ingots, coins, pendants, lozenges; some cute and almost edible came in little cubes, fat and yellow like processed cheese. How extraordinary that so much treasure should be produced from the deep, black, stony heart of their country.

This reverie was broken by a chauffeur in smart green livery who carried a sign reading 'Reverend Blanchaille' and announced that he had instructions to transport them to 'the big house on the hill', where a friend awaited them.

Who were they to argue? Alone and unloved in a strange land? However close to the end of their journey they might be (for after all 'the big house of the hill' was a tantalising description) offers of friendship from whatever quarter were difficult to resist.

It is a sign of the desperate state to which the once-powerful security men had been reduced that they, seeing Blanchaille and Kipsel escorted to a great limousine, should have decided to follow them, despite Nokkles' warning that these men were deluded pilgrims come to Switzerland to seek Kruger's dream kingdom and that they were in real life a disgraced traitor and a renegade priest. As Chris Dieweld put it: 'We're lost without someone to follow.'

The chauffeur pointed to the grey Mercedes keeping discreetly behind them. 'We'll lose them,' he promised.

The road ran for miles along the lakeside. The lower slopes of the mountain were thickly crammed with vines, every inch of land terraced to its very edges, the dense greenness tumbling down to the roadside, vine leaves stirring in the passing breeze their car made. Then on the other side of the road the vines continuing their downward plunge to the very water's edge. Up ahead were larger mountains folding one into another and covered in a thick dark fur of vegetation. It amazed him, the roughness of this vegetation, its harsh contours. No doubt it was different in the winter when the snows softened and smoothed away the detail, but now, under the sun hot and high, under a light-blue sky, there was a rough, wiry, raw determination about the way these shrubs and trees clung to the mountain side, a lack of softness, an absence of prettiness that reminded him very strongly of Africa. After running some way along the lakeside they began climbing steeply. The driver pointed to the town of Montreux below and to a small tongue of land jutting out into the lake, that was the prison castle, Château Chillon, very famous. They climbed through the thick fuzz of bush and forest, the harsh unlovely vegetation. Here and there boulders broke through the dark green and nearer the summits were ridges of grey stone, mountain skulls, patched and balding. And even higher still was the snow, even in this June heat, last year's snow, icy grey.

And here was a grand house, a castle within its own walls, but no rearing bulk of dull stones, more of a *Schloss*, a château, white-washed, trim and solid. Then they were driving through the great wrought-iron gates with their chevrons and swans intricately worked, along a gravel drive up to great oaken doors.

Their host in his big solid house at the end of a long drive, behind high walls and wrought-iron gates, awaited them on the steps. With his hand outstretched, wearing the dark business suit, the well-shaped smile so familiar from a thousand press photographs and television, with his head cocked to one side, sparse grey hair neatly combed, the round intelligent face with bright eyes that gave him the look of an intelligent gun dog, the characteristic quick shrewd glance from behind thick lashes, the quiet, formidable air of authority. It was very difficult for them to suppress their astonishment.

'What? Himmelfarber, you!' Blanchaille said.

Kipsel said, 'It really is another bloody exodus. It's a diaspora. If Himmelfarber the mine-owner has left, then it's all finished. Everyone will leave. You won't be able to move anywhere overseas for fleeing South Africans.'

'But I haven't left,' said the mine-owner. 'This is merely my summer place. I spend the African winter here.'

Blanchaille turned on his heel. 'Have a happy holiday,' he said.

'I have a proposition,' said Himmelfarber.

'We're not open to any proposals,' Blanchaille said very firmly.

'We may as well hear what he has to say,' said Kipsel, 'now that we're here.'

'Let's talk inside,' Himmelfarber led them through the house into an enormous lounge furnished in white leather with thick pink carpets on the floor, a large generous room looking through french windows onto the lawn and large circular lily pond. Himmelfarber stood at the bar at the far end and poured them drinks. A little fruit punch, he said, of his own making, light and refreshing.

On the walls of this room were blow-ups of black and white photographs of miners working below ground, drilling the rock face, or loading the ore, coming off shift. Happy pictures of a classroom full of new recruits learning Fanagalo. Other photographs, far more disturbing, showed men terribly mutilated, crushed and bleeding; they also saw corpses lying on sheets in what must have been a morgue, rows of them, they stared at the ceiling wide-eyed and with quite terrible, unfrightened detachment. Why should Himmelfarber keep these reminders about him?

Blanchaille considered the entrepreneur. Curtis Christian Himmelfarber was the brilliant son of a brilliant family. The family had been established by the remarkable Julius Himmelfarber, a penniless Latvian emigrant to the South African goldfields who had founded a great mining empire. Old Julius had been an intimate of Cecil Rhodes and Milner, a drinking companion of Barney Barnato, a sworn enemy of Kruger who had called him '*Daardie Joodse smous*' . . . that Jewish pedlar . . . Julius Himmelfarber had bought Blydag, his first mine and one of the premier producers of all time, for a little more than was now paid for one single ounce of its gold, and the foundation of a great financial empire had been laid.

Frank Harris, the noted Irish philanderer on a visit to South Africa shortly before the Boer War began, had been favourably impressed.

Harris had met Julius Himmelfarber and liked him well enough to leave a portrait of him: '. . . cultured, urbane, very pointed in conversation, a gentle Croesus, a philosopher miner, a flower of the Semitic type, markedly superior to your Anglo-Saxon sportsmen.' But then Harris, of course, had held a long-standing prejudice against the Anglo-Saxon sportsman, for, as he told Cecil Rhodes in a bizarre meeting which took place on top of Table Mountain while Rhodes presumably gazed from this fairest Cape in all the world towards distant Cairo, it was perfectly understandable that God in his youth should have chosen the Jews for his special people, for they were after all an attractive, lovable race. But that later he should have changed his mind in favour of the English, as Rhodes contended, showed that he must be in his dotage.

Curtis Christian Himmelfarber, who was now handing out drinks in the pink and white room to Blanchaille and Kipsel, would not have been described by Harris as the flower of the Semitic type. In any event, the Himmelfarbers had long since severed the connection. Curtis Christian was an Anglican and this faith, along with his mines, had been part of his inheritance. The change in faith had taken place when his fierce grandfather, Aaron, always a mercurial man, the ne'er-do-well of the family, had persuaded investors that a local mine under his control was capable of producing richer amounts than anyone had suspected, and displayed samples to prove it. Alas, a surveyor's report revealed that the mine was likely to produce far less than promised and Aaron found himself in jail, awaiting trial. It was there that he underwent a spectacular conversion at the hands of a travelling Baptist minister. Naturally the entire family followed suit. They did not long stay with the Baptists but moved instead, down the years, by degrees, with a stately assurance that reminded one of a luxury liner heading for its home port, from the choppy seas of Baptist rhetoric into the calmer, shallower waters of the Church of England and in these pacific waters had floated ever since.

The Himmelfarbers were the closest thing to a Royal family the country had. Each member of this family received adulatory notice in the media. Everyone in the country was familiar with the little vagaries of the Himmelfarbers. There was Waverley, C.C.'s wife, tall, tanned and fit. She appeared often at fund-raising dinners, drove jeeps for famine relief, organised milk for the townships and free school books for the kids. There was Elspeth, the eldest daughter and the 'serious one', a lawyer. There was Cookie, the madcap gadabout youngest, with a taste for high living and drugs, a kind of painter, and reportedly a great strain on her parents. And then of course Timmo, the son and heir, dashing, eligible, often pictured behind the wheel of a racing car, or in his yacht off Cape Point. Photographers had accompanied him on his first day of military service. That service was later to be marred by a scandal when it was rumoured that Timmo, who had trained with a crack paratroop squadron 'The Leopard's Claw', had been excused jumps over hostile territory. The chiefs of staff took the unusual step of refuting the rumour and reported that young Himmelfarber always jumped with his comrades and, what was more, he had one of the highest 'score' rates (the name given to the jump/kill ratios), in the entire regiment.

'I see you're examining my photographs,' said Himmelfarber. 'These pictures, you know what they are? They're photographs of my workers and show the full extent of their employment. The dangers of mining are not disguised. Accidents at the rock face, drilling accidents, men hurt in rockfalls, or ramming, that is to say when loading the trucks with gold-bearing rock. I wonder if you have any idea what a mine looks like underground? Imagine a buried Christmas tree, the trunk is the mine shaft plunging down hundreds of meters. Off the shaft the stopes radiate like branches. At the far tips of these branches is the thread of gold. Think of it rather like tinsel that you drape over the branches of your Christmas tree. Gold mining is deep, dark, hot, dangerous work. You must break a great deal of rock to claim a little of the glitter, a couple of tons of ore give you little more than twenty grammes of gold. I keep these pictures on my wall to remind me where I come from, how I live and what it costs.' Himmelfarber brought their drinks across. 'This is a good light punch. I hope you'll enjoy it. Fruit juice spiked with rum and lemon, mixed with a little pomegranate, satsuma segments, some passion fruit and thin shavings of watermelon. Shall we drink to the health of our President? I believe he needs our good wishes,' Himmelfarber smiled, and raised his glass. 'But that's another story. I haven't got you here to talk about poor Bubé.'

'Why are we here?' Blanchaille demanded.

Himmelfarber looked surprised. 'To listen to a few stories of my own. Such as the story of Popov.'

'Do you really mean that?' Kipsel demanded incredulously. 'Do you know the true story of Popov?'

This is where Blanchaille waded in. 'Now just a moment,' he said. 'Let's get this straight before you start swallowing everything he tells you. Himmelfarber here and his firm, Consolidated Holdings, have propped up successive governments for as long as anyone can remember. Himmelfarber buys defence bonds, sits on armaments boards, advises the Regime on its business deals, he even plays golf with Bubé.'

'That's one way of looking at it. I also fund the Democratic People's Party, I'm a public supporter of racial freedom and Consolidated Holdings is one of the most enlightened employers in the country. It has more black personnel managers than any other, it was the first to employ Indian salesmen, our coloured cost accountants are internationally known and bright young Liberals join us in the sure knowledge that their ideas will be welcomed and acted upon.'

'For God's sake, Ronnie, you're not going to stand there and swallow that stuff, are you? Why don't you ask him about Popov?'

Kipsel's eyes widened. 'You knew Popov?'

'Knew him! Himmelfarber ran him!' Blanchaille shouted.

'I asked Mr Himmelfarber, Blanchie, let him answer for himself.'

Himmelfarber placed four fingers over the rim of his glass and put his mouth to the liquid and laughed softly, a frothy resonance. 'Now you see the trouble with our holy friend here. He's very much the obsessive South African type. He's more of a danger to our country than the entire Total Onslaught. And d'you know why? It's because he combines this horrible puritanical streak on the one hand with an absolutely crusading ignorance on the other. Your friend Blanchaille suffers from the characteristic South African disease. He wishes to blame people. No, Mr Kipsel, I can't promise you the true story of Popov. But I can give you my version.'

'That will do,' said Kipsel, and he helped himself to more punch.

'But before you can understand the importance of Popov, you must listen to my story of why we love the Russians.'

'Do we love the Russians?' Kipsel asked.

'In our own way, yes we do. We have something in common which completely overrides our political differences – our gold sales. This is only natural since the Soviet Union and the Republic between them possess most of the gold in the world. It's obviously in our mutual interest to regulate the supply of that gold to the world markets and thereby to control the price. Remember that every fluctuation of a few dollars up or down is a total gain or loss of millions to our economies. Let me give you an example of the sort of co-operation I have in mind. For years gold sales were handled in London. But we found that successive British governments were becoming too damn inquisitive about our sales. So we pulled out. London till then was *the* gold market, the next moment we were gone. On our side naturally it gave the Regime great pleasure to kick the Limeys in the teeth, it's an extension of the Boer War, of course – I quote to you President Bubé's choice remark: "We've got nothing against the British – it's the English we hate." The Russians also had their reasons for pulling out. They said they were concerned about security at Heathrow. But they weren't really worried about the stuff being stolen, although it happens from time to time. What they really objected to was having people sniffing around their gold because word might get out about the amount they were selling. So off we went to Switzerland and there, with the price doubling and redoubling like crazy, we had a high old time in our Zurich years. In fact so much gold was sold that the Swiss threw caution to the winds for once, and seeing a chance of making even more money the Government slapped on a sales tax, something a little over five per cent I seem to recall. It's a long time ago now.

Well, that was a very bad mistake. It wasn't that we objected to the Swiss becoming even richer but having that tax meant that the dealers had to show how much gold they were selling, from which could be calculated the amount that we were putting onto the market. We were right back where we were before. And the amounts of gold we were making available were in danger of being anticipated, even discounted. Even then we might have hung on, but the price crashed as it does every few years and the Swiss dealers, who had grown fat in the good years, dragged their feet over selling our newly mined metal at a much lower price than in the old good gilded days of yore. So back we went to London with some of our business. We and our friends. Not all our business. Never again all of it. What a welcome! Kisses on both cheeks from the Bank of England, no unseemly taxes, or too close a scrutiny of sales – our friends were most insistent about that – and everything looked like sweetness and light.'

Blanchaille turned to Kipsel. 'You hear what he says? He admits to working with the Russians and he expects us to clap. And yet we know people who did the same thing and were hanged. Look at the first commandment of our country: the Regime kills people who help the Russians. That's the rule. Everyone knows it. Everyone obeys it. Go up to the man in the street and ask what will happen if you help the Russians and he'll draw his finger across his throat. He may even kill you himself. People live and die according to the rules the Regime makes – so how can they change them?'

'Why not? If it suits them,' Himmelfarber demanded brutally. 'They're their rules.'

'But what about Popov, the spy?' Kipsel asked. 'You still haven't said.'

'He was no spy,' said Blanchaille. 'He was a Russian banker who got arrested by mistake. Van Vuuren showed me that.'

'Correct,' Himmelfarber acknowledged. 'First inkling I had of it came in a call from Zurich, the Wozchod Handelsbank, and my contact Glotz on the line, screaming at me: "Just what the hell have you done? You stupid, fucking Boers! You morons! What in Christ's name have you done with Popov? I've just had Vneshtorgbank on the line – that's his headquarters, Bank for Foreign Trade in Moscow – absolutely frantic! They say their man has gone cold. Do something!" Well? What could I say? Nothing – at the time and just as well, too. Imagine his reaction if I told him – yes, look I'm sorry about this Ivan, but your man is at the moment languishing in a cell in Balthazar Buildings having been beaten within an inch of his life. Because he was, you know. The Security Police got so drunk when they realised they'd caught a live Russian that they didn't refer the matter to the Bureau, as they should have done; instead they gave poor Popov the treatment. They strung him up by his toes, they tied him to a broomstick and gave him the catherine wheel, they put an uncomfortable voltage through each testicle. Then they threw a party. They went to the press and issued self-congratulatory statements. Popov by this stage was past knowing or caring. He didn't tell them much. He *couldn't* tell them much! His English has never been any good and he was in a state of profound shock. Besides that he'd lost his false teeth which fell out when these buggers dangled him from an open window on the tenth floor. They frightened him to within an inch of his life and that put paid to any chance of communication. Fear and the lack of teeth ensured that Popov was talking to no one. But as far as the papers were concerned, as far as the rest of the country was concerned, our boys had caught a Russian and of course the Regime had to play along with it. They had to confirm that their brilliant Security Police had pulled off the most extraordinary capture of a Russian spy, they made him a full colonel in the KGB and they went round saying proudly how clever they'd been. Well they had to, hadn't they? The Government had been warning for years that the Russians were working to destroy us, that they sent their spies into the country all the time, that they had armed and supported the black armies on the borders, that their agents had infiltrated the townships, and the resettlement camps, that their submarines cruised off our coasts and that they were working day and night for the destruction of our country. Now they'd gone and proved it! Well, I had to take some hard decisions. I started taking flack from both directions. The Regime wanted to know what I was going to do about smoothing relations with the Russians. The Russians were muttering darkly about treachery and threatening to end co-operation on gold sales. The Regime, while publicly ordering its ministers to dance in the street, was telling me that I was the only one who could sort out matters with Moscow. In the end I did what I had to.'

'What was that?' Kipsel asked.

'I sent my nephew to Moscow.'

'Just like that?'

'He's been before. Popov was the Russians' man here. Bennie was our man there.'

'Bennie?'

'My nephew. A bright boy, Craddock. A few years ago I was

happy to make him a director of Consolidated Holdings. He's been running missions to Moscow for years.'

'What happened in Moscow?' Kipsel asked.

'He was arrested the moment he stepped off the plane.'

'You shopped him,' declared Kipsel wonderingly.

'It was my duty,' said Himmelfarber. 'I had to give Moscow something to hold. He was a kind of deposit against the safe return of Popov. We knew it was necessary.'

'We?' said Kipsel.

'Those of us who will seize the chance of a change in our country. Real change! Consider, Ronald, our previous history. Once the Regime consisted of men who believed themselves chosen by God to bring light to a dark place. They were known as the Dark Men, or the Old Guard. In time they were replaced by a new breed, the so-called Men of Light, or New Men. Now the New Men believed also that God had chosen them, but they also believed that the country couldn't be protected by faith alone. They must be protected by rocket launchers and useful business contacts as well as the proper deployment of troops on the borders. Of course the New Men are no longer frightened of the outside world. They want to carry the fight to the enemy, they want to meet the world and beat it. They refuse to see the options closing one by one. They want to get out and do things. It was the New Men who were behind Bubé's foreign tours, and I'm not just talking about the European tour that got all the publicity, the six capitals in five days, or whatever it was. No, I'm talking about the tours, the secret tours that have been going on for years, the clandestine diplomacy on which the President has been engaged for almost a decade now. Why, if I told you the number of countries he had visited you'd be absolutely amazed. Then there's also been a publicity campaign mounted by the Department of Communications and the quite stunning work which Trudy Yssel has done, buying into, buying up, and buying off opinion makers in the West. I tell you there's not a place from the Vatican to the White House where Trudy, yes little Trudy Yssel from the back-of-beyond, a poor little country girl who went to school barefoot, is not welcomed and fêted. Fêted! Do you see the nature of things? Do I make myself clear? Do you see the chances to which I refer? The old ways have gone, or at least are going and others are being adapted. Yes, of course we still believe in God. Yes, of course, we still believe that under certain circumstances a platoon ambushed must fight to the last man for the glory of the country and to add substance to the ancient belief that the entire country would do so, in need. Yet gradually the realisation has come about, that what we need is not God and bombs, though they may be very useful, but gold. And we have it! By God, we have it and we use it. Hell, can either of you imagine what it's like to turn on your TV and see one of our warlike black presidents in one of the states to the north of us threatening to blast us off the map of Africa and know that not twelve hours before the same guy has been pouring you a whisky and soda in the VIP's guest-house and inquiring after your wife and kids? That's progress! The Regime sees the options and uses them, that's all,' said Himmelfarber, 'and so do I.'

'You're saying it's possible to do a deal with the New Men?' Blanchaille asked.

Himmelfarber gave the wolfish smile of one who has scented the approaching kill. 'I don't know about dealing with the Regime. That comes later. But sure, I'll deal *for* them. I already did. More than once. Let me give you one example. The Regime has a lot of trouble securing various supplies which we regard as essential. A little guy from the Department of Commerce comes to see me. Can I suggest a way for our country to acquire certain strategic supplies overseas? Well that's a bit of a problem because you see foreign countries don't exactly like the idea of penetration by South African interests, still less by South African Government agencies. So what did we do at Consolidated Holdings to resolve this difficulty? Well, we did our buying using a group of Panamanian companies which could not be traced back to us. And having bought our way in to certain target industries abroad we left the local management structures very largely intact and operated through a series of interlocking boards. This was a wise move because it's always better not to disturb the people on the ground. But since you have your own directors in there and these directors are linked, and controlled, say from your New York office, you maintain a fairly useful oversight of your operation. Perhaps you might buy a forest in Scotland, because we need pit props in good supply, or a British insurance company, or take over American interests in coal, copper, uranium and so on. Look, believe it or not, and I'd probably be shot if anybody knew I'd told you, but so vital does the Regime consider this programme of strategic acquirements that they're investing millions in its long-term strategy for buying up or buying into key interests abroad. Somebody has to do it for them.'

'But you'd still consider yourself an opponent of the Regime?' Kipsel asked.

183

'Greater opposer is there none,' said Himmelfarber, directing his eyes heavenward. 'My family has opposed this Regime and all its neolithic predecessors. Consolidated Holdings is in the forefront of the struggle to reform the labour laws, electrify the black townships, promote the inter-racial arts and encourage more black mothers to breastfeed. Yessir, we are opponents! But as opponents the question we must ask ourselves, if we are serious, is do we merely wish to condemn the Regime, or do we want to destroy it? Look, I work with the Government on certain ventures, but that doesn't make me a Government man. I also make donations in an indirect fashion to the Azanian Liberation Front – but that doesn't make me a guerrilla. It's really just a question, as I say, of exploring all the options. This is now Government policy. And believe you me it's going to sink the bastards! Already it has started. Yssel and Kuiker are gone. When you get people using a lot of money, travelling, living well, it's perhaps not surprising that they begin to acquire expensive tastes. They start enjoying certain wines, they become fascinated with a house with a particular view. These things happen. As for President Bubé, I've no reason to doubt that he's abroad because he's ill and he's seeking treatment, as the reports say. As to the rumours – well, I also know that when gold sales were switched from London to Zurich a number of Swiss dealers competed for President Bubé's friendship and co-operation and made concrete signals of their gratitude when he was able to help them. But before you jump to conclusions let's consider that in a way perhaps his motives might have been good. According to the rumours we hear, any money that President Bubé may have acquired has been set aside as a kind of insurance fund against the day when, possibly for military reasons, the Regime finds it cannot any longer operate safely from home base and they have to set up somewhere abroad. In other words, Bubé has set aside funds for the establishment of the Government in exile. Now why should this be a scandal? Surely it's not an ignoble gesture. It might even be quite sensible. You see what forces in the end will destroy them? They will smash on their own logic.'

'Yes,' said Kipsel. There was a strange light in his eye. 'I follow you now. What you're saying is that if you are genuinely committed to exploring all options, then among the options you're going to have to consider is the one that has you disappearing down the plug hole.'

'You've got it,' Himmelfarber beamed, clearly believing that in Kipsel he had found a recruit. 'I appeal to you. Leave off this foolish travelling. Come back with me. Come back home and make the new changes work for us. The old consensus is smashed. The bastards are on the run. They say they're being modern. In fact they're merely terrified. They say they want to look ahead. In fact they daren't open their eyes.'

'Join them,' said Kipsel, 'join them and then destroy them – isn't that it?'

'Exactly.' Himmelfarber was clearly exulted by the thought. 'You understand.'

'Indeed I do. I have friends who did the same thing once. To me,' Kipsel said. He stood up. 'Come Blanchie, it's time we were on our way. I'm sorry but I suppose by rights I belong to the Old Guard. I will never be a New Man.'

And Blanchaille, his heart pounding with relief and gratitude, followed his friend through the french windows and down the drive before the astonished Himmelfarber could collect his wits.

'Thank God!' muttered Blanchaille. 'For a few moments I thought he had you. You see what he does to people, don't you? You see his own miners on the wall and how he's destroyed them. You think of the bright-eyed idealists who go to work for Consolidated Holdings in its Art-Deco palace in the capital with their new suits and their dreams of multi-racial progress. Of how they will become personnel officers and drive their new BMWs proudly home to the townships at night to show that they have succeeded in a white man's world because they work for kindly, liberal, rich, decent Curtis Christian Himmelfarber.'

'Think of his nephew,' said Kipsel.

Behind them C.C. Himmelfarber stood in the window screaming: 'Preachers! Prudes! Sermonisers! My God, if there's anyone worse than racists – it's people like you!'

'Of course we should never forget what Himmelfarber gets from this for dealing on behalf of the Regime,' said Kipsel, unexpectedly revealing how sure his grasp of the complexities of the mine-owner's position had been. 'What he gets out of it is increased clout with the Regime and he gets business put his way. Perhaps most important of all, he gets a number of channels for exporting his own funds abroad, currency regulations hold no fear for him, if they ever did. Since he's doing business abroad on behalf of the Regime, secret, valuable business, he can transfer as much capital abroad as he wishes. He can build up his interests in Europe and in America. Should he ever have to leave his native country he wouldn't have to pack more than a travelling bag. It's just another option, you see.'

'You know,' said Blanchaille as they neared the end of the drive, 'it's always the same with the Himmelfarbers. I suppose Julius, the founder of the whole firm, was all right. But C.C.'s great-grandfather, Julius Himmelfarber, kept on best terms with the Boers right throughout the war, kept supplying them with gold. And when the British marched into Johannesburg he was on best terms with them too. Now you have C.C. with his liberal politics and his Government contacts. He really does mean to destroy them. And if he does, he wins.'

'And if he doesn't?' Kipsel asked.

'He still wins.'

A grey Mercedes travelling at speed spat gravel at them as it raced up the drive. It carried Ernest Nokkles and Chris Dieweld, Emil Moolah and Koos Spahr.

'For a moment back there I thought Himmelfarber was getting through to you,' Blanchaille said.

'I suppose it's betrayal that sticks in my gullet. We're old-fashioned, Blanchie. That's why we're finished. We never got the point of it all. As true as God sometimes I think we knew about as little as Mickey the Poet. It's a joke, really.'

'Yes, I think it is a bit of a joke,' said Blanchaille sadly, recalling his lost love, remembering Miranda's words. 'I'm beginning to get it now. If it's any consolation, you can say you were betrayed by your enemies. Now the New Men can expect to be betrayed by their friends.'

Kipsel gave him a strange, twisted look. Blanchaille did not know whether he meant to laugh or cry. 'But, Blanchie, that's just it! The joke. There are no New Men.' Then he laughed. 'O.K. now where?'

Blanchaille remembered Lynch's last words, '. . . to the left and above the town . . .' but the beginning, as the girls at the Airport Palace had told him, was Clarens and the official Kruger house by the lakeside, preserved as a national monument by the Regime. 'Where Uncle Paul finished seems as good as a place as any to begin.'

Kipsel continually turned back to stare behind them, though Blanchaille implored him not to do so. Himmelfarber was best forgotten. He was even then presumably pouring punch for his new guests.

'The men in the Mercedes, Nokkles and others, who were following us,' Blanchaille said.

'I thought we'd lost them,' said Kipsel.

Blanchaille shook his head. 'People like that will always find their way to Himmelfarber.'

What proposition the mine-owner put to Nokkles and his colleagues can only be guessed at – whether they returned to work in South Africa on Himmelfarber's behalf, or remained abroad to look after the Swiss end of his operations, or were dispatched on secret missions to buy coffee plantations in Brazil, or weapons systems in Germany, or computers in Silicone Valley, or excavation equipment in Scotland on behalf of shadowy Panamanian companies, I cannot say. But having entered into Himmelfarber's employ, certainly it was the last that anyone ever saw of them.

CHAPTER 18

She stood upon a platform, dais, podium, rostrum, elevation of some kind, he could not tell precisely what it was, looking back, as if petrified by the bright light which hit her. Raised above her adoring public clamouring to touch her, she was surrounded by dignitaries who sat in gilt chairs in rows behind her on the stage. Of course she was not petrified. She was loving it! Smiling proudly, radiantly.

It took Kipsel a moment before he recognised her photograph in the French newspaper in the Café of The Three Poets, where they paused on the road to Clarens. (He did not know it then but she was in fact standing upon the stage of the newly-completed Opera House on the Campus of the University of National Christian Education which had so recently eaten up the defunct parish of Father Lynch.) That too he did not know. Nor did he know that at that same venue, some nights before, at the official opening of the Opera House with a production of *Madame Butterfly* in the presence of the new President, young Jan 'Bomber' Vollenhoven, terrible scenes had been witnessed when the famous soprano, Maisie van der Westhuizen, 'our Maisie', appearing in the title role, arrived on stage to find the front rows packed with orthodox Jews in yarmulkas waving placards reading SAY NO TO MAISIE'S NAZIS!, and she rushed from the stage in tears and disappeared forever. But that was another story.

In a stunningly low-cut evening gown with plaited shoulder straps, aglitter with diamonds, she wore a high choker around her neck, as well as some sort of ribbon and medal, an official military decoration pinned below her right breast. Her head was turned away from the camera, chin slightly raised and the frozen look was no more than a pose she had struck. And for what possible reason? Not vengeance, as with Lot's wife, who also looked back, but fame! And yet it could be said she stood so still, she seemed so studied in her stillness that she might have been stone, or a pillar of salt. Kipsel had the impression he was witnessing some tableau in which an actress impersonated a woman he knew, or had once known. Among her adoring audience were men in uniform, saluting. Others, in evening dress, were raising glasses to her in excited acclamation. The women present were wearing big picture hats

188

identifying them immediately as wives of Government ministers. They gazed in rapture at their heroine upon her raised platform and she half-turned graciously as if she had been on the point of leaving this gathering or reception or perhaps tumultuous welcome, or whatever it was, and stopped for a final wave, turned once again, perhaps to acknowledge the applause of the crowd and it was in this half-turn that the flash caught her.

Kipsel had found the newspaper rolled around a long stick in the cordial manner of continental cafés, and unfolded it idly as they sat among the remains of their excellent lunch, fillets of fera, a succulent fish found in Lake Geneva. The photograph was on the front page. Kipsel passed Blanchaille the newspaper and asked for a translation of the headline.

Blanchaille, barely able to contain his horrified astonishment, pointed out to his friend that although he descended from a Mauritian sailor and his mother had had high ambitions for him in the France she had never seen, although he carried a French passport, his knowledge of the language was elementary. None the less, after much muttering in a voice from which the tones of horror could not be eradicated, he stared at the headline: La Grande Espionne Sud-Africaine Rentre.

'Big, grand or great South African spy returns,' Blanchaille offered reluctantly.

'Returns?' said Kipsel wonderingly. 'That means she's been with them all along. It is Magdalena – isn't it?'

'I'm sorry, Ronnie.'

Inside the paper there were more pictures. They showed Magdalena's secret life in colour photographs. Here was a picture of her spymaster, Brigadier Jim Langman, taken in Magdalena's garden, Blanchaille announced after some deciphering. It showed the Brigadier in what appeared to be a uniform of his own making, a rather strange tan tunic with great big buttoned breast pockets and a collar of exceptional size. Brigadier Langman sat on the swing in the garden. The swing was painted lemon yellow. Langman wore black shoes and white socks which clashed noticeably with the tan uniform. He gazed soulfully out of the photograph, a round, fleshy face with soft, rather pouchy dark eyes with a glint to them that reminded Blanchaille of an ageing watchdog. Brigadier Langman's nose was large, veined, his moustache curved out and downwards from each nostril to bracket the corners of his mouth. What was the Brigadier doing, perched on the swing in this odd uniform? No matter. It made a startling photograph in what was an amazing series. Here was Magdalena taking the sun by her poolside. Here she was at pistol practice wearing ear-protectors, the tip of her tongue clenched between her teeth in an effort of concentration, her tailored jumpsuit covered in zips, her hair caught behind her head in a bow. Here was Magdalena in Red Square, white fur collar around her ears, the same photograph which hung on the wall in her flat. Here was Magdalena in a recently bombed refugee camp somewhere north of the border wearing military uniform, identification disc pinned to her chest, inspecting the damage following a South African air raid. Here was Magdalena with a group of black students in Mombasa, a row of grins and clenched fist salutes. Here was Magdalena arm-in-arm with Kaiser at an Azanian Liberation rally in Hyde Park and here she was again at a barbecue in a suburban garden in the company of a number of men whose very long shorts, bullet heads, stony eyes, the curious way the hair was shaved well above the ears and vigorously oiled, revealed them to be policemen. Here was a photograph of Magdalena's favourite weapon, a Beretta Parabellum which it seemed she now carried everywhere in a hand-tooled leather case. The reasons were clear, even with their limited French. The Front for the Liberation of Azania, enraged at its humiliating penetration, had sworn revenge. Its eradication squad, the mysterious Strike Kommando No. 3, had vowed to kill her. Here was a photograph of Magdalena attending the christening of the youngest child of Kaiser's cousin, in St Martin-in-the-Fields, where she had become the child's godmother. Was there no end to her capacity for deception? It seemed not.

Now I saw Kipsel struggle to an elbow and with glazed eyes begin to speak: 'Look, let's get this straight – I never set out to be what I am. Hell, no! I mean a guy starts off at home as a rugby player, most guys do, but if he's got more than a smidgen of brain someone comes along who tells him there's more to life than playing ball, there's politics which is just as dangerous, intellectually satisfying and pulls girls who start thinking about these things from an early age being more mature than boys. So before I knew it I was investigating the living conditions of our cook and pressing my old folks to increase her wages – and this while still at school, such is the pace of political development. At university, well, you find yourself leading a protest march on the police station, or picketing the profs for free medicals for black lab assistants, you go on marches, join demonstrations, engage in sit-ins and get arrested when failing to disperse after being ordered to do so by a police officer, but after a while it palls, or at least disenchantment sets in, you don't feel that you're really doing anything, you're simply not scoring, so you get active, you start a trade union for gardeners and you dream of becoming a para-medic in the starving homelands. Jesus! you even send for the home-tuition course and you run a literacy night-class for black taxi-drivers and *still* you don't feel you're connecting. I mean there's no one cheering in the stands and so you become desperate for action, and of course you're reading like mad, Marx and Dostoevsky and Gide and Fanon, and you suddenly realise that what is needed is the lonely gesture of self-affirmation, that freedom is to be seized in a single act, authentic existence must be deliberately chosen, so what do you do? You get a few guys together and form a secret revolutionary cell, that's me and J.J. Bliksem and Len Silberstein and Magdalena, but not Mickey the Poet, he was never in the cell, he was just roped in to drive because Silberstein's stupid bloody Volvo wouldn't start on the last morning of our campaign. Off we went, clutching our dynamite snitched from the explosives store of the gold mine where Silberstein's uncle was compound manager, and found some power pylons in the veld outside town. They had to be outside town because we didn't want to hurt anyone. We drew the line at casualties, hell we drew the line at everything you can think of! We wanted to make an impact but we didn't want blood, or maiming. I mean we were naïve middle-class people, we gave up our seats to old ladies on buses, so we weren't about to scatter arms and legs across the place. Silberstein laid the charges because he'd leant how to do it having been a sapper during his military service. I helped him. Back at the car Magdalena engaged Mickey the Poet in conversation and took him for a walk. Mickey said in court that she seduced him and I believe him. It was her usual response when conversation flagged, and that when the blast went off she told him these were the reverberations of his inner being. Mickey would believe anything. But I noticed that next night when we had to go off and blast the electrical pylons in the black township Mickey was unavailable to drive us and Silberstein had to borrow his father's car. We went to bomb the other pylons after a pretty heated argument. I said two was enough but Silberstein and Magdalena said it would expose us to a charge of racial division if we hit white stuff only. As the Regime decreed separate lavatories it was only right that we hit separate black pylons; anything else would look like crude anti-white prejudice. The next morning the police picked me up. They knew everything; they knew Silberstein's uncle, they knew how many sticks of dynamite, dammit they even knew poor Mickey's poem. They played me tapes of the fool Silberstein's telephone conversations. After we got back from the township bombing he spent hours phoning people around the country hinting at what we'd done, telling them to read the papers in the morning, like it was a picnic we'd been on, or a party. I didn't think to ask myself how they knew. I just knew they knew and I tried to save Magdalena. They locked me in a room upstairs at the police station with the curtains drawn with a Special Branch killer called Vuis. He hit me until I fell down. Then he kicked me. In those days they didn't bother to be subtle, no electrodes on the balls, no strangling with the wet towel. Fists and feet, drowning, doorways, steep stairs, high windows. They didn't care if the marks showed. Dammit, they *wanted* marks to show! That was one of the perks of being a security policeman, you got to hit people often. Tried to tell them that Mickey had nothing to do with the explosions, but they laughed. Told them not a syllable about Magdalena and they beat me some more. For interrupting! You see, they knew the lot! They didn't want my confession, true or not. They wanted to be left alone to go on with the beating. Arnoldus Vuis was also captain of the police hockey team; on his days off, he told me between punches, he played left back. It's funny what you remember when you're bleeding heavily and seeing double. We used electric detonators on the pylons. Silberstein read all about them, that's the useful thing about lawyers, they read. Captain Vuis knew about Silberstein's reading. He knew about things even I didn't know about, like the fact that it had been Looksmart Dladla who did the recce and supplied the map of the power pylons in the township. They slipped there, of course, because Looksmart happened to have been hauled in before the attacks on the electric pylons and when the dynamite went off he was being savagely beaten and had his head banged against the wall, so he could not have been present. His alibi was unshakeable. They had to release him temporarily and were about to pick him up when someone tipped him off and he skipped to Philadelphia. Anyway, I shopped myself and Silberstein, reckoning we were for the high jump anyway, but I said nothing about Magdalena and I defended Mickey as best I could.'

Here Kipsel broke down and began to stab Magdalena's picture with his fork and Blanchaille had to lead his friend from the café before the proprietor became too angry.

'I wasn't the traitor. Magdalena was with the Regime all the time. She set me up, and you. And even Kaiser. Christ! But Kaiser must feel sick.'

'So do I,' said Blanchaille, 'Magdalena was Apple One. It's so obvious it hurts.'

'Well,' said Kipsel, 'maybe at last we know something.'

'Maybe,' said Blanchaille.

But it wasn't much and it came too late.

CHAPTER 19

They wandered about in the general area of Clarens until they struck the little road set back from the lake and lined with large nineteenth-century villas, one of which they knew immediately from a hundred slides and photographs Father Lynch had shown them over the years. Then, too, there was the familiar flag flying from a first-floor balcony. It was growing dark, the sun was setting behind the further mountains lighting the clouds from below so they seemed not so much clouds as daubs of black and gold on the deepening blue of the sky. Even though there were lights in the upper storey of the house, the shutters on the lower floors were closed. The last of the tourists had departed. They would not gain entry until the following morning.

As it happened there were a number of garden chairs and a small, circular steel table at the bottom of a short flight of stairs which led from the front of the house into the garden. Here, though cold, they slept until some time after midnight when they were roughly awoken.

They knew him even though he wasn't wearing one of his Hawaiian shirts with the golden beaches, the coconut palms and the brilliant sunsets, even though he carried a revolver which he waved at them ordering them into the house.

Once inside, Blanchaille marvelled at his outfit. A raw silk suit extremely crumpled as if it had been slept in, no tie, shirt collar twisted, his laces undone as if he'd just shoved his feet into his shoes before coming outside and wafting off him good and strong were waves of liquor. He'd been drinking, drinking most of the night, Blanchaille guessed. He was aware of a hallway, the smell of polish, photographs on the walls, Kruger everywhere, and to his right a staircase which carried the large warning: *No Admittance to the Public*. At the top of the stairs stood a woman in a blue dressing-gown.

'What have you got there, Gus?' she asked grumpily.

They recognised her immediately, of course, that slightly imperious, dark, faintly hawk-like profile – those handsome rather beaky good looks, the eagle priestess, Secretary of the Department of Communications, Trudy Yssel.

'Oh Ernie Nokkles where are you now?' Kipsel whispered.

'Spies are what I've got here,' said the big wild man.

'Tourists,' Blanchaille countered.

'Normal times for that. Normal opening times. It's rare that pilgrims, whatever their fervour, camp in the grounds. Isn't that so, Trudy – isn't that so?' he appealed to the haughty figure in blue above them.

'I'd say, from the look of them, you've picked up a couple of bums, that's what I'd say. Who are you boys?'

They told her.

'Not *the* Kipsel?'

Kipsel sighed and admitted it.

'And I know you,' said Kuiker to Blanchaille. 'You used to be Father Theo of the Camps.'

'And you used to be Gus Kuiker, Minister of Parallel Equilibriums and Ethnic Autonomy.'

Above their heads Trudy Yssel laughed harshly. 'You really picked a couple of wise-guys this time. As if we don't have problems! When will you learn to leave well alone?' She spun on her heel.

'Come on, Trudy,' the Minister implored. 'Give a man a break. I caught 'em.'

But she was gone.

Another woman bustled along the corridor. Frizzy grey hair and a cross red face. She carried a broom and a pan. She looked at Kipsel and Blanchaille with horror. 'Now whom have you invited? I told the Minister that he can't have any more people here. This house isn't designed for guests, it's a museum. I'm sorry but they must go away, they can find a hotel, or a guest-house. The Minister must understand, we can't have no more people here.' She began sweeping the floor vigorously.

'I'm sorry, Mevrou Fritz, but you see, these aren't guests,' said Kuiker, 'These are prisoners.'

'Prisoners, guests, it's all the same to me. Where will the Minister put them? I keep trying to explain to the Minister. This house is not made for staying in. It's made for looking at. Every day at ten I open the doors and let the people in to look. They look, sign the visitors' book and leave.'

'I'll lock them in the cellar,' said Kuiker.

Kuiker took his prisoners down into the cellar, which turned out to be a warm and well-lit place built along the best Swiss lines to accommodate a family at the time of a nuclear blast and was

195

equipped with all conveniences, central heating, wash-lines, food and toilets. Kuiker producing a length of rope, ordered Blanchaille to tie Kipsel to the hot-water pipes and then did the same for Blanchaille, despite the complaints of Mevrou Fritz who pointed out, not unreasonably, that she would be extremely put off when she did her ironing by the sight of these two men trussed up like chickens, staring at her. Kuiker's response was to turn on her and bellow. His face turned purple, the veins stood out in his neck. Mevrou Fritz flung aside her broom and fled with a shriek.

Kuiker whispered rustily in Blanchaille's ear. 'Soon the house will be open to tourists. You will hear them passing overhead. Examining the relics, paying their respects to the memory of Uncle Paul. Make any attempt to get attention and you'll be dealt with. That's a promise.' And to prove it he struck Blanchaille across the face with his pistol.

They sat trussed like chickens all day. At one stage Mevrou Fritz came in and used the ironing table, complaining increasingly about their presence and of the trouble which the arrival of Gus Kuiker and Trudy Yssel had caused her. 'This is Government property. I'm here as a housekeeper, I see to it that the tourists don't break things or take things. I sell them postcards. I polish the floors. I dust the Kruger deathbed and I straighten the pictures. It is dull and lonely work, far from home and the last thing I expect is to have to share my extremely cramped quarters with a jumped-up little hussy who's too big for her boots and a Government minister on the run who spends most of the day drinking. And now I have prisoners in the cellar.'

Blanchaille and Kipsel were not fed. They were released from their chairs only to go to the lavatory and then only under Gus Kuiker's gun.

Later that night Trudy Yssel lay in bed. Down the corridor from the small spare bedroom they could hear the continual low grumblings of Mevrou Fritz now relegated to this little corner of the house, as if, she said, she were a bloody servant, or a skivvy.

Minister Gus Kuiker poured whisky into a tooth glass. Trudy Yssel looked at him. It was hard to believe that this unshaven drunk was the Minister confidently tipped to succeed President Bubé. But then she considered her own position. Despite the attempt to maintain appearances, the carefully groomed nails, the chiffon négligé, the impeccable hair, it was hard to believe that she was the Secretary of the Department of Communications.

'What do you recommend, Trudy?'

Trudy looked at him pityingly. 'Why ask me? You brought them in here. Now you deal with them. Why couldn't you have left them in the garden? Then they would have come in at the official time, with all the other tourists, looked around and left. None the wiser.'

'Maybe they're spies,' said Kuiker. 'Maybe the Regime sent them to find us.'

'Well, that doesn't matter now – does it? You've found them. They know who we are. Worse still, they know *where* we are. What's to be done?'

'Get rid of them, I suppose,' said Kuiker.

The blood had dried on Blanchaille's face and on the ropes that strapped him in. He blamed himself for not anticipating something like this. Kipsel was hard put to find anything to say that would cheer him up. When Kuiker arrived the general mood of gloom darkened still further. He pulled up a chair and sat opposite them, he swung his pistol around the finger guard in a manner so casual Kipsel would not have expected it in a police trainee. He was very drunk. His midnight blue dressing gown was monogrammed with a great G gulping down a smaller K. The stubble on his chin was longer and tinged with grey. His feet were bare and the pyjama trousers which protruded beyond his dressing-gown creased and rather grubby around the unhealthy whiteness of his ankles.

'Why are you here? Who sent you?' Kuiker demanded.

Blanchaille ignored him.

'If we'd known you were holed up here we'd never have come,' said Kipsel. 'Come to that – what are you doing here? The papers said you were in Philadelphia.'

'We were betrayed in Philadelphia. That black shit Looksmart dropped us in it. He and that oily priest bastard brother of his got together and destroyed us in America. Years of work wiped out in a few minutes. Our plans broadcast all over the bloody country. Now, at home, they've turned on us. We heard today that there are warrants out for our arrest, it seems that the Regime, desperate to find somebody to blame has settled on us. It is we, it seems, who have been rifling the treasury, absconding with public funds, hiring executive jets and wining and dining our way around the world, all for our own selfish ends. They are saying that we went abroad once too often and were seduced by foreign ways and luxuries. But they, *they* stayed at home, they are the only ones who remained pure. They will preserve racial amity, only they can withstand the Total Onslaught, they have never been corrupted. They are no longer pretending that we are in Philadelphia, they have officially announced that we are on the run and what's more the bastards have taken credit for making the announcement, for setting up an enquiry into the misuse of public funds, for the dismantling of the Department of Communications, they have resurrected the dead official, Ferreira, they have announced that this good and faithful official discovered the beginnings of this rotten business, as if small peculiarities in the movements of Government funds which we handled are worth twopence compared to the much larger, one could say total, distortion and perversion of reality the Regime has organised against us.'

'Do you know who killed Ferreira?'

'Who? You mean *what*! What killed Ferreira? I'll tell you what killed Ferreira. Curiosity killed Ferreira, and ignorance and the refusal to operate within the parameters of the practical. The mind of an accountant. The insistence on perfection, his own perfection. The stubborn desire to go by the book. His book. *His* books! The refusal to recognise that we were just proper people doing what we could to change things for the better, to win our country a place again in the world. To fight. And we had to fight because we were at war, see. And you can't behave like you're in a monastery garden when you're at war with the rest of the world. But ignorance and pig-headed fucking stubborness chiefly – that's what killed Ferreira. He wouldn't listen, he wouldn't learn, he wouldn't adapt. So he died.'

The Minister lurched forward waving his revolver and perhaps in his rage might have killed the prisoners had not Mevrou Fritz bustled in at that moment with a fresh pile of ironing and complained that the prisoners were beginning to smell.

'They'll stink a lot more when they're dead,' said Kuiker.

Kipsel kept perfectly calm. 'This place as such is of no importance to us, it's a shell, a ghost house. We only came here because it's the start of our mission. We're not fighting the war against you. We're looking for the other Kruger House, we're retiring.'

Kuiker made a sound, somewhere between a belch and a laugh. 'There is no safe house, no garden of refuge, no asylum, no home for the likes of you – or me. And shall I tell you how I know? For one very good reason. If there were such a place you can be damn sure I would have found it by now.' He swayed and almost fell, ran a hand through his hair, pounded himself several times on the chest and hawking phlegm turned abruptly on his heel they heard him clumping upstairs.

That night when Kuiker got into bed he said, 'There's no

persuading them. They're mad. I tried to explain this is the end of the road. This is where we turn and fight. But they seriously believe in some promised land. We'll have to finish with them.'

'Let me try,' said Trudy Yssel.

Early next morning she fetched the prisoners from the cellar. Blanchaille and Kipsel were unshaven and smelt badly and after days without food they were weak on their feet. But Trudy smiled at them as if she were taking them on a picnic. Before the first visitors arrived at Uncle Paul's House she wanted to take them on a little tour, she said. She wore a spotted blue dress with pearl ear-rings and was unnaturally cheerful, relaxed and chatted to them as if she might have been any houseproud wife showing off her establishment and not the mistress of a hunted Government minister with a price on his head and she the disgraced and vilified civil servant accused of spiriting away thousands upon thousands of public money.

'Don't you think, Father Blanchaille, that the tour is nowadays the chief way we now have of communicating information to busy people? We have a tour of the game reserve to learn about animals. We tour the townships to show our black people living in peace. We tour the operational areas of our border wars to discover how well we are doing. Talking of war, do you know I have toured forward areas where it felt as if the war had been turned off for the day, like a tap, or a radio broadcast, or a light. You expected when you got back to your tent at night to find a small note on your pillow saying –"The conflict has been suspended during your visit by the kind agreement of the forces concerned", but of course you knew that wasn't so when you heard of American senators caught in the bombing raid, or a group of nuns from one of the aid organisations like "Catholics Against Cuba", had been ripped to pieces by shrapnel. Follow me, gentlemen. Don't hang back.'

The place was kept spotless, a gleaming polished purity, it seemed to them that Mevrou Fritz must have caught the Swiss passion for cleanliness. It smelt of elbow grease, it smelt of floor wax. It was heavy, dark, depressing and virtually empty. Their footsteps echoed on the smooth boards. 'Of course none of the furniture remained when the old man died. It was sold off. The house now comes under the Department of Works and they've replaced what they can with copies, or pieces of the period. But it's still pretty bad. A bit of a tomb really. When the old man died his body was taken back to South Africa, again on a Dutch warship, and given a hero's burial. That was the end of his association with Switzerland. There was no money left here, the furniture was sold off, the house given up and any talk of the missing millions was simply a myth. And it remained, as General Smuts said, merely something "to spook the minds of great British statesmen". The time has come to stop talking of these dreams. We must wake up. We've been woken up, the Minister and I. We're considering our position. When we're ready we will move.'

'I think you're on the run,' said Blanchaille.

'You're in hiding,' said Kipsel. 'We read the papers.'

'Bullshit,' said Trudy pleasantly. 'This house is Government property. As Government people we're entitled to stay here.'

'You said you were getting ready. For what?' Blanchaille asked.

'Our President is expected shortly. Once he arrives we'll be in a position to put certain thoughts to our Government at home. We plan to hold talks with our Government.'

'What makes you think they'll talk to you?'

She smiled again. 'We would rather talk to them than to the world press.'

'Blackmail,' said Blanchaille.

'We won't be blamed for having done our duty. When we've cleared our name we shall return in triumph.'

'And until then?' Kipsel asked.

'We will wait here. In the Kruger House. You believe in the sad story of a rest home for the refugees the Old President set up. You should be the first to understand the use we put this place to. Uncle Paul would have understood.'

'You don't understand what has happened back home,' Kipsel said. 'They've dispensed with you. When Ferreira found the figures, publicised them and died, he blew the matter wide open. The Regime stepped away from its anointed Minister and his favourite. First they covered for you. But now they're joining the crowds calling for your blood. You should be going where we're going.'

'There is no place where you're going,' said Trudy. She led them into a small bedroom. 'This is Uncle Paul's death room. Here is the actual death bed. Well no, not the actual death bed, but a replica.'

They saw the dark wood of the bedstead. The sturdy head board, the starkly simple bulk of the bed with its white linen counterpane. On a small bedside table stood a vase of pink carnations. Thick green drapes in the window and fuzzy white net curtains strained the sunlight to a weak, pallid wash. A huge old-fashioned radiator stood in the corner and a large carved chair stood very prominently by the bedside. The seat and back of the chair were decorated in bold floral patterns and surmounted by crossed muzzle-loaders. This was a recurring emblem throughout the house, the Boerish equivalent of the fleur-de-lis. Other popular symbols about the house were powder horns, ox wagons and lions. Lions had always been associated with Uncle Paul. Hadn't he wrestled one to death before his thirteenth birthday? Or outrun one? And had he not been known as the Lion of the North? Or was it of the South? Blanchaille couldn't remember. All presidents had been identified with larger powerful beasts, or weapons. President Bubé had been known as Buffalo, or more colloquially as 'Buffels Bubé', while the young and thrusting Wim Vollenhoven, 'Bomber' Jan Vollenhoven as they called him, the Vice-President, continued the old tradition.

Trudy sat on the bed. Blanchaille was struck by the ease with which she committed this sacrilege. Here indeed was one of the new people. He pushed open the french windows and stepped on to the veranda where the flag gave its leathery rattle.

'Our belief, our brief, our mission was straightforward. In this matter of putting across our country's position we should attack. Fuck sitting on our arses any longer. Get out there and sell the bastards our bag of goodies. Don't try and win through to the big men overseas, spot the young ones in advance, pick them when they begin to come up the tree, and gamble. Don't expect the foreign newspapers to print nice stories about you, the only reason they like producing stories about you is because you're so horrible. So don't wait for them to tell your story, buy a space and tell it yourself. If possible buy the fucking newspaper, radio station, investors' bulletin, whatever. If that won't do then buy the owners lunch, dinner, drinks as often as possible, have them around to your place for confidential chats. If governments are against you, fly their MPs over, show them the game reserves, the war zones, the beer halls, peace in the townships. Play golf with them. Did you know we were the ones who got Bubé to play golf with the newspaper owners? We made him take lessons, even though he moaned like hell at the time. Well, today, they're saying back home that we stole the money for the golf clubs. They say it was Government money. Well of course it was bloody Government money! Where else would it come from? And what's more the Government knew it was Government money, because that was the deal. I said to them, I spoke to half the damn cabinet, that half of it which matters: Kuiker, the President himself, Vollenhoven and of course General Greaterman, the

Defence Minister. I said to them, look, I want permission to go ahead on a propaganda offensive. O.K. they said. Wait, I said, till I finish. It's going to cost a bomb. If I need to send an editor away with his mistress to Madeira, then I'll do it. If I have to bribe a newspaper editor, then I need the funds immediately. No questions asked. If I need to hire an executive jet to fly a party of journalists into the country via Caracas or Palm Springs or anywhere else on the globe, then I want the wherewithal to do it – without anybody raising an eyebrow. Bubé was there and he wanted to know how much this campaign would cost. I gave it to him straight. Millions, I said. He took it on the chin. I should start as soon as possible and the funds would be forthcoming. So I went ahead, and I stress this, with full official backing. And I've done so from that day to this. They all knew. President Bubé knew. Vollenhoven knew. Greaterman knew. And approved. The money was raised from various departments so as not to cause too great a dent in individual budgets. So much from Defence, so much from Security, so much from Tourism, everybody had to cough up their share and the money was then transferred to Switzerland and passed through various Swiss banks. And let me here say a word for the Swiss banks which have been bloody unfairly slandered. We have a great debt of gratitude to the Swiss banks. They have raised loans for us when nobody else would and we were damned hard up for foreign capital. They've safeguarded difficult deposits, overseen delicate payments and observed the strictest confidentiality in sensitive matters such as the volume of gold sales. To suggest that we bribe certain Swiss banks to hold secret funds is a gross lie. And a nonsense. They did it for nothing. Well, for a small holding percentage. And even there we get a discount from them. No, I won't hear a word said against the Swiss banks. Where would South Africa be today without them?'

'Why were you denounced then? Why have you made a run for it? Why are you hiding out here?' Kipsel demanded, scratching blearily at the thick stubble on his jaw, and shivering slightly in the early morning damp rising from the lake.

'We were fingered by the Regime! They were frightened to own up to a mission they had sanctioned. They wanted scapegoats.'

'And the story about the missing money, the Swiss accounts, the house in Capri, the apartment on the Italian Riviera?'

'The houses were part of the job, safe houses for our people, reception centres for new recruits, entertainment bases for important visiting VIPs who didn't want the world to know that they were spending the weekend with South Africans. The houses were used in the course of operations, they weren't holiday cottages, you know. As for the money we're supposed to hold – what money?'

Blanchaille looked out across the big green lawn to the lake. It was on this balcony the old man had sat, the Bible open on his knees, peering blearily across the water at the big blue mountains on the other side. The locals had paused, he knew, as they passed by and pointed up at the famous old exile, Uncle Paul on his balcony. The lake lapped at the bottom of the garden. The gulls made their skidding contact with the water, claws angled for the landing as if not knowing for certain where they were putting down until they had actually landed, distrustful of the medium. The old man had sat on his chair, solid as the mountains, deep as the lake. Perhaps he had seen and admired this tireless energy of the gulls, this compulsion to take off and land, but that energy always tempered by caution, their wildness calmed into life-preserving habit. Away to the right was the town of Montreux, it crowded down to the water's edge along a gentle crammed curve of densely packed buildings on the shore, pretending to be a small Mediterranean port. But here was no sea, this was still water, a great placid lake lying in the bowl of the mountains. Those mountains in the distance, the big blue ones across the water that he knew were in France, if one screwed up one's eyes and gazed blindly until they began to water, they were vaguely reminiscent of mountains in the Cape Peninsula. But of course the old refugee and his rented accommodation wouldn't have known the Cape mountains either, he'd seldom been out of the Transvaal veld until, that is, he began his great last journey into exile.

The flag-pole on the balcony was slanted at an angle of forty-five degrees and from it hung the familiar blue and white and orange colours. Very carefully Blanchaille lowered the flag to half-mast.

'Any more questions?' Trudy asked jumping up and smoothing the white coverlet on the death bed. 'Oh yes, I know – you're dying to ask me if I'm Gus Kuiker's mistress. So, then – do I sleep with Gus Kuiker?'

'No,' Kipsel protested weakly, 'we were not going to ask you that.'

'But I insist. Sleeping with Gus Kuiker means that once or twice a week he gets into bed beside me. I lie on my back and spread my legs. He puts a cushion under my backside because, he says, he doesn't get proper penetration otherwise, and then he pushes himself into me with some difficulty and moves up and down very fast because he gets penis wilt, you see. He can get it up but he can't keep it up. You can rub him, suck him, oil him. It doesn't help. While he's going he's O.K. The moment he stops, it drops. So about two minutes later, that's it. Overs cadovers. So much for sleeping with Gus Kuiker. He's also heavier now, sadder, he drinks almost all the time and he seldom shaves. But, as you say, we do indeed sleep together. Though I hope next time you use the phrase you will think hard about its implications.'

Back in the cellar Blanchaille was gloomier than ever. 'What if I'm wrong and the Kruger story ends with this house?'

'It doesn't.'

'But say it did.'

'No, dammit. I won't say it did! You know the story as well as I. This is just another stage on the journey which began in Pretoria, went on to Delagoa Bay, touched Europe and Marseilles, and then moved on to Tarascon, Avignon, Valence, Lyons, Mâcon and Dijon to Paris, as Uncle Paul travelled Europe to win support for the Boer cause. He pressed on to Charleroi, Namur and Liège, he called at Aachen and Cologne and Düsseldorf, Duisburg and Emmerich, and then he went on to Holland, stopping at over half a dozen cities before pitching up at the Hague. December 1901 saw him in Utrecht, nearly blind, 1902 he was in Menton for the warmth. He was in Hilversum in the following year and then back to Menton for the sun. Only in 1904 did he come here to Clarens, to this house which he did not buy, but rented from a M. Pierre Pirrot – some doubt has been cast on the existence of this man – notice the similarity between his name and the French pantomime character with the white face, Pierrot. The picture we have of the solidity of this house, of his living here in exile, of the near-blind old man in his last days looking out across Lake Geneva to the mountains, it all sounds like a drama, doesn't it? Or a tragedy? And it suits the people to give the legend weight and durability, to make it solid and believable. The bourgeois respectability of this house aids that delusion. But it's not a drama, or a tragedy. It's a pantomime! Everybody's dressed up, everyone's pretending. For instance, he wasn't here alone, Uncle Paul. His family was with him, his valet, his doctor, countless visitors called. And he was by no means finished either. He had his plans. The last act of the pantomime was not yet played out. And he had to hurry. He came here in mid-May of 1904 and by the end of July he was dead. But in those short months he was busy, sick as he was, planning a place for those whom he knew would come after. He knew that many of his people would collaborate with the enemy. But he also knew that some would hold out, escape, and would have to be accommodated. He wanted a place, an ark that should be made ready to receive the pure remnants of the *volk*.'

But a black passion had seized the ex-priest and he said stubbornly. 'Yes, but what if there is no such place?'

'Then,' said Kipsel, 'all I can do is to quote to you again the mad old Irish priest who knew a thing or two – if a last colony, home, hospice, refuge for white South Africans does not exist, then it will be necessary to start one.'

That night Trudy lay beneath Kuiker who was hissing and bubbling like a percolator and had his tongue clenched beneath his teeth in a frenzy of concentration as he entered her, trying to ensure that his erection lasted through the entry phase.

'I think,' said Trudy, 'that you are going to have to get rid of our guests.'

Kuiker did not reply. He had begun moving well and did not want to break his intense effort to remain upright and operational. Instead he shook his head, not to indicate his refusal, but to show her it was not the time to talk of these things.

'Now,' said Trudy, cruelly tightening her exceptional vaginal muscles.

Kuiker shrank, he fell out of her, he sat back on his haunches and said, 'Damn! That's lost it.'

'We can't hold them much longer, Augustus. Something is going to have to be done. They claim they don't care about us. They say they're above all this. But they might just give us away.'

But he was not interested. He considered his failed member. The brandy he had drunk had befuddled him and was making him very sleepy. He reckoned he had at least one chance to make it inside Trudy that night and he was going for it. Such determination, such single-mindedness had been the mark of his political success in the days when he was tipped as the next prime minister. Desperately he seized his penis and began rubbing it firmly. It stiffened perceptibly. There was no time to lose. With a grunt he pushed her back on the pillows, thrust his hands under her buttocks and rammed himself home.

'First thing in the morning,' he promised. 'Crack of dawn, I'll finish them.'

Downstairs in the cellar Kipsel was in a bad way. Trudy's knots cut so deeply into his wrists that the circulation had gone and try as he might to loosen the cord he only succeeded in cutting more deeply into the flesh and making his wrists bleed. He'd not been able to contain his bladder either and a pool of urine spread beneath the chair.

It was then that Blanchaille had a brainwave.

'Ronnie,' he said suddenly, jerking upright in his chair, 'Jesus what an idiot I am! I've been sitting here for days putting up with this crap and all the time I had a way out of here.'

Kipsel licked his lips weakly. 'Good. Only hurry, Blanchie.'

Sometime later Mevrou Fritz arrived with a pile of ironing. She grimaced at the sight of the urine and wrinkled her nose.

'Mevrou Fritz,' said Blanchille, 'do you get well paid?'

'Are you joking?' the concierge demanded. 'I work for the Department of Works, that's who this house comes under, through the Embassy in Berne, that's who I work for. I thought I told you. Do I get well paid? Bus drivers get better paid! Then there's my accommodation here, for free, so they dock the salary accordingly. Why?'

'What would you say if we disappeared?'

Her grey eyes stared into his unblinkingly. 'Hooray. That's two less to worry about, I'd say. This house isn't meant for people, you see. Not living people. At the moment I've got the attic full of guests, and you men in my cellar.'

'I think we can help you on both counts,' said Blanchaille.

A few minutes later they were on their feet and Mevrou Fritz was stroking the necklace threaded with Krugerrands with which Blanchaille had been presented in the Airport Palace Hotel by the beautiful Babybel – a key she had said which he would know how to use when the time came.

Mevrou Fritz took them to the front door but to the old woman's horror they would not go until they signed the visitors' book. Trembling she took them to the book and begged them to hurry before the big boss upstairs, as she called him, woke up and shot them all.

Very carefully, Kipsel wrote this message in the book: TO THOSE WHO COME AFTER US – BEWARE! THIS IS NOT THE HOLY PLACE YOU THINK. THIS IS THE HIDE-OUT OF ESCAPED MINISTER GUS KUIKER AND TRUDY YSSEL. THEY ARE LIVING RIGHT ABOVE YOUR HEADS. TELL OUR EMBASSY IN BERNE. YOU WILL BE RE-WARDED.

Blanchaille wrote simply: WHERE ARE THE KRUGER MILLIONS?

And then to Mevrou Fritz's intense relief the two fugitives slipped into the night.

CHAPTER 20

Now I saw in my dream how the travellers wandered the lakeside in the manner of those wild tribes who are said once to have populated the shores of Lake Geneva in Neolithic times. They looked, it must be said, no less savage being red-eyed from lack of sleep, tousled, dirty and smelling to high heaven.

It was fine weather all that day with the sky high and blue, full of rapidly scudding thick woollen clouds, and the shining freshness of the prospect increased the feelings of relief and freedom which Blanchaille and Kipsel enjoyed as they made their way along the lakeside towards the town of Montreux. Kipsel wanted to stop at an hotel to wash and eat a meal but Blanchaille allowed only a brief pause by the water's edge where they splashed themselves, dunked their faces, ran their fingers through their hair and Kipsel at last got rid of the strong ammoniac smell of the dried urine that clung to him. Blanchaille removed his underpants and threw them into the rubbish bin. This was after all Switzerland and the trim sparkle of the countryside insisted on respect. Nothing could persuade Kipsel to do likewise. 'I simply cannot walk about without underpants, it gives me the oddest, most uncomfortable sensation. Sorry, Blanchie, I know I pong a bit. Where to now?'

'Up into the mountains, above the town. Remember the readings from Kruger's book old Lynch gave us so often? Remember the story?'

And Blanchaille quoted exactly as he could remember, the passage from *Further Memoirs of a Boer President*:

'Travellers approaching their journey's end will find themselves as it were between heaven and heaven, one as deep as the other is high. They will think themselves close to Paradise, and they will be as close to it as faithful servants are permitted on this earth, for the country answers to the heavenly ideal in these several instances; to wit, it possesses elevation; it is a republic; it respects and honours the memory of John Calvin; and, not least, honesty prevailing over modesty requires the recognition that it has taken to its bosom this servant of his broken, scattered people, Stephanus Johannes Paulus

Kruger. That it is not the divine country itself but its reflection will be apparent to those who walk in its mountains and still lose their way. But help is at hand for those who seek their true homeland. Scouts will be posted by the camp kommandant as I did always when establishing a concealed *laager*, or Boer strong-point . . .'

'Between heaven and heaven, the book said,' Blanchaille pointed to the deep blue lake on their right and the bright sky above. 'I'm sure that's what he meant.'

'Scouts will be posted, I remember that.'

'Well, then, shall we start climbing? They'll be expecting us.'

'Bloody well hope so. You could wander in these mountains forever without a guide.'

Blanchaille surveyed the great blue lake, smooth as a dance floor. He saw the flat brown pebbles neatly packed beneath the clear surface, the brown ducks daintily dunking their heads, the roving sea-gulls, the sailing swans. At his feet miniature waves slapped tidily against the rocks. A few palms stood by the lake. Palms in this place! It cheered him faintly. Some sleek crows scavenged an old sweet packet and a sparrow carefully shadowed a gull and ate what it dropped. A duck dived and showed its purplish under-feathers, two swans pecked at each other viciously. The water of the lake began with pebbles and clarity at his feet and turned grey-blue under a gentle rippling surface and then still further out showed itself in pure grey slicks bounded by great shadows, flat and full it stretched into the mist of the further shore line where blue mountains reared; if he half closed his eyes they reminded him eerily of Africa. But this wasn't Africa: Africa was dead and gone for him. He was here now, and here he must keep his feet firmly planted. At his feet there floated a split cork from a wine bottle, several shredded tissues, a fragment of the *Herald Tribune*, a Pepsi-Cola can, several orange peels swimming in a bright school, wisps of swansdown, an old pencil, the filters of many cigarettes, and all the few small signs of life washed in by the tiny waves which arrived with gentle decorum. The lakeside was broken up by stone jetties and small coves and he noticed how cunningly the trees and shrubs had been introduced among the rocks: saw the ivy which crawled down to the waterside, the huge willow flanked by palms, those shrubs planted in pots and cunningly blended among the rocks, saw everything was arranged, everything cemented into place. The apparently haphazard grouping of rocks into natural stone piers and causeways was an illusion, he saw that they were actually propped with wooden stakes and iron bars beneath the surface. He could see the steel cables that held these structures in place. Everything was at once so natural and so skilfully arranged. Here was a country which lent itself to such paradoxes. Here, you felt, everything was allowed providing it could be properly arranged. A family, mother, father and two sons in a red paddle boat, with knees going like pistons, floated by. They waved. It was time to be getting on.

In Montreux they paused at a camping shop to buy two knapsacks which they filled with chocolate, bread and milk and a couple of bottles of cherry brandy – they also bought two stout walking-sticks, walking-boots and then struck into the mountains.

Here in this corner of French Switzerland they admired the clipped serenity of the countryside, its villages, vineyards, hotels and castles. They noted how well all things were accommodated, the way in which the country entered towns and villages in the form of carefully mown lawns and artful gardens, while the towns tiptoed into the countryside never disturbing the settled neatness. Here everything was made to fit but given the semblance of casualness. They passed orchards of heavily laden apple trees and burgeoning vineyards and had no qualms about raiding the fields of fruit, snatching apples and bunches of grapes as they went.

The road above the town of Montreux climbs steeply and soon leaves vineyards and orchards behind. The day was hot. They were soon pouring with sweat. The lake was now a long way below.

It was here, in the late afternoon, that they were met by four men wearing walking-boots, short leather trousers, thick red woollen socks and walking-sticks decorated with brightly coloured tin badges showing the coats of arms of all the cantons thereabouts.

The men said they were shepherds.

Kipsel rejected this and in fierce whispers told Blanchaille why: 'One, they don't have any sheep; two, they're carrying sticks and not crooks; three, this is cow country, you don't get sheep here; and four, they're countrymen of ours, right? Well, you don't get South African shepherds. I vote we be careful.'

Blanchaille secretly agreed. Something in the manner of these men reminded him of the policemen in their shiny orange mackintoshes who had stopped him on the road to the Airport Palace Hotel. Yes, he was fairly sure of it, their heavy and rather aggressive manner suggested representatives of the Force. Or at least ex-policemen, who were now going straight. But he confided none of this to Kipsel.

'Scouts have been posted,' he reminded his friend of the clues in the Kruger book. 'We can but hope.'

By way of breaking ice Blanchaille told the shepherds that they had helped themselves freely to grapes and apples and water from the streams along the route and he hoped that there was no objection. The shepherds replied that walkers had been coming this way for so many years and that some of them wandered for so long among the mountains that the owner of the big house to which they were bound, this was delicately put, had an understanding with the neighbouring farmers under which any of his people who came that way were free to help themselves from orchards and vineyards, in moderation of course, and providing no damage was done or camp fires lit, since the Swiss were a particular race and, like farmers everywhere, took a dim view of strangers tramping on their land. However, the procedure had worked well enough for many years and just as well for there were travellers who had come from great distances and who were tired and hungry and parched, not to say absolutely bushed and clapped out, by the time they got this far. And besides, the altitude got to one, if one was not used to it.

'Is this the road then to the big house?' Kipsel asked.

'Keep straight on,' came the answer. 'You can't miss it, set high on a hill in the last fold of this range of mountains, you'll know it when you see it.'

'How much further?' Blanchaille asked.

Here the shepherds were less forthcoming. 'Too far for some,' they said. 'Not everyone makes it. There are accidents.'

'What sort of accidents?'

'Climbing accidents. Heat-exhaustion in the summer. Cases of exposure in the winter,' said the shepherds. 'People arriving from Africa often underestimate the ferocity of the winter.'

Now I saw in my dream that the shepherds questioned them closely, asking exactly how they found this route, and how they'd come so far without maps, directions or luggage. But when they heard of Father Lynch, of the death of Ferreira, of the betrayal of Magdalena, they smiled and said, 'Welcome to Switzerland.'

The shepherds had fierce, flushed jaws, hard, cold eyes like washed river stones, hair blond and thick, necks thick too, and muscles everywhere. Their names were Arlow, Hattingh, Swanepoel and Dekker and they took the travellers to one of the travellers' huts which the thoughtful Swiss provide in the high mountains for those who need them. This they found well stocked with tinned food, a paraffin stove, blankets, bunks and all necessities, and here after a meal the travellers went to bed because it was

210

very late.

In the morning they rose and breakfasted on beans and bacon and although they had no razors and could not shave, there was running water so they enjoyed the wonderful luxury of a good wash. They breathed the clear mountain air and wondered at the fierce gleam of the rising sun on the snowy peaks of the distant Alps.

A little later the shepherds arrived and, taking Blanchaille and Kipsel back inside the hut, they drew the curtain and showed them slides on a small portable projector. 'We would just like to clear up a few points which may have been puzzling you boys,' they said. The first slide showed battle casualties fallen on some African battle-ground. The troops appeared to have been caught in some terrible bombardment, artillery perhaps or an air strike because they were hideously wounded, limbs had been torn away and there were many soldiers without heads. The soldiers, they noticed, were young, no more than boys.

Then Blanchaille said: 'What does this mean?'

And the so-called shepherds, who by this time had produced flasks of coffee and kirsch and were drinking heavily, replied: 'These are innocent boys who were called up to fight for their country and for Christian National civilisation and for the Regime and for God and for the right of all people of different races to be entitled to separate toilet facilities, which is the custom of that country, as well as for every family's rights to a second garden boy and for the freedom to swim from segregated beaches, and who now lie where they have fallen in the veld because on the day on which these pictures were taken the troops suffered a reverse and were forced to retire owing to the perfidy of the Americans who having persuaded the Regime to launch an invasion of an adjacent country then left them in the lurch and so these children lie here in the sun. What you see here is the death of a nation. Civilisations have died of old age, of decadence, of boredom, of neglect, but what you are seeing, for the first time, is a nation going to the wall for its belief in the sanctity of separate lavatories.'

'It is a tragedy,' Blanchaille said.

The shepherds nodded. 'And a farce,' they said.

Further slides showed the Kruger lakeside villa at Clarens they had so recently vacated. And the shepherds said, 'We wanted you to see crowds of deluded pilgrims visiting what they're told is Uncle Paul's last refuge abroad, though it was nothing more really than a stage prop. At the heart of their delusion is the belief that the

Regime is the true heir of Uncle Paul and will preserve the white man's place in Southern Africa forever. Whereas the poor sods are no more than tourists and the site they visit may be compared to an abandoned stage, or the deserted set of some old movie and the Regime of course is busy selling out everything and everyone in the service of the only reality it recognises, survival.'

In the pictures parties of the faithful arrived in coaches, flocking into the house with looks of awe and reverence. They wept when they saw the ugly bust of old Uncle Paul, they wept when they saw the death bed, they wept at the President's last message to his people, set in stained glass, encouraging them to look to the past, they admired the view from the balcony where the old man had sat, and they wrote of their feelings in the visitors' book. Examples of their messages were also shown in a variety of different colours of inks and hands: *Uncle Paul your dream is alive and well in South Africa*; *We will never surrender!*; *The Boer War goes on!* There were angry threats: *Kill the Rooineks* and *God Give Us More Machine Guns* and *We Will Die on the Beaches*; as well as more frivolous slogans such as *Vrystaat!* and *Koos Loves Sannie . . .*

At this point in the proceedings the shepherds, having become rather drunk on the large quantities of kirsch consumed during the slide show, withdrew to relieve themselves at a discreet distance from the hut and Blanchaille and Kipsel met each other's eyes and blushed to think that even they, who should have known better, had been unable to resist a visit to this empty shell of a house and had paid dearly for their foolishness by spending days under the whip of Gus Kuiker and his paramour.

Kipsel, perhaps to deflect attention from that humiliating episode, again expressed his suspicion of the so-called shepherds. And despite Blanchaille's attempts to dissuade him he met the four men on their return with these words:

'I don't believe you're shepherds at all. I've got a feeling for these things and I think you're policemen.'

And Swanepoel replied: 'If you're talking about what we were, you may have a point. But if we were all judged by what used to be then who would not be damned? Weren't you Kipsel the Traitor, once? The only thing that matters is what we are now.'

'And we're shepherds now,' said Dekker.

'Oh yes?' exlaimed Kipsel. 'In that case where are your sheep?'

'You are our sheep,' came the reply.

Blanchaille stepped in to prevent further embarrassment and told the shepherds that they were eager to continue their journey. Then the shepherd Arlow said to the shepherd Hattingh, 'Look, since these guys are on the right road wouldn't it be an idea to give them an indication of their destination?' And Hattingh agreed, so they stopped at a typical mountain hostelry, perched on a promontory and called the Berghaus Grappe d'Or with a wonderful view of the mountains, where there was a telescope, as is the custom in such places. And here, after the insertion of one franc, they were invited to 'lay an eye against the glass'.

What they saw differed considerably. Blanchaille said he could see what he thought was a big house surrounded by a wall and it reminded him of a hospital, or perhaps a school. Kipsel said he could see no wall at all, but he made out a gate, a garden and many tall trees and a tall building 'like a skinny palace'. Then their time ran out.

Would the shepherds give them more precise directions?

'Keep on the way you're going and you can't miss it,' said Arlow.

'Look out for Gabriel,' Swanepoel advised.

'Our Gabriel?' Blanchaille was astonished.

'Ain't no bloody angel, that's for sure,' said Hattingh.

And the shepherd Dekker said nothing at all, just laid a finger alongside his nose, and winked.

CHAPTER 21

On that hot, never-ending Sunday beneath the Tree of Heaven, among the wreckage of Father Lynch's church, while the baleful yellow earth-moving machines baked in the heat, I slept again and dreamed of the two travellers, gipsy spirits one would have liked to have said, carefree, happy voyagers – except that they looked in fact like two increasingly tired, dirty, bearded and hungry men (a two-legged pear and his lightly furred friend), trudging through the Swiss mountains towards they knew not what – some great house or palace, or castle, château, hotel, hospital which they had glimpsed, or thought they had glimpsed through the telescope of Berghaus Grappe d'Or; some retirement home, or refuge, or whatever it is where white South Africans must one day fetch up, if they are to fetch up anywhere. What is the old joke? When good South Africans die they go to the big location in the sky. When bad South Africans die they go into government.

I saw how, as the climb grew steeper, the road winds back on itself to lessen the upward slog and gives a clear view behind and below. It was then that they saw another traveller straggling behind them in a queer sideways crab-like shuffle. Imagine their astonishment as he drew closer and they recognised Looksmart Dladla, last heard of in exile in Philadelphia.

Their old friend was smartly turned out in a dark blue suit and shining black shoes, quite unsuitable for the rough road he followed and he stopped every so often and knocked his forehead with his fist as if it were a door and he wished to be let in, or at least attract the attention of whoever was inside. He gave no sign of surprise, or of recognition, but Kipsel, all his old fears and guilt returning, had become terrified and had quite unashamedly hidden behind Blanchaille.

'Looksmart! What, you here? Hello, it's me, Blanchie!'

The black man peered. There was no surprise, no anger, not even a quickening of interest, merely a blank cursory inspection. 'I do not remember.'

'You must remember the old days.'

'Why?' Looksmart asked.

214

Kipsel, now bolder, stepped forward: 'Well, you remember me.'

Looksmart stared at him. Perhaps his eyes narrowed fractionally. But then his head was continually cocked to one side and he appeared to suffer from a facial tic.

Blanchaille seized his hand. 'For God's sake, Looksmart – it's Blanchie. How are you? I thought you were in Philadelphia.'

There was a slow nod of the head. 'Yes. I was in Philadelphia.' He spoke very slowly, as if searching for the words, rounding them up like wild ponies from the canyons inside his head. He spoke thickly, clumsily, with little whistles and splutters. It seemed there was something vaguely familiar about the two men who had stopped him, especially the one with the fish face, the thick lips and the agitated manner. He hadn't time now. He took a red handkerchief from his breast pocket, bent and polished his black shoes. Then he straightened. 'Goodbye,' he said. 'People are waiting for my news.'

What happened to Looksmart before and after his flight to America has been the stuff of wild rumour, legend and conflicting stories. But it was given to me in my dream to see the truth.

Looksmart escaped to New York on a ticket acquired by his brother Gabriel (as was his passport, US visa, and a pocket full of money), a step ahead of the police and unbeknown to himself, in the company of the famous Piatikus Lenski, the defence lawyer. This flight was ever afterwards regarded as having been *planned*. People marvelled at its audacity and gave credit for its brilliant execution to Gabriel Dladla. Gabriel Dladla, everyone agreed, was an absolute marvel. On the one hand he was a priest and so forbidden to take part in politics. On the other hand he was known to be openly sympathetic to the Azanian Liberation Front. Yet he continued a free man. In fact his political sympathies and connections, far from endangering Gabriel, increasingly won him admiration and respect. It was whispered in some quarters that if ever, and it was a big if, the Government were to attempt some form of dialogue with its sworn enemies in the Azanian Liberation Front, then Dladla might be the man to talk to, and through; there was widespread agreement that Dladla was the sort of man with whom one could 'deal'. Of course the official view was that there was absolutely no question of dialogue, or of dealing with the ALF and its murderous terrorist wing, the Azanian Strike Kommando No. 3. Even so, people felt obscurely comforted by the knowledge that if, and it was an enormous if (everybody always stressed this), the need should ever arise and the Regime should wish to talk to the Front, Gabriel was the man. The Regime were careful to discourage any such speculation. Bubé himself had given the official response, when, in the course of a particularly strident political meeting, he had responded to the repeated jibe of 'Yes – but what *if*?', with the remark that people could believe what they liked and the Regime could not stop people believing in fairy stories – but, speaking for himself, *IF* was a dangerous country which he did not visit. Everyone knew what he meant.

The famous defence lawyer, Piatikus Lenski, was equally unaware of Looksmart's presence – but the two were forever afterwards associated in the public mind. Thus do haphazard conjunctions become established as historical facts in the story of our country. Lenski had made his reputation in the trials of such notables as the saintly pacifist leader, Oscar Amandla and the martyr, Joyce Naidoo. Lenski's reputation stretched from the great show trials of the anti-pass laws demonstrators of the early years to the increasingly frequent hanging trials of black guerrillas which more and more occupied the courts as time went on. Piatikus Lenski defended his clients with passion and brilliance. He invariably lost the case but this never affected his reputation as a formidable opponent of the Regime. He was, as he himself said, if one was to judge by results, a complete failure. He never accused the judiciary of any bias. The judges, Lenski had said, were quite objective in their interpretation of the law but since the Regime was thoroughly perverted, corrupt lawgivers and objective judges made an unbeatable combination. He was a short, curly haired, vain little man with dark eyes and a high querulous voice which drove court officials to distraction and struck fear into the witnesses for the State. Nothing scared Lenski. When the prosecution scored a point he would turn to his junior and in his high, carrying tones exclaim: 'Now *that* was well done. But do we care?' He'd been terrorised by the usual methods applied to public opponents of the Regime. His house had been shot at, his children threatened, his wife abused – and he had yielded to none of it. Instead he gave an interview to the papers explaining how these efforts ensured that he would never falter in his appreciation of the lengths the Regime was prepared to go in order to get its way. Finally, Piatikus was placed under house arrest for 'associating with known terrorists and violent opponents of the State'. The Government thus found in his connection with his clients an unanswerable logical reason for banning him. And in so doing they had at last done really well, and even Lenski had to admit it, and did, by showing that yes, finally, they had made him care, for

216

when the police arrived with the signed order of his banning at his gracious residence in the northern suburbs, Piatikus had fled.

On board the Pan Am flight to New York, Looksmart knew nothing of his illustrious travelling companion. He'd never flown before, he had got into conversation with the passengers, he was rather drunk, and the recent beating he had received had left him in a disturbed and agitated frame of mind. Besides, Lenski travelled first class, behind a beard and dark glasses, and his presence on the plane only came to light when they arrived at Kennedy Airport and the press thronged the concourse. Lenski left the airport immediately after the press conference for a secret destination in Colorado where he went to work on his memoir of the most celebrated of his deceased clients. Called *The Last Days of Oscar Amandla*, it was to become a minor classic. The American press, and through them the wider world, concluded that this eminent lawyer and the black activist must have escaped together. That was the impression Piatikus never chose to correct and Looksmart was never asked to do so. Not that it mattered for he was so incoherent with his rasping voice and the terrible roaring in his right ear since the cell beatings that he would have been unable to convince them otherwise.

Looksmart had left the country abruptly. His brother had collected him and taken him to the airport in a great big black Chrysler. Looksmart had tried to get some information: 'How –' he began.

'How did I get you the passport? These things can be done, my dear Looksmart. Of course your visa only gives you three months. You'll have to think of something else by then.'

'Yes, but how –' Looksmart tried again. His tongue sat wooden in his mouth, sluggish, thick and unable to respond to signals from his brain. 'But . . . how?' It wasn't quite what he had wanted to say, but it would have to do.

Gabriel said, 'How what? How did I do it? Please, give your brother some credit.'

'How?' asked Looksmart again.

'Forget it,' snapped Gabriel. 'Better you don't know.'

Here Looksmart wept. He didn't mean to weep but it had become an uncontrollable response after weeks of interrogation. Anyone raising their voice to him got that response from the tear ducts. There was a furnace in his right ear and a subterranean rumble which reminded him of the rockfalls on the gold mines which from time to time shook the city and set the cups complaining on the shelves and windows shivering in their panes.

He paused at the barrier at the airport and waved. Gabriel raised an encouraging thumb. Looksmart squared his shoulders and shuffled through fully expecting to be stopped and turned back but feeling in the face of Gabriel's efforts that he ought at least go through the motions, if only to please his brother.

Gabriel had this gift of making people want to please him. He had a honeyed charm, a lightness, a fleet delicate mind, he was little, gracious, winning, not at all dark but golden. There had always been this contrast with his brother ever since their days in Lynch's garden when he called them his greyhounds, his porcelain slave boys, his unlikely pages. Gabriel was deft and surefooted, Looksmart was heavy, solid mahogany, his lips pink and full as inflatables, a lump beside Gabriel's vaulting allure. Gabriel forged ahead effortlessly in the seminary towards ordination and a brilliant career while Looksmart stumbled and floundered in a bog of black theology, making passionate speeches about 'The first Kaffir Christ', and burning his Bible on the seminary steps as the white man's bank book, and thereafter departing in a kind of glory.

'My vocation,' Gabriel sweetly told friends, 'is the priesthood. Looksmart's is prison.'

Indeed it was. Looksmart proceeded there by the usual route: demonstrations, marches, plots, arrests and bannings and all the blood-warming activities which opponents of the Regime practised in the hope that somehow, someday, they might have some effect. At last grey and despondent he went underground and dreamed of bombs.

When Kipsel's bombs went off he would have been a prime suspect had he not had a cast-iron alibi. He was already in prison at the time, in the cells of the Central Police Station being beaten with a length of hosepipe by a blond young man called Captain Breek, that very same Arrie Breek who was later to become so close to wresting the world middleweight boxing crown from the American Ernie Smarf in their memorable encounter in the amazing amphitheatre hewn from solid rock in a newly independent black homeland cum casino, run by the Syrian entrepreneur Assad, before a ferocious crowd of 75,000. As Breek later told the papers, his heart had never been in his police work and this may explain why the young man with his great blond cows-lick and the open fresh looks of a serious young accountant should have so forgotten himself during the interrogation of Looksmart that he seized the prisoner's head and banged it repeatedly against the wall, a method as clumsy as it was inadvisable, since it broke the cardinal rule of police interrogation which is never to leave discernible marks on a live victim and on a dead one only such marks, bruises, lesions, or breakages as would accord with the kinds of fatal injuries the coroner could reasonably expect to find on a dead prisoner who has fallen from a high window, or down a steep flight of stairs, or has hanged himself in his cell.

This Breek was to go on to become a famous entrepreneur and promoter himself, with his own casino and his own homeland and his own international pro-am golf tournament.

Looksmart had been stretched to his limits by Captain Breek. There had been electric shocks to his testicles and when this failed, the current was passed from his nape to his coccyx to render him more pliable. Then he was taken swimming. In this procedure his head was dunked in a bucket of water for a period determined by the swimmer who could obtain release before he drowned by tapping the floor with his foot thereby indicating that he wished to talk.

His lungs burning, Looksmart tapped. Breek hauled him out. Looksmart took a few, deliberately deep breaths while Breek waited impatiently. 'I forget the question,' Looksmart confessed. It was true, although even if he could have recalled it he couldn't have answered. He did not know what Breek wanted, but then neither did the policeman. He kept demanding that Looksmart tell him all he knew. He swore that he would get at the truth. But what he wanted to know, and what he imagined the truth to be, he never made clear and Looksmart found it impossible to guess. Looksmart's tears mingled unnoticed with the water streaming from his nose and ears. Angrily Breek seized his hair and plunged his head back into the pail. Looksmart prepared to die. He would not tap. He waited for unconsciousness. He welcomed death. Deliberately he thrust his head further into the pail. His chest felt as if it were collapsing, he felt the terrible burning pressure grow. He could hear his heart firing away crazily. Just another few seconds, another few moments and he would open his mouth and suck water into his lungs. He would cheat Breek. He would die in front of his eyes. Breek realised almost too late what was going on. Furiously he yanked Looksmart's head from the pail and in his rage began banging it against the wall until Looksmart passed out.

The next day he was released, his head swathed in bandages, an eye closed, an intense burning feeling in his right ear, a deep rumbling groan deep in the eardrum together with a rather strange inertia of the tongue which simply wouldn't obey him, baulked at even easy words, no matter how he whipped it up to them, refused like a horse at a jump. He was recovering in Gabriel's house when the police came and asked about the bombings of the electricity pylons.

'He was in jail. How could he be involved?' Gabriel asked them.

The police went away.

The papers headlined the story. LUCKY LOOKSMART! 'JAIL ALIBI'.

The next day Gabriel suddenly said he must leave. He had heard that the police were coming back. That they were definitely after him even now, whether or not he had been in jail at the time of the bombing. They had other reasons for looking for him. He must skip the country.

'How do you know they won't arrest me as soon as I show them my passport?' That had been the question he had wanted to ask Gabriel. After all if the police were looking for them, then the airport officials would know and would turn him back.

But they did not. His passport was cursorily checked and he was waved through. An hour later he was airborne over the baked brown veld of Africa. This was even more puzzling still. For if the police wanted him they would have been watching the airport. Since they weren't, he had to conclude that they were not looking for him yet. Was it not a miraculous sign of Gabriel's power and prescience that he had known that the police would be looking for him before the police knew themselves? Thus Looksmart was long gone when the police issued a warrant for his arrest, citing information supplied which revealed that he had a hand in the maps showing the locations of the electrical pylons in the townships destroyed by Kipsel, Zandrotti and others.

DOUBLE BREAK FOR FREEDOM, the papers said. DLADLA – LENSKI, FLEE COUNTRY!

Now he stood on that Swiss mountainside did Looksmart Dladla, in his blue suit and black shoes and his odd mode of sideways locomotion, and his odder cranial rumblings, insanely beaming, turning on them a look Blanchaille later described as one of radiant ignorance. Had Blanchaille not seen examples of such deluded sweetness of temperament many times before during his years in the camps in old men and women who after their sufferings should have been eaten with rage and bitterness, he might have wept. Instead he turned patiently to Looksmart and asked about his time in America.

Looksmart beamed. 'In America I began as a humble student of history and rose to become president of several radio stations, a news magazine and a cable television station.'

'America is still the land of opportunity, then?' said Blanchaille politely, without the least sign of surprise at Looksmart's meteoric rise.

'Oah yes,' said Looksmart with another series of rapid smacks of the head as if to keep his word-hoard flexible. 'But it was never ambition that took me to these positions.'

'What then?' demanded Kipsel sceptically.

Again the seraphic smile. 'Patriotism. Oah yes! Without a doubt. I am part of the new order. Now I really must go. As you can see, I walk slowly. The result of an old injury. Now forgotten. And forgiven. I must give the good news.'

'What is the good news?' Blanchaille asked.

Looksmart produced a piece of paper from his suit pocket and waved it. 'We are saved. I have here a treaty signed by the President himself granting to me and my dependants a territory on the east coast of Southern Africa, in *perpetuity*.' He stressed this word with reverence.

'You're going home?' said Blanchaille. 'But, Looksmart, you're a wanted man.'

The other laughed delightedly. 'We are all wanted men. We are needed to rebuild our country again. What good does it do to hide in some mountain lair, some hospice, some institution set up on Boer charity for lonely exiles, frightened of their shadows? We must reinvent our country. Set out like Van Riebeeck in reverse to rediscover South Africa.'

'The only territory they'll give you back home is six feet deep,' said Kipsel.

Looksmart gave him a look which though no less joyous was tinged with pity and a hint of scorn. 'As his nephew wrote of the late great Benjamin Franklin, so with Looksmart, believe you me. "My resolution is unshaken, my principles fixed, even in death." ' – and he banged himself on the right ear for emphasis. 'We have been given our African Pennsylvania, in which we will found our new Philadelphia, a city of brotherly love, and from that perhaps we shall make a new Africa, a revolution like that of the Americans, a triumph of sensible, pragmatic, independent people. They did it. So will we.'

'We already have a Philadelphia,' said Kipsel. 'And plenty of Pennsylvanias. Only we call them Homelands and Bantustans, Tribal Reserves and Resettlement Camps . . . We tried it, Looksmart, and it didn't work. And we don't have any sensible people.

221

Never mind pragmatic ones. Looksmart, don't go back!'

'I have it in writing,' repeated Looksmart waving the paper again. 'It has been promised to me in exchange. Now you must not delay me, I am on my way to the place on the hill to convey the good news. Step aside if you will. This is the freedom route. They will cheer when they see me. "Come home with Looksmart," I will say. Permit me to give you a small memento of our meeting.' He handed them a coloured postcard showing a big brass bell with a crack in it. 'The famous Liberty Bell. I have seen it with my own eyes. Soon we will have one of our own hanging in our country.' And with a cheerful wave, the black man set off on his slow, shambling progress.

They watched him helplessly.

'Bell's not the only thing that will hang back home,' said Kipsel. 'Tell me, Blanchie, what is this new order he muttered about?'

Blanchaille remembered his meeting with Van Vuuren in Balthazar Buildings and the pathetic outcasts in the holding cells. 'The New Order is actually the old order, adapted. Under the old order they refused to compromise. Under the New Order there is nothing they won't compromise.'

And thinking these things over in their minds they walked on, soon overtaking Looksmart who moved at half their pace, boxing his ears, muttering and stopping to polish his shoes, but he showed no sign of recognition and they had soon left him far behind.

CHAPTER 22

Now I saw how our pilgrims, climbing ever higher, came suddenly upon a party of police manhandling a captive by the roadside. The prisoner was a plump, elderly tramp in handcuffs who must have been hiding out in the countryside for some time because he was very dirty and even more thickly bearded than Blanchaille and Kipsel. He was very frightened and kept crying that he was a diplomat of the highest standing and entitled to immunity according to all known protocols. The police, while not dealing with him harshly, bore him relentlessly towards a waiting police car. Despite the dirt, the beard, the matted, filthy hair, the travellers knew him immediately.

Blanchaille asked permission to speak to the prisoner and the Swiss police turned out to be perfectly amiable despite their appearance, for they wore rather a menacing grey uniform and carried large pistols in their belts. Perhaps it wasn't too surprising that Kipsel shrank back when one considered his dealings with policemen but I saw that it was the prisoner himself who most disturbed him, sending him scuttling for cover. Later, he was to claim that the need to relieve himself had carried him behind some large roadside boulders, but I think we know better. The wretched fugitive in the hands of the Swiss police was none other than Adolph Bubé.

Here perhaps it is fitting for me to pay tribute to the humanity and innate democratic sensibility of these Swiss officers who must have been hard put to distinguish between the large tramp who approached them and the hysterical hobo they had taken into custody. Perhaps they were influenced by their long experience in administering the Red Cross, as well as the admirable ideals enshrined in the Geneva Convention for the treatment of prisoners of war. In any event, the officer in charge granted Blanchaille's request for a few words in private with the prisoner and he and his men withdrew to their vehicles and occupied themselves by polishing windscreens and clearing the roadside verges of unsightly weeds and performing various other useful activities.

I saw in my dream an astonishing sight. The ex-priest and the former President cloistered at the side of the road in the attitude of a father-confessor and penitent, while Kipsel hid from sight and the Swiss police tidied up the landscape. In hoarse whispers Bubé made his confession while Blanchaille listened gravely, nodding at times and comforting the old man when grief overcame him. An odd couple, to be sure, but both men were experiencing the painful dislocation of reality which had pitched them onto this Swiss mountain and so felt a curious kinship and Blanchaille listened with every sympathy, stirring only to offer his handkerchief when the tears became a flood and once intervening to restrain the old man when he attempted to dash his head against a rock. And on another occasion, he drew something in the sand with his finger and the old man beat his breast and called on God to forgive him.

When at length they finished I saw Blanchaille lead the prisoner over to the police. And as he turned I saw, as did Kipsel, now bold enough to peer over the boulders, a sign on his back which read A. BUBI.

As the police car disappeared down the mountain road Blanchaille returned to Kipsel and told him the amazing saga of that unlikely renegade, former President Adolph Gerhardus Bubé.

'He's in serious trouble. He has committed the gravest offence this country recognises –'

'Wait, don't tell me,' said Kipsel raising his hand. 'He's broken financial regulations.'

Blanchaille nodded. 'Yes, but it's worse than that –'

'It's something to do with the missing millions, isn't it? The money Ferreira was looking for, the discrepancies in the books? The money he sent here?'

Blanchaille had to smile at his friend's naïvety. 'Heavens, Ronnie, that's no crime! Not here. It's widely expected that the heads of various regimes should squirrel away large sums in Swiss accounts against a rainy day, the sudden coup that will pitch them into exile, or just for insurance. Hell, no, the Swiss don't get offended about that. They consider it quite natural that foreign regimes should screw their people, empty the banks, siphon off the aid cheques into secret accounts in Geneva and Zurich. African regimes especially. And to them Bubé is just another African. No, what the Swiss have set their faces firmly against is anybody diddling the Swiss.'

Kipsel blew harshly between his teeth. 'Wowee!'

'Precisely,' said Blanchaille, 'though "Wowee!" hardly covers the complexities involved. It has to do with gold sales. We might have guessed that. You remember Himmelfarber telling us about the switch from the London gold market to Zurich in what he called the gilded days? Well Bubé was largely responsible for the move. And the Swiss bullion dealers were impressed. Some of his best friends were bullion dealers and they were very grateful to get our gold. Some of them were very grateful before they got our gold and showed their gratitude. As we say back home, they "thanked" the Minister.

'But when gold sales returned to the London market the love went out of Bubé's relationship with the dealers. It did no good to explain that it was the Swiss Government's fault for imposing the sales tax, thereby forcing the dealers to show their volumes of sales and upsetting our other friends, the Russians. As far as the dealers were concerned, one moment they had all the gold and the next moment they didn't. They insist Bubé gave them to believe that South African gold was here in Switzerland to stay. They feel aggrieved. And behind the dealers are the banks. Because of course they lent the money to the dealers. And as that pleasant young police officer from the Commercial Division of the Swiss police told me back there – in Switzerland when the banks speak the cantons tremble. The banks are very bitter. After all, they argue – who was it who arranged loans and credits to the Regime when no one else would touch them?'

'Then the stories about the President are true?' Kipsel asked. 'He has money stashed away?'

'Quite a lot. Perhaps as much as twenty million. Perhaps more. Bubé himself isn't sure.'

'That's a fortune!'

'That what I said. Bubé became pretty peevish. "You don't plan for a government-in-exile on peanuts," he said. "It's not like arranging a skiing trip." It's this money that is the subject of the dispute. The bullion dealers claim that it was amassed using their contributions, their commissions, so they're laying claim to it. Meanwhile the Regime, having got wind of it, is also after the money. They say it belongs to them having been improperly acquired. Bubé says he's sick to death of this nonsense. He says that there have long been plans to establish a government-in-exile should the Regime fall. It was, as Himmelfarber told us, just one of the options. Various South American countries have been selected. as suitable where of course there are communities of the many descendants of those Boer exiles who originally fled to South America after the Boer War. Bubé referred to this money as a contingency fund. A hedge against the day when, like it or not, the Regime may have to transfer to Paraguay or Bolivia. What's more he says that everybody in the inner ring of the Cabinet has known of this fund for years, approved of it, encouraged it. Yet when he arrived in Switzerland he found the Regime was denouncing him for fraud. They were demanding his extradition – with all the money. And the Swiss bullion dealers are demanding that what they call "earlier undertakings" must be honoured and the banks are talking menacingly of this insult to the soul of the nation; this cancer in the body of the Helvetian State – this is dangerous stuff because the banks are to Switzerland what I suppose the Roman Curia is to the Vatican, director and guardians of the faith . . . Bubé's alleged crime is not only that he has injured Swiss banks, but by turning up in person on Swiss soil he has added insult to injury. Not only are they determined to get their money back, but they want to make an example of him. I expect he will be paraded in the market squares of all the towns between here and Geneva.'

Kipsel understood. 'Hence the notice.'

'Right.'

'I've got little sympathy for him,' Kipsel commented. 'But I wonder how firm their evidence is when they can't even spell his name.'

'It's very common in the German-speaking cantons of Switzerland to find names ending in "*i*" – Matti, Jutti and so on. That young policeman's name was Mitti. They've spelt it the way they heard it – BUBI.'

'How come you know so much about the Swiss arrangements, Blanchie?'

'Well, I was incarcerated for some time with a wild Swiss priest back at home. His name was Wüli. There's a case in point. Wüli had often been arrested in Switzerland and he was something of an expert on the subject.'

'What was he doing in South Africa?'

'Much the same sort of thing. Getting arrested. He had an overwhelming desire to expose his genitals to unsuspecting civilians. This simply didn't cut him out for parish work. So the Church confined him to one of those *gulags* in the mountains. But that didn't stop old Wüli. He was as fit as could be and would saunter off, up hill and down dale, like a bloody mountain goat in search of some sympathetic soul to whom he could make his personal revelations. Wüli warned me about the horror and detestation with which economic crimes were regarded in Switzerland. Each nation has its love, Wüli told me: the Regime dreams of naked black women; the English are a nation of child molesters; the Swiss have exchanged their soul for financial security, they worship the franc and hold sacred the bank account.'

'And Bubé has abased the sacred rites?'

'It's worse than that. The account was found to be empty, it's tantamount to religious blasphemy. He's in deep trouble.'

'All of it – gone? But Blanchie – where? How?'

'Bubé was very cagey about that. He kept trying to defend himself. Said he had no option. He was a victim. The Swiss would wring him out and hand him back to the Regime who'd spent so much time washing their hands of him they had to wear gloves. They were going to blame him for their own decisions, crucify him for saving his country. I put it to him straight. You've transferred the money to the other fund, I said. He was ready for this. He looked almost triumphant. There was a flash of the old Bubé, the truculent jeerer of the political platform, scourge of the press, whirlwind diplomat, baby creator – "How could I?" he asked. "There is no *other* fund." What about the Kruger fund, I asked. He laughed. "You don't believe that old story, do you? There were no millions, there is no fund."'

'Clever,' said Kipsel.

'The President's vanishing trick. Where are the missing millions? Now you see them, now you don't. Like Kruger, like Bubé. Clever, and inevitable,' said Blanchaille. 'The old man may suffer in the short term, because the Swiss are convinced he's got the money stashed away. But they won't find it since the other fund doesn't exist. And that's official. The Regime denies the story of the Kruger millions. The Swiss deny the existence of a Kruger asylum here. Therefore it's not possible for Bubé's treasure to have joined it. After a while the Swiss will convince themselves that the money Bubé owes them never existed. They never bribed Bubé and he never welshed on his promises to them. The banks will absorb their losses stoically and save face. The Regime will appreciate the value of this. If the money does not exist, nor the secret accounts, then neither does the fraud or the defection of the President, nor the plan for a government-in-exile.'

'Yes,' said Kipsel, savouring the beauty of it, 'and I won't be surprised if the Regime starts threatening anyone who tells these stories of the missing Bubé's missing millions. People will get into trouble for telling stories.'

'The chances are,' said Blanchaille, 'that Bubé will be completely cleared, his name will be incised on all the war monuments and the attacks upon him cited as further evidence of the Total Onslaught against our country. The missing presidential millions have their uses.'

Kipsel nodded emphatically. 'What would we do without them?'

They sat by the roadside and gazed down at the lake far below. A tiny white steamer moved in a wide arc across the still blue water, it followed a great circle, creeping round like the second hand of a watch. Running down the sides of the lake the vineyards seen from this height stretched out with a green and metalled regularity.

After some while I heard Kipsel ask: 'Blanchie, what were you drawing in the sand when you were talking to Bubé?'

In reply, Blanchaille drew in the dust the letters ASK 3. 'When I was in London, before Van Vuuren was killed, we met Father Lynch. He had been following us. Don't ask me how. We talked about death. His and ours and Ferreira's. Having explained to us why the price of shares fell after Tony's murder we asked if he knew who'd killed him. He said he didn't. But he said something interesting. What if the letters scrawled on the wall did not stand for the Afrika Straf Kaffir Brigade, or the Azanian Strike Kommando No. 3? What if those letters had not been written by his killers, or even by someone wanting everyone to think they'd been written by his killers? What if they'd been written by Ferreira himself? I remember his words, "If you can read the writing on the wall you may be close to the killer." Back there, when we saw the police with Bubé, something suddenly occurred to me. Look at the letters again – ASK 3. Now imagine someone writing them in a hurry, someone in a state of shock, in pain, someone dying. Maybe he would write clearly. Look at the number 3 – and remember that the people who saw it said they "thought" it looked like a 3. But say it wasn't. Say the dying man had been trying to write not 3 but B.'

'All right, say they were,' said Kipsel. 'All it does is to make the message even more mysterious. You can't make sense of B. At least ASK 3 can be made to fit the initials of two known organisations both of which were capable of murdering a Government official who had discovered something nasty about them.'

'Exactly,' said Blanchaille triumphantly. 'Those letters can be *made* to fit. Your words, Ronnie! And they were made to fit. They made possible a theory to explain Ferreira's death. So we grabbed it. But we were being too clever by half. We were forgetting the first rule in African politics, the principle which dominates the way we are.'

228

'Which is?' Kipsel asked, amused.

'That what begins as tragedy turns into a farce at a blink. That in all Government activities you must suspect a cock-up. We forgot that rule. Why should the letters on the wall stand for anything? Why shouldn't they mean exactly what they say?'

Kipsel jumped up and began to turn around in excited circles banging his foot on the ground as if to try and anchor himself, as if he might spin too fast and fly off the mountain. 'Blanchie! Of course!'

Blanchaille leaned forward and completed the message in the sand. ASK BUBÉ, the message read.

Kipsel stopped spinning and sat down. The little steamer now circled the lake like a racing car. He closed his eyes. 'And so you did just that. You asked Bubé?'

'Yes.'

'Well, don't hang on to it – tell me, who killed Ferreira?'

'I wish I could make this something you'd like. Something you could respect. I apologise in advance for what I have to say. Entirely typical. In a way I prefer the earlier theory of the political organisations. It's more elegant, more serious. And it makes the killing seem more important. Something to look up to. Hell, we *need* something to look up to.'

'Blanchie, please!'

'His killer was a small-time English thug named Tony "the Pug" Sidelsky, from Limehouse.'

'You're pulling my leg. From Limehouse, England?'

'I'm perfectly serious.'

'Then why are you smiling?'

'I can't help it. According to Bubé, Sidelsky drove to Ferreira's house on the appointed night knowing what he had to do. It was supposed to be professional, clean and quick. But it wasn't. Sidelsky, it seems, was none too bright. For a start he behaved as if he were going to knock off an old-age pensioner in Clapham. He didn't seem to realise that in South Africa houses are barred, wired, and fortified against night attack, that some of them even have searchlights. Now Ferreira didn't have all that security. He didn't even have a dog, which was most unusual and lucky for Sidelsky. But Ferreira was no idiot and naturally he was armed. Sidelsky found himself unable to enter the house without breaking a window. Ferreira was waiting for him. I don't know what Sidelsky expected. Perhaps he expected Tony to put up his hands and get shot. Instead he got hit himself a couple of times before he got Ferreira.'

Kipsel turned on him a look of intense suffering. 'But you still haven't told me – why get an Englishman to kill him?'

'It's really not so surprising,' Blanchaille said. 'Not when you think about it. English killers have been used for one job or another for many years in South Africa. It's almost traditional. Do you remember the shooting of the racehorse, Golden Reef? That was done by that bookie fellow from Ealing. Who was it again? Sandy Nobbs. He had been secretly commissioned, for reasons I don't remember, by the manager of the Tote. They caught him, remember? And then there was the killing of the fairy mining-magnate, what was his name?'

'Cecil Finkelstein.'

'That's right, Finkelstein. He was gunned down one night when he opened his front door. You remember the story?'

'Yes, I remember the story,' Kipsel said. There was immense weariness in his voice. And contempt. 'Years later some English guy in Parkhurst prison confessed to Finkelstein's murder after he got religion. Of course I remember the old story. It's the story of imported labour. It's the story of our country. Lack of muscle power in some areas, lack of skilled technicians in others. So you import them, engineers, opera singers, assassins. It's always the same – the butler did it, or the cook, or the gardener. Anybody but ourselves.'

'I said you wouldn't like it, Ronnie. I'm just telling you what I know.'

'Who ordered the killing? Bubé?'

'He swears not. He says that this was a *Bureaucratic* decision, as he puts it. He says the order came directly from Terblanche.'

'– who may not exist.'

'Correct. Bubé's story is strengthened by the fact that men from the Bureau were the first to arrive on the scene after the murder. I believe they probably expected to find Ferreira neatly dispatched and the place turned over and robbed so as to make it look like some sort of violent burglary. But what did they find instead? They find Ferreira dead, or damn nearly, and Sidelsky dying on the carpet. You can imagine the problem this gave them. I believe, at least Bubé says, they came close to panicking. You see it meant they first had to dispose of the killer and then return to the house and pretend to discover the body of the dead accountant. It was a very hairy business. Bubé's story had the ring of truth to it. You should have heard the way he sounded off about the Bureau. He says that the Bureau chose Sidelsky because he was broke and unemployed in England and they got a real bonehead for their pains. False

230

economy. He says the money they saved on the contract then got eaten up by the burial costs of the dead Sidelsky and they couldn't even claim on his return ticket because they'd booked him Apex, or something like that. Cost-cutting costs money, Bubé told me, showing a flash of the old financial brain that made him the big wheel he was. He was absolutely scathing!'

'For Christ's sake, you can't swallow that! Bubé controls the Bureau. He is or was the President and the Bureau is his army.'

'In a manner of speaking that's right – but to say that is to say very little. What exactly is the Bureau? We like to think of it as the Secret Police, run by the mysterious Terblanche – who probably doesn't exist. Well, I've got news for you, Ronnie. Not only does Terblanche not exist, but neither does the Bureau. Not as a single entity; some super-secret unit. The Bureau is simply a term, a useful fiction which we use to describe a whole range of options – the police; the Hand of the Virgin; the Ring; the Papal Nuncio; the New Men; the New Order; the Old Guard; the Straf Kaffir Brigade; the Azanian Strike Kommando; the Department of Communications; the Bureau is all of them and none of them. It's Bubé and Kuiker and Yssel and the entire establishment which controls our view of reality. It exists so that we have something to fear. But more importantly, it exists so we have someone to *blame*. It is that force which the Regime as much as its enemies needs to believe in. It gives clarity and purpose to what is otherwise a long, ugly, dirty grab at power. We need the Bureau, we love the Bureau. We would be lost without it. You ask if the Bureau killed Ferreira? The answer you want is, yes. All right, the Bureau killed him, they paid the incompetent Englishman who pulled the trigger. But Ferreira stumbled on the truth and every new discovery was a nail in his coffin.

'Ferreira took three hammer blows to his faith. Firstly he believed in books, in fact, in figures. One day he was taking a routine look through the books. He began by checking the budget figures of the various departments of the Regime and in those figures he found discrepancies. Consider what this did to him. His whole life depended upon a single premise. The Regime might be mad, it might be stupid, it might be cruel – but it was sincere. It was honest. Tony believed that utterly. Well, the books told another story.

'To begin with he found that some of the monies listed in departmental spending had actually been channelled elsewhere, they appeared to him to have gone to Minister Gus Kuiker. It disturbed him. He went to Sidleman, the Government Accountant, and reported his discovery. Sidleman hit the roof. He was another Government man. He didn't understand why the official figures did not reflect the truth. Apparently he asked Ferreira if he was suggesting that elected officials were setting up secret funds of public money. Ferreira replied that he wasn't suggesting anything of the sort, but he wanted to know why the figures didn't add up. Sidleman went to the President who promised a full investigation. In the meantime he told Sidleman to call off Ferreira and to stop his enquiries. But that was impossible. He had to follow where the figures led. There was no stopping Ferreira. Everywhere he looked he uncovered further mysteries. Not only did he find, as he went through the files of the various Government departments, that there was money leaving the country for unexplained reasons, there were also funds reaching Government coffers which he couldn't account for. The figures led him abroad. To South America, Bermuda, France. He was shown houses on the Italian Riviera, farmhouses in the South of France and learnt they belonged to Gus Kuiker and Trudy Yssel. The Department of Communications was waging a foreign war against secret funds. He travelled on, to Rome, Washington and then Switzerland. Everywhere he went he heard the most astonishing stories. He heard of wild nights in Montevideo, week-long sex parties in Las Vegas, of private jets for American politicians and free holidays for British editors. He learnt about dummy companies set up in Bermuda and Panama which were used to buy up or buy off political commentators; he found deals as bizarre as the plan to arrange a tour of Japan by our rugby players in exchange for a tour of the casino nightclubs by Japanese sumo wrestlers and for the tour to be extensively covered by a Taiwanese news agency which would circulate the story as evidence of our racial tolerance; in Switzerland he found companies set up to translate South African currency into American dollars, apparently an expensive business, and he found that this accounted for some of the millions he had detected draining out of our foreign reserves; in Switzerland too he came across disturbing rumours of deals between important men of the Regime and the whole raft of currency manipulators, he learnt of promises not kept, of secret deals, secret accounts, gold sales and Russian contacts. Perhaps he unearthed the true story of Popov. By the time he got to London he was shattered. He got in touch with Zandrotti. Perhaps he needed to talk to a friend. He got drunk, he probably told Roberto more than he'd intended. Of course Zandrotti got it in one. Ferreira still didn't realise the full implications of his discoveries but Zandrotti did. I think with that wild, anarchic mind of his he probably got it in a flash, saw the horrible black farce it was. Ferreira was overwhelmed by the tragedy. But Zandrotti saw the joke.'

'And Zandrotti went home – to find out for himself?' Kipsel asked. 'He couldn't believe it.'

Blanchaille looked surprised. 'Oh no, he went home because he refused to believe it. I remember how he was in Balthazar Buildings after he'd been caught by the police. Zandrotti was broken, he'd lived his whole life in the belief that the Regime was genuinely, thoroughly, consistently and impressively, let's face it, evil. He grew up in that belief, he'd suffered for it, he'd gone to jail for it, he'd lived in exile for it. It was, when you think about it, a very high expectation. He had a worthwhile enemy. You can imagine what it did to him when Ferreira told him he was dealing with a bunch of crooks. He hadn't been a hero. He'd been a fool. He was not going to have that. My guess is that he booked his flight home and then saw Magdalena.'

'Who shopped him, of course,' Kipsel snapped.

Blanchaille understood the anger of his friend; how the business of Magdalena's betrayal still hurt.

'My feeling – guess – is that was just what he wanted. Heaven knows what came pouring out between bursts of the litany in the bar where Ferreira told Zandrotti his story. Some clue, perhaps, which gave Magdalena's double game away. And Zandrotti used her.'

'It makes a change,' said Kipsel.

'Ferreira believed in figures. He also believed in the integrity of the Regime. Mad it might be, but honest. Negative, but sincere. Narrow, but forthright. The Regime had set its face against blacks, Communists, Jews, Catholics, against compromise, liberalisation, democracy. This might be narrow, foolish even, but it was a question of principles. And he could admire people with principles, who would die for those principles. As for himself, well somebody had to do the sums, as he liked to say. He had kept the faith. Now he found the Regime dealing with the Russians through Popov and Himmelfarber –'

'And Himmelfarber's nephew, left in Moscow on deposit,' Kipsel reminded him gloomily. 'Blanchie, this gets blacker.'

'And Himmelfarber was supposed to be an enemy. But gold as we know is more important than principles. The Regime had dealt with Moscow when they moved bullion dealings from London to Zurich. In Switzerland he'd heard rumours that some big man in the Regime had cleaned up on the move. Then he discovered money going to the Israelis! Now the orthodox teaching was that at least half of the Regime was of the unshakable opinion that Hitler got a bad press and was really a sensitive, patriotic house painter at heart who became Chancellor and was looking for nothing more than sweetness and light and that any stories to the contrary were products of commy, pinko Jews, who wished to destroy the white man's way of life, his religious beliefs, and to sleep with his daughters – and yet here was the Government supporting whole teams of Israelis and concealing them in the countryside. Israelis who wore baseball caps the wrong way round and disturbed the peace of the countryside, cost a fortune to police and protect and then desecrated the Calvinist Sabbath by drinking and whoring in sleepy country towns. Most important of all, he'd been taught that the President was the father of his country and its stay and protection in times of trouble, that he would lead the nation in the flight to the beaches when, and if, by some horrible catastrophe, the savages prevailed and the last white tribe in Africa faced extinction. Then, with his back to the sea, the President would hand round the poison to the kids and begin shooting the women before the enemy troops arrived. That's what he believed, and then blow me down, he goes out and finds that the old fox has been salting money away for years in a Swiss account against just such a contingency, against that rainy day which might carry him off to Bolivia or Paraguay.'

'Then he goes back to his books and finds he isn't looking at figures, he's reading a horror novel,' Kipsel broke in. 'He finds not one financial nightmare but three or four. There are the funds creamed off the various Government departments and sent abroad secretly for Kuiker and Yssel's Department of Communications to fight its propaganda war. There is the money Bubé has been collecting in his secret accounts against a rainy day.'

'And there are the funds entering the country which presumably baffle the hell out of him until he interviews the brokers Kranz, Lundquist and Skellum. And his last and most cherished belief collapses. He finds out about the *Manus Virginis* with their strategic charity, how the Ring collaborates with them in tactical investments in the future of the Regime.'

Kipsel sighed. 'Poor Tony. Finding that the Church was in it too will have hurt more than anything.'

'Yes, but not for the reasons you think. What crucified Ferriera when he discovered the links between the Regime, the Ring and the Hand, with the Nuncio Agnelli acting as flyhalf, was that the Church really was powerful after all. Tony had never accepted Lynch's theories about the structure of power. He rejected the Church as played-out, ineffectual, unimportant. And he was wrong. Everywhere he looked he found a policy of outright deception. There was the Church going around the country issuing statements about embracing its black brethren in Christ. There was Bishop Blashford publicly deploring the shipment of human populations to the transit camps and relegation of entire tribes to desolate "homelands", and defying the Regime to arrest him. There were the charitable bodies shipping in dried milk and penicillin and designing new churches in the beehive style and attacking the Regime for being in league with the devil and preaching that the programme of separate freedom for ethnic groups was a crime against humanity, an economic nonsense and a sin against the Holy Spirit. While this was going on, here was the Regime whose followers took an oath of loyalty to Calvin before they slept and believed the Pope feasted on baby meat and sucked the marrow from the bones of orphans, meeting with certain Italian Societies, and here were its loyal followers in that most secret of societies, the Ring, those ultra-Calvinists, sitting round a table with a bunch of genuine opera-loving flesh and blood holy Romans, fresh from the Vatican, representing the *Manus Virginis* and discussing share portfolios. One by one, every belief he held had been destroyed. Lynch had been right. And if Lynch had been right about the deceptions, he was right about all the other things too – including the missing Kruger millions, right about the house on the hill. It was in this despairing state that he phoned me.'

Kipsel was very pale. 'I didn't know he phoned you.'

'Just before he died. I was one of the last people to speak to him.'

'What did he say?'

'That I should get out. That he had found the City of God, or Gold. The line was bad. He was slightly hysterical, said he was planning a trip himself. He sent me money. Next thing I knew he was dead.'

'And here you are?'

'And here we are.'

Kipsel swore bitterly, then scrambled to his feet and picked up his stick and rucksack. 'Let's get on. I don't want to know any more. Tony "the Pug" Sidelsky! The whole thing's a horrid cheap little pantomime. Do you think it's much further?'

'I hope not, I hope not,' said Blanchaille fervently. 'I've had about as much as I can take. All my prayers are that God preserve me from any more of my itinerant, wandering, bemused, addle-brained countrymen, from policemen, rugby players, patriots, accountants, priests and presidents.'

'Amen,' said Kipsel.

CHAPTER 23

And so I saw in my dream how they hurried on their way, anxious to arrive somewhere, anywhere, elsewhere, the pear and the fish, strange partners.

Fearful imaginings crowded in on Blanchaille and left him weak and uncertain of his true direction, characteristic phobias, indigenous phantoms, familiar demons arose from the catalogues every South African recites before sleep and loves to recall with horror. Black men hunted with huge home-made knives beaten out of oil drums or made from railway steel ripped from the sleepers, flattened by a maniac, hammered, honed to a scalpel's edge, metal machetes called *pangas*, slicing the air; he remembered white boys, so huge, so long and lanky they reminded him of giraffes, against whom he had played rugby, boys with strangely dark complexions and moustaches, surely men, and not that *white*! They raced down the rugby fields towards you with that stiff-legged giraffe gait, their hooves wrenching the turf. These monsters were surely never the babies which loyal white mothers had had for Bubé? No, these boy giants were born with full moustaches – wearing rugby boots. Their call-up papers were delivered to the maternity wing, they leapt from their cradles, kissed their new mothers goodbye and went off to defend their country's borders against the Total Onslaught. Thus the dreams of misplaced, wandering white Africans, each with his own compendium of horrors, stories of *tokoloshes*, green and black mambas, murdered nuns. Each has his favourite, but most fearful for Blanchaille was the memory of a crop of graves he had watched growing in the camps. Growing and growing. If there was a symbol that scared him, it was not the gun nor the knife nor the snake – but the spade. In the camps he had learnt to dig. He had stood in the big trench grave and thrown red sand up onto the parapet, mounting higher and higher. He had felt he was digging in for a great war. What he now feared most as he slogged along an obscure Swiss track towards an improbable destination was not ambush or betrayal, but arrival. In the old story, the Regime was regarded by its opponents as utterly evil, by its supporters as divinely good. Everyone dwelt among absolutes and was happy. Now it seemed that the Regime was no better or worse than two dozen other shabby little dictatorships north of the border. He stole a glance at Kipsel, a tousle of curls falling over the shallow brow, the fish lips making their silent, pouting little *o*'s. Had it occurred to him that if the hell he had left behind wasn't as bad as they had believed or hoped – then might not the place to which they travelled be no better than anyone might imagine?

What do you do when you find that the world you imagined to be bad, decently evil and have judged this so by observation and report and legend, fact and figure, is none of these, but is instead flat, dull, ordinary and very much like anywhere else? You have believed in its evil, trusted in it, you have been convinced by friend and enemy alike of its horror, have had it whispered to you in the cradle, written on the bodies of men in the cells, the message is one which has reassured the condemned as they are led to the gallows and made for an enemy worth fighting against – but, what if everything turns around suddenly, turns upside down and becomes in truth, banal? When it reveals to you that thing which you can least bear? That it is, in reality, very ordinary? Well, what you do is to keep climbing, and to dream, and to come in your dream, as Kipsel and Blanchaille did now, to the crossroads.

And into my dream there now steps a strange figure, his perfect teeth flashing like a sword. The teeth are noticeable for they are all that can be seen behind the African mask he wears, a wooden mask with black lines incised on the cheek bones and a fuzz of hair made from sacking falling down almost to the eyes and where the ears should be.

The travellers stared at this strange figure. Their road was little more than a track. The tree-line was ending. The pines that had been climbing steadily beside them had grown thin and feeble and were now tottering to a halt. It was from behind one of these ailing trees that there stepped the figure in the mask and unsheathed its smile. The lake below was lost in a distant blue haze and might have been the sky. It might have been that the whole world turned suddenly on its head.

The creature before them was dressed in tribal finery of an African chief, though of which tribe neither of them could say, but certainly he looked very regal, war-like and confident, and most bizarre on that green mountainside. He was planted squarely on the spot where the roads divided. There was, it occurred to Blanchaille, something vaguely familiar about his costume though he couldn't put his finger on it.

'We're looking for the road to Uncle Paul's place,' said Kipsel politely. 'Perhaps you can direct us?'

Blanchaille examined this strange tribal creature. He wore a kind of cap of fur with the arms and tail dangling round his head, a monkey pelt across his shoulders, he carried a short stabbing spear and a cowhide shield. Beneath it all he wore a black morning suit and highly polished shoes.

'How would you describe the place you're looking for?' the stranger asked.

'A place of rest,' said Blanchaille.

'A holiday home,' said Kipsel.

'Retirement village, old-age home, hospice,' said Blanchaille.

'A home-from-home, hide-out, colony, camp,' said Kipsel.

The figure nodded. 'Follow me.'

And he led them along the road which turned to the right and passed along the shoulder of the mountain. The sun was setting and a small chill wind was blowing. They followed him in silence and so compelling was his presence that they covered considerable ground before they realised the road had levelled out and was beginning to descend.

'Wait,' said Blanchaille. 'This can't be right.'

'I'm doing you a favour,' said their guide. 'Don't argue. Keep moving. Don't look back.'

'But we're going down,' said Blanchaille. 'We're not supposed to be going down.'

'Where does this road lead?' Blanchaille asked.

The stranger stopped. He turned and confronted them and very slowly removed his tribal mask.

'Gabriel!' Kispel said.

'I tried to help. It's the least I can do for old friends. I want to help you.'

'Where does this road lead?' Blanchaille asked again.

'To Geneva, the airport and home.'

'But that's the way we've come,' Kipsel said.

'Of course it is. I asked what you wanted and you said home, hotel, hospice, guest house, retirement village. That's what you're wanting and this is the road that leads to it. This is the *only* road that leads to it.'

'That wasn't the home we had in mind.' Blanchaille objected.

'It's the only home you have. There is nothing where you are going. Believe me, trust me.'

Despite himself Blanchaille laughed.

Gabriel became angry. 'Yes, laugh! Maybe you won't get another chance. The joke's over. Come home with me. Face up to reality – or go on and fall off the edge of the world.'

'If you want to help someone, what about your brother? He's still wandering about here. He's got a piece of paper in his hand that he believes will give him the title to some fabulous strip of land where he'll be king and everyone will be equal and live happily ever after. Why not take him home?' Blanchaille asked.

'My brother is in a real sense quite unreachable,' said Gabriel. 'My brother's on another plane. He imagines himself as a great explorer. He thinks he can reverse history. He believes he can set out with his piece of paper and imagines he will discover the New World. Like he's Columbus in reverse. Or Van Riebeeck going the other way to rediscover the Cape of Good Hope. He plans to reopen the Garden of Eden, which he thinks has just been closed for repairs.'

'We saw the guarantor of his dream of Eden being led down the mountain in chains,' said Blanchaille.

Gabriel shrugged. 'Correction. You've seen Dubé in chains. What Looksmart sees is another matter.'

'You sent Looksmart to Philadelphia.'

'Another correction. I didn't send him to Philadelphia. He took up with some girl and landed there. All I did was to get him on the plane to America, one step ahead of the police.'

'So you warned him the police were coming?'

'Of course.'

'And who warned you?'

Gabriel shrugged.

'You don't deny it then?'

'Why should I?'

Kipsel who had been listening to this exchange in bewilderment now broke in. 'What are you saying, Gabriel? That it was you who talked to the police?'

'How else do you think I got him out? Sometimes,it's necessary to talk, to deal.'

'But the police hurt your brother,' said Kipsel. 'They nearly killed him.'

For the first time Gabriel showed signs of impatience. 'Jesus you guys are so tiresome. I've tried to help you before, Blanchie. I got you into Pennyheaven. To do that I talked to Blashford. But then I've talked to the Afrika Straf Kaffir Brigade and to the Liberation Front, in my time. But you guys won't have it, will you? I'm the only

239

one who understood it wasn't enough to hear what Lynch taught us. We have to act on it! I am brave enough, desperate enough to do what's necessary, because we plan to win.'

'So do the other side.'

'Naturally this gives us something in common. So we talk to each other. It's a complex balance.'

'Gabriel. What are you saying?' Kipsel was aghast. 'People are dead. Mickey, Ferreira, Van Vuuren – friends!'

'Van Vuuren was no friend. Besides he brought it on himself. If you want to blame somebody, blame the Regime. You can't send policemen snooping around the Azanian Front. If the Regime wants to talk they know the way of getting through to us.'

'But he wasn't with the Regime. He was one of you!' Blanchaille cried. 'Kaiser Zulu sent for him. Van Vuuren came because the ALF called him in.'

'That's his story,' said Gabriel. 'I'm beginning to wonder if you guys have understood a damn thing.'

He left them then, striding away rapidly into the gathering dark.

Then Blanchaille remembered where he'd seen the tribal dress before. 'In Balthazar Buildings there was a portrait of Bubé hanging on the wall. He wore ceremonial tribal finery, the skins, the spear, the shield. He wore it to visit the tribes of which he was honorary chief. Gabriel was wearing the same get-up.'

'As a kind of disguise,' Kipsel suggested, ever naïve.

'No. Not a disguise. It shows Gabriel is presidential material.'

Kipsel said he wished he could identify the tribe from which it came.

Blanchaille said it didn't matter. 'They probably have a big box of fancy dress tribal finery, or a props cupboard and drag out some vaguely appropriate costume when a ceremonial visit crops up. Something that makes you look vaguely chieftain-like and impressive.'

'The only thing that worries me is that Bubé, of course, wore it when he made these visits to some wretched tribe who were about to be dumped in the middle of nowhere.'

'God, how he must have terrified them!' said Kipsel. 'Imagine Bubé stepping out of the presidential limousine in that get-up. Imagine what the God-forsaken tribe felt when they saw him. It must have been like getting a sign, the arrival of the messenger of doom,' said Kipsel.

'Remember the shepherds warned us about Gabriel,' Blanchaille pointed out. 'They said he was no angel.'

'I still say they weren't shepherds,' Kipsel insisted.

'Please Ronnie, is this the time to argue about shepherds?'

Kipsel agreed it was not perhaps the time.

And I saw in my dream how the two friends began the long haul, retracing their steps back to the crossroads as darkness fell.

CHAPTER 24

Blanchaille and Kipsel heard, rather than saw, Looksmart, for it was quite dark by the time they had regained their position at the crossroads, deeply regretting the distance travelled and the time lost in the vain detour into which Gabriel had tricked them.

They heard the scrape and scrabble of his dragging walk while he was still some distance behind them and they heard him muttering to himself. They heard the name 'Isobel'. They heard how he addressed himself in a language composed of grunts and clicks, in a dialogue between the foreigner and the lunatic.

'Here comes Looksmart,' whispered Kipsel. 'Poor bastard. If he saw Bubé it will have finished him. Let's wait.'

'Perhaps he really does imagine himself to be another Columbus. Listen how he argues with himself. Do you think he could be talking about Isabel of Spain? Didn't she send Columbus off to discover the New World?'

'Isabella,' said Kipsel. 'It was Queen Isabella and Ferdinand who sent Columbus off.'

Looksmart approached. 'Isobel,' he said firmly, 'who sent me to find America.' Here he took out a tiny, weak torch and examined their faces. What a strange couple, the big round one with a face like kneaded dough and the other, thin, big-lipped, with hands that sliced the air like fins. Though it was many years ago they still retained the familiar shapes of the boys he remembered toiling in Father Lynch's parish garden. In his curious click language he muttered their names.

'He really knows us now,' said Blanchaille.

Of course he knew them now. They were the altar servers whose heads Lynch had filled with stories of vanished millions, of Uncle Paul's promised land across the sea, of gold and secret colonies and lost souls, of the illusions of politics and the sole reality of power. Above all he remembered the pleasure he felt at seeing how hard those white boys were made to work in a garden which would never be got right, by an Irish priest leaning on an elbow on a tartan rug on a hot day drinking something from a thermos flask. But these memories returned in bits and pieces, now bright, now fading, like light glimpsed through a smashed windscreen. The work done by the policeman Breek on Looksmart's head had been thorough, the damage to the brain irreversible, but these glimpses remained of the old days. 'Blanchie, and Kipsel . . .'

'Odd that he should know us by night and not by day,' Blanchaille reflected.

The weak, yellow flickering torch-light searched their faces, assembling sections for process and developing in the dark room of Looksmart's brain.

'Did you meet with the President?' Kipsel asked.

The torch went out. 'Looksmart saw him, oah yes. What a traveller! He must be on another diplomatic tour. He had been given a special police escort. I approached the car with my treaty and asked for ratification that this land belongs to me and my descendants, in perpetuity.' Looksmart had trouble getting the word out. 'The President looked at me. He pushed my pen away. "No need for me to sign. You have it anyway. You and your descendants, forever". Then he went away, the President and the police. Perhaps they planned to show him to the people of all the towns he passed through '

'Perhaps,' said Kipsel drily.

Blanchaille felt his pity mounting. This shambling wreck in the darkness with his weak little torch and his insane ideas. This shadow of Looksmart. The real Looksmart had been a holy terror. This was a mumbling ghost. 'Who is this Isobel you're talking about? Tell us, please.'

On went the little torch again, probing their faces as if verifying the authenticity of this request. 'It's a good story,' said Looksmart. 'Oah yes.' And switching off his torch he began.

If Looksmart had been ignorant of his famous travelling companion, Lenski, on his flight to America, he had not wanted for company. In the seat beside him sat Isobel. And before we are too quick to condemn Looksmart for his failure to recognise the treachery of which he was a victim we would do well to remember the fate of other black exiles who went to America, reached New York, and later jumped to their deaths from sky-scrapers, or bridges; and the white exiles had come to no happier conclusions. Their patron saint is probably General Cronje, who earned a few dollars at the World Fair in St Louis in 1904 by re-enacting for gawping tourists his disastrous defeat and surrender at the Battle of Paardeberg. That Looksmart arrived in Philadelphia and discovered the roots of the American revolution was an advance due

243

entirely to Isobel. That he drew strange conclusions from what he learnt must be laid at the door of the salvationist delusions of all South Africans.

Pretty Isobel, in her caftan, cowboy boots and soft generous ways had come to Southern Africa as a mere tourist intending to visit the famous game reserves including, of course, the Kruger National Park. Instead she had fallen into conversation with the man who carried her cases to her hotel bedroom soon after her arrival in the country and had been converted. This radical spirit had taken her on a tour of the townships, to the resettlement camps, had taken her to meet those who had been detained, mothers whose children had died in front of them, people under house arrest and discarded people of all sorts. The high point of her visit had been taking part in the great student march on the Central Police Station in the capital to protest against the detention without trial of student leaders. It was this that suddenly radicalised Isobel, plump, pretty and so pleasant, so cordial in her peppermint caftan and cowboy boots, who found herself sitting beside Looksmart on the flight to America. He had never met anyone so thrilled to hear he had been in prison. Her face puckered, she cried for some moments before pulling herself together and then defiantly ordered champagne. She felt utterly privileged, she told him. He liked her, too. She did not make his eyes water. Over the champagne he told her he was also fleeing the country. After that they never looked back.

Isobel carried his luggage and refused to comment on his behalf when the reporters encountered him in Kennedy Airport after their interviews with Piatikus Lenski. It had been Isobel who dealt gruffly with the surly immigration officers over the matter of Looksmart's presence in the United States. It was Isobel who got the tickets for the train to Philadelphia and who moved him into her apartment on Walnut Street.

It was Isobel who took him into her wide soft bed beneath the eiderdown decorated with signs of the zodiac and its sky blue sheets.

She removed his clothes, she took his penis between her breasts and massaged it. It had been Isobel who straddled him. She was an odd girl, he remembered thinking. Political commitment made her misty-eyed, stimulated her, while he looked on quizzically with his one good eye caught between the desire to help and the vague feeling that he ought to apologise, wondering whether this was quite the career Gabriel envisaged for him in America. She took his now rampant member and kissed it, crooning to it between kisses, pulling and patting the foreskin gently as if trying to get it to lie

244

down, as if it were the corner of a shirt collar she'd been ironing and which refused to stay neat. She took him inside her and began rising and falling, her face tightening with concentration, her forehead shiny with effort. He tried to move with her, to make some gesture of communion, but her knees gripped his hips and kept him still. He lifted his hands to her breasts but she took them down and pressed them flat on the bed, gripping his wrists hard. She had told him on the plane how she loved Africa, how joined to it she felt however vast it was and with this her grip on him tightened. He wished he were more substantial beneath her, he did not feel very large or even very African. She was riding him more swiftly now, her breath coming in short hisses. He realised that his role at this particular point anyway was to lie still. He realised from something in the movement of her body that what was happening was in some sort a further dimension of her tribute to him, both to his person and his cause, as she had taken it to herself, now she took him. Looksmart's good eye watched the triangular patch of pubic hair rising and sliding, felt the contractions of her vaginal muscles, felt himself swell and spurt within her as she came to a shuddering, panting conclusion, dropping her head onto his chest and resting on her arms which curved outwards at right angles to her body like staves, or hoops, cutting half moons out of the white walls behind her. Afterwards it was Isobel who told him that this was her commitment to a vision of freedom. It was a vision to which Looksmart felt he had been permitted to make only an involuntary contribution. It was rather like giving to some mysterious, distant charity, he decided. You felt better for it after you had done it, though you couldn't help wishing you had a clearer idea of where the money went.

A few weeks later it was Isobel who arranged their marriage by 'the turkey who lives on the hill'. The turkey turned out to be a pleasant young Methodist minister; the hill, Society Hill. It wasn't so much marriage, Isobel explained to him, as the question of his visa, his freedom to stay in the United States. She said this very delicately as if she feared he might take offence. Afterwards she took him to lunch at a fish restaurant called Bookbinders and ordered him lobster. The waitress produced a huge paper towel which she tied around his neck and Looksmart felt very embarrassed to be wrapped like a parcel. With his knife he tapped an anxious tarradiddle on the red beast's back. Isobel asked about his mother.

Looksmart's mother had been called Agnes. That much he did

remember. Up from the kraal, a raw farm girl, she came to the capital in search, not of work, but of her husband who worked on the gold mines. Which mine? No one knew. One day her husband's letters had stopped. Worse still, so had the money he used to send. So Agnes brought her sons to the city and failed to find him. She was told to go home and wait. But she couldn't do that, her children had no food. She looked for work. Those to whom she applied warned her, threatened her: she had no papers, no permission, no future, no business to be there. Tap, tap went Looksmart's knife on the lobster's gate of bone behind which the beast hid and would not let him in, knock as he might. The hot, salt, sea flesh inside steamed in his nostrils. He realised then what was to be done in order to eat a lobster, why the huge paper bib, the finger bowl. You were supposed to tear it apart with your bare hands. His mother would have fled from this monster. The lobster fixed him with hard, unblinking eyes. Never mind, he would outstare it, using his bad eye.

Agnes, Looksmart's mother, arrived at Father Lynch's front door clutching Gabriel's hand and Looksmart, then still a baby, strapped to her back. Lynch took her on immediately, impressed on the one hand by her inability to do any cooking or washing or ironing or sewing. These were deficiencies he approved of heartily. Coming into contact with the white madams who taught these things was the ruination of many a good person, he liked to say. Lynch was delighted by the impressionable enthusiasm she showed and her lack of bad culinary habits. He taught her to cook what he called Irish food, plain and solid, stews and roasts and soups and plenty of potato with everything, since that was the way it was done in Ireland, his country, God help it, a tiny island no bigger than the tip of a finger nail, and here he squeezed between thumb and forefinger the requisite area of nail for her inspection. A little place so full of priests it would sink beneath their weight into the sea one day.

So much for the wedding lunch and Looksmart's mother. It was Isobel who acknowledged that she would awake one morning and find him gone, having slipped away in the night, summoned by his comrades to return home and fight for the cause of freedom.

And it was Isobel, above all, who sent him out one day with instructions to cast an eye over 'our revolution'.

Down Walnut Street Looksmart scrabbled towards that amazing rectangle bounded by Second Street and Sixth, by Larch Street and Spruce, the launching pad of the American revolution. He visited the Declaration Chamber in Independence Hall along with a bunch of tourists. Their guide was a bluff young man who wore what looked to him like a scout's uniform, but who turned out to be a Ranger in the Parks Department. He discovered that the area of Independence Hall was designated a National Historical Park. How strange America was! In his country the national parks were full of animals; here, they were full of people. The crowds stood behind the railing which enclosed the sacred area where the furious debates about independence had taken place. They stared at the tables covered with green baize and the crowded, spindle-legged Windsor chairs, the papers, the quills, the inkstands. They saw the Speaker's Chair with its rising sun motif and heard how Benjamin Franklin sat day after day, during deliberations that led to the Declaration, wondering whether that sun was rising or setting. He gazed at the silver inkstand designed by Philip Synge for the Speaker's Table, he learnt that unlike most of the other furniture, the inkstand was original; from it had come the ink that had loaded the quills that signed the Declaration of Independence adopted by this rumbustious, Second Continental Congress of 1776. The tourists stared at the crowded tables and chairs in that silent, empty chamber and tried to imagine the bells, the bonfires, the cheers and the shots with which the revolution began. Most of them were dressed in jeans or slacks and had this shifty, almost guilty look about them, Looksmart thought, as if try as they might they simply couldn't imagine that such climactic matters had begun in this small place. Afterwards, Looksmart bought a copy of the Declaration Document and a postcard of Trumbull's painting, *The Signing*, with its bouquet of American flags and its serried racks of bewigged and utterly respectable gentlemen who beneath their composure and their wigs had proved to be wild and redhot revolutionaries.

Looksmart visited, that same day, the House of Representatives Chamber in Congress Hall, as well as the Senate Chamber. He stared at the great star-spangled eagle painted on the ceiling overhead with its claw full of arrows. He admired the creamy symmetry of the old Supreme Court Chamber and he walked across Market Street and joined the crowds thronging the Glass Pavilion where the Liberty Bell hung.

He arrived home that night loaded with papers. He had gone out a tourist and come back a recruit to the American revolution. Something had caught fire within him and the roar of its flames competed with the deep internal cranial rumblings and explosions inside his damaged head and sometimes, hallelujah! overcame them and drove them out, even quietened the continuous buzzing in his ear, warmed his stiff and stupid tongue, disciplined the feet that each went their stupid, separate ways. He carried brochures, postcards, maps, prints and an armful of books he had discovered on sale at the Visitors' Centre on Second Street. Isobel was amused by this enthusiasm. He lay there that night staring up at her sizeable breasts, swinging like bells. Later, while Isobel slept, he got up and went through his papers.

The next day he was back at Independence Hall. He admired the style of the ground-floor rooms which he now knew to be in the English Renaissance style, with graceful pilasters proceeding heavenwards in strict proprietorial order, Doric on the first floor, Ionic on the stair landing, Corinthian cornice beneath the tower ceiling. When the guide asked the tourists whether anyone could identify the rather skinny-looking chairs crowding the Declaration Chamber, Looksmart said right out loud that they were Windsor chairs, adding in his slow and rather baffling tones, that legend had it several of the chairs had been borrowed to accommodate the delegates who crowded into the Chamber on those heady days in July, 1776. The guide stared back at him, thunderstruck.

In the Liberty Bell Pavilion across the road, a plump lady in furs and dark glasses asked why the bell was cracked.

'It cracked when they rang it,' said the guide, an innocent girl staring with big eyes at the huge brassy bell.

Looksmart stepped forward. 'The bell has always been cracked,' he said, rejoicing that his tongue obeyed him. 'It's been cracked from the day it was born. Since 1752 when it arrived from England and they hung it up on trusses in State House Yard. It cracked on the first bang. Pass and Stow cast it again. But this time it didn't sound right. Too much copper. The third time –' Looksmart held up three fingers '– they got it right. The bell rang for the Declaration of Independence in 1776, and for another fifty-nine years until, in its eighty-second year of service it rang out for the death of Chief Justice Marshall in 1835, and cracked for the last time . . .' He leaned over and with his knuckle knocked on the bell. It gave off a dim and distant echo. His audience stared. It's doubtful they understood much of this explanation, for though he pronounced quite perfectly the words came out a trifle rough and slurred and sluggish perhaps. The tourists backed away from him. The guide and the plump lady in furs beckoned frantically to the two heavy gents in green standing at the door, doubtless the guardians of the bell, and up they came and very firmly requested Looksmart to leave the Pavilion.

Looksmart sat on a bench in Independence Square and read a copy of the Declaration of Independence and I saw in my dream how the scales fell from his eyes, poor fellow. America appeared to Looksmart rather in the way that the Angel of the Lord appeared to the Virgin Mary. In Philadelphia, the cradle of revolution, an idea of an African redeemer was born.

Of course he quickly realised that the American Declaration of Independence was a document so advanced in its political thinking that, had it been promulgated on that day in his own country as the manifesto of some new party or movement, it would have been shredded on the spot and its adherents exiled or arrested, banned, imprisoned, or tortured as wild men beyond the civilised pale. It rang with phrases, any one of which would have brought blood to the eyes of the followers of the Regime; it spoke of equality, of inalienable rights, of Life, Liberty and the Pursuit of Happiness. It spoke of Just Powers, and, most startlingly, of the 'Consent of the Governed'.

It must have been likely that in the years that followed the Revolution some news of its occurrence would have travelled abroad, even as far as Southern Africa. But to judge from all the evidence no such thing occurred. Of course it was not unusual nowadays to claim kinship in retrospect. It was put out by the Regime that they too had fought for their freedom against the Imperialists, to say that 'we were fighting for our freedom from the British at about the same time as the Yanks, you know.'

In fact they hadn't stayed to fight at all, they had not been set afire with a light of freedom. Instead, deeply unhappy about the loss of their slaves and chafing at the English overlordship, though they had settled the country with their first colonists at about the same time as the Americans, they put up with successive overlords for years – until damn busybodies got between them and their slaves, and the disgruntled Boers migrated northward with God as their guide and their guns loaded, set the whips cracking over the backs of oxen, and the covered wagons rolling north into the interior in search of fresh grazing, uninterrupted privacy, and plenty of servants, in search of a heaven in the middle of nowhere. A Garden of Eden free of English and full of garden boys. Over half a century had passed since the time the Massachusetts militiamen shot it out with the British at Lexington. But no news of these great events appeared to have reached the Boers. Or if it had, Looksmart suspected, they wouldn't have liked what they heard. The early Americans wanted a nation free and independent among the nations of the world. The Boers had no nation, distrusted freedom and cared nothing for the world. The very idea would have had your average Boer choking into his brandy. What he wanted was to be left alone and to put as much distance between himself and the English enemy as possible, to trek until he reached that magic land, the land of Beulah, where the game was limitless, grazing good and armies of black slaves kept him in clover. That was the cloud-capped summit of the dream towards which they had trekked. Trekked once more. And Uncle Paul had trekked yet again.

In the end they had to stand and fight. They found you could never go far enough. It wasn't just that the English were following them, it was history that stalked them down and chased them and in time overtook them and ran them to earth. They fought and lost. But when the Dutch farmers lost the war to the English rednecks at the turn of the century, and Uncle Paul Kruger fled into exile, it was the end of the Boers forever. Those who replaced them, that is to say those who remained, and never took the one-way ticket to the remote Paradise on the Swiss mountains set aside by Uncle Paul for his dispersed people, those who remained got wise. If you couldn't out-gun the English, you could out-vote the bastards. And they did. And scooped the board and so in exchange for the two Boer republics they had lost, they gained the whole damn southern sub-continent and as many servants as any reasonable man could wish to flog in a lifetime.

On through Philadelphia Looksmart trekked, to Betsy Ross House with its spinning wheel and its first American flag; then to Franklin's Tomb in Christ Church, to Carpenters Hall and to the Tomb of the Unknown Soldier of the Revolution where Looksmart laid a dozen red roses. And towards evening he set off back down Walnut Street, forgetting, as Isobel had prophesied he would, where home really was, to Penn's Landing where he fell on his knees to the amusement of a man selling pretzels and gave thanks for his salvation. And he began to plan in his mind his 'holy experiment', his own Pennsylvania, his own Philadelphia, City of Brotherly Love, which was to absorb him utterly from then on and dreamt in Franklin's words that he might one day set foot on its surface and say, 'This is my country.'

It was Isobel who remained loving and true even when he fell so deeply into these reveries that he forgot who he was or where he lived and spent the winter nights in the streets crouched over the iron gratings from which the hot wind blew, like any other bum. And of course it was Isobel who, when the invitation came to present himself at the Barclay Hotel where 'he would hear something to his advantage' encouraged him to go at once.

'You've heard of the wandering Jew, well you're the wandering African. Finding ways to go home.'

Isobel was a dreamer. And a bit of a dope. But she loved him. And though there are some who say that Looksmart would have learnt more of the genius of America in her arms than in all his researches into Benjamin Franklin, they forget how far gone he already was when he met her.

Looksmart's head had been repeatedly knocked against the wall by Captain Arrie Breek, who today imports famous crooners and entire Las Vegas girlie line-ups to perform in his Mountainbowl Auditorium, and arranges pro-am golf tournaments at his Palace in the Veld, with million dollar prizes, and his part in the little matter of Looksmart's head should not be forgotten. When you twirl a glass of water, the glass moves but the water stays still; unfortunately, when the head is struck and moves violently this rotation means the brain tries to move with it, with calamitous results for concentration, pronunciation, locomotion.

Looksmart crossed Rittenhouse Square in brilliant sunshine and went up to a suite on the tenth floor where he met a certain Mr Carstens and his friend, Estelle. Mr Carstens said he was an American with plenty of available capital. Estelle was a friend of his from Looksmart's country. Carstens wore a vivid green and orange shirt. Estelle was dark, authoritative, and her features were chiselled, determined and pert.

Now again, there are those who say Looksmart should have known the score. He should have spotted who Carstens was. And anyone who had looked at a newspaper in the months past would have identified Estelle as Trudy Yssel. But Looksmart did not know the score and he did not read newspapers, not when he had the mountainous literature of the American Revolution to consume.

'Mr Dladla,' said Estelle, 'we are here with a revolutionary plan.'

'Mr Dladla,' said Mr Carstens, 'you may or may not know that there is in our country a new dispensation. A New Order. Changes are occurring.'

'Mr Dladla,' said Estelle, 'I have here a letter of introduction from your brother, Gabriel. He is one terrific guy. And a friend.'

Again, there are those who charge that Looksmart should have known Carstens was a phoney, that his accent was ridiculous, and, anyway the shirt he wore with its mango sun floating above some palms should have been a dead give-away. But Looksmart had long passed beyond the petty day-to-day treacheries of the Regime. He was out of all that. He had entered a new world.

And they overlooked the letter from Gabriel.

Dear Looksmart,
This is to introduce you to a couple of friends of mine, useful contacts and deep down, I believe, supporters of the cause. They have proposals to put to you which I genuinely believe can promote our struggle for liberation. I urge you to listen carefully to what they have to say and to act quickly.
Remember me in your prayers.
Your brother in Christ, Gabriel Dladla.

'We represent a force so radical we cannot reveal ourselves,' said Carstens, 'so secret it speaks only through its appointed agents. The Regime wouldn't tolerate our liberal aspirations or pragmatism. The Americans will not believe them. We have a problem. We wish to invest in several of the communications media in this town to promote our message. A couple of radio stations, a closed-circuit TV station and a news magazine.'

'What can I do for you?' asked Looksmart.

'Scepticism, cynicism, downright suspicion of our intentions is what we have to combat. If we are to buy into these businesses, our enemies would cry foul. But if you were to bid, or to allow us to bid for you –'

'You want me to buy some radio stations?'

'We will do the actual buying,' said Carstens.

'We will do the actual paying,' said Estelle. 'But you'll be the owner.'

Looksmart stared at them, wonderingly. This they misinterpreted.

'Of course, we would make it worth your while. I understand you are a student of history here. We believe you wander the streets. Sleep rough.'

'I'm a student of revolution,' said Looksmart proudly.

'Aren't we all?' said Carstens politely.

'Don't want money,' said Looksmart.

'That's up to you. Maybe you want something else. You just tell us and we'll see if we can help.' Estelle smiled sweetly.

'Do you know anyone in the Regime?' Looksmart demanded. 'Do you know President Bubé?'

252

After some hesitation Carstens said he had met the President, briefly, on one of his foreign tours, he thought.

'O.K.' said Looksmart. 'Now this is what I want.'

In the darkness on the mountainside Blanchaille and Kipsel heard him waving what he had got, his slip of paper, his dream. 'Here it is! Here it is! Pennsylvania here I come!' The little torch was switched on, the light pale on the paper.

'You fool,' said Blanchaille. 'You idiot!' Blanchaille yelled. 'You'll never do it. Our country is already torn into independent kingdoms, homelands, reserves, group areas, Bantustans, casinostans, tribal trust lands and all you're proposing to do is to fucking well found another!'

'Mine will be different!' Looksmart's voice cracked and trembled. At Blanchaille's raised voice he could feel the tears beginning to start. 'We'll have no racial separation, no servants, no gold mines, no Calvinists, no faction fights. In my country the Boer will lie down with the Bantu.'

'Numbskull!' Blanchaille shrieked. 'They're *all* different. All these places. That's why there are so many of them. Everybody who is different has got to have one. The one thing we have got in abundance is difference. Difference is hate. Difference is death. I spit on your difference.' And he did, spitting noisily into the night. 'You've been gypped, by your brother, by the Regime, by yourself.'

They heard the scrabble of paper as Looksmart returned the precious document to his pocket. 'You can't scare me,' he replied through his sobs, 'I will continue. Oah yes, right on to the end of the road, as the song says. I will enter Uncle Paul's place and lay my case for a new republic before the lost souls. And they will hear Looksmart, and return with me to our homelands leaving you behind, Blanchie, like the last bit of porridge clinging to the pot.'

Here I truly believe Blanchaille would have leapt at Looksmart and killed him if Kipsel hadn't pulled him off. The two friends turned to their path again and by starlight continued on up the mountain, soon leaving the sobbing, crippled, cracked visionary far behind.

CHAPTER 25

So I saw in my dream how they arrived by night at the high stone wall and the big iron gates and read by moonlight the name of the place:

BAD KRUGER

On each of the gateposts crouched enormous stone lions, much weathered; rain, snow and wind having smoothed away their eyes and blunted their paws; their crumbling manes were full of shadows. And I saw in my dream how priest and acolyte, or detective and aide, dish and spoon, fisherman and fish, call them what you will, pushed at a big iron gate which opened easily on well-oiled hinges and closed behind them soundlessly. Without any idea of the sort of place they had entered but too tired to stand any longer, they lay down on the grass and slept.

They awoke to a morning full of bird-song to find themselves in an extensive garden thick with flowers, ornamental ponds, gravelled walks, fountains and orchards and beyond, a small, thick wood. Kipsel identified several familiar blooms: blazing Red-hot Pokers, magnificent specimens standing five feet high, their full, tubular heads of red and yellow swinging like flaming bells; the rare Red Disa, Pride of Table Mountain, as it was called, with its little trinity of reddish-purple petals framing a third which turned the opposite way showing a cup veined in purplish ink. Blanchaille knew nothing of flowers but this identification of plants and blooms recognisably African excited him as the first definite sign that they had truly arrived. The water in the ponds was a cold green. The ponds were fringed with reeds and carpeted with blue water-lilies and these in particular made Kipsel exclaim: 'Amazing! You see them? Blue! *Nymphaea* those are, blue-ridged leaves! Blanchie, they barely exist any longer. You used to find them in the Cape Peninsula many years ago. But not any longer. To find them here . . . they're virtually extinct! And look – masses of Red Afrikanders. It's far, far too late for them, surely?'

'Virtually extinct,' Blanchaille repeated, wondering at Kipsel's floral knowledge and thinking that sociologists, like cold green pools, sometimes possessed hidden depths.

Small turtles swam across the lily ponds pushing a film of water before them. They watched a brilliantly coloured bird, its plumage a dancing gloss of green and purple, its bill and forehead in matching orange, its throat bright blue, hunting elegantly among the reeds and when it caught something it would pause to feed itself with its foot with the aplomb of a fastidious diner.

Through the small thick wood they pushed and came at its edge to a wide and well-kept lawn and across it saw a great building presenting a broad and sturdy front to the world. Here Kipsel and Blanchaille drew back into the trees, for walking on the lawn were groups of people. Some were in wheelchairs attended by nurses, some walked with sticks, others seemed fit and well and played a game of touch-rugby. The scene reminded Blanchaille of a convalescent home, of pictures seen of veterans home from a war, recuperating. Though the strains of music coming from the big loudspeaker mounted high on the pediment of the house gave to the scene something of the convivial quality of a village fête. Only the bunting was missing. They withdrew more deeply into the wood. At their waists were Kaffir-lilies, three-foot high at least with great trumpeting mouths of deep crimson; hip-high Chincherinchees, big white flowers with chocolate hearts; spotted velvet Monkeyflowers; and golden banks of the misleadingly named Snow-on-the-Mountain; all of which caused Kipsel further perplexity as such flowers were found only in African gardens. The music the loudspeakers relayed was a medley of light classics: Strauss marches mingled with traditional *boere-musiek*, or farmers' music, of which the old favourite 'Take your things and trek Ferreira' seemed very popular, with its wicked thudding refrain:

> My mat-tress and your blan-ket
> And there lies the *thing*!

If the music seemed appropriate to the establishment they'd expected, the house did not. It was a solid, assertive building: a strange mixture of grand hotel, railway station and museum, built on two storeys, squat, bulky and prodigiously solid, perhaps eighty feet high and crowned by a great dome of coloured tiles, pierced by oval windows. A flight of stairs in two graceful stages climbed majestically to the bronze doors. The windows on the ground floor were arched and comparatively simple while those on the second storey were flanked by columns and surmounted with medallions and above it all, and for the whole of its length, the pediment was crowded with statuary: Greek gods, perhaps; venerable old men with philosophers' beards; horsemen; griffins; wrestling cherubs and other fancies intended to give an aura of substance and dignity, but this was undermined by the big loudspeakers mounted on poles which framed the statuary.

They drew even deeper into the wood, aware of how strange they must look, two ragged fugitives, eyes pink from lack of sleep, bodies smelling of sweat, chocolate, cheese and brandy.

'We should go forward. Introduce ourselves. We should see if this is the right place after all,' Blanchaille spoke without conviction.

'Or we could wait until we felt a bit stronger,' Kipsel suggested.

Blanchaille appreciated his trepidation but knew it wouldn't do. 'We'll never feel as strong again.'

'Excuse me, but I need a swaz,' said Kipsel and disappeared hurriedly.

A swaz! How many years was it since he heard that expression? One had to admit it was precisely onomatopoeic, echoing perfectly the zip and gush against the rock in the dusty veld, or the business of drilling muddily into a garden bed, but it pained and discomfited here in its buzzing directness. Accuracy of observation, whether of the names of flowers or of the sonic effect of urination did nothing to help; what was needed was not description but meaning!

When Kipsel returned he challenged him accordingly.

Kipsel shrugged. 'Fall into a small pool of words early on and you'll spend the rest of your life splashing around in it. For example, I had a girlfriend once, by name Karina. She had five brothers, all cricketers. I think her father played, too. Her life was taken up with starching shirts, whitening boots and keeping score. As a result she was a child of the pavilion. There *was* no other world. Her bag of words came straight out of the changing room. She had no other terms of reference. Everything was described in cricketing language. Even sex. She was forever making jokes about maidens. When we were in bed she would cheer me on if I looked like flagging with cries of "only another sixty to go or you have to follow on"! And when she was coming she'd cry "how's that?" and stick a finger in the wind like an umpire giving his man out.' Kipsel banged his fist against his forehead to still the extravagant memories of these exhausting matches. 'Going to bed with her was like going into bat without a box. She took that as a compliment when I told her. See what I mean? It wasn't so much that she was really interested in cricket itself but it provided her with a life she could get hold of. And beat. Cricket was her way of living, her get up and go, her entry into the life of action settlers must have, because doing gives an illusion of winning. Her way of grappling with life.'

'And going forward,' said Blanchaille. 'No illusion is more precious.'

It is interesting to note that they themselves did not go forward at this point but walked away from the house until the music from the loudspeaker faded. They found themselves in an apple orchard. The fruit beckoned them, the crispness of the huge pale green apples tempted them. They must have eaten half a dozen each, tearing at the tight sweet flesh as if their systems needed it, as if it was some sort of antidote to the poison of too much travel, a diet of brandy, chocolate, cheese and a constant series of shocks to the system.

I saw also that there was a vineyard nearby and this, too, they invaded, gorging on the plump white grapes until they could eat no more. I watched Kipsel who lay on the ground with his fingers over his eyes to keep out the sun and let the juice run down his throat, spitting the pips into the air, even though Blanchaille had asked him politely to stop. And then with full bellies and pleasantly overcome by the walk they slept, restlessly muttering of home, heaven and angels and policemen, no doubt believing themselves safe in the privacy of their dreams.

Then I saw that they weren't alone.

He stood up among the vines. A big broad man in a floppy straw hat, waring faded and patched brown dungarees, with his thumbs hooked into his belt. He stood watching the sleepers from a little distance away, listening to them; a big man with freckled arms and a considerable tan, attending closely, taking notes in a small book with great rapidity. And when he saw me watching him, he looked up and smiled and said: 'What's so puzzling? They come here, they're tired and hungry, they eat, they relax, they sleep. In their sleep they talk. It's a habit of people like this, terrified of speaking aloud what they think, they confine their comments to this sort of dream talk. Dreams are the only underground left.'

'And you? Is your note-taking also a habit?'

He didn't answer me, but I had my suspicions.

So I saw when the sleepers woke they found the man watching them, though he no longer carried his pencil and notebook.

'Who are you?' Blanchaille asked.

The big man smiled, he rubbed his neck, he cracked his knuckles, he flexed the muscles in his freckled arms and he said: 'I'm a gardener. At least I help to keep the place up. Of course I've got under-gardeners with me. This place is too big for one man.'

'I hope you didn't mind us helping ourselves to your fruit,' said Kipsel.

The gardener smiled. 'That's why it's there. Only I wouldn't stay here very much longer, it's getting on towards evening. You'll be wanting dinner soon. The others have already gone in, the music has stopped.'

'Are they expecting us – up there?' Blanchaille nodded his head towards the big house beyond the wood.

The gardener nodded. 'Anybody who gets this far is expected. They'll be looking out for you all right. The worry always is that people who make it this far might get lost again.'

'We weren't lost,' said Kipsel. 'A few detours, perhaps. A few hedges and ditches to jump. But not lost.'

The gardener smiled. 'If you hadn't been lost, buster, you wouldn't be here.'

'What's your name?' said Kipsel.

'Happy.'

'Happy!' Kipsel laughed, genuinely rolled about. Blanchaille was embarrassed.

In fact it wasn't too difficult to understand Kipsel's amusement or his friend's sheepishness, since, after all, the term 'Happy' was used in their own country as one of the many derogatory terms in the rich vocabulary of racial invective the ethnic groups enjoyed directing against each other. Mutual abuse was a mainstay of political life. The pleasure of calling supporters of the Regime, Happies, with all the ironical strength the insult carried was matched only by the enjoyment with which the Regime declared its opponents to be Kaffir-loving Jewish Commies who should go and live in Ghana . . . Hence Kipsel's laughter and the embarrassed silence which followed.

The big man stood by impassively watching. 'There've always been Happies here,' he said. 'Ever since the old man started up the place.'

'I think I see what he means.' Blanchaille cleared his throat with the air of a man anxious to prevent misunderstanding. 'This word "Happy" I think is a corruption, or at least a mutation, of the name of Kruger's valet, a certain Happé. You remember? He was the one who was with Uncle Paul when they found whatever it was they found.'

'Came at last to the place in question,' said Kipsel.

'Quite.'

'Which was this place.'

'Very likely. Happé is supposed to have taken down the notes dictated to him by Uncle Paul, which became the *Further Memoirs*. Our friend says he's a Happy. I think what he means is that he descends from an unbroken line of the Happé family. Is that right?'

The big man did not offer to enlighten them. Instead he indicated where their direction lay with a jerk of his chin towards the big house. 'They'll be expecting you.'

He walked them through the wood; perhaps marched would be a closer description of their brisk determined progress.

As they came to the edge of the wood the windows of the big house scintillated in the afternoon sunshine which gave an equally rich lustre to its gutters and drain-pipes which Blanchaille realised with a start were made of copper and polished to this ruddy sheen.

'This is the place?' he asked, '*Bad Kruger?*'

'Is *Bad Kruger* the place?' Kipsel demanded more subtly.

He was more than a match for both of them. 'This is it. *Bad Kruger*. Of course it's the place. Where else would it be if it wasn't *Bad Kruger*? It's *Bad Kruger* or nothing.'

I saw how the gardener knocked on the door which was opened immediately and he handed over his companions to a pair of bare-legged attendants most curiously dressed in what looked like checked pyjamas; short pants, loose fitting shirts without arms and big white buttons. I watched as these two attendants took Blanchaille and Kipsel firmly by the hands and drew them inside, the enormous bronze doors closed behind them and the great house presented once again its look of massive solidity as it presided over the perfect lawn flowing past the front steps like a tranquil green river which the gardener now crossed, giving the occasional chuckle to himself as he went, amused no doubt at the foolishness of those who did not know the place when they found it.

Blanchaille and Kipsel were escorted through the great entrance hall with a vaulted roof. Old-fashioned iron lamps hung overhead from long chain pulleys; the walls were decorated with frescoes showing knights on horseback, boys on dolphins, dying dragons, naked maidens, castles, rivers, holy grails and mermaids wearing large golden ear-rings. The place was vast and silent; the only sound their own footsteps, for their barefoot companions made no noise at all. There was a very strong smell, too, a strange mixture of sulphur, mud, salt and above all of soap, and a certain peculiar dampness pervading everything. They made their way down an extraordinary corridor off which led handsome arcades flanked by tall Corinthian columns. The frescoes became more extravagant as they proceeded; angels struck rocky outcrops with golden wands and jets of crystal water burst into the light of day. The mermaids combed their long blonde hair on high rocky promontories, turning their angelic faces to the high-flung spray from the pounding seas below. Plump olive-skinned bathers with a faintly Roman or Grecian look to them, were shown taking to the waters, moving in stately fashion – noses rippling the surface like sea-lions, and their eyes shining like dates.

Blanchaille and Kipsel asked their companions where they were taking them.

'For a bath,' came the wholly unexpected answer. 'We are the bathing attendants here to introduce our facilities to all the newly arrived guests.'

Here they began to descend a steep flight of stairs where the smell of soap and sulphur was even more pungent and the damp, mouldering air of the place clogged the nostrils.

Kipsel began to show signs of panic. 'I don't need a bath,' he whispered furiously to Blanchaille, despite the fact that his need, and that of Blanchaille, had long been apparent and increasingly unpleasant, even to themselves. The stairs grew even danker and saltier until they issued at last in an enormous underground cave or bathing chamber in the centre of which was a huge bath, a large sunken swimming pool lapping at its tiled lips.

'Step into the water,' the bathing attendants invited, 'as if you were Roman emperors.'

Then I saw Blanchaille and Kipsel remove their heavy walking boots and Blanchaille took off his clothes, though it is true that Kipsel at first attempted to walk into the water fully dressed and had to be restrained and it was only with considerable difficulty, after assuring the attendants that he would undress only if they went away, that he could be persuaded to take off his clothes and, with Blanchaille, stepped into the water which proved far hotter than they had expected and took some time to get used to.

The attendants meanwhile had withdrawn to a small glass booth and were watching them steadily. These attendants in their barefooted, flapping obsequiousness reminded Kipsel of warders, he said, or actor convicts who'd escaped from an old Charlie Chaplin movie. Blanchaille said this was probably because they were dressed in some costume of an earlier period. Kipsel said that one of Blanchaille's less likeable traits was his pedantic streak. He christened the attendants Mengele and Bormann, a joke which

Blanchaille found to be in very bad taste.

Kipsel gained sufficient confidence to float on his back. 'Have you noticed how the water gets suddenly deeper? In some places I can't stand.' He drifted idly in the water with just his nose and his toes visible. Blanchaille stared at Kipsel's toes which were very white and seemed to fold in on themselves, reminding him of white roots, or of strange mushrooms. The two attendants in their glass booth continued to watch them closely.

When at length they stepped out of the bath it was to find their clothes had disappeared. The attendant stepped forward and Mengele explained that the clothes had gone, as he put it, for the burning. The attendants offered towels. They were shown the row of saunas, the Turkish baths and the Turkish showers which were followed by the freezing plunge bath one reached by climbing a steep steel ladder and then dropping into, breaking a film of ice. They were shown a choice of soaps, the hairdriers, the pomades, creams, colognes, razors, sponges, scrubbing brushes, loofahs, and invited to make use of some or all of these. The waters in which they had been bathing were highly effective for oto-laryngological ailments, said Bormann, radioactive of course and slightly odorous, and so showering was advisable after taking the waters. They might feel rather tired a little later, said Mengele, but this was quite usual. They should go and lie down if they felt tired. There would be a place for them to lie down.

After their showers they were directed to the relaxation room, a chamber of the utmost modernity carved into the rock, glass-walled, softly and luxuriously furnished with leather loungers and a variety of ultraviolet sunbeds. There was also on offer, it seemed, among the many therapies: massage, electric roller-beds, acupunture, aromatherapy, colonic irrigation, physiotherapy, meditation and drinks, both hard and soft, as well as mud baths, a gymnasium, and, for those who felt they needed them, a valuable course of rejuvenating, fresh-cell injections. At short notice, the attendants also offered to arrange for inhalations and osteopathy.

These offers were declined. And as he stepped into the shower I heard Blanchaille put it with simple dignity, 'to be clean is enough.'

Afterwards, with their hair clean, freshly shaved, deodorised and shining, they were dressed in soft and fluffy cream towelling robes with the golden letters B.K. prominently blocked above the breast pockets. I saw them led back up the stairs and through the corridors and arcades and then up a further flight of stairs into the dining room.

Kipsel could not help trembling in his towelling robe as he stood in the doorway of the crowded dining-room feeling, as he confessed to Blanchaille with a half-apologetic, rueful smile, that he really hadn't believed that he'd ever see the light of day again when the attendants marched them into the sunken bathing hall. 'This notion of washing before entry is a bit bloody quaint, not so? I mean, you know Blanchie, it reminds me of going swimming, when they used to have one of those freezing foot baths with disinfectant you had to slop through. I hated that. I always hopped it.'

'There is no hopping here,' said Blanchaille briskly. 'Here I get the feeling that they do everything by the book. Unless you go into the baths you can't join the others.'

'It reminds me of Lynch's thoughts on salvation. Do you remember his Clean Living Fallacy?' Kipsel said.

Who could forget it? This was Lynch's answer to the morbid teachings of the Margaret Brethren on sudden death and inevitable damnation. The Margaret Brethren taught them that by going about in a state of sin knowing not what the day brought forth they risked the wrath of God: a motor car accident, a sudden electrocution, asphyxiation, choking, or one of the hundred hidden ways in which God might strike and send the sinner to judgement unshriven, unprepared and irredeemable. Death in the state of mortal sin would deprive the sinner of any chance ever again of heavenly bliss, and even a venial sin would plummet the sinner to purgatory where sufferings were just as bad and the period of confinement so vast that by comparison all the time which had passed since the creation of the cosmos to the present day seemed no longer than a millionth of a second. Lynch savaged this doctrine by pointing out that precisely the same fear possessed people who hoped, if knocked down by a motor car, to be wearing clean underpants. In the eschatology of the Margaret Brethren, Lynch explained to them, God was reduced to a bad driver, the human being to a hit-and-run victim and the soul to the status of an article of underwear.

This mere mention of Lynch made them both wonder and look around them as if hoping that they might spy the little priest lurking about. Perhaps they might ask him whether he thought people here lived by the book and if so whether the book was any good and life lived by it worth the trouble?

They were in the dining-room now, a magnificent iron and glass pavilion which looked rather like a huge bird cage. There were many tables and many diners. Obligatory portraits of President Kruger hung on the walls. In the centre a fountain kept its awkward watery balance in a great stone basin shaped like a giant baptismal font. All the diners wore the same creamy towelling robes and all looked freshly scrubbed. A short, square, capable looking woman in a dark blue uniform which gave her the look of a nurse, though there was also something vaguely military about her, stepped forward. There were black epaulettes on her uniform and silver stars that served as buttons and her bearing was upright and disciplined. Clearly someone not to be trifled with. But her smile was open and genuine and her welcome warm. She was smoking a short, thin black cheroot.

Though there were none of the faces they half-hoped, dared perhaps, in their wildest imagination to find, there were all around them familiar countenances. Surely that grey-haired old gentleman was a former prime minister who was said to have retired to his farm in Swellendam to raise bees? And was that a necklace of golden coins he was wearing threaded on a piece of string around his neck? (As they were to discover it was not string, but fishing tackle that served best for this purpose.) Here surely was the origin of the legend of the golden crowns which all who reached the last refuge would receive. Some of the women, with considerable ingenuity, had designed jewellery, elaborate harps or butterflies made entirely of gold coins, and some of the rougher looking men, perhaps farmers or rugby players in former lives and who could hardly be expected to go in for bodily decoration or for fancy jewellery, had fashioned their coins into large gold rings, chains, and chunky medallions which nestled in the thick black hair of their chests. A few held golden flutes and some played on them, rather badly but with great enthusiasm.

The matron followed their glances. 'Patience. We have such a wide variety of people in *Bad Kruger*. We are many things to many people – a club for retired gentlefolk, an old folks' home, an old boys' reunion, a retirement village, a sheltered accommodation scheme, a hospital, a shelter for the incurably desolate and an asylum for patriots. You are perhaps looking for people you know? It will take a while to recognise all those who are here, and not everyone comes down to dinner. Some stay in their rooms. You'll have time enough to look for them. *Bad Kruger* was never built to hold our present numbers. We must arrange two or three sittings for each meal – just as they did on the trains.'

The food was served and the wine went round. The meal was good, if rather heavy. Soup, followed by veal in a thick cream sauce, fried potatoes and solid wine which they took from a carafe at the table. The waiters wore black trousers and rather grubby white bunny jackets fastened with a single brass button, their black bowties were scruffy and they lounged against the walls and muttered things among themselves in the manner of waiters the world over, bored between courses. They looked as if they had once worked on the trains, Blanchaille thought. They had that characteristic air about them, a truculent and a rather rough *bonhomie*. Also there was a slight roll to the way they walked, as if the room were moving.

In the centre of the room the fountain played. Matron explained: 'The fountain is known as the *Afrika Stimme*, or the African Voice. When Uncle Paul arrived here with his valet Happé he found the place in ruins. It had been a spa once, it was to have been a palace of health visited by the crowned heads of Europe and was founded by one Pringsheim with casinos above, baths below. Built in 1875 at a time when the great spas of Europe were beginning to draw the rich and famous to them, Pringsheim knew of the link between wealth and power as well as the incessant interest aroused in rich and successful people by their bowels, their colons and their irrigation systems. He understood their obsession with health. He understood that the rich and beautiful and powerful needed to purge themselves of the grime which inevitably accumulated in mastering the world. This spa was founded upon an incredible hot-water spring. Such was its heat that it was known to the locals as the *Afrika Stimme*. You've seen the bathing halls below, those enormous, moist, echoing places. The curative properties of the steaming, radioactive waters were believed to be miraculous and have been known since Roman times when legionaries were said to have bathed here in the reign of the Emperor Diocletian. Pringsheim planned for these healing waters to wash away the sins of the worldly. Pringsheim was ambitious. He built wonderful new bathrooms, steam rooms, mud rooms, inhalatoriums. There were nozzles and sprays and dunk baths, plunge pools, massage rooms, radon chambers. There were waters for drinking, for irrigation, for warming, curing, strengthening, purging, saving. Alas, tragedy struck. The great casino was no sooner built, where we now sit, than the spring died. Stopped dead one day and would not flow again. Pringsheim shot himself. For a time the place was empty and I believe after that an asylum was established for a short while. However it was quite unsuitable for lunatics who drowned in the mineral water swimming pool, choked in the mud baths, strangled one another with inhalant tubes. The building fell into disuse, into ruin – and that is how Uncle Paul and his valet Happé found it.

'Uncle Paul did not hesitate. He knew the curative properties of the water, these had been analysed and found to contain various chemicals: lithium, manganese, phosphoric acid, fluorine, caesium, and even a tiny touch of arsenic, besides, of course, being radioactive. Fifteen mach units of radon was the measurement, good for the blood, for breathing problems, for arthritis, rheumatism, for just about anything you care to mention. He knew this, but that wasn't the main attraction. The main attraction was the hot spring, the African Voice. It seemed fated. Intended by God. It was a sign. Of course they told him that the spring had failed. That it would never flow again. The old man is reported to have said nothing, merely to have asked Happé to help him over to the base of the fountain you see there, and proceeded to strike it with his walking stick. And the spring flowed again. Those around him understood the significance of that gesture, they read their Bibles regularly, they knew the story of Moses striking the rock in the desert and finding water. They knew of the wanderings in the desert of the Israelites in search of the Promised Land. They knew the old man had made his choice. In a sense he had come home, he had realised his dream. The spring flowed again. He had made a home for others to come home to.

'Two events were crucial in driving the old man to this place. The story of the Thirstland Trekkers of the 1870 haunted Kruger, Happé writes. Perhaps you know it? The Thirstland Trekkers were not content even with a pure Boer Republic. Even there they felt the lack of freedom, even there they felt constrained, even there when they had what they wanted of Africa they dreamed of yet another Promised Land, a heavenly Republic beyond the horizon. They dreamed, in a word, of Beulah, the Promised Land, Eden, Shangri-La. It was a vision which drew this particular party of Boers to trek forever onwards to the sacred *laager*. It carried this small desperate party of six hundred or so men, women and children through the Kalahari Desert "dying as they went", according to one historian. The end is sad. The dream drew them not to Beulah but to a steamy, fever-ridden province owned, not by Jehovah, but by Catholic Portugal. They set off, as Uncle Paul told Happé, those poor haunted brave Boers in search of heaven only to end in the hands of Portuguese market-gardeners! The special significance of this trek, said Uncle Paul, exposed the vital character of the Boers. They were destined to trek, but the mistake of the Thirstland Trekkers was that they trekked away outward, whereas the true trek was not one which covered territory but one that moved forever inward. An interior trek, an internal journey to the centre of themselves. This was the paradox at the heart of the true Boer, that he must continue to trek and yet he could never expect to arrive in the Promised Land. Kruger saw the fate which awaited his people if the trek failed. He saw it in the two colleagues closest to him, he saw it in Smuts who turned from general to bank robber overnight, and, worse, went on to show considerable flair for world diplomacy. Kruger did not know which was the greater scandal. And then there was General Piet Cronje, whose defeat in the Battle of Paardeberg and his subsequent surrender to the British enemy had been one of the most cruel calamities of the war and hastened the end of the struggle against the British Empire. He saw his enemies, the foreign outlanders, the gold bugs, throwing parties and buying beers all round, inviting Boer generals to sit on the boards of their companies. And then in the final months of his life he heard of General Cronje's horrible plans in St Louis, Mississippi. For what was the old general preparing to do? He was preparing to stage, for gawping tourists, his Last Stand at Paardeberg. According to Happé this distressed the old man terribly. "Can you imagine it, can you imagine it?" he is supposed to have said. "Can you see, these Americans, queuing up to see this great disaster inflicted on our suffering people?" The knowledge tortured him. Visitors to the Kruger House in Clarens gave him graphic descriptions of the preparation for Cronje's little piece of theatre in faraway St Louis.'

The matron drew deeply on her cheroot and puffed creamy smoke. Her voice sharpened and quickened in an American drawl. 'Roll up! Roll up! See the *Boojers* meet the British in mortal combat! See General Kitchener's final triumph! See the Boojers digging nests of trenches! See the Lydite shells blasting their positions! Read Cronje's courteous request for a truce to bury his dead and for British doctors to treat his wounded. Listen as Field-Marshal Roberts pronounces his niggardly refusal. Then hear General Cronje's noble response, which was in essence, *Then bombard away*. . . ! Now watch the great Boer military genius De Wet harassing the British from Kitchener's *koppie* which with supreme daring he has snatched from under their noses. See him command the strong point of Paardeberg for three days. But it is too little, too late. Now see everything lost. See General Piet Cronje and his four thousand men surrendering to Roberts. See him stepping down from his white horse, the Boer in his big hat and his floppy trousers and see the triumphant Roberts, neat and dapper, stepping towards him while in the shade Cronje's broken troops watch impassively from their wagons, and all around them sit the British in their khaki, wearing their funny hats with those strange protective peaks back and front to keep the sun off those long, thin noses, those red necks . . .' The matron's impersonation using hands and napkins impressed a number of the diners who applauded politely. She acknowledged the compliment with a nod of the head. 'You can imagine the old man's agony when he heard of Cronje's preparations at the World Fair, of his old friend's plan to make money while the bones of the Boer dead whitened on the slopes of the mountains their General had lost. But it spurred Kruger on. He told his doctor, according to a story that has come down to us, "You take care of the bodies, but someone must take care of the souls. We must make a little hospital, a little spirit hospital, ready for them." Well this is that little hospital. By July of that year, 1904, Uncle Paul was dead, but *Bad Kruger* was alive and well.'

'And what do you do here?' Kipsel was bold enough to ask.

'What do we do? We tell stories, of course.'

'More stories!' Kipsel protested. 'I'm tired of stories. Will we never get to the end of stories?'

Matron turned on him sternly. 'Never. And what would you do if that happened? Stories have brought you this far. From the most powerful member of the Regime to the lowest gardener, cook or nanny, we all need stories. We owe our lives to stories. Would I be here now? Or you? Or any of these people if it weren't for the stories of another place, of Uncle Paul's arrangements for the likes of us? Do not spit on stories, Mr Kipsel, or stories might spit on you.'

Kipsel hung his head. 'I'm sorry, it's just that we never seem to get to the end.'

'The end? Mr Kipsel – *we* are the end of these stories. I see you're puzzled. You fail to understand – even now.'

Sweets were brought, great big dishes of *koeksusters*, golden plaited sweetmeats oozing oil, and milk tarts as big as wagon wheels, fig jam, watermelon conserve, raw sugar cane, fly cemetery, coconut ice and, of course, peach brandy with the coffee.

'Fail to understand what, precisely?' Blanchaille asked.

'Everything,' came the laconic reply. Matron nodded her head towards the first speaker who had got up and was preparing to address them. 'Listen and you'll learn.'

A thin man with a nervous manner. His cream towelling robe

made him look rather like a chemist, a little drunk, and he tugged nervously at his ear-lobes while he spoke.

'My friends, my name you know.'

'I don't,' whispered Kipsel.

'It's Peterkin, Claude Peterkin, the radio producer,' said Blanchaille, 'from home, I knew him immediately.'

'From home!' Kipsel echoed in hot sarcastic tones. 'Where's that?'

Matron banged on the table with her spoon. 'Let him tell his story,' she ordered.

Peterkin bobbed his chin gratefully towards her. 'I was by trade a radio producer and rose in time to become Head of Broadcasting. My motto had always been – "choose the middle way". Useful advice to myself, working on the State radio you might say, since it meant I could steer between what was on the one hand a public broadcasting facility and on the other a Government propaganda service. You could say I'd been happy and moderately successful. Then one day I made a mistake. I allowed myself to be persuaded by Trudy Yssel that times were changing. "Produce plays," she said, "which display our adaptiveness to new political perceptions, which are modern, which are of today!" I went out and commissioned a play by none other than Labush Labuschagne. The Labuschagne you all know with his Eskimo wife and his interest in Zen and his quivering attacks upon the Regime's race policies and his impeccable Boer credentials, being a descendant of one of those heroes in Piet Retief's party who were murdered by Dingaan. And what did Labuschagne give me? He gave me an attack on the Catholic Church in Africa. Fair enough, you might say. The play was entitled *Roman Wars* – and not, let me stress, *not Roman Whores*. That was an incredibly stupid printing error. The same combination of bad luck and mechanical error which has pursued me all my life. Be that as it may, my intentions were good. Could I have made a better choice of playwright than Labush Labuschagne? His radicalism was unchallenged and yet his Government connections were superb. He wrote a play about a Church which is far from popular and he portrayed its missionary activity on our continent as hypocritical, self-serving and deceitful. What better way of encouraging a debate? Why then did the Regime put out a statement saying that while it was true they had differences with the Roman Church in the past, there was now no room in the new South Africa for religious or racial bigotry and they deplored the irresponsibility of those, they did not say whom, who attacked other religious groups? Now if this wasn't enough, at the same time stories of my homosexuality began appearing in the newspapers. It was suggested that I had a particular taste for young police reservists. Readers' letters choked the columns of the newspapers demanding that this faggot be neutered on the spot. Then the Board of Governors of the Broadcasting Service put out a statement that I was considering, quite voluntarily, whether I shouldn't perhaps take early retirement. The first I knew of this was when I heard it on the "Six O'Clock News". Then the Chairman of the Governors organised a farewell party. And who do you think he invited? He got in Bishop Blashford, the Papal Nuncio, Agnelli, and half a dozen pretty young police reservists. And this was to be my retirement party – a surprise retirement party! I walked in and found myself on the way out. Of course the cameras were there and the whole thing was shown live on television. I was presented with a farewell memento. I have it here.' Peterkin reached inside his robe and withdrew a large knife. 'It's a hunting knife, for those of you not near enough to see it. It has a sheath of genuine kudu-hide, its blade is fashioned from a piece of steel taken from one of the original rails from the Delagoa Bay line which carried President Kruger to exile. Its handle is made of rhino horn. This is inset with four golden studs, representing the four major racial groups in South Africa. I accepted the gift. After that I was escorted to the door and shown into the night. And so I came here, like so many of you. One morning the gardener found me wandering in the vineyard, and here I am. I thank you for listening to me and most of all I thank our President who made this place ready for us.' And with that he lifted his glass towards the portrait of President Kruger on the wall. The old man with the tufty beard, the sashes, the rows of medals, stared broodingly down upon his displaced children.

Another then rose, a bulky man with a bristling moustache, a big belly beneath the robe. Of course they all knew him, Arnoldus Buys, the nitrate millionaire. Even Kipsel knew him.

'I was a Government man, through and through. I was amongst the chief sponsors and backers of the New Men in the Regime. I was something of a rough diamond, but I was modern, tough, pragmatic. I backed the new dispensation. I believed in the new vision. I supported the principle of Ethnic Parallels, Plural Equilibriums, Creative Differentiation, all the terms, all the ideas, all the words. I also believed that we could fight our way back into history. I was one of the original backers of Minister Kuiker and his Creative

269

Sterilisation Campaign. I backed the propaganda war. But my friends I was asleep. We have all been asleep so you know what I mean. I was asleep and when I woke up I found I'd been taken to the cleaners. My story is brief and tragic and may be encapsulated in a few words; I fell victim to our own propaganda, I believed in it because I was paying for it.' And here Buys, the businessman, sank back into his chair and buried his face in his arms and a sympathetic hush descended on the room.

Then there rose a man who Blanchaille and Kipsel knew immediately – and who would not? For here was Ezra Savage, the novelist, the most notable writer the country had produced, described by some as a sad, thin old lay-preacher. Savage was the dogged champion of a Christian, liberal multi-racial vision of the future, author of a shelf of books amongst which the most famous were of course, *My Country 'Tis Of Thee; Come Home Dingaan!; Our Land Lies Bleeding;* and *White Man Weep No More*. It was extraordinary to see him here. He who had proclaimed that *Emigration is Death*! A man who had stood up for years against the harassment of the Regime, had survived countless arrests, imprisonment and privation, had seen his house set on fire by gangs of white youths wearing ruling Party sashes, an attack which his asthmatic wife barely survived and which undoubtedly contributed to her death soon afterwards. A man who had withstood this and yet now stood here in this room full of fugitives.

'What the Regime had been unable to achieve, my daughter accomplished. Some of you will be familiar with the extraordinary events surrounding the elopement of my daughter, Mabel, with Sunshine Bwana, the black taxi driver. When Mabel and her lover set up house in open defiance of the laws against interracial cohabitation, the pressure on me of course increased. Some of you will perhaps have read my *Letters to a Daughter of the Revolution*, in which I tried to set out, as calmly and dispassionately as I could, the difficulties which her behaviour had caused me. Mabel's reaction was to give an interview to a Government paper in which she identified people like myself with "liberals who thought left and lived right". We owned large comfortable houses in the white suburbs, preached racial harmony to our black servants and were in reality the true enemies of the revolution. Mabel said she preferred the Regime to us, that if she were made to choose she would have found more in common with those who ruled the country than she did with these vague and sentimental politics, these liberal chimeras, these values of a damp English rectory. But of course Mabel knew the thing was not to talk about the world but to change it. And so, though perhaps this is not widely known, my daughter Mabel led a second charge on her father's house at the head of a gang of black youths, and they attempted to set it on fire. Considerable damage was done. The Regime's newspapers took pleasure in reporting this, as you can imagine and there was a lot of speculation at the time, probably mischievously put about, that I was thinking of selling up at last, leaving the country and moving to a home for retired clergy on the Isle of Wight. It was then that I made my declaration – emigration is death! Well then, you must be asking yourselves, what is he doing here in this room full of fugitives? What drove him? I'll tell you what drove me. What I wasn't prepared for, what I think many of us were not prepared for, was the impact of what are called the Young Turks, or sometimes the New Men, or the Pragmatists, or whatever term you chose to designate that dangerous breed personified by the likes of Minister Gus Kuiker and Trudy Yssel. What was at the heart of their programme? It was to talk to us, persuade us, delude us into the belief that substantial changes were under way. It depicted a new deal in race relations in which people of goodwill and of good sense were seen working together in a society based on synchronised ethnicity, equal freedoms and plural balances. So it went. New names, old ideas. You might have laughed. I might have laughed. But my daughter accepted the challenge and that wasn't amusing. She took a job in Gus Kuiker's Department on the understanding that she was totally free to work for its destruction from within. She justified her job by saying she was genuinely interested in power and since this was the case it made sense to get as close to the centre of it as possible. If working for Kuiker meant getting her hands dirty, well that was too bad. Working with power meant coming to grips with it. That's what I didn't understand, she told me. That's what I was too frightened, too pure to grasp. Was there any greater test of a man's resolve than to realise he was fighting a regime ready to die for the sacred right to segregated lavatories? Well, yes, actually there was. As Mabel said: what I couldn't face was the fact that they had no intention of dying at all! Well, that's when I went away. You understand I couldn't take that. I think I would've preferred my daughter to shoot me, it would have been kinder than preaching at me from the Government benches.'

There were sighs all around the dining hall and an evident feeling of sympathy translated itself into an audible hum. Several diners wiped their eyes with their sleeves. Savage sat at his table clasping and unclasping his hands, a look of intense puzzlement on his nut-brown, wrinkled, intelligent, simian face. Every so often he shook his head and they knew the rage to understand what had happened to him still went on inside him.

Next there arose two ladies who introduced themselves as the Misses Glynis Unterjohn and Moira Schapp, the noted lesbians. They rose, not to tell their own story, at least not then, but to introduce a third friend, the journalist Marie Hertzog, whose pioneering study of the working conditions of black domestic servants entitled *Matilda: Venus of the Servants' Quarters* had caused a considerable stir some years before. The study had been notable not only for its original work on the conditions in which black women were forced to live but also because Hertzog herself was a card-carrying member of the ruling Party. Her book, which revealed the women she studied to be serfs in a male-dominated world, victims both of their drunken, brutal husbands as well as of their white mistresses and masters, had been promoted by Trudy Yssel and Minister Kuiker, both at home and abroad, as an indication of the new mood of liberalisation and self-examination sweeping the country. The book was held up as an example of the way in which members of the Regime were turning the microscope upon themselves, fearlessly analysing their weaknesses, changing the system from within.

Marie Hertzog spoke in a low, angry growl. 'It was my feminist investigations that took me to the Misses Unterjohn and Schapp because they came and complained to me that their houses were being raided by the police. Imagine my horror one Sunday morning when I discovered a photograph on the back page of the paper. This photograph purported to show what was described as "an illicit love-in" in a house of sin. It showed leather-clad women scrabbling suggestively, and among the tangled legs and tongues and other phantasmagoric elements I glimpsed my own face. No names were printed beneath the photograph, I wasn't identified. But then it was hardly necessary. Those who printed the photograph knew I would recognise myself. Quite obviously someone had decided to discredit me and since they were unable to do so publicly – my uncle was after all Attorney General for many years, and my connections with the Party were good – they had turned to this means. Naturally I suspected the Bureau, for what reasons I couldn't be sure, but it smacked of their taste and planning. Naturally I said so, right out loud. I had no intention of keeping such news to myself. The Bureau immediately denied it and to prove their good faith to a loyal daughter of the Party, offered to investigate themselves. They did. And they produced the culprit.' Marie Hertzog's head drooped, she found it difficult to continue. 'It turned out to be my own domestic servant, Joy, whom I'd invited to the party believing that she was as much entitled to go as I was. It seems she took along a camera, just because she thought it might come in useful. And it was. The picture she took turned out to be worth a lot of money and poor Joy needed money. She had a sick mother, she was a working girl. What else was she to do?' Marie Hertzog threw back her head. 'Friends and colleagues, everyone of you has lived through a similar experience. That isn't what's brought us here. No, I'm afraid the trouble with us is that we've all expected to win. We're on the right side, we said, so we've got to win. Well that sort of dreaming is all right I suppose provided you win. You can say a lot of things about us. You can say we've been foolish, that we've been sentimental, we've been misled, we've been badly treated. Maybe all these things are true, but truer than them all, simpler, ordinary, horrible, is the truth that given the way things are – we've been dead wrong.'

Many were the stories they heard that night, terrible, heart-rending. Consider the tragedy of Maisie van der Westhuizen, a singer synonymous with local opera, a well-loved soprano, 'Our Maisie', a familiar figure, somewhat bulky in flowing electric blues and acid greens, with elaborate black bangs and her huge sapphires, a wonderfully successful artist, best known of our singers abroad, making regular appearances with the Vienna State Opera. Fame and a soft heart and an excellent command of German; thereby hung her tale and her downfall. For Our Maisie was one of the chief supporters of the Benevolent Fund for Forgotten Germans, which, as everybody knew, was a front organisation for the support of elderly Nazis, a group of demanding old pensioners for whom, generally speaking, holidays were difficult to arrange. To this end Our Maisie had founded a group of sunshine homes on the South Coast to which these loyal old soldiers could be flown for a few weeks, to bask in the sun in the evening of their lives. Maisie told her story:

'One day a party were turned back at the airport when they arrived. And the reason given? Because they were National Socialists. I couldn't believe my ears! So were half his Government, I told Gus Kuiker, who had signed the exclusion order against my old gentlemen friends. It did no good, they were turned back, flown out, sobbing some of them, back to their little flats in Düsseldorf and Frankfurt, to die of disappointment. And if this wasn't enough, when I returned to the country some while later to open the new opera house in the great University of Christian National Education I walked out onto the stage to discover all the front rows were crammed with Jews, wearing yarmulkas and carrying placards: SAY NO TO MAISIE'S NAZIS! My voice snapped like a pencil, I stormed off the stage, I walked to my dressing room, I fetched my car, I drove to the airport and here I am, as you see, finished . . .'

Then there was the pathetic little tale of Hans Breker, the long-service South African spy who had worked for years in London under cover of a stringer for Dutch and South African newspapers, passing back information, mostly pretty low-grade stuff, to Pretoria, without interruption for almost two decades. His material had been rather pedestrian, nothing in comparison to the jewels of information achieved by the likes of Magdalena. Breker had culled the newspapers for reviews and articles by South African exiles, photographed them secretly at political rallies, looked up information on suspect organisations, kept his eye on peripheral figures, supplied biographies, checked addresses, filed descriptions and generally carried on the boring everyday business of undercover surveillance. This loyal agent lived in a flat in Hackney and in the normal course of events could have expected to see out his time and return home and spend the rest of his life in a special settlement for retired spies on the South Coast, with his pension sufficient to keep him in gin and cigarettes. Alas, Breker had fallen in love with an artist. She taught him to paint. The results were fatal. He sold his large flat in Hackney and took a room in Chelsea. He began to be seen in art galleries. His shoes were hand-made. He entered paintings for the Royal Academy Summer Exhibition, he even began learning French. By this time the woman had left him, but the damage was done. Breker was seen around town frequenting the oyster bars, he even signed his name in a letter to *The Times* about the fate of the Turner paintings.

'In short, I committed the worst sin of an agent – I became known. When the Government ordered me back I refused. I said I wasn't going back to some holiday home for senile spies in Bronkhorstspruit. Well, that did it. I was as good as dead. I came here – where else?'

And many more were the stories they heard that night. Too many to be recounted here, though mention must be made of the odd little history of Bennie Craddock, C. C. Himmelfarber's nephew, whom Blanchaille had last seen in a photograph weeping in Red Square. No wonder! He spoke briefly and movingly of his arrest in Moscow and of his eventual freedom which was achieved when Popov was exchanged for several agents who had been held in the Soviet Union, to wit a Briton, two Frenchmen, an American and a German. This young man, with his thin face and shaking hands, gave no indication that he had once been on the board of Consolidated Holdings, his uncle, Curtis Christian Himmelfarber's right hand. He produced copies of the Regime's propaganda magazine *Southern Comfort* (free to all foreign embassies, colleges, doctors' waiting rooms worldwide), its cover-story the exchange of Popov in Berlin and he pointed to his uncle, Curtis Christian, among the smiling observers of what was widely regarded to be a sensational coup for the Western intelligence services and not least, of course, for the Regime.

It would be unfair not to mention also the appearance of the former opposition leader, Sir Glanville van Doren who didn't in fact tell his story at all but instead gave a repeat performance of his farewell speech to Parliament, the one he made before he disappeared. The speech ran as follows: 'With happy memories of a full and useful life, conscious of having fought the good fight, I leave this House now to return to my farm, Morsdood, near my hometown of Glanville, which those of you who know your history will remember was named for my grandfather – and there I plan to devote myself, as a good dairy farmer, to rebuilding my herd.'

Matron gave a little bow when she heard this. 'Brave words, and absolute utter nonsense. What he was saying was that he was a shattered man. It was only a question of time before he left his cows and came to us.'

So it was, in the silence that followed the recounting of these cruel events that Blanchaille had time for reflection. He remembered what Kipsel had said about the plants and flowers growing in the garden; it was that most of them were found only in Africa and some were extinct. Was there something on this mountainside, in the quality of the air, or the soil, or some strange trick of climate that enabled them to survive here and only here? He found himself remembering the balcony of Uncle Paul's other house in Clarens, his heart went out to the old prophet, sick and tired, sitting on his front veranda staring blindly at the blue mountains across the water, those mountains which looked so curiously African. How sharply they must have reminded him of home! And then he found himself studying the waiters, or stewards, or whatever they were (he didn't really like to give them any other titles or descriptions). Waiters would do. Waiters sounded safe. They stood there against the wall in their white jackets and trousers, observing the diners. He knew there was nowhere else to go now, this was where the Last Trek ended, in this refurbished bathing establishment, this decrepit one-time spa on a Swiss mountainside attended by a matron and surrounded by Happies . . . They had indeed come home, they had all come home. They had come home with a vengeance.

Now let it be remembered that in this great dining-room there were many hundreds of people; that Blanchaille and Kipsel were excited, disturbed and that the alcohol had had some effect on them; and let it also be said that the stories they'd heard moved them very deeply and unsettled them more than they wished to admit. For one thing it was quite clear that they too would be expected to tell their stories, if not that night, then soon. It was in this unsettled, bewildered state that one must treat Kipsel's extraordinary claim, made in a choked whisper to Blanchaille, that sitting in a small group of men near the door, a group who he had not noticed until they got up to leave the room, hadn't wanted to notice, hadn't looked at really, who were partly masked by the fountain anyway and had their backs turned . . . that in this group of men he had recognised Ferreira.

It was a claim which Blanchaille dismissed out of hand. And a short angry conversation was conducted between the two men in whispers which the matron pretended not to hear.

'Perhaps you were mistaken. It's the light. There were a lot of people in here. It could not have been Ferreira.'

'I tell you it was.'

'How do you know?'

'What do you mean – how do I know? Of course I know! I know Ferreira. As well as you do. I'm telling you it was him!'

It clearly excited and delighted Kipsel to think he'd spotted his friend. The implications were astonishing! If Ferreira was here then why not others? Why not Father Lynch (only to be expected, surely?), Mickey the Poet, Van Vuuren? Or any of those who had gone before.

The possibility excited Blanchaille too. If Kipsel had been right then they would find their friends here. Now a second realisation occurred to him which he preferred not to contemplate, which he put out of his mind almost as soon as it had made its insidious, chilling entry. For if Ferreira was here it told them something about themselves which Kipsel hadn't thought of yet. Because the point about Ferreira which really alarmed was not that Ferreira was there – but that Ferreira was dead.

Despite the implication of this he couldn't stop himself from scrutinising with ever great intensity the faces of his fellow diners.

'You are perhaps looking for somebody?' the matron asked.

Blanchaille nodded. 'A friend. A friend I knew once.'

'I'm sure you'll find many of your friends here.'

'Her name was Miranda, I knew her some years ago. She – she went away. Do you know if she's here?'

Matron blew jets of steely smoke from her nostrils. 'Regret I can't answer. I'm not at liberty to disclose the names of our patients. That's up to them. Rights of privacy are paramount in our little community. It's up to people themselves to decide whether they want to be known, or whether they want us to know who they are. And if they do, they tell us their story. In fact it's very often by telling us their story that we find out who they are and they find out why they're here.'

Then I heard Kipsel ask Matron a question which went to the heart of the mystery. 'Where did Kruger hide the gold he brought with him?'

On this subject she was forthcoming. 'Oh yes, the gold. Do you remember the scenes you so often enacted, where you played the old President in the railway saloon waiting to be taken to the coast and the ship which was to carry him off into exile? Well most conveniently he had with him a number of Bibles. They were big family Bibles. Very heavy. Each capable, I suppose, of holding a few pounds of gold – once the pages had been removed of course.'

Kipsel shook his head incredulously. 'He would never have done that! Never! Not in the Bibles.'

'Why not?'

But Kipsel would not bandy words, simply shouted, red in the face, 'Not in the books!'

She shook her head. 'You don't understand. You see for him the gold was no longer money, treasure. It was his sacred trust. He wasn't stealing it. As far as he was concerned he was safeguarding it. And where better to do so than God's holy book? Nobody would have thought of looking there, nobody would have thought of searching an old man's Bibles. Of course many realised that the gold had gone. The British knew it had gone. And when he was out at sea, on board the man-of-war, the *Gelderland*, a curious incident occurred. As they steamed between Cairo and Corsica five British men-of-war were sighted and they gave every impression of being about to attack. Certainly the Dutch captain thought so. He prepared to fight. But at the last moment the British ships turned away. The story is that somebody big in London decided to let it go. Perhaps even Chamberlain himself. They called it off at the last moment. It wasn't worth an international incident. It would have looked like the worst sort of bullying. "Let the old man have his few dubloons which he's tucked into his socks," Chamberlain is supposed to have said.'

'So he got his millions after all?' Kipsel asked.

'Not exactly. The amount has been grossly exaggerated. He collected a few hundred thousand in total when the gold was sold but hardly the fortune of myth and popular imagination. I hate to spoil a good story but the money didn't amount to that much. Not even with the sums flowing into the house at Clarens from Boer sympathisers and charities from all over the world. But it was enough for him to do what he had to do. Enough for him to buy this place. And remember he was a man of simple faith. He believed that once he had the place, the funds to keep it going would follow. And he was right.'

Blanchaille said softly, 'Then there never were any Kruger millions.'

She looked at him now, and she laughed, broad and rich. 'Oh yes, there were Kruger millions all right. Just that they weren't the sort you think. You see, we are the Kruger millions.'

And then I saw the whole company of diners stand up and quite spontaneously sing several verses of the National Anthem; after which I watched the Happies going around drawing the curtains of the great dining-room with its living fountain and its lost souls and I wished, as the curtains closed one by one, that I too was inside with that strange company of story tellers before I woke from my dream to find myself, as of course I knew I would find myself, alone in Father Lynch's ruined garden beneath the Tree of Paradise waiting for the earth movers to close in.

Perhaps one last thing should be added. Unknown to Blanchaille and Kipsel, a traveller arrived at the big wrought-iron gates and was met by the gardener. Looksmart Dladla produced his slip of paper ceding him the strip of land for his new colony in Southern Africa. The gardener took his piece of paper and asked as well for Looksmart's passport, and his pass, and his book of life, documents which contain between them every single item of information about what are often otherwise quite unremarkable existences. Looksmart innocently handed these over, explaining to the gardener that he wished to enter and make a short address to the inhabitants of *Bad Kruger*. Asking him to wait, and promising him speedy attention, the gardener made a telephone call while Looksmart confidently anticipated admission and ran through the speech he had prepared.

But instead, clattering out of the sky came a police helicopter and Looksmart was arrested. For what was he in the cold light of day but an illegal immigrant, a black man without papers of any sort, a refugee from justice, an African lunatic abroad on Swiss soil, a man suspected of a variety of currency offences, a man who gibbered incomprehensibly of freedom and liberation. The lips of the policemen tightened when they heard this tirade.

I saw Looksmart frog-marched to the helicopter and watched as the machine took off and headed down the mountain. And then I knew that poor Looksmart though he had read Jefferson the philosopher of the American revolution, and Franklin and others, was beyond saving. He had fallen into the extraordinary delusion that given energy, ingenuity, bravery and just a modicum of goodwill, a people of sufficient determination can survive and prosper, even in South Africa. And as I saw him turned away from the gates of Uncle Paul's great white location in the sky, expelled from the sacred Alp, I realised that it's a long way down at the best of times and that the pit may wait at the end of the American rainbow, or open beneath the feet in some seeming Swiss paradise just as surely as it does in the city of destruction where I was born.